Praise for *New York Times* Bestselling Author
Jennifer Crusie and Her Novels

Bet Me

"A sassy and entertaining modern-day romance filled with witty sarcasm and snappy repartees. *Bet Me* has it all: laugh-out-loud lines, novel characters, and a torch-hot ending."   —*Rocky Mountain News*

"Twisting plot and the snap and flash of witty dialogue . . . Crusie navigates it with assurance and outright brio."   —*The Washington Post*

"Few popular writers handle light romantic comedy as deftly as Jennifer Crusie."   —*The Boston Globe*

"Crusie's growing success as an author is built on a list of funny, tantalizing contemporaries such as *Welcome to Temptation*, *Tell Me Lies*, and *Faking It*, that have readers laughing out loud. Min is bold, sassy, and funny—a combination that Cal and the reader will find to be irresistible."   —*Oakland Press* (Michigan)

"With multiple references to Chicken Marsala, Krispy Kreme donuts, and Midwestern brats . . . Crusie's latest should delight romance readers with a penchant for sinful foods."   —*Publishers Weekly*

"*New York Times* bestselling Crusie maintains her winning streak in another wickedly witty, deliciously sexy contemporary romance. Finding exactly the right balance between cynicism and optimism, Crusie deftly blends snappy dialogue; quirky, irrepressible secondary characters; and two beautifully matched protagonists struggling against their romantic fate."   —*Booklist*

"Utilizing her own unique brand of humor and panache, Crusie delivers yet another amazingly fun and funny novel. Eccentric characters abound in this book, making each new situation slightly offbeat, touching, and always hilarious."   —*Romantic Times*

"A sure bet . . . Jennifer Crusie's rollicking romance hits the jackpot."   —*BookPage*

Welcome to Temptation

Welcome to Temptation

Bet Me

Also by Jennifer Crusie

Crazy for You

Tell Me Lies

Fast Women

Faking It

Don't Look Down
with Bob Mayer

Welcome to Temptation

Bet Me

Jennifer Crusie

 St. Martin's Griffin ☙ New York

WELCOME TO TEMPTATION Copyright © 2000 by Jennifer Crusie Smith and BET ME Copyright © 2004 by Jennifer Crusie Smith. All rights reserved. Printed in the United States of America. No part of this book may be used or reproduced in any manner whatsoever without written permission except in the case of brief quotations embodied in critical articles or reviews. For information, address St. Martin's Press, 175 Fifth Avenue, New York, N.Y. 10010.

Map of the town of Temptation illustrated by Mollie Smith

ISBN-13: 978-0-312-36683-4
ISBN-10: 0-312-36683-3

First St. Martin's Griffin Edition: September 2006

10 9 8 7 6 5 4 3 2 1

Welcome to Temptation

For
Meg Ruley,
the world's greatest agent,
who believed in this book
when it was called *Hot Fleshy Thighs;*

and for
Jennifer Enderlin,
the world's greatest editor,
who said, "Why don't we get another title?"
and then waited with the patience of a thousand saints
until it was done.

Acknowledgments

I must thank
Valerie Taylor,
who has read in manuscript every book I've written since 1993
and who has made them all immeasurably better with her critiques;
and *Chene Heady,*
who read all of my MFA work and still managed to write the
magnificent "Salvation in Thirty Seconds or Less."

My thanks also go to
Tom Stillman,
who taught me how to play pool;
Jeff MacGregor,
who taught me how to make pornography;
Monica McLean,
who told me how to hide money offshore;
Laurie Grant,
who told me how to almost kill people;
Jack Smith,
who taught me how to electrocute people;
and *John Finocharo,*
who told me how to get away with killing people.
Without the help of these fine people, this would have been a book
about lemonade, ice cream, and wallpaper.

"I wrote the story myself.
It's about a girl who lost her reputation
and never missed it."

—MAE WEST

One

Sophie Dempsey didn't like Temptation even before the Garveys smashed into her '86 Civic, broke her sister's sunglasses, and confirmed all her worst suspicions about people from small towns who drove beige Cadillacs.

Half an hour earlier, Sophie's sister Amy had been happily driving too fast down Highway 32, her bright hair ruffling in the wind as she sang "In the Middle of Nowhere" with Dusty Springfield on the tape deck. Maple trees had waved cheerfully in the warm breeze, cotton clouds had bounced across the blue, blue sky, and the late-August sun had blasted everything in sight.

And Sophie had felt a chill, courtesy, she was sure, of the sixth sense that had kept generations of Dempseys out of jail most of the time.

"Slow down," she told Amy. "There's no need to rush." She stared out the window as she twisted the rings on her middle fingers. More riotously happy, southern Ohio landscape. That couldn't be good.

"Oh, relax." Amy peered at Sophie over the top of her cat's-eye sunglasses. "It's a video shoot, not a bank heist. What could go wrong?"

"Don't *say* that." Sophie sank lower in her seat. "Anytime anybody in a movie says, 'What could go wrong?' something goes wrong."

A green sign that read *Temptation ¼ Mile* loomed ahead, and Sophie reviewed her situation for the eleventh time that hour. She was going to a small town to make an unscripted video for a washed-up actress she didn't trust. There were going to be problems. They'd show up at any minute, like bats, dive-bombing them from out of nowhere. A strand of her dark curly hair blew across her eyes, and she jammed it back into the knot on top of her head with one finger. "Bats," she said out loud, and Amy said, "What?"

Sophie let her head fall back against the seat. " 'We can't stop here. This is bat country.' "

"Johnny Depp," Amy said. "*Fear and Loathing in Las Vegas*. Stop quoting. There's nothing to be nervous about, you're just overreacting." She turned off the highway and onto the old road that led into Temptation. The exit was marked by a shiny new gas station and a less shiny but still-plastic Larry's Motel.

"Colorful," Amy said.

"Trouble," Sophie said.

"Oh, for heaven's sake," Amy said. "It's not the Bates Motel."

"You have no idea how dangerous small towns are." Sophie scowled out the window. "You were only ten when we moved to the city. You can't remember what hell all those little places we lived in were."

"Sophie."

"And it's not as if we have a plan." Sophie stared with deep suspicion as they passed a blackened, log-built bar that sported a rusting neon sign: *Temptation Tavern. Beer. Music.* "It's all very well for Clea to say, 'We'll improvise,' but even if this is just an audition video, I need more of a script than, 'Clea goes back to her creepy hometown and meets her long-lost love, Fred.' "

"Frank." Amy shook her head. "I don't believe you. We're finally filming something besides a wedding, and all you can say is, 'Trouble ahead,' and, 'Why can't we stay in Cincinnati?' and, 'I don't trust Clea.' Face it, the only reason you don't like Clea is because she dumped Davy to marry a TV anchorman. That's very sisterly of you, but it's time to get over it."

"That's not it," Sophie said. "I don't know what it is, it's just—"

"Come on, Sophie. This is good for you. It gets you away from Brandon."

Oh, yeah, sure this is good for me, Sophie thought, but Amy couldn't help it. It was in her blood to turn everything into a con.

"Why you're dating your therapist is beyond me," Amy was saying. "Your health insurance covered his fees."

"My *ex*-therapist." Sophie squinted at the deserted tree-lined road before them. Ominous. "It saved a lot of time. You don't know what a relief it was not to have to explain the family to him."

"You know, sometimes I think it's just our destiny to be bad." Amy took her eyes off the road to smile at Sophie. "What do you say we quit making wedding videos and fall like the rest of the Dempseys?"

"No," Sophie said. "The fall will kill us."

She waited for an argument, but Amy was already distracted. "Oh, wow." She leaned forward and slowed the car. "*Gotta* love these road signs."

Sophie read the battered white-and-black signs: *Temptation Rotary Club, First Lutheran Church of Temptation, Temptation Ladies' Club, Temptation Nighttime Theater*. The last one was a corroded green-and-cream metal sign that said, *Welcome to Temptation*. Under it a smaller sign in the same rusted antique green said, *Phineas T. Tucker, Mayor*. And under that, a newer but still battered sign said, *We Believe in Family Values*.

"Get me out of here," Sophie said.

"Can you imagine how old Phineas T. must be if the sign is that rusted?" Amy said. "Older than God. Hasn't had sex since the Bicentennial. Do you think the Church of Temptation is like the Church of Baseball?"

"Not if it's Lutheran," Sophie said.

Then they crested the hill and there was Temptation.

"Pleasantville," Amy said, taking off her sunglasses.

"Amityville," Sophie said.

The town proper was on the other side of a muddy river that streamed sullenly under a gunmetal bridge at the bottom of the hill. Beyond the bridge, the land rose up green and lush behind smug little brick-and-frame houses, and as the hills rose, the houses got bigger, much bigger. Sophie knew the kind of people who lived in houses like that. Not Her Kind. " 'It's quiet,' " she told Amy as they started down the hill. " 'Too quiet.' " But Amy was gaping at something in the distance.

"Oh my God!" Amy pulled off the road. "Look at that water tower!"

"What?" Sophie leaned forward to look.

The flesh-colored, bullet-shaped tower thrust through the trees at the top of the hill, so aggressively phallic that Sophie forgot to fidget with her rings as she stared at it. "Hello. Do you suppose they did that on purpose? I mean, you couldn't *accidentally* paint it to look like that, could you?"

"Maybe Phineas T. is compensating. I don't care. *I love this town.*" Amy handed Sophie her sunglasses, yanked her orange tube top into place, and reached between the seats for her camera. "My God, the visual opportunities. Change places with me."

"Why?" Sophie said, but she climbed over the stick shift and into the driver's seat as Amy got out of the car. "Okay, the water tower is cute, but 'I bet the Chinese food here is terrible.' " When Amy gave her a dirty look, she said, "I'm not whining, it's a line. *My Cousin Vinny.*" Sophie squinted out at the road. "I *will* bet they don't have a decent pool table. Probably outlawed them. Where are we going now?"

"Back to the beginning." Amy got in the passenger-side door. "I have to get all of this. The Church of Temptation, Phineas T. Tucker, and that big hard-on of a water tower. This is our opening-credits crawl."

"Can we film in public without a permit?" Sophie put on Amy's sunglasses with only a brief thought as to how pink plastic and rhinestones would look with her plain white blouse and khaki shorts. She double-checked the road and then pulled out and made a U-turn. "Because breaking the law is out."

"They'll never know," Amy said, sounding way too much like their father. She braced the camera on the window and added, "I'll keep watch this way and you keep an eye on the rearview in case somebody comes up behind us. Go about five miles an hour. I want to get all of this."

Sophie drove back to where the signs began and turned around, keeping an eye on the rearview mirror as Amy filmed. All they needed was to get rear-ended by some irate Citizen of Temptation—

Then, as they reached the crest of the hill, the beige Caddy zoomed out of a side road that Sophie hadn't even seen and smashed into their front fender.

Sophie hit the brakes as she felt the impact, and the sound of crunching metal tore through her head at the same time Amy's sunglasses flew off her nose and hit the dashboard. She tasted blood as she bit her lip, gagged once as the seatbelt cut into her stomach, and then it was over, and they were sitting in the wrong lane with Dusty singing "I'll Try Anything" as if nothing had happened. There was no one coming the other way, so Sophie breathed deep, licked her bleeding lip, let go of the steering wheel, and turned to deal with the situation.

Amy was bent over, her head at a funny angle under the dashboard. "*Amy!*"

Amy straightened, holding the video camera. "It's okay. I dropped it but it's fine." She scowled at the dash and picked up her glasses, and the broken lenses fell out. "But my sunglasses are history, damn it."

Sophie swallowed her panic and tried to stop shaking. "Oh. Good. Good. The camera's okay. Good. Sorry about the glasses." She turned Dusty off in the middle of "Playing it safe is just for fools," and said, "How are you?"

"Me?" Amy scowled out the window. "I'm pissed as hell at the asshole who hit us."

Sophie peered through the window at the asshole. A bulky, white-haired, fifty-something Pillar of the Community stalked around their right front fender, thick with righteousness. "Oh, no, I hate these guys. He's going to try to make this our fault." She fumbled in her purse for her insurance card, thanking God it wasn't their fault since Amy's previous disregard for the laws of the road had already hiked their premium. "You keep quiet. I'll get us out of here, and the insurance people can handle everyth—"

"Well, actually, it is our fault." Amy dropped her sunglasses back on the dash. "We sort of ran a stop sign."

Sophie froze, clutching her insurance card. "We did *what*?"

"If I'd told you, you would have stopped," Amy said reasonably. "I was *panning*."

"Terrific." Sophie took a deep breath as the Pillar showed up at her window. She got out, making him step back as she did so.

"That was extremely reckless driving, young lady." The Pillar drew himself up to his full, blue-suited, stern-jawed height which, since Sophie met him eye-to-eye, was about five-seven. "You were speeding. Do you have insurance?" His hands were shaking, Sophie noticed, but before she could ask if he was all right, Amy stuck her head out Sophie's window.

"No way in hell were we speeding. We weren't going any faster than five miles an hour, tops. This is your fault, Grandpa."

"Shut up, Amy," Sophie said, thrusting the insurance card at her. "Copy that information down and do *not* say anything else." Then she turned back to the Pillar, determined to escape without giving him anything. "I'm so sorry," she said to him, flashing her family's stock-in-trade gotta-love-me-give-me-what-I-want smile.

The Pillar stopped glaring at Amy and turned back to Sophie. Amy said, "Hey—" but shut up when Sophie held up one finger behind her back. *One: Make the mark smile.*

"Someday my sister's brain will catch up with her mouth," Sophie said, "but until then I apologize for her." She deepened her smile and looked at the Pillar through her lashes.

"Well, I don't know," the Pillar said, and his scowl faded a little.

Sophie held up two fingers behind her back. *Two: Get the mark to agree with you.* "We're new here so we don't know the roads,"

Sophie went on. "You know how confusing it can be driving in a new place."

"Well, yes," the Pillar said. "But that doesn't—"

Three: Make the mark feel superior. "Of course, you're probably never confused." Sophie smiled up at him, no mean trick since they were the same height. She widened her eyes. "I bet you always know where you're going."

"Well, of course," the Pillar said, relaxing now. "However—"

"And now we've stopped you in the middle of all this heat," Sophie went on, apology thick in her voice. She nodded to the Pillar's trembling hands. "And we've upset you." *Four: Give the mark something.* "We really should let you go on. Standing here waiting for the police isn't going to do any of us any good." She smiled again at the Pillar, who began to smile back, looking a little confused.

"Well, that's true," he said. "It could be hours before Wes or Duane comes by."

Great. He knew the cops by their first names. Sophie kept her smile in place. *Five: Get what you want and get out.* "Amy, do you have the insurance information?"

The Pillar looked past her to Amy, and his face darkened. "What is that?"

Sophie turned around to see Amy checking the camera.

"That's a video camera," the Pillar said, sputtering. "What are you doing?"

"Making a movie, obviously." Amy looked at him with patent scorn. "And I'm telling you, you better have insurance because this is a classic car and it's not gonna be cheap to restore."

The Pillar flushed in fury, and Sophie thought, *Oh, thanks, Ame.* She moved to block Amy and sidetrack any debate over the classic status of an '86 Civic. "So we'll just—"

"This is outrageous." The Pillar expanded as he blustered. "You ran a stop sign. My wife is very upset. What kind of movie are you making? You can't do that here."

"Your wife?" Sophie abandoned the con for the time being and looked past him to see a faded-blonde woman leaning against the back fender of the other car, her chubby face a pasty white. "What are you doing over here if she looks like that?" Sophie turned her back on him and pointed her finger at Amy. "Do not talk to this man. Hand him the information, roll up that window, get the car off the road, and wait for me."

"Your lip's bleeding," Amy said, and handed her a Kleenex.

Sophie took it and blotted her lip as she walked around the still-protesting Pillar and crossed the road. The poor woman had made her way to the Caddy's passenger door, and Sophie bent to look in her eyes. "Are you hurt?"

"Oh." The woman seemed dazed, her pale blue eyes blinking up at Sophie in the sun as she plucked at the collar of her Pepto-Bismol pink suit, but her pupils looked all right. And there wasn't a hair on her head out of place, although that might have been the hairspray.

Sophie took her arm anyway. "You'd better sit down." She opened the passenger door, and the woman got in obediently. "Put your head between your knees." Sophie blotted her lip again. "Take some deep breaths."

The woman put her forehead on her plump knees, which she kept clamped together, and began to gasp.

"Not that deep," Sophie said, before she hyperventilated. "If you spread your knees apart, you can get your head lower."

"Virginia, what are you *doing*?"

Virginia straightened with a jerk, and Sophie turned on the Pillar in exasperation. "She's trying to get some blood back to her head." *If I was married to you, I'd keep my knees together, too.* "Did my sister give you the insurance information?" she asked, and then saw the paper trembling in his hand. "Fine. I understand that you want to get your wife home, and that's no problem for us." He started to protest, and she added, "We'll be at the Whipple farm until Sunday. After that we'll be back in Cincinnati."

"Your insurance agent—" the Pillar began, but this time his wife interrupted him.

"Are you friends of Clea Whipple's?" Virginia said from the front seat, her color returning. "Is she home again? Oh, Stephen, did you hear that? We haven't seen Clea for over twenty years. Except in the movies, of course."

Movie, Sophie wanted to say, since Clea had only made one, but the last thing she wanted was more conversation with the Pillars. She began to back away. "She's home, but only until Sunday. Now, please, don't let me keep you."

"Well, that's so exciting." Virginia trilled. "Is she still married to that handsome Zane Black? We watch him every night on the news." Sophie turned to make her escape, and Virginia raised her voice to compensate. "You tell her Virginia Garvey said hi!"

"They've got movie equipment," Stephen bellowed. "And they're filming on public land which is *clearly illegal.*"

"A movie?" Virginia's face lit up and her voice rose to a shout. "Oh, wait, tell me—"

Sophie reached the other side of the road, pretending not to hear. Ahead of her, a torn and faded campaign poster fluttered on a tree: *Tucker for Mayor: More of the Same.*

"Dear God, I hope not," she said under her breath. She got in the car and maneuvered it back on the road while Stephen Garvey glared at her and Virginia fluttered her hand. The front fender scraped against the tire as she searched for the lane to the farm, touching her lip with the Kleenex to see if the bleeding had stopped.

"What a butthead that guy was," Amy said. "Are you all right?"

"No." Sophie looked for the Whipple mailbox. "I've got a smashed car, a moving violation, a sister who screws up my getaway, and a dead white male telling the whole damn town we're making a movie." She slowed as the bridge loomed ahead, and scowled over the steering wheel. "And we must have missed the turnoff for the farm because we're almost in town now."

"No, there's the mailbox." Amy pointed with her broken sunglasses. "Turn left."

Sophie turned down the farm lane Clea had promised them was a good half-mile long. "This place gives me the creeps. . . ." Her voice trailed off as the dusty yard of a dilapidated farmhouse came into view. "Didn't Clea say the farmhouse was a long way off the road?"

"Maybe they moved the road," Amy said as they pulled up in front of the house. "It's been twenty-four years since she's been back." She peered through the windshield at the farmhouse. "Understandably."

Sophie tried to be fair as she turned off the ignition. The paint was peeling in dingy white strips from the side of the clapboards, and the gutter hung loose across the front of the peaked roof, but the house wasn't a complete loss. There was a wide front porch across the entire front with a swing. And there was . . .

Sophie looked around the dusty, barren yard. Nope, the porch was about it. "Great place to film. Yeah, we can trust Clea. I smell trouble."

Amy sniffed the air. "That's dead fish. Must be the river."

She opened her car door as the screen door banged, and Clea Whipple came out onto her porch, her lush body straining at her bright blue sundress, her white-blonde hair almost incandescent in the sun. She shaded her cameo-perfect face with her hand and called, "You're late."

"And hello to you, too," Sophie said, and got out of the car to unload their supplies, starting with their cooler. It was full of Dempsey life essentials—lemonade and Dove Bars—and she was in need of immediate essential comfort.

Amy went toward the house with the camera. "Isn't this going to be wonderful?"

Sophie looked at Clea, the most self-absorbed woman in the universe, staring blankly back at her from the derelict front porch. "Oh, yeah," she said as she hauled the cooler out of the car.

Nothing but good times ahead.

Eight miles up the road, in Temptation's marble-and-sandstone courthouse, Mayor Phineas T. Tucker wondered not for the first time why he was cursed with a council made up of a blowhard, a doormat, a high-school English teacher, the town coroner, an amateur actor, and his mother. The combination was depressing to contemplate even with the blowhard and the doormat missing, so while Hildy Mallow waxed poetic over the aesthetic benefits of reproduction vintage streetlights,

Phin leaned back from the oak table to distract himself with his council secretary's legs.

Rachel Garvey had excellent legs. Of course, with only twenty years on them, they were too young for him no matter what his mother and hers thought, but they were still fine to look at.

". . . and since their beauty would discourage vandalism, the extra cost will pay for itself over time," Hildy finished, confusing Phin until he remembered that Hildy was talking about streetlights and not Rachel's legs.

"That may be a little optimistic." Liz Tucker's voice was as cool as her champagne-tinted hair. "Of course, our alternative is those horrible modern lights that would clash with the nineteenth-century architecture."

Phin winced. The only nineteenth-century architecture in Temptation was in the wealthy part of town. Grateful that only a few citizens were sitting in the front row listening to his mother forget the little people once again, Phin sat up to head her off before she could offer them cake.

"Yeah, but the good streetlights would go everywhere, right?" Frank Lutz said before Phin could intervene.

"Right," Phin said.

"Okay." Frank sat back and ran his hand over his matinee-idol hair, clearly relieved that the new development he'd built on the west side of town would have class lighting, too. "I'm for it. Let's vote."

"Can we do that without Stephen and Virginia?" Liz said, and Hildy straightened her cardigan and said, "Certainly. If we all agree, we'll have a majority no matter how they voted. And we all agree, right?"

She stared pointedly at the fourth member of the council, Dr. Ed Yarnell, who gazed back, unfazed, armored with thirty years of council experience. If Phin thought about Ed too much, it depressed him, knowing that thirty years down the line he could *be* Ed: bald, sixty-something, and still staring at the same WPA mural of *Justice Meeting Mercy*. It was not how he wanted to spend his sixties. Hell, it wasn't how he wanted to spend his thirties. He glanced guiltily at the sepia-toned photos of three of the four previous mayors—Phineas T. Tucker, his father; Phineas T. Tucker, his grandfather; and Phineas T. Tucker, his great-grandfather—all staring down their high-bridged noses, with cold eyes, at their latest and laziest incarnation.

"Then we'll vote," Hildy said.

"Call the roll, Rachel," Phin said, and Rachel called Lutz, Mallow, Tucker, and Yarnell and got four yeses. "Motion passed. What's next?"

"The water tower," Liz said, and Hildy said, "I don't see why—" and then the double doors from the marble hall opened and the Garveys came in.

"There was an accident." Virginia plopped herself down in her chair, looking like a wad of bubblegum with big hair. "Hello, baby," she said to Rachel, reaching across to pat her daughter's hand. "This car came out of nowhere and *didn't stop*. Two women, a snippy little redhead, Stephen says, and a nice brunette who was sweet to me. Curly hair. Low-class. They're staying at the Whipple farm. And they're making a *movie....*"

Phin watched Liz draw back, probably because "low-class" was such a low-class thing to say. "I'll never understand why Stephen married one of his counter clerks," he'd heard her tell his father once. "His mother must be revolving in her grave."

"Enough," Stephen said now. "We've held up this meeting by coming late, let's not waste more time with gossip."

"Are you all right?" Liz asked, and Virginia nodded.

"Wait a minute, they're making a movie?" Hildy said, and Virginia transferred her nod to her.

"The water tower is on the table," Phin said, deep-sixing his own interest in the news so he could get the meeting over with. If somebody really was making a movie, the whole town would have the details by nightfall anyway. "Stephen, you put it on the agenda."

"I certainly did." Stephen collected himself. "That water tower is a disgrace."

"Well, white looks so drab a few weeks after we paint it—" Hildy began.

"I have an appointment at four-thirty at the Whipple farm, and a rehearsal at six," Frank told Phin under his breath as Hildy elaborated on the "drab" problem. "*Carousel.* I'm the lead." Phin nodded as he spoke, trying not to picture forty-two-year-old Frank walking through a storm with his head held high.

"—and so I thought it would look better in peach," Hildy finished.

Stephen said, "Hell, Hildy, it's not your laundry. It's a water tower, it's supposed to be white—all water towers are white."

Hildy sniffed. "The water tower in Groveport is blue."

"Well, my God, *Groveport*." Keeping one eye on the four constituents in the front row, Stephen turned back to Phin. "A competent, *concerned* mayor would do his *civic duty* here. We have *family values* to protect."

Here we go again, Phin thought. There had been a time when Stephen's blatant pandering had enraged him, but after nine mind-numbing years as mayor, nothing made him lose his temper anymore. He let Stephen wind down, and then he said, "Hildy, I agree that only people with dirty minds would think it looks like anything but a water tower, but there appear to be a lot of people with dirty minds. We're going to have an accident any day now, what with all the people pulling off the highway with their Polaroids. It's a safety issue." Phin tried to look sympathetically into Hildy's eyes.

Hildy looked at him as if he were a Republican.

"This is a disgrace," Stephen said, playing to the front row again. "You call this leadership?"

"I've got an appointment and then rehearsal," Frank announced. "I'm playing Billy Bigelow. *Carousel*. I can't be late."

For this I spent six years in college, Phin thought. "Let's vote."

"You gotta have a motion," Rachel said, still bent over her pad.

"I move we repaint the water tower back to the old red-and-white we always had," Stephen said. "School colors. That's what it should have been all—"

Phin sighed. "Just move we repaint the water tower, Stephen."

"I move we repaint the water tower red and white," Stephen said.

"I second," Virginia said from beside him, pleased with herself.

The vote went three to three, with Stephen, Virginia, and Liz voting for the new paint job, and Hildy, Ed, and Frank—"I'm putting a sign out there for the theater, good advertising"—voting to keep the peach.

"Did you ever think about being anything but a yes-woman?" Hildy snapped at Virginia, who straightened and fussed with her jacket.

"Virginia votes her conscience, Hildy," Stephen said.

"The motion is tied," Rachel said over Hildy's snort. "The vote goes to the mayor. Tucker."

"Yes," Phin said. "Sorry, Hildy."

"Motion passes, four to three," Rachel said, and Hildy smacked her notebook down on the table, and said, "So now I have to do this all over again."

"Just tell the Coreys to charge the new paint at Stephen's," Phin told her. "They know what to do."

"Funny how Garvey's Hardware is getting twice as much business because of this." Hildy sat back and crossed her arms. "Clear conflict of interest, if you ask me. He shouldn't have been voting."

"That's a good point," Frank said, visibly struck by the argument. Whenever Frank had a thought, it was visible. "Why didn't you refuse to sell her the peach paint?" he asked Stephen.

"I sold Hildy the paint," Rachel said as her father began to sputter with indignation. "It was, like, all my fault."

Five different council members fell all over themselves telling Rachel it certainly wasn't her fault, while Ed sat silent and smiling at her, and Phin marveled at the way big blue eyes and taffy-blonde hair could snow the hell out of people.

"Well, it doesn't matter now anyway," Rachel said. "I got the vote recorded."

"If there's no new business—" Phin began, but Stephen said, "Wait. We need to talk about this movie."

"Well, Stephen, I *tried* to talk about it—" Virginia began, and Stephen spoke over her.

"Not gossip. We need to consider the impact on the town. The pitfalls." He looked slyly at Phin from the corner of his eyes, and Phin thought, *What are you up to now?* "The *dangers*," Stephen went on. "We're a town that believes in *family values*, and after all, you remember Clea."

Phin definitely remembered Clea. The last time he'd seen her in the flesh, he'd been twelve and she'd leaned over to give him the money on his paper route. He'd looked down her blouse and fallen off his bike and ended up with nine stitches in his chin, but it had been worth it. He was fairly sure she'd jump-started his puberty.

"I don't see any dangers." Frank stood up to go. "And I have to leave. I'm late."

"Sit down," Stephen said. "Some of us think of other things besides *acting*." He sent a dismissive glance at Phin. "Or playing pool."

"Yeah, like painting the water tower twice to double your profit," Frank said.

"There is that," Hildy said.

"Could you forget that so we can speak to the *issues*?" Stephen said.

"I think that making double your profit at the expense of the taxpayers is an issue," Frank said.

"Oh, for heaven's sake, I'll *give* you the damn paint!" Stephen said, and Phin said, "Thank you, Stephen, we accept. Now if there's nothing else—"

"This *movie*." Stephen put his hands on the table. "Clea made that one movie, remember? We don't want that kind of movie made here."

"*Always Tomorrow*." Virginia nodded. "But I really think the nudity in that was for artistic purposes, and it wasn't very much. And she died in the end so she was punished."

Phin spared a brief thought as to what it must like to be married to Virginia if she thought nudity was punishable by death, but then Stephen caught his attention again.

"No, not *Always Tomorrow*," Stephen was saying, and Frank said, "Oh," and sat down again.

Virginia looked mystified; Rachel looked intrigued; Liz and Hildy looked at the ceiling; and Phin remembered *Coming Clean*, a plotless, straight-to-video movie set in a car wash that Clea undoubtedly did not have on her résumé since she'd been billed as "Candy Suds." He didn't know how Stephen had gotten hold of it; Phin had only seen it because Ed had it in his extensive pornography collection.

"Stephen, I doubt she's shooting porn here," Phin said, and Rachel said, "Clea Whipple made a dirty movie? Fabulous."

Stephen nodded. "There. See? That's what I'm talking about. Family values. We let Clea make this kind of movie here, and our children will think it's all right because we approved of it. And those women with the camera looked loose."

Excellent, Phin thought. At last, some *good* news.

His mother shot him a sharp look.

"We should have a policy on this," Stephen went on. "We won't give a filming permit to anyone unless they sign a no-nudity clause."

"How many movies do you think Temptation is going to get?" Phin said, but Frank said, "Hey, it could happen. Although, with a no-nudity clause—" He shook his head. "That's too strict, Stephen. We don't want to stifle the film industry here."

Stephen zeroed in on Phin. "Responsible leadership demands responsible legislation. It's our civic duty—"

The problem, Phin thought—not for the first time, as Stephen ranted on—wasn't that Stephen was a fathead and Virginia was a gossip, it was that Stephen was a driven fathead with a large conservative following, and Virginia talked to everybody. Phin could hear her now: "Well, of course Phin's a lovely boy, but he was actually for pornography, can you imagine?" Yeah, that would get out the votes in November.

On the other hand, there were some things that Phin was willing to fight for. "I'm against censorship, Stephen," he said, interrupting the older man in mid-tirade. "It comes with owning a bookstore. No banned books."

"How about a pornography clause?" Virginia said. "That's not nudity, and it's not censorship because pornography is bad. We have to protect our children." She gave Rachel her usual obsessively loving smile, including Phin in it, too, as her future son-in-law. *Such a nice couple,* her smile said. *What lovely grandchildren they'll give me. And they'll live right next door.*

Phin's answering smile said, *Not a chance in hell,* while Rachel gazed at Justice and Mercy, pretending she'd never heard of pornography or sex, or Phin, for that matter.

Phin said, "And how would we define 'pornography'?"

"Everybody knows pornography when they see it," Stephen said.

"There's some difference of opinion on that," Phin said. "I don't think we should make law on 'Everybody knows.'"

"Stephen may be right," Liz said, and Phin thought, *Oh, hell, Mom, shut up.* "We have an obligation to the citizens of Temptation." She cast a calculating look at the four citizens in the audience, undoubtedly sizing up the situation in terms of getting her son reelected in November. "We could pass a no-pornography ordinance, and stipulate that 'pornography' is to be defined by the council."

"I think that's unconstitutional," Phin said. "You can't make a law that gets defined later. People have to know what they're breaking."

"It's not a law," Stephen said. "It's an ordinance. I move that Temptation adopt an antipornography ordinance."

"No," Phin said. "I'm not going to have you going through the bookstore and throwing out *Lady Chatterley*."

"I move that Temptation adopt an antipornographic *movie* ordinance," Virginia said, and Stephen said, "I second it."

Phin looked at his council and thought, *Why do I put up with this?* It was a stupid ordinance, and probably unconstitutional, and definitely a waste of time. On the other hand, talking the council out of it would take another hour which would cut into the semiregular late-afternoon pool game he played with Temptation's police chief. And, since it was highly unlikely that anybody but Clea Whipple would ever want to make a movie in Temptation, and, in fact, highly unlikely that Clea Whipple *did* want to make a movie in Temptation, he'd be fighting for a principle that was never going to be tested. "Call the roll, Rachel."

The vote went four in favor of establishing the ordinance, to two against, with Frank voting no to defend the infant Temptation film industry and Ed dissenting without comment. Hildy should have voted against it as an anticensorship English teacher, but the look she shot Phin as she voted made it clear that this was payback time.

Stephen said, "I'll draft the ordinance tonight and we'll call a special meeting to pass it."

"No, we won't," Phin said. "We'll vote on it next Wednesday, same time, same place. And now, if there are no objections, I move we close this meeting."

"Second." Frank stood up to go. "And by the way, Stephen, we voted to buy the fancy streetlights while you were gone."

"You *what*?" Stephen's roar was outraged.

"You're late for your appointment, Frank." Phin stood up. "This meeting is dismissed." When Stephen drew breath to protest, he added, "Everybody *leave*."

Rachel snickered and closed her notebook.

"We shouldn't wait on the ordinance," Stephen said, as the others left, and Phin said, "Sure we should. Legislate in haste, repent at leisure. Next week is fine."

"Well, then, we're going to reconsider those streetlights next week, too." Stephen shook his head, clearly disgusted with the state of politics in Temptation.

Phin smiled at Rachel as he headed for the door. "Thank you, Rachel, for taking the blame for the paint. That was very noble."

Rachel grinned at him, and Phin saw his mother waiting for him by the door, relaxing into a half-smile as she watched the future daughter-in-law of her choice. *Fat chance*, he wanted to tell her, but that was another argument he didn't want to have. He'd already told his mother that it was out of the question—Rachel said "like" a lot, she didn't read, and she played lousy pool—but Liz Tucker hadn't gotten to be First Lady of Temptation by taking "no" for an answer.

"Wait a moment," she said to her son now as he went past her, and he shook his head.

"Can't stay. I'll talk to you at dinner." He escaped into the marble hall only to find himself waylaid by Ed Yarnell, who looked at him with naked contempt.

"Interesting council meeting you missed just now, Phineas," Ed said. "You just sit there staring into space with your thumb up your butt while Stephen rams through a censorship law."

"Thanks, Ed," Phin said, trying to move away. "Can't stay—"

"You're getting to be too much like your old man, rolling over for Stephen."

Phin felt his temper rise and repressed it from long practice. "Dad never rolled over, he was just careful. This is politics, Ed."

"This is crap," Ed said. "I thought it was a good thing you'd cooled your jets some over the years, considering what a reckless dumbass you used to be, but now I don't know. It's been a good long time since I've seen you break a sweat over anything."

Phin clapped him on the shoulder. "Well, thanks for the advice, Ed. Have a nice evening."

Ed shook his head as Phin escaped again, this time through the wide-arched door of the little courthouse. An architectural gem, a tourist had once told him. "Well, we like it," Phin had said, but it was hard to be impartial since he'd grown up in the place. Generations of Tucker mayors had run the courthouse and Temptation, except for those two dark Garvey years when Stephen's father had wrested the office from Phin's father over the New Bridge controversy.

That was what Stephen was looking for now, Phin knew as he went down the marble steps to the old-fashioned storefronts of Temptation's Main Street. Some controversy that he could exploit the same way his father had exploited the New Bridge. The water tower had been small potatoes, and Stephen wasn't getting anywhere on his anti–new streetlight campaign, but the way he'd jumped on the porn thing, he might be thinking that was his ticket. Which only went to show how desperate Stephen was.

Of course, having your Cadillac hit by loose, low-class women could rattle a man.

Phin reached the pale green Victorian that housed Tucker Books, climbed the wide wooden steps to the porch, and flipped over the sign that said *Back at 4:30* in childishly skewed, crayoned printing. Then he sat down in one of the cushioned porch chairs and thought of the upcoming election with fatalistic distaste. He didn't care if he won; it was losing that would make him crazy. Tuckers didn't lose. Especially since losing would carry with it the extra burden of watching Stephen Garvey run Temptation into the ground with his nutso family values. God forbid there should be another Garvey Reign of Error. Phin was still sitting there half an hour later, lost in thoughts of streetlights, water towers, and porn permits, when Temptation's police chief pulled up in front.

"Stephen stopped by the station," Wes Mazur said as he got out of the patrol car.

"Don't tell me, let me guess," Phin said. "He wants me arrested for un-mayorlike conduct. Dereliction of civic duty."

"Close." Wes came up the steps looking as unconcerned as ever behind his heavy black glasses. "He wants me to go out to the Whipple farm and investigate some women that ran into him."

Phin nodded. "He mentioned them. They're loose women. And possible pornographers."

"Really?" Wes looked encouraged as he sat down. "And we know this how? No, wait, I've got it. The Whipple farm. Clea Whipple. *Coming Clean.*"

"There you go." Phin put his feet on the porch rail and leaned back in his chair. "The keen mind of the law at work."

"So Clea's coming here to make a movie." Wes looked almost enthusiastic. Then reality set in. "Why?"

"Excellent question. If only Stephen would ask it occasionally."

"He can't. It would slow down the leaps he makes to get to his conclusions." Wes frowned out at the street. "You know, I was considering just letting the insurance agents handle the accident, but now I think I better go out there, make sure everything's okay."

"Check out Clea in the flesh."

"My civic duty."

"Not to mention the loose women."

"That, too." Wes stood up, checking his watch. "It's five. You want to close up and come with me?"

"Oh, yeah," Phin said. "My civic duty, too. We can play pool later."

"We live to serve," Wes said.

"I just want another look at Clea," Phin said.

Sophie unpacked their supplies and organized the dingy kitchen while ignoring the truly ugly cherry wallpaper on one wall, and Clea talked to her the entire time, not helping at all. "Frank's going to be here any minute," she kept saying, sounding almost excited, which was unlike her; she'd been beautifully bored for the five years Sophie had known her.

After half an hour, Sophie had heard enough about Frank the football star; Frank the high-school-theater leading man; Frank the wealthy developer; Frank, the generally magnificent. "Interesting wallpaper," she said, trying to change the conversation.

Clea looked at the wall and shrugged. "My mom put it up. She got that one wall done and my father saw it and made her take the rest of the wallpaper back. He was a tight old bastard."

Sophie looked at the huge ugly bluish cherries. "Maybe he just had good taste."

"No." Clea turned her back on the cherries. "He was just a bastard. He was lousy at taking care of us, but he was a real pro at saying no." She seemed bored by the change of subject and drifted out the door, leaving Sophie to scrub the sink.

When Sophie finished the kitchen, she put her suitcase in a sweltering bedroom that included a hideous blue china dolphin lamp, and then she cleaned the bathroom, although she couldn't manage to unclog the showerhead or find a replacement for the pink-and-blue-fish-covered, mildew-encrusted shower curtain. Finally she went back to the kitchen, put *Dusty in Memphis* on their CD player, and made ham-and-cheese sandwiches to "Just a Little Lovin'."

"The plumbing works, sort of," Sophie told Amy when she came in. She rinsed out a glass in the kitchen sink and then watched the water seep down the drain. "Although showers will be a problem. I haven't checked the electricity—the basement looks like the pit of hell—but the refrigerator is on again and we're leaving Sunday. We can stand anything for five days."

"You haven't met our leading man." Amy picked up a ham sandwich and bit into it. "A charter member in Buttheads Anonymous."

"This would be Frank?"

"This would be Frank. He got here half an hour ago, and already I want him dead." Amy dropped into one of the dingy white wooden kitchen chairs in front of the mutant-berry wallpaper. "He looks like Kurt Russell did in *Used Cars*, I mean, he's wearing a *green suit*, for heaven's sake, and he's drooling into Clea's cleavage."

"The police and the mayor are here," Clea said from the archway, making Amy choke on her sandwich. "Frank says he'll handle it."

"Oh, no he won't," Sophie said.

When she went out on the porch, tensed for battle, a guy in a green suit was talking with a cop in uniform, but they looked manageable. It was the third man, leaning bored against the passenger side of the squad car, who sent every instinct she had into overdrive.

He had broad shoulders, mirrored sunglasses, and no smile, and Sophie could hear ominous music on the soundtrack in her head as her heart started to pound. His fair hair shone in the late-afternoon sun, his profile was classic and beautiful, the sleeves of his tailored white shirt were rolled precisely to his elbows, and his khaki slacks were immaculate and pressed. He looked like every glossy frat boy in every nerd movie ever made, like every popular town boy who'd ever looked right through her in high school, like every rotten rich kid who'd ever belonged where she hadn't.

My mama warned me about guys like you.

He turned to her as if he'd heard her and took off his sunglasses, and she went down the steps to meet him, wiping her sweaty palms on her dust-smeared khaki shorts. "Hi, I'm Sophie Dempsey," she said, flashing the Dempsey gotta-love-me grin as she held out her hot, grimy hand, and after a moment he took it.

His hand was clean and cool and dry, and her heart pounded harder as she looked into his remote, gray eyes.

"Hello, Sophie Dempsey," her worst nightmare said. "Welcome to Temptation."

Two

Sophie's nightmare had a good six inches on her, and it was hard to smile looking that far up into cool eyes while her heart tried to pound its way out of her rib cage. "Oh. Thank you."

He nodded down at her, his eyes never leaving her face as he favored her with a politician's practiced smile. "I'm Phin Tucker, the mayor, and this is Wes Mazur, our police chief."

The cop had come to stand next to them, shorter than the mayor and pale in his white shirt and black pants. Under his brown crewcut, he peered out of serious, heavy black-rimmed glasses.

"We came about the accident. . . ." the cop began, and then his voice trailed off and Sophie turned to see Clea floating down the steps, looking as blonde and lush as ever.

"Did I hear you say you're Phin Tucker?" Clea drifted past Sophie to take the mayor's arm. "I can't believe it. The last time I saw you, you fell off your bike." She let her eyes slide up to his.

"I'm having the same feeling now. Hello, Clea. Welcome home." The mayor looked down into Clea's blue eyes, but he didn't sound off-balance in the slightest. He was probably never off-balance. Sophie felt annoyed with him for that.

"And who's this?" Clea gazed past his shoulder at the police chief.

"Police chief," a deep voice said from behind Wes. "They want to know about some accident."

Sophie turned. Medium, dark, and smug, the green suit had too much hair mousse and a slight paunch, and he'd slung his suit jacket over one shoulder in a misbegotten attempt to look cool. His shirt had green and white stripes, and his tie was bright yellow.

"You must be Frank," Sophie said.

"That's me. Now don't you worry about a thing." Frank winked at Sophie. "I can handle this for you. I'm on the council."

"Nothing to handle," the cop said mildly, and Sophie shot Clea a look that said, *Do something with this guy.*

Clea took Frank's arm. "Why don't we go up on the porch and discuss your scenes for tomorrow?"

Frank looked stunned, as if he couldn't believe she was touching him, and let her tow him off.

One confirmed jackass out of the way. Two possible wolves to go.

"Well, that's the car," she told the cop, and the mayor looked at her one last time and then left them to walk over to it, evidently having seen all he needed. "It's registered to my sister and me." She turned back to the dilapidated porch where Amy was now leaning against the post, chewing her ham-and-cheese sandwich and looking exotic in her orange tube top and purple capris, her red hair flaming in the sun. "That's my sister."

"Oh," the cop said, looking at Amy.

The mayor called the cop over, and he went as Amy put her sandwich on the porch rail and came down the steps.

"I told you so," Sophie said to Amy under her breath. "The Pillars reported us to some outback nazi law-enforcement agency and now they've run us down like dogs—' "

"*Fear and Loathing* again. You're getting boring." She studied the two men. "So that's Phineas T. Tucker. We were wrong. He's having sex. And he can have more with me."

"Concentrate," Sophie said. "The cop's name is Wes Mazur. Get over there and give him anything he wants so he'll go away and we can get to work."

"I'd rather give it to the mayor." Amy sighed. "Unfortunately, he appears to want it from you."

"What?" Sophie said. "Amy, *concentrate.*"

"I was standing in the doorway when he said hi," Amy said. "And from the look on his face, what he has for you is not the key to the city."

"There was no look on his face," Sophie said. The mayor was now gazing at the car with the same lack of expression he'd been sporting since he'd arrived. Clearly a product of too much inbreeding. "I don't think he has anything for anybody. Go get rid of them."

Fifteen minutes later, after the cop had gone back to the patrol car, gotten a crowbar, and pried the fender off the tire, Amy came back to the porch with the two men behind her. "Wes has a few questions."

Wes? "Questions?" Sophie clasped her hands together to keep from fidgeting and then began to twist her rings instead.

The cop gestured to the swing, and she sat down. When he started to sit on the porch rail, Sophie said, "No!" and lunged for the rail, grabbing Amy's sandwich before he sat on it. "Sorry," she told him, handing the sandwich to Amy.

"Thank you." He sat on the rail while the mayor leaned on the post behind him, looking amused, which did nothing to endear him to Sophie. He was starring in *The Philadelphia Story*; she looked like an extra from *The Grapes of Wrath*. Life was so unfair.

"Just tell me what happened," the cop said.

Sophie turned her back on the mayor and told the nice policeman everything, and when she was finished, she said, "I just wasn't looking and missed the sign. We didn't break the law on purpose."

The mayor stirred a little. "Actually, you did." He sounded as if he didn't care. "You left the scene of an accident."

"Understandable under the circumstances," the cop said before Sophie could speak. "Amy says we can have the tape of the accident if we bring it back tomorrow, so we'll bring the accident report for you to sign then."

"Amy asked you to come back." Sophie bit her lip, wondering why her mother had insisted on having three children.

"She also mentioned something about the electricity and plumbing," the cop said, smiling at Amy.

"A good reason to call an electrician and a plumber," Sophie said brightly. *Not the police and the government, Amy.* "Really, there's no need—"

"Not a problem," the cop said. "My pleasure."

"—certainly not for both of you—" Sophie began again, hoping at least to avoid the mayor. But when she looked at him, he was staring at her mouth, and she blushed and then felt her temper rise.

"Did you get hurt in the accident?" he said, and Sophie blinked. "Your lip. It's bleeding."

"Oh." Sophie licked her bottom lip and tasted salt. "I bit it when he hit us. It'll be all right."

His eyes lingered on her mouth for another moment, and then he nodded.

It was time to get rid of the mayor.

One. "But thank you for asking," Sophie said, smiling the Dempsey smile.

The mayor looked startled for an instant, and then his lips quirked a little.

Two. "But I think my mouth will recover, don't you?" Sophie said, flirting up at him.

"Oh, yes" he said, meeting her eyes.

Three. "I'd forgotten all about it," Sophie said, truthfully. "You must be very observant."

"I try," the mayor said, openly appraising her now.

Four. Sophie stood up, including the cop in her smile. "You've been wonderfully kind, and we really can't ask you for anything else; certainly not another trip out here. So I'll come in tomorrow and sign the accident report and—"

"I can ask them," Amy said from behind her. "I want plumbing that works and electricity that won't kill me."

Sophie tried to keep the exasperation off her face but the mayor must have seen it anyway because he grinned at her, a real smile this time, and she thought, *Of course you'd be gorgeous.*

"We'll be back tomorrow," he said, straightening away from the porch post, and all Sophie could say was, "Thank you."

When they were gone, Sophie turned to Amy. "Let's review the plan. It's going to be just the three of us and *we're not going to attract attention.*"

"You know there's such a thing as being too cautious," Amy said. "We need the plumbing and electricity fixed and they'll do it for free."

"The hell they will," Sophie said, thinking of the mayor. "We'll pay one way or another."

"And I don't care what you say," Amy went on. "The mayor is hot."

"I didn't say he wasn't hot." Sophie stood up and let the swing bounce behind her. "I said we were going to stay away from him. He's trouble, it's in his eyes. He's a hard mark."

"I bet he is," Amy said.

"Will you concentrate? We stay away from the mayor."

"Yes, but will the mayor stay away from us?" Amy said.

"God, I hope so," Sophie said, licking her lip as it started to bleed again, pretty sure she meant it.

Phin sat in the passenger seat of the squad car and considered running the Dempsey sisters out of town on a rail. He had no legal grounds, of course, but it was his job to ensure the peace, and he had a feeling that getting rid of the Dempseys would be a good start, even if it was only for *his* peace. There was something wrong there.

Besides the brunette's lush, red, swollen lip.

He shook his head to get rid of the image and Wes said, "What?"

"The brunette. She bothers me. Why is she so tense?"

"That's not why she bothers you."

Phin ignored him. "The way she twisted her rings, I thought her fingers were going to fall off. And then she turned on the charm. She'd have had me, too, if she hadn't been so abrupt about it."

"She had you anyway," Wes said. "Her name's Sophie. I like her, but it is hard to believe she's Amy's sister."

"Amy's a hot little number." *Sophie hadn't been hot,* he thought, concentrating on the older sister's shortcomings so he could forget about her mouth. She'd had the potential to be as attractive as Amy—all that dark curly hair knotted on the top of her head, and a good-enough ivory-pale face with those big brown eyes—but the tension had radiated off her so hard that it had been exhausting just standing next to her. "Sophie's wound so tight she doesn't even breathe," he told Wes. "That cut on her lip had to hurt like hell, and she never mentioned it, never even touched it." He shook his head. "She's trying too hard to pretend everything's all right. Which means she's up to something, and it has to be about that movie." He didn't like women who were up to something. Not that they all weren't. "Which reminds me, you're going to have a new ordinance to enforce next week. Antiporn. So if they're shooting sex, you get to arrest Amy and her tube top."

Wes closed his eyes. "Oh, fuck, why didn't you kill it?"

"Because the majority of the council wanted it, and we're not likely to see a lot of movie companies coming in here, so—" Phin shrugged.

"I don't think Clea Whipple should be discouraged from making pornography," Wes said. "That's just wrong."

"Yeah, well, you run for mayor and fight the good fight." The vague uneasiness Phin had felt about the porn ordinance returned and made him cranky. "I thought I handled it pretty well, considering."

"Nobody died." Wes drove across the New Bridge and surveyed the town as it spread out before them with satisfaction. "That's pretty much my bottom line. No blood, no death, no sweat."

"It's an elemental life, law enforcement." Phin said.

"Beats mayor."

"Right now, yes."

Wes was quiet for a moment, and then he said, "That Amy is something."

"Go for it," Phin said. "You've got until Sunday." That was a cheering thought, that the Dempseys would be gone that soon. "Maybe once they're gone, Stephen will give up on this porn thing."

"I wouldn't underestimate him," Wes said. "The election's coming up." He slowed and made a U-turn to park in front of the bookstore.

"In two months," Phin said in monotone. "As I keep telling my mother. Plenty of time."

Wes shook his head. "Stephen's determined not to lose this time. It's been twenty years since his father won and made a mess of everything. People forget. He could win if you just sit on the porch and watch the world go by, and I don't even want to think about what could happen then."

Phin felt a real stirring of alarm. "Are you saying I should be campaigning? Okay, we'll put the posters up early."

"I'm saying," Wes said carefully, "that Stephen is standing on years of Garvey defeats. Losing over and over again like that wears on a man's soul. He's obsessed, Phin. I think he'll do damn near anything to win this time, and if he does he'll spend the next two years trying to drag us back to the Stone Age."

Phin got out of the car. "There's irony for you. I've had enough mayor to last me a lifetime, and Stephen wants it bad, and we're both stuck."

"That makes it worse," Wes said. "You don't even want what he craves. And you won't give it to him, either. At least, I hope you won't."

Phin looked down the street to the sandstone-and-marble courthouse. Tuckers did not lose. "Okay, we're watching that movie company, then, since that's where Stephen seems to be going with his latest dumbass legislation. Especially we're watching what's-her-name. Sophie. A woman that tense and devious is going to be trouble for anybody who gets involved with her." Phin thought about her mouth again, and the smile she'd hit him with when she'd decided to snow him. If she ever relaxed, she'd be the kind of woman his father had warned him about, the devil's candy, a woman who'd ruin you as soon as look at you. Phin had been enthusiastic about the idea until he'd run afoul of one.

"You're safe, then," Wes was saying as they went up the steps to the bookstore. "Seeing as you're not getting involved."

Phin nodded as he unlocked the door. "Yeah, but I'm going back with you tomorrow to find out what she's up to with this movie."

"That's what you're going back for, huh?"

"That and to see if Georgia Lutz strangles Clea Whipple when she finds out what Frank's up to." Phin held the door open for Wes.

"Don't even joke about it," Wes said. "We haven't had a murder here for forty years, and I don't want the next one on my watch." He glanced up the street, which was as empty as usual for the dinner hour. "Do you have to get home to Dillie or do you have time for a game?"

"I always have time for a game." Phin motioned him inside. "It's my reason for living."

"I thought that was politics," Wes said as he went in.

"No, that's my mother's reason for living. I live for pool."

"Loose women would be good, too."

Phin thought of Sophie, wound so tight she vibrated. "Yeah, well, if you find any, let me know. In the meantime, we play pool."

Before dinner that night, when the sun had gone down and the air had cooled off a little, Amy made them go out on the porch to talk. She'd grouped what looked like a thousand candles on the porch rails and the upper windowsill near the swing, and Clea reclined on the end that had the candlelight, which was fine by Sophie. She sat in the relative dimness at the other end, listening to the crickets and the soft wash of the river, calming down in the twilight as she swung them back and forth with the tip of her foot. Even the creak of the swing was nice. Maybe all her premonitions had been just funk after all, since the police chief had turned out to be a human being. She tried not to think about the mayor at all. She heard "I Only Want to Be with You" start in the kitchen which meant Amy had put on *The Very Best of Dusty*. That felt right, too.

"Don't you guys ever play anything else?" Clea said.

Sophie shook her head. "Dusty is comfort music," she told Clea. "My mom used to sing along with Dusty every night." She let her head fall back against the swing, sang along softly, and thought of Davy and Amy when they'd all been together, and the last of her tension slipped away.

"Sorry," Clea said. "I didn't meant to sound bitchy. Zane called while you were out in the yard. Doesn't mean I should take it out on you."

Sophie stopped swinging. "Something wrong?"

"I left him. So now he wants to come down here and talk to me about it." Clea rolled her eyes, and Sophie thought, *This is not good.*

Amy came out on the porch with a pitcher of cider and three tall glasses, and smiled at her. "Cider and peach brandy."

"Ooooh," Clea said after her first sip.

"So is Zane coming?" Sophie said as she clutched her glass. "Because we don't need any more people here." Especially angry, semi-famous people. Virginia Garvey would be out like a shot to see her favorite news anchor.

"Who?" Amy said, and Sophie filled her in.

"I told him not to," Clea said. "I already filed for divorce. What he's upset about is the money."

Sophie's tension doubled. "Money?"

"I'm selling the farm," Clea said. "There's a big chunk of land on this side of the highway and this house." She frowned as she looked around. "It doesn't look like much, but Frank says it should bring close to three-quarters of a million."

Sophie sat up. "For this house?"

"No, for the land." Clea pushed the swing, and Sophie slumped against the back so she wouldn't fall off. "My dad sold the biggest part of the farm right after I married Zane five years ago. I inherited almost two million dollars from my dad, and it's gone now." Clea took a deep breath and added, "Zane did something with it in the past six months, spent it, I don't know. We had a big fight about it and that's when I filed. My lawyer says he's going to have to explain in court where that money went. And that's not going to do his career any good at all." She set her jaw. "I want that money back."

"Well, Amy always said—" Sophie looked around for her sister. "Amy?"

Amy had faded off into the darkness of the yard, and Sophie could see her moving in the bushes beside the porch. "What are you doing?"

"Just checking to make sure we put the equipment away." Amy came back on the porch, picked up her drink, and she and Clea began to talk about the video.

"I want the tape to send to L.A." Clea said. "To a producer I know out there, Leo Kingsley."

"That sounds familiar," Amy said to Sophie.

Sophie nodded. "Davy used to work for him. That's how he met Clea." *And then he brought her home to meet the family and she dumped him for Zane.* Sophie took another sip of cider and brandy. She should get over that since Zane had turned out to be enough punishment all by himself. She let her head fall back and listened to Dusty and looked out into the lush green darkness of the trees that separated the house from the river.

"So what about this Frank?" Amy said.

"Frank." Clea didn't sound nearly as excited about Frank as she had earlier in the day. "He called about a month ago, and it made me . . . nostalgic. He said, 'Why don't you come home, we'll talk about the deal here, it'll be just like old times,' and I thought, what a great idea to film for an audition tape—going home, meeting my old high-school flame, sort of a love story/documentary, you know?"

Amy nodded. "How long did you and Frank go together?"

"One night." Clea emptied her glass and reached for the pitcher to pour another. "I, of course, thought it was going to be forever."

"One night?" Sophie thought of Frank: pudgy, badly dressed, and annoying as hell. One night would be plenty.

"I was in love." Clea made it sound like, *I had the plague.* "And he *acted* like he was. And he was so good-looking—"

"Frank was good-looking?" Sophie said.

"It was twenty-four years ago," Amy said. "Shut up and let her talk."

"—and we were doing *Taming of the Shrew* for the senior play,"

Clea was saying. "And you know how it is whei
rehearse and pretend you're in love. Except I real
everything back then."

If Temptation was a place where Frank was jus
was leaving town. Somebody smart, good-lookii
somebody like the damn mayor, that made sense.

"He'd been dating Georgia Funk forever," Clea said. "But on Saturday night, after the cast party, Frank took me out to the Tavern for
a Coke, which, let me tell you, was big stuff. And he parked in the
back which is pretty much Temptation's lovers' lane, and he made his
move, and that's when I lost my virginity." Clea drained her second
glass.

"Ouch," Sophie said.

"He promised me he was through with Georgia," Clea said. "But
when I got to school on Monday, she was wearing this tiny chip of an
engagement ring."

"Maybe we could film a murder mystery," Amy said.

"He said she was pregnant," Clea said, "and they got married fast
enough. And then eleven months later, sure enough, she had a baby."
Clea reached for the pitcher again, and Sophie held out her glass.

"So she lied or he lied," Amy said.

"She lied," Clea said, as she poured Sophie's cider. "Their wedding
picture was in the paper. You've never seen a more miserable-looking
groom." She took a sip from her glass and then topped it up from the
pitcher. "And that's how I lost my virginity and went to Hollywood to
become a movie star." She laughed, but she looked grim, even in the
candlelight.

"Does anybody ever have a good losing-my-virginity story?" Amy
said. "I lost mine to Darrin Sunderland after the homecoming game my
junior year, and it was lousy." She sipped her cider and brightened.
"Fortunately, sex got better."

"It was pretty good with Frank," Clea said. "I mean, the sex wasn't
wonderful, but he was nice to me. And really grateful."

"Darrin was too drunk to be grateful," Amy said. "Which taught me

st lesson about sex: They have to be sober. It's one of the 'Classic
nders,' right up there with 'never get involved in a land war in
Asia.'"

"My first lesson was not to believe anything a guy tells you when
he wants it," Clea said. "The best guy I was ever with was a crook, so
that tells you about my taste in men."

"You didn't know Zane was a crook," Sophie said.

"No, Zane's a mistake," Clea said. "*Davy's* a crook." When Sophie
sat up fast and rocked the swing, she added, "And you know it, so
don't even try to defend him. I know you love him, but he's as crooked
as everybody else in your family tree."

"Excuse me?" Sophie said, ice in her voice.

"Except for you and Amy," Clea said. "And sometimes I have my
doubts about Amy."

"Everybody does," Amy said cheerfully.

"But I have no doubts about you, Sophie," Clea went on. "You'll
never do anything wrong. I've never met anybody as straight as you. I
bet you even lost your virginity well. Elegantly, with no trauma." She
toasted Sophie with her glass. "I bet you didn't even get your clothes
mussed."

"I lost it to Chad Berwick in Iowa, one month before school was
out, my junior year," Sophie said, trying to keep her voice even so she
wouldn't spit on Clea. "I thought I'd con him into taking me to prom
because I wanted to be 'in' just once, and nobody was more in than
Chad. Except it was awful, and when I got to school on Monday, everybody knew. And when I went to the cafeteria at lunchtime, his best
friend came up and stuck his finger in the pie on my tray and scooped
out this big, gloppy cherry and said, 'Heard you lost this, Sophie.' And
then everybody laughed." Sophie kept her voice flat, but she felt sick
all over again as the memory came back; smelled the bread-and-butter
smell in the cafeteria, saw the gray linoleum floor and turquoise wall
panels, and heard the smothered laughter.

After a minute, Amy said, "Jeez."

"I knew better," Sophie said, trying to sound offhanded. "Mama
warned me about the town boys. They had to be nice to the girls they

knew, so they'd go after the outsiders like me instead. And then I thought I'd be so smart, trick this town boy into taking me to prom." She shook her head. "Clearly *not* my father's daughter. Can't even run a decent con."

"I didn't know," Amy said, sounding miserable for her.

"You were ten," Sophie said. "I didn't feel like sharing. But I did make Dad leave us in the next town we stopped in so you and Davy could finish growing up in one place. And by the time you were a high-school junior, you belonged." She smiled at Amy to reassure her. "To the wrong crowd, of course, because you're a Dempsey, but still."

"And then I ended up with Darrin Sunderland," Amy said.

"I can't do everything," Sophie said. "You have to pick your own guys."

"Well, that explains why you were so cold to Phin Tucker," Clea said.

Sophie frowned at her. "What?"

"Town boy." Clea gestured with her glass. "The high-class town boy to end all town boys. You're making him pay for Chet Whosis."

"Chad," Sophie said, thinking of Phin Tucker and his perfect face and perfect body. "Chad was tall and blond, but that was it. The mayor doesn't look anything at all like him."

"Doesn't matter," Clea said. "Frank's still the guy I lost, and any town boy is going to be the guy who fucked you over. That's history. It keeps repeating on you."

"So you're making this film to get Frank back?" Sophie said, trying to get the conversation off town boys and Phin Tucker.

"No." Clea shuddered. "Did you see him today? What a fathead he grew up to be."

"We noticed." Amy sounded a lot more concerned than the occasion warranted. "You still want to do the video, right?"

Clea nodded. "All I need is film that shows I'm still bankable." "When I talked to Leo, he sounded interested because he has this sequel he wants to make, but I don't want to do that."

"He wants to make a sequel to *Always Tomorrow*?" Amy asked doubtfully.

"I thought you were dead at the end of *Always Tomorrow*," Sophie said.

"Not *Always Tomorrow*," Clea said. "Look, all you guys need to do is make me look good on tape."

"That's not hard," Amy said. "As long as we get the light right, you still look great."

"Thanks," Clea said, as if she wasn't sure that was a compliment.

"And I'm still up for murder," Amy said. "Although I think Chet in Iowa deserves it more. Maybe we could go on a spree. We knock off Frank, and then on the way to Iowa to kill Chet, we find Darrin and break his kneecaps." She stopped, caught by a thought. "You know, that would make a great movie."

"Chad, not Chet," Sophie said. "And that was fifteen years ago. I'm over it."

"You're never really over it." Clea looked out into the night. "You just learn to live with it." She sighed. "Don't you wish you knew then what you know now? Don't you wish you could go back and fix it?"

"I'm not sure I'd know what to say even now," Sophie said. " 'Get your finger out of my pie' doesn't seem enough."

"How about 'Yes, and he was lousy'?" Amy said. "You could at least make sure Chet didn't get any more."

"Chad," Sophie said. "It's all right. Really. *I'm over it.*"

"And what would you do if Chad showed up in the path of your speeding car?" Clea asked.

"I'd run him down like the dog he was," Sophie said. "And his little best friend, too."

"Well, don't get confused and go after the mayor instead," Amy said. "At least not until the video is done."

"I won't do anything to the mayor." Sophie thought of him as she said it, so carelessly confident that he was barely conscious. She found herself gritting her teeth, so she relaxed her jaw, took a deep breath and added, "No matter how appealing that might be."

While Sophie was drinking cider punch, Phin had gone home to his mother's brick house on the Hill and found his little blonde daughter waiting for him on the spacious, empty porch, her hands on her non-existent hips.

"You're very late," Dillie told him in her precise, Tucker voice as he climbed the white stone steps. "Dinner is waiting."

"I apologize," he said. "Did you take your vitamin today?"

Dillie sighed with the exaggerated patience of a nine-year-old. "Yes. A Wilma. Jamie Barclay doesn't have to take vitamins."

"Jamie Barclay is going to be sorry about that someday." He kissed her on the top of her head and let his cheek stay there for a minute before he said, "Who is Jamie Barclay?"

"Jamie Barclay moved in two houses down across the street on Monday. Jamie Barclay gets to walk lots of places alone. I'm old enough to do that. I could walk from here to the bookstore by myself." Dill stuck her chin out, and her long pale hair fell away from her odd little pointed face.

"Don't even think about it."

"Well, when *can* I walk by myself?"

"When you get your driver's license."

"You always, always say that." Dillie scowled at him. "That's when *everything* happens."

"It's going to be a busy day," Phin agreed. Since he wasn't planning on letting her get her license until she was twenty-one, he wasn't worried.

"Well, I already know about babies so we won't have to do that," Dillie said. "Grandma told me some stuff a long time ago, but then Jamie Barclay told me a lot more today."

Phin bent down to look at her. "Is Jamie Barclay a boy or a girl?"

"A girl." Her voice was full of admiration. "She knows *a lot.*"

"Wonderful." Phin straightened again. "I thought I told you not to talk to strangers. And she's probably wrong, so don't worry about it."

"Okay. I have an idea," Dillie said, switching gears on him. "A *good* idea."

"Okay," Phin said cautiously. The Tucker porch didn't have any chairs because the Hill was not the kind of place where people sat on their front porches and chatted, so he sat down on the top step, and

Dillie sat down beside him, a featherweight in a white T-shirt and tan shorts.

"I was thinking," Dillie said, "that you and I could go live over the bookstore. Where you used to live."

"Dill, there's only one room that's livable up there. The rest is storage. We couldn't get all your stuff in there, let alone mine."

"I could get rid of some of my stuff." Dillie stuck her chin out nobly.

"That would be tragic."

Dillie shifted in her chair. "It could be just us. We could be . . ." She stared into space, searching for the right word, narrowing her gray eyes and pursing the cupid's-bow mouth she'd inherited from her mother, and Phin felt the instinctive parental ache that still took him by surprise after nine years: *How was I lucky enough to get this child, and how can I ever keep her safe enough?* He hadn't wanted to get married, he hadn't wanted a baby, and he sure as hell hadn't wanted to be a single father. And now he couldn't imagine life without her.

"We could be *private*," Dillie said finally.

"We're not cramped here," Phin pointed out. "There are fourteen rooms. It's a wonder we don't lose each other."

"We have to be with Grandma Liz all the time," Dillie said. "I really love Grandma Liz but I would like it to be just us family. If it was just us, we could have hot dogs. And paper napkins. And dessert when it's not the weekend." She put her hand on his arm, and said, "Please?" looking up at him with intense gray eyes, and he looked down to see a smear of purple on his shirt sleeve.

"Blackberry?" he said.

Dillie pulled her hand back. "Grape. I had toast 'cause you were late." She turned her hand to look at the jam-smeared edge of it. "It was goopy."

"So it was." Phin handed her his handkerchief. "Paper napkins, huh?" This wasn't one of Phin's priorities, but if it had come to loom large in his daughter's life, it had to be dealt with.

"That's just an example." Dillie licked her hand to dissolve some of the jam and then scrubbed at it with Phin's handkerchief.

Phin sat back and considered the situation. It had made sense to move in with his mother when Dillie was born because somebody had to take care of the baby. But Dillie wasn't a baby anymore. And it must have taken a lot for his preternaturally polite daughter to say, "I want out."

They could rent a house, he supposed, but since he owned the house by the river his mother-in-law lived in, and the bookstore house, and Liz had this semimansion on the Hill, it seemed like a waste of money. And if he and Dillie moved, who'd take care of her during the day while he ran the bookstore? She'd end up back here on the Hill with Liz anyway, which was the way his mother wanted it. "She'll be a Tucker," she'd told Phin when he'd brought the baby home from the hospital. "Leave everything to me."

Thinking about it now, he could see Dillie's point. Being a Tucker was often a pain in the ass.

"Compromise," he said, and Dillie sighed. "How about if we stay at the bookstore one night a week? Like a sleepover. We'll have hot dogs and dessert and no napkins. And we can try to put the overstock into two rooms instead of three so you can have your own room."

Dillie tilted her head, considering it, looking pensive and delicate in the evening light. Phin knew she was a tough little kid, he'd seen her on the softball field, but still her thinness shook him. "You looked just like that when you were her age," Liz had told him. "You were six foot at fourteen and didn't stop then. She'll fill out when the time comes."

"How about," Dillie said in her patient, measured voice, "if we try that for a little while and then if I'm good, we always stay there?"

"How about you take what you can get?"

Dillie exhaled. "It needs to be just us."

"Why?"

"Because I need a mom."

Phin went very still. "A mom."

"Jamie Barclay has a mom. Jamie Barclay said her mom said I needed a mom, too."

"Jamie Barclay's mom is wrong," Phin said grimly.

"I don't think so." Dillie's voice was thoughtful. "I think I need one. I think I'd like it. But I don't think I want my mom to be Rachel."

"Rachel?" Phin's temper flared. "Who—"

"Grandma Liz says Rachel is just like a mom when she baby-sits me," Dillie said. "And Rachel's mom keeps saying maybe someday she'll be my grandma and won't that be nice. But I don't think Rachel's *practical* enough to be my mom. And I really don't want her mom to be my grandma because her mom is mean to Grandma Junie all the time." She fell into her maternal grandmother's southern Ohio drawl as she added, "She's just *naasty.*"

"Rachel's not going to be your mom," Phin said. "You can stop worrying."

"Well, I don't know." Dillie sighed and straightened. "That's what Grandma Liz wants, and if we stay here, that's what'll happen because we always end up with what she wants."

"Trust me, Dill," Phin said. "There's not a chance in hell that Rachel will be your mom." He heard his mother call, "Dillie?" and he raised his voice and called back, "We're out front."

Liz came around the house from her garden, her gloved fist clenching blue-violet roses, her pale hair refusing to move in the summer breeze. The Tuckers did not let nature push them around. "Why are you sitting out here?"

"Because it's nice," Phin said. "What did you want to talk to me about?"

Liz stopped at the foot of the steps. "I want you to spend more time with Stephen Garvey instead of turning your back on him and rushing off like that. You'll never build a consensus giving him the cold shoulder."

"I don't want to build a consensus, I want to run a bookstore," Phin said. Dillie poked him and he added, "And eat hot dogs with my kid. Dillie and I are going to have a sleepover at the store tomorrow night."

"What?" Liz frowned at them both, two ridiculous children. "She can't. Her piano lesson is at six and then there's dinner, and she has to be in bed at eight-thirty. There's no point in her sleeping there."

"Friday, then," Phin said.

"Ballet," Liz said. "I don't understand this at all."

"What night don't you have a lesson?" Phin said to Dillie.

"Mondays," Dillie said glumly.

"That's the only night?" Phin turned back to Liz. "When did that happen?"

"You stay at the bookstore past six most nights," Liz pointed out. "She's not missing quality time with you. And we want her to be well-rounded."

Phin looked down at his angular little girl. "She's rounded enough. We're staying at the bookstore on Monday."

"That's the first day of school so it would be impractical—"

Dillie looked at him anxiously and he broke in. "We like impractical. Dillie and I live on the edge."

Dillie beamed at him, joy radiating from every cell in her body, and he thought, *I have to spend more time with this kid. She's the best.*

Behind Dillie, Liz opened her mouth again and Phin met her eyes. "Monday we stay there."

"Very well," Liz said, clearly thinking it wasn't. "Just for this Monday, though. We have to be practical about school nights. Come on, Dillie, let's go get changed for dinner."

Dillie took one yearning look back at him, which would have wrenched his heart if he hadn't known what an actress she was. "All right," she said plaintively, and took her grandmother's hand, dragging her feet as she went up the stone steps.

"For heaven's sake, Dillie," Liz said, and Phin laughed.

Dillie jerked her head up and grinned at him, pure kid again, and then she went inside with her grandmother to go without dessert because it was a weeknight.

Diane would have given her dessert for breakfast, he thought, and then stopped, surprised that he'd thought of Diane at all. They'd been together for so short a time, he wasn't sure he could remember what she'd looked like. Round, he remembered, because that was what had gotten him into trouble in the first place. That, and she'd been so warm. Warmth had been in short supply at the Tuckers', especially when he'd come home to help his mother cope with his father's second heart attack and his father cope with his own mortality.

Then one night he'd gone to the Tavern to get away from all the manufactured optimism at home, and Diane had sat down beside him. "So you're Phin Tucker," she'd said. "Heard about you." He closed his eyes and tried to call up her face, guilty that he'd cared so little for her that he couldn't even get that back. Warm brown eyes, he remembered, and dark tumbling hair, and that cupid's-bow smile that Dillie could use to twist him around her little finger. He tried hard to put the features together, but instead of Diane, he saw Sophie Dempsey, who didn't look like Diane at all, her brown eyes wary and her dark hair twisted in that tense curly knot on top of her head. And her mouth was full and lush, not bowed like Diane's—

He felt a flush of heat thinking about her mouth and stood up, wondering what the hell was wrong with him that he could forget the woman who'd given him a daughter and get hot for a woman he didn't know and didn't like.

"Dad, *dinner,*" Dillie said from the doorway behind him, and he went inside, dropping another kiss on the top of her head when he reached her.

"You are my favorite woman in the whole world," he told her, and she said, "I know," and led him into his mother's immaculate, air-conditioned, dessert-free dining room.

Three

On Thursday morning, Rachel Garvey went out to the Whipple farm, a woman on a mission: She had to get out of Temptation before she went crazy and became her mother.

Her plan was simple; she was going to offer Clea Whipple her services on the movie, and then she'd make herself indispensable, so that when Clea left, she'd take Rachel with her. Her mother was always telling her what a treasure she was, so now she'd be Clea's treasure. Rachel felt no guilt at all about deserting her mother. Her two older sisters were still in town and they could be treasures after she was gone. It was way past time for their turns anyway.

When she pulled up to the porch, Clea was sitting on the top step, beautiful in the sunlight. More than beautiful. Drop-dead, sky-eyed, magnolia-skinned beautiful. So when Clea said, "Hello?" in a voice that sounded like music, Rachel said, "God, I've never seen anybody as gorgeous as you."

Clea smiled and became more gorgeous.

Good start, Rachel thought, and went toward her. "I'm Rachel Garvey," she began, holding out her hand. "And I was thinking maybe you could use—"

"Garvey?" Clea lost her smile. "Any relation to Stephen Garvey?"

"I'm his daughter," Rachel said. "Um, I came out to see if you could use some help."

Clea shook her head, but before she could say anything, the screen door slammed, and Rachel looked up to see a redhead in tight jeans and a pink T-shirt knotted above her belly button.

"Hi." The redhead looked at Rachel with naked curiosity. "I'm Amy."

"I'm Rachel. I came out to help." Rachel held out her hand and then noticed that the redhead's hands were full of paint scrapers. "You're painting?" she said, hope rising.

Amy jerked her head to the right side of the porch. "Just the porch wall white for a background." She handed one of the scrapers to Clea, who looked at it as if she'd never seen one before.

"No," Rachel said. "First of all, the paint's almost off that wood, so it's going to suck up the first six coats of white paint you put on. You need a coat of primer."

"Oh." Amy squinted at her. "Listen, we don't want this to be a *good* paint job, we just want a nice background."

"Then you don't want white, either. White isn't very flattering." Rachel smiled sweetly at Clea. "You want something warm that will bounce color back at you."

"She's right." Clea reexamined Rachel, head to toe, and Rachel stood with her smile fixed, thinking, *I don't like you, but if you take me to Hollywood, I'll learn to deal with you.*

"So what do you suggest?" Amy sounded wary, and Rachel turned back to her, figuring she'd be easier to charm, anyway.

"I can get you a great deal on some peach paint," she told Amy. "We ordered a lot for a project that got changed in the middle. I'll get it for you at cost, and I'll help you for free. I just want to learn to do what you're doing." Rachel smiled up at Amy again, grateful Amy was on the top step so it was easier for Rachel to look small and innocent and appealing.

"You're hired," Amy said, and handed her the other scraper.

Rachel handed it back, sure of herself now. "You scrape, I'll go get the paint." She turned to go before Amy could argue, and Amy called, "Wait, do you need money?"

"Oh, no," Rachel said. "I'll set up an account for you at the store."

"Fantastic," Amy said.

"That would be Garvey's Hardware, right?" Clea said deliberately.

"What?" Amy said, and Rachel waved and left, determined to be such a treasure that Amy wouldn't dream of letting her go.

The peach paint turned out to be too dark for the porch, but mixed half-and-half with the white Rachel had brought, it was perfect, so pale it was more blush than peach. Rachel primed the wall, and while Amy and Clea talked out in the yard about reflectors and camera angles, she listened and learned and began to paint the porch rail. Peach for the posts and rails, blush for the spindles, white for the detailing.

"Wow," Amy said when she came up to the porch at noon. "That looks good. It's even pretty."

"Thanks," Rachel said, but she watched Clea closer because Clea was frowning.

"We should do the whole house," Clea said finally, and Amy said, "No, we should not. Are you nuts?"

"This film is a business expense," Clea told her. "Tax-deductible. This paint therefore becomes part of that business expense. And I want to sell this house." She nodded to Rachel. "Do the whole house."

"No," Rachel said. "We can do the whole front porch if you want to film on both sides, that won't take long. But I do not paint whole houses. I can call the Coreys for you, though. They'll paint anything."

"Are they expensive?" Clea said.

"It's a tax deduction," Rachel said.

"Let me think about it." Clea walked out to the edge of the yard to see the porch from a distance.

Rachel turned back to find Amy grinning at her. "I like you, kid," Amy said. "You remind me of me."

The screen door banged again and a brunette came out, saying, "If you want lunch—" She stopped when she saw Rachel, and Amy rushed to fill in the silence, saying, "This is my sister, Sophie," to Rachel, explaining Rachel's ideas and the paint to Sophie, all without ever mentioning the name Garvey.

Sophie smiled politely at Rachel. "Well, it's nice of you to offer to help, Rachel, but—"

Rachel went tense, but Amy said, "Wait a minute. Come here."

Amy towed her sister out into the yard, and Rachel thought she'd never seen two more different women in her life, Amy in tight pink and Sophie in loose khaki. Then Amy turned Sophie around and said, "Look at the porch."

Sophie folded her arms and studied the porch, and Amy did the same beside her, just like her big sister, and that's when Rachel saw how alike they were. Same big brown eyes, same curly hair, same full mouth, same incredible concentration, even the same white Keds, although Amy's had pink shoelaces and were painted with gold spirals. They stood close, leaning into each other a little, and Rachel was struck by how together they were. She'd never stood that close to her sisters, ever, but Sophie and Amy were a team.

"You think?" Sophie said.

"I think," Amy said.

"Your call," Sophie said. "The color is wonderful."

"Just one thing," Amy said. "Her last name is Garvey."

Sophie started and Rachel thought, *That's it.*

"Give her a chance," Amy said. "Why should she pay for her father's crimes?"

"Hey." Sophie stepped back. "Don't pull that on me."

"I'll work really hard," Rachel said from the porch.

Sophie came toward her. "I know you will, honey." She looked at the painted porch rail, gleaming warm in the sunlight, then nodded. "Come have lunch with us. Then you can paint the porch wall this afternoon and help Amy with whatever she needs. But if your father shows up, you're fired."

Rachel relaxed as relief flooded through her. "He won't ever know. And I'll be a huge help, you wait and see. I'll make things so much easier for you."

But after lunch, in spite of Rachel's best intentions, things got difficult because Rob Lutz showed up with his parents. Clea almost had a heart attack when she saw Rob, and Rachel could understand why, since it was hard to see he was a moron when you looked at that face. That was how Rob had talked Rachel out of her virginity, by not talking, just by smiling at her with that face. There was a lesson learned, for sure.

Clea had said, "This is *your son?*" to Rob's dad, Frank, and Frank had grinned down at her like a dork, standing really, really close to her. That made Rob's mom, Georgia, mad, which Rachel could also understand except that if she'd been married to Frank, she'd have been *looking* for somebody to take him away. Then Clea put her arm around Georgia and called, "Sophie, meet Georgia."

Georgia squinted at the porch where Rachel and Sophie and Amy were standing, and she looked about twenty years older than Clea, probably because she'd been baking her skin into shoe leather all her life so she could be a Coppertone Blonde. That was what she'd said to Rachel every summer since Rachel had started dating Rob: "Come on and lay out with me, honey, and we'll be Coppertone Blondes. People will think we're sisters."*Right.*

Then Clea said, "Georgia and I graduated together, Sophie! Isn't that something?" and Sophie said, "And neither one of you has aged a day," and glared at Clea to make her behave, and Rachel liked her more.

Clea just laughed and called back to Rob, "Why don't you come up on the porch?" and that must have been the first time Sophie saw him because she said, "Oh, Lord."

"What?" Amy said.

"Look at the way he's looking at Clea," Sophie said.

Amy nodded. "Like she's whipped cream and he has a spoon."

Well, that was Rob for you. Always looking for sex. Rachel didn't know if sex in general was bad or it was just bad with Rob, but as far as she was concerned, Clea could have him.

Sophie moved to the top of the steps and called, "Come on up to the porch, we have lemonade," and when she had Clea, Frank, and

Georgia settled on the right side of the porch with a warning to stay away from the blush-painted wall, Amy began to shoot.

Rachel handed Rob a scraper and said, "We need to scrape the other side of the porch," and Rob said, "Cool." As he worked, he kept his eyes on Clea, who sat perched on the porch rail looking adorable. Clea watched Rob from the corner of her eye while Frank sat opposite her, laughing and flirting, and Georgia sat between them on the porch swing, looking like a Coppertone Toad.

Sophie had gone out into the yard to talk to Amy, and she looked concerned. Even after a few short hours, Rachel knew Sophie liked things calm and organized. So when Phin Tucker walked up behind her and said something, and she jumped a mile, Rachel could have told him that was a bad move. He and Wes had parked behind the Lutz's van, and Wes had said something to Amy and gone in the house, but Phin went to Sophie and stayed. So he wanted something—three guesses what—but he was doing it all wrong. Well, he'd figure it out. Phin got everything he wanted sooner or later.

"Hey," Rob said behind her. "Get busy."

"Right," Rachel said, and crossed her fingers that Phin would do his usual good work.

Her future depended on it.

"I'm a little worried about Clea," the mayor had said to Sophie out in the yard. "I had nine stitches because of her. She could put Frank in the hospital."

Sophie watched Frank making a fool of himself on the porch in front of his wife, who looked homicidal. "Clea's not the only one who could hurt him." She turned back to the mayor. "How did she give you nine stitches?"

"I looked down her blouse and fell off my bike."

Sophie looked at him with contempt and he said, "Hey, I was twelve. She leaned over. Not my fault."

He was as immaculately handsome as ever in the sunlight, and it was even more annoying now that she knew he'd been a pervert at twelve. She started to tell him so and decided she didn't want to get personal, she just wanted to get rid of him. "Did you say you wanted to look at the electricity?"

"No," he said. "I said Amy wanted me to look at the electricity."

"Right this way," Sophie said, leaving Amy to handle the mess on the porch. Five minutes later, she was in the dark farmhouse basement, wishing she was back on the porch. At least in the sunlight she could see what the mayor was up to. "Uh, what are we doing, Mr. Tucker?"

"Phin," he said. "And this is your fuse box. We're looking at it to see if it's going to burn your house down."

"Where are the little switches?" Sophie squinted around his shoulder in the dim light. She'd expected to get a whiff of some expensive cologne as she leaned closer, but instead he smelled of soap and sun, clean, and she swallowed and concentrated on the fuse box.

There were no switches, just little round things that looked sinister.

"Switches would be circuit breakers." Phin said. "For which you need circuits not fuses. This is the old way."

"Is this better?"

"No. But it's more exciting."

"I don't want exciting." Sophie took a step back. "I want functioning, nonshocking, neat little switches. I've always depended on the kindness of strangers. You do it."

"That's the problem with you city folk. No sense of adventure. Let me explain how this works."

"No," Sophie said firmly. "I don't want to know. I want switches. I know how they work."

"You can't have switches. Get over it."

Sophie shook her head. "I've heard about these things. You stick pennies in them, and they shock you."

"You do not put pennies in them." He sounded as if he were trying not to laugh. "If you put pennies in them, you deserve to be shocked. Not to mention have the house burn down. Do not put pennies in them."

"Not a problem. I'm not going near that thing." Sophie started up the stairs. "Thank you very much, but no." When she realized he wasn't following her, she stopped. "You can come up now. The electricity lesson is over."

He grinned at her in the light that filtered down the stairs from the kitchen. "Quitter," he said, and her pulse skipped a little at the challenge in his voice.

"Only on the stuff that will get me electrocuted," she told him. "I believe in safety first." She escaped back up the stairs and put on *Dusty in Memphis* to calm her nerves.

Phin followed a few minutes later.

"They're all working," he told her, washing his hands at the sink. "If you have trouble, yell, and Wes or I will come out and fix it."

Sophie blinked at him. "That's extremely nice of you."

"We're extremely nice people." Phin smiled at her, and Sophie had a brief moment where she thought he might be a good guy after all before he said, "So tell me about this movie," and she took a step back.

"I told you, it's just an audition tape," she said. "It was Clea's idea, and she hired us because we did such a good job filming her wedding. Amy's shooting it on the porch because it's easier to light." Even as she said it, the lights in the kitchen went out, and she heard Amy out on the porch say, "Oh, *damn*."

"If there was a switch," Sophie said, "I could go throw it now."

"But there's a fuse instead." Phin pointed at the basement door. "So you can go replace it. Like an adventurous adult."

"Not in this lifetime," Sophie said, and Phin sighed and went downstairs, shortly after which the porch lights evidently came back on because Amy called, "Thank you!"

"You do very nice work," she told him when he came back upstairs, trying to be nice since he wasn't Chad. Exactly. "For that, you get lemonade."

"You know, a little adventure in your life wouldn't kill you," he said as he sat at the table. "Especially if it's just replacing a fuse."

"I had enough adventure as a child," Sophie said firmly as she poured. "I'm having a staid adulthood to make up for it."

"That's a waste," Phin said. "Do you make staid movies, too?"

Sophie slapped a glass of lemonade down in front of him so that some of it slopped out on the table. "What is it with you and this movie?"

"What is it with you and this hostility?" He got up and pulled a paper towel off the roll by the sink and mopped up the spill. "You've been tense from the minute I said hello."

"It was the way you said it," Sophie said. "And I've told you. The movie is a short, improvised film for Clea which Clea asked us to do because she likes Amy's work."

"Not your work?" Phin sat down and sipped his lemonade. "This is very good. Thank you."

"Don't patronize me, just drink it," Sophie said. "Clea wants Amy because I don't do improvised. I shoot all the necessary parts of the wedding and manage the business, and Amy gets the weird stuff around the edges and cuts the video. She's the artist."

" 'Weird stuff'?" Phin said.

Sophie folded her arms and leaned against the sink. "People can get the stuff I shoot from any video company, but they can't get the stuff that Amy finds. But if they only got what Amy shoots, they'd be mad because people like things like their vows in their wedding videos. So we work together."

"And why is Clea making this video?"

Sophie scowled at him. "Why do you care so much about this movie?"

"As long as you're out of here before Wednesday, I don't."

"Well, we're out of here on Sunday."

"Fine," Phin said. "And I wasn't patronizing you, the lemonade really is good."

"Thank you," Sophie said, feeling slightly anticlimactic.

"And for whatever I did in a former life to make you so damn mad, I apologize." Phin smiled at her, clearly used to charming everyone in his path. "Now, will you please stop spitting at me?"

"Considering that former life, an apology is not nearly enough. 'My name is Inigo Montoya' on this one."

"Who?" Phin said.

Sophie picked up the pitcher and said, "Lemonade?"—sounding more threatening than she meant to.

Phin pushed his glass back. "No, I've had enough, thank you."

He got up and went back to the porch, and Sophie felt a little guilty for taking her frustrations out on him. She put his lemonade glass in the sink and went out onto the low, wide, back porch to calm her nerves. If she could get just get rid of that constant feeling that something awful was bearing down on her—

Something furry brushed her leg and she looked down and screamed.

There was an animal there—a big one, it came halfway up to her knee—and it had matted red-brown fur on its barrel-like body and short white legs with little black spots on them, and Sophie had never seen anything like it in her life. It was crouched now that she'd screamed, in the attack position she was sure, and when it moved, she leaped back against the wall of the house and screamed again.

Phin slammed the screen door open as he came out onto the porch. "What?" he said, and Sophie pointed down. He let his shoulders slump. "You're kidding. You scream like that for a dog?"

That's a dog? "They bite," Sophie said in her own defense. It seemed feasible.

"Some do," Phin said. "This one appears not to."

Sophie followed his eyes down to the dog, which had rolled over on its back with its four stumpy white legs in the air. "It looks weird."

"It's built like a Welsh corgi." Phin craned his head sideways to get a better look at the prostrate animal. "And a few other things mixed in to keep it interesting." He squinted at it. "God knows where the black spots came from. It's probably a highway dog."

"A highway dog." Sophie looked down at the dog, which was now looking up at them from its back. It was splashed with mud and quivering, possibly the ugliest living thing Sophie had ever seen. Its huge, black-ringed brown eyes stared at her pathetically, and she felt bad for thinking it was ugly.

But dear Lord, it was.

"People dump the dogs they don't want along the highway," Phin said, a thread of anger in his voice, neatly repressed like everything else about him. "They think the dogs will be free and wild, but most of them get hit right away, looking for their owners' cars."

"That's terrible." Sophie stared down at the dog, outraged, and the dog stared up at her, upside down with those huge, melting brown eyes, comic and pathetic. "Is it hungry?"

"Probably, but if you feed it, you'll never get rid of it."

But there were those eyes. Sophie watched the dog for a minute while it watched her back, still upside down, and then she went into the kitchen to get some ham.

Five minutes later, Sophie was sitting on the back-porch steps, cautiously feeding ham to the grateful dog. "I never had a dog," she told Phin.

"We always did." Phin leaned against the porch post. "My dad never turned a highway dog away. If we had too many, he found homes for the ones we couldn't keep."

Sophie held out another piece of ham, and the dog took it gently. It looked up at her with the ham dangling from its mouth like an extra tongue, and she laughed because it looked so funny and sweet with its brown snout and black-ringed eyes. "Too much mascara, dog," she told it, and the dog opened its mouth and barked at her, dropping the ham. "Goofus," she said, and fed it again while the dog looked at her adoringly, completely ignoring Phin. Sophie held out another piece of ham.

"That dog's a real politician," Phin said. "Goes right to the pork barrel and hunkers down."

"Maybe I could keep him a couple of days, until we leave."

"Sure," he said. "Just don't name it. That's always fatal."

"Okay," Sophie said. "Here, dog, have some more ham."

Phin's voice was casual when he spoke again. "So do you take care of the whole world, or just dogs and Amy?"

"Just Amy and my brother." Sophie fed the dog again.

"And who takes care of you?" Phin said, and Sophie looked up, startled. "You're here because Amy and Clea want to do the video, and you're feeding ham to a dog you're not sure you like. Who takes care of you? When do you get what you want?"

"I take care of me," she said, scowling at him. "I take very good care of me, and I always get what I want." *Back off, buddy.*

"Of course you do." Phin straightened. "Lots of luck with the dog."

He went back to the front porch, and Sophie felt guilty for driving him away again, but then the dog nudged her hand with his nose, and she went back to feeding him. When the last of the ham was gone, Sophie patted the dog gingerly on the top of the head and the dog looked at her as if to say, *You're new at this, aren't you?* "I never had a dog," Sophie told it, and it sighed and settled in next to her, smearing mud on her khaki shorts. She patted it again and then went back into the kitchen and opened her PowerBook to block out a plan for the video now that the Lutzes were creating some story conflict on the front porch. The dog sat outside the screen door and watched her, and she sat behind her PowerBook and watched it back.

She couldn't remember ever having wanted a dog. It would have been impossible on the road anyway; the last thing she and her mother had needed was something else to take care of. And then she'd been stuck in that little apartment at seventeen, trying to raise Davy and Amy, and a dog was *really* the last thing she'd needed.

But there was something in the patient way this dog looked through the screen door at her, not trying to get in, just watching her. From the outside.

It rolled over on its back outside the screen door so all she could see was four stubby white feet pointed to the sky. "Okay," Sophie said, and let him in. "But you're covered with mud, so don't get on the furniture or anything." The dog sighed and lay down at her feet, and when Amy called her name and she went out to the front yard, it followed her.

Amy was standing behind the camera, talking to Phin, but she stopped when she saw Sophie coming. "We've got a problem," she said as Sophie got close, and then she saw the dog. "Cool. A dog." She looked at it more closely. "I think."

The screen door slammed as Wes came out. "You now have a new bathroom showerhead," he said to Amy as he came down the steps. "But the shower drain still needs work. I'll come back tomorrow."

"Oh, well—" Sophie began, but Amy said, "Fantastic."

"Your guests need work, too," Phin said, and Sophie turned to look at the porch, where the Lutzes were having one of those intense, whispered conversations that married people have before they kill each other.

"Yeah, that's the problem I called you out here for," Amy said to Sophie. "We may have pushed this too far."

"I'm blaming this on you," Phin said. "Before you got here, they only did this when they'd had too much to drink."

"Good," Sophie said. "Now they're out in the open. We're clearing the hypocrisy out of Temptation."

"A little hypocrisy never hurt anyone," Phin said.

"So were you born a politician?" Sophie started off for the porch. "Or did you have to work to achieve this level of immorality?"

"Oh, I was born to it," Phin said, sounding a little grim.

Sophie went up the porch steps to the Lutzes, with the dog at her heels. "We were so grateful that you were helping us with the filming that we forgot to feed you. Can I make you a sandwich?"

"Oh." Georgia straightened a little. "Oh, no, we have to be going anyway. But how nice of you to offer."

"Well, we're supposed to cater to the talent." Sophie smiled at her, and Georgia flushed with pleasure and smiled back.

"That's a good one." Frank looked at his wife with contempt.

"Amy says you both looked great on camera," Sophie lied. "Maybe you can come back out tomorrow."

"You bet." Frank perked up, and even Georgia began to look less fried around the edges.

"We'll do anything we can to help." Georgia looked at Sophie with unqualified approval. "And maybe you can use Rob, too."

Sophie looked into the yard to the minivan, where Clea was laughing up at a dazzled Rob. "I'm sure we'll be using him," she said flatly.

"That was kind of you," Phin said, when the Lutzes had gone and Sophie was sitting on the porch steps with the dog at her side surveying the yard as if it belonged there, its mascaraed eyes half-lidded in complacency.

"I'm a kind person," Sophie said, her chin in the air.

"You know, all evidence to the contrary, I think you are." He leaned over to pat the dog, his face was close to hers, and Sophie's pulse kicked up. "What I can't figure out is why you're so damn nervous."

"I've been under a lot of stress." Sophie scooted up a step, and the dog climbed to stay with her. "And I come from a very tense family." She thought about her father and Davy and Amy, all of them absolutely nerveless, and honesty made her add, "Well, some of the Dempsey women have been high-strung."

"A weekend in the country should take care of that," Phin said, still watching her as he scratched the dog behind the ear. "There's nothing stressful in Temptation."

Just you, Sophie thought, and he grinned at her as if he'd read her mind.

"Nice seeing you, Sophie Dempsey," he said, and straightened to go out to the car where Wes was waiting for him.

"Same to you," Sophie said, as her pulse slowed again. "And if I don't see you again, thanks for all your help."

"Oh, you'll see me again," Phin said without turning around.

"Terrific." Sophie watched him go, appreciating the fact that he was leaving while admiring how good he looked from behind.

Amy came to enjoy the view with her. "Helluva day, huh?"

"Explain to me again," Sophie said, "what happened to 'just the three of us'?"

Amy shrugged. "You're the one who invited the dog."

Sophie looked down at the dog who looked back up with its Cleopatra eyes, adoring her.

"The dog stays for a while," Sophie said. "The mayor goes."

When Sophie took her shower that night, blessing Wes the entire time for their new flexible showerhead, the dog put its feet on the edge of the tub and whined. It was covered with dried mud and looked so pathetic that Sophie said, "Oh, okay," and hauled him in with her, hosing him down while he squirmed in ecstasy under the water, and then sudsing him up with eucalyptus-and-lavender shampoo. Half an hour later, they both sat blow-dried in the kitchen, enjoying the semicool night air that came in through the screen door, the dog keeping one eye on the Dove Bar Sophie was eating. Sophie licked the ice cream and worried again about the accident, the movie, and the mayor.

She was still obsessing when Amy came down the stairs in her baby-doll pajamas, looking a lot like she had when she was ten. She sat in the chair across from Sophie and drew her knees up to her chin.

"We need a love scene," Amy said. "Clea wants one."

"A love scene." She should have figured on that, it was so like Clea. Sophie gave the wallpaper a dirty look in place of Clea. "I can't write a love scene. Especially not with those damn things staring at me."

"You cannot blame writer's block on giant mutant cherries," Amy began. Then she stopped, and said, "Oh. Cherries."

"What?" Sophie said, and Amy said, "You know. Cherries. And Chet."

"Chad," Sophie said, but she sat back, a little jolted. "I'm sure that's not it." She should ask Brandon. He knew everything about her subconscious. She frowned at the wall phone. She should have called Brandon before now, but she kept forgetting him.

Amy shifted uneasily. "Clea's decided that Rob is the love interest. She says it's better for what she has in mind."

"I bet it is." Sophie thought about it and nodded. "So she comes back to meet her old boyfriend and falls for his son. Lot of conflict there." She thought it through. "Oh, hell, *a lot* of conflict there. Frank's going to have a fit."

"If we do this right, he'll never know," Amy said. "Just write a nice seduction scene, and we can finish this up."

Sophie sat up and tapped her PowerBook out of sleep mode. "Who seduces who?"

"Are you kidding? Clea's an old-fashioned girl. He seduces her."

"So we're not doing a documentary." Sophie began to type in the scene log line, and Amy jerked away and stood up. "Hello?" Sophie said. "What?"

"Nothing," Amy said.

Sophie pointed at the chair. "Sit."

Amy sat, her feet on the floor this time.

"I've been very patient," Sophie told her, "but there's something you're not telling me which is dumb because you know I'll stand behind you no matter what you want.·What are you doing?"

"I'm making a documentary," Amy said.

Sophie sat back. "You're making a documentary about Clea coming home to Temptation?"

"No, I'm making a movie of that. I'm making a documentary about making the movie." Amy leaned forward. "This is so cool, Soph. I didn't want to tell you because I wanted you to be natural in the footage—"

Footage? "Wait a minute."

"—but you wouldn't believe how great this is already. That virginity stuff we talked about last night came out great—well, a little dark, but very moody with Clea all lit by those candles, and I can use the stuff she said as a voice-over—"

"Amy!"

Amy stopped and Sophie reminded herself to be supportive. "You filmed me on the porch last night?"

"All of us," Amy said. "I set up the camera in the bushes. It's good stuff, Soph. And then today I interviewed Frank and got him to talk to the camera and he really comes across as the butthead he is."

"Is that fair? Did he realize—"

"He knew he was on camera. He signed a release. And we're going to have so much stuff to cut together, it's going to be great."

Sophie leaned forward. "Amy, you're conning these people. They're signing releases because they think they'll look great, and you're—"

"I'm not conning them," Amy said, indignant. "And even if I am, I'm not taking anybody's money. I'm just filming what they say. I'm not changing their words. I'm just getting what I want."

"You have to think about other people," Sophie said, and Amy said, "No, that was you and Mama, trying to save everybody. Davy and Daddy and I, we know you can't save anybody so you might as well take care of yourself. And I'm not hurting anybody here. They all *want* to be in this movie."

She was so much like their father—all redheaded innocence, suckering people in with the Dempsey smile—maintaining to the end that it wasn't his fault if they trusted him, and that he never, ever lied.

But everybody he met lost something to him, just the same.

"Sophie, this is real filmmaking," Amy said, leaning closer, radiating sincerity. "Doing the wedding videos has been great, but it's been seven years, and I've learned everything I can from them. This is what I want to do now. This is my chance to get out. Maybe the only chance I'll get."

Amy's heart was in her eyes, and Sophie took a deep breath and thought, *I knew she'd get tired of those dumb weddings someday.* The thought of Amy leaving was painful, life without her was almost unimaginable, but the thought of her staying when she wanted to go was worse.

"I want to cut the documentary and go to L.A. and use it to get work there," Amy was saying. She looked as if she were holding her breath waiting for Sophie to say something.

Are you out of your mind? wouldn't seem supportive. "L.A.'s a tough town."

"I know." Amy bobbed her head up and down, eager to agree. "But Davy's out there. He can help me. It's his turn anyway." Her smile faded. "So what happens to you, now that I'm leaving?"

Sophie shrugged. "I don't know. I guess I'll have to think about what I want for a change." *After I get finished worrying about you.*

"Don't you have any dreams?" Amy said. "Isn't there something—"

"No," Sophie said. When she thought about it, it was sad. Thirty-two years old, and she had no idea what she wanted from life. She thought of Phin on the back porch. Maybe his question hadn't been so smart-assed after all.

"Are you going to sell the business?" Amy said.

"Probably," Sophie said.

"Can I have half?"

Sophie blinked at her. "Of course. What were you thinking?"

"I was thinking you needed the money more," Amy said. "I'm going to have a career. You're sort of stuck."

Ouch. "Take half the money," Sophie said. "I can get myself unstuck."

"Thank you," Amy said. "I mean it. Thanks."

"You're welcome," Sophie said. "Now get some sleep."

Amy stood up, hesitating as if there was something else, and then she bent and wrapped her arms around Sophie's neck.

"I love you so much, Soph," she whispered.

"I love you, too, Ame," Sophie said, patting her arm as she tried to breathe. *That's the only reason I'm letting you go.*

When Amy had gone upstairs, Sophie sat back and thought about her future. She wasn't worried; smart, organized people who worked hard always found jobs. But she didn't want a job, she wanted what Amy had, a career that fulfilled her.

It occurred to her that the reason she'd never figured out what she wanted to be was that she'd spent so much time concentrating on what she didn't want to be: a Dempsey. She let herself think about doing what Davy did, conning slightly crooked rich people out of their shady gains, but it held no appeal. Well, that was good. But maybe if she opened her mind, she could channel the Dempsey genes into something productive and fun, like Amy had, getting people's weak spots on film.

Maybe if she just opened herself to life, she could have fun. There must be something in her life that was recreational. She thought of the mayor, smiling lazily at her, detached and undemanding and her pulse kicked up. *He'd be fun.*

It was a dangerous thought, so she only entertained it for one rebellious minute before straightening herself out and heading up the stairs to bed, the dog on her heels.

The last thing she needed was the mayor.

On Friday, Phin's hassles started early.

First his mother gave him grief at breakfast because he'd been out to the Whipple farm twice.

"Associating with those movie people can do you no good," Liz had told him across the white linen expanse of her dining-room table. "Stephen has mentioned it to me several times already. Don't give him any leverage, Phin."

"What's 'associating'?" Dillie said around a mouthful of bran muffin.

"Hanging out with," Phin told her.

"Do not talk with your mouth full," Liz told her. "It's rude and disgusting." She transferred her attention back to Phin. "Don't go out to that farm again." She didn't add, "It's rude and disgusting," but the implication was clear.

"I did not associate," Phin said as he buttered Dillie another muffin. "I went out on Wednesday with Wes to see about the accident, and I went back yesterday because Wes roped me into looking at their electricity." Liz started to say something, and he added, "And I would also like to point out that I'm over twenty-one, so you can stop hassling me about my peer group. Talk to Dillie about this Jamie Barclay. I have grave doubts about Jamie Barclay." He grinned at Dillie and handed her the muffin.

"Jamie Barclay is an *excellent* person," Dillie said, taking it. "I should associate with her."

"Jamie's stepfather is the new vice president at the Third National," Liz said. "Her mother joined the Ladies' Club and is very nice. Dillie is allowed to associate." She smiled at Dillie and leaned forward to wipe the butter off her granddaughter's chin. "You missed your mouth," she told her, and Dillie grinned back. Then Liz turned back to Phin. "Now about these movie people—"

"I have to go to the bookstore now." Phin pushed back from the table. He kissed Dillie on the top of the head and said, "Behave," but Liz followed him out onto the broad front porch before he could escape.

"I didn't want to discuss this in front of Dillie," she said, "but I know you and women. It's one thing for you to conduct most of your liaisons out of town, another thing to do it here with a woman we know nothing—"

" 'Liaisons'?" Phin turned around, incredulous. "I replaced a fucking fuse, for Christ's sake." Okay, he'd lusted after a hostile woman, too, but he hadn't done anything about it.

"Don't look so outraged," Liz said. "I know you, and I worry about you. It's past time you settled down. Dillie needs a mother, and I want to see you married to a decent woman this time. You're almost forty, Phin."

"I'm thirty-six," Phin said. "And I have no intention of getting married again, and if I did, it wouldn't be to Rachel Garvey, which I know is where you're going with this. Which reminds me, stop talking about Rachel in front of Dillie. You're upsetting her."

"I never said anything to Dillie," Liz said.

"Well, she has big ears, and she's not stupid. Just forget the whole Rachel idea." He shook his head at her. "What is it with you lately? You never used to be this nuts."

"I think you should get married before the election," Liz said. "Weddings are popular. And—"

"Have you been hitting the cooking sherry?"

Liz stopped, two spots of color high on her cheeks. "Phineas Tucker, that is no way to talk to your mother."

"Well, this is no way to talk to your son." Phin met her eyes, and she had the grace to flush. "Have you listened to yourself? You want me to marry a woman I don't love so you can win the next election and get a grandson to win the one that'll come up thirty years from now."

Liz's blush deepened. "If you'd find somebody acceptable on your own, I wouldn't interfere. But I don't see the problem. You like Rachel, she's a lovely girl, she's very intelligent, and she's wonderful with Dillie."

"Dillie doesn't think so, and Rachel has no more interest in marrying me than I do her, so knock it off."

"Rachel's mother says she does." Liz moved in for the kill. "She says Rachel is shy, but she cares about you."

"Rachel is shy?" Phin laughed. "Rachel is a barracuda. And she does not want to marry me. If I know Rachel, what she wants is to get away from Virginia and Stephen."

"Nonsense," Liz said. "Rachel is very close to her parents."

"That's why she wants to get away." Phin turned to go down the

Hill. "I'm going to work now. Try to regain your sanity before I come home."

"I just want what's best for you," Liz called after him.

"The words every son hates to hear," he called back.

It was a good thing he loved his mother, he thought, as he walked down the Hill to the bookstore. If he didn't, he'd have put her in a home for the politically deranged long ago. The problem was, she'd bought too far into the Tucker legacy. His dad had been hipped on it, but that was at least understandable since he'd been raised with a box of *Tucker for Mayor: More of the Same* posters as a booster seat. But Liz was a Yarnell. Hill people. She should have had some proportion on politics.

Except that she'd loved his father so very much. Phin slowed a little as he remembered them together, so wrapped up in each other and politics that they'd almost forgotten they had a son. He could re-member a few times he'd had his parents' full attention—like the day he'd told his kindergarten class he wanted to be a fireman; they'd spent hours with him that afternoon—but mostly it had been the two of them, together against the world.

And now she was alone. He turned to look back at her and was distracted by the water tower, thrusting through the trees behind the houses.

It was bright, bright red.

"Oh, Christ," he said, and walked faster to the bookstore to find out what had gone wrong this time.

Four

*I*t looks like the Whore of Babylon," Phin told Wes later that afternoon as they sat on the bookstore porch at closing time.

Wes said, "You should hear Stephen. He came into the station and told me Hildy had conspired with the Coreys to humiliate him."

"Yeah, I can see Hildy meeting two high school kids in a dark alley just to give Stephen heart failure." Phin sighed. "Which, unfortunately, he didn't have."

"Hey," Wes said. "I told you. No death."

"I don't want him to die," Phin said. "I just want him sick enough to resign from the council and take his rubber stamp of a wife with him. He's still trying to block the new streetlights because they're too expensive."

"He'll resign when they pry his cold dead hands from around his campaign posters," Wes said. "Which will now read, *Paint the Water Tower White and Buy Cheaper Streetlights.*"

"Forget the campaign," Phin said. "Tell me something new."

"I watched Amy's tape," Wes said, and the way he said it made Phin pay attention. "There were a couple of interesting things on it."

"I don't need any more suspense in my life," Phin said.

"The Garveys ran their stop sign, too," Wes said. "Clear as day on the tape; they didn't even do a rolling stop, just went right through."

"And they hit the Dempseys, so Sophie had the right of way," Phin said. "Although they both ran the signs, so fry them both, that's my advice."

"Well, there's one other thing," Wes said. "Stephen wasn't driving, Virginia was."

Phin frowned at him. "Why would they lie about a thing like that?"

"Don't know," Wes said. "I'm looking into it. But it's interesting, isn't it?"

"I don't want 'interesting,' " Phin said. "I want boring and calm." He looked away from Wes and caught sight of the water tower again, glowing like a bloodred bullet in the sun. "Why did the Coreys paint the tower red, anyway? I couldn't find them to get any answers."

"They're out painting the Whipple farmhouse," Wes said. "And they painted it red because Stephen gave them the cheap stuff the school buys in bulk for the athletic department, and the white wouldn't cover."

Phin leaned back in his chair and put his feet on the porch rail. "You know, I think I like it red. Perks the place right up. And it annoys Stephen. I can't see a downside here."

"Amy and Sophie are perking the place up, too," Wes said, and Phin kept his face expressionless.

"Yeah, my mother thinks so. Have you got anything out of Amy yet?"

"I'm biding my time," Wes said.

"I meant about the movie," Phin said. "Your sex life is your business."

"It appears to be a love story," Wes said. "Frank seems to think he's the lead."

"And he's not?"

"Judging from what I saw Amy shoot today, that would be Rob."

Phin winced. "Frank's going to be real unhappy about that."

"Yeah," Wes said. "The perfect start to your midlife crisis: Your son sleeps with the woman you always wanted and takes your part in the movie you've been waiting for all your life."

"But are they shooting porn?"

"I don't know," Wes said. "If they are, I hope they let me watch."

"That'll be a major consolation if Stephen uses that to throw me out of office," Phin groused. " 'At least Wes got to watch,' that's what I'll say."

"You're being irrational," Wes said. "You haven't even voted in the permit yet. And you said yourself, Sophie doesn't look like the type."

"I changed my mind," Phin said. "Sophie is capable of anything except changing a fuse and reading. She's obsessed with film. I don't think she's ever picked up a book."

"The movie-quote thing? Amy says she does that when she gets nervous. It was a game they used to play when they were little." Wes leaned back. "I get the feeling that they didn't have a great childhood."

"I can tell you that sometime during it, somebody like me did a job on Sophie," Phin said. "She spits every time she sees me."

"Maybe she just doesn't like you," Wes said, and Phin said, "Thank you. I'm sure that's it."

Wes stood up. "Got you mad, did I? Good. Let's play pool. Maybe I can beat you, now that you're distracted."

"Don't count on it." Phin stood up. "You going to look into this Stephen thing?"

"Have to," Wes said. "Insurance companies like to have the whole story. And so do I. I'm thorough. Which reminds me, we're going to the Tavern tonight."

"On a Friday?" Phin thought about the development crowd that came in on Fridays. He liked his bars quiet and dark. "I don't think so."

"You're driving," Wes said. "So you can leave and strand me there, and I can catch a ride home with Amy."

Phin closed his eyes. "I have to go through this hell so you can get laid?"

"No," Wes said. "I just want to get closer."

"She's leaving on Sunday," Phin said.

"She's just going back to Cincinnati," Wes said. "I can drive an hour to make my move. Nine o'clock. You can tuck Dill in and then go play with Sophie."

Sophie. "And I'd want to play with Sophie because she's so warm and cuddly? No."

"Just play with her until I hook up with Amy," Wes said. "We're buddies. You're supposed to come through for me."

Sophie. And that mouth. "I'll pick you up at nine," Phin said. "No earlier. There's only so much Tavern and Sophie I can stand."

When Rachel got home, her mother was sitting at their red-checked-plastic–covered kitchen table, snapping beans, waiting for her as always.

"Hello, baby," Virginia said, "I ran into Georgia Lutz today," and Rachel thought, *Uh-oh.* "She told me what a good job you were doing at the Whipple Farm. I'm not sure that's a good place for you to be." Rachel started to protest and Virginia added, "But your father seems to think it's a good idea, so I guess it's fine."

"Daddy does?" That couldn't be right.

"I called him after I talked to Georgia, and he said we should let you go out there. He seemed pleased."

That *definitely* couldn't be right.

"And that nice Sophie said they were going home on Sunday," Virginia said. "So you won't be out there that much anyway."

Rachel eyed her mother and risked her next move. "Sophie's going back to Cincinnati, but Amy's not. I'm sort of hoping Sophie might hire me to take Amy's place in their video business."

Virginia's hands stilled over the beans, and Rachel rushed on. "Wouldn't that be wonderful, for me to get a job so close to home?" She had no intention of ever coming back to Temptation, but her mother didn't have to know that.

"I don't think so, dear." Her mother smiled as she began to snap the ends off the beans again. "Your father wouldn't let you go that far."

I'm twenty, Rachel wanted to say. *I can go wherever I want.*

"And besides, he needs you at the store." Virginia stopped to smile lovingly at her. "And I just don't know what I'd do without my baby. I'd worry so much if you left. You don't want me to worry, do you?"

Rachel felt a flush of resentment. "What if staying here makes me unhappy? You don't want me to be unhappy, do you?"

"Your father and I know what's best for you, Rachel. You've always wanted things that weren't good for you. Remember when you used to ask for two cotton candies at the fair? And we never let you have two because we knew you'd get sick."

"This isn't cotton candy," Rachel said, trying to keep the desperation out of her voice. "This is my life."

"Why don't you find something here in Temptation?" Virginia put the last of the beans in the bowl and stood up. "Let's see, what could you do? Not something too demanding because you'll be raising your own children soon." She picked up the bowl, and Rachel revised her plan.

"I suppose it's possible Sophie will stay here and work," Rachel said, watching her mother from the corner of her eye. "Phin's interested, you can tell, and if he decides he wants her, she'll have to stay."

"That's ridiculous," Virginia said, clutching the bowl to her breasts. "The two of you are practically engaged."

"Mother." Rachel took a deep breath. *Now or never.* "Look, Phin and I were never engaged, we never wanted to be engaged, and we're never going to be engaged." Her mother's eyes narrowed, and Rachel backtracked fast. "And anyway, I'm sure he's after Sophie now. He gets that look in his eye whenever she's around. He never gets that look for me." *Thank God.*

"That's just physical," Virginia said primly. "He made that mistake with that Diane but he won't do it again. Liz'll see to that. I'll call her and tell her about this Sophie and she'll put a stop to it." She nodded at Rachel. "You're the right one for him, and Liz knows it. The two of you have known each other forever. That's a real foundation for a marriage. Now, come peel potatoes, and then you can do some weeding."

"Fabulous," Rachel said, more determined than ever to get out of town.

———

By nine, the Tavern was as bad as Phin had thought it would be: Too many people determined to have a good time if it killed them, and Billy Ray Cyrus on the jukebox. He and Wes took their beers back to one of the initial-scarred booths along the back wall; half an hour later, he had a second beer and a headache, and he was ready to strand Wes for real.

"It's after nine," he told Wes. "They're not coming. Let's go back to the store and play pool."

Then Wes smiled past him, and he turned and saw Amy in a blue tube top.

And behind her was Sophie.

Sophie's hair was in loose, dark ringlets on her shoulders, and her cheeks were flushed, and she was wearing a short pink dress that fit tightly under her breasts, and it wasn't until Phin had taken it all in that he realized he had no idea what she'd been wearing the rest of the week. Something brown, he thought. Nothing like this.

He hadn't even noticed she'd *had* breasts until this. Just what he needed, something else to think about besides her mouth.

"Now what?" she said, looking at him warily as he tried to keep his eyes on her face.

"Cute dress." He slid over to make room for her since Amy had already taken a seat on the other side of the booth next to Wes.

"It is not cute." Sophie slid in beside him and put her drink on the pitted table. "I am never cute. But thank you for the compliment anyway. I borrowed it from Clea. She wore it in high school." Sophie stared down at herself doubtfully. "I think it was in style then."

"If you don't like being called cute, don't wear pink." Phin looked down the scoop neck of her dress. Excellent cleavage.

Sophie tugged up on the neck. "It's not pink, it's magenta. Or maybe watermelon."

"It's pink," Phin said. "As is your bra, I see."

"Those nine stitches didn't teach you a thing, did they?" Sophie gave up on the neck of her dress and picked up her drink.

"What is that?" Phin said, fearing the worst.

"Rum and Diet Coke," Sophie said. "And no cracks about what a wimpy drink it is. I like it."

He was sitting next to a woman with such lousy taste in alcohol that she'd mix good rum with aspartame. He looked across the table at Wes, who shrugged and made a small motion with his head that said, *You can go now.* Amy was talking a mile a minute about lights and camera angles, and Wes went back to listening to everything she said, his arm draped behind her across the back of the booth. One happy police chief.

Sophie was looking around the bar as if it were a zoo. " 'No point in mentioning those bats,' " she said to Amy, and Phin frowned. Then she added, " 'The poor bastard will see them soon enough,' " and he said, "Oh. Hunter S. Thompson."

Sophie frowned at him. "That's Johnny Depp. Who's Hunter S. Thompson?"

"Author," Phin said. *"Fear and Loathing in Las Vegas.* Great book. Who's Johnny Depp?"

"Actor," Sophie said. *"Fear and Loathing in Las Vegas.* Mediocre movie."

"So you're nervous," Phin said, and tried not to watch while Sophie wet her lips with her tongue.

"Me? What do I have to be nervous about?" Sophie said, and spilled some of her drink.

Phin pulled a wad of napkins from the holder and dropped them on the spill, just as Wes patted his shirt pocket and said to Amy, "I've got something for you." He pulled out a glasses case and gave it to her.

She opened it and said, *"My sunglasses,"* the way another, less interesting woman might have said, *"My diamonds."*

"I found them on the dashboard," Wes said. "Seemed like the least we could do to make up for such a lousy welcome."

"You're kidding," Sophie said, as she mopped up the last of her drink.

Amy put the glasses on. They were bizarre: thick pink plastic cat's-eye frames studded with rhinestones in the corners. Even the lenses were pink.

"You got pink lenses!" Amy was so delighted she was almost in Wes's lap.

He looked pretty delighted, too. "I couldn't tell what color the old ones were," he told her. "But Mindy at the optometrist's said pink would be best."

"Mindy is a genius," Amy said from behind her glasses. "These lenses are *much* better than the old ones."

"Got those turned around pretty fast, didn't you?" Phin said quietly to Wes as Sophie leaned forward to see the glasses better.

"I sent Duane to Cincinnati to one of those one-hour places," Wes said, not taking his eyes off Amy.

"You sent your deputy to Cincinnati so you could get—*ouch!*" Phin rubbed his shin as Sophie leaned back and smiled at Wes.

"You are obviously one of the good ones," she told him. "We're very impressed here."

"We certainly are," Amy said. "These are *great*."

Phin's work as a best friend was done. A smart man would leave. He turned to ask Sophie to scoot over so he could go, and look down her dress again.

On the other hand, if he left too soon, the whole setup would look as contrived as it was. It wouldn't kill him to stay a couple of minutes longer so Amy wouldn't catch on. "So how's the movie going?" he asked Sophie over the din, and she shot him a suspicious glance.

"Just fine, thank you," she said, and sipped her disgusting drink.

"You never did tell me what it's called."

"*Return to Temptation*."

"Catchy title. I don't suppose I could talk you out of using the name of the town."

Sophie shook her head as she looked out over the crowd, and he watched the way her curls bounced on her shoulders. "I don't think so. Who are all these people?"

"People who live in Temptation," Phin said. "What did you think, we bus them in on Fridays?"

"I didn't think there were this many people *in* Temptation."

"Over two thousand," Phin said. "And every one of them contrary and stubborn as mules."

"And you know them all," Sophie said. "Who's the cute guy in the green windbreaker over there, talking to Georgia?"

Phin bent closer to her to see where she was pointing, trying to ignore how her hair smelled like lavender. "Pete Alcott. He's part of their theater group. He moves a lot of scenery."

"I can understand that. He looks really strong."

"Not that strong."

"He's built very well."

"He can't play pool worth a damn. No position play at all. Fixates on whatever ball is in front of him." Phin looked down to see her frowning at him. "Sorry. Of course you don't know pool. Amateurs just knock the balls in one at a time. Pros use position play which means they always know not only how they're going to play the ball in front of them, but how they're going to play the next two or three balls, too. That way every shot they take positions them for the next one."

"And Pete Whatsis takes it one ball at a time." Sophie nodded at him, her eyes wide. "That's very interesting. Thank you."

She smiled at him, full wattage, and every political instinct he had went on alert. He looked down into her big brown eyes and said, "What are you up to?"

"Nothing." She nodded over to where Frank stood at the bar with his back to his wife and his front to Clea. "How's Frank play?"

"He likes trick shots," Phin said, still wary. "Bank shots, combination shots. Frank plays in the moment. He thinks pool is a performance. And he loses a lot."

"How about Rob?"

Sophie pointed over to the neon blue jukebox where Rob was arguing with Rachel.

"Rob tries to think ahead, but he never practices the basics. So he plans ahead four balls and then miscues on the second one and that throws him off so much that he panics and just starts banging balls around."

"You play with Stephen Garvey?" Sophie asked.

"Why are you so interested?" Phin said.

"Because I never thought about pool like this." She sounded sincere. "It's so smart of you to figure this out. That you could tell what kind of person somebody is by the way he plays pool. I'd never have thought of that."

"That's because you can't," Phin said. "Some people are very sharp, but they never learned to play the game right. So they screw up, but it's not a function of personality."

"But Rob and Frank learned right?"

Phin nodded. "My dad taught all of us. And Ed Yarnell plays us, too. Good training."

"So how does Stephen Garvey play?" Sophie said, smiling at him, lush and warm and round in the dim light, and Phin gave up trying to figure out what she was up to.

"He plays position, but he hits the ball too hard. The harder you hit the ball, the smaller the pocket gets, so it's easier to miss. He thinks it's macho to slam the cue into the ball which is why he loses a lot."

"But not always," Sophie said thoughtfully.

Phin shrugged. "Sometimes you have to hit the ball hard. In those cases, he wins."

"Sophie!" Georgia slid in beside her and jammed her into Phin.

"Sorry," Sophie said to him. "Easy, Georgia, we're a little cramped here."

She shifted to make more room, and Phin could feel the warm length of her thigh against his. *Thank you, Georgia.* Not that he intended to do anything about it, that would be dumb, but having Sophie pressed up against him even briefly was a pleasure. He let his arm fall along the back of the booth.

"Amy showed me some of the tape today," Georgia was saying as she beamed across the table at Amy. "I was *so* impressed. There I was, right there on the television. You have to come back from Cincinnati to tape our theater productions from now on."

"I'm not staying in Cincinnati," Amy said, and Phin winced at the look on Wes's face. "I'm going to drive to L.A. as soon as I have the tape edited." She leaned across the table to Sophie. "I forgot to ask. Can I take the car? To L.A., I mean?"

"Oh." Sophie looked taken aback. "Sure."

And what are you going to use for transportation? Phin wanted to say, but the last time he'd suggested she think about herself, she'd gotten hostile.

"Well, *you* have to come back here to visit," Georgia was saying to Sophie. "We just really like you a lot."

"That's very sweet of you, Georgia. I like you all a lot, too." Sophie looked up at Phin, imploring instead of hostile: *Get me out of this.* Then she drained her rum and Coke.

Phin thought about offering her a ride home and decided to keep her trapped there a while longer. For one thing, she felt really good pressed up against him, which was selfish of him but fortunately, he didn't have a problem with selfish. For another, if she got tanked, maybe she'd come across with more information about the movie. He looked down her dress again. It was a real shame he wasn't in a position to encourage her to come across with some other stuff, too. That was the trouble with dangerous women: They were almost always attractive. "The devil's candy," he remembered. "Women who would ruin you as soon as look at you."

Sophie looked up at him pitifully, but before he could say anything, Georgia bellowed, "Frank!" and Frank turned around from Clea to scowl at her. "Sophie needs a drink, honey."

"No, really," Sophie said, but Frank nodded and came over a minute later with another rum and Coke.

"Clea said this is what you're drinking," he told her, delighted to be reporting that he'd had conversation with Clea, and Phin thought, *Frank, you're a moron and your wife is going to kill you.*

"Thanks," Sophie said. "But really, you shouldn't have."

"Well, we're all so pleased you're here." Frank smiled at Sophie and Amy.

"Yes, we are." Georgia toasted Sophie with her drink and spilled some of it on the table in the process.

"And that you brought Clea back to us," Frank finished.

Georgia put her glass down.

Frank looked back at Clea and Rob. "That boy of mine," he said. "He's so starstruck, he doesn't know which end is up."

Phin looked around Frank and saw Rob at the bar being dazzled by Clea, who looked pleased to have him there.

"If he's not careful, Rachel's going to get jealous," Frank said. "I better go tell him to take care of what he's got."

"Good advice," Georgia said, but Frank was already heading back to the bar. She turned to Sophie, "I'm sorry, but Clea Whipple is a fucking bitch from hell."

Phin winced, but Sophie just said, "Cheers," and drank another slug of rum and Diet Coke.

"She's still trying to get him, that bitch," Georgia said. "She's never gonna learn. She tried to get him in high school, bet she didn't tell you that, did she?"

"Uh, yeah, she did," Sophie said into her drink, but Georgia wasn't listening, which was about par for Georgia, Phin thought. Center of the universe, at least in her own mind, that was Georgia.

"Thought she was going to get him, but she didn't. I fixed that. I fixed that good." Georgia drank again. "You gotta keep men in line or they'll just run all over you."

Phin spared a moment of sympathy for Frank until he looked back and saw him at the bar, leaning into Clea's cleavage. *Get a grip, Frank,* he thought, and then he looked down Sophie's dress and thought, *Never mind, Frank.*

"But I got what I wanted," Georgia said. "You can get what you want, too." She squinted at Sophie. "What do you want?"

"World peace," Sophie said, and tried to move away from Georgia a little.

Since that pressed her up even closer to Phin, he tried to think kinder thoughts about Georgia, but it was hard.

"I got everything I wanted," Georgia said. "Except a little girl. I never got my little girl. Boys aren't the same."

"This is true," Sophie said, and shifted on the booth seat again.

Very true, Phin thought gratefully, as the lavender in Sophie's hair drifted up to him again. Of course, if he'd been born female, there'd be blood in his brain right now, but a little light-headedness seemed a small price to pay for the rush he was getting every time Sophie moved. He tried not to think about that, but that was hard, too. Everything was hard.

"I really wanted a little girl," Georgia said. "I really did. But we never got one. When that bitch got her big Hollywood break, Frank said we could try, and we tried and tried but I never did get my girl. And I had the *cutest* clothes already bought for her."

"Oh, God," Sophie said into her drink. When Georgia went on in detail about the cute little dresses—"smocked with little tiny roses"— Sophie let her head fall back against Phin's arm, and he started calculating square roots so he wouldn't lunge for her mouth.

"He's still mad because we had to get married," Georgia said, looking back at the bar. "That's why he's doing this. That's why."

"You didn't have to get married," Sophie said.

Georgia straightened. "No, we certainly did not."

Phin had heard all about Georgia's eleven-month pregnancy when Diane's rabbit had died. "She's lying just like that Georgia Lutz," his mother had said, but when Ed confirmed it, even Liz had been defeated. Too bad Frank hadn't had a Liz in his corner.

"We did not have to get married," Georgia repeated, staring now at Frank and Clea. When she turned back to Sophie, her face was tragic. "You do what you have to do," she told Sophie quietly, not sounding drunk at all. "You fight for what's yours, for your family, for the family you were meant to have. And they never forgive you for it, *they never do*. You just keep paying and paying."

Sophie put her drink down. "Are you all right, Georgia?"

Georgia looked back at the bar. "I'm just fine. I've got everything I want. And nobody's going to take it away. I'm Frank's leading lady, he needs me." She straightened. "Did he tell you we're doing *Carousel*? I'm the lead, of course, and . . ."

For the next two hours, Georgia rattled on, and Phin watched Sophie knock back her third and fourth drinks. She was pressed up warm against him, her curls brushing soft against his arm, and he'd long ago given up caring about the movie and was now seriously reconsidering his stand on dangerous women. It wasn't just Sophie's cleavage and her mouth; when she tilted her head to talk across the table, her neck curved so beautifully into her shoulder that it made him dizzy. The temptation to lean down and bite into that curve was becoming overwhelming, to lick his way up her throat and take that mouth, and then Wes said something and she laughed and turned her face up to him to share the joke, and he fell into her huge, warm, brown eyes and his mind went blank.

"Are you all right?" she said.

"Nope." He caught his breath and drained his beer. "Hot in here."

At midnight, when Sophie reached the bottom of her fourth glass, she put it down and said, "I didn't need that."

She was drunk, he realized; not obnoxious drunk like Georgia, but still too drunk for him to move on. He didn't mind seducing women whom drink had made cheerful, but he drew the line at those whom drink had made stupid.

Amy leaned forward. "You can't drink worth a damn, Soph. You ready to go?"

"I can walk it." Sophie nudged Georgia with her hip. "It's not that far."

"Honey, it's dark out there," Georgia protested, but she moved out of the booth.

"I have Mace," Sophie told her as she slid across the seat. "And I'm not afraid to use it."

"Tell you what." Phin slid right behind her, chasing her heat. "I'll take you home.

"You sure?" Amy said. "I'm almost done here."

Phin smiled at Amy. "No problem. If you'll take Wes home when you're ready to go, I can drop Sophie off."

Amy nodded, and Phin steered Sophie to the door. "Give me the Mace," he said. "I don't want any accidents."

"Wimp." She walked away from him toward the door, and she looked as lush from behind as she did from the front.

I am a civilized man, he told himself as he followed her out the door. *I am not going to touch that inebriated woman.*

At least, not tonight.

The rum had made Sophie's knees loose, and as she sat in the dark in Phin's car—he had a Volvo, of course, tastefully expensive and under-stated—she was terrified the problem might spread to her lips and she'd say something stupid. Like, *Take me.*

She stole a glance at him as he drove down the main road in the dark, his hand draped over the wheel, oblivious to her there beside him, and she felt a little shiver at how dark it was and how close he was and how damn sexy he was.

That was not a good thought so she tried to squelch it, but the fact was that she was in the dark with a powerful man, a *town boy,* and he was gorgeous and Not Her Kind and it was a real turn-on. She squirmed a little with guilt and pleasure, and Phin said, "You okay?"

"Sure," she said. "Why wouldn't I be?"

"All that rum and Coke," he said. "If you're going to throw up, let me know and I'll pull over. I just had the upholstery cleaned."

"Oh, that's romantic," she said, and he shot her a startled glance.

Right. They weren't supposed to be romantic. See? This was what loose lips did for you. "That's not what I meant. I meant that wasn't polite or something. What's the word I'm looking for?"

"I have no idea," Phin said, as he slowed to turn into the farm lane. "Your thought processes elude me."

"Oh, really?" Sophie knew that was lame, but she'd left her verbal skills in the last rum and Coke. "I fail to see why my thought processes are of any interest to you at all." There. That was pretty good.

"They're not until they interfere with my town," Phin said as the Volvo bumped down the short lane. "This movie of yours is disrupting things."

"Hey, *not* our idea," Sophie said. "*We* did not ask for volunteers from the populace. They just"—she waved her hands, almost smacking Phin in the eye—"showed up on their own."

Phin had ducked to avoid her hand. "Right." He pulled the car up in front of the porch and cut the ignition, and Sophie could hear the crickets creaking in the darkness. Lovely.

"You okay?" Phin said, interrupting the crickets.

"Will you quit saying that? I'm not drunk." Sophie swung open the door and almost fell out. "I'm just not used to alcohol. It'll evaporate off in a minute."

"No, it won't." Phin got out and came around to her door while she was trying to get her bearings. "Give me your hand."

"Why?" Sophie said belligerently.

"So you don't fall on your ass," Phin said.

"Nice way for a mayor to talk." Sophie took his hand. It was warm and firm and strong—he almost lifted her out of the car with that one hand alone—and when she was standing, she found herself inches from a broad chest that blocked out the moonlight. "You're like a total eclipse," she said, and tried to detour around him.

"Yeah, I get that all the time." He let go, and she began to walk toward the house, escaping before she did something *really* stupid.

"Thank you for the ride, Phineas," she called back over her shoulder. "You may go now."

The wind rustled through the trees and made her shiver because it was so warm and alive on her skin. When she stopped to feel the breeze, she heard the wash of the river and thought how good it would be to cool off listening to the river in the wind in the moonlight. She turned and headed for the path at the side of the house.

"A little higher and to the left," Phin called after her. "You're missing the porch."

"All part of my plan," she called back. "Good night."

"Oh, great." She heard the car door slam behind her. "Where are you going?"

"Not your concern," she said. "I'm not disrupting anybody. You can go home now."

She rounded the corner of the house and it was dark, the trees blotting out the moonlight as effectively as Phin had, and she shivered because she was alone in the gloom.

"What are you doing?" Phin said from behind her. She started and tripped over a tree root, and he caught her arm before she could fall.

"I've told you a million times, stop sneaking up on me like that. I'm going to see the river in the moonlight." She pulled free and headed for the path again.

"Oh, good. The river. Excellent place for a woman who can't walk without falling over."

Sophie came out behind the house into a silvery blue landscape that fell away to the water like a movie set. "Oh," she said and stopped so that Phin bumped into her from behind. She spread her hands apart to frame the scene, flexing her fingers so that her rings glinted in the moonlight. "This is beautiful."

"Yeah," Phin said. "It is." For once he didn't sound exasperated or bored, and she looked over her shoulder to find him watching her.

"You get this all the time," she said. "You live in this movie set of a town, and you belong absolutely and everybody loves you and I bet you don't even appreciate it because you're too busy being cool and powerful."

"Do you have *any* idea of what you're talking about?" Phin said.

"Yes." Sophie started down the slope to the river. "I'm talking about what you have and what I don't. All you see is politics and problems. I bet right now you're thinking about how liable you'd be if I drowned."

"Well, I wasn't until you mentioned it," Phin said. "Try not to fall in."

"Maybe I will." Sophie turned around and walked backward so she could face him while she argued. "Maybe I'll just walk right in to see what it feels like."

"It feels cold and wet," Phin said. "Much like your bathtub, only with fish stink." He reached out and grabbed her dress at her stomach.

"Hey!" she said, but he had her stopped in her tracks.

"Two more steps and you'll be wearing the fish stink," Phin told her. "We haven't had rain for a while and the river's low. It gets muddy here." He tugged her closer to him but took a step back at the same time, a semi-gentleman. "Stay on the grass."

"You're no romantic," Sophie said, as she pulled his fingers off her dress.

"I certainly am," Phin said. "When the occasion calls for it. This occasion calls for the rescue squad."

"Prove it." Sophie looked around for a dry place to sit and headed for the dock. No mud there.

"Fall in the river," Phin said from behind her. "I'll pull you out."

"No, prove the romantic part. Tell me one thought you've had out here that didn't have to do with lawsuits or fish stink or river hazards." Sophie stepped up on the dock, kicked her shoes off, and went to sit on the edge.

"Julie Ann," Phin said. "And I was kidding. Do not fall in."

Sophie eased her feet into the cool, cool water and sighed before turning her attention back to Phin. "Julie Ann is somebody you had sex with here, I gather. That doesn't count. Romantic is not sweaty."

Phin sat down on the dock behind her. "It is if you do it right. Julie Ann's from a song. My grandma used to sing me to sleep with it."

"My mom used to sing us to sleep with 'I Only Want to Be with You.' It's pretty when you sing it slow." Sophie leaned back on her hands and looked up at the stars. "Was 'Julie Ann' a pretty song?"

"Yes," Phin said from behind her. "One line was about Julie Ann in the moonlight, with her silver rings on her hands. When you held your hands up, your rings picked up the moonlight."

"That is romantic," Sophie said. "I concede. Sing the song."

"No," Phin said.

"So much for romance." The sky overhead was dark as velvet, and the moonlight was luminous blue. "Why was she out in the moonlight?"

"Her lover betrayed her and she wandered off into the mountains."

That sounded lovely, wandering off into the dark, looking for a dangerous, hot lover to replace the old, boring one. "Did she find someone in the mountains?" She leaned back farther just to feel her body stretch.

"A bear."

Sophie jerked her head around to look at him. He had stretched out on the dock with his hands behind his head, and he was looking at the stars, too, pretty much ignoring her.

"She fell in love with a bear?"

"No, a bear ate her." Phin rolled his head to look at her. "Appalachia is not big on silly love songs."

"A bear ate her." Sophie shook her head. "Leave it to you to think that's romantic."

"The song's beautiful." Phin looked back at the stars. "It ends with her ghost wearing a crown of sorrow. Very romantic."

"Dead women are not romantic," Sophie said flatly.

"Okay, she's not dead," Phin said. "The bear ate her, and she came her brains out."

Sophie felt her laugh spurt before she could stop herself. "Oh, *very* nice. That's not romantic, either."

"It is if you do it right."

Sophie thought about it. "I must not be doing it right."

"It wouldn't be you that isn't doing it right," Phin said. "It'd be the bear."

"No picking on the bear," she said. "Liberated women take care of themselves. 'I've read *The Second Sex*. I've read *The Cinderella Complex*. I'm responsible for my own orgasm.' "

"Why?"

"What do you mean, 'Why?' That's a line from a movie. *Tootsie*. It's a famous line. I can't believe you didn't recognize it."

"I don't watch movies," Phin said. "I read. And I repeat, why would your orgasm be your responsibility during oral sex?"

Sophie sat up a little. His tone was matter-of-fact, but his subject matter wasn't. "I don't think I want to talk about this."

"Okay," Phin said,

Sophie splashed her feet in the river and tried to think of something else. Talking about oral sex with Phineas T. Tucker was not something a smart woman would do. If you talked about sex with men, they often took it as a sign you wanted to have some. And then where would she be? She let her mind slide off that one fast, and it ended up back on his question.

Of course she wanted to be responsible for her own orgasm. She was an independent woman in control of her own life. She wasn't about to throw herself at some man and selfishly demand that he satisfy her while she just lay back and *enjoyed* herself—

No, that wasn't right, either.

"It's because I'd have to depend on somebody else to give me what I want," she said, and Phin rolled his head to look at her. "I'd be one of those clingy women like Virginia Garvey or Georgia Lutz who just wait for men to take care of them and then are disappointed when they don't. If I take responsibility, then I can't be disappointed with anybody but me. I have control."

"And you see that as an improvement."

"It's empowering," Sophie said uncertainly. The rum and Coke were wearing off and so was the river. It still sounded and felt wonderful, but the fish stink was there, too. Reality, making its usual appearance just when she was getting somewhere.

" 'Empowering.' " Phin didn't sound impressed.

"Well, it's better than just lying back and hoping for the best." Sophie kicked the water.

"Ever tried that?" Phin said.

Sophie kicked the water again. "I don't want to talk about this."

"Okay," Phin said, and went back to watching the stars.

The amount of water she was splashing was ruining the peaceful effect of the river so she stopped and let it flow past her ankles. The silence stretched out until all she could think of was Phin lying behind her. He wasn't that attractive. He was a pain in the butt. He probably thought she was uptight just because she was independent. He didn't even know what he was talking about. Her heart pounded harder the more she thought about him.

"Sex isn't what's important anyway," she said loftily. "It's the relationship that matters, and relationships take work." He didn't say anything, so she went on to fill the silence. "I mean, sure, it sounds good to just hand everything over to somebody else, but that's not how it works in real life." She felt angry about that, which was totally inappropriate, and she was pretty sure it was the rum and Coke betraying her, but it might have been her life.

"Depends on the version of real life you're using," Phin said.

"Well, in my version, you have to be careful all the time and you get nothing for free," Sophie said waspishly. "Especially orgasms."

"Then you need another version."

Sophie lost her breath as the silence stretched out again. Well, if he made a pass, she'd say no. She'd just turn around and look at that great face and better body, and say no. Who did he think he was, anyway? She certainly knew who she was, and she wasn't the kind of woman who—

"Come here," Phin said, and Sophie felt his voice in the pit of her stomach.

She shook her head.

"You've got nothing to lose," he told her. "Day after tomorrow you're gone, and we'll never see each other again. This is your one shot at being selfish. Let somebody take care of you for a change." She swallowed as she tried to get her breath, and he said, "Come here and let me give you an orgasm you don't have to work for."

The heat spread fast and low in her, and Sophie bit her lip and tried not to feel anything. *Don't be dumb*, she told herself. *You are not this kind of woman, this is not what you want*, but her breath came faster and it was what she wanted, *he* was what she wanted. She opened her mouth to say no, but what came out was, "Why would you want to do that?"

"So I can touch you," he said. "I've wanted to since the first time I saw you on the porch."

There definitely wasn't enough air by the river. The heat was driving it away. If she turned around and looked at him, she'd probably asphyxiate. "You didn't even know me on the porch. You don't know me now."

"That's the beauty of it," Phin said. "No guilt. No responsibility. Just pleasure."

She did turn to look at him then, and he met her eyes coolly. He had propped himself up on one elbow, but there was no tension anywhere in his body—she closed her eyes because he had such a beautiful body—no pressure there on her at all. He could have been offering her dinner and his voice would have sounded the same.

"You wouldn't care if I said no, would you?" Sophie said, and he looked surprised.

"It wouldn't ruin my evening." He sat up slowly. "Okay, not a good idea. I apologize. Let me walk you back to the house, and we'll forget—"

"I'd have to be depraved to say yes to something like that," Sophie said, and her voice sounded thick. "I'd have to be . . ."

She stopped because she couldn't get the words out, and he watched her for a moment and then he leaned closer. "Wild," he said, softly. "Reckless." He was so close his lips were almost touching hers, and she knew he was going to kiss her. But then he whispered, *"Satisfied,"* and bit her lower lip, and the ache made her moan, and then he did kiss her, tasting her mouth as if she were candy, easing her down onto the dock as she clutched his shirt and arched into him, depraved and abandoned after all.

Five

*P*hin's mouth was hot on hers where Sophie had been sure it would be cool, and she tasted the beer he'd been drinking and something else that she thought might be the intoxicating promise of sex without responsibility, or maybe it was just Phin. Then he pulled her hand off his shirt and put his hand on her breast, and the world swung around.

She broke the kiss and tried to catch her breath even while she clung to him. The river gurgled away under the rough boards of the dock, and the breeze was warm, and his hand was hot on her, and when he kissed her again, this time teasing her lips with his tongue, she opened on a quick breath and let him take her mouth completely.

This is wrong, she thought, but she couldn't remember why anything that felt this good would be wrong unless it was just because it felt so good. He kissed his way down the curve of her neck, into the hollow of her shoulder, and found a nerve there she didn't know she had and brought it alive as he pressed her onto the dock with the hard length of his body, and when she rocked under him, she heard him suck in his breath and that made her hotter, too.

Then his hand was on her thigh, and she felt him slide the short skirt of her dress up, and the slipperiness of the fabric and the weight of his hand and the prickle of her skin made her shudder. He kissed her again, and his mouth was as hot as before, his tongue as tantalizing, but his fingers were moving across her hip, under her dress, and she couldn't concentrate on his mouth anymore. He eased the elastic of her underpants down, and then his fingers slid against her, between her legs, and she went mindless.

She closed her eyes at his touch and said, "Oh"—too hot to feel embarrassed—and he kissed her again as he stroked her over and over. Then he slid his finger inside her and made her body jolt from the pure pleasure of it. "Tell me when it feels good," he whispered in her ear, and she said, "Oh my *God*," and he laughed—the first time she'd heard him laugh—and said, "No, when it feels *really* good," and moved his finger to curve it inside her. "Here?" he said, and she shook her head, wanting to tell him that the clitoris wasn't inside, that he'd passed it on his way in, but he said, "Wait," and slipped a second finger in. He moved higher this time until he hit something so good that Sophie jolted against him and said, "Oh, God, *there*."

"I'll be back," he said and slid down her body, shoving her dress up at the same time so that the breeze that had been so warm chilled her stomach. And then he bent and licked into her, finding her clitoris with no problem at all, while his fingers made her crazy from inside.

She gave one fleeting thought to panic, and then she crossed her arms over her eyes and let her body take her where he wanted her to go, living in the heat of his mouth and the rhythm he built in her and the shudder and the shake of her breath as the tension twisted tighter inside her. He pressed her down, holding her to the dock as she moved mindlessly against his mouth and hand, letting him do it all, and the pleasure built and built and built until she felt the first surge in her blood. She cried out in the darkness, shuddering against his mouth, and he brought her back again and again while she did absolutely nothing at all, and it was glorious.

When he finally stopped, she lay there, letting her mind seep back in, feeling every muscle and nerve in her body celebrating. He pulled her underwear back up and kissed her stomach, and she felt the nerves there jump, and then he smoothed her dress down with the flat of his hand, and the weight of it felt wonderful, and through it all, she lay there thinking she should be feeling guilty, should be feeling grateful, but instead feeling too damn good to move.

Phin stretched out beside her, and she rolled her head to see him, almost surprised that it was him. The mayor, no less. "So, it's you," she said, her voice thick and satisfied.

"Yep," he said. "It's me. How soon we forget."

It was odd, not feeling the need to take care of him after sex. No relationship to foster. No ego to stroke. She looked back up at the stars, content to float in postorgasmic mindlessness. "Well, you were gone for days."

"I had work to do," he said. "Everything okay up here?"

"It was incredible," she said politely.

"I know," he said, and she thought about how nice it was that they weren't in a relationship so she wouldn't have to kill him for being arrogant about being right all the time.

"I think this is the part where you say something nice about me," Sophie said, not really caring.

"Why?" Phin said. "You didn't do anything."

Sophie smiled dreamily up at the stars. "I like you after all. You're consistent. And competent. You know, you don't get stars like this in Cincinnati."

"There's a lot of stuff here you don't get in Cincinnati," Phin said. "In fact, you just got some."

"I could tell Br—" Sophie began. "Oh, *no*." She sat up, cold with guilt, sandbagged by reality once again.

Phin sighed. "What now?"

"I just cheated on my significant other," Sophie said. "I didn't even *think* about him, I just invited you right on in and cheated on him. I'm scum."

"You didn't cheat on him," Phin said. "Although you might have mentioned him sooner."

Sophie looked at him with all the scorn she felt for herself. "Like you care."

"I don't," Phin said. "I just like having all the information I can get."

He turned his head to meet her eyes. "And the damnedest thing, Sophie, I always have this feeling you're holding something out on me."

"Clearly I wasn't holding out tonight," Sophie said, not liking the look in his eye or the turn the conversation was taking. "I can't believe I cheated on Brandon. I am *not* a cheater, but boy, I sure rolled over for you."

"Many women have," Phin said. "And you didn't cheat, so stop beating yourself up. Unless you enjoy it."

"How is this not cheating?" Sophie demanded. "We had sex. Right here on this dock. I was here. I remember."

"We didn't have sex," Phin said. "I was here, and I didn't have sex. You're too drunk to have sex. I'd be taking advantage of you."

"What? That's the dumbest thing I've ever heard." Sophie stood up and closed her eyes as her body remembered what a good time she'd just had. Which was wretched of her, she reminded herself, and then she stretched a little so her muscles would remember some more. "We had sex," she said, and her body telegraphed back, *Sure did.* She looked down at Phin, still stretched out on the dock, and the thought of what his body could do for her made her want to kick him. And then jump him. She looked away. "And now I'm going to call my lover and tell him what a scum I've been and hope he'll forgive me. Thank you very much for a lovely evening. Let's not do it again."

She walked off the dock and felt the cold grass on her toes just as Phin said, "Hold it, Julie Ann. Nice exit, but you forgot your shoes."

She turned and watched as he rolled to his feet and picked up her shoes. He strolled toward her and held them out, and she met his eyes and saw heat there and wanted him again.

Sophie took her shoes. "I'm not Julie Ann. I'm still alive and I'm staying that way." She looked into his eyes one last time, and then she turned back toward the house, toward safety and away from temptation.

"Maybe," Phin called after her as she walked away from him. "But the bear got you just the same."

Sophie closed her eyes and kept walking. The devil wasn't inside her after all. He was back there on the dock, making her crazy.

The dog greeted her with rapture when she came in, which made her feel even worse, keeping him shut up inside while she was having sex on the dock. She was a terrible mother. She took him outside and told him what an wonderful canine he was, and then she went upstairs for a long shower to scrub away the guilt. It didn't work; she could still feel Phin everywhere. *And hooray for that,* her body said, *let's do it again.* Then she put Dusty on for comfort and crawled into bed to call Brandon so guilt would give her some perspective. It worked pretty well: When he said, "Hello," she felt like throwing up.

"It's me." She swallowed.

"Sophie?" Brandon sounded as if he'd been drugged.

"Brandon, I'm a horrible person," Sophie said. The dog jumped on the bed and she patted its solid little barrel body.

"No, you're not," he yawned. "What happened?"

"I had sex," Sophie said. "Of course, he says it wasn't sex, but it was, and now I've called you and made you feel awful in the middle of the night so I won't feel so guilty, and that's worse."

"What do you mean, 'he says it wasn't sex'?" Brandon said, not yawning. "Who was this?"

"A guy I met here. The mayor. We were talking and then he kissed me, and then things got . . . out of hand."

"If all he did was kiss you, he was right. You didn't have sex." Brandon sounded a little grumpy, which wasn't quite the reaction she'd been expecting. "Look, I know you think I haven't been paying enough attention to you and I should have called before this but—"

"You've been paying plenty of attention to me," Sophie said. "And it was more than one kiss. It was—"

"You're just tired of walking the straight and narrow." He sounded exasperated. "So you went for a little harmless excitement by necking with an authority figure."

"Excuse me?" Sophie said.

"You didn't even give this man a name. You said he was the mayor. That's obviously more important than who he is as a person."

"His name is Phineas Tucker," Sophie said. "And I think you're missing something key here."

"I'm not missing anything," Brandon said. "You're rebelling against the oppressive social structure that's made your family outcast, by corrupting its most powerful and popular adherent. And now you're sending me a wake-up call—literally—that I'm not paying enough attention to you."

"I don't think this is about you," Sophie said. "Brandon, I came all over that dock. Guilt and all, and I still came."

"Guilt can be an aphrodisiac," Brandon said automatically.

"Brandon, pay attention here. He went down on me and I loved it. I wanted to . . ." Sophie searched for the words that would make him pay attention and finally borrowed Phin's. "I wanted to *fuck his brains out*." Her voice rose as she thought about it, and anger made her honest. "As a matter of fact, I still want to fuck his brains out. Really, I do. And call me crazy, but I think this is a bad sign for our relationship."

"You don't have to shock me with language to make me pay attention," Brandon said, and Sophie wanted him dead. "When you get back home, we'll have a long talk and get you straightened out."

Sophie gritted her teeth. Maybe she didn't want straightened out. Maybe she liked being bent. Maybe she'd go find Phin and invite him to bend her some more. "And we did have sex. I came, that's sex."

"You come with a vibrator, too," Brandon said. "Stop dramatizing yourself."

Sophie gripped the receiver until her knuckles went white. "I'm telling you, I had sex!"

"Good for you," Amy said from the doorway. "Who are you bragging to?"

"Brandon," Sophie said.

"Yes!" Amy plopped herself down at the foot of the bed, bouncing with satisfaction, and the dog moved closer to Sophie, the epitome of annoyed canine. "Sorry, dog. This was Phineas T., right?"

Sophie nodded.

"And now Brandon is explaining to you why you did this, and he isn't mentioning lust and satisfaction."

Sophie nodded again.

"Who's talking to you?" Brandon said.

"Amy," Sophie said. "She just recapped your entire conversation."

"Oh, yes, your sister, the psychological genius." Brandon sounded annoyed for the first time. "Definitely listen to her."

"Let me get this straight. You don't care that Phin went down on me, but you're jealous that I'm listening to my sister instead of you?" Sophie gave up. "Brandon, I think this is an indication that this relationship isn't working for us."

"Yes," Amy said.

"Of course the relationship is working for us." Brandon sounded really annoyed now. "You're just acting out a little—"

" 'A little.' " Sophie shook her head. "I'm not acting out *a little.* I'm getting my brains blown out by the river by a guy I hardly know."

"I *love* this," Amy said.

"Sounds like acting-out to me," Brandon said. "Go get some sleep and sober up. You'll be back to normal in the morning."

"Wait a minute—"

"Good night, Sophie," Brandon said, and hung up.

"I don't believe this." Sophie stared at the receiver.

"Who cares about him?" Amy said. "You had great sex."

"Not according to Phin and Brandon." Sophie put the receiver back on the cradle. "It's not sex at all, according to these yahoos."

"Wait, I get it. You only had oral sex." Amy rolled her eyes. "How Clintonesque of them."

"Well, it's an out for me," Sophie said. "Evidently I didn't cheat, after all. And Brandon says when I get home, he'll straighten me out."

"Does he now?" Amy's voice was cold, and Sophie said, "Yeah."

"I don't like Brandon," Amy said. "The mayor, however, I might approve of. On a short-term basis only, of course."

"I don't," Sophie said, and thought about Phin in the dark, and his hands and his mouth, and she shivered all over. "I just want him again. Only this time, I want the whole thing, the entire phallic variation."

"The Phallic Variation." Amy grinned. "Sounds like a techno-thriller. Tom Clancy's *Phallic Variation.* I think you should go for it."

"I can't." Sophie slid down into her pillows and tried not to think about going for it and thought about it anyway. "I can't cheat again. But, oh God, Amy, it was good."

"You know, I never heard you say, 'God, it was good' after Brandon," Amy said. "And now here's the mayor, who seems to know his thumb from a clitoris."

Sophie felt her lips quirk in spite of herself. "Oh, yes. He went places no man has gone before. He also seems open to direction."

"Your future is clear." Amy grinned at her. "Dump Brandon and move on to the Phallic Variation. Of course I'd emphasize that it's a variation, and he has to slide down your stomach first before he gets his."

Sophie stopped smiling. "I can't. Phin was sort of a kinky fantasy, sex with a guy I don't know, swept away in the dark by the river, all that stuff—" She felt a little dizzy just thinking about it. "But I'm not even sure I like him—" *Although I like what he does, dear God, I do.* Sophie dug herself deeper into the bed and shoved all thoughts of Phin away. "He probably won't even come back. I don't think he had that phenomenal a time. Mostly we argued."

"You have so much to learn about men," Amy said. "If he talked you out of your pants, he had a good time. And even if you're all right in the morning, you'll be wanting him again in the dark. That's what the dark is for. Wanting guys like Phin."

"Good *night*," Sophie said, and Amy laughed and left the room.

Guys like Phin. Sophie thought of him again, so relaxed next to her, careless and cool, and then she thought of the way his mouth had moved down her body and made her shudder, thought of his hands hot on her, his fingers inside her, thought about what he would feel like moving hard into her—

Sophie put her pillow over her head.

He'd been so hot. *She'd* been so hot. That was so wrong of her. But, oh God, it had felt so *good*. After an hour, she gave up and relived the whole thing all over again, dwelling lavishly on the moments that were particularly perverse and unlike her, fixing the awkward parts. By the time she'd reviewed it a couple of times, it was so glossy, it could have been a hot scene in a movie.

Hello.

That would be wrong, she told herself, but her mind clicked along, rewriting her night, and after a few minutes, she gave up and went downstairs and opened her PowerBook, the dog sighing and following her to lie down again at her feet.

"Sorry," Sophie told him.

And then she began to type.

"Beautiful morning," Phin said when he came down to the breakfast table. He kissed Dillie on top of her head. "You gonna beat 'em today, kid?"

Dillie straightened her softball shirt. "Yep. I'm ready."

"The Tuckers are always ready." He sat down, picked up his glass of orange juice and met his mother's narrowed eyes. "What?"

"Good time last night?" she said.

He put his orange juice glass down. "I beg your pardon?"

"I said, did you have a good time last night at the Tavern with the movie people?" Liz said.

Dillie frowned. "You didn't say all that."

Liz handed Dillie a buttered muffin. "Eat, please." She turned back to Phin and smiled her cobra smile.

"Yes," Phin said, returning her smile with an equal lack of warmth. "An excellent time. What else did Virginia have to say?" He snagged a muffin and buttered it while he reoriented his brain from smug satisfaction to defense alert.

"She suggested you take Rachel to the movies."

"I don't go to the movies," Phin said. "Especially with Rachel. I have a major softball game this morning, and it needs all my attention."

"It's just the Blue Birds," Dillie said. "We can beat them no problem."

"Never let your guard down, Dill," Phin said, keeping one eye on his mother. "The ones that look harmless are the ones that take you by surprise."

"You really thought nobody would talk?" Liz said.

"Not before breakfast," Phin said. "It's Saturday, for Christ's sake."

"You're the mayor," Liz said. "You have standing. People are interested in what you do. You have a *responsibility* to this town."

"Lucky me. Could I have some eggs?" He handed Liz his plate, and she filled it while she talked.

"As I said, it's not a good idea, associating with the movie people. Virginia's told everybody by now—"

"Told everybody what? That I had a couple of beers at the Tavern? There's breaking news for you." Thank God, Virginia hadn't been on the Whipple dock. "What does she—" he began and then froze at the belated memory of where the Whipple dock was.

Across the river from the Garveys'.

Not directly across. Upstream a little. But still too close.

"What else did Virginia say?" he asked his mother.

"That was it." She handed him his plate. "I gather she missed something?"

Phin sat back in his chair, stared at the ceiling, and regrouped. He must have been out of his fucking mind. Three or four beers and Sophie saying, "I'd have to be depraved" with that mouth, and he'd forgotten where he was and who he was and lunged for her.

Of course, she'd forgotten she had a boyfriend, so he wasn't alone. Lust could play hell with a person's memory. And morals. And common sense.

"What did you do?" Liz said.

Phin sat up and ate a forkful of eggs. "Excellent breakfast. Thank you."

Liz closed her eyes. "Am I going to be hearing something horrible?"

"Nope," Phin said. "You'd have heard it by now."

"What's horrible?" Dillie said.

"Nothing," Phin said. "Everything's great. But I still think you'd better watch those Blue Birds."

"Stephen will make capital of this," Liz said.

"Stephen sleeps with Virginia," Phin said. "He has to find something to do for excitement."

"Don't get cocky," Liz said. "Don't give him *any* advantage. And stay away from those movie people."

The phone rang, and Phin escaped to get it. When he came back, Liz said, "Who was it?"

"The movie people," Phin said. "They need fuses. I'm taking some out to them this afternoon."

"Don't do this," Liz said, with an edge in her voice.

"Don't push me," Phin said, just as sharply.

"Can I have more muffin?" Dillie said, and when he looked at her, her eyes were anxious.

"If you have more muffin, will you throw it up on third base?" he said.

"No." Dillie looked from Phin to Liz and back again. "Are you guys fighting? You never fight, but this sounds like a fight, and I don't like it."

"It's okay, Dillie," Liz said. "Your father is being a dummy, but we're not mad."

"Grandma's not minding her own business," Phin said. "But we're not mad. We don't get mad. We're Tuckers."

"Okay," Dillie said. "It sounded mad, though."

"About the Blue Birds," Phin said, and distracted his daughter with softball strategy.

Across the table, his mother regarded him coldly, not distracted at all.

When Sophie came downstairs again, it was almost noon. She'd shoved the memories of the night before away, tried to call Brandon and got his machine, buried the pink dress in the back of the closet, and resolved to be A Better Person now that the sun was up.

"Late night last night, huh?" Amy said, as Sophie came into the kitchen. She was eating toast slathered with butter, sitting at the worn wood table where Clea was reading pages of script. Dusty was singing "Mama's Little Girl" in the background, the sun shone through the kitchen windows, and the dog looked up, panting, and wagged his stubby tail when he saw Sophie.

It was hot as hell, but Sophie began to feel better. "Hello, baby," she said to the dog, and bent to pet it. Then she went to the fridge to pour herself a glass of juice. "I was up until about four—" She stopped, realizing what Clea was reading. "Oh, about that. It's—"

"It's phenomenal," Clea said. "My God, I had no idea you could even *think* like this."

"She's right." Amy opened her eyes wide. "You were obviously *inspired.*"

"Don't start," Sophie said.

"Of course, we can't *film* this—" Amy said, and Clea said, "Well, maybe—"

"—but Clea and I were just talking," Amy went on, "and we think you should write another one, a full love scene this time." Amy took a huge bite of toast and then said, with her mouth full, "Like a Phallic Variation, you know?"

"We have no time to film a Phallic Variation," Sophie said crushingly. "We're going home tomorrow. We have work—"

"Not really," Amy said, and Sophie stopped with her juice glass halfway to her mouth. "I sort of canceled everything before we left," Amy said. "But it's okay, I got everybody booked with other places, I just—"

Sophie sat down hard. "Other places." All that work. All that income. Gone.

"I wanted time to do this right," Amy said, talking faster. "And now we can take our time and film a really great Phallic Variation. You can, uh, write it tonight."

"No," Sophie said.

"Amy's right," Clea said. "We need to build to a big finish." She held up the script. "This is good, but it's not the whole nine yards, you know?"

"I know," Sophie said. "Believe me, I know." She watched Amy, who concentrated on her toast, defiantly cheerful about having dismantled their business. "But this is a *short, nonpornographic* movie. It does not need a sex scene." She tried to take the script pages from Clea, who put them behind her back.

"Don't be a prude, Sophie," she said. "Sex is not necessarily porn."

Amy said, "Yeah, don't be a prude, Sophie. Maybe that's something else about you Brandon can straighten out when you get back to Cincinnati."

Then a car door slammed outside and Clea said, "Rob," and evaporated through the door.

"So you shut down the business," Sophie said.

"I set you free," Amy said. "If I hadn't, you'd have tried to go back and do it all alone. Now you're free to figure out what you want—"

"Thank you," Sophie said. "I want to be employed. Don't do me any more favors."

"Hi!" Rachel bustled into the room, making Sophie drop her toast. "Guess what I found!" She dumped a paper bag on the table and a tub of wallpaper paste rolled out, endangering Sophie's juice. "The rest of the wallpaper!" Then, to Sophie's horror she pulled out eight rolls of ancient wallpaper. "When you said Clea's mom had taken it back, I figured it had to be to our store, so I went and looked in the old stock and it was there. Isn't this great?"

Rachel looked so pleased that Sophie said, "Absolutely," and tried to smile. Just what she needed. A whole kitchen of snotty mutant cherries.

"Wait a minute," Amy said, picking up a roll. "These aren't cherries."

"I know," Rachel said. "The label on the roll says, *Apple Blossom Time.* But it had *Whipple* written on it, and how many rolls of kitchen wallpaper could Clea's mom have bought?"

"Apples?" Sophie studied the wall. "Those are apples? No, those are cherries."

"No, they're not," Amy said, squinting from the roll to the wall. "They're apples. This is the same paper. The ones on the wall just faded. The yellow went, for some reason, so they're sort of a blue-pink. That's why you thought they were cherries."

"They're not cherries?" Sophie opened a roll and spread it out. Definitely apples on the roll. Ugly, orangey red apples, but still apples.

"Whatever," Rachel said. "You can do the whole kitchen now, and then you can write."

She looked so pleased with herself that Sophie didn't have the heart to disappoint her. "Thank you, this was very sweet of you, Rachel."

"My pleasure," Rachel said. "Oh, and somebody else is here, too."

"The Coreys," Amy said. "Clea hired them yesterday to paint the house. You gotta see 'em. They look like Laurel and Hardy in high school."

"No," Rachel said. "The Coreys are already out there. This is some new guy who pulled up in a black Porsche just as I came in. I didn't see him—"

Sophie's heart sank. "Zane."

"Oh, no," Amy said.

"Zane Black, the anchor guy?" Rachel said. "Cool."

"You have a lot to learn, Rachel," Sophie said and headed for the front porch.

Sophie thought she'd seen all she'd needed to of Zane Black when she'd filmed his wedding to Clea, but now, as he came toward the porch across the sunbaked yard, a newscaster's smile pasted on his lips in spite of the fact that Clea was glowering behind him, she was struck by how much he looked like Frank. He was better-looking and not as smarmy, but the resemblance was still strong. "I'm starting to see a pattern here," she murmured to Amy, who said, "Yeah, add in Davy and Rob and you've got a four-pack of dark-haired guys you can't trust."

"Stephanie!" Zane said.

"Sophie," Sophie said.

"Right, right, Sophie." He came up the steps and took a deep breath. "Nothing like country air."

"That's dead fish," Amy said. "We haven't had much rain lately and the river's low," but Zane had already lost interest, staring past her, his smile widening.

"And who have we here?"

Sophie turned. Rachel stood inside the screen door, looking like a blonde cupcake. "Oh. This is Rachel, our production assistant."

Rachel's tentative smile for Zane spread all over her face when she heard her title. "Hello, Mr. Black," she said, but her smile was for Sophie.

"Call me Zane, everybody does," Zane said.

"Not everybody," Amy said under her breath. "Some of us call you 'dickhead.' "

They followed Zane and Clea in, as Clea said, "I told you not to come."

"Don't be ridiculous," Zane said. "You're my wife."

"You should have thought of that before you took my money and slept with the weather girl," Clea said, and went into the kitchen.

"Weather girl?" Amy said.

Zane followed Clea, a stiff smile pasted on his face.

"Okay, we should go out onto the front porch now and let them have this argument in private," Sophie said to Amy and Rachel.

Out in the kitchen, Clea began to tell Zane what she thought of him. She had a nice turn of phrase and the delivery of an auctioneer.

"Or not," Sophie said, and the three of them sat on the couch and listened, the dog at their feet with his head cocked, too.

About ten minutes into Clea's list of Zane's offenses which included theft, adultery, not waiting for Clea to come, preventing her from reestablishing her career, and not providing her with a warm, nurturing environment, Amy said, "This would be better if we had popcorn."

Five minutes later, as Zane was explaining that it was Clea's fault that he'd cheated on her because she was cold and withholding which was not what he expected from his wife because he wanted a warm, nurturing environment, too, Sophie said, "This would be better if we had alcohol."

And shortly after that, at the height of the argument, when Zane told Clea that she'd never see her money again if she left him, Amy said, "The hell with the popcorn. Let's get Sophie's Mace and take the bastard out."

"My mom thinks he's the coolest," Rachel said. "Wait'll I tell her about this."

Out in the kitchen, Zane was taking the righteously indignant route.

"I can't believe you thought I'd spend that money. Hell, I'm not that damn Dempsey guy you used to be with, I'm honest."

Sophie straightened on the couch, and Amy said, "Easy, girl."

"Yeah, well, I should have stayed with him," Clea said. "He never took anything from me, and he took care of me, too. Only you said you could do it better, remember? And I was such a fool I went for it."

Amy said, "See? She's sorry," and Sophie relaxed.

"I've taken care of you," Zane said. "For God's sake, Clea, you live in one of the biggest houses in Cincinnati."

"How is stealing my money keeping me safe?" Clea shrieked at him.

"Not to mention the weather girl," Amy said.

"I didn't steal it," Zane said. "I told you, I've got it in an offshore account, and it's going to stay there until I move it, so if you want it, you're going to stay my wife."

"That's it, isn't it? You knew I was tired of your crap, so you hid the money so I couldn't leave."

"You're my wife—"

"Well, it's not going to work," Clea said. "Because my lawyer is going to make you give it up. And I'm selling this farm, too, and Frank says—"

"Oh, God, not Frank again," Zane said. "Frank the Great. Frank the Wonderful. Get over high school, Clea, he's not—"

"He's a developer here," Clea said. "He bought land from my dad before, and he said he'd give me seven hundred and fifty thousand dollars for the rest of the land around the farmhouse. When I get back what you stole, I'll have almost three million dollars, and when I send this tape to Leo—"

"*Leo*? No wife of mine is going to work for Leo Kingsley."

"He seems to be missing something key here," Sophie said, as Clea said, "Zane, I'm not your wife anymore. We're over."

"Not unless you want to give me half of that three million," Zane said, and this time there was a long silence from the kitchen.

"You wouldn't," Clea said.

"The hell I wouldn't," Zane said. "If you'd left me before you got the money, you'd sure as hell have taken half of *my* assets. Well, I get half of yours, too, sweetie." When Clea didn't say anything he went on. "Now, there's nothing to be upset about, I have all the money safe in an offshore account. If we ever need it, it's just a phone call away."

"Prove it," Clea said. "I want to see a bank book or something. I want—"

"What good is that going to do you?" Zane said. "God, you know nothing about finance. Trust me."

"Oh, please," Amy said.

"You need me, Clea," Zane wheedled on. "You think you can take care of yourself? You never have. There's always been somebody around to be your daddy. And I'm the best one of the bunch. You think Leo is going to take care of you? The only reason's he's even talking to you is because he wants to make *Coming Clean Two*. You want to do that?"

Sophie frowned at Amy and said, "*Coming Clean Two?*"

Amy shrugged.

"No, I don't want that," Clea said. "But there are other projects I can do with Leo. Sophie's written some great stuff and she's going to write more. She—"

"Sophie couldn't write for *Sesame Street*, let alone Leo Kingsley," Zane said, contempt dripping from his voice. "Hell, look at her, she's about the least exciting woman we know. She's so repressed, she's sexless."

Sophie felt herself flush. "Definitely the Mace."

"Besides, I told you, my wife does not make movies for Leo Kingsley," Zane was saying to Clea. "Now you go get packed. I'll wait for you on the porch, and then we'll go home together."

They heard Clea stomp up the kitchen stairs and then her bedroom door slammed.

Zane came into the living room, looking mad as hell but triumphant. "Did you get all that?" he asked them, and Amy said, "Pretty much, but we have a few questions. About the weather girl, did—"

"You can pack up your video shit," he said. "My wife is not making this damn movie, she's coming home with me."

"Oh, *no*," Rachel said, and Sophie said, "We'll just wait to get the good word from her."

Zane shook his head. "My wife does what I tell her to. Someday you'll understand that."

" 'And someday you'll drop dead and I'll come to your funeral in a red dress,' " Sophie said.

Zane snorted and went out on the porch.

They heard a car come down the lane, and Rachel got up to look. "It's the Lutzes."

"Nothing but good times ahead," Amy said, clasping her hands in front of her.

They sat on the couch and listened to Frank and Georgia fawn over Zane on the porch—"A real celebrity right here in Temptation," Georgia said over and over—until Rob came in from the porch looking annoyed. "That guy," he said, and Rachel nodded.

"We know." She made room for him on the couch.

"What a loser," Rob said as he sat down.

Sophie waited for him to elaborate, but he seemed to feel he'd said it all. Okay, so Rob wasn't deep. Looking like that, he didn't need to be. Except someday he wouldn't look like that, and then he'd be Frank.

"You know, Clea might be up there packing," Amy said, but then Clea came down the stairs in her red-and-white dress, ready to film, and smiled at Rob when she saw him.

"Well, hello there," she said, and he leaped from the couch, elbowing Rachel in the process.

"You look great," he said.

"So we're still making a movie?" Amy said.

"Well, of course," Clea said, and went out onto the porch with Rob to torment her husband.

And more power to her, Sophie thought, loathing Zane more than she ever had in her life.

An hour later, Sophie was exhausted from watching all the raging egos in the dusty yard. Georgia flirted obnoxiously with Zane (keeping one eye on Frank), while Zane flirted obnoxiously with Rachel (keeping one eye on Clea), while Rachel politely did not tell him he was a jack-ass. Through it all, an oblivious Frank continued to drool on Clea, who flirted obnoxiously with Rob and kept an eye on everybody else to make sure she was the center of attention. It gave Sophie a headache, but Amy filmed it all with delight, including shots of the now bright red water tower. "It looks like a lipstick with a nipple," she told Sophie. "Very female." Sophie looked at Clea and said, "I've had enough 'fe-male' for a while," and went back into the house.

She sat at the kitchen table with the dog at her feet and tried to work on the Phallic Variation, but Zane's voice kept interrupting her thoughts.

"She's sexless," she heard Zane say again, and she thought, *You son of a bitch, I am not sexless.* Okay, maybe she wasn't exciting, but she wasn't sexless. Zane should talk to Phin, that's what he should do.

Although what would that prove? As Phin had pointed out the night before, he'd done all the work. She hadn't exactly taken a walk on the wild side. It was more like she'd been walked.

Which didn't mean she couldn't take a walk over there, it didn't mean she couldn't be sexy and exciting. When she thought about it, Temptation was the perfect place to go to the devil.

Thinking about the devil made her think about Phin, and thinking about Phin made her sure. That's what she'd do. The hell with Zane, she'd just go find Phin. And be exciting.

She got up to call Brandon to tell him things were definitely off, and got his machine again. Well, she'd just work on an *exciting sex scene* for now and call him later.

Two hours of anguished composition later, she'd tried to call Bran-don four times and erased the words on her screen six times because they were so stupid, which proved Zane was right, damn him. Plus the temperature had risen at least ten degrees, and she was drowning in her own sweat. Even the dog had rolled over on its back and was panting heavily. Sophie looked at the words on her screen and thought, *And that's the only heavy breathing this garbage will ever hear,* and deleted it all again.

The problem was trying to write a love scene and stay a lady at the same time. It wasn't possible. The minute you started thinking that writing sex was cheap and disgusting, your mind froze up and you wrote boring dreck. It was sort of like having sex. You either threw everything you had into it, or it wasn't worth the bother.

Which was probably why most of the sex she'd had up till now hadn't been worth the bother.

She sat back and stared at the wall as she contemplated this new thought, and the cherries sneered back again. Evidently they hadn't gotten the good news they were apples.

"Amy called and said you needed these," Phin said from behind her, and Sophie leaped in her chair.

"I *hate* it when you do that," she said, trying to get her heart out of her throat.

Phin dropped a box of fuses on the table and pulled out a chair. "Why are you so nervous?"

"I'm not nervous." Sophie refused to meet his eyes. "I'm annoyed. I hate those damn cherries, and now it turns out they're apples. If you want to bring me something I really need, get me a gallon of white paint."

"If you don't like them, don't look at them," Phin said. "Look at me."

"The cherries are beginning to look better," Sophie said, staring at the wall.

"You want to explain why you're mad at me?"

"I'm not mad at you," she said, and made the mistake of looking at him.

Even sitting in an ugly kitchen in the heat, he was gorgeous: cool and immaculate in another one of those damn perfect white shirts.

"Good," Phin said. "Amy says you're coming to the Tavern tonight. Of course, this time you'll be drinking Diet Coke without the rum."

Sophie forgot how gorgeous he was. "I'll be drinking whatever I want. And give me one good reason why I'd want to go back to that dump."

Phin grinned at her, and Sophie's heart betrayed her and kicked up a beat. "You had a good time last night, didn't you?" he said.

"Why do you give me an opening like that?" She turned back to her PowerBook, trying to ignore the sizzle that was making her dizzy. "You're just begging me to say something crushing."

"You won't." Phin leaned back in his chair. "You're too honest."

She wanted to wipe that smile off his face, to tell him it had been lousy, tell him he was entirely forgettable, tell him that she wasn't honest, that she came from a long line of crooks and liars and deviants, that she'd been *using* him. . . . But when she met his eyes, she couldn't do it. "Okay. It was phenomenal."

"I know," Phin said.

Sophie's irritation rose again. "You know, women don't find arrogance all that attractive."

"Giving me pointers on my technique?"

"It could use some work."

"It got you on your back last night."

Sophie lifted her chin. " 'When you first came in for breakfast, when I first saw you, I thought you were handsome. Then, of course, you spoke.' "

"So I make you nervous," Phin said.

"Not at all."

"Because that's a movie quote, right? You know, if you do that with books, people think you're intelligent."

Sophie lowered her chin. "If this is your pathetic attempt to seduce me again, you're failing miserably."

"I don't seduce women." Phin shoved back his chair and stood up. "They just fall into my open arms."

"Clumsy of them," Sophie said, feeling relieved and disappointed that he was going. She turned back to her empty screen and hated it that Zane was right. "A guy just called me sexless," she blurted.

"He's wrong," Phin said. "So, I'll see you at the Tavern tonight?"

There he stood, tall, blond, and capable of giving her not only the Phallic Variation and all the intense satisfaction that went with it, but also her love scene. And she wanted him. She was not sexless. She was practically hyperventilating because he was standing next to her. She was *hot*.

"Yes." Sophie swallowed. "We'll be there." He started to leave, smug as ever, so she said, "By the way, love the water tower. Looks like a giant lipstick with a nipple."

He turned back. "What?"

She smiled at him. "The water tower. It looks like a lipstick now. Except there's that bump on top."

"Catwalk," Phin said. "It was harder to see when it was peach."

"It's not hard now," Sophie said. "In more ways than one. Gotta love it."

"Glad you like it," Phin said, and left, not nearly as smug.

Sophie went back to her PowerBook. She should be able to put all this heat to good use. *Concentrate*, she told herself, and tried to write the sex scene again.

At seven, she put her head down on the kitchen table in despair, which was how Amy found her a few minutes later.

"Not going well?" Amy said. "Not to worry. I asked Phin if he'd fix the slow drain in the kitchen sink tonight after the Tavern. And once you get him in the kitchen, how hard can it be to lure him upstairs?"

"I don't lure."

"Concentrate, Sophie," Amy said. "Your insignificant other will be back tonight. What are you going to do about it?"

"I have no idea." Sophie thought about Phin, and blushed in the heat. "Maybe he'll just take over like he did last time. And the earth will move, and then we'll both look beautifully moist without being too disheveled."

"You don't want to have sex," Amy said. "You want to have sex in the movies."

Sophie thought about it. "No, I want to have sex. I've been trying to call Brandon all day to break things off so I can have the mayor tonight without guilt, but he won't pick up the phone."

"He knows you too well," Amy said. "He knows you won't cheat, so if he doesn't give you the chance to dump him, you'll have to be faithful."

"I don't have to be faithful." Sophie thought again about the night to come, and began to have doubts. After all, this would involve taking her clothes off in front of a semi–complete stranger. "But I probably will be anyway. I have no moves, and I don't see the mayor making one on his own. He's not the aggressive type. The only reason he moved last night was that we were sort of talking dirty."

"So do that again," Amy said.

"I don't think I can," Sophie said, looking at the mess on her screen. "I can't even *write* dirty."

"It's easy. Just say, 'Fuck me.' He'll take it from there."

" 'Fuck me.' " Sophie tried to imagine saying that to Phin. It sounded so unlike her. "I'll think of something else."

"Simple ways are best," Amy said. "Go with 'Fuck me' and get that scene."

Oh, right, Sophie thought. Then she thought of Zane. The least exciting woman he knew, huh? Then she thought of the dock. And Phin. And the heat rose again. *Fuck me*. "Fuck me," she tried out loud.

"There you go," Amy said.

"Fuck me," Sophie said again, and went upstairs to practice while she put on Clea's pink dress.

Six

At nine that night, Phin sat in the booth across from Wes and watched Sophie, stuck at a table with the rest of the crowd from the farm. She looked as fuckable as ever.

"Amy's over there," Wes said. "We should—"

"No," Phin said, still watching Sophie. "As soon as Amy realizes she needs you, she'll come over here and we won't have to put up with Frank and Georgia. Although since you gave her that showerhead, she may not realize that anytime soon. Never give a woman an appliance that replaces you. She'll use it and turn on you."

"She's smart as hell," Wes said, ignoring him. "And she's funny and sharp, and she lays it right on the line. I like her."

"Try to think about something else," Phin said.

"I went to see Stephen Garvey this afternoon," Wes said obediently. "He said he was going to take care of the Dempseys' car to avoid negative publicity before the election. He seemed to think I was there because you'd sent me."

"Me?" Phin frowned at him. "Why would I—"

"He said he knew if he went after the Dempseys, you'd be vindictive and use it against him, you being so closely tied to the movie people."

" 'Closely tied'?" Phin said, his mind drifting to rope and Sophie.

"His words, not mine. He's up to something and it's got something to do with that movie."

Across the room, Sophie stretched, and Phin lost interest in Stephen. "Maybe if I ask nice, Sophie will tell me about the movie."

Wes rolled his eyes. "That's good. Concentrate on the important stuff. What happened to her being a dangerous woman to get involved with?"

Phin watched Sophie nod at Frank. *Forget him, come over here to me.* "I'm not talking about getting involved with her. I'm talking about seeing her naked."

"I'm against you using Sophie for sex," Wes said. "I like her. Also, I think she's dangerous as long as Stephen's got this movie thing going. Besides, she has a boyfriend back in Cincy. Amy says he's a big-shot therapist."

Phin took his eyes off Sophie to frown at Wes. "That was a real hot conversation you had with Amy. Conversations like that will get you in the sack about in time for Y3K."

"Amy also said that, based on what Sophie tells her, the guy is extremely boring in bed. So you might be able to talk her into the naked part, but it would be a really stupid thing to do since she's going to leave tomorrow."

"Since when did you become the Chastity Patrol?"

"I like Sophie," Wes said. "Do not seduce and abandon her or I'll arrest you for something."

"Police brutality," Phin said. "Which reminds me, if I get lucky with Sophie, can I borrow some handcuffs?"

"You've still got the last ones you borrowed. Phin, I'm not kidding. Sophie deserves more than your hit-and-run, and Stephen's too damn pleased that you've been out there twice. Just stay away from her."

"Hey," Amy said, as she bounced into the booth beside Wes. "What's new in crime and government?"

Phin watched Wes turn toward her, his world a better place. *Great*, he thought. *She's going to leave and break his fucking heart.*

Across the bar, Rachel was standing, and Sophie looked unhappy.

"Later for you two," Phin said to them, and went to see what Sophie needed.

Half an hour earlier, Frank had sat down across from Sophie, friendly-drunk but not reeling, and said, "So how's it going?"

"Just great," Sophie had said, pretending not to notice Georgia crawling into Zane's lap beside them. It was difficult because she was also pretending not to notice Phin sitting across the room. She'd planned to play hard-to-get, but if that got her Frank's conversation and Georgia's seduction in stereo, she was going to get a lot easier very soon.

Georgia said loudly, "You really are some man, Zane Black, you really are," and Frank shrugged at Sophie and gave a little laugh.

Five minutes, to be polite, and then I'm heading for that booth. "And how's your life?" Sophie said, trying to make conversation, realizing too late that it was a dumb thing to ask at that particular moment.

Frank drank some beer. "Oh, pretty good." He started to peel the label off his bottle. "That's all I ever wanted anyway. Pretty good." He let his eyes drift over to Clea at the bar, laughing up at his son.

" 'Pretty good' 's not bad," Sophie agreed, wishing there was someplace she could look that didn't have evidence that Frank's life was pretty terrible.

"You know, growing up, I knew exactly what I wanted," Frank said, expanding into contemplative used-car salesman mode. "A good job, a nice house, a pretty wife, a son, and two cars, a Jeep and a big luxury car to take the wife places. I had it all planned out by eighteen."

"Well, you got that," Sophie said. "Of course, I'm guessing on the cars."

"I got it all," Frank said. "And it is not a bad life, not at all. Except..." He looked over at the bar again and took another swig of beer. Then he leaned forward, and Sophie leaned forward a little, too, to get farther away from Georgia. "Did you ever one day look up and realize you'd been staring at the ground when there was a whole sky on top of you? Just one day, realize that there was more out there than you could have imagined?"

"No," Sophie said. She'd always known there was more out there than she could imagine, that was why she was so careful not to look up. Bat country.

"By the time I was a senior in high school," Frank said, "I had it all lined up. Even the job with my future father-in-law." He stopped and stared at the bar. "And then one day there was Clea." He shook his head. "Sure, she's beautiful now, but you should have seen her at eighteen, Sophie." He leaned back. "We were in the school play together, you know."

Sophie nodded to be polite, and stole a look at Phin. He was talking to Wes, looking as detached as ever. She wondered if anything ever made him sweat, and then she thought, *I could*. No matter what Zane thought.

Frank was still talking. "And after the last performance, she said, 'Let's go out to the Tavern, Frank,' and we sat out in back, with a thousand stars over us, and she said, 'We could be like that, Frank, we could be stars. We could go to Hollywood.'" Frank laughed, a little shamefaced. "Yeah, I know it sounds corny."

"Not as much as you'd think," Sophie said. "Everybody needs dreams."

"Yeah, but Hollywood?" Frank leaned forward, serious again. "The thing is, I believed her, Sophie. When I was with her that night, I believed *I* could make it. I mean, I'm a damn good actor, and I have a really great voice. I might have . . ." He looked back at Clea. "No, I wouldn't have. *She* didn't even make it, really. But, boy, it was a hell of a night. We were going to have it all."

"I heard you got it all," Sophie said.

Frank looked down at his beer. "She told you that?" He shook his head. "Finest moment of my life when she said, 'I want it to be you, Frank.'"

Sophie frowned. This story was not the one Clea had told. She let her eyes slide to the booth in the back and saw Phin watching her and her pulse kicked up.

"You know . . ." Frank looked back at the bar and Clea. "It wouldn't be so bad if I hadn't thought, for just that one night, that there was more. You know? If I just hadn't seen what . . . It's like losing something you never had. You can't really be sorry, but you can't ever really forget it, either. Even when you've got everything you ever really knew you could get. Sometimes, it still comes back."

"In this case, literally," Sophie said, looking at Clea, who was flirting with Rob, oblivious to the carnage at the table behind her.

"Yeah," Frank said. "I was ready to go to Cincy to make the land deal, but she said she wanted to come here. And I thought . . ." He sighed. "Oh, hell, you know what I thought." He drained his beer.

"Yeah," Sophie said. "I know what you thought."

"Dumb," Frank said. "Jesus, I'm dumb."

"Well, human," Sophie said.

"No, dumb." Frank finally looked the other direction, away from Clea and toward Georgia, now hanging all over Zane.

Sophie opened her mouth to say something comforting, but she couldn't think of anything. The man's lost love was at the bar moving on his son, his wife was molesting a TV anchorman, and he was stuck nursing a warm beer in an ugly bar in a creepy little town. About the best thing that could happen to Frank would be a direct hit from an asteroid.

"We'll be gone in a week," she said finally, and Frank said, "That calls for another beer," and got up.

Rachel slid into his seat, looking miserable.

"Are you okay?" Sophie said.

Rachel rolled her eyes. "Oh, yeah, I'm great. I'm in Temptation, how bad can it be?" She was trying to come on cool, but she sounded a little shaky.

"Yeah, I heard you want out of town pretty bad, Rachel," Zane said, as he leaned toward her across the empty chair between them. "I told you, if there's anything I can do—"

Rachel leaned back.

"Want to trade places with me, Rachel?" Sophie said. "I have Mace."

"You wouldn't need it," Zane said.

"What are you *talking* about?" Georgia nudged Zane with her shoulder and batted her eyes at him. "Go on, now. You were telling me about being a news anchor. I just think that's so *sexy*."

Zane leaned back and began to talk about the joys of being a celebrity, and Rachel looked even more miserable, so Sophie leaned forward and said, "Okay, what's wrong?"

"I want out of this town," she finally said. "I was lousy at college and I'm not good at anything else, and my mom and dad are hipped on me getting married and living next door to them forever, and if I don't get out of Temptation I'm going to go crazy, and I'm not kidding."

Sophie nodded. Given Rachel's parents, she wasn't exaggerating.

"And I thought, like, maybe the movie thing would get me out, but you're going back to Cincinnati, and Amy said no, and Clea hates me." She shot a look of loathing across the table at Zane. "And I talked to *him* about it for maybe two seconds, and he stood real close and put his hand on my butt and told me we could talk about it in private."

"Stay away from him," Sophie said. "He's a complete loss as a human being."

"I know," Rachel said. "But he's telling people how much I want to leave, just like I told him, only he's making it sound like I offered him something that I didn't. And he keeps touching me."

Sophie picked up her purse and took out her Mace. "Just in case he goes deaf when you say no," she said, and handed the lipstick-sized can to Rachel.

Rachel cheered up a little bit as she turned it over in her hand. "I've never had Mace."

"Well, now you're armed and dangerous," Sophie said. "And I'd be so delighted if you used it on Zane. Really. Use all of it."

Rachel grinned at her, almost back to normal. Sophie let her eyes drift back to Phin. He was looking at her with a half smile on his face.

Sophie's pulse give a little surge of lust and panic.

Okay, there was no reason to get rattled just because he was looking at her as if he wanted her. She wanted him, too, right now, no waiting. That sounded slutty, so she told herself it was for the movie. It really wasn't sex—she took her eyes off Phin so she could think better—not sex, that would be depraved, it was work. That was it. She had work to do tonight. Important work to do tonight. *Imperative* work to do tonight. And it was just *sitting* over there *waiting* for her—

"Sophie?" Rachel said.

"We'll think of something for you," Sophie told her, babbling a little. "We've got an extra week, we'll think of something."

"Really?"

Sophie looked back at Phin. "Absolutely."

Frank came back to the table and put another rum and Diet Coke in front of Sophie, and Georgia said loudly to Zane, "Tell me more about being a big TV star." She pressed her breast against Zane's arm, and Sophie thought he was going to say something rude. Then he smiled and said, "What do you want to know?" and she realized what he was doing.

"Georgia, would you show me where the bathroom is?" Sophie said, and Georgia jerked her thumb over her shoulder.

"Behind the bar, sugar."

Zane leaned closer to her. "Sophie wants you to go with her so she can tell you what a bad man I am."

Georgia widened her eyes and giggled. "I *love* bad men."

"Georgia," Frank said quietly. "You're drunk."

Georgia leered at him. "Oh, you're a real rocket scientist tonight."

"I think I'll go home," Rachel said, and stood up.

"Wait." Sophie nodded to the bar where Rob was leaning close to Clea, clearly not leaving soon. "Rob brought you, didn't he? How are you getting home?"

"I can walk," Rachel said, and Sophie stood up and said, "No, you can't. I'll get the keys from Amy."

"I'll drive her," Phin said from behind them. "You want a ride home, too?"

Sophie turned and caught her breath. "Oh. Yes. Sure. If it's on your way." *Of course it's on his way. Jeez, Sophie.*

"I've had about all the Tavern I can stand for one night," Phin said. "We can take Rachel home and then go back and fix your kitchen."

"Sounds good." Sophie looked across the room at Amy, who waved her on and turned back to smile at Wes. Clea and Rob were practically in each other's laps. Georgia was whispering something in Zane's ear. Frank looked confused and sad.

"Get me out of here," Sophie said, and Phin said, "Thought so," and gave her a gentle push toward the door.

Half an hour later, Sophie leaned on the kitchen sink with a glass of wine and tried to calm her pounding heart while Phin worked on the plumbing. With his head under the sink, she could scope out his body without having to face the distance in his eyes, and, having reacquainted herself with how very nicely he was put together, she felt a lot better about having fallen the night before, not to mention her plans to fall again tonight. Clearly this was quality stuff. If she could just get him to shut up, he'd be perfect.

"That's it," he said, pulling his head out from under the sink. "Turn on the water."

She walked over to the sink and turned on the tap. "Very fast," she said as the water swirled down the drain. "Nice job, Mayor."

"Yeah, well, we do it all." He got to his feet. "Now, I'll have some of that wine."

She poured him a glass while he washed his hands, and then sat at the table with him in uncomfortable silence while he took his first sip. "Interesting," he said, looking at the glass. "Did you make this in the basement?"

"We bought it at the grocery," Sophie said.

"The grocery here in Temptation?" Phin said, appalled.

"It's the only one," Sophie said. "Of course, the grocery here."

He started to laugh. "What, you couldn't afford the Ripple?"

"Fine, don't drink it." Sophie reached for his glass, but Phin held on to it.

"I'm sure it'll be fine once I get used to it." He took another sip and shuddered. "Never mind," he said, and passed it over to her. "So tell me about the movie."

"No." Sophie looked at him with naked exasperation. "That's all you ever ask about, and I've already told you everything. What is it with you?"

Phin shrugged. "Okay, tell me about your life. How did the therapist take the news last night?"

Sophie raised her eyebrows. "You know he's a therapist?"

"This is Temptation," Phin said. "Stay long enough, I'll know everything about you. Of course, since you're leaving tomorrow, you'll get to keep most of your secrets."

"We're not leaving tomorrow," Sophie said. "We're going to shoot some extra footage for the movie, so we're staying over until next Sunday."

"Really." Phin's face was as impassive as ever. "And how did the therapist take that?"

"I didn't tell him." Sophie sipped her wine and gathered her courage. "I told him I wanted to fuck you, and he told me I was trying to shock him with language." There, that was the ticket, just say it really fast, like swallowing medicine or pulling off a Band-Aid.

Phin frowned his disbelief. "You told him you wanted to fuck him, and he yelled at you for talking dirty?" He shook his head. "This guy is dead below the waist."

"No." Sophie picked up his glass and moved to the sink to dump it. Then she swallowed and said carefully, "I told him I wanted to fuck *you*, and he said—" She stopped because this time he'd gotten it. "That wasn't a pass," she said, backing up a step. "I was merely—"

"The hell it wasn't." Phin stood up, and Sophie thought, *Oh, jeez, it's working, now what do I do?*

"Well, not really." She backed up again and bumped into the wall. "It was more . . ."

He followed her to the wall and bent to look her in the eye. "Sophie."

"What?"

"That was a pass."

She shrugged. "Maybe, subconsciously, a small one."

"Sophie."

She shut her eyes. "Okay, it was a pass, but—"

He kissed her, and she didn't have to finish the sentence, which was a damn good thing because she had no idea where she'd been going with it. She kissed him back, clutching at his shirt, and he broke the kiss to say, "Don't wrinkle the cotton," and pried her fingers off. She thought, *Well, the hell with you.* Then he pulled her close again, and she pressed herself against all that lovely muscle and bone and thought, *As long as he shuts up, this is going to be good,* and then his mouth was on hers again, and she stopped thinking at all.

Ten minutes later, when her dress was unbuttoned and so was his shirt, and she was dizzy and tight with the heat and even he looked a little mind-whacked, he said, "Where's your bedroom?"

"What?" Sophie blinked at him, coming back from all that good lust.

"Bed. Room," Phin said distinctly, sliding his hand inside her dress. "Or we can do this on the kitchen table, but I'm pretty sure I just heard somebody pull up outside. I don't care if Wes and Amy watch, but having Zane in the room would definitely put me off my stroke."

"Oh, no." Sophie stepped back, and he followed her, his hand tightening on her waist. "That would be bad with people . . ." She looked around vaguely. ". . . here." She caught sight of the phone and said, "Oh, *damn*, I have to call Brandon."

Phin looked at her incredulously and took his hand out of her dress. "Now?"

"I have to break up with him before I fool around with you," Sophie said. "That's only right."

"You're a little late." He gestured to her open dress. "The fooling-around is pretty much under way. Come here." He reached for her again, and she ducked away to grab the phone. "I don't believe this," he said, and sat down on the edge of the table, disheveled and gorgeous, looking at her as if she were demented, while she dialed and then waited for Brandon to pick up the phone.

"Brandon?" she said when it finally clicked, but it was his machine again. "Listen, Brandon, I did not want to leave this message on your machine, but since you're avoiding me—" She looked back over her shoulder at Phin, who was shaking his head at the ceiling. "—I think we should break up. And see other people. So that's what I'm doing. Seeing other people."

Phin put his head in his hands.

"Of course, they're not sensitive, understanding people like you," Sophie said pointedly.

"You want sensitive and understanding, stick with the therapist," Phin said. "You want great, headbanging sex, get off the fucking phone and come with me."

"I have to go now," Sophie said breathlessly into the phone. "I'm sorry if this hurts you but I don't think it will. You always seemed sort of clinical anyway."

"Oh, yeah, that'll soften the blow," Phin said. "Remind me never to get involved with you."

"Um, have a nice life," Sophie said brightly, and hung up. She walked over and boosted herself onto the table next to him, willing herself to stay cool, and reached for her wineglass again. "So you're not getting involved?"

He took the glass away from her. "No. I'm just going to have cheap sex with you and then run like hell."

"Chicken," she said.

He stood up and put her glass in the sink, and then he came back to stand in front of her, parting her knees with his body. He said, "You bet," and she lost her breath again.

He kissed her, sliding his hand into her dress to cup her breast, and she thought, *A semi–complete stranger is groping me*, and smiled against his mouth.

"What?" he said, and she gave in to the devil and wrapped her legs around his waist.

"It feels good," she said, and he said, "Well, that's why I do it," and kissed her again, running his hands down her back to lift her off the table.

"Where's the bedroom?" he said, and she said, "Second door on the left upstairs."

"Upstairs?" He put her back on the table. "Then you walk. And make it quick, before the therapist calls back."

She was going to argue, but she heard Amy and Wes on the porch, so she slid off the table and headed for the stairs and all that head-banging sex she'd been promised.

Twenty minutes later, she was suffocating on top of him in the heat of her unair-conditioned bedroom, the ancient box springs squeaking under them like a bad accordion, and her head was unbanged because the sex was lousy.

It wasn't Phin's fault. He was as thoroughly competent at the Phallic Variation as he'd been orally the night before. *So it must be me,* she thought, as he moved under her, doing absolutely nothing for her. She felt embarrassed by the whole situation. Zane had been right. She just wasn't the type for headbanging sex. She was too detached. She was too prissy and straight. She was doing this to write a sex scene for a movie she wasn't even sure she wanted to make. She was hot and sticky and she could feel her hair kinking in the heat even as Phin breathed under her, so she knew she looked awful. She was *unexciting.* Whatever the reason, it didn't matter, she was never going to get anywhere at this rate.

She thought briefly about faking it, and then dumped the idea when she realized that Phin would probably see through it and make fun of her performance. That pretty much left her with no option except tapping him on the shoulder and telling him to play on through because she was out of the game. *Sorry,* she'd have to say. *I'm not even close.* Or she could let him figure it out on his own, except guys never did. They just—

"You're not even close, are you?" Phin said, breathless below her, and she refocused back on him.

"What?"

"Hi, I'm Phin Tucker, and I'm inside you. I know how these things slip your mind." He didn't sound annoyed, but she felt bad anyway.

"I'm sorry," she said, and he slid his hand down her back and rolled to one side so that they lay face-to-face on the damp sheets, the springs protesting under them.

"Don't apologize." He brushed back a curl that was stuck to her forehead. "Thinking about the therapist?" He moved against her to bring her closer, and her nerves kicked into gear.

"Who?" she said, trying to figure out what the hell he was talking about.

"Well, at least you forgot us both," Phin said. "That was very democratic of you." He used a corner of the sheet to wipe sweat off her forehead. "Remind me to get you an air conditioner before we do this again. I'm dying here."

She wanted to say, *What are you talking about, AGAIN? This is a disaster*, but it didn't seem polite. "Maybe we should just call it a night," she said, and moved back from him, and he followed her to stay inside her, and that made her shiver under his hands.

"Maybe we should give it another shot," he said as she trembled. "That's at least one nerve you've still got working." He kissed her in the damp curve where her neck met her shoulder, and she took a ragged breath and moved against him again without thinking. "And that one always works. I noticed that last night."

"Last night was different," she said.

"Yeah, you came," Phin said, and she laughed in spite of herself.

"Not that. I'm distracted tonight. It's not your fault."

"Do me a favor." Phin slid his hand down her sweat-damp back again. "Don't be understanding. There's nothing worse for a guy's ego."

"Your ego is in fine shape," Sophie said crushingly. "Along with the rest of you. Really, this isn't going to work. Could we go watch TV now or something?"

"No." Phin kissed her in the curve of her neck again, and she shivered and said, "Stop that."

"See?" he said in her ear, which made her shiver, too. "Progress. Now tell me your fantasies."

"What?" She tried to squirm away and he rolled again, trapping her under him. He was heavy and sweaty which should have been a turn-off, but her body rocked against his, independent of her mind, and she closed her eyes as he slid deeper into her.

"I think it's time we got to know each other," Phin said, laughter in his voice. "What do you think about when you masturbate?"

"Okay, I'm out of here." Sophie tried to roll out from under him, but he pressed down on her with his hips, and she stayed just to feel him hard inside her.

"What do you think about, Sophie?" he whispered in her ear, and she said loudly, "I don't think about anything."

"You are such a lousy liar." He rolled again, this time so that she was on top, his body sliding slickly under hers, and Sophie felt herself flush.

"Bondage?" he said, his voice husky as he rocked against her, his hands on her hips, and she caught her breath and said, "You come near me with a rope, and I'm history."

"Okay, later for that," he said. "Rape fantasy?"

"Tacky," she said, and he said, "Not if you do it right. You want to dominate?"

"Oh, yeah. Like you'd let me." She started to laugh, only to stop when she heard people in the kitchen downstairs. "Shhh."

"Why?" Phin stopped moving. "It's just Wes and Amy."

"Yeah." Sophie looked over her shoulder at the door.

"Did you lock it?" Phin said in her ear, and he sounded amused.

"I forgot." She tried to pull away from him, but he rolled and trapped her again, sliding deeper inside her and making her gasp. "Stop it," she said breathlessly. "I'm not even sure it's closed all the way. Let me go lock it and I'll come back."

"Bothers you, huh?" Phin started working his way down her neck again as he pulsed inside her, and Sophie felt the heat spread low as her blood pounded.

"No," she lied.

"They could walk in anytime." He nibbled on her shoulder, and she twitched under him and felt her breath go. "Walk right in and find us naked." He slid his hand up to her sweat-dampened breast, and the heat rolled across her as she moved to his rhythm. "Find *you* naked. With me inside you. *Nothing* you could do about it."

She caught her breath and said, "*Stop* it," and he said, "Nope, I think we're getting somewhere."

She squirmed under him to get away, and their bodies slid together. He said, "Oh, God, yes, do that," and she smacked him on the shoulder because he was so impossible, and arched into him at the same time because he was so hard moving inside her and he felt so good.

"Maybe I can get . . . somebody else . . . to open that door," he said in her ear, and she said, "No!" a lot louder than she meant because it was part moan. She heard Amy say, "Sophie?" downstairs, and she tensed. Phin laughed down at her, his face as damp as hers.

Beautifully moist, Sophie thought. *Be careful what you wish for.*

Amy called her name again, and Phin said, "Excellent." He rocked higher into her, and she bit her lip to keep from moaning and then moaned anyway. "Louder," he said, and she shook her head as the heat built and his rhythm began to make her mindless.

"Then it's up to me." He sounded breathless. "The guy always has to do everything."

He leaned over her to the bedside table, and she bit into his shoulder from the sheer pleasure of feeling him against her. Then he stopped, and she looked up to see him holding the alarm clock.

"I'll buy you a new one," he said, and threw it against the wall.

"What are you *doing*?" she screamed as it crashed and went off clanging. Amy called up, "Sophie?" and Phin moved again, rocking harder, and she shuddered under him and gasped, "*Stop* it."

"This close? Not on your life." He was moving faster now, and she clutched at him and breathed hard as the pressure built. She said, "No . . . no . . . we're not . . . close," and he rolled across her again, making her jerk against him. He picked up the dolphin lamp, yanking the cord out with it, and she realized what he was doing and shrieked, "No!" just as he threw it against the wall.

It shattered and fell on top of the clanging alarm.

"Sophie?" Amy called, and started up the stairs, and Phin said, "This is it," and moved high into her, grabbing her wrists and holding them over her head, sliding hot on top of her, rocking hard inside her, whispering in her ear that Amy'd catch them, any minute, any minute, any minute, now, now, *now*, and Sophie twisted under him, caught in the heat and the slide and the panic and the throb he was pounding into her, and then Amy said, "Sophie?" and pushed open the door, and Sophie cried, "Oh, *God*," and came so hard she almost passed out.

"Oh," Amy said, and shut the door.

Sophie heard Amy go down the stairs, with only a fraction of her attention. The rest was consumed with how good she felt everywhere as the aftershocks made her twitch, how much she needed her breath back, and how she was going to strangle Phin when he let go of her wrists and she was done feeling incredible. And even as she had the thought, he shuddered on top of her and let go, collapsing with his face in her pillow.

"You *pervert*," she said minutes later, when she could talk.

"You came," he said, his voice muffled by the pillow.

"I don't *believe* you did that."

"I don't believe you're not grateful."

"Grateful?" Sophie struggled to sit up, and for once he let her slide out from under him, rolling to get rid of the condom as she moved away from him. "*Look* at this." The alarm clock was smashed next to the baseboard, and the dolphin lamp was in a million pieces, and it was just a *mess*, but try as she might, she couldn't work up any real indignation. Total satisfaction did that, she supposed, just sort of made everything else irrelevant. Still, he'd been impossible, so she concentrated on the carnage while she used the sheet to blot the sweat from her happily throbbing body. "I mean, just look at it!"

Phin draped his arm across her shoulders and pulled her back down on the bed, his face still in the pillow. "Did you come?"

Sophie crossed her arms over her breasts and glared at the ceiling, ignoring the hot weight of his arm across her and all the cheering her body was doing. "Yes."

"Did you like it?" he said, his voice still muffled by the pillow.

She started to grin in spite of herself. "Yes."

"Say, 'Thank you, Phin.'"

"Oh, please."

"Say, 'Thank you *very* much, Phin.' "

"I don't think so."

"Say, 'You are a great lover, Phin.' "

"I'm out of here." She rolled to swing out of bed, and his arm slipped down to her waist and pulled her back against him.

He felt good, solid against her back, and she had to concentrate to remember she was annoyed with him for making her come.

That couldn't be right.

He pulled his face out of the pillow and rolled to cuddle her to him from behind, kissing her damp hair and holding her close. "Discovery fantasy," he said, and she relaxed into the hot curve of his body.

"What?"

"You have discovery fantasies. Very common among women." He yawned in her ear. "Men don't have them. We like to watch."

"I do not have discovery fantasies," Sophie said. "That's kinky."

"You're kinky."

Sophie tried to pull away in outrage. "I am *not* kinky."

He sighed. "Sophie, your soul is a corkscrew." He held on to her and kissed her neck again, and she gave up to stay curled in his heat, guiltily flattered that he thought she was kinky. Not sexless after all. In fact . . .

"So . . . I'm exciting?"

"Heart-stopping," Phin said into her neck. "And you definitely have discovery fantasies. I foresee us having a lot of sex in public places." He yawned again and shifted on the bed. "Anyplace would be more comfortable than this mattress. Not to mention quieter."

"I don't see us having a lot of sex anywhere," Sophie said, trying to get her control back. *But I'm exciting.*

"That's because you're repressed," Phin said. "Which is why God sent me to save you."

"God did not send you," Sophie said. "The devil sent you. And we're not having sex in public."

"Sure we are," Phin said. "You want to know why?"

He kissed her neck again and her pulse kicked up again. "No."

"Because you like it," he whispered in her ear, and she shivered against him.

"I don't think so," she said, and put her hand on the edge of the bed to push herself out of his arms before he talked her into sex on the kitchen table.

He caught her right hand to stop her, and then he brought it close to their faces to look at it. "Your ring has writing on it." He sounded sleepy, and she gave up trying to escape, enjoying the way his voice felt in her ear.

"They both do," Sophie said. "One says *free will* and the other one says *destiny*. They were my mother's." She looked at the ring in the moonlight, and at Phin's fingers intertwined with hers, and thought, *That's nice.*

Phin turned the ring until the *destiny* was centered on her finger and yawned. "Free will and fate?"

He didn't sound as if he cared, and Sophie rolled in his arms so she could look at him. He smiled when she turned, a sleepy, lazy smile just for her that had nothing to do with politics or charm, and she thought, *Wow.* She almost rolled closer and kissed him, but that would make things more complicated, so she concentrated on his question.

"There are things you can change . . ." Sophie held up her left hand with the *free will* ring to watch it glint in the moonlight. "And things you can't change." She pulled the *destiny* hand free from his.

Phin recaptured the hand with *destiny* on it. "I don't believe in destiny," he said, as he pulled her hand down. He kissed her knuckles, and Sophie shivered at the heat from his mouth.

"Mama said that family is your destiny," she said, trying not to fall again, "because they shape your life."

Phin shrugged against her. "Maybe at first—"

Sophie shook her head, her curls brushing his chest, and watched as he caught his breath. It was such a little thing, but she thought, *I did that.* "Your worldview is established by six," she said, watching him. "You don't have any choice in that. You just get it." *I think I want it again.*

"And then you grow up and move away. You have free will." Phin met her eyes and looked a lot less sleepy. "You can choose whatever you want. I choose this." He began to work his way down her neck again, his lips tickling hot on her skin.

Sophie's pulse kicked up. "Well, that was Mama's point," she said, her voice a little higher than before. "Your family is your destiny, and then you make what you can of that." She thought about her mother for a minute, about all those dreams lost because of her bad choices, and she pulled away. "And then sometimes, destiny comes along and slaps you again anyway."

Phin stopped. "What happened?"

"There was a car accident," Sophie said, remembering the sound of the crunching metal, now confused with the sound from the Garveys' accident, so it seemed new all over again. "She died. She'd spent all those years following Dad around the country, waving her rings and saying, 'Everything will be fine,' and Dad saying, 'Nothing but good times ahead,' and then—" She stopped for a moment, and Phin pulled her closer. "One day there was the accident, and Dad stopped talking about the good times and it was pretty much the three of us and Dusty Springfield."

"That explains a lot," Phin said.

She lifted her chin and flashed her mother's rings in the moonlight. "So then I'd say to Amy, 'Everything will be fine,' and Davy would say to her, 'Nothing but good times ahead,' and Dad would tell us to shut the hell up and we'd be off again."

"Your dad was a salesman?" Phin said.

"Sort of," Sophie said, and rolled away.

He pulled her back against him. "But now everything is fine," he said in her ear. "Davy and Amy are grown up and you're all safe and happy. You made it come true for them."

Sophie nodded. *Just not for me.*

"So let me make it true for you tonight," he said, and when she turned to him, amazed, he kissed her, so gently that she gave herself up to him completely, no doubts at all this time. "Nothing but good times ahead," he said against her mouth, and began to kiss his way down her body again, fulfilling his promise with every move he made.

The phone rang the next morning just as Sophie was typing the end of the lamp scene. She hit SAVE and answered the phone, only to hear Brandon say, "I'm returning your call."

Sophie winced. "Oh. I'm really sorry about that. But you're really better off without me. I know it's painful—"

"But are you better off without me?" Brandon said.

Sophie looked at the phone incredulously. "What?"

"I don't think you've thought this through. You're going to be home this afternoon and we can—"

"Actually, we're staying another week," Sophie said.

"—discuss the situation and help you deal with your denial."

"*My* denial?" Sophie said.

"Another week?" Brandon said.

"Brandon, the only one in denial here is you," Sophie said. "Really, I think we just got used to each other. I think it's time we found other people who will meet our needs." She closed her eyes as she thought of some of the needs Phin had met, could meet, would meet in the next week with any amount of encouragement at all.

"We can meet our needs," Brandon said. "We've always met our needs."

"I think I've discovered new needs," Sophie said.

"If this is about sex, don't be childish. Tell me what you want and I'll give it to you."

"My freedom," Sophie said. "I'm trying to do this the civilized way, but I really want out of this relationship. In fact, I am out."

"I'll call you again at the end of the week," Brandon said. "I'm sure the thrill will be gone by then and we can talk."

"The thrill might be gone, but I will be, too. Really, Brandon—" Sophie began, but he'd already hung up.

"Is the new scene done?" Amy said from the door into the living room.

"Yeah." Sophie hung up the phone and shoved the PowerBook toward her. "That was Brandon. He thinks—"

"Shut up so I can read this," Amy said, and Sophie jerked her head up at the tone in her voice. She watched Amy read from the screen, looking a lot tenser than the scene deserved.

"This is great," Amy said when she finished, but she didn't look happy. "And this explains a lot. I couldn't figure out what all the crashing was about."

"He's very inventive." Sophie frowned at her. "What's wrong."

"Nothing," Amy said. "I have to show this to Clea—"

"No," Sophie said and closed the PowerBook. "What happened?"

Amy bit her lip. "That dickhead Zane," she said finally. "He just told me that if I don't quit doing the video so Cleo will go home with him, he's going to tell Wes about my juvenile record." She swallowed hard. "So I told him to go ahead. I told him Wes already knew and didn't care."

"Does he?"

"No," Amy said. "And I think he'd care—he's a cop, isn't he? But I don't care. I'm going to make this video and the documentary no matter what, and I don't care what that dickhead does, but—"

"But Zane must die," Sophie said, nodding. "I understand. We'll think of something horrible to do to him."

"That would help," Amy said, cheering up a little.

"Too bad Davy isn't here," Sophie said. "He always did the best revenge."

"Let's call him," Amy said. "Because I want something really bad to happen to Zane. Which reminds me, Clea wants another love scene. And that's bound to piss Zane off, so—"

"We should play along." Sophie tried to look blasé. "You want me to sacrifice myself to the mayor again."

"From what I saw last night, it was no sacrifice." Amy managed a weak smile. "And see if he's got a letter sweater we can borrow. He looks like the type who'd have one."

Sophie frowned at her. "A letter sweater?"

Amy nodded, not happy. "Clea wants to do this thing where she's driving up the road on her way home remembering Frank in high school so that when she sees the real Frank, everybody will understand the shock. And then when Rob shows up as his son, it'll make sense that she falls for him."

"I still don't get the lett—"

"She wants Rob to play Frank in her high-school memories." Amy wrinkled her nose. "Corny as hell, but she's calling the shots."

"Right," Sophie said. "I'll ask the mayor for a letter sweater." *And great sex.* She stopped breathing for a moment just thinking about it.

"Soon," Amy said.

Sophie tried to look noble. "I suppose I could go visit the bookstore now. He said he was going to be working there today. And maybe if I can't find anything in the books, he'll have some ideas." *I have some ideas.*

Amy looked down at the lamp scene. "I'd count on it." She still seemed down. "You're just toying with the mayor, right? You're not getting involved?"

"No," Sophie said, cooling off a little. "It's pretty much mutual toying."

"Because I don't need a scene if this is going to be another Chad thing," Amy said. "I really hate it that that happened to you. And the mayor has Chad written all over him."

"He's not," Sophie said. "He was very sweet last night."

"I hate Zane, too," Amy said, not really listening.

"We'll take care of Zane," Sophie said as she got up to go. "Really, nothing but good times ahead."

For once, at least for the rest of the afternoon, she was pretty sure that was true.

Seven

*T*hat same afternoon, Rachel's father called her out of the garden onto the cement patio behind their house. She sat gingerly on the steel garden chair beside him, her weeding gloves on, wary of both the sun-warmed metal and her father's topic of conversation.

"So you're working on this movie," he said. "What are they doing?"

"Just shooting people talking on the porch," Rachel said.

"Oh." Her father seemed disappointed. Then he said, "You let me know what they're doing. It's important for the town."

"Why?"

"It's my civic duty to know what's happening in this town," her father said, puffing up a little. "These outsiders, they could be bad influences. So you tell me everything, you understand?"

"Yes, Daddy," Rachel said, having no intention of doing any such thing. "The Coreys are painting the house this weekend and after school. There's some news."

Her father didn't look interested. "Maybe I should drop by, see for myself. Phin Tucker's out there a lot, isn't he?"

"He showed Sophie how to change the fuses," Rachel said, although she was pretty sure that wasn't the only thing Phin was showing Sophie how to do. Even from the backseat of Phin's convertible the night before, Rachel had picked up on the sexual tension in the front seat. When her mother had met her at the door and said eagerly, "Was that Phin Tucker who brought you home?" she'd said, "Mom, he didn't even know I was there."

"So he's involved with the movie people," her father was saying, and without thinking, Rachel said, "Oh, yeah."

"Does that upset you? Does it upset you that I'm running against him in the election?"

"Why would I be upset? You do it every two years." Rachel stared out at the garden, the garden she'd have to go back to weeding soon, the garden she'd weeded every summer for her whole life.

She wanted to go someplace where somebody else did the weeding.

"I don't want you to be hurt if he's spending time with other women," her father said. "And I don't want you to think you have to choose between your father and your husband."

"*Husband*?" Rachel said. "Not in a million years. Mom's got it in her head that we're going to be together, but she's wrong."

"I'm sure she—" Stephen began, but Rachel cut him off.

"Look, Daddy, it's *Phin*, for God's sake. He taught me to ride my bike and stuck Band-Aids on me when I fell off, and he coached me in softball and yelled at me when I fell over third base in the tournament game. After that, it's kind of hard to get hot looking at him."

"Oh." Stephen looked uncomfortable, and Rachel added, "Sorry, Dad. More than you needed to know."

"No, no, you know you can tell me anything," Stephen said, but his expression added, *Just not that.* "It would be a good match. You could hyphenate your last name. Garvey-Tucker." He looked out into the distance. "Your son could take that name, too."

"Son?" Rachel said.

"Phin needs a son, and you need to stop running around and be settled."

"Running around?" The unfairness of this was criminal. "Where do I run around?"

"I don't like you going out to the Tavern," Stephen said. "You're underage. Of course, I know you go with Rob and he's a gentleman. Too bad his father's an idiot. You're not thinking about marrying Rob, are you?"

Rachel thought about spending the rest of her days in Temptation and the rest of her nights with Rob. "No."

"Well, you have to marry somebody," Stephen said. "You think about Phin. He's a good-looking man. You'd have good-looking sons."

Enough of this "son" talk. The last thing she needed was a baby, for cripes' sake. She was *twenty*.

Her father was still talking, nodding to the house to their right. "And you'd live right next door, so we could help you out whenever you needed."

"Phin wouldn't kick Junie Miller out of that house," Rachel said. "That would be mean."

"There's no reason for him to house his ex–mother-in-law," Stephen said, and Rachel cast a wary look back at the kitchen in case her mother heard. Her mother could go on for hours about how Diane Miller had made Phin buy the house next door to the Garveys just so she could rub their marriage in Virginia's face.

"Just don't wait too long to decide," Stephen was saying. "Or you'll end up like Clea Whipple, not getting married until you're over thirty, no children, living all over the place and never coming home until you're middle-aged. . . ." He went on, and Rachel thought, *God, that sounds great.*

Her father talked on, about family values and her living next door and how they'd see each other every day and how her son would grow up to be mayor, too, and Rachel decided that she was definitely going to L.A.

Whatever it took.

When Sophie peered through the glass front door of the bookstore in the heat of the late afternoon, she saw Phin frowning at papers on the counter. Then he saw her and his face cleared, and he let her in. "Hello, Sophie Dempsey. What brings you here?"

"Amy needs to borrow a letter sweater. And I might buy some books." Sophie turned away so she wouldn't have to meet his eyes and discovered that she was in a really nice bookstore. It was the downstairs of a converted Victorian house, but it had been opened up with support columns so that what had once been four rooms was now one big room. There were a couple of comfortable chairs and four fireplaces, but mostly the room was filled with walnut bookcases, neatly labeled with copperplate signs. "It's beautiful," she said. "Really beautiful."

"Thank you," Phin said, without any of the cynicism that could make his voice grate on her. "My grandpa did it all."

Toward the back, there was an open doorway, and she said, "What's back there through that door?"

"My pool table," Phin said, and she went to check it out.

The kitchen and a breakfast room had also been opened into one big room, and the pool table sat in the middle of it.

"It's pretty," Sophie said when she saw it, knowing what a massive understatement that was. It was a magnificent nine-foot hand-carved oak table, with rosewood rails inlaid with pearl and gold silk fringe on the pockets. Phin winced at the "pretty," but he said, "Thank you," like the gentleman he was.

She went to the cue rack and put her hands behind her back so she wouldn't touch anything. The temptation was terrible. The rack was old and very beautiful, an Eastlake design that had *New England Pool Cue Company* lettered in gold across the top. "This is really pretty, too." She backed up a step and almost fell over a stack of boxes behind her.

"Careful," Phin said. "Campaign posters."

There were cartons of them stacked all along the wall. "You planning on running a big campaign?" Sophie said, and Phin said, "No, my grandma made a mistake."

"My grandpa wanted these for his second campaign, back in 1942. He told her to order a hundred of them. So she did, but she didn't notice that they came in lots of a hundred, so she ordered a hundred lots and Grandpa ended up with ten thousand posters. We've been using them ever since."

"You haven't changed posters since 1942?"

"Only once. After Gil Garvey beat my dad because he'd built the New Bridge." Sophie frowned and he went on. "Gil made a big deal out of what a waste of money it was because we had to buy that right-of-way from Sam Whipple to put the new road in, but by the time the next election came around, people had noticed that there weren't as many car wrecks and the driving was easier. So my dad had bumper stickers printed that said *He Built the Bridge* and he and my mom and I sat here one night and stuck them over the *More of the Same* part of the poster and then went out and hung them the next day."

"And he won," Sophie said.

"In a landslide." Phin stuck his hands in his pockets, a clear give-away, Brandon would have said, that he was repressing his emotions.

"So what's the rest of the story?"

Phin shrugged. "He served his term, had a heart attack, served four more terms, had another attack, and died a year later from his third attack. He got the office back but he was never the same."

Sophie frowned. "I can't imagine wanting anything that much."

"I don't think it was the wanting," Phin said. "I think it was the years of tradition he felt he'd broken. And then he thought he had to play it safe after that so he wouldn't lose again. It finished him."

"Just because he lost one election." Sophie shook her head.

"Tuckers don't lose," Phin said. "Which is why I'd like to know if you're shooting porn out there."

Sophie blinked. "Porn? Good grief, no. I wouldn't do that." She looked down at the posters and thought, *I don't want to be his New Bridge.* "We're shooting a sex scene, though." *Maybe two, if this afternoon goes well.* "About at the level of the *NYPD Blue* stuff on TV. It's not porn, I swear, but some people might think it was."

Phin relaxed a little. "Not if it's something you could show on TV. If that's all you're doing, we don't have a problem." He smiled at her, and Sophie felt the heat kick in just because he was close.

"So I . . ." she began, and he moved closer, and she met his eyes and went dizzy at the heat there.

"Tell me what you want and you've got it," he said.

"I don't know what you're talking about," Sophie said, trying not to fall against him.

"I'm talking about that look in your eyes. I've seen it three times now, and it makes me cheerful."

Sophie looked at the ceiling.

"Forget it, Soph," he said. "You don't want to do it, fine, but don't try to tell me you don't want it."

She met his eyes. "Oh, I want it," she said, and he kissed her, running his hand up her side to her breast while she leaned into him.

Fifteen minutes later, she was stretched out beside the pool table with her blouse open, her zipper down and her body ready. Phin stopped to get his breath and said, "You know I have a bed upstairs," and then the front door opened, and she clutched at him.

"I locked that," he said. "*Fuck*, it's my mother."

Sophie grabbed for her blouse while Phin rolled to his feet and tucked his shirt in.

"Hey, Mom," he said as he walked toward the front of the store, and Sophie heard a cold voice say, "What were you doing back there? You've left papers all over the counter. People can see this mess from the street."

"It's Sunday," Phin said. "There are no people in the street. That's why you came in here?"

"I'm on my way to pick up Dillie, but I wanted to talk to you alone first."

I shouldn't be listening to this, Sophie thought. She tucked in her blouse and then, just as Phin's mother said, "Virginia Garvey came by," she stood up and walked toward the front of the bookstore, saying, as nonsexually as she could, "Well, thanks for the help." She let her eyes drift to Phin's mother, casually, no big deal, but when she got a good look, she froze in place.

Liz Tucker was tall, elegant, blonde, and expensive, but mostly she was terrifying. And with the chill she was radiating right now, if they could get her to sit in the living room at the farmhouse, they wouldn't need central air. Ever. Sophie took a step back.

"This is my mother, Liz Tucker, who is just leaving," Phin told her. "Mom, this is Sophie Dempsey. I like her, so be nice."

"How do you do, Miss Dempsey." Liz Tucker held out a perfectly manicured hand that had a diamond on it that could have paid off any young doctor's college loans. Sophie looked at her left hand. The diamond there was even bigger.

"Pleased to meet you," Sophie said faintly, and took her hand. It was cold and dry and the handshake Liz gave her was the equivalent of an air kiss, sliding away before any real contact could be made.

"You're one of the movie people," Liz said. "Virginia said you were working hard." Liz's eyes went to Phin. "And interacting with the community."

"You know, I should be going," Sophie said. "Lots to do."

"You're not going anywhere." Phin opened the front door. "Goodbye, Mom. Give my best to Virginia and tell her to get a life."

Liz looked as if she wanted to argue, but Phin opened the door wider and pointed to the porch, patiently staring his mother down until she gave up and went out the door, giving Sophie one last, cool look before she went.

"Boy," Sophie said when she was gone.

"She wasn't always like that," Phin said. "My dad's death hit her hard. She has a good heart."

Sophie wanted to say, *How can you tell?* But it was his mother, after all. "I'm sure she does."

"No, you're not." Phin came closer. "But I don't care. I was about to be in the middle of you. Pick a place, anyplace, and lie down."

Sophie caught her breath and took a step back. Anyplace. Something that would be good in a movie. "The pool table." That could make up for the bad rep pool tables had gotten in *The Accused*.

Phin stopped in his tracks. "Are you insane? Do you know what that would do to the felt?"

As a matter of fact, Sophie did, but she was surprised he'd think of it now. "So much for adventure," she said to him, and he said, "Any adventure you want, as long as it doesn't screw up my pool table. Let me show you the upstairs. You can pick out a letter sweater and take off your clothes."

The bedroom at the top of the stairs was sloppily comfortable, and the bed was wide and rumpled. "Is this where you live?" Sophie said, looking around, and Phin said, "Not anymore," and kissed her, taking her down into heat.

"I want something exciting," she said breathlessly, as she came up for air. "I want something exciting and different and depraved."

He laughed as he stroked his hands down her back. "Talk's cheap. Give me details."

He kissed her neck, finding that good place, and she felt dizzy. *Concentrate.* "I can't think of anything," Sophie said, which was true; her mind was going south again.

"Handcuffs."

"I don't think so."

"Just as well, I can't find them anyway." Phin tugged her toward the bed and tipped her onto the quilt. "Ice cubes. Feathers. Whipped cream."

"What?" Sophie scooted over on the bed, her heart pounding as he took off his shirt. "Never mind. No."

"I could call Wes over for a threesome." He stripped off his pants and rolled onto the bed beside her.

"No, you could not," Sophie said, and shivered as he put his arms around her.

"He wouldn't do it anyway," Phin said against her hair, as his fingers moved down her blouse. "Private kind of guy, Wes is. Why are you still dressed?"

"What?" Sophie said. "Oh." She sat up and realized she was unbuttoned again. "I was thinking of something more—" She shivered as he pulled her blouse off her shoulders and the air-conditioned air hit her.

"More what?" he said, sliding her zipper down, and she tried to organize her thoughts and said, "You know. Erotic but not embarrassing."

He stopped at that. "Let me get this straight. You want something exciting but not weird, different but not kinky, and depraved but not embarrassing."

"Yes," Sophie said, trying not to notice that he was naked. God, he was beautiful.

He sighed. "Can't we just have sex? It's not as if we've known each other long enough to get bored."

"No," Sophie said. "I'm learning a lot from you. This is like college." *Touch me.*

"College," Phin said.

"I never got to go," Sophie said. "And I always wanted a degree. So I'm getting it from you." *Give it to me.*

"In sex," Phin said.

"Well, you're a master at it, aren't you?" Sophie said, batting her eyelashes at him as she shoved off her shorts. *Take me.*

"Don't even try to charm me," Phin said, but he sounded distracted.

Sophie put her arms around him and pulled him close. "Teach me something new," she said, and he bent her back onto the bed and she shivered as his body slid against hers.

"Okay," Phin said. "But pay attention, Julie Ann, there'll be a quiz."

Sophie woke up alone. She stretched, sliding across almond oil–soaked sheets, which was disgusting, but she felt terrific, so what the heck. She squinted at the clock beside Phin's bed and realized that she'd been asleep for over an hour. Those quizzes took a lot out of a woman.

She wrapped herself in the slippery top sheet and tiptoed down the hall until she found the bathroom, and then she showered until she was sure all the oil was gone. The stuff was everywhere, so it took her a while.

Then she went back to Phin's bedroom and dressed, and, because she couldn't stand the mess, she stripped the oil-stained bottom sheet and mattress pad from the bed. Something clanked as she pulled them off, and she stooped to look under the bed to see what had fallen.

Handcuffs.

She held them up, and they glinted back at her, and she thought grim thoughts about what Phin had been using them for and who he'd been using them with.

It wasn't that she was jealous at all, she told herself.

It was just that he was a *perv*.

"Would these be yours?" she asked Phin when she got downstairs.

He turned from the register, looking sleepy and satisfied in the late-afternoon light, and said, "Oh, good, I've been looking for those."

Sophie held the cuffs higher, hoping to instill some sense of shame, if not in him, then at least in herself. One look at him and she wanted him again. "I found them in the bed."

"That makes sense," Phin said. "That's where I lost them."

"I'd ask what you were doing with them," Sophie said, trying not to sound bitchy, "but I probably don't want to know, do I?"

"Sure you do. It was exciting and different and depraved." Phin nodded toward the stairs. "Go put them someplace we can find them, and I'll show you later. How do you feel?"

"Unsure," Sophie said, looking at the cuffs with growing curiosity.

"Not about them, dummy," Phin said. "This is the part where you get frosty and turn on me."

"What part?" Sophie said.

"The part after we have sex," Phin said. "When you remember that I'm a pervert, and you're not this kind of woman, and it's all my fault." He sounded pretty cheerful about it.

Sophie looked back at the cuffs, now definitely intrigued in spite of herself. There was no point in being disgusted with him; she'd loved everything he'd done to her. And if she was going to be honest, she was open to discussion about the cuffs. "I think we can skip the frosty part from now on. So exactly what do you—"

The front door opened, and Sophie tried to hide the cuffs, too late.

Wes looked more startled than she did. When he recovered, he said, "Those are mine, thank you." He took the cuffs from her and put them in his back pocket. "Why does it smell like salad in here?"

"I had plans for those," Phin said, at the same time Sophie said brightly, "Well, I've got to go."

She tried to sidle out the door, but Phin blocked her. "Wes was just going back to the pool table," he said, and Wes said, "Right. I'll just go back to the pool table."

When he was gone, Phin said, "So we can skip that part from now on."

"What part?" Sophie said, and he bent and kissed her, gently this time, and she leaned into him and felt her breath go, just because he was so close and so gentle and so hot.

"We can skip the frosty part," he murmured against her mouth. "And go straight to the good stuff."

"Right," she breathed. "Absolutely." She slid her arms around his waist and pulled him closer, falling into his kiss again, and when he came up for air, he said, "You know, I don't have to play pool right now."

"Oh. Sure you do." Sophie stepped away from him. "I have to get back. I have . . . work to do."

"Work." He let his breath out. "Okay. So I'll see you tomorrow."

"Yeah," Sophie said, drifting toward the door. "Tomorrow's good." She closed the door behind her and stood on the porch looking dazedly out at Temptation's Main Street baking in the late-afternoon sun.

Nice little town, she thought. *Pretty.*

The door rattled behind her and Phin came out, holding a white sweater. "Forgot to give this to you." He handed it to her just as a car went past.

It slowed down, and Phin waved.

"Anybody we know?" Sophie said, shaking the sweater out. It had a large red *T* with a red-and-white basketball in the middle of it.

"I know them. You don't," Phin said, and Sophie thought, *Story of my life, town boy.*

"We'll be very careful with the sweater," she told him, and he said, "Don't bother, I have more."

"Of *course* you do," Sophie said, and started down the steps.

"Frosty," Phin said, and went back inside.

"Satisfied," Sophie said to nobody, and went back to the farm.

———

"I suppose you had to," Wes said when Phin went back to join him at the table.

"Pretty much. She seduced me."

"Yeah, right," Wes said. "She said, 'Please fix the kitchen drain,' and you interpreted that—"

"She said, 'Fuck me.'" Phin put two balls on the table and picked up his cue. "I interpreted that to mean she wanted sex."

"Oh." Wes picked up his cue. "That would have been my call, too." He squinted at the table. "Why would she have said that?"

"On a guess? Because she wanted sex." Phin bent to shoot, and Wes did the same. They stroked the balls to the opposite cushion and then watched them roll back. Both balls hit the second cushion, but Wes's stayed an inch behind Phin's.

Phin racked the balls for him and stepped away from the table. "She's not as uptight as she looks. She wants to be a straight arrow, but she's bent as hell."

Wes slammed the cue ball into the rack and the balls scattered, two finding pockets. "So you're helping her find the real Sophie."

"I'm pretty much doing whatever she tells me to," Phin said. "That's working out well for me. She called the therapist last night and broke it off, so you can forget giving me grief on that account."

Wes made the next ball and walked around to the other side of the table. "So thanks to you, her relationship is over."

"Is this going to be a long conversation?" Phin said.

"I just want to know why she's giving up a solid relationship for seven more days of sex with you." Wes stopped to chalk.

"I have no idea," Phin said. "I'm just grateful."

"You said that first day she was up to something." Wes pocketed the second ball. "I think you were right. And Stephen is very hot to find out what and link you to it, and Zane Black thinks he knows."

Wes chalked again as Phin said, "Zane Black?"

Wes nodded. "He came in today. Tracked me down on a Sunday to say I should look into Amy's background. He said I should close down the movie because he was pretty sure it was something we

wouldn't like, and once I got a look at Amy's history, I'd know it for sure."

Phin felt his old unease about the movie come sneaking back. "Did you check?"

Wes nodded again. "She's clean. But I'm still worried about Stephen." He bent to shoot again, adding, "Especially since you appear to lose your mind every time you get near Sophie."

"So, you getting anywhere with Amy?" Phin said, and Wes miscued.

"You want to play pool or talk?" Wes said.

"I want to play pool," Phin said, and began to run the table, trying not to think about what kind of trouble Sophie could be getting into out at the farm with that damn movie. He'd just have to watch her more closely, he decided.

His civic duty.

The next morning, Sophie handed Amy the almond-oil scene.

"This is good," Amy said when she'd finished reading. "Almond oil, huh?"

"It wasn't so much the oil," Sophie said, "as what he did with it. I think he reads a lot." She paused and then added, "I met his mother, too."

"That bad?"

"Angela Lansbury in *The Manchurian Candidate*. I kept waiting for her to say, 'Why don't you pass the time by playing a little solitaire?' and then the last thing I'd see would be Phin's eyes glazing over."

"That would explain a lot about Phin," Amy said. "There's a considerable chill factor there."

"That would be because his mother is a Frigidaire," Sophie said.

"One of the Hill Frigidaires?" Amy said. "These old families sure know how to repel outsiders."

"Yeah," Sophie said, feeling a little depressed. "They sure do."

They heard a car come down the lane, and Amy went to look. "Who do we know that drives a blue BMW?" she said, and Sophie said, "Us? Nobody," but when the car stopped and a champagne blonde got out, she said, "Oh, no."

Amy squinted out across the yard. "Who is that?"

"Phin's mother," Sophie said, and pushed past her to go out onto the porch.

"My son is an important man in this town," Liz said carefully, when they were sitting on the swing alone, Amy and the dog having taken one look at Liz and retreated into the house. Sophie was melting in the heat—she could feel the sweat trickling between her breasts—but Liz wasn't even flushed, even in her silk suit. "The Tuckers have always been important here."

Sophie nodded. The woman had to be an alien.

"I'm sure that seems amusing to you, coming as you do from the city—"

"No," Sophie said. "I'm not amused at all. He told me about the New Bridge. I understand how important it is."

Liz nodded. "Thank you. That makes what I have to say much easier." She pressed her lips together. "I realize that you and my son are involved in a liaison, and that is none of my business. But the political well-being of this town is my business, has always been the business of the Tuckers, and it's my duty to make sure that it is not threatened. Your association with him is unfortunate from a political perspective. When are you leaving Temptation?"

Sophie drew back, stung in spite of herself. Well, what had she expected? *Welcome to the family?* "Next Sunday," Sophie said, holding her temper.

"Will you be seeing him in Cincinnati?"

Sophie took a deep breath. "We haven't talked about it."

"I see." Liz stared out across the barren yard, her face like stone. "But if he decided to pursue the relationship once you went back to Cincinnati, you would agree."

"I have no idea," Sophie said. "By this time next week, I may loathe him." She thought about Phin, and fairness made her add, "Or not."

"He doesn't have any money, you know."

Sophie jerked around to look at her, all the anger she'd been repressing breaking through. "What?"

"He doesn't have any money." Liz stared out at the yard. "The Tuckers have never had money. The money comes from my family."

I'm not after his money, you ice cube. Sophie shook her head, willing herself to stay calm through her fury. "You know, you're not thinking this through."

"Really, Miss Dempsey—"

"I realize your view is clouded on this because you're his mother, but he's gorgeous and smart and funny and kind and skilled. He's fixed half the stuff in this house. Do you know how attractive that is?"

"His father was like that," Liz said, taken aback a little.

"Then you know how attractive that is. But mostly, he's just sexy as hell." Liz flinched, and Sophie thought, *Good.* "Trust me, if Phin were standing on a street corner in a barrel, holding a cup with pencils in it, women would still be lying at his feet." Sophie stopped, caught by the image. "Okay, that's a little weirder than I meant it to be, but you get my drift. He doesn't need money to be attractive. In fact, he's a lot more attractive to me without it. Rich people are usually lousy human beings."

Liz raised an eyebrow at her.

"Well, you haven't impressed me much so far," Sophie told her. "I still don't know why you're here. If I was after him for his money, what would you do? Buy me off? I'm warning you, I'm expensive."

Liz smiled at Sophie and Sophie wished she hadn't. "I can offer you—"

"Forget it," Sophie said, cutting her off with pleasure. "You keep your money, I'm keeping him. As an investment."

Liz's eyes grew colder, if that was possible. "Don't underestimate me."

"Don't underestimate me, either," Sophie said, just as sharply. "I'm sure you're out here to protect your son, and I can sympathize. My family is important to me, too. But I'm tired of being insulted. So let's cut to the chase: I know he doesn't have any money, which is fine by me because it's not his money I want. We low-class women are like that. We just go for the cheap thrill. So the only thing you have that I want is your son. Sorry."

"Clearly I made a mistake by coming out here." Liz got to her feet. "I was hoping to make you see reason."

"No, you weren't," Sophie said. "You were hoping to intimidate me so I wouldn't try to get into your world. Well, you can relax. I wouldn't have your world as a gift."

"You don't get my world as a gift," Liz told her, her voice slicing through Sophie's bravado. "You earn the privilege of entering, so don't even try to get in on your back."

"That's it," Sophie said. "I'm tired of you. Go sell paranoid someplace else. We're all stocked up here."

"Good morning, Miss Dempsey." Liz drew herself up even straighter, if that were possible. "Have a pleasant trip back to Cincinnati. And don't even think about trying to trap my son. I'll see you in hell first."

When she'd gone, Amy came out onto the porch and said, "Wow."

Sophie nodded, trying not to shake. "Yeah. 'They'll see and they'll know and they'll say, "Why, she wouldn't even hurt a fly." ' "

Amy nodded with her. " 'We all go a little mad sometimes.' "

"Except Phin's not Norman."

"If that gave birth to him, he's not normal, either," Amy said. "Stay away from both of them."

"No, really, I think I might like her," Sophie said. "If I had some time to get to know her, bond, do the mother-daughter thing."

"Like, a thousand years," Amy said.

"Maybe not that quick." Sophie tried to relax. "God, she did everything but mention my good bag and cheap shoes."

"As long as she didn't invite you to the house for a nice Chianti and fava beans."

"She'd never let me in that house." Sophie shivered. "She'd fillet me on the front steps."

"Good thing we're leaving on Sunday."

Sophie thought of Liz Tucker and nodded, and then she thought of Phin, smiling at her with heat in his eyes, fixing everything she had that was broken and then making her laugh while he licked almond oil off her in bed.

"Yeah, good thing," she said.

After lunch, an irate Zane went back to Cincinnati and the news, and Amy took Rachel and Clea off to film the driving-into-Temptation footage, and Sophie went out to the kitchen with the dog to work. But once she was alone, all she could think of was Phin. She was pathetic, that's what she was. He certainly wasn't mooning over her. When she'd told him that night in the kitchen that she was staying another week, he hadn't even said, "Good." You'd have thought he could have at least given her a "Good."

Well, that was men for you. She glared at the cherries across from her. Took what they wanted and then—

It occurred to her that this thought wasn't getting her anywhere. It was the same thought she'd been having for fifteen years without any insight or growth, it was the thought that had led her into two years of mind-numbing security with Brandon, it was the thought that had kept her from having the kind of wickedly abandoned sex she'd been having since she'd met Phin. It was, in short, nonproductive.

Worse than that, it was boring.

"I'm through with you," she said to the cherries. "It's a brand-new day."

When Phin showed up at five-thirty, he found her teetering on an old ladder, wrapped in apple wallpaper, sticky from the paste and sweaty from the heat and frustrated because the old paper kept tearing.

"You've never looked better," he said as she shoved a paste-matted curl out of her eye. "What are you doing?"

"Hanging wallpaper," Sophie said waspishly.

He reached up and peeled a torn strip off her sleeve. "It's supposed to go on the wall."

"You know that 'frosty' part you were talking about yesterday?"

"Get off the ladder, Julie Ann," Phin said. "I'm good at this, too."

"Of course you are, you do everything well," Sophie said, feeling surly as she climbed down.

"My mother has a house with fourteen rooms," Phin said. "And one summer she decided to paper twelve of them. My dad called it the Summer from Hell. You know, I don't mean to be critical—"

"Then don't be."

"—but that is ugly paper."

"You can go now."

He smiled at her and her pulse kicked up even though she didn't want it to.

"I can't go." He picked up the paper. "You want to wallpaper, we'll wallpaper. Then we'll do what I want to do."

Sophie tried to ignore the heat his voice flared in her. "You have to be kidding. I'm hot and sweaty and sticky and I look like hell and—"

"I know," Phin said. "I don't care. Get out of the way so I can hang this wallpaper."

Sophie put her hands on her hips. "Listen, if you think I'm—"

She stopped because he'd put the wallpaper down and was trapping her against the wall, one hand on each side of her head, his face close to hers. He started to say something and then he closed his eyes and laughed.

"What's so funny?" Sophie said, but she already knew. She looked awful and he was laughing at her, and she didn't need this from him, she didn't need it from anybody but certainly not from—

"Me," he said. "Christ. I met you six days ago and you've got me so crazy, I'll hang wallpaper so I can touch you."

Sophie blinked. "What?"

"What do you want, Sophie?" he asked, smiling down at her. "Fuses, books, wallpaper, flowers, candy, diamonds—whatever it is, you get it, just as long as I get you."

She was pretty sure he was kidding, but not completely, not with that look in his eye and that heat in his voice.

"Six days," he said and shook his head. "Hell, one day. One minute. One look at that mouth. The devil's candy." He bent his head to kiss her and she ducked under his arm and away from him as she began to realize he was serious.

"Let me get this straight," she said, as she put the corner of the table between them. "You want me."

"In every way possible," Phin said, moving around the table to get to her, and she moved just as he did, beginning to smile as he came after her.

"You can't resist me," Sophie said.

"Not since I saw that mouth," Phin said, following her. "Come here."

"I had you at 'hello,' " Sophie said, still moving back, and Phin stopped and said, "What?"

"I *love* this," Sophie said, beaming at him. "I look like hell and you're chasing me around the kitchen. This is great."

"I am not chasing," Phin said.

Sophie undid the top button on her blouse.

"I'm chasing," Phin said, and moved faster than she'd planned on. She'd made a dash for the stairs but he lunged for her, grabbing her around the waist and lifting her off her feet to drag her back against him. She lost her breath because he'd knocked it out of her, and then he turned and trapped her against the table and pushed against her with his hips and she knew exactly how much he wanted her. "We'll do the wallpaper later," he said in her ear as his hands moved to her breasts. She tried to squirm away and he whispered, "Oh, Christ, Sophie," and slid his hand under her shirt, pulsing against her from behind, and she closed her eyes because he felt so good.

"We should go upstairs," she said breathlessly, as he buried his face in her neck, making the nerve there go wild.

"Here," he said, and she felt his hand slide down her stomach to her zipper. "Right here, against the table, I'm going to fuck your brains out."

She shivered and said, "Don't talk dirty," and he laughed low and said, "I could feel you get hotter when I said it. You are so bent, Sophie."

He slid down her zipper and she said, "No, I am not," and tilted her hips into his hand, and then as his fingers went into her shorts and between her thighs, she put her hands on the table and pushed back against him, taking the sharp intake of his breath for the tribute that it was.

Then she lifted her head to tell him how good he felt and looked through the screen door into Stephen Garvey's eyes.

"No!" she said, and tried to get away from Phin, but he said, "Yes," into her neck and pushed back, sliding his fingers lower, and when she twisted to get away, he held her tighter which would have been erotic as hell if Stephen hadn't just put ice water in her veins. "Stephen!" she

said, and Phin said, "What?" and stopped long enough for Sophie to gasp, "Back door," as she tried to turn away and pull her blouse back together.

Through it all, Stephen stood there with his mouth open.

Phin didn't let go, although he did take his hand out of her shorts and swing them both around so she was shielded behind him. "Stephen, we're busy here," he said over his shoulder. "What the hell do you want?"

Stephen straightened, still looking confused. "I came to see Rachel, and I certainly didn't expect—"

"Well, we didn't expect you, either," Phin said. Sophie tried to move away again, and he tightened his grip on her. "Rachel's not here. Go away."

"I was wrong. This is exactly what I would have expected from you," Stephen said, and left.

"I think that was an insult." Phin slid his hand into her shorts again. "Although this is what I would have expected from me, too."

"Oh, no," Sophie said, and twisted away, and Phin said, "Oh, yes," and caught her again.

"Trust me, Stephen just killed *any* interest I have in discovery fantasies," Sophie said. "There's a shower upstairs. With a showerhead that Amy says is illegal in most Southern states." Phin stopped fighting her and she pulled him toward the stairs. "Imagine the possibilities."

"I want you to know," he said as he followed her, "that once I get laid, I'll be back in control here."

"Think so?" Sophie turned and kissed him, licking into his mouth and making him shudder under her hands.

"For at least fifteen minutes," he said against her mouth. "Then I'll need to fuck you again."

She shivered, and he laughed and said, "You are so easy."

"So are you," she said, and he said, "And there's our problem right there. We're both crazed until this wears off."

Sophie straightened. " 'Wears off'?"

"This stuff never lasts." Phin pushed her toward the stairs. "We'll be sane again someday, so let's enjoy it while we've got it."

"Been here before, have you?" Sophie said, feeling cranky because she hadn't.

"Actually, no," Phin said. "Not like this. Get a move on, will you?"

"You have to say that," Sophie said, starting up the stairs. " 'No, Sophie, nobody else has ever been like you.' " She picked up speed because she was mad and because she still wanted him, and he hooked his fingers in the back of her shorts and pulled her down a step against him.

"Not like you," he said in her ear. "Which is why you scare me. But I keep coming after you anyway."

She leaned back against him and said, "I would like to be memorable, if that's possible."

"Try 'unforgettable,' " Phin said. "And no, I did not have to say that. Now, can I please have you?"

"Yes," Sophie said. "You can have anything you want."

Two hours later, Phin kissed Sophie good-bye in front of Amy, who was frowning at the kitchen wall, newly papered in apples.

"I've got to go," he told Sophie. "I'm late to meet another woman."

"That's a joke, right?" she said, and he said, "Nope,"

" 'You men are all alike,' " she told him, deciding to believe it was a joke. " 'Seven or eight quick ones and you're off with the boys.' "

"What are you talking about?" he said, and Amy said, "Movie quote. You must know that one."

"I don't watch movies," Phin said. "I'm an intellectual." He kissed Sophie again and said, "Calm down. Stop quoting." Then he left before she could think of something cutting to say, like, *You remind me of your mother.*

"So exactly what were you doing in the bathroom?" Amy said.

"Exactly what you thought we were doing," Sophie said, still trying to assure herself the other woman was a joke. "Remind me to thank Wes for that showerhead. Oh, and Phin swears the mildew on the shower curtain was watching us and we should get a new one."

"Did you mention his mother had tried to run you out of town?"

"No." Sophie sat down at the table and opened her PowerBook

again. "Although she'll no doubt be buying a bigger rail to do it on tomorrow. Stephen Garvey caught us in the kitchen."

"How bad?" Amy said.

"Oh, bad," Sophie said, and then smiled in spite of herself. "And really, really good."

"Sophie, you're not getting serious about the mayor, are you?" Amy said. "Because that would be bad. He's not going to love you the way you deserve—"

"Nope," Sophie said, but she felt a chill even as she said it. "Not serious at all. I have it on good authority that this will wear off."

"Okay," Amy said. "Uh, well, then. In other news . . ."

Sophie tensed. "What?"

"We're getting some company tomorrow," Amy said. "Zane appears to have lit a fire under Clea and she called L.A. and that Leo guy is coming out here to see what we're doing."

"Leo Kingsley," Sophie said, her instincts breaking through her satisfaction. That was the problem with great sex. It dulled your survival tools. "Davy's old boss, the producer."

"Right."

Sophie considered it. "I don't see how this could be trouble." *But it will be.*

"I don't, either," Amy said and they looked at each other doubtfully.

"Let's assume it's not until something goes wrong," Sophie said.

"Good." Amy turned back to the wall, not looking cheered at all. "Now, explain why ugly apples are better than ugly cherries, and all my questions will be answered."

Eight

*T*his is excellent," Dillie said that night at the bookstore as she and Phin stretched the new mattress pad across the bed. "Except that you were an hour late getting me, so I should stay up an extra hour even though it is a school night."

"Works for me," Phin said, knowing she'd be out like a light five minutes after her bedtime anyway. "We'll read in bed that extra hour." He snapped the bottom sheet across the bed and Dillie caught her end of it. "So what's new with you?"

"Jamie Barclay is in my room at school." Dillie tucked the elastic corner under the mattress like a pro. "Grandma fixed it for me."

"Grandma's not supposed to do that," Phin said. "No special favors for Tuckers."

"Dad," Dillie said. "This is my life."

"Right." He flipped the top sheet across and she caught that, too.

"And besides, Jamie Barclay is new and needs a friend so it's really for her." Dillie smoothed her side of the sheet down. "Do you have new friends?" She said it with such elaborate disinterest that Phin stopped.

"There are some people visiting in town," he said cautiously.

"The movie people?" Dillie smoothed the already smooth sheet, her chin in the air to show how unconcerned she was.

Phin picked up the quilt and shook it out before he flipped it across the bed. "What do you want to know, Dill?"

Dillie caught her side of the quilt and pulled it straight. "I just think it's nice that you have new friends."

She sounded so much like the way Liz talked to her, Phin laughed. "Thank you."

"Are they nice?"

He tugged the quilt smooth over the bed where he'd poured almond oil on Sophie and thought of her, hot and round and slippery in his arms. And then that afternoon in the shower—

It seemed wrong to have those thoughts with Dillie in the room, so he shoved the memory away. "They're very nice. Okay, this is your night. We have hot dogs, we have paper napkins, we have dessert, and it's not a weekend. What else?"

Dillie shot a look at the armoire across the room. "TV?"

"What is this, Go-to-Hell Night?" Phin picked up a pillow and tossed it to her and she caught it.

"Jamie Barclay watches TV," Dillie said. "*All* the time, not just for special things." She plumped the pillow and put it at the head of the bed. "She watches it with her mom." She looked at Phin out of the corner of her eye. "It would be nice to watch TV with a mom."

"I'm so glad Jamie Barclay moved here," Phin said, picking up another pillow. "Yes, after dinner you can watch TV. With a dad."

"Would you like to meet Jamie Barclay?" Dillie asked, much too innocently.

"Sure," Phin said cautiously.

"And then I could meet the movie people," Dillie said.

"No," Phin said.

"Dad." Dillie put her hands on her hips. "I should know your friends."

"They're leaving in a week," Phin said, tossing the last pillow to her.

"Well, I'm really glad the movie people came here," Dillie said as she caught it. "Friends are important. Don't you think?"

"What do you want on your hot dog?" Phin said.

After lunch on Tuesday afternoon, a cab came bouncing down the lane to the farm. "Company," Sophie called back into the house, and then went out to meet Leo Kingsley. He was bent over talking to the driver, and she waited patiently, but then the cab door opened again and somebody tall, dark, and Dempsey got out of the backseat.

"Davy!" Sophie shrieked, and threw herself off the step into his arms, and he swung her around and hugged the breath out of her. "I didn't know you were coming, why didn't you tell me you were coming, I'm so *glad* you came—"

He kissed her on the cheek, a big, brotherly smack that was loud and loving, and said, "I didn't know, either, until Leo called me. What the hell are you up to?"

"We're making a video," Sophie said. "Amy wants to come to L.A. I am *so glad* to see you."

He looped his arm around her neck and said, "I'm glad to see you, too, babe. Amy's not going to L.A. She'd hate it. Now, explain to me why you're making—"

"Don't let me get in your way," a mournful voice said from behind him. "Just because it's the Mojave here and I'm about to have a coronary, don't let that—"

"Leo, this is my sister, Sophie," Davy said, and Sophie looked around him to smile at Leo politely.

Leo Kingsley was an attractive man, healthy and fit in his middle forties, beautifully dressed and styled to the teeth. His hair was thick and brown, and he had kind eyes and a good face. But Leo Kingsley was also clearly a man who'd seen too much and wasn't getting over it.

"Welcome to Temptation," Sophie said, and he nodded sadly and said, "Catchy title. Nice to meet you. I need central air."

"Sorry," Sophie said. "It's primitive here."

"That figures," Leo said gloomily. "It's Ohio."

"Why don't you come in and have some lemonade?" Sophie said.

"Lemonade?" Leo said. If she'd offered him arsenic, he couldn't have been more appalled.

"Diet Coke?" Sophie said. "Peach brandy? Ice water? Beer? Ham sandwich? Dove Bar?"

"Ice cream?" Leo said, and Sophie relaxed.

"Right this way." She held the door for him and he went in, stepping neatly over the dog that had flopped down in the doorway, saying, "Look out, Lassie," as he did.

Sophie said, "*No*, don't name it," but it was too late. She looked down at the dog and said, "Lassie?" and it stood up and wagged its stubby tail.

"You have a dog?" Davy said.

"Is this a problem?" Leo said.

"No," Sophie said to both of them. In a way it was a relief. She'd been getting the sneaking suspicion that the dog's name was Dog, and that would have been much worse.

"So," Leo said. "Clea here?"

"Of course I'm here, Leo, darling," Clea said, coming in so on cue Sophie would have bet money she'd been listening in the kitchen. Amy trailed behind her as Clea embraced Leo gracefully if not warmly and said, "It really is good to see you." Clea ignored Davy completely, and he watched her with no expression on his usually mobile face.

Leo patted her arm and said morosely, "Nice to see you, too, kid."

Then Amy caught sight of Davy and shrieked, and Sophie pushed them both into the kitchen so Clea and Leo could talk.

"I can't *believe it*," Amy said and hugged him as Sophie got Leo's Dove Bar from the freezer. "I didn't think we'd see you until Thanksgiving."

"I didn't, either, until Leo told me you were making porn," Davy said, and Sophie dropped Leo's ice cream.

"What?" Amy said, as Lassie grabbed the bar.

"Getting the news that you two were making a skin flick brought me right home. Have you lost your minds?"

"Skin flick." Sophie sat down. "We're not making a skin flick."

"Clea wants Leo to distribute it," Davy said.

"Right."

"Leo only does porn," Davy said. "That's why they call him the Porn King."

" 'Porn King'?" Amy said.

"He doesn't look like a Porn King," Sophie said. "Are you sure?"

"Harvard MBA," Davy said. "They don't mention him much in the alumnae mag. So what's going on?"

"Good question," Sophie said, and went into the living room to find out.

"It's not real porn," Clea said when they'd cornered her in the living room. "You've been filming it, Amy, you know that."

"Okay, well, fine," Leo said. "So what the hell am I doing here?"

"It's a new kind of porn." Clea sat down next to Leo on the couch and smiled at him. She looked beautiful. He looked doubtful. "It's called vanilla porn and it's very hot right now, it's just flying off the video-store shelves, and I think you should make it, Leo, I really do. We've got a great story, about me coming home to meet my old high-school lover and being disillusioned, and then meeting his son, who seduces me and sets me free of my past, and I drive off into the sunset with him, getting everything I've ever wanted. It's a real woman's fantasy, Leo, you'll make a mint—"

"I think I should make *Coming Cleaner*," Leo said.

"What the hell is *Coming Cleaner*?" Amy said.

"I don't want to make *Coming Cleaner*," Clea said. "I want to make *Return to Temptation*. I swear to God, Leo, this is good stuff. You could make a lot of money here. Don't blow it by being old-fashioned."

An old fashioned Porn King, Sophie thought. An old-fashioned Ivy League Porn King. Her world was getting weirder by the minute.

"What is *Coming Cleaner*?" Amy said again, and Davy said, "Clea's second film. Set in a car wash. Lots of soap."

"Oh, *bleah*," Sophie said. "Clea, how could you?"

"How do you think I met your brother?" Clea said. "Working for Disney?"

Amy rounded on Davy. "You were in a porn film?"

"No," Davy said. "I worked for Leo who made porn films. Forget about me. Concentrate. You're making porn."

"No," Sophie said.

"Yes," Clea said. "Porn about a woman achieving all her dreams. Classy porn."

"Sort of like 'military intelligence,'" Davy said.

"Shut up, Davy," Clea said without looking at him. "This is completely different. It's not gross stuff, it's straight-to-video erotica for women."

"No," Sophie said.

Clea exhaled. "Sophie, what's your favorite scene in *The Big Easy*?"

"'Your luck's about to change, *cher*,'" Sophie said automatically.

"And what's the only thing you don't like about it?"

"It's too—" She broke off when she saw where Clea was going.

"Short," Amy finished for her. "I got it." She cheered up some. "I like it."

"It'll be romantic, not crude," Clea said. "I was thinking maybe we should change the title, maybe to something like *Cherished*, because it's about emotion, not sex."

"You want me to do a movie called *Cherished*?" Leo looked at Davy. "Get the cab back."

"The cab's halfway to Cincinnati by now," Davy said. "Look at my sister's tape."

Leo sighed and moved to the monitor, and Sophie went to get him a Dove Bar, feeling sorry for him even if he was a porn king.

"It's going to need some work," he said, when the last screen was dark again. "But Clea was right, you've got a good start there. It needs a lot more sex, of course."

Amy looked at Sophie and said, "We have somebody working on that."

"No, we don't," Sophie said.

"And the score will add a lot," Leo went on, and Amy winced.

"I don't know how—" she began, and Leo waved her away.

"We can do that in L.A.," he said. "No problem. Along with the titles and credits. You just shoot the footage and let us handle the details."

"The sound is a detail?" Sophie said, but Amy shushed her.

"But mostly you need more sex," Leo said. "A lot more nudity."

"Leo," Clea said. "Don't forget what I told you. This is women's porn—"

"Oh, no," Sophie said, and Amy kicked her ankle.

"Don't get in Clea's way," she whispered to Sophie. "This is my chance."

"—so it's not going to be vile like the other stuff you do," Clea finished.

Leo sighed. "I need skin."

Sophie winced, and Amy whispered, "He's a real producer, Sophie, *please*."

"Jesus," Davy said. "The Dempsey morals at work again."

Leo smiled at Clea, which didn't look natural at all on him. "Now about *Coming Cleaner*—"

"Later, Leo," Clea said. "We're making *Cherished* now."

"*Cherished*," Leo said, and looked more depressed than ever.

Rachel was out in the front yard watering what little grass there was when Leo came down the porch steps. He didn't look like a big Hollywood producer. He was only a couple of inches taller than she was, and even though he was good-looking in a Hollywood kind of way, he looked tired and depressed. So when he said, "Are you the gofer around here?" she squeezed the water out of the front of her T-shirt and said, "That's me," without trying to be anything special.

"I need a place to stay," he said.

"Sure." She dropped the hose and started for the car. "Get in the car. I'll take you to Larry's Motel out by the Tavern."

"Larry's Motel."

She turned back and saw his look of pain. "It's all we've got." Rachel opened the car door for him. "Just be grateful you've got me for a driver because we don't have a taxi, either. You could be, like, walking."

"No, I couldn't," Leo said, and got in.

"So you know Clea from L.A.?" Rachel said when they were on the road.

"Yes." Leo peered out the window

"Cool. I want to be the next Clea."

"No you don't," Leo said.

Rachel flipped the neck of her damp T-shirt back and forth to get some breeze going there, too. "Why not? She's rich and successful and she got out. Sounds good to me."

Leo didn't answer, and she looked over in time to catch him staring at where her T-shirt was stuck to her chest.

He caught her eye and said, "Sorry," and she shrugged and said, "Hey, I was the one flapping the wet T-shirt."

"I still shouldn't be leering. Sexual harassment." Leo sounded mournful. "Life's no fun anymore."

"Tell you what," Rachel said. "You can sexually harass me if you want. I'm having a slow summer anyway. Want to look down my shirt?"

Leo sighed. "So this is what it's come to, teeny-boppers doing me favors. Middle age is hell."

"I'm not a teeny-bopper," Rachel said. "I'm twenty."

"Oh, shit." Leo put his head in his hands. "Contributing to the delinquency of a minor."

"I'm not a minor," Rachel said. "I'm twenty. You can sleep with me and not go to jail. Of course, you have to, like, take me to L.A. first. I've had all the lousy sex in Temptation I can stand."

"But lousy sex in L.A. is okay?" Leo shook his head. "Lousy sex is lousy anyplace, kid." He stopped and considered. "I don't think I've ever had lousy sex."

"That's 'cause you're a guy." Rachel turned into the motel driveway.

Leo stared at the motel with distaste as she parked in front of the lobby door. "So who runs this, Norman Bates?"

"It's okay, the showers don't work anyway. Think of it as an adventure."

"I don't want an adventure," Leo said. "Adventures are for the young. Comfort is for the old."

"What time do you want me to pick you up, old guy?" Rachel said.

"Soon," Leo said as he got out. "Very, very soon."

"I'll pick you up at five, then," Rachel said. "Dinnertime."

Leo poked his head through the window. "Five is dinnertime here?"

Rachel sighed. "When is it dinner in L.A.?"

"No, no," Leo said. "Five is fine. I missed lunch anyway." His face changed suddenly from vaguely worried to downright apprehensive. "You do have restaurants here, right?"

"Sure," Rachel said. "There's a restaurant in town and a diner, too. The food's pretty good. It's not fancy but it's good."

"Okay."

He still looked doubtful, so she smiled at him and said, "And if you promise to buy, I'll come have dinner with you in a blouse with the top button undone and you can harass me until dessert."

"Oh, yeah." Leo nodded as he straightened away from the car. "That'll go over great at Granny's Home-Cooked Restaurant. Forget it, Lolita. I'll eat alone."

For some reason, that hurt. "Okay."

She put the car in gear just as he put his head down next to the window again.

"Hey," he said. "I was kidding. I didn't mean to hurt your feelings."

His eyes were kind, and she was so surprised she let the car die. "You didn't. Really. I just wanted to eat dinner with you. And hear about Hollywood."

He nodded. "Okay. Pick me up at five with all your buttons buttoned."

"You don't have to—"

"At five, kid. I'll tell you what a big shot I am. You're the only one who'll believe it anyway."

Rachel nodded. "Okay. Thanks."

Leo waved her off, and she watched as he headed for the motel door, shaking his head as he checked out the turquoise panels near the entrance. He wasn't really upset, she realized as she pulled back onto the road. It was just his way. Like Eeyore. She should tell him that at dinner. "You're the Eeyore of L.A.," she'd tell him, and he'd have to laugh. Getting a laugh out of him wouldn't be easy, but she'd do it before dessert. He should take her back to L.A. with him just for the laughs—

She slowed the car. There was an idea. She could be his personal assistant and make him laugh and help him relax and drive him places and take care of him. Of course, he'd say no at first, but he'd said no to dinner and she'd talked him into that.

It really was a great idea. She could take care of him and he could take care of her.

And she could finally get out of Temptation.

When Phin pulled up to the porch that evening, he saw Sophie sitting on the swing with a good-looking guy whose curly dark hair and dark brown eyes reminded him of someone. *The therapist*, he thought, and it bothered him a lot more than it should have. After all, he had nothing permanent with Sophie. He just needed to touch her on a semiregular basis or he couldn't finish his sentences. It was just lust. It would go in time.

He was going to have to get rid of the therapist.

Sophie waved to him, and the dog barked from under the swing as he got out of the car.

"Come meet my brother, Davy," Sophie said, glowing with happiness.

"Your brother." Phin regrouped, sizing Davy up again as he patted the shaggy panting dog who had come out to greet him. Now that he was closer, Davy looked like Sophie's twin, same ivory skin and generous mouth, but a lot more jaw and more height. And his eyes were colder than Sophie's ever could be. "Good to meet you, Davy." Phin went up on the porch and held out his hand.

"This is Phin Tucker, the mayor," Sophie said, and Davy freed his arm from around her and stood to shake Phin's hand with a firm, dry grasp.

"Pleased to meet you," Davy said. "What's the mayor doing so far out of town?"

Phin raised his eyebrows. "Just being neighborly."

Davy looked at Sophie and then back at Phin. "That's real nice of you."

"I try," Phin said.

"Whatever you guys are doing, knock it off," Sophie said.

"You never learn, do you?" Davy said to her before he turned back and smiled at Phin. "So, can I get you a drink, Phil?"

"Phin," Sophie said. "Stop it."

"I'm fine, thanks," Phin said.

"I bet you are," Davy said. "Could I see you for a minute, Sophie?"

"No," Sophie said. "Go harass Amy. She's dating a cop. And remember, you brought Clea home and we never said a word."

"Good point." Davy opened the screen door to go inside. "I'll be right back, Phil. Don't do anything stupid."

"What the fuck was that all about?" Phin said, and Sophie pulled him down on the swing beside her, the dog at her feet again.

"We moved around a lot when we were kids," Sophie said.

"And he's still hostile about it today?" Phin said.

"We didn't have a lot of money and the rich kids weren't our pals," Sophie said.

"Sorry," Phin said. "I still don't see how I figure in here."

"I told you, we took a lot of grief from rich kids."

"I'm not rich," Phin said, as Davy came back out on the porch with a beer.

"You're not poor," Davy said. "Have a beer." He handed it to Phin who took it as the easiest move at the moment, and then Davy sat down on the porch rail and folded his arms and stared at Phin.

Sophie looked from him to Phin and back again. "Okay, stop it."

"I'm just saying," Davy said, "that I've paid less for entire suits than he spent on that shirt."

"Well, it's been swell," Phin said, standing up.

"Armani, right?" Davy said.

"Right." Phin handed the beer back to him. "Great meeting you."

"Davy."

"Okay." Davy got up and turned back to the door with the beer. "I'll go, Harvard. You stay. Sophie makes her own choices." He grinned at Sophie who ignored the pun and glared back. "Right. You try to do the brotherly thing and nobody appreciates it."

When he was gone, Phin said, "Interesting guy, your brother."

"You should talk," Sophie said. "Your mother gives me frostbite every time I see her."

"What 'every time'?" Phin sat down beside her again. "You've only met her once." Then he grew very still. "Haven't you?"

"Anyway, Davy's just protective," Sophie said. "He thinks all guys are only after one thing."

"He's right," Phin said. "So my mother dropped by, did she?"

"Social call," Sophie said. "So you only want me for sex?"

"No, I'm nuts about your golf game. What did my mother do to you?"

"Maybe I'll go inside." Sophie started to get up, but Phin caught her arm and pulled her back down on the swing.

"Okay, sorry about the golf crack. Give me the right answer and I'll say it. I'm too tired to come up with it on my own."

" 'No, Sophie, it's not the sex,' " Sophie said. " 'It's your wit, your beauty, your warmth, your intelligence, the cute way your nose crinkles when you laugh, your sunny, funny face.' "

"Your nose doesn't crinkle," Phin said. "I'm good for the rest of it."

"But mostly it's the sex, right?" Sophie said.

"And you want me for what?" Phin said. "The third day I knew you, you lay down for me on the dock. The next night I came back with a plan to get you down again, but you said, 'Fuck me,' before I could make my move. The next day, I'm thinking about heading out to see you and you deliver to the bookstore before I can find my car keys. I won't even mention what you did with the showerhead yesterday because I'm grateful. Now, what is it you want me for?"

Sophie sighed. "The sex."

"So we're on the same page here."

"I doubt it," Sophie said. "You're wearing Armani."

"I really like your brother," Phin said. "Is he leaving soon?"

"Don't pick on my brother. Your mother thinks I'm after your money. I told her it was the cheap thrill."

"Oh, fuck," Phin said. "I'm sorry."

"Yeah, well, I'll forgive you your mother if you forgive me my brother. They're just looking out for us."

"Christ, it's not as if we're sleeping with lepers," Phin said.

"Well, in a way we are," Sophie said. "We're both with people who are Not Our Kind. Davy looks at you and sees every guy who pushed us around when we were kids. Your mom looks at me and sees every gold-digger who ever went after you because of your name and your shirts. How are they to know we're just using each other for the physical thrill and have no interest or affection beyond that?" She folded her arms and stared out across the dusty yard.

Phin sighed and sat back. " 'Go out and see Sophie,' I told myself. 'You've had a rough day, she always makes you feel great, treat yourself. Go out and see the woman.' "

"Human Valium, that's me," Sophie said.

"Hey," Phin said, and when she looked up, her beautiful lips parted to say something horrible to him, he kissed her, long and slow and deep, and she kissed him back, and he felt human again instead of harried, just because he finally had his arms around her and she was so warm and sure against him. "We're more than just the sex," he whispered, and she closed her eyes and whispered back, "I know, I know."

He kissed her again, and then rocked the swing with his foot, and she put her head on his shoulder and said, "So tell me about this lousy day," and he told her while they watched the sun go down, and everything that had been awful seemed funny when he told her about it. He listened to her laugh in the twilight and felt the tension seep away. When it was dark, he sighed and said, "I have to go," but he didn't want to.

"What about the sex?" Sophie said. "Usually you have me naked by now."

"Davy's staying here, right?" Phin said, and when she nodded, he said, "I don't think so."

"You're kidding," she said, and he said, "Tell you what. Come on up to the Hill, and we can do it with my mother in the next room."

"Oh, God," Sophie said, and he laughed and kissed her and said, "I've got a council meeting from hell tomorrow anyway. I'll really need to release some tension after that."

"You're such a romantic," she said, and he kissed her again and then again until she laughed against his mouth, and he drove away feeling all the comfort he'd come for.

Maybe her brother would leave soon.

"You never fucking *learn*," Davy said when Sophie went inside.

"What?" Sophie plopped down on the sofa, and Lassie plopped down at her feet. "Thanks to you, he left early, so this is not a good time to yell at me." She looked at Davy, standing indignant by the fireplace, and had to smile. "I'm so glad you're here, even if you are being a butthead."

Davy came over and sat down beside her. "Let me explain to you again about town boys."

"Go away, Davy." Sophie let her head fall back against the couch and smiled, thinking about her town boy. "He's not like that."

" 'This can only lead to tears,' " Davy said in a comic voice, and when Sophie rolled her head on the back of the couch, he said, "*Anastasia*. The bat."

"Bat country," Sophie said. "What are you nervous about?"

"The way you look at him," Davy said. "The way he looks at you. You're in love. He's in heat. It's an old story and a lousy one."

"That's what I keep telling her," Amy said, coming in with three Dove Bars. " 'This is Chad all over again,' 'he's got "town boy" all over him,' but—"

"Chad?" Davy said.

"An old mistake," Sophie said, taking her Dove Bar. "And Phin is not Chad. And I'm not in love."

"I still think we ought to go to Iowa and make Chad pay," Amy said, and bit into her ice cream viciously.

"This would be Chad Berwick, right?" Davy shook his head and bit into his bar, too. "Not necessary," he said around the ice cream.

Sophie blinked at him. "How did you know—"

Davy looked at her with affectionate contempt. "I was a freshman in the same school, dummy. Everybody knew."

"Oh, *ouch*," Sophie said, and ate more Dove Bar for comfort.

"Yes, but the last month of Chad's senior year was not a good one," Davy said. "Poor guy."

Amy collapsed cross-legged on the rug in front of them with her ice cream dripping, looking about ten. "Ooh. Ooh. What did you do?" She licked the drips away and grinned up at Davy adoringly, moving her ice cream as Lassie took an interest and waddled over.

"Many things," Davy said airily. "Too many to recall now."

"Come on, Davy," Amy said. "Sophie needs to know."

Davy leaned back on the couch and ate more ice cream as he thought. "Mostly little stuff. I taped a cheat sheet in his notebook and then snitched on him to the English teacher. I started a rumor he had head lice and put lice shampoo in his gym locker. I stuck a bunch of Hustlers in his regular locker and he got busted and had to see the counselor."

"That's it?" Amy sniffed, and ate her ice cream, holding the stick above Lassie's reach.

"Well, let's see, *was* there anything else?" Davy pretended to ponder, and Sophie started to grin.

"I love you, Davy," she said, and leaned into his arm.

Davy put his arm around her. "I love you, too, babe. Oh, yeah, wait. It's all coming back to me now. There was that cherry-red Camaro he got for graduation. His folks gave it to him early so he could take it to prom." He grinned and bit into his ice cream again.

"He was driving a clunker when I . . . knew him," Sophie said.

"He drove it to prom, too," Davy said. "I put shrimp in the Camaro."

Amy frowned. "Shrimp?" But Sophie started to laugh, hiccuping on her ice cream.

Davy nodded. "I put shrimp down in the seats, in the wheel well, shoved some down into the screw holes under the carpet, anyplace it would be hard to find them. Shrimp are small, you know." He began to smile, remembering. "And it was the end of May so we were getting some hot weather." He shook his head. "Chad never did get to use that car. For a week, whenever I went by the Berwick house, that car was sitting in the driveway with all the doors open. Then finally, it just . . . disappeared."

He laughed and bit into his Dove Bar again, and Amy said, "Oh, *yes.*" Sophie thought, *I love my family, I really do.* "What else?" she asked Davy.

"He destroyed the guy's Camaro," Amy said. "What do you want?"

"Dempsey revenge, Ame," Sophie said. "A car is not enough." She looked at Davy. "Right?"

"Well," Davy said. "There was prom."

"Oh, tell us about prom," Amy said.

"He was dating this really hot senior girl named Melissa Rose," Davy said. "Boy, she was something. She wore this silky blue thing to prom that sort slipped around whenever she—"

"I thought this was supposed to cheer me up," Sophie said.

"And because Chad was an asshole, he took a flask to prom," Davy said. "Big man around town, sneaking Boone's Farm into the gym. So around midnight, I put ground-up sleeping pills in it."

"So he went to sleep at prom and that's it?" Amy said.

"No," Davy said. "He got groggy at prom, and Melissa got disgusted because she thought he was drunk and made him take her home, except he was too out of it, and I just happened to be there in the parking lot. So I helped her." Davy shook his head as he finished his Dove Bar. "He got a little banged-up when we tried to get him into the backseat. Melissa was not a nice person, so she did most of it."

"Good for Melissa," Sophie said, entertaining her first thoughts about Chad that didn't involve guilt.

"That's good," Amy said. "That's enough—"

"Then we took him home and left him on his front-porch steps with his flask in his hand and his fly unzipped," Davy said. "Melissa suggested he should have something else in his other hand, and I just happened to have Dad's Polaroid with me. The pictures were a big hit at school on Monday."

Sophie was laughing into her Dove Bar now. "Thank you, Davy," she said, and his arm tightened around her.

"Okay, *that* was enough," Amy said. "You did good—"

"And then I drove Melissa home," Davy said. "And we were feeling warmly toward each other at that point, being sort of united in our distaste for Chad, so I asked if there was anything else I could do for her."

"And was there?" Sophie said.

"You weren't the only Dempsey who lost yours in the backseat of that clunker," Davy said. "I remember Melissa fondly to this day. That girl knew things. Wonder what happened to her?"

"Something wonderful, I hope," Sophie said.

"She already had something wonderful," Davy said. "Me."

"Beyond that," Sophie said. "I like a woman who knows how to get even."

"So do I, as long as she's not getting even with me," Davy said.

Lassie whined at their feet, and Sophie looked down into his pathetic brown eyes. "Poor baby," she said, and then he rolled over with his legs in the air and she laughed and leaned down so he could lick the rest of the ice cream off the stick.

"Con dog," Davy said.

"What?" Sophie said, still smiling at her baby.

"Con dog," Davy said. "Look pathetic, make the mark feel superior, get what you want. He just ran a con on you for that ice cream."

"My dog conned me?" Sophie said.

"What the dog is doing to you is not your problem," Davy said. "It's what the mayor's doing to you that worries me. Which brings us back to now. If I have to fill a Volvo with shrimp, I will, but I'd just as soon you wised up."

Sophie stopped smiling. "I'm wise. He's not a Chad. I'll be fine."

"Yeah," Davy said, "Right. Well, I'm telling you now, when he screws you over, I'm kicking his butt."

"I love you, Davy," Sophie said.

"I love you, too," Davy said. "You dumbass."

The council meeting the next day went so badly that Phin was still reeling from it when his mother cornered him in the empty council room.

"About this woman," she said. "You can't see her again."

"I did my damnedest to stop that permit vote, and Stephen got it through anyway because *you* turned on me." Phin sat down on the council table, fuming. "What the *hell* were you thinking of?"

"That movie company can do us no good," Liz said. "Zane Black visited everybody on the council this morning, trying to get them to stop the filming, and that's made everybody suspicious. I don't want us to do anything that aligns us with them. You cannot go back out there. That woman—"

"I like that woman," Phin said. "She's a hell of a lot more comfort than you are. You knew damn well—"

"Will you at least think of Dillie?" Liz said.

Phin frowned at her. "What's Dillie got to do with this?"

"You might think of her future while you're unzipping your pants," Liz snapped.

"You have to be kidding me," Phin said. "If every parent thought about his kid before sex, the race would die out."

"What happens when she finds out about this? What happens when she wants to meet this woman?"

"She's not going to meet her," Phin said. "And I get to have a life, too, you know."

"You put your child first," Liz said flatly.

"You never did," Phin said, just as flatly, and Liz took a step back, as if she'd been struck. "And you know it," he said when she didn't say anything. "You didn't even know I was there if Dad was in the room. And when he wasn't, I only had half your attention because you were waiting for him to show up."

"Phin," Liz said.

"It's all right." Phin sat back, trying not to take his frustration out on his mother, no matter how much she deserved it. "The older I get, the more I envy what you and Dad had. I'd watch him come up those steps at night, looking old and tired and miserable, and then he'd see you, and his face—" He stopped because Liz's face had crumpled and he thought she might cry. *It's about time*, he thought, and when she didn't, he said, "You made the world go away for each other."

Liz tightened her jaw. "Don't."

"I thought I was going to get that, too," Phin said. "I thought it just came with the wedding ring, that feeling that the world was all right because two people were together." He laughed shortly. "Found out I was wrong about that."

Liz rallied. "That was not your fault. That was—"

"That *was* my fault," Phin said. "I thought what you had was easy. Now I know better, and I'm not settling. I get what you had or I don't get married. Which doesn't mean I can't have a good time while I'm waiting for the right woman."

"Damn few people get what we had," Liz said. "And you pay for it. You pay a lot for it."

Phin shook his head. "So you just gave up."

"I never gave up," Liz said. "We're still—"

"Not 'we'," Phin said. "I'm not talking about the fucking court-house. I'm talking about you. You just cut that part of your life off completely. There are great guys in this town, but you won't even look at them."

"I have no intentions of getting married again," Liz said.

"I don't either," Phin said. "But you're pushing me at Rachel Garvey just the same." He leaned closer. "You really think if I marry Rachel, I'll start to love her? That she'll love me?"

Liz swallowed. "People do come to care for—"

"Is that how it happened for you? Is that what you and Dad had?"

Liz shut her eyes tight, and then the tears did start. "I'm sorry, Phin. I just can't stand thinking about it. I just can't. I've lost everything except you and Dillie and—"

She broke off and he said, "And that's not enough. We're a lot, but we're not enough. You need your own life."

Liz sniffed and said, her voice strangling with pain, "I just want him *back*."

"I know." Phin walked around the end of the table and put his arm around his mother, and then she did start to cry. "I know you do. I know." He patted her shoulder until she stopped crying, which was about thirty seconds, and then he said, "Listen, I don't know what's going to happen with Sophie. It's only been a week, so who knows?"

"I knew right away," Liz said, pulling back a little and wiping her eyes with her fingers. "The minute I saw your father in high school, I knew. If you don't—"

"Yeah, well, that's easier in high school," Phin said, handing her his handkerchief. "Nobody has any sense then."

"But I knew," Liz said. "And so did your father, he knew, too. And if you and this woman—"

"Her name is Sophie," Phin said as he sat on the end of the table. "And there's something there, because I do not want to be involved with her, but I am still going back out there tonight."

"That's sex," Liz said, almost her old self again.

"Don't knock it," Phin said. "You guys used to do all right there as I remember, so don't even try to tell me you were above all that."

"No," Liz said. "We weren't above anything."

"I don't want any details," Phin said. "I got enough just walking into rooms at the wrong time. If I had a nickel for every time I caught Dad with his hand on your butt, I'd have a lot of nickels."

"That's enough," Liz said, but she gave him a watery smile.

"You had a good marriage," Phin said. "Respect and passion and good times and love."

"Yes," Liz said.

"Well, Sophie gives me respect and passion and good times," Phin said.

"No," Liz said. "Listen to me, that woman is all wrong for you. She's low and she's rude and she's callous. She's *terrible* for you."

"Talked back to you, did she? I don't blame her. You probably started it."

Liz froze up on him again, and Phin said, "You know, you were almost human there for a minute."

"Just because I'm looking out for the people I love—"

"Don't." Phin stood up. "Obsess about the election if you must, but don't even try to pretend you're doing it for me and Dillie. For some reason, you've got it stuck in your head that it's the most important thing in your life, and I'll be damned if I know how to talk you out of it. So I'm not going to try. Just back off and let me live my life."

"I will do *anything* to protect you," Liz said, all her tears gone. "Anything."

"You know, when you talk like that, you scare me," Phin said. "Knock it off. I'll go get Dillie. You get a grip."

He left her sitting there then, alone in the marble council room, under the portrait of his great-grandfather, and his grandfather, and his father, because he didn't know what else to do.

He just hoped he never found out exactly what "*anything*" meant.

While Phin fought the good fight, Sophie was brushing Lassie on the dock and trying to get her life back on track. Somewhere back at the beginning of time, she'd had a plan, but now Amy was out front with Rachel filming Clea and Rob in what was turning out to be a porn flick while Davy watched and shook his head. Georgia was planning to do God-knew-what with Zane when he came back that night, Leo was planning to talk Clea into *Coming Cleaner*, and the Coreys were painting the house a lighter version of the water tower. Amazing. "A cast of thousands," she told Lassie, bending down close to him. "But that's it. We don't let anybody else in."

"Are you talking to that dog?"

Sophie jerked her head up. A pale, thin child with long blonde hair stood at the end of the dock in neatly pressed blue shorts and an immaculate white T-shirt. "Where'd you come from?" Sophie said.

The girl pointed across the river. "My grandma's house is over there."

"Not the Garveys."

"Certainly not." The little girl examined the end of the dock and evidently found it satisfactory because she sat down. "My grandma Junie."

"Oh. Does she know you're here?"

"She's napping." The girl stared at Sophie, and Sophie felt a little uneasy. "I'll go back before she wakes up. If you don't mind that I visit, that is."

"Oh. Sure." Sophie gestured to the yard. "Visit away."

"Because you said you weren't going to let anybody else in," the little girl pointed out. "You said that to the dog."

"Well, you're just visiting, not staying." Sophie tried to find her place in the conversation. "I'm Sophie."

"I know," the little girl said. "That's why I came."

"Okay, now you're weirding me out," Sophie said. "Who are you?"

"Dillie Tucker," the girl said, and Sophie said, "Tucker? Are you related to Phin?"

"He's my daddy," Dillie said, and Sophie lost her breath.

"Your daddy." Sophie regrouped and tried to keep her voice light. Well, Amy and Davy had warned her. Always listen to family. "And how's your mommy?"

"She's dead," Dillie said, and Sophie tried hard to feel sympathetic about that instead of relieved. The poor kid was motherless, for heaven's sake. "She died a long time ago," Dillie went on. "I was a baby. It was very sad."

"Oh," Sophie said. "Yes, I'm sure it was. So, uh, you live with your dad." *There's something he might have mentioned.*

"And my grandma Liz," Dillie said. "But I would like to move." She turned to look at the farmhouse, and Sophie had one strange moment when she thought Dillie might be house hunting. She seemed organized enough for it.

"How old are you?" Sophie said.

"Nine," Dillie said. "How old are you?"

"Thirty-two," Sophie said. "Explain to me again why you're here."

"Don't you want me?" Dillie made her eyes huge and pitiful, and Sophie said, "That's pretty good, kid, but you're out of your league, I grew up with a pro. What are you up to?"

"What's a pro?" Dillie said.

"Dillie," Sophie said warningly.

"Jamie Barclay says her mother says that she heard that you're my dad's girlfriend," Dillie said. "Are you?"

"No," Sophie said. "Who's Jamie Barclay?"

"Because it's okay if you are," Dillie said. "I can stand you."

"That's very generous," Sophie said. "I'm not his girlfriend."

"Why not?" Dillie said.

Sophie decided there was nowhere the conversation could go that wouldn't be dicey. "How about some ice cream before I walk you back to your grandma's?"

"Yes, thank you," Dillie said, and then she grew very still as Sophie stood up, and Lassie got to his feet and yawned.

Sophie watched Dillie watch Lassie. "Are you afraid of dogs?" she asked gently.

"No." Dillie stuck her chin out and just for a moment she looked so much like Phin that Sophie sucked in her breath. "I'm just not accustomed to them."

"This is a very nice dog," Sophie said. "His name is Lassie Dempsey. But if you're unaccustomed, I can make him stay out here while we go inside."

"No." Dillie seemed uncertain. "What kind of dog is he?"

"A con dog," Sophie said. "It's all right, Dillie. I promise he won't hurt you."

"All right," Dillie said, and then Sophie walked off the dock with Lassie close behind her as always and stopped next to the rigid little girl.

"Do you want to pet him?"

"Maybe." Dillie swallowed and gave the dog a gingerly pat. Lassie looked up at her with his *You're new at this* look. "His legs are short."

"But his heart is large." Sophie held out her hand. "Come on. We'll get you a Dove Bar and walk you home to your grandmother."

"What's a Dove Bar?"

"An insanely good ice cream bar."

Dillie looked at her for a long moment and then took her hand. "There's no hurry," she said, and they went up to the house.

An hour later, after extended conversation about school, softball, Dillie's driver's license, dessert, Lassie, Jamie Barclay, Grandma Junie, Grandma Liz, Dillie's dad, her hopes, her dreams, her past, her present, and her plans for the future, Sophie had a new respect for Phin. The kid never shut up; clearly nobody had ever turned on her and told her to put a sock in it. That took massively patient parenting skills. Phin really was good at everything.

Dillie also ate like a horse. When they'd gotten to the kitchen, Dillie had looked at the bag of potato chips on the table and said, "I missed lunch, you know." Sophie made her a ham sandwich, followed by potato chips, followed by an apple and a banana, washed down with lemonade. "This is excellent," Dillie said, reaching for another chip. "Is it time for dessert?"

They were finishing up their Dove Bars and singing along to the sixth replay of "I Only Want to Be with You" so Dillie could learn the words and Sophie wouldn't have to hear any more about Jamie Barclay, when Amy came into the kitchen.

"It's hot as hell out there," she said, and Sophie said, "Meet Dillie Tucker and stop swearing."

Amy blinked at Dillie. "Hello."

"Dillie is Phin's daughter," Sophie said.

"*Hello.*" Amy sat down at the table. "I knew it. I told you so."

"This is my sister Amy," Sophie told Dillie. "Ignore her."

"I don't have any sisters," Dillie said around the last of her Dove Bar. "Or a dog. It's very sad."

"Tragic," Sophie held her stick down so Lassie could lick the last of the ice cream off.

Dillie turned huge gray eyes on Amy. "I don't have a mommy, either."

"That's a relief," Amy said, sitting back, and Dillie looked shocked.

"I told you," Sophie said. "We're pros. Don't try it on us."

"Well, it is sad," Dillie said in her regular voice. "I love Grandma Liz, but I've had enough."

"I sympathize," Amy said.

"I'm not following here," Sophie said. "What do you want?"

"I want to live with my dad by ourselves," Dillie said. "But he says we have to live with Grandma Liz because somebody has to take care of me."

"Couldn't he get Nurse Ratched?" Amy said. "That'd be a step up in warmth."

Dillie concentrated on Sophie. "So then Jamie Barclay said you were Daddy's girlfriend."

"I'm not," Sophie said. "We're leaving next Sunday."

"You don't have to," Dillie said. "You could stay here. I like you. And I think I need a mom." She surveyed Sophie, who was trying to think of something to say, and added, "Maybe you. I don't know."

"Don't get confused because of the dog and the Dove Bar," Sophie said. "I'm really not mom material."

"I don't know," Amy said. "They might be pretty good indicators."

"You're not helping," Sophie told her.

"She raised me, you know," Amy told Dillie. "She was great."

Dillie frowned. "I thought you were her sister."

"My mother died when I was little," Amy said. "It was very sad."

"Don't try that on me," Dillie said. "I'm a pro, too."

"I like you, kid," Amy said. "Was your mom a Dempsey?"

"No, a Miller," Dillie said. "Her name was Diane. She was very pretty. Grandma Junie has pictures. She looked like Sophie."

"Time to go home," Sophie said, suddenly feeling depressed.

On their way out, they ran into Davy. "This is my brother, Davy," Sophie said.

"I don't have any brothers," Dillie said, looking up at him. "It's very sad."

"Not necessarily," Sophie said. "This is Dillie. Phin's daughter."

"Is it?" Davy smiled down at Dillie. "Very nice to meet you, Dillie. And how's your mama?"

"She's dead," Dillie said. "It's very—"

"The mayor gets to live another day," Davy told Sophie. He smiled down again at Dillie. "I was just going to teach this dumb dog how to play Frisbee. Want to help?"

"Yes," Dillie said, and then looked at Sophie.

"Ten minutes," Sophie said. "Lassie's legs are so short, that's all she's going to last anyway."

"That's about my attention span, so it should work out nicely," Davy said. "Come on, kid. Let's see what you've got."

"Davy?" Sophie said, and watched her brother take her lover's daughter out to play.

She had the sinking feeling Davy would be critiquing Phin's parenting technique all through dinner.

When Phin picked Dillie up from Junie's, her T-shirt had a chocolate smear on it. "What happened?" he said, and chunky little Junie said, "She must have found some chocolate while I was napping. She won't say."

"She won't, huh?" Phin looked at his daughter, who stuck her chin out.

"I'll tell you about it when I get my driver's license," she said.

"Get in the car," Phin said. "You'll tell me about it now."

But in the car, Dillie stonewalled him. "You have lots of stuff you won't tell me about. So now I do, too."

"Dill," Phin began warningly, but Dillie began to hum to drown him out. She had no musical ability whatsoever, so he couldn't tell what she was humming. "You know, you're asking for it here," he began, but then she threw back her head and belted out, *"Now listen, honey,"* to really drown him out, and he pulled off the road.

"Where," he said, "did you learn 'I Only Want to Be with You'?"

Nine

Sophie met Phin at the door that evening, still not sure how she felt about that afternoon. "Hello, Dad."

"It never came up," Phin said. "Or I'd have told you."

"She's a pretty big deal to never have come up," Sophie said.

Phin looked past her into the living room. Amy and Davy were on the couch, listening with a great deal of interest.

"How you doin', Harvard?" Davy called. "Or is this a bad time to ask?"

"Can I talk to you alone?" Phin said to Sophie, and she said, "Anyplace but a bedroom," so they went down to the dock.

"It's all right," Sophie said when they were sitting, watching the river muddy by. "It was just a shock. Especially when she said I looked like her mother. I mean, it explains a lot about why you—"

"You don't look like her mother," Phin said. "Diane had dark hair, but she was shorter than you are, and younger than you are, and her face was different. Most of the pictures Dillie has are from far away. She just sees a woman with dark hair."

Sophie turned away. "I didn't even know you had a wife. I know you Tuckers are detached, I know you're going to forget my name before I'm back on the highway—"

"I married Diane because she was pregnant," Phin said, his voice flat. "She got pregnant because she thought I had money."

Sophie drew back a little. "Women don't get pregnant all by themselves. Men help. And of all the men I've slept with, you are the most Johnny-on-the-spot with a condom—"

"She told me she was on the pill and I believed her." Phin drew back, too, until they were sitting apart like strangers. "I don't make the same mistake twice."

Sophie's temper flared. "You think I'm trying—"

"Of course not." Phin bit off the words. "Christ, Sophie." He took a deep breath. "I don't think about her much. We were only together a couple of months, and she died in an accident three months after Dillie was born."

"An accident," Sophie said. "The Old Bridge?"

"No." Phin stared out across the river. "She died over there. She came home in the middle of the night and fell down the porch steps and hit her head and bled out before her mother woke up and found her."

"It must have been awful for Dillie."

"Dillie never knew her," Phin said. "Diane had complications after Dillie was born, so I took the baby home to my mother. Diane never came after her when she got out of the hospital."

"You weren't living with her?"

Phin closed his eyes. "My marriage lasted about two months, and they were the worst two months of my life. When my dad died, I moved back to the Hill to stay with my mother because she collapsed. I thought I was going to lose them both."

Sophie thought of Liz's frozen face. "That could explain a few things."

"And I never went back. Mom was rocky, and Diane was happier without me as long as she could keep the river house." He shook his head. "She'd moved up with the in people. She didn't want me, she just wanted my name and my house."

Sophie said, "I'm sorry."

"It's all right," Phin said. "I didn't want her, either. I was stupid, and I paid. But I got Dillie, so I'd do it all again in a heartbeat. Dillie's worth everything."

Sophie nodded. "I can't believe Diane didn't want her baby."

"She wasn't the maternal type," Phin said. "And I think there was another man by then. She was spending a lot of money and she wasn't getting that kind of cash from me."

Sophie felt awful. Some guy that soon, right after . . . She straightened. That couldn't be right. No woman wanted to date right after she'd given birth. "*Right* after the hospital? And you never heard who the guy was?"

"No. I didn't care. I don't care now."

Sophie looked at him in exasperation. "Phin, this is Temptation. Everybody in town would have lined up to tell you who the guy was."

"Sophie, I didn't care. I had a mother who was half crazy with grief and a baby I didn't know how to take care of and a brand-new job as mayor to fill out my dad's term. Diane was the least of my problems."

"She was the least of your problems once she moved back to the river house and let you alone."

He frowned at her. "What are you talking about?"

Your mother bought off your wife. "Never mind. It doesn't matter what you did nine years ago." Sophie stared at the river. "So Dillie told you she came to visit. Are you upset?"

He nodded, and she felt like hell. "It makes things more complicated. She's decided she needs a mother, and I don't want her getting attached and thinking you're it."

"I think I want to go in now," Sophie said. "This conversation is depressing the hell out of me."

"I know," Phin said. "It's not doing a damn thing for me, either."

Neither of them moved.

"So other than that, how was your day?" Sophie said.

"Stephen got the porn permit pushed through," Phin said. "It's the first time I ever opposed something that the council still voted for. He's also managed to convince damn near everybody that I'm involved in this movie, so if anything goes wrong out here, you're taking me down with you."

"Good to know," Sophie said.

"And my mother thinks you're the new Diane. She warned me Dillie would find out. That's the thing about my mother. She's always right."

He made it sound as if he'd been doing something vile, and Sophie flinched. "You know, nobody's forcing you to come out here and play with the unclean. Nobody's making you cross the tracks."

"I think I'll go home now," Phin said and stood up. "I'll call you."

Sophie nodded and didn't turn to watch him walk away, trying hard not to cry. She didn't turn at all until Lassie poked her cold nose at her. "Hey," she said, blinking tears back fast, and turned to find Davy standing there with the dog and two unwrapped Dove Bars.

"Want me to beat him up?" he said, handing her one of the ice cream bars.

"No." Sophie sniffed once and took the bar, patting the dock with her free hand. "Sit down and stop talking big."

Davy sat beside her, and the dog took her other side and looked longingly at the Dove Bar.

"He was mad because you met his kid, right? You're good enough to screw but not to bring home to the family." Davy bit into his Dove Bar as Sophie winced. "Okay, that hurts," he said around his ice cream. "But cop to it now while there's still time. He's not right for you."

"Nobody's right for me," Sophie bit into the sweet chocolate and let it melt in her mouth. It was a great comfort, but it wasn't enough. She thought of Frank saying, "It wouldn't be so bad if I hadn't thought, for just that one night, that there was more." *Right there with you, Frank.*

"Are you okay?" Davy said.

Sophie nodded. "I know you're right. If he's that upset about me seeing his kid, he doesn't deserve me."

"I don't want to be right, I want you to be happy," Davy said.

"I don't think that's one of the choices at the moment," Sophie said, and finished her Dove Bar in silence, leaning on Davy's shoulder, concentrating on the good stuff she could have instead of the great stuff she'd just lost.

For the next three days, Sophie watched as Rachel threw everything she had into convincing Leo to take her with him while avoiding her mother, who had begun to drop by frequently. At the same time, Amy threw everything she had into the video. Amy was the most successful. On Thursday, Leo had gone back to L.A. alone with the rough cut of *Cherished*—"Gotta change that title," he said on his way out the door— and Amy was deep into cutting her documentary. "I'm going to call it *Welcome to Temptation*," she told Sophie. "Just like the sign when we came in."

"Cute," Sophie said. Then Zane cornered her and threatened to tell Phin all her secrets if she didn't stop the movie so Clea would go home with him. Since the only exciting or deviant things about her were the things she'd been doing with Phin, she wasn't worried. Of course, he could tell Phin they'd been shooting vanilla porn, but if he did, then at least Phin would have to call. She hadn't heard from him since the afternoon on the dock, so clearly he'd decided that his kid was more important than great sex, a decision Sophie applauded in the abstract but resented in the specific.

So when Amy blew fuses, Sophie took a deep breath and went down and changed them the way he'd showed her. Then she cleaned the house to distract herself, putting the ugliest of the furniture in the barn and airing out the rooms. It was a lovely little place, she discovered, as she cleared it out. The rooms were cozy and the windows were wide and she couldn't help but picture it painted and papered and beautiful. It was already beautiful on the outside; the Coreys had finished painting, and the house glowed blush and peach in the sunlight. Sophie looked at it and thought, *I'm going to lose this, too.*

Even so she asked Rachel to get her some green paint for Saturday, something that matched the leaves in the wallpaper. "I just want to see one room done before I go," she said, and on Saturday they papered halfway up on the other walls and added two apple green stripes for a border, and then painted all the woodwork and cabinets apple green, too.

"It's pretty," Rachel said, when they were done. "I didn't think it would be, but it is." She began to pack the empty cans and used brushes into a garbage bag.

"Yeah, it is," Sophie said, and then pulled herself together. "Have you heard from Leo?"

"Oh, yeah, he calls every day, but it's always about business, and what's going on here. I mean, he never says he misses me."

"Rachel, if he calls every day to talk about business, he misses you. There is no business in Temptation."

"Well, he's not saying, 'Rachel, honey, come out to L.A., I need you.'"

"You may be asking for too much," Sophie said.

"Just a job. I'd be a great personal assistant."

"Oh, just a job," Sophie said, feeling sorry for Leo.

"It'd be a great job and I'd get out of here." Rachel dropped into a kitchen chair and surveyed her green-stained manicure. "My mother is driving me nuts because of all the rumors about you and Phin. That's why she keeps dropping by here. That and to see Zane." Rachel rolled her eyes.

"Rumors," Sophie said, feeling the chill again.

"The town knows you're doing it," Rachel said, and then added hastily, "Phin hasn't been bragging or anything or taking you to dinner to show you off. It's not his fault, he's kept you real quiet."

Yes, he has, Sophie thought, and then kicked herself for feeling wounded. She hadn't wanted to go to dinner anyway.

"But my mom is hipped on me marrying him so she hates you," Rachel finished. "That's why she keeps showing up here."

"Oh. Well, tell her she can stay home. Phin's lost interest. Doesn't call, doesn't write, what the hell."

"That can't be right," Rachel said frowning. "Phin's not like that. He's a gentleman. He wouldn't just walk off. And he really wants you. The last time I saw you guys together, he looked like he was going down for the third time."

"Well, his mother threw him a rope," Sophie said, getting mad just thinking about Liz and the rest of the insiders.

"You should talk to him," Rachel said. "He'll probably be at the Tavern tonight. You should go."

"Maybe," Sophie said, wanting to see him again, which was too pathetic for words.

"Definitely you should go," Rachel said.

Outside, thunder rumbled in the distance.

"Okay," Sophie said.

Back in town, Phin flipped over the CLOSED sign and thought about Sophie. Davy had made it acidly clear when Phin had called that Sophie never wanted to see him again, and when he remembered the things he'd said to her on the dock, Phin could understand that. But that didn't mean he couldn't seduce her back to him if he could just get her alone. Maybe he could drug Davy—

Somebody knocked on the glass door, and Phin turned to see Zane. Since it was unlikely that Zane had felt a sudden need to read, Phin opened the door with fair assurance that he was about to be the focus of Zane's next dumbass move to get Clea back.

"Heard you had a pool table," Zane said. "That's my game."

This should be good, Phin thought, and said, "Table's in the back."

Zane went past the table, picked up a cue and sighted down the length of it, scowling, then put it back and picked up another, settling on one wrapped with red tape.

"They're all good," Phin said. "But that's the break cue."

Zane nodded. "Good." He racked the balls, scrubbing the rack up and down on the felt until Phin thought he'd have to take it away and smack him with it. When he lifted the rack, the front ball was a sliver of an inch from the rest, but either Zane didn't notice or he didn't care. Then Zane went to the head of the table, put the cue ball a good six inches behind the head string, and bent to shoot, gripping his cue until his knuckles went white.

I'm playing with an idiot who doesn't even know you don't rack your own balls, Phin thought, and sat down, nodding when Zane's break bounced the head ball and left the most of the balls barely scattered. Nothing went in, and he cushioned only three balls, two of them stripes that ended up near pockets. *And now I have to open that mess*, Phin thought, and picked up his cue again, but Zane said, "Stripes," and bent to shoot.

Phin sat back down again, wondering whether Zane knew he was cheating or if he just didn't know eight-ball. Both, he decided as he watched Zane flounder around the table, pumping his stroke from his shoulder and hitting the two stripes into their pockets at warp speed. On his third ball, the cue ball brushed Phin's two before it smacked into the thirteen, but Zane didn't seem to notice. *That was a foul and I have ball-in-hand*, Phin thought about saying, but it was more instructive to watch Zane bash the balls and the game around.

On his fourth shot, Zane jawed the twelve in the corner pocket and it bounced out. "Tight pockets," he said to Phin.

You're a moron. "They can be," Phin said, and picked up his cue. "Solids, huh?" He scanned the table, which Zane had broken up for him with his blundering, chalked his cue, and began to pocket balls on plain vanilla draw-and-follow shots.

"I think there are some things about that video you should know," Zane said as Phin played. "Especially since you put in that film permit."

Phin ignored him and pocketed the six.

"It's pornography, Phin," Zane said. "I know you don't know that because I know Sophie lied to you. Her whole family is crooked. Davy's a con man out in L.A. Amy's got a juvie record that would turn your hair white. The cops want her dad on a fraud charge right now. Sophie's playing you—"

Phin straightened and met his eyes, not amused.

"I'm just saying," Zane said, stepping back, "that it would be smart of you to stay away from the Dempseys because people tend to lose things around them. Like money. And elections."

Phin shut him out, chalked his cue, and bent back to the table to work his way to the eight, concentrating so he wouldn't grab Zane by the throat.

"You don't believe me? Look up Leo Kingsley, that producer they've got out there. You know what his production company is? Leo Films. He only makes porn. You check it out. You'll see. She's lying to you if she told you that movie isn't porn."

Phin ignored him and put the one ball in the side pocket with a draw shot that brought the cue ball into position for the eight in the corner pocket. It was a lovely, simple shot, but then, the simple shots were always the prettiest, restoring his faith in physics and the world in general, something he needed right now since what Zane was saying was probably true. Anything that could be checked as easily as that had to be true. Except for Sophie playing him. She wasn't like that.

Of course, that's what every guy who'd ever been played had probably thought.

Phin chalked his cue and bent to put the eight ball in, and Zane said, "So you'll stop the movie?"

Phin pocketed the eight. "No," he said as he straightened. "That's game. You can go now."

"I'm thinking about your family," Zane said. "I can understand family, I'm trying to save my own here. My wife—"

"My family is fine," Phin said, putting his cue back. "Good-bye."

"Your wife isn't. She's dead." Zane leaned closer. "You know, the police reports from her death are pretty interesting. A little more digging there, and I could have a real news story. And you could have a real scandal."

"And you could have real lawsuit," Phin said. "My wife's death was an accident.

"The police chief was your father's cousin, and the coroner is a relative of your mother's." Zane put the break cue down on the table. "I start digging and you'll have no place to hide. You confiscate that video and send Clea home, or the Dempseys won't be the only family with a jail record."

"Don't fuck with my family," Phin said. "I will cut you off at the knees."

Zane stepped back and said, "Women can sure make fools out of smart men," and left, a lot faster than he'd come in.

Half an hour later when Wes showed up, Phin was sitting on the porch, sorting out the mess as lightning played in the sky and thunder growled in the distance.

"Looks like we're finally going to get that rain," Wes said as he dropped into his chair.

"Zane Black just tried to blackmail me into closing down the movie. Accused me of killing Diane."

Wes frowned. "He's not too smart."

"He also told me Sophie is lying to me and making porn."

"Hell. Is she?"

"I don't know. I've been warned to stay away from her."

"Her brother?"

Phin nodded. "And you and my mother and now Zane."

Wes sighed. "So knowing you, that means you're going to the Tavern to see her tonight."

The thunder rumbled again, closer this time.

"Oh, yeah," Phin said. "Got to."

Sophie didn't see Phin when she walked into the Tavern, but as she looked around the dim interior and recognized most of the faces there, she realized that in the past ten days, she'd become a regular without belonging there herself. It was sort of like being with Phin. She was there and interacting, but she wasn't a part of him, not somebody he'd introduce to his daughter or take to dinner.

She moved toward the jukebox, where Garth was singing "Baton Rouge," a perfectly good song, but too much like Temptation was before she got there and would be after she left. She started searching the song lists for Dusty, and after a minute she felt someone come to stand beside her.

"I've been looking for you," Phin said, and before she could stop herself, she said, "Don't stand too close. Your mother will find out." She flipped over another jukebox card.

"Forget my mother," Phin said. "Could you look at me for a minute? In fact, I'm the one who should be mad here. In the future, I'd appreciate it if you'd dump me in person instead of sending your brother with the message. That was downright—"

"What?" Sophie said, jerking her head up.

They stared at each other for a moment.

"Davy said you didn't want to see me again." Phin said. "And I was stupid enough to believe him."

"Oh." Sophie turned back to the jukebox. "Well, you sure gave up easy." She flipped over another jukebox card, and Phin took her chin and made her look at him.

"Talk to me," he said, looking her straight in the eye.

Sophie swallowed. "You made things pretty clear on the dock when you didn't want me near your kid. And then I realized that I'm not part of anything here, except now I'm part of the gossip, which is why you haven't been taking me to dinner, because you've been hiding us so Dillie wouldn't find out—"

"I haven't been hiding us," Phin said. "I just haven't been standing on Main Street shouting. 'I'm having great sex with Sophie Dempsey.' It didn't seem like a gentlemanly thing to do."

"You're right, you're right." Sophie turned back to the jukebox and flipped another card.

"Sophie, if I've screwed up, I'll pay for it, I'll even take you to dinner, but I'm damned if I'll pay for my mother and Davy."

He sounded annoyed which was cheering. Why should she be the only angry person in the bar? She flipped over another card.

He sighed. "What are you looking for?"

"Dusty," Sophie said. "I can't believe this stupid bar doesn't have—"

Phin took out some change and put a fifty cents in the box. Then he punched in a number combination and said, "Can we go sit down now?"

The first chord sounded from "Some of Your Lovin'," and Sophie said, "Oh. Thank you."

"Don't mention it." Phin nudged her away from the box and toward the booths, and she moved away, swaying a little bit to the music, caught between misery and hope, but mostly glad just to be with him again, which was pathetic. One of the men by the bar caught her eye and smiled, and she stopped swaying. She was already enough of an outsider without calling attention to herself.

Phin put his hand on her back and said, "Over there," and she saw Wes and Amy in their usual booth, far back in the corner.

Dusty sang behind her, soft and low, and she thought, *No matter what I do, Liz and the others are going to hate me, and I'm going to be an outsider stuck in a booth in the back.*

"Sophie?" Phin said, and Sophie said, "I'm tired of this. Make your mother a happy woman. Go on without me."

She moved to the center of the dance floor and began to dance, losing herself in the gentle swing of the music until the guy at the bar got up. *Not you,* she thought, and turned away from him to see Phin shaking his head.

"Care to dance?" he said.

"That'll start talk," she said, and moved away from him.

"No, dummy." Phin slid his arm around her waist and pulled her back. "This is the part where you fall into my open arms and never stand a chance."

He smiled down at her, and Sophie relaxed into him, so glad to have his arms around her again that she didn't care what he said next. She moved with the music, and he pulled her closer.

"It's too late to stop the gossip anyway," Phin slid his hand down to the small of her back and moved his hips into hers. Sophie felt the heat start again and took a deep breath. "Anybody who's seen us knows we've been together," Phin whispered in her ear, making her shiver. "That's how the gossip started. They just looked at us and knew."

"Oh." She moved with him, letting her cheek rest against his shoulder, and he held her tighter and her breath came faster. "This is the sexiest song in the world," she said a couple of minutes later, through so much heat she was blind with it.

"It is now," she heard him murmur, and when she lifted her face to smile at him, his eyes were dark and hot. "It's been four days since I've touched you. You're driving me crazy."

"Good," she said, putting her face against his shirt again, and he kissed the top of her head.

"Careful with that," she said.

"Hey," he said, and when she looked up, he bent and kissed her on the mouth, a quick kiss that turned into something longer, as rich and sweet as the song they were dancing to. He stopped moving and held her close, right there in the middle of the dance floor, and she forgot everything and kissed him back, clinging to him as the heat spread and her knees went weak.

When he broke the kiss, the music had stopped and he looked as mind-whacked as she felt. "If they didn't know before, they do now," he said, and then he looked past her shoulder, and his face changed. "Oh, Christ."

"What?" she said, still dizzy from his kiss, but he was already pulling her toward the crowd around the table where Frank and Zane were squaring off.

"Family values," Zane was sneering. "You and your town council brag about your family values, but you won't do a damn thing to stop a porn film right in your own backyard."

"I'm not making a porn film," Frank shouted back, and Sophie said, "Oh, no."

"And nobody wants to do anything about it," Zane said, talking to the crowd now. "You all just sit home, holding on to your secrets, pretending there's nothing wrong. Well, there's a lot wrong, and I know it all. I've warned everybody and nobody listens, so I'm telling you all now: You stop that damn movie, or none of you will have a secret left. Especially you, Lutz."

Frank stepped closer. "I told you, I wouldn't make porn. I support family val—"

"Your family values?" Zane's laugh spurted out. "Hell, your kid is fucking my wife, and your wife is fucking me."

Frank went white, and Phin said, "Okay," and pushed through the enthralled crowd to Zane.

"Not that she's any good," Zane said, looking at Georgia, and when she made a little cry of protest, he added, "Hell, Georgia, even Jell-O moves when you eat it."

"You're done," Phin said to Zane as he reached him. "Go home."

Zane toasted him with his glass. "And here's your mayor who is fu—"

Phin had him by the throat before he'd finished. "I said, go home," he said, and then Wes was there, too.

"Let go of him," he said, and Phin did, and Zane tried to say something through his bruised throat. "I wouldn't," Wes said to Zane and hustled him protesting to the door, making it look like no effort at all, and Davy followed them both out.

Frank was staring at Georgia as if he'd never seen her before, and Sophie went to her. "Zane lies all the time," she said to Frank, putting her arm around a still-frozen Georgia. "He—"

"He's not lying about you, is he, Georgia?" Frank said dully. He turned to look through the mass of fascinated faces. "Where's Rob? Was that true?" He looked at Sophie. "Was that true about Clea and Rob?"

"I don't know," Sophie said. "I really don't. I just know I wouldn't trust anything Zane says. He's awful, Frank."

"It's all true," Frank said, and left without a backward glance at Georgia.

"Frank!" she cried, and it came out like a mew.

"We'll take her home," Phin said from behind Sophie, and she nodded.

"Well, that was ugly," Phin said, when they'd dropped Georgia off at home and made sure she was marginally all right. It had started to rain as they left the Tavern, and Georgia had cried right along with it, the mascara running in black tracks down her face while the rain ran silver down the windshield and Sophie thought vicious thoughts about Zane.

"What is *wrong* with that man?" Sophie said now.

"He's trying to hold on to his wife," Phin said. "Men get tense when their women leave."

"Not Frank—Zane."

"I'm talking about Zane." Phin slowed to take the turn out of the Frank's development and onto the main road. "Sophie, are you making porn?"

"No," Sophie lied, and felt like hell. The rain was sheeting down, and the wipers clicked back and forth, and she tried to concentrate on how happy she was to be back with Phin again, but guilt got in her way. "Zane just wants Clea's money," she said, to change the subject.

"He wants her, too." Phin squinted through the windshield. "I've never heard one man say 'my wife' so many times. He's all but branded her."

"She is spectacular."

"Yes, she is," Phin said. Sophie lifted her chin and he added, "Don't even try it. You know I wouldn't have her."

"Just wanted to hear it," Sophie said. "Not that I have any right to assume—" She broke off as Phin pulled to the side of the road and cut the engine. "What? Is the rain—"

Phin turned to face her in the light from the dash. "Okay, I know you've been mugged by my mother, but you've got to get past this. You want me to tell you I love you?" Sophie opened her mouth and Phin said, "Because I've known you ten days. That's too damn fast to start planning futures, don't you think?"

The rain pounded on the roof and Sophie felt lost. "Well, ye—"

"And you're mad because I wasn't happy you'd met Dill," Phin said. "Well, you're going off to Cincinnati day after tomorrow. I'm not happy about seeing my kid lose somebody she likes."

"She only spent a hour with me," Sophie said.

"You got me in the first minute," Phin said, and she flushed. "I'm so nuts for you, I'm not even asking the questions about that damn video that I should. I don't care. I just want you. Can I come see you in Cincinnati?"

"Yes," Sophie said, her heart racing as fast as the rain.

"Can I see you Monday before you go?"

Sophie smiled in the dark. "Yes."

"Can I see you tomorrow?"

"Yes."

"Can I see you naked tonight?"

"Oh, God, yes," Sophie said, and met him halfway for his kiss.

Several minutes later when they were both breathless and the car was back on the road, he said, "Listen, that stuff you said on Wednesday, about me crossing the tracks to get to you, that was just to annoy me, right?"

"Well, you're definitely crossing a river," Sophie said.

"Don't buy into that, Sophie. That's so damn dumb, I can't—"

"That's because you're the one on the Hill," Sophie said. "I understand from a very good source that you're either born there or you earn your way in."

Phin was quiet for a long moment. "I may be a little late coming to see you tomorrow," he said finally. "I'll be killing my mother first."

"Yeah, well, if I'm a little late coming to the door, it'll be because I'm disarming my brother."

"Still hates me, huh?"

"I cried some when you left."

"Oh, fuck." He reached for her hand in the darkness. "I'm sorry."

She laced her fingers with his and closed her eyes because it was so nice to be alone with him again, in the dark, just talking. "Not a problem. Davy's not that good a shot anyway."

"Screw Davy. Are you okay?"

"Yeah," Sophie said. "I'm excellent, actually."

"That you are." He turned down the lane to the farm, taking his hand back to park in the sea of mud that was the yard. Then he curled his arm around her neck and pulled her close and kissed her again, and she fell into him, warm and safe. Everything she'd felt while they'd danced came back and she gave in to it, knowing it would only get better. "You do that *so* well," she whispered, and he said, "We do it well. Imagine if we practiced," and kissed her hard again.

An hour later, they were in her bedroom, damp from the rain that came in the open window and from each other, tangled in her sheets on her lumpy, noisy mattress, gasping in each other arms. "We're getting good at this," Phin said between breaths, and Sophie nodded, too satisfied to do anything but agree. He stroked her back, and she stretched like a cat, feeling all her muscles because he'd made them throb. "I could stay like this all night," she said, and then realized what she'd said. "I didn't mean—" she began, and he cuddled her closer and said, "Good idea. How do you feel about sex in the morning?" She said, "With you?" and he said, "No, with Wes. Of course with me," and she smiled, but then somebody knocked on the door and broke the moment.

"Go away," she called, but Davy said, "Sophie, I have to talk to you."

"If he's trying to do the brotherly thing and warn you that I'm only after one thing, it's too late. I just got it." Phin drew the tips of his fingers down her back and made her shiver. "Get rid of him, and I'll try getting it again."

"Sophie, *now*."

She'd never wanted to leave a bed less. "Hold on," she called, as she rolled out of Phin's arms and grabbed his shirt from the floor.

"That's my shirt," he said, but she shrugged into it and held it closed as she opened the door.

"Amy has a problem." Davy's voice was low and his face rain-spattered and dead serious, and Sophie felt a chill. "Get rid of him and come with me. Fast."

"Okay," Sophie said, her heart pounding, and closed the door.

"About my shirt," Phin said. "Take it off and come back here," and Sophie slipped it off and threw it to him.

"All yours," she said, and picked up her dress. "Thank you for a lovely time—let's do it again real soon."

Phin sat up. "I was planning on doing it real soon. Where are you going?"

She threw him his pants. "I forgot, Davy and I have plans, and I can't stand him up just to have more incredible sex with you. That would be antifamily."

"What kind of plans?" Phin said, and she shoved his shoes closer to the bed. "So I gather we're in a hurry here?"

Sophie leaned over and kissed him, staying in the kiss a little longer than she should have because he felt so good, "I really have to go," she whispered against his mouth. "But I really do want this again. I missed you so much. I'll call you later tonight, I swear."

"The telephone is so impersonal," he said, and caught her to him, pulling her back down on the bed, and if it had been anybody but Davy and Amy who needed her, she'd have fallen. But it was Davy and Amy, so she said, "Thank you, I have to go," and rolled off the bed.

She left him sitting there, looking puzzled and not a little grumpy, and when she got to the landing where Davy was leaning against the wall, she whispered savagely, "This had better be good."

"Where's Harvard?" Davy said. "We need him off the premises."

"He's getting dressed," Sophie said. "And he's not in a good mood, so don't call him Harvard. And by the way, next time, *I* get to dump the guy I'm sleeping with."

"Later for that, we've got trouble," Davy said, and Sophie felt chilled again.

Phin came out of the bedroom, buttoning his shirt. "Just like the Waltons," he said, as he walked past them.

"No, we have better music than the Waltons," Davy said, and then held Sophie's arm until they heard the front door slam. "You can make it up to him later," he told her as he pulled her down the stairs and out the back door.

Sophie followed him as the instincts of disaster that had been dogging her from the beginning kicked into high gear. He led her around the side of the house in the pelting rain into the dark of the trees, and she saw Amy standing there, hugging herself.

"I'm sorry, Sophie," she said, looking like a soaked little cat. "Davy says this is a screw-up, but I didn't know what else to do."

"What?" Sophie said. "I still don't know—" Then she went cold as she saw the old blue-and-pink-fish shower curtain at Amy's feet, wrapped around something that looked horribly like a body. "Tell me that's not a—"

"That's Zane," Davy said, turning his collar up against the rain. "And thanks to Amy, he now sleeps with the fishes."

There you go, her instincts said. *Told you so.*

Ten

Sophie said, "What??"and Amy said, "*No*, I didn't kill him. I just sort of . . . moved him."

"Moved him?" Sophie turned back to Davy. "What—"

"Amy found him on the dock," Davy said, his exasperation with his sister plain. "And being a Dempsey, she thought first of her own interests and realized that if she wanted to film a sex scene tomorrow without the police, she'd have to move the body. So she dragged it up here, and I found her when she was wrapping it in the shower curtain."

"Oh, jeez, *Amy*." Sophie looked down at the rain-spattered bundle and saw Lassie sniffing it. "Lassie, get away from there." The whole situation was surreal. It couldn't possibly be true. She nudged the shower curtain gingerly with her foot. "Are we sure he's dead?"

"God, Sophie, you're worse than the dog. Don't kick him." Davy shoved Lassie away from the body with his knee. "I checked. He's dead." Davy sounded mad about that.

"Well, what did he die of?" Sophie tried to pull herself together. This was real. She had to think. Then she was going to be sick, but first she had to think.

"I don't know," Davy said patiently. "Here's what I do know: Zane is dead, Amy moved the body, and we should do something soon before people start to notice and make comments."

"Okay," Sophie said. "Okay." *There's a dead man at my feet.* "Okay." This was no time to panic. She could panic later. Panic later, plan now. The rain came down heavier, pelting them even through the trees. She cleared her throat. "Okay. We can take the body back to the dock and call Wes, we can leave it here and call Wes, or we can take it someplace else. I vote for the dock and Wes."

"No," Amy said, wiping the rain from her face, and Davy said, "As much as I hate to admit it, I vote no on that one, too."

Sophie said, "Why?" and he said, "Because they're going to know somebody moved the body. They can tell that, and they'll wonder why. Once she moved the body, we were screwed."

"Hey," Amy said, sharply. "We were screwed anyway. It's that dickhead Zane. Who else but us would want to kill him?"

"Half the town," Sophie said. "Moving a body is a felony or something, isn't it? This is bad."

"We have to put it someplace else," Amy said, her hands on her hips. "Some ditch maybe."

"Boy, dating the law hasn't taught you a thing, has it?" Davy said, exasperated. "We cannot put it in some ditch. And we're going to have to get this damn shower curtain off it, too." He turned to Sophie. "I'm assuming Harvard is acquainted with the shower curtain."

"Intimately," Sophie said. "He's had conversations with the mildew. Wes knows it, too. He fixed the showerhead." She looked down at the bundle again, trying to make the situation less surreal, but there was a body wrapped in that ugly shower curtain, the rain beading on the fishes. Vincent Price should be there. "Maybe Zane just had a heart attack. We could take him to an emergency room."

"Yeah, good idea," Davy said. "Except he's *cold*. He is obviously *dead*. They're going to wonder why we didn't notice that." He shook his head at his sisters, glowering at them through the downpour. "Generations of Dempseys must be rolling in their graves, watching you two."

"They're probably too busy hauling coal in hell to worry about us," Sophie said. "Okay, I'm against the moving the body someplace else, *really against*, moving the body. And I'm really, really against lying to . . . people."

Amy frowned at her. "Sophie, I need your help. How can—"

"Shut up, Amy," Davy said. "You're right, Soph. You're finally getting a life of your own and here we come to screw it up by making you lie to the mayor. Go back inside, we never should have dragged you into this."

"Wait a minute," Amy said.

"She doesn't even have a motive," Sophie said to Davy. "We could tell them—"

"Zane was leaning on everybody to confiscate the film," Amy said. "He tried everything to screw up this project while he was alive, and he's not going to do it now that he's dead. I'm going to finish this video. I'm moving him."

"Go back inside, Sophie," Davy said. "I've got this covered."

Right. "You want the head or the feet?" Sophie said.

"You sure?" Davy said.

Sophie nodded. "I think this is a mistake, but I'm damned if I'll let you do it alone. This is no time to break up the family."

"If you ask me, it's the perfect time," Davy said. "Amy, get the car and back it up as close to the trees as you can." When she'd splashed off into the yard, Davy said, "She's not going to make it in L.A."

"Thank you for sharing," Sophie said. "Can we worry about that when we've gotten rid of this body?"

Once they had Zane in the trunk, Davy said, "Okay, where?"

"Someplace where they'll find him fast," Sophie said, hugging herself against the downpour. "I am not covering up a crime if this is one."

"I'm pretty sure this is one," Davy said. "You need someplace dark with a lot of people. Temptation have a lovers' lane?"

"Oh, not there," Sophie said, and Amy said, "That's perfect. I'll drive."

Any lingering thoughts Rachel might have entertained about ever going back to Rob were vanquished after an hour and a half spent parked with him behind the Tavern with the rain drumming on the roof.

"You know, Rache," he said. "We're really not together anymore."

"I *know* that," she said. "I don't want you. But Zane was so awful—" She drank another slug of the scotch Rob had brought for her and wished for the four thousandth time that Leo wasn't out of town.

Rob frowned at Rachel. "I still don't get what happened."

"I told you, I went out behind the house to meet you, and he was there," Rachel said. "He was staggering and he grabbed me and—" She took another drink and sniffed. "Thank God my mom doesn't know about that. Thank God my *dad* doesn't know about that."

"He'd kill him," Rob said.

"I just need a chance to calm down," Rachel said. "I just need to be calm before I see my parents again because you know—"

"Yeah," Rob said. "But I think you should tell your dad."

"Why?" Rachel said, and then she got it and looked at him with contempt. "So he can kill Zane and you can get Clea. Get real." The idea was so dumb, she stopped shaking and took another drink. "You know, you have to get over her. She's going to eat you alive."

"She already did," Rob said, his voice smug with satisfaction.

"Oh, *gross*," Rachel said. Then, after a moment, she said, "So you're doing it."

"Yeah," Rob said.

"Fabulous," Rachel said. *You are such a dumbass.* Strangely enough, hearing about what a fool Rob was being was calming her down faster than anything. "So is she going to leave him for you?"

"If she can get the money back." Rob sounded truly disturbed. "If she can get the money, we can go anywhere, but without it, she's stuck with him." He pounded his fist on the steering wheel. "Man, I hate that guy."

"Whatever happened to true love being all you need?"

"We're talking over a million here, Rache," Rob said, sounding like a man of the world. "You don't just walk away from that kind of capital."

Rachel was willing to bet that was a direct quote from Clea, and she had to admit it was a lot of money. But if she cared about somebody, she'd go with him without the money. If Leo got wiped out and asked her to go to L.A. to help him rebuild, she'd do it in a second, and she wasn't even in love with him. She could waitress to support them while Leo found his feet again.

Rob said, "So are you okay now? Because I got things to do," and Rachel gave up her rescue fantasy and said, "Yeah. Take me home. And thank you. For this."

"Hey," Rob said. "I owe you that much. I dumped you for Clea, and you're being great."

"Oh." Rachel thought about clueing him in to the fact that she'd already dumped him, and decided there was no point. "Well, if you love her, you love her."

"I love her," Rob said, and his voice was sure as he put the car in gear.

"Good luck," Rachel said. *You're gonna need it.*

Rob pulled out from the back of the Tavern through the sheeting rain, and the car bumped over something. "Shit," he said, and stopped the car. "I think I hit a dog."

"Oh, no." Rachel looked back, but it was too dark. "I didn't hear a yipe."

"Stay here." Rob slammed the door and she could see him splash around to the back of the car and bend down. Ten seconds later, he was back in the driver's seat, drenched and shaking.

"I hit Zane."

"What?" Rachel froze. "What do you mean, you hit Zane? I didn't see anybody! We didn't hit anybody!"

"I hit Zane. He's dead." Rob was sweating now. "Oh, God. They'll think I did it on purpose to get Clea."

"He's dead? Get us out of here," Rachel said.

"I just—We can't—"

Rachel grabbed his T-shirt and pulled him to her, nose to nose. "Get. Us. Out. Of here. *Now.*"

Rob nodded and put the car in gear. And when they peeled out of the parking lot, Rachel said calmly, "Slow down. We don't want Wes picking us up for reckless op."

Rob shook his head and slowed down. "What are we going to do?"

"We're going to do nothing." Rachel felt panic rise and stepped on it. There was already one loser in the car; they didn't need two. "We're going to go home and go to bed like good children. And we're going to be really surprised in the morning when we find out he's dead."

"I killed him," Rob said.

"Clea will be so grateful," Rachel said.

In the green light from the dashboard, she saw Rob's face change from panic-stricken to panic-thoughtful.

"There you go," she said. "Always looking on the bright side of life."

At eleven-thirty Phin was in bed, staring at the ceiling, listening to the drumming rain and waiting for Sophie to call, when the phone rang. He picked it up and said, "If this is an apology, you better be naked."

"It's not an apology," Wes said. "I'm at the Tavern. Pete Alcott just ran over Zane Black."

"Oh, Christ," Phin said. "I suppose Zane was too drunk to move out of the way."

"Too dead," Wes said. "He appears to have been murdered first. Ed's going to do a preliminary right away and an autopsy tomorrow."

"I'll meet you at the infirmary," Phin said. "Maybe Ed'll decide Zane died of a heart attack."

"I wouldn't count on it," Wes said. "There's a bullet in his back."

Zane didn't look good dead. He was damp and pasty and slack-jawed and squashed as he lay on Ed's table under the unforgiving florescent light.

"He was wearing your letter sweater," Wes told Phin when he came in.

"He can keep it," Phin said.

"A lot of people didn't like this guy," Ed said from behind the table.

"Nobody liked him," Phin said. "But I didn't think they'd kill him because he was an asshole."

"You taking this down, Duane?" Ed said, and Wes's deputy nodded. "Starting at the top of the head, there's a contusion on the left temple with wood fragments in it."

"Somebody hit him with a club?" Wes said. "What about the bullet hole?"

"Getting to that." Ed pointed to Zane's eyes. "Somebody also sprayed a corrosive at him. See the red patches around the eyes? Probably Mace, but not necessarily."

Mace. Sophie.

"And there are bruises on his throat where somebody choked him," Ed went on.

"That would be me," Phin said. "He was still alive after that."

Ed looked at him with the contempt he deserved. "Thought you'd gotten over that temper."

"He annoyed me severely," Phin said.

Ed nodded and went on. "Then there's the bullet hole in his shoulder. A .22. Which appears to have been fired at close range from behind and below."

"Close range? Somebody shot him in the shoulder with a popgun?" Phin shook his head, incredulous. "Why? To get his attention?"

"And there are also several cuts and scrapes on his arms and hands," Ed finished. "And his ankle is swollen. Looks like a bad sprain."

"That's not funny," Wes said.

"No, but it's true," Ed said. "And here's something else you're not going to like: None of that would have killed him. But he was definitely dead when Pete and somebody else ran over him."

" 'Somebody else'?" Wes looked annoyed.

"Looks like two different tire tracks to me. Pete's truck and somebody's car."

"Then what *did* kill him?" Phin said. "The combination of wounds?"

"I'll do the autopsy tomorrow," Ed said. "My best guess right now, given the state of his clothing, is that he drowned."

Wes scowled. "Very funny."

"No. His clothes are damp clear through. He spent some time in the water."

"It's raining like hell out there," Phin said.

"No," Ed said. "He's been underwater, not just rained on."

"River or bath?" Wes said, and Ed said, "What am I? A magician? After the autopsy, maybe; when the lab report comes back, definitely."

"That'll be Monday, at least," Wes said gloomily. "Probably later. It's Labor Day."

"Okay, then," Ed said. "Here's a guess: The river. That would make sense with all the scratches, that he fell through some brush."

"Yes, but who'd do all this?" Phin said. "If you tried to kill somebody by shooting him almost point-blank and missed, you wouldn't drop the gun and reach for the Mace. You'd shoot him again. And if that didn't work, you wouldn't pick up a club. And you sure as hell wouldn't drown him."

"More than one attacker?" Wes shook his head. "Okay, Zane pissed off everybody in town, but I find it hard to believe they all decided to get even in the same two hours."

"Maybe they, like, planned it," Duane said.

"Conspiracy?" Phin snorted. "You couldn't get four people in this town to agree to kick him on the shin on the same day, let alone kill him."

"I heard he caused a ruckus at the Tavern," Ed said.

"A ruckus, yes," Wes said. "But nothing to make anybody shoot him."

Phin thought about Georgia, white with rage and shame. "Maybe."

Ed pulled the sheet back over Zane's body. "Could you two go argue someplace else? I have to operate on this guy in the morning."

Phin looked back at Zane lumped on the table under the sheet and felt a confusion of sympathy, regret, distaste, and exasperation. Zane had done nothing but make trouble since he'd come to town, but he didn't deserve to die for it. And now here he was, with people who didn't like him arguing over his body, and nobody to mourn for him. "Clea's his next of kin. Somebody should tell her."

"That'll be me," Wes said, standing up.

"Want some company?" Phin said.

"Oh, yeah," Wes said.

Sophie had showered and was knocking back her second cider and peach brandy when the squad car pulled up. She'd been okay until they'd unwrapped Zane, and then he wasn't a fish-covered bundle anymore, he was Zane, cold and stiffening with his eyes wide open, wearing Phin's letter sweater. They'd left him propped on the slope behind the Tavern in as lifelike a position as they could manage, but as they'd pulled away, Davy had said, "Damn. He fell," and Sophie had gone green again.

Davy looked out the screen door now. "It's Wes. And Harvard. The gang's all here. Suck it up, Soph. You're a Dempsey."

"Right," Sophie said, and hit the brandy again.

Phin didn't look happy to see her, and he didn't say much. Wes asked to see Clea, and when Amy went up to check Clea's bedroom, she was there, alone. That was so strange as to make anybody suspicious, but Clea's performance after that was so good that even Sophie had to give her points. She didn't play the grief-stricken widow, but she looked shocked, stunned, and all the other appropriate emotions on being informed that somebody she'd once slept with on a regular basis was now sleeping permanently.

"I can't believe it," Clea said. "He was always having those blackouts, but I thought that was just for attention." She put her hand to her eyes as if to block out the pain, and Sophie saw Davy's face twist just for a moment. *He can't still care about her*, Sophie thought, and then Wes took her attention again.

"Uh, we're pretty sure it wasn't a natural death, Clea," Wes was saying. "He was assaulted before he died."

"Assaulted?" Clea blinked up at him, her china-blue eyes opening and closing like an expensive doll's. "But why?"

"We're working on that," Wes said. "Right now we're just trying to get some information. When was the last time you saw him?"

"At the Tavern." Clea sniffed. "He was so awful, and I couldn't stand it anymore so I had Rob bring me here."

"And you didn't see him after that?" Wes was patient but not stupid.

"I saw him," Davy said. "About nine. I followed him back after that mess at the Tavern, but he was being a real butthead, so I left him alone. He took that sweater and went out the back door and headed out past the dock."

"Toward the Old Bridge?" Wes said.

Davy shrugged. "Toward something. He wasn't wandering. He was going somewhere, although he seemed a little . . . sluggish."

"Sluggish." Wes nodded. "Like he'd been hit?"

"Or he was drunk." Davy shook his head. "I didn't get close. He pretty much walked through the house and out again."

Wes turned to Sophie and she thought, *I have the blood of a thousand felons in my veins. I can lie to the police.*

"Did you see him, Sophie?" Wes asked, Sophie shook her head and hugged Lassie to her. She hadn't seen him. That thing with the staring eyes hadn't been anyone she knew.

"I came back with Phin." She swallowed and said, "I can't believe he's dead. I hate this."

"I know," Wes said, and Phin told him, "We came back to the farm about nine-thirty and I was here until almost eleven. We didn't see him at all."

"You left before eleven," Wes said, and Phin turned to look at Davy and said, "Yep."

"I came and got Sophie," Davy said. "That dumb dog had jumped in the river again and was mud all over. So we put him in the bathtub and washed him off."

Phin got very still, and Sophie remembered her lie to him, that she'd forgotten something she had planned with Davy.

Next time she moved a body, she was going to make sure all the stories were straight.

"So the last time anybody saw Zane he was heading out the back door," Wes said. "About . . ."

"Nine-thirty maybe," Davy said. "Phin and Sophie came in after that, so before they came in, he left."

Sophie risked a look at Phin and met his eyes. He wasn't buying any of it.

"One other thing." Wes looked at Sophie. "Anybody here have Mace?"

"Mace?" Sophie blinked at him and clutched Lassie harder. *Rachel.* "Mace. No."

"Okay." Wes nodded. He began to ask Clea about Zane's life in Cincinnati, and Davy faded up the stairs as Phin crooked his finger at Sophie. "Could I see you a minute, please?" he said, and she went out on the porch with him.

Lightning split the sky and the thunder followed it as the rain pelted down. "What happened?" he said to her over the storm, and she thought, *I wish I could tell him everything.* But he'd have to tell Wes to protect his job and his family of politicians, and there was no way she was going to betray her family of felons. For the first time, she wished she didn't have quite so much family.

"Nothing. Davy and I washed the dog and that was it."

"You're lying," he said, not angry, and she shrugged. "Where's your Mace?"

"I don't have any Mace."

"You said, that first night at the Tavern—"

"It was a joke," Sophie said. "I don't have Mace."

Phin leaned down to her. "Believe it or not, I'm on your side."

She felt the tears start. "I know," she whispered, and he kissed her until she stopped crying.

"Yell if you need me," he said when Wes came out, and then they left.

When Sophie went back inside, Clea had gone back upstairs, and Davy was there.

"Her mourning was pretty much over when Wes left," Davy said. "What did Harvard want?"

Sophie said, "He told me to yell if I need help."

Davy leaned in the doorway and looked out into the stormy darkness. "He didn't believe a word we told Wes, and he never said a thing. He's got money, right?"

"No," Sophie said. "Forget him. Somebody killed Zane. Concentrate."

"Forget Zane, he's dead." Davy came to stand in front of her. "You concentrate. Harvard has money, right?"

Sophie flopped back against the couch. "No. He owns a bookstore but it can't make much, stuck out here. Don't even think about running a con on him."

"His shirts are Armani," Davy said. "And he drives a classic Volvo."

"His mother probably bought it all. Forget it."

"What are you talking about?" Amy said. "Zane—"

"He could take care of you, Sophie," Davy said, ignoring Amy. "He'd be good at it. He wants to do it. I've changed my mind. You can have him."

Sophie shook her head. "I don't need anybody—"

Davy nodded. "Yeah, you do. You're tired and you're not happy and you're still putting your butt on the line for us. It's time we set you free."

"Sophie doesn't feel that way," Amy said. "Sophie always says, 'Family first.' "

"He is family," Davy said. "He's her family—"

Yes, Sophie thought.

"—and she's not going to lose him because you and I are screwups. We've been dragging her down long enough." Davy nodded to Sophie. "It's time somebody took care of you, Soph, and that's Harvard. He was in real agony there, trying not to care tonight, covering your ass."

"Sophie?" Amy said. "He's wrong, isn't he?"

"I don't want to talk about this. I'm going to bed." Sophie stood up and then said, "Oh, damn, no I'm not. We have to do something with that shower curtain."

"You could just let Sophie run her own life," Amy said to Davy. "We did just fine after you left. We take care of each other."

Davy looked at her with contempt. "Oh, yeah, you take care of her. That's how she ended up making videos of other people's weddings and sleeping with a therapist and moving a dead body."

"Excuse me?" Sophie said. "*The shower curtain.*"

"I'll take care of it," Amy said, ignoring Davy. "I got us into this, and I can get the shower curtain out."

When she was gone, Sophie said, "We're not going to put it back in the bathroom, right?"

"*I'll* take care of it," Davy said.

"You'll take care of it, just like that." Sophie folded her arms. "You know, while I was standing out there trying not to throw up, you were making *Godfather* jokes. That worries me."

"Well, somebody had to be cool," Davy said. "Would you just forget that? We have your future to fix now."

"That wasn't your first dead body, was it?"

"I've never killed anybody, if that's what you're asking," Davy said.

"I'm letting Amy go to L.A. because you're out there," Sophie said. "But if you're mixed up in—"

"You're not 'letting' Amy go anyplace," Davy said. "She's twenty-five, she can go anywhere she wants." He scowled at her. "Just not L.A."

"If you're there to watch out for her, I won't worry," Sophie said. "Unless you're getting rid of bodies—"

"I'm not going to be there," Davy said.

"What—"

"Okay," Amy said as she banged through the screen door, the shower curtain bundled in her arms. "I've got it." She looked at Sophie. "What do we do with it?"

"I'll take care of it." Davy took the curtain from her and looked back at Sophie. "For once, *I'll* take care of all of it. Everything's going to be fine."

Sophie shook her head, sure nothing was ever going to be fine again.

———

"So what's the plan?" Phin said to Wes as they headed back to Temptation in the rain.

"Look for a gun, a club, and a can of Mace and a car with some Zane in its tires," Wes said. "Try to figure out why the angle of that shot was so awkward. See if we can find somebody who will admit to seeing Zane after he left the farm but before Pete ran over him so we can narrow the time of death. And start checking alibis of anybody who might have a motive." He looked over at Phin. "Did Sophie come clean about the Mace?"

"Come on, Wes, you don't suspect Sophie."

"She might not kill him, but she'd use the Mace if he attacked her," Wes said. "Hell, that's why she carries it."

"But he wouldn't have attacked her," Phin said. "They'd known each other for years."

"Women are usually attacked by men they know," Wes said. "I'd bet anything the Mace was self-defense. It's such a lousy offensive weapon, it almost has to be."

"If it was self-defense, she'd have said so," Phin said. "No reason to lie. Maybe it was Amy's."

"I asked. She said no."

"Maybe Amy's lying."

"No," Wes said. "She isn't. Not about the Mace, anyway."

"About something else?"

Wes shrugged. "Oh, yeah. There's something big there. I haven't quite got it yet."

"I have to say," Phin said. "I don't think anybody we've talked to tonight has told you the whole truth about anything." *Including me, damn it.*

"Welcome to the wonderful world of law enforcement," Wes said.

Phin had a hard time sleeping, and things got worse when he woke to an increasingly stormy Sunday morning. The word had spread fast, and everybody in Temptation wanted to talk, even though the store was closed, but it was the strangers that got to him. The *Cincinnati Enquirer*, the *Columbus Dispatch*, the Dayton *Daily News*, and even some of the smaller papers, had sent reporters who'd slopped through the continuing storm, hoping for something juicy about the murder of a news anchor. "This is southern Ohio," Phin told one of them. "Nothing of interest ever happens here. Go away." But they stayed to dig dirt and gather gossip and by the end of the afternoon, Phin was sure they'd all have the scene at the Tavern at the very least and probably a line on the movie, too. None of that was good, but the worst was the original fact: Zane was still dead.

By late afternoon, Wes hadn't come by, which meant he was swamped, and part of being a best friend was the automatic obligation to dig out swamps. Phin turned the lock on front the door, but then he saw Davy with his jacket over his head against the rain, climbing the steps. He unlocked the door, and Davy shook out his coat and said, "Heard you had a pool table."

Phin said, "The last guy who said that got killed."

"Yeah, they said you were good," Davy said, and Phin let him in, wondering what he wanted and not caring much unless it was going to help solve the Zane mystery and get life in Temptation back where it belonged.

When Davy saw the table, he said, "Hello. *Beautiful* piece of furniture." His voice held real admiration as he walked around the table, and Phin tried not to like him for it. "Late nineteenth century, right?"

"Yep. It was my great-grandpa's."

Davy touched the rosewood rail. "It's like being in church. And you play on it every day."

"But I never take the privilege for granted," Phin said.

Davy met his eyes. "Harvard, you may not be a complete loss after all. What's your game?"

Phin shrugged. "Your choice."

"Straight pool," Davy said, and Phin thought, *Oh, hell, I don't want to like you.*

Davy added, "To fifty?"

"Works for me."

Davy went over to the rack, picked up a cue, bounced it on its end and checked the tip.

"They're all good," Phin said.

"So I see," Davy said. "Should have known. I beg your pardon." He sounded sincere.

Phin won the break, and Davy racked for him without comment, keeping the front ball tight against the rest and treating the felt with the respect it deserved, and Phin picked up the break cue, interested to see what Davy had going for him.

An hour later, the score was 32–30 with Phin in the lead, but that was pretty much meaningless. Davy's position play was flawless, and his concentration was complete: he'd been in stroke since his first shot. Even more impressive was his safety play. When he turned the table over with the cue ball frozen to the rail for the second time, Phin said, "Where did you learn to play?"

"My dad," Davy said. "He has few skills, but the ones he has are sharp and profitable."

Phin raised his eyebrows on the "profitable." "We playing for money here?"

Davy shrugged. "We can. Makes no difference."

Phin looked at the mess on the table. "How about twenty?"

Davy nodded. "Good bet. Enough to make you care but not enough to make you broke."

Phin studied the table and decided that a safety was the better part of his valor, too. "So your daddy was a hustler."

"Still is," Davy said. "And not just at pool. He's on the lam right now from a fraud charge."

Phin caromed the cue ball off the four and buried it in a cluster, and Davy said, "Damn."

"Thank you," Phin said, and moved away from the table. "Zane Black mentioned your dad was . . . uh . . . colorful."

"Zane did?" Davy looked thoughtful. "Now, why would he share that with you?"

"He was being helpful," Phin said. "Explaining why Sophie was a bad influence."

Davy's face darkened, and for the first time Phin realized that he wasn't just a slacker; Davy Dempsey might be dangerous. "Now that annoys me," Davy said softly. "He shouldn't have been talking about my sister."

"Well, he's dead, and I'm open to bad influences," Phin said. "You going to take a shot here?"

Davy bent to the table and did a bridge shot over the two ball, a beauty of a shot that did exactly what it was supposed to, and Phin shook his head in admiration. Then Davy picked up the cue ball and handed it to him.

"Foul," he said. "I brushed the two with my hand. That's what I get for letting Zane in my head."

Phin took the ball and said, "I didn't see it."

"I did," Davy said, and moved out of Phin's sight line.

Phin nodded and studied the table. If he could pocket the two, there was a possibility he could run the table. He put the cue ball down in position so that he could draw it back after he hit the two.

"That's what I would have done," Davy said ruefully from the side, as the two went in. "So you think my sister's a bad influence?"

Phin studied the table. "I think your sister's a hell of a woman, but I don't want to talk about her."

"Well, we're going to have to," Davy said. "Because that's what I came for."

"And I was hoping it was for the pool." Phin took his shot, but his ball missed the pocket by a fraction of an inch. *Concentration is everything*, he thought, and wondered if Davy had brought up the subject of Sophie to break his.

"Here's the deal with Sophie," Davy said as he took the table. "She's the finest person I know, so she should get everything she wants. Now, for some reason, she wants that ugly farmhouse, that stupid dog, and you." Davy chalked his cue. "None of which I would have picked for her, but then, Sophie has always walked her own path." He shot a plain vanilla draw shot with such elegance that Phin forgot about Sophie for a minute.

"It's a pleasure to watch you play pool," he told Davy, and Davy said, "I know. It's the simple shots that make you love the game."

"I really don't want to like you," Phin said.

Davy nodded. "I don't want to like you, either, Harvard, but we're stuck with each other because Sophie loves us."

"I went to Michigan," Phin said. "And Sophie doesn't love me."

"You know," Davy said as he chalked and shot again, "if you paid as much attention to your personal life as you do to your pool game, you wouldn't make these stupid mistakes. She's in love with you. And you'd better love her back."

"Is that a threat?" Phin said.

"Pretty much." Davy scowled at the table as his next ball missed the pocket. "And that's what I get for trying to talk and play at the same time. Look at that table. Don't say I never gave you anything."

"Davy, I care about Sophie, but that's it," Phin said. "And I never promised her anything at all, so you can back off now." Then he looked at the spread Davy had left him. "Christ, it's Christmas."

"Yeah," Davy said. "I had plans for that table." He sat down out of Phin's sight line. "I'll be over here in case you go blind and miss something. Now, about Sophie."

"I'm finished talking about Sophie," Phin said, and bent to make his shot.

"I'm not," Davy said. "She never told you about how we grew up, did she?"

"Yeah, she did." Phin made his shot and straightened to chalk his cue. "At least, she told me about your mom dying."

"She did." Davy seemed impressed. "So you know she's been taking care of us ever since."

Phin nodded.

"Well, it's time she found a man to take care of her, and you're the one she's picked. You're not my choice, Harvard. But you're Sophie's and you're going to marry her."

"No, I'm not." Phin bent to take his shot.

"Why not?" Davy said. "Think about it. You could go home to Sophie every night."

Phin looked at the ball, thought about Sophie at night, and miscued. Just a fraction of an inch, but pool is not a forgiving sport.

"Fuck," he said, and Davy said, "That was my fault, talking to you like this."

"No shit," Phin said, and walked away from the table, annoyed with himself for falling for it.

"Take another shot," Davy said.

Phin glared at him, and Davy said, "Right. I apologize for even saying it," and took the table back.

"It was the Sophie-at-night bit, wasn't it?" Davy said as he lined up his shot. "Sorry. It's what I miss most about her. That quiet bit at the end of the day when we talked about everything." He grinned at Phin over the top of his cue. "Of course, your nights with her are probably different."

Phin thought about the hours he'd spent talking with Sophie. Before he fell into bed with her and lost his mind. "Slightly different."

Davy nodded and began to run the table. When he was five balls from victory, he straightened and chalked his cue. "Here's the thing. I learned early that life is full of cheats and liars." He bent to the table and said, "I don't believe in Santa Claus," and hit his first ball into a pocket. "I don't believe in the Easter Bunny." Another ball went in. "And I don't believe in the innate goodness of mankind." A third ball went in.

"But I believe in Sophie."

He pocketed the fourth ball and straightened to chalk, something that he should have done three times before but that would have ruined the effect. Dumb pool but interesting psychology.

"And that's why I'm going to make sure Sophie gets what she wants." He smiled at Phin. "And what she wants is you, God help her." He bent back to the table and said, "Game ball," and Phin watched as he lined his cue up for the easy draw shot into the corner pocket that would take the game. Then Davy moved the cue a fraction of a fraction of an inch to the right, and shot.

And the ball jawed and bounced out again.

"I should never talk while I play this game," Davy said philosophically, and walked away from the table.

Phin picked up his cue, chalked it, lined up the shot, and made the ball. Another rack later, he had the game. Then he turned to Davy, who was taking a twenty out of his wallet, and said, "On the very outside chance that we might play again, you should know that pool is the closest thing I have to a religion. Don't you ever throw a game with me again."

Davy went still and then nodded. "Fair enough. My apologies." He put the twenty back in his wallet.

"You really thought that would make a difference?" Phin said.

"Well, it seemed like a smart thing to do," Davy said. "Generally speaking, if you want something from somebody, it's best to give him something, not beat him at his own game. I just didn't realize who I was dealing with. Now I do." He nodded at Phin. "It was a damn good game, Harvard. Thank you."·

Phin looked back at the table. "Yeah, it was. But I'm still not marrying your sister."

"Why?" Davy said, and Phin blinked at him. "You have a great time with her, the sex is obviously terrific, she's smart, she's funny, she's kind, she's a wonderful mother, your kid's crazy about her, and she loves you." He shook his head. "I don't see why you're fighting this. You can't say no to her anyway, or you'd have stopped coming out to the farm by now."

"You can go now," Phin said, annoyed.

"That would be best," Davy said. "I think my work is done anyway."

"And what work would that be?" Phin said as he followed him to lock the door behind him.

"I broke your concentration," Davy said. "Sophie was already in your head, you just weren't paying attention. Now she'll be there all the time."

"Don't come back," Phin said, and Davy laughed and went down the steps to the street.

Phin turned off the lights in the store and headed for the stairs to his apartment. He was late to meet . . . Sophie. His steps slowed as he realized the rhythm he'd fallen into. Close the store, go out to the farm, kiss Sophie, and end the day. No wonder Davy thought he was the marrying kind. He was practically there already.

Well, the hell with that. Tonight he was staying home. Maybe Wes would want to play a little pool.

Oh, right, Wes would be dealing with the murder.

He picked up his car keys and went out into the rain to the police station, a little rattled that the murder wasn't the most pressing thing on his mind.

Eleven

$\mathcal{E}$d got the autopsy done," Wes said from behind his desk when Phin came into his office. He didn't sound happy. "There's water in the lungs and it's river water, but Zane didn't drown."

Phin dropped into the chair across from him. "So what killed him?"

Wes tossed the report onto his desk. "Heart attack."

Phin leaned back. "That a joke?"

"No." Wes poked the folder with his finger. "It's in there. Necrosis in the heart muscle. Ed says his heart was a mess and probably had been most of his life."

"He had blackouts," Phin said. "Clea talked about them. She thought he did it for attention."

"He did it for oxygen," Wes said.

"So it's not murder?" Phin shook his head. "That can't be. A lot of people took a poke at this guy before he died. One of them must be responsible."

"Ed said to wait for the forensic report on Monday, but none of the attacks would have been enough to kill him, and we can't prove that any of them triggered the coronary, so we'll have a hell of a time getting a murder conviction." Wes's jaw was tight and he looked mad-

der than Phin had ever seen him. "Which doesn't mean I'm not going
to go after assault convictions, even though I have no clear motive, no
weapon, and—oh, yeah—no fucking crime scene."

"He wasn't killed at the Tavern."

"No," Wes said. "That's the good news. We've narrowed down our
options. He was killed somewhere in southern Ohio, but *not* behind
the Tavern."

"You may be taking this too hard," Phin said. "Davy said Zane was
heading out the back door. And Ed said he'd been in the river. Did you
look at the dock at the farm?"

"What a great idea," Wes said flatly.

"Okay," Phin said. "If you're going to be surly, I'm going to leave."

"I checked the farm dock, the Garvey dock, your dock, and Hildy's
dock, everything within walking distance given that Zane was drunk,
and all points in between. Sent some samples to Cincinnati, but I'm
not hopeful."

"My dock?" Phin said. "I don't—Oh, Junie's dock. I don't think
Junie killed him, Wes."

"I think he went in on that side of the river," Wes said. "That would
be consistent with the scrapes and cuts, if he fell off the high bank
and through the brush. The bank on the farm side is just mud."

"So he went out the back door and took the Old Bridge to the other
side?" Phin shrugged. "Easy enough, but why?"

"That's according to Davy," Wes said. "I don't think the truth is
anything Davy Dempsey holds sacred."

"The only thing Davy holds sacred is his sisters," Phin said.

"Yeah," Wes said, and waited.

"Sophie was with me from nine at the Tavern to about ten forty-
five."

"Pete ran over him a little after eleven-thirty," Wes said. "That gives
her forty-five minutes, but it doesn't give her a motive. I ran a background check on everybody I could think of, which, by the way, solved
our earlier mystery of why Stephen lied on that damn accident report.
Virginia's been picked up for reckless op several times in Cincinnati.
Evidently traffic in the city makes her nervous."

"Lot of points?"

"She'd have lost her license," Wes said. "So Stephen took the heat and tried to bully the Dempseys."

"Had he but known," Phin said. "Wrong family to bully. Why wasn't Stephen driving?"

"Don't know," Wes said. "I got the police report back on the Dempseys, too. Davy has a record."

"Since Zane wasn't defrauded to death, I think Davy's still in the clear."

"So you knew." Wes picked up a pack of cigarettes from the mess of papers on his desk and shook one out.

"I knew he was on the con," Phin said. "That didn't seem relevant."

"Anything is relevant," Wes lit the cigarette and inhaled. "As you damn well know. Amy has a juvie record which is, of course, sealed. But the cop I talked to in Cincy remembered her well. And then, just for the hell of it, I checked Dad, too. The guy has a record you wouldn't believe."

"Temptation has a 'no smoking in public offices' ordinance," Phin said. "And you kicked the habit two years ago."

"You got a real genius for the obvious," Wes said.

"So how do you feel about Amy's juvie career?"

Wes frowned. "Really turned on."

Phin nodded. "I'd have taken it that way, too. Still, falling for a bent woman is no reason to give yourself lung cancer. And since the Dempseys aren't violent—"

"If the Dempseys were being blackmailed, they could turn that way." Wes took a drag on the cigarette and then exhaled on a deeply-felt sigh. "I used to think the Tuckers were crazed about family, but you guys can't hold a candle to those three out at the farm. I think Zane was blackmailing people, and they'd have been prime candidates."

"He tried with me," Phin said. "He wasn't too bright."

"What every town needs," Wes said. "A stupid blackmailer. I think he went after Frank, too. He was in today. He does not look good."

"Well, he's married to Georgia, who was fucking Zane," Phin said.

"Although, evidently not very well. You know, if Georgia could have killed Zane at the Tavern last night, she would have."

"And, of course, there's always Clea," Wes said. "She's capable of damn near anything, and so far I haven't found that bank book everybody was talking about that she wanted so much and that I'm sure Davy was interested in, too. I'm going to Cincy tomorrow to look at Zane's apartment, talk to the people at his work, but if that book's not there, I'm going to have strong suspicions about Clea Whipple and Davy Dempsey." He took another hit on the cigarette and added, "Zane talked to your mom, too. Yesterday afternoon, right after your pool game."

"And we know this because . . . ?"

"Because that's what Frank came in to tell me," Wes said. "He also said Zane had talked to the Garveys and insulted Rachel and had something on the Dempseys. He was pretty much casting suspicion everywhere but at his family, although he did mention that Georgia was unstable."

"Like that's news," Phin said. "I don't suppose he mentioned his kid, who wants Zane's wife."

"No," Wes said. "Didn't mention that."

Phin shook his head. "Christ, what a mess."

Wes took another drag on the cigarette and then looked at it. "I wonder if we've confiscated any grass lately."

"You could go bust the Coreys," Phin said. "They paint stoned."

"Dangerous of them," Wes said. "The water tower is looking strange. Sort of bubbly. They're going to have to paint it again. Wouldn't want an accident up there."

"Taking their stash would be for their own good," Phin agreed.

"So what aren't you telling me?" Wes said.

Phin sat there for a long moment, balancing loyalties, and then he said, "I didn't leave voluntarily last night. I got kicked out when Davy came for Sophie."

"He needed help," Wes said.

"Or Amy did," Phin said. "My bet is Amy. She's the one they always rescue."

"Amy wouldn't kill anybody," Wes said. "I don't think. So, we talk to Davy Dempsey again."

"If you think you're going to break Davy, forget it. Especially if he's protecting Amy."

"Or Sophie," Wes said.

"Let's go bust the Coreys," Phin said.

Half an hour earlier, Sophie had been facing down Dillie through the screen door. "Dillie, your daddy *really* doesn't want you to be here."

"But don't you want me to be here?" Dillie said, looking rejected and heartbroken.

"Oh, honey, of course—" Sophie began, and then she frowned. "Nice try, kid. You almost had me."

Dillie looked exasperated. "Well, I know you want me here. You're just being difficult. Let me in."

"How come you're so sure I want you?"

"Because I'm delightful," Dillie said.

Sophie sighed and let her in. "You're father tells you this, I assume?"

"No, my dad tells me I'm spoiled rotten and not to pull that stuff on him." Dillie didn't look too abused by this. "My grandma Liz says it. She says, 'Dillie Tucker, you are the most delightful child in the world.' She thinks I'm smart, too. I'm a real Tucker."

"Lucky you. Dill—"

"I have a reason for being here," Dillie said hastily. "An important reason." She sat down at the table and fished a torn piece of notebook paper out of her back pocket. "Jamie Barclay and I made up a mother test."

"How cute of you," Sophie said. "No."

"It's just four questions," Dillie said, her cupid's-bow mouth drooping with disappointment. "Four little questions. *Please.*"

Sophie sighed. Maybe if she flunked Dill's test . . . "Shoot."

Dillie straightened in her chair. "Okay. These are multiple choice to make it easy."

"Thank you. We potential mothers appreciate all the help we can get."

"One. Should a nine-year-old's bedtime be (*A*) eight-thirty; (*B*) nine-thirty; (*C*) ten-thirty; or (*D*) whenever she gets tired?"

Sophie said, "(*A*). Or even earlier. Six, maybe."

Dillie nodded and made a mark on the paper. "Two. A child should watch TV (*A*) only when there are educational specials on; (*B*) only on weekends; (*C*) whenever she wants."

"What happened to (*D*)? Shouldn't there be a 'never' on there?"

"Sophie," Dillie said, and Sophie said, "(*A*)."

Dillie made a mark on the paper. "Three. A girl is old enough to get her ears pierced when she's (*A*) ten; (*B*) twelve; (*C*) sixteen; or (*D*) twenty-one."

"(*D*). Or when she gets her driver's license, whichever comes last."

Dillie shot Sophie a look from under her lashes and then made another mark on the paper. "Four. When a girl grows up she should be (*A*) a ballerina, or (*B*) a mayor."

Sophie straightened, not amused anymore. "(*C*). Whatever she wants."

Dillie sat back. "Perfect score."

"What?"

Dillie nodded. "My dad picked the exact same answers. Even the different answer on number four."

"You gave your father a mother test?"

"No, I gave him a father test," Dillie said. "Jamie Barclay said I have to find a good match for him so he won't get divorced. She's had three dads so she knows. And since my dad likes you, I figured I'd start here." She looked at the paper. "We need to talk about some of this stuff, though."

Sophie stood up. "We're walking back to your grandmother's now."

"Without ice cream?" Dillie sounded truly distraught, so Sophie got two Dove Bars and several wet paper towels and took her down to the dock, Lassie on their heels. The river rushed past them, high and fast from the rain. "As soon as this is gone, you're gone," she told Dillie, who began to eat her Dove Bar slowly, chattering the entire time.

"My dad says that I'm his favorite woman in the whole world," Dillie said when she was finally licking the stick. "But I bet you're second." She thought for a minute. "Or maybe third. There's my grandma Liz."

"I'm just honored to be on the short list," Sophie said. "You have to go back now, Dill."

"But I just got here," Dillie said, imploring. "And it was a long way. My feet hurt. I'm just a child, you know."

"I have my suspicions about that," Sophie said.

"I shouldn't have come," Dillie said sadly. "It's because I don't have enough supervision. I need a mother. Really bad."

Sophie stood up. "Come on, Meryl Streep. We have to get you back before anybody notices."

Dillie ignored her to stare up the hill.

"Dillie?"

"Too late," she said in a small voice, looking genuinely pitiful this time.

Sophie turned and saw Phin coming toward them, looking like thunder. Dillie moved closer to Sophie and Sophie put her arm around her.

"I could have sworn," he said to Dillie when he reached them, "that I'd told you not to come here. You want to explain this to me?"

"You were unreasonable," Dillie said, sticking out her chin from the circle of Sophie's arm. "Sophie is my friend." She put her hand on Lassie's head. "And you won't let me have a dog, and she has one and I can play with him." She went into orphan-child mode. "This is probably the only dog I'll ever get to play with in my whole life. Ever."

"Where does she get this from?" Sophie said. "I can't believe she learned it from you or your mother."

"Her mother was one hell of an actress," Phin said grimly.

Dillie looked up, and Sophie said, "Well, she's damn good at it, and it's a useful skill, once she learns to stop overselling it. Since you're here, can she stay a couple minutes and play with Lassie?"

"You want me to reward her for disobeying me?" Phin said.

Sophie leaned closer to keep Dillie from hearing, and whispered, "I want you to stop being such a tightass and let the kid play with the dog."

"Yeah," Dillie said.

"Don't push your luck, young lady," Phin said. "I told you not to come over here and you came anyway."

"Grandma told you not to come out here and you did anyway," Dillie said.

Sophie looked out across the river and pressed her lips together.

"Go play with the damn dog," Phin said, and Dillie went. "If you're laughing, I'm going to shove you in."

"Well," Sophie said, and then she laughed out loud. "I'm sorry, I'm sorry. But she had you on that one."

"She has me on all of them. Spoiled rotten kid."

Sophie watched Dillie run up the hill with Lassie. "You know, it'd be worth it to stay in Temptation just to watch you when she starts to date."

"She's never going to date."

"Not even when she gets her driver's license?" Sophie sat down on the dock and put her feet back in the rushing water. "She's a good kid."

Phin sat down behind her. "I know she's a good kid."

Sophie leaned back until she touched his shoulder. "I should warn you, she gave me a mother test which I tried to flunk. I passed."

"You pass all my tests, too," Phin said, and she turned her head just as he dropped a kiss in the curve of her neck.

"Hey," she said, alarmed. "Dillie."

"She just went around the house," Phin said in her ear. "Look at me."

She turned to him and he kissed her thoroughly. "I'll be back tonight," he said against her mouth. "Bed check. And you'd better be here."

"I thought your mother told you not to come here anymore."

"She's being unreasonable," Phin said. "You're probably the only Dempsey I'll ever get to play with in my whole life. Ever."

"Lucky for you," Sophie said, and he kissed her again, and she put her hand on his arm and felt safe and fine. "Is this what we're going to do tonight?" she said, her eyes still closed.

"No, we're going to wax my car," Phin said.

Sophie opened her eyes. "What?"

"Then I'm going to fuck you on the hood," Phin said, and took her mouth again.

"That was a *really* rude thing to say," she said a few moments later, trying to get her breath back.

"Yeah, but it turns you on every time," Phin said. "I go with what works."

"We have to stop necking on this dock," she said a minute later. "Stephen Garvey's probably taking Polaroids right now."

"See if you can get copies." Phin leaned toward her again, and then Lassie barked and they both jerked around to see Dillie coming down the hill, elaborately unconcerned with them. "Remind me to stay away from you," Phin said as he stood up.

"What did I do?" Sophie pulled her feet out of the water and drew them up under her.

"It's not what you do, it's what you are." Phin raised his voice and called, "Say good-bye to the dog, Dill. We have to get going."

"I could go out in front again," Dillie bargained, as she came up to the dock. "You could kiss Sophie some more."

"I had something in my eye," Sophie said. "We weren't—"

"I'm finished kissing Sophie," Phin said. "Say good-bye."

"Good-bye," Dillie said, the orphan child once more. "I had such a nice time, but it was too, too short."

"That's the good times for you," Sophie said. "They never last."

Leo came back Monday afternoon, splashing through the front yard and talking about arks and Labor Day traffic, and Rachel was so glad to see him she couldn't stand it. Her life was so awful, so out of control, but now Leo was back. She could tell him about the Mace and he'd tell her what to do. She'd wait until he was done at the farm and then—

He showed them his cut of *Cherished*.

"I changed the title, of course," he said as the video began to play. A cartoon lion in a smoking jacket appeared and the words *Leo Films* scrolled across him, and Rachel thought, *This is so cool, he's got to make me his assistant if I don't go to jail for giving Zane a heart attack.* But then the credits started.

Gone was Amy's carefully filmed approach to Temptation, panning up to the water tower. Instead two curvaceous-to-the-point-of-chunky legs straddled the words *Leo Kingsley Presents* which dissolved to flaming letters that read, *Hot Fleshy Thighs*.

"What?" Clea shrieked, " *'Thighs'!*"

But the title change was the least of it. Leo had kept most of the film, but he'd added some of the raunchiest sex scenes Rachel had ever seen, not that she'd seen many.

"I'm going to be ill," Amy said, when they'd hit the second one. "Look at that grain. It's not even the same film quality," and Rachel and Sophie looked at her in disbelief.

"Film quality?" Sophie said, her voice going up an octave. "The fact that this is *pornography* doesn't bother you? My dog shouldn't be watching this."

"Leo, this is disgusting," Clea said. "Did you do this all the way through?"

"Of course," Leo said, not the least insulted. "This is what I sell. This is what makes money. This—"

Oh, Leo, Rachel thought, torn between anger and disillusionment. *This is so wrong.*

"I don't care about the money—" Sophie began.

"You ruined my film—" Amy began.

"Leo, you pervert—" Clea began.

He wasn't a pervert, Rachel knew, growing calmer even as the bodies flailed on the screen. He was a darling. He just wasn't thinking, that was all. Sometimes you had to point things out to Leo. The big sweet dummy.

"Now, look," Leo was saying. "You knew I wasn't Disney. And I told you it needed—"

Rachel turned off the television and popped the cassette out of the player. She took a red magic marker and wrote *Smut, Smut, Smut,* on it in big letters and handed it to Leo.

"Rachel, honey, be—" Leo said.

"This is *not* going to happen, Leo," Rachel said firmly. "We had a deal. You were going to try vanilla porn. You were going to be classy this time."

"Rachel, baby," Leo said, very avuncular. "You don't understand—"

Rachel pointed her finger at him. "Don't you 'baby' me. A deal's a deal. You don't put garbage like that in a quality film." She put her hands on her hips and stared down into his eyes, making him pay attention. "That's just wrong, Leo. You should be ashamed."

The silence stretched out until Amy said, "Yeah."

Leo sighed. "Look, you girls did a fine job, but you have to be practical. I couldn't sell what you made to high-school kids, it was that tame."

"So we'll make it hotter," Rachel said, making him meet her eyes again. "This is not a problem. But *we* make it hotter, not you. Jeez, Leo, what did you think? That we'd say, 'Oh, good, Leo put in some cheesy sex scenes for us?' "

"I thought you'd be reasonable," Leo said.

"You thought wrong," Rachel said. "Give us a week."

"Rachel—"

"A week. That's not too much to ask, Leo. Not after what you just did." Rachel stared him down, implacable, and Leo sighed again and said, "Okay, a week. But I need skin and I need sex. And if you don't give it to me, I'll cut it in myself."

"Deal," Rachel said, and then stepped back as she realized what she'd just done. "Uh, if that's okay with Amy and—"

"It's okay with me," Amy said.

"You can make all our deals," Sophie said.

"Especially with Leo," Clea said, looking at her appraisingly.

"Come on," Rachel said to Leo, feeling magnanimous now that she'd gotten her way. "I'll take you out to the motel and you can drop off your stuff. And then we'll go get something to eat, and you can tell me what this movie needs."

"I am not going to talk dirty to you in a restaurant," Leo said.

Rachel shrugged. "Then we'll go to Dairy Queen and eat in the car."

"Fabulous," Leo said, but he followed her out when she opened the screen door and gestured, just like she knew he would. He was a good man, really. He just needed *managed*.

Rachel got in the driver's seat. "Dairy Queen or the diner?" she asked, and Leo sighed and said, "You choose."

"Dairy Queen," Rachel said, putting the car in gear. "You like their ice cream. And tonight we'll go watch the Labor Day fireworks, and you'll feel better. I'll take care of everything."

Beside her, Leo groaned, and Rachel thought, *Not a good time to tell him about the Mace.*

She'd just tell him later, then.

When they were gone, Sophie said. "I'd give her a raise but we're not paying her anything."

"Forget Rachel," Clea said. "She's bought us another week, but it's up to us to come through. We need sex scenes. And we're going to have to film them fast."

Sophie shook her head. "We signed that porn permit—"

"Sophie," Amy said. "For God's sake, this is my video. When we signed the permit, we weren't making porn. Exactly. And were not filming on public property, so we're innocent."

"Amy, we're never innocent," Sophie said. "I said this place was trouble. Remember? That first day, when we *were* filming on public property?"

Amy looked back, unblinking. "You sorry we came?"

Sophie stopped and thought of Phin. "No." Then she thought of Clea and Zane's sightless eyes and the lying and making porn. "Yes." Then she thought of Phin again. "No. Okay, we'll do this fast, but this is the end. No more." She met Amy's eyes. "I'm not lying to him again, not even for you."

"So much for family," Amy said, and stalked off into the kitchen.

————

At nine that night, Sophie stood with Amy on the bank of the river while Clea and Rob took their places on the dock. There wasn't much light from the quarter moon, so Amy had set up reflectors and side lights, and the dock looked like a carnival to Sophie. Trashy.

"This is too bright," Sophie said. "Way too bright, somebody's going to see."

"Stop whining," Amy told her. "Everybody's at the Labor Day picnic. We're going to shoot this very fast and get out of here before the fireworks are over. Right, guys?"

"Well, I like to take a little time," Rob said, and Clea said, "Very funny. Not tonight."

She stripped off her sundress and stood naked on the dock, looking even more beautiful in the moonlight than she did in the sun, and Rob said, "Whatever you say, Clea." He pulled off his shirt and threw it on the grass next to her sundress, and then unbuttoned his jeans, and Sophie turned away.

"I don't want to see this," she said, as she heard his jeans hit the ground, and Amy said, "Oh. Yes, you do."

Sophie turned around and blinked. It wasn't just youth that drew Clea to Rob.

Amy looked at her. "We're going to need a bigger dock," she said, and Sophie turned away again, trying not to laugh. Fireworks exploded beyond the trees, and she stopped to watch them sparkle gold and blue and red in the sky. Beautiful. Then she caught a glint from the trees across the river upstream. At first she thought a spark had caught a tree, but it wasn't that kind of glint, and she froze as she saw it again.

"Somebody's watching us," she told Amy quietly, and Amy clutched her camera tighter. "There, see that? Somebody's got binoculars or a camera or something. That's glass reflecting back light. Turn those lights off now."

"No, I can't." Panic made Amy's voice tight. "We can't stop, we have to get this. We're running out of time." She grabbed Sophie. "You have to go see who it is, maybe it's nobody, maybe nobody's there."

"Are you nuts?" Sophie pulled away. "Turn off those damn lights."

"*Please,*" Amy said. "Just go see. And then come right back if somebody's watching and we'll stop, I swear, but it's probably nobody, and I don't want to stop if it's nobody."

"Amy, somebody just got murdered here. I'm not going—"

"It was *Zane*," Amy said. "Everybody wanted him dead—nobody wants to hurt you—just go look. Oh, please, Sophie." Sophie hesitated and Amy said, "*Please*. This is my chance, please help me."

Sophie closed her eyes. "If I get killed, I'm haunting you."

"Oh, thank you," Amy said. "Thank you, thank you, you always come through for me, Sophie."

And I'm getting a little tired of that, Sophie thought, as she headed for the main road and the other side of the river. The Old Bridge was just too creepy this late at night.

When she turned off the road and began to walk down the river path, she realized the whole place was creepy at night, thick with trees with the swollen river rushing below. *Just find out what that glint is and go*, she told herself. Once she knew for sure what was going on—

She stopped when she was behind the Garvey's house because somebody was moving on the path above the dock. She stepped into the shelter of the trees and saw Stephen, binoculars at ready, staring across the river.

They were screwed.

She bent to look through the trees to see the dock so brightly lit they could have counted Clea's freckles from the courthouse.

They were completely screwed.

Then her Dempsey instincts kicked in and she realized she wasn't alone, but before she could turn, somebody shoved her hard, and Sophie tripped and fell into the trees, smacking her head hard on a branch and toppling down the steep slope half-conscious, grabbing instinctively at branches that ripped at her hands until she plunged headfirst into the river.

She hit the water hard and went under, and it was cold, ridiculously cold, and that helped bring her back from the head blow. The pull of the current was strong as she fought her way to the air, shuddering and gasping as the river took her. She was past the farm dock by the time she surfaced. She saw Junie's dock off to her left, and kicked off her shoes and began to swim for it, cutting diagonally across the current, but the water was so cold and her head hurt and she missed the dock, slipping under the water twice as she almost lost consciousness.

I'm not going to die, she thought, and kept fighting her way across the current, and then the current was weaker, and there was another dock and she managed to get close enough to shore that the river took her against the pilings. She clung to the edge of the dock, feeling herself slip away, and then she thought, *No*, and pulled herself up, painfully, to collapse on the splintery boards. *You can't stay here*, she told herself, and put her hand to her head where it hurt the most. It was wet, she was wet all over, but when she brought her hand down, it had blood on it. *I'll get help*, she thought. *I'll get help in a minute.*

And then there was nothing.

Phin was opening the bookstore the next morning when Wes came up the steps. "I got the lab report and I'm heading out to the farm," Wes told him, biting off the words. "You coming?"

"I have this store I'm running," Phin frowned at him. "What are you so mad about?"

"The lab report." Wes stopped on the top step. "And the Dempseys. They're going to tell me the truth this time or I'm going to fry them, and that includes your girlfriend. I don't care how banged-up she is."

He started down the steps, and Phin said, "What?"

"Sophie," Wes said. "She didn't call you? Somebody shoved her in the river last night. She's got the same wound on her forehead that Zane had. Ed's pretty sure they both hit their heads on the same tree."

Phin flipped the sign *Back at 4:30* over, slammed the door to the bookstore shut, and went down the steps past Wes. "Drive," he said.

When they got to the farm, Phin was out of the car and at the door faster than he'd ever moved in his life. He didn't bother to knock.

"Oh, hi," Sophie said from the living-room couch. She had a livid scraped bruise on her forehead and blue circles under her eyes, and she looked like hell. Davy and Amy stood over her, scowling at each other, but when they heard Phin come in, their faces smoothed out to bland.

"What the hell did you think you were doing?" Phin said to Sophie, not caring that everybody was listening. "It's *dangerous* out there."

"What?" Sophie frowned at him and then winced and put her hand to the bruise, and Phin wanted somebody dead. "Whoever killed Zane doesn't want me, unless you think you've got a serial killer on your hands, which doesn't seem—"

"If you ever do that again," Phin snapped, "you won't need a serial killer. I'll do you myself just to get the suspense over with."

"It's just a scrape," Sophie said. "It's no big deal."

"The hell it isn't," Phin said. "And you were in the river. Tell me Ed pumped you full of penicillin."

"Yes," Sophie said. "I'm *fine.*"

She sat there with her chin in the air, and he said, "No, you're not. You're too dumb to live," and went out and sat down on the porch steps and put his head in his hands and thought, *I almost lost her.*

Davy came out and sat down beside him.

Phin braced himself. "If you're coming out here to kick my ass because I yelled at your sister, go right ahead."

"No, I think you pretty much summarized the situation for her," Davy said. "She's just used to taking care of everything. Sophie's not one for waiting around if the family's in trouble."

"Wes said she says she just went for a walk." Phin raised his head and looked at Davy. "Tell me she's not *that* damn stupid."

"I wasn't there," Davy said. "As I understand it, they were shooting on the dock, and Sophie thought she saw somebody watching, so she went to see. Amy would like that to be Sophie's idea, but my bet is, Amy leaned on her. The movie is making Amy crazy, but it's family that makes Sophie stupid. You should be able to relate."

Sophie came out on the porch. "You still here? I thought you'd have gone back to the smart people by now. Davy, Wes wants us."

Phin looked at the bruise on her forehead and the misery in her eyes and felt like hell. "You are not allowed to leave the house again until you get your driver's license."

"I already have a driver's license."

"That's what you think," Phin said, turning to stare back across the yard. "I'm making Wes take it."

Davy stood up. "Don't scare the mayor again," he told his sister and went inside.

After a moment, Sophie sat down beside Phin. "I'm sorry if I upset you."

"You didn't upset me," Phin said. "You took ten fucking years off my life." She leaned into him a little, and he felt her warm weight against his shoulder. She was so close and so important, that he put his arm around her and kissed her, very softly because she'd been hurt.

She closed her eyes. "I'm sorry if I scared you. I scared me, too. I even lost my rings." Her voice shook a little and he kissed her again.

"I'll get you new rings," he said against her mouth, and then Wes came out and said, "I want Sophie in here now."

Phin sat on the arm of the couch with Sophie close against him, and Amy leaned on the fireplace and stared malevolently at him. *Warm little family you got, honey*, he thought and then remembered his mother. *Never mind.*

"A couple of things," Wes said. "Somebody filled Zane full of sleeping pills."

Sophie straightened against Phin, and he thought, *Great*, now *what did they do?*

"Enough to kill him?" Phin said, and Wes scowled and said, "No. But there's more." He turned back to Amy. "There was mildew smeared deep into that letterman sweater. I'd like to see your shower curtain."

Amy froze, and Davy said, "I made them get rid of it. It was so gross I couldn't stand it."

"You know," Wes said, "you're pissing me off." He looked at Amy. "You got anything you want to tell me?"

Amy stuck her chin out. "No."

Wes nodded. "I know damn well you moved that body, and I need to know where you found it." He never took his eyes off Amy's face. "Don't lie to me."

Amy flushed, and Sophie looked miserable.

Phin took her hand. "Sophie's sick," he said, and pulled her outside, away from her family. "Okay," he said, when they were back on the porch step. "You don't have to tell me a damn thing, but don't go down for them. There's a limit to what you do for family."

"I don't think there is," Sophie said miserably. "We didn't kill him, Phin, I swear, we didn't."

"Okay." He put his arm around her. "Don't get upset. How's your head?"

"It hurts," she said, and he kissed the scrape. "We moved the body," she blurted, and he looked back over his shoulder to see if Wes was close enough to hear. "I can't *stand* lying to you."

"That why Davy came for you," he said, and Sophie nodded.

"Amy wanted to film on the dock, but the body was there, so she moved it into the trees, and then we moved it to the Tavern."

"Amy's been leaning on you for too damn long," Phin said grimly. "When are you going to let her clean up after her own mistakes?"

"When are you going to let Dill?" Sophie said. "When she gets her driver's license? I don't think there's an age where you say to the people you love, 'You're on your own.'"

"No, but there's an age where you say, 'I'm on my own,'" Phin said. "And you're there. Can I tell Wes?"

Sophie closed her eyes. "I don't want to betray my sister."

"As long as she didn't shoot Zane, you won't," Phin said. "Wes isn't going to arrest her for moving the body, he's after bigger fish."

She shuddered. "That damn shower curtain. I see it in my dreams."

"You don't think she shot him, do you?" Phin said, and Sophie was quiet for too long.

"No," she said finally. "But I think she might have given him the sleeping pills. Davy got revenge once using sleeping pills, and we'd just been talking about it. I don't know." She put her hand to her head. "You know, this really hurts."

"You need quiet," Phin said and stood up. "Come back with me. I'll have Ed give you some stronger pain stuff and you can sleep upstairs at the bookstore."

Sophie closed her eyes. "I can't leave Amy."

"You have to leave Amy," Phin said. "It's the only way you're going to survive."

The council meeting the next day was depressing, even more depressing than telling Wes the Dempseys had moved the body or leaving Sophie at the farm with her conniving sister. Stephen asked to table the streetlight vote for another week so he could present more evidence of Phin's fiscal depravity and neglect of civic duty. Then, during the new business, he tried to pass a formal thank-you to Phin for working so closely with the movie people, said thank-you to be printed in the Temptation *Gazette*. The motion went down when only the Garveys voted for it, the rest of the council viewing them with deep suspicion. Stephen fumed, his hands shaking, and then he played his last card.

"I have an announcement," he said. "I've talked to the people at Temptation Cable and they've agreed to preempt their usual programming so that we can show the "Return to Temptation" video at eight next Tuesday night."

"Uh-oh," Rachel said from beside Phin.

"Have you asked the people who made the movie, Stephen?" Phin said. "They have rights, too."

"I'm sure they'll be thrilled," Stephen said smugly. "Why wouldn't they be? A chance to preview their film to a receptive audience. And besides"—his voice dropped a little—"We should see what they've done. We gave them a permit, after all. I'm just doing my civic duty."

You *watched them film on the dock*, Phin thought. *What do you know?*

But he already knew.

They were making porn.

Half an hour later, Phin stopped by the police station and told Wes about the cable premiere.

Wes stubbed his cigarette out on the edge of one of the coffee cups that littered his desk "They know about this out at the farm?"

"I doubt it," Phin said. "I haven't heard any screaming. Rachel will tell them when she gets out there. You want to go out?"

"No," Wes said, sourly. "Amy won't tell me anything anyway. When you go, find out if they have a .22."

"Everybody has a .22," Phin said. "Hell, I have a .22, or at least, my dad did."

"I know," Wes said. "I ran the registration forms. There are almost four hundred of the damn things in this county alone."

"An armed populace is a secure populace," Phin said. "Also, this is southern Ohio. What did you expect?"

"You have one, Frank has one, Clea's dad had one, which could mean it's still at the farm, Ed has one, Stephen has one, hell, even Junie Miller and Hildy Mallow have one—" He stopped, caught by an idea. "Your entire city council is armed."

"That, I didn't need to know," Phin said, standing up.

"I went to Cincinnati today," Wes said, and Phin sat down again. "No bank book anywhere, although Zane showed it to a couple of people on Friday."

Phin winced. Missing money and Dempseys were a no-brainer.

"Also, he had the whole council investigated." Wes tossed a thick folder across the desk to him. "He had a crackerjack research team. The people at the station thought a lot of him. Evidently he was a damn good reporter. He'd been an investigative journalist before doctors found his heart problem and made him quit, but he trained the research team. They thought he was God."

Phin picked up the folder and began to leaf through it. The top sheaf of papers had his name on them: a list of everybody he'd slept with for the past ten years, with significant details. "Fuck you, Zane."

The next set of papers was Hildy Mallow's arrest record.

"Everybody at the station hated Clea, though," Wes was saying. "Said she was a conniving, manipulative bitch."

"That sounds like Clea," Phin said, still reading. "Hildy went to jail for protesting the war?"

"Often," Wes said. "She said Zane tried to talk her into stopping the video on the basis of family values, and when that didn't work he threatened to do her arrest record as part of a human-interest story. She offered him his choice of pictures of her behind bars from her scrapbook and asked him for a copy of the arrest records because she wants to frame them."

"Good for her." Phin flipped through her records, his respect for Hildy growing. "Man, she was busted everywhere. She—" He stopped when he came to the next set of papers: Virginia Garvey's record. "He knew about Virginia's driving citations."

"She says he never mentioned them, but he did come by the house. She said he asked Stephen to stop the video on the family-values grounds again, and Stephen said he'd look into it." Wes shrugged. "He probably didn't use the records because he didn't need them. They came on board without the threat."

"Did he have anything on Stephen?" Phin said, stopping to frown at an invoice from an online video-porn distributor. "He didn't really think he was going to blackmail Ed for porn, did he?"

"He tried," Wes said. "Ed told him everybody in town knew he had the best porn collection in southern Ohio."

Phin flipped the invoices over and found a medical record. "What the hell? So Frank Lutz had a vasectomy in 1976. Who cares—" Then he heard Georgia again, talking about the little girl she didn't get. "Frank, you moron."

"Yeah," Wes said. "Frank's revenge."

Phin looked at the Cincinnati address on the top of the form. "Georgia would have left him if she'd known. How the hell did Zane find this?"

"Look at the next one," Wes said. "Stephen has Parkinson's disease."

"That's why his hands have been shaking," Phin said, reading the next medical record and feeling sorry for Stephen for the first time in his life. "They don't always, so I thought it was just rage." He looked up at Wes. "That's why Virginia was driving. He didn't want to have an attack while he was driving."

"It's more than that," Wes said. "He didn't want anybody to know because of the election."

"Why? I don't—"

"Because he thought you'd use it against him," Wes said, and when Phin jerked his head up, outraged, Wes added, "He'd have used it against you."

Phin sat back and stared down at the folder. "Christ, what a mess."

"You know, this might be pretty much the last chance for him," Wes said. "Parkinson's is progressive, and he's getting older. He only has to keep it a secret for another two months to win this time. But another two years, in this town—" Wes shook his head. "It's not like Temptation's ever given him a break before."

Phin winced. He'd never thought of it that way, and for the first time he wondered what it must be like to be Stephen Garvey in Temptation. While he'd been trapped under the weight of dozens of Tucker victories and one loss, Stephen had been carrying dozens of losses and one victory. What must it be like to be destined to strive for something you were lousy at, that your father had been lousy at, and his father before him? What would that do a man?

What would a man do to end that?

Phin met Wes's eyes. "So did Zane threaten him with the medical report?"

Wes shook his head. "Stephen swears it was all family values and agreement."

Phin spared one last sympathetic thought for Stephen and then flipped through the rest of the papers, through Davy's record, and a page on Sophie's relationship with the therapist that he definitely didn't want to read, and a much thicker sheaf of pages on a Michael Dempsey that had to be dear old Dad. At the bottom of the Dempsey stack was a final clip of papers, and Phin stopped when he saw the newspaper article on top.

Mayor's Wife Dies in Accident.

"He really was going after that, then," Phin said, shuffling through Ed's autopsy report and the police report with crime-scene photos and the newspaper report and Diane's obituary. He tried not to look at the photos, at her pale face lit starkly against the dark of the grass. "What did he find?"

"I don't know," Wes said. "But I don't think Zane bluffed anybody. I think everything he said was true. Had a real nose for secrets, Zane did, not that there's anything there to show Diane's death wasn't an accident."

Phin tossed the folder back on Wes's desk. "So what do you con-
clude from this?"

"There's a thorough report in there on all four of the Dempseys,"
Wes said. "And there are reports on you and all the council members.
Except one."

Phin felt sick. "Maybe he just couldn't get anything on her. She's
damn near perfect."

"Nobody's perfect," Wes said. "Not even your mother. If he took
Diane's file to her and told her he was going after you—"

Phin thought of Liz saying, *"anything."* "What do you want?"

"Bring me your dad's .22," Wes said.

"Fuck," Phin said.

Out at the farm, Sophie stared miserably across the kitchen table at Davy
while Lassie sniffed his suitcase by the door and Amy glared at them
both. "You really have to go?"

"Yes," Davy said. "I'm catching a ride with Leo, but we'll both be
back Friday, so stop looking so tragic."

"I'm not tragic," Sophie said, and Amy said, "Sure, go ahead, just
desert us," but then the phone rang, and when Sophie picked it up, it
was Brandon.

"Are you all right?" he said. "Amy called and said you'd fallen in a
river. I think I should come down there."

Sophie glared at Amy, who looked at the ceiling. "No, you should
not come down here. I'm fine. Brandon, you should stop calling. I appreciate your—"

"Sophie, I've been doing a lot of thinking, and I think you should
come back home," Brandon said. "I realize you feel the need to act out
your anger with this man—"

"Brandon, you're a wonderful man," Sophie said. "You deserve
somebody who loves you completely, not somebody who love you
comfortably. I—"

"Comfort lasts," Brandon said. "The kind of passion you're talking
about doesn't. A year after you marry this man—"

"We're not getting married," Sophie said, looking at the pretty apples on the wall. "He's not that serious about me."

"This guy needs his ass kicked," Davy said, and Amy said, "Which one, Phin or Brandon?"

"Both," Davy said. "The two of you have terrible taste in men."

When the silence on the other end of the line lengthened, Sophie said, "Brandon?" and he said, "You deserve more than that, Sophie."

"I know." Sophie swallowed. "I'm working on it. But—"

"Sophie, I think Amy's right I should come down there—"

"I have to go, Brandon," Sophie said. "I'm sorry. Good-bye."

She hung up and said to Amy, "Do *not* call him again. Stay out of my life."

"At least he loves you," Amy said. "He's boring, but he's committed. The mayor doesn't even—"

"Yes, he does," Davy said. "He gets my vote. Now, let's discuss the stupidity of a Dempsey getting involved with a cop."

"I'm not involved," Amy said, trying to sound tough and only sounding more miserable because of it. "He hasn't even called since he yelled at me." She shoved back her chair. "It doesn't matter, I have a real problems. I have to finish cutting a documentary. I don't have time to worry about some guy."

When she'd gone, Sophie sighed. "Do you really have to go?"

"Things to take care of," Davy said. "But I'll be back. Don't let her shoot anybody till I get here."

Sophie swallowed. "You don't think—"

"I don't know," Davy said. "I wish the cop would just take her over. She needs a strong hand, and you've baby-sat her long enough."

"Hurry back," Sophie said.

Phin's next two days were lousy with problems and frustration, alleviated only by the time he spent with Sophie. Phin watched Wes move up to two packs a day and thought, *We have to finish this before he gets lung cancer.* It didn't help that his dad's .22 was gone from the locked gun cabinet. "Anybody could have taken it," he told Wes. "The key's on the top, up where Dillie can't reach it, but we weren't trying to keep anybody else out. I haven't looked in there for over ten years. It could have been gone that long."

"Great," Wes said, and turned down a pool game to obsess over his lack of evidence again.

The premiere took over the townspeople's attention, possibly because Zane had been such an outsider, probably because the video was more interesting because it was about them. Stephen suggested the schools assign it as homework. "I have to write a report," Dillie said on Friday, "so I *have* to watch TV. Jamie Barclay said I could watch at her house and then we could do our reports together—isn't that a good idea?"

"Oh, yeah," Phin said, and thought, *I hope to hell they've got a G-rated version of that video.*

"I'm going out to the farm," he told Liz, who looked at him with frozen contempt. He went out to the car, grateful that it had finally stopped raining, and then caught sight of the water tower on the Hill above him.

It was peeling.

"What the hell happened?" he said, when he'd tracked down the Coreys.

"It's that stupid cheap paint," the older one said. "When that hard rain hit, it just peeled right off."

"It's cool," the younger one said. "Looks like blood dripping off. The newspapers were here taking pictures."

Phin looked back up the Hill where the tower did indeed look like a huge bleeding phallic symbol. "Can you get that red off and paint it white?"

"Oh, yeah, like we're gonna strip the water tower," the older Corey said. "Just give it a couple of days and it'll be off anyway. The tower's gonna be a weird color, though. That red doesn't stick, but it stains."

That would explain why the tower looked rosier this time, even more like flesh than before. Wonderful.

He let the Coreys go and drove out to the farm for sanity and comfort, and by the time he'd slammed the car door, Sophie was on the porch. He went toward her, feeling better just looking at her, but she shook her head and whispered, "This isn't a good time."

"Now what?" His irritation married his frustration and made him snarl. "Amy build a bomb? Davy decide he hates me again? Or are you just playing hard-to-get because you want to go out to dinner? Come on, Sophie, I've had a lousy day. Fuck me."

Sophie winced, and he frowned at her, wondering when she'd turned into a prude. The screen door slammed as he said, "What's wr—" and then a fist slammed into his eye and he was on his back in the dirt, his head throbbing.

"Brandon." Sophie said, and Phin looked up through the pain at a guy the size of a tank.

"You son of a bitch," the therapist said.

Twelve

Sophie moved in front of the guy, blocking Phin's view which was pretty hazy anyway. "All right, stop it, Brandon. He didn't mean it the way it sounded—"

"*Nobody* talks to you like that," Brandon said, and Phin sat up and tried to figure out how he'd ended up the bad guy.

"It's his idea of foreplay," Sophie said uncertainly, and Phin felt like hell.

"It's his idea of diminishing you so that you know you're not important to him," Brandon said. "He's abusive, and you're enabling him."

Wait a minute. Phin tried to stand up but the world swooped around him, so he sat back down in the dirt again.

"He's not abusive," Sophie said. "He's in a bad mood. He can be perfectly lovely when he wants to be."

"Ouch," Phin said.

"And what do you have to do to make him lovely?" Brandon said. "Sophie, I know he's been exciting, but if this is the way he treats you—"

"He treats me just fine," Sophie said, and Brandon looked down at Phin in the dust and said, "He treats you like a whore."

"Brandon!" Sophie said, and Phin leveraged his way up, grabbing the porch rail to keep what little sense of balance he had.

"I will never understand why women stay with abusive men," Brandon was saying. "Especially somebody like you. You're a sensible woman, Sophie. Surely—"

"Oh, not really," Sophie said, watching Phin warily. "Brandon, I think you'd better go."

"Sophie, you can't—"

"Yes, I can," she said to Brandon. Then she looked at Phin, frowning. "Don't move until I get back." She prodded Brandon over to his car, and he went, still explaining her abusive relationship to her. Phin squinted at the car. A late-model Toyota. Practical of him. Then Sophie stretched up to kiss the giant therapist good-bye, and Phin scowled, which hurt, and leaned against the porch post, which also hurt, until the enemy was gone.

"Let's get some ice on that eye," Sophie said, as she came back to him and took his arm.

"I don't like him," Phin said, still dizzy.

"I know, bear," she said. "He doesn't like you, either."

Fifteen minutes later, Phin was stretched out on the dock by the rushing river with his head in Sophie's lap, ice on his eye, and Lassie sniffing his ear.

"This is all my fault." She leaned down and moved the ice to kiss his bruised eye, and he felt some of his tension seep away. "I never should have told Brandon about you."

"Yes, you should have." Phin watched her face hover above him, concern wrinkling her forehead. *She's mine*, he wanted to tell Brandon, preferably on the phone. "You might have told me he was built like a truck."

Sophie put the ice back on his eye. "He played second-string football for Ohio State. He says he would have been first-string but he kept going to class."

"Don't tell him I played golf for Michigan. Although, if I'd had my four iron, this would have ended very differently."

Sophie's laugh bubbled out and he smiled at her because he loved her face when she laughed. "Why the hell did he hit me anyway? I thought you'd told him it was over."

Sophie's smile faded. "It was that crack you made about dinner and the . . . language you used."

Phin frowned and then winced as his face protested. "He doesn't want me to take you to dinner?" he said, as he moved the ice away from his eye. "Too damn bad, but that's not a reason to punch somebody. And you never minded my language before."

"He doesn't want you making me feel cheap," Sophie said. "I have a history of that."

He scowled up at her and said, "What?" and then he listened with increasing guilt as she told him about the louse she'd lost her virginity to.

When she'd finished, he said, "This is the town-boy thing."

She nodded.

"Fuck. I'd have hit me, too. Maybe I can still catch him, and we can go to Iowa together. Beating up a middle-aged businessman would make us both feel better."

"Thank you, but no," Sophie said. "Davy took care of Chad a long time ago."

"Good for Davy," Phin said. "I'm sorry, Sophie."

"You didn't mean anything when you said it," Sophie said, smiling at him.

An "enabler," Brandon had said. "Call me on it when I'm being a son of a bitch," he told her. "Don't take that crap from me just because I'm tired and I can be nice when I want to be."

"Call yourself on it," Sophie said, a little waspishly, and he said, "Fuck," and moved the ice pack up to cover his eye.

"I'm sorry about Chad," he told her. "I'm sorry about every guy who ever fucked you over. God knows, I probably did it to some girl, too." *"Probably," hell. Definitely.*

"No, you didn't," Sophie said. "You married Diane."

"I used Diane to get what I wanted, and then paid for it," Phin said. "I don't think I get any awards for being a sensitive male on that one."

"I don't want a sensitive male," Sophie said. "I want you."

"Thank you," Phin said. "Damn good thing you have lousy taste in men or I'd be out in the cold."

"Oh, cheer up." She kissed him on the forehead and he frowned and then winced again.

"I'm sorry about the 'fuck me,' too," he said. "The therapist is wrong. You're important to me. You know that."

Sophie glared down at him, exasperated.

"Well, you do, right?" He squinted up at her again.

"Sure. Yeah." Sophie took a deep breath. "Forget Brandon. Let's make you feel better."

"The only thing that would make me feel better at this point is headbanging sex," he told her, guilt making him cranky. "But since Brandon pretty much banged my head for me, I think sex is out." *Probably part of his plan, the son of a bitch.*

"Well, then, talk dirty to me," Sophie went on, now relentlessly cheerful. "You like that. What about *your* fantasies? We never talk about you."

Phin stared at the sky. The last thing he needed right now was Sophie being chirpy. Under ordinary circumstances, he'd have told her to can it, but that "abusive" bit had stung. "My fantasies," he said. "Most of them start with you naked."

Sophie nodded. "Okay, then what?"

"Handcuffs, whips, chains, butter, the usual."

"Stick or tub?" Sophie said.

"What?"

"The butter."

Phin closed his eyes and gave up being sensitive. "Sophie, I know you're trying to be cute, but shut up. I have a headache." He felt his eye and winced and then tried to sit up.

"No, I'm serious." She put her hand on his stomach to stop him, and he stopped moving to appreciate it. "Tell me a fantasy."

He looked down at her hand. "About six inches lower."

"A *fantasy.*"

He sighed, and her hand rose and fell with his stomach. "Okay.

Let's see." He closed his eyes and let his head fall back into her lap. She was going someplace with this, so he went for something easy. "I'm sitting in a bar, being my usual cool, sophisticated self . . ."

"That's it," Sophie said. "A fantasy."

". . . and this incredibly beautiful woman sits down beside me."

"This has to be something I can do," Sophie said.

"Stop fishing for compliments. And she says, 'I want you, I need you, I must have you, and by the way I'm not wearing underpants.' And then we go someplace, and she fucks my brains out." Actually, that sounded pretty damn good, now that he thought about it. The pain receded a little.

"You have no imagination," Sophie was saying. "That's like the oldest cliché there is."

"Don't say 'like,' " Phin said. "You sound like Rachel."

"That one's even been in the movies a couple of times," Sophie said. "Don't you have anything—"

"Hey." Phin opened his eyes and glared at her. "You asked, I told. I have others involving hardware and dairy products, but you made mock."

"You're not taking this seriously."

Phin closed his eyes again. "Christ, no. You should never take sex seriously. Terrible idea. Do you have any aspirin?"

Sophie sighed. "Okay. Meet me at the Tavern tonight at eight."

Phin opened his eyes. "You're kidding."

Amy came out on the porch and called to her, and Sophie gritted her teeth.

"Tell her to take a hike," Phin said.

"She's having a rough time." Sophie lifted his head to slide out from under him. "Wes hasn't called since that day he yelled at her for lying to him. And then there's this cable premiere thing. She's under a lot of stress."

"Who the fuck isn't?" Phin said.

"You, tonight." Sophie bent over and kissed him as she got up. "The Tavern at eight, bear."

Phin let his head drop back onto the dock, missing her warmth. "Cool."

"Now *you* sound like Rachel," she said, and headed for the house and her sister, the problem child.

"Leo, I have to talk to you," Rachel said that night after she'd picked him up at the airport and they'd dropped Davy off at the farm. "This is really, really, *really* important."

"I'm not taking you to L.A.," Leo said automatically.

"I have to get out of Temptation," she began, and he said, "I know, I know," and she said, "Because I think I might have killed Zane."

"Pull over," Leo said, and Rachel did. "Tell me."

"I went out back of the house to meet Rob," Rachel said. "And Zane was there, sort of stumbling, and he grabbed me, and wouldn't let go and I had Sophie's Mace so I Maced him, and then I pushed him and he fell in the river and had a heart attack and died and I think it's my fault." She stopped, breathless.

"What were you doing meeting Rob?" Leo said, sounding cranky.

"He called me," Rachel said. "He wanted to break up with me because he's sleeping with Clea now. You're missing the point, Leo. What about Zane?"

Leo shook his head. "You're okay, kid. It was self-defense. They won't arrest you."

Rachel shook her head and leaned toward him. "He told people I was chasing him. He told people I offered to sleep with him to get him to take me to L.A., and I *didn't*. I know that's hard to believe, but I wouldn't have crossed the street with him—"

Leo put his arm around her as she started to shake. "I know, I know."

"—but nobody's going to believe that," Rachel wept into his shoulder, "because I've been chasing everybody, trying to get out of here, and they'll think he said no and I killed him because I was mad—"

"They won't." Leo patted her shoulder. "That's ridiculous."

"—and then we ran over him—"

Leo stopped patting. "You what?"

"Rob and I ran over him at the Tavern. We didn't know he was there. I don't even know how he *got* there—"

"Shut up for a minute," Leo said, and Rachel was so surprised, she shut up. He'd tightened his arm around her when he'd told her to shut up, and that felt good, too, to have him holding her that tight and sure, and, for the first time since Zane had grabbed her, she felt safe. If she could spend the rest of her life with Leo's arm around her, she'd be okay.

"L.A. is not your answer," he said. "We'll just go to Wes and tell him everything and you'll get points for being so honest."

Going to Wes sounded like a lousy idea, except he'd said "we'll go," and that sounded wonderful.

"But we should get there first, before anybody else. Who else knows about this?"

"Just you," Rachel said, feeling almost cheerful. "Rob knows about the Tavern because he was driving and he knows Zane grabbed me, but he doesn't know I Maced him and pushed him."

"You only told me?" Leo sounded amazed.

"You're the only one I trust," Rachel said. "Besides, you'll know what to do. You know everything." It sounded dorky when she said it, but it was true.

"Oh, great."

Leo tightened his arm around her, so she leaned into him a little more, and that felt so good she put both her arms around him and hugged him to her.

"I know I'm a pain," she said into his chest. "I know I drive you crazy, but you're the only one I—"

"Rachel, don't—" He let go of her but she held on.

"I need you," she said. "I need you and I trust you and I love you." She hadn't meant to add the last part, but there it was and it was true, and she felt wonderful as soon as she said it. "I know you think I'm just a hick kid, but I really love you. I just didn't realize until this happened and you were the only one." She swallowed and then raised her head so she could look in his eyes. "I want to be with you. It's okay if you don't—"

"I'm not what you think I am," he said. "Nobody could be what you think I am."

She shook her head. "You can be. You are. You're the best."

He closed his eyes, and she pressed closer, afraid of losing him.

"I should let go of you," Leo said.

And then she kissed him.

Phin sat at the bar—the only guy in the Tavern in a linen jacket—wondering if Sophie was going to go through with her promise. He pressed his cold beer to his bruised eye and thought about Sophie and his fantasy, such a great thing for her do, slink into the Tavern with half the town watching and tell him she wanted him while he grinned down into those big brown eyes. . . .

He looked at his watch.

Fifteen minutes past eight. Sophie was never late. She'd chickened out. He tossed a ten on the bar to take care of his tab, and then turned to go, and that's when she slid onto the stool next to him. "Promptness is a virtue—" he began, but the rest of his sentence died in his throat as he got a good look at her.

She was wearing a bright red tube dress that started low on her breasts and stopped halfway to her knees, a narrow red ribbon tied behind her neck holding it up. Her hair was loose in dark ringlets on her shoulders, and her cheeks were flushed, and she'd put on a lot of lipstick so that her usual pink mouth was a red slash that matched the dress. The only jarring note was the bruise on her forehead, and she'd mostly covered that with makeup. He looked down at her breasts again, stretching the red fabric of the dress far past any safe point, and his palms itched to jerk that dress down and set her free. "Very hot dress."

"Literally." Sophie tugged at the top, making everything shift beautifully. "It's Clea's. This stuff doesn't breathe and it *itches*."

"I don't think that was your line," Phin said. "Are you sure that's going to stay up?"

"No," Sophie said. "That's why I'm tense and forgetting my lines. Wait a minute." She frowned in concentration and he grinned at her, and she said, "Knock it off. You're not supposed to patronize me, you jerk." She took a deep breath, which he appreciated, and then she leaned closer to him, and he almost fell into her cleavage.

"I saw you across the room," she said throatily. "I want you, I need you, I must have you, and I'm not wearing—"

"Phin, I need to talk to you," somebody said behind him, and Phin said, "No, you don't," but Sophie had looked over his shoulder and was already sliding off the stool, taking her breasts with her.

"Are you all right, Georgia?" she said in her normal voice, and Phin shook his head to get his mind back to where it belonged.

"I just need to talk to Phin," Georgia said, as she looked at Sophie's dress, and then she hopped up on Sophie's stool and smiled at Phin.

"Oh." Sophie looked a little taken aback. "Uh, I'll just be over . . . here." She gestured behind her, and Phin looked past her to where several assorted townsmen were watching her with great appreciation.

"Do not talk to anybody," he told her.

She nodded, and went down to the end of the bar, and Phin craned his neck to see her go.

"Phin?" Georgia said, leaning forward to smile weakly at him and then she blinked. "What happened to your eye?"

Sophie's end of the bar began to get crowded as a general migration headed in her direction. "Make it fast, Georgia," Phin said. "I'm in the middle of something here."

"Oh," she said. "Okay. It's about Frank. I'm really worried—"

"Georgia, I don't do marriage counseling." He tried to see Sophie at the end of the bar, but there were too many people. Male people.

"I think he might have killed Zane," Georgia said, her voice shaking. "He wasn't home that night, he didn't come home at all, and he was so mad when he found out—" She dropped her eyes. "You know."

"I know," Phin said. "Try not to fuck other men, and he won't get so mad."

"Well, he was doing it with that bitch Clea," Georgia said, stung. "What was I supposed to do?"

"Not have sex with Zane," Phin said, trying to see around her. "Georgia, go home. Get some rest, talk to Frank, apologize, he'll probably tell you he spent the night at Larry's, and things will be fine in the morning."

"You think so?" Georgia hiccuped. "Oh, Phin. I'm so worried." Her voice dropped an octave. "And I hate that bitch Clea."

"Right." She started to lean into him, and he took her arm and helped her off Sophie's stool. "Good night, Georgia. Careful going home. Do not drive."

Georgia nodded and wobbled off, and Phin caught Sophie's eye. She sidled out from the group at her end of the bar and came slinking unsteadily back, teetering, he saw for the first time, on ridiculously high, red spike heels.

Her legs were flawless. And they went all the way up to where she wasn't wearing underwear, if she was telling the truth. Given how short that dress was, Phin wouldn't have been surprised if she'd hedged her bets on that one.

"Hello, gorgeous," she said as she slid onto the stool. "I saw you across the room—" She met his eyes and grinned, which shouldn't have been sexy at all but was, and he grinned back and thought, *Hell of a woman, my Sophie.*

"—and I want you—" She licked her lips and leaned closer. "I need you, I—"

"Phin, I have to talk to you," Frank said from behind him, and Phin said without turning around, "Get out of here, or I will hurt you."

"It's about Georgia," Frank said, and Sophie said in her normal voice, "I'll just be at the end of the bar."

"No you won't," Phin said.

"I'll just be at the jukebox." Sophie slid off her stool, and Phin looked down at her round butt in that tight dress and saw no panty line. In that dress, he'd have seen a birthmark, so she wasn't wearing underwear. And she was walking away from him.

"This better be good, Frank," he said.

Frank took her place on the stool, and Phin sighed, resigned to at least another two minutes of Lutz.

"I saw you talking to Georgia," Frank said. "And—" He frowned at Phin. "What happened to your eye?"

"Frank, what do you want?"

"What did Georgia say?"

"She's afraid you killed Zane," Phin said. "Why don't you go discuss that with her?"

"I think she did it, Phin." Frank looked pasty in the dim bar light. "I think she went after him after that Jell-O crack. She went for me with a knife when we were first married and I told her that it was okay to move in bed, and let me tell you, she wasn't kidding."

Phin watched Sophie at the jukebox. "I don't want to know this, Frank. Tell Wes. Human interaction fascinates him."

"And it was that time of the month, too." Frank shook his head. "Georgia and PMS are a bad combination. Plus she was drunk. She's a mean drunk."

"Frank."

"I'm just saying, you be careful believing what she tells you. She's crazy. And Zane, he was crazy, too. You wouldn't believe the lies he was telling. Probably told some about me." Frank laughed.

"That would be the vasectomy."

Frank closed his eyes. "Oh, crap, don't tell Georgia."

"I don't plan to," Phin said. *You stupid son of a bitch.*

"Jesus, if she knew," Frank said, leaning against the bar, going weak at the thought, "she'd kill me. She really is crazy, Phin."

"Well, the good news is, she'd kill you, not Zane," Phin pointed out.

Frank frowned, not seeing why that was good news.

"Zane's the one who died, Frank. If you were dead, she'd be a good candidate, but since you're still with us—"

Frank perked up a little, "Right."

"—she evidently doesn't know about the vasectomy."

Frank began to get a little color in his face. "Right, right."

In the background, the jukebox started playing "Some of Your Lovin'," and Phin lost what little interest he had in Frank. "Well, I have things to do. Go talk to your wife. Save your marriage. Whatever." He took Frank's arm and helped him off the barstool.

Frank nodded and wandered off, slightly happier than he had been when they'd started, and Sophie came back and boosted herself up on the stool, making everything bounce, including his libido. Then she leaned forward, stopping his heart with the view, put her hot little hand on his thigh (*Higher*, he thought), and said, "I saw you across the room—"

Then she stopped, caught by something from behind him.

He turned and saw Rachel searching the crowd with Leo close behind her. *No*, he thought, and then Sophie grabbed him by the knot in his tie, and he had to turn back to her to keep from choking.

"I'm not wearing any underwear," she said, nose-to-nose with him. "Want to fuck me?"

The room swung around as all the blood left his brain. "God, yes," he said, and pulled her off the stool to drag her to the door.

"I'm sorry, that wasn't your fantasy," she said from behind him.

"Not a problem," he said, dodging people like a demented quarterback with Sophie in tow. "Yours was better."

Behind him, Rachel called, "Phin!" but he didn't stop until he had Sophie at the car and he'd opened the door to the backseat.

"Backseat?" Sophie said, and he said, "I'll make this up to you later. Get in there and strip."

She slid across the seat and he slid in after her, reaching for her before the door slammed closed. He shoved his hands up her thighs, pushing her rubber band of a dress up as he went, and when his hands moved over her naked butt, he said, "I'm going to last about five seconds here." Sophie wriggled to slide under him, and he added, "Maybe not even that."

"Your fantasy, bear," Sophie said, twining her hands around his neck. "Do with me what you will."

He tugged at the top of her dress, and she let go of him to reach behind her neck and untie the straps so he could pull it down. Her breasts popped out as if they were as glad to be free as he was to see them, and when he'd filled his hands with them, and she'd arched her hips into his, he said, "I swear, I'll make this up to you later," and reached for his zipper for the best fast fuck of his life.

And then Sophie said, "Ack!" and slid out from under him, tugging her dress up and down at once.

"What?" he said, trying to pull her back and she said, "Window," and gestured with her elbow.

When he turned, Rachel was peering at them.

He rolled it down and said between his teeth, "Get out of here, Rachel, this is not the time," and she said, "Please, Phin."

"No," he said, and started to roll up the window, and she said, "I think I killed Zane."

He froze, a thousand thoughts colliding in his head, half of them to do with plunging hot into Sophie and the other half to do with Rachel in big trouble and the inevitability of the choice in front of him.

"We tried to find Wes, but he's out, and we don't have his pager number and we knew you—"

"*Oh . . .*" Phin searched for words vile enough to vent with and then banged his head into the seat in front of him and went for the classic, "*Fuck!*"

Rachel took a step back, and Phin took a deep breath. Then, in his normal voice, he said to her, "I'll call Wes. You follow us to the station." He rolled the window up and took another deep breath and then turned to Sophie, who was trying unsuccessfully to put everything back where it had been. "You know, before you came here, I never screamed like that."

Sophie put her chin in the air and tried to look superior, which was difficult considering her hands were full of her breasts. "You were repressed. Which is why God sent me to save you."

"It wasn't God," he said, watching her trying to stretch fabric where it would never go again. "It was the devil." He thought about just ripping the damn dress off her, but then he'd never get to the station, and Rachel needed him there.

"I have to go to the police station," he said.

"I picked that up. Uh, could I borrow your jacket? I don't think this is ever going to work again."

He took off his jacket and passed it over and watched as she gave up the good fight and the breasts he wanted appeared within reach again, only to be covered by his linen jacket. He thought about the smooth silk lining of the jacket sliding over all that smooth, warm flesh and felt light-headed again. "We have a minute," he said, and reached for her, and she blocked his hand.

"Rachel," she said, and he gave up and moved to the front seat to call Wes on the car phone and tell him about their latest disaster. "I'm sorry this didn't work out," Sophie called to him from the backseat.

"The night is still young," he said, trying to see her in the rearview mirror, and then Wes answered, and he concentrated on the problem at hand instead of the pleasure in the backseat.

The only part of Rachel's confession that Phin found even vaguely interesting was that Rob had called her to meet him exactly where Zane had turned up. From the look on Wes's face, that was the only part that interested him, too. When he'd sent Rachel off with Leo and a stern warning to tell the police everything from now on, Wes turned back to Phin and said, "I want to talk to that dumb fuck Rob."

"Me, too," Phin said. "But not now. I have unfinished business with Sophie."

"How's Amy?"

"Miserable. Call her. Hell, you knew she was bent."

"She lied to me," Wes said.

"She lies to everybody," Phin said. "It's part of being a Dempsey. You want the excitement and the tube top, you have to take the lies, too."

"I don't want them that bad," Wes said miserably, and Phin said, "Sure you do," and went out to find Sophie.

When he got to the farm, everything was dark and the door was locked. Given the turn the crime rate had taken in Temptation, that was smart, but it wasn't helping him get to Sophie. He stood out in the front yard and considered trying to climb the front porch to her window and rejected it for the moment. No point in killing himself for sex unless he had to.

Instead, he picked up a stone from the yard and threw it at her window. Unfortunately, it was open, but on his next one he got lucky and hit Sophie, who had come to the window.

"Ouch," she said as she stuck her head out. Her shoulders were pale and naked in the moonlight, and he realized she was wrapped in a sheet.

"Are you naked?" he said.

"You threw a *rock* at me," Sophie said.

"Think of it as foreplay," Phin said. "Come down and play."

"It's midnight," Sophie said, and pulled her head in.

Well, he'd tried. He sat down on the hood of the Volvo and decided to give her five minutes in case she changed her mind, but she surprised him by showing up almost immediately, wearing his jacket and nothing else, Lassie padding sleepily beside her.

"You're a biddable woman," he said, as she boosted herself up on the hood beside him, and the dog stretched out in the dirt and fell asleep.

"There's generally a payoff if I do what you tell me," Sophie said. "Also, it seemed weird tonight not arguing with you flat on my back, so this is sort of closure."

"Closure?" *She's leaving*, he thought, *she's going back to the therapist*, and panic kicked up his pulse even though he knew it was stupid.

"We never did finish your fantasy," she told him. "We were building to a climax there, and then you wandered off. How's Rachel?"

"Not guilty of anything but self-defense," Phin said. "How are you?"

Sophie smiled up at him. "I have a fantasy."

"If it takes a lot of energy, it may stay a fantasy," Phin said, and thought, *Anything you want.*

Sophie let his jacket fall open so that she sat pretty much naked on the hood of the car. " 'Right here,' " she said in a Brooklyn accent, patting the hood. " 'On the Oriental.' "

"It's a Volvo," Phin said, trying to be cool. "It's Swedish." Then he looked at how round and hot she was and gave in. "A naked woman on an expensive car. I think this is *my* fantasy. Without the movie quote, of course."

Sophie leaned closer and said, "Tell me where the quote's from, and I'll go down."

"Let me take a rain check," Phin said. "Plain vanilla is all I have the energy for."

"Also you have no idea where it came from," Sophie said.

"Don't bust my chops tonight," Phin said. "Are you really going to let me have you on the hood of this car in the front yard?"

"There's no moon," Sophie said. "Not much to see."

"Unless your brother looks out the window," Phin said. "Then I'm a dead man. How about the backseat?"

Sophie moved her knees apart and leaned back on her hands.

Phin sighed. "Or right here."

She leaned over and kissed him, and he felt a lot better. "If you could make this day go away for a while," he whispered. "I'd be really grateful."

"I thought that might be the case," she said, and climbed into his lap to straddle him, and he caught her to him, sliding his hands under his jacket and over all her smooth softness, and buried his face in the hollow of her neck.

"It's just you and me, bear," she whispered in his ear. "Nobody else."

And then she made everything go away.

Three hours later, Phin was sleeping like the dead beside her, and Sophie was trying to find a comfortable place on her mattress. There was one errant spring in particular that was torturing her. She tried to shift over, but Phin was taking up most of the double bed, and the rogue spring dug into her even as she tried to shift him.

Phin murmured something in his sleep, and she tried to climb over him. If he was that fast asleep, he could sleep on the damn spring. But when she was on top, his arms went around her, and even though she said, "No, go back to sleep," he rolled her to one side—the good side of the mattress—and kissed her, still half asleep, and she thought, *What the hell*, and kissed him back.

Half an hour later, with the mattress rattling like a tambourine under them, Sophie felt her blood boil and dug her fingernails into him and said, "Oh, God, *yes*, *now*," and he rolled so that he was on top, and the spring gouged into her again and cooled her blood on the instant. "Ouch!"

She tried to squirm so her spine was off it, but Phin was oblivious on top of her, rocking fast into her, making the bed bounce hard. She tried to bounce her hips over when he pulled back, but he was too fast, so they only hit the mattress harder in the same place. She said, *"Ouch"*—really loud this time—and tried to shove him away before her spine went, and Phin jerked up, finally hearing her, at the same time she heard a sharp *crack* with a whine behind it.

He rolled them both off the bed onto the floor, and she landed on top of him.

"Ouch," she said again, trying to sit up, and he pulled her head back down and rolled on top of her.

"Stay down," he said, breathless but not mindless anymore.

"What are you doing?" Sophie said. "Get *off* me—" and then Davy slammed the door open and said, "Sophie?"

"She's okay," Phin said from the floor. "I'd stay away from the window if I were you."

Davy stepped back into the hallway. "Sophie?"

"I'm okay," Sophie said from under Phin, as he stretched his hand to find his boxers. "What did I miss?"

"Sounded like a gunshot to me," Davy said from the hall. "I thought maybe the mayor had gotten tired of you." He was trying to keep his voice light, and failing.

Phin retrieved his boxers and stood up away from the window. Sophie pulled the sheet from the bed and wrapped herself in it.

"What are you doing?" she said as she propped herself up on one elbow, keeping an eye on the window. "If somebody shot at us—"

"At you—so you stay down," Phin told her as he put on his khakis. "Remember the river? Somebody may be trying to kill you. The only person who wants me dead is Davy."

"I've decided to let you live," Davy said, back in the doorway. "Where'd it come from?"

"I'm still not sure it was a shot," Phin said. "My mind was on other things." He looked around the room. "But it sure as hell sounded like one and it was in this room." He looked back at Sophie. "You stay there."

"Through the window?" Davy said, coming in and looking at the wall opposite the window. "I'm not seeing a bullet hole."

"Maybe it hit the mattress." Sophie crawled away from the window in her sheet to get her clothes, trying to unscramble her mind from interrupted sex and the new knowledge somebody had just tried to kill her. "Or maybe a car backfired," she said, going for normality.

"No," Davy and Phin said at the same time.

She had crawled almost to the door when she saw the hole, a little one, about two feet up from the floor. "There," she said, still on her knees, pointing to it, and Phin and Davy both bent to look.

Phin said, "Hold on," and went to the bedside table to rummage through the drawer. "Here," he said, going back to Davy, and handed him a pencil.

Davy put the pencil in the hole as far as it would go, and it stuck straight out.

"I don't get this," Sophie said from where she was sitting by the door, but they both ignored her to follow the line of the pencil.

"You're kidding me," Davy said, and they both moved to the bed.

Phin pulled up the quilt and said, "Nope."

Sophie squinted over at the bed. There was a hole in the side of the box spring.

"Go out in the hall," Phin told her, and they both went to the other side of the bed, while Sophie scooted out into the hall.

"No hole on this side," Davy said, bending over.

They grabbed the mattress at the same time and pulled it off the bed.

"No wonder my back's been killing me," Phin said, and Sophie craned her neck around the doorway to see a box spring so ancient, the top fabric had rotted to ribbons.

Davy looked at the wall and then back to the box springs and said, "Someplace about here." He began to peel the rotted ribbons of fabric from a section of the spring in line with the hole, and after a moment he stopped. "Son of a gun."

"Literally," Phin said.

Sophie stood and inched her way over to the bed, trying not to trip over her sheet. A small gun lay caught in the box springs, pointing toward the wall. It was so surreal, she felt detached from the moment, as if she were watching a movie. "Somebody booby-trapped my bed?"

"No," Phin said.

"Somebody stuck a gun under your mattress," Davy said. "And then you and Harvard fucked it into the box spring and set it off."

"Beautifully put," Phin said, looking at him with distaste.

"Somebody's trying to frame you, Soph," Davy said.

Sophie looked down at the gun again. "Well, somebody's not too bright. It's been decades since anybody looked under this mattress."

"So somebody's still waiting for this to be found." Phin looked at Davy.

"And getting anxious," Davy said, nodding at him. "So now what?"

"What do you mean, 'now what?' " Sophie said, fear making her cranky. "We call Wes."

"Quietly," Phin said. "Because we don't want anybody to know about this."

"You really think somebody's going to believe I killed Zane?" Sophie said.

"No, he really thinks somebody's going to go nuts waiting for the damn gun to be found," Davy said. "And the crazier somebody gets, the more likely it is he'll overplay his hand."

Sophie looked back at the gun. "I can't believe I've been sleeping on that."

Phin looked back at the mattress. "I can't believe I've been having sex on that. From now on, we do this in my bed."

"I don't want to know about this," Davy said. "She's my sister." He left the room without a backward glance, and Sophie looked back down at the gun.

"Somebody really hates me." The thought made her cold, and she drew in a long shuddering breath.

"Not necessarily." Phin picked up his shirt. "Somebody may just want you out of the way."

Yeah, your mother, Sophie thought, but even she couldn't imagine Liz sneaking into the house to plant a gun. "How'd it get in here?"

"Anybody can get in here." Phin buttoned his shirt and tucked it in. "The damn place is always full of people, and they all came upstairs to use the bathroom. Go sleep with Amy." He looked back at the mattress. "I'm assuming you're out of the mood."

"Maybe forever," Sophie said, picking up her shorts.

"Just until tomorrow," Phin said, and went to tell Wes.

"What happened to you?" Phin's mother said to him when he came down to breakfast after three hours of sleep.

"What? Oh, the eye?" He looked at Dillie. "I ran into a door."

"Really?" Dillie said, pushing back her softball cap.

"Sophie's ex-door," he told Liz, under his breath. "No cap at the table, Dill."

"You ran into a therapist?" Liz said, and Dillie put her cap by her plate.

"Yes, it surprised me, too," Phin said. "Next topic."

"What's a therapist?" Dillie said.

"Like a guidance counselor," Phin said.

"Sophie has a guidance counselor?" Dillie said.

"No," Phin began and then stopped as his mother's face darkened.

"Do you know Sophie, Dill?" she asked.

"Oh, ye—" Dillie began, and then stopped, just as her father had. "A little."

"You took your daughter to meet your . . . friend?" Liz said, her voice taut as piano wire.

"No," Phin said. "My daughter went to meet my friend on her own after talking with Jamie Barclay. I told you that kid was no good."

"Jamie Barclay's mother said that Sophie was Daddy's girlfriend so I went to see," Dillie said. "Sophie said she wasn't. It's perfectly all right."

"You went to see." Liz's eyes softened a little as she turned to her granddaughter, but she still wasn't happy. "All by yourself?"

"While Grandma Junie was napping." Dillie looked from her father to her grandmother. "It's all right. I'm perfectly safe. I've done it dozens of times."

"What?"

"You have not done it dozens of times," Phin said. "You've been there twice." After Dillie was silent for a moment, he added. "That I know about."

"This stops now," Liz said. "Dillie, you do not go back there. Ever."

"But—"

"Never," Liz said. "Do you understand?"

"No," Dillie said, and both Phin and Liz zeroed in on her.

"Don't tell your grandmother no," Phin said.

"Well, I *don't* understand." Dillie looked scared but determined. "Sophie's my friend. She likes me. She's *expecting* me. I go on Sundays and Wednesdays when I'm at Grandma Junie's and Sophie likes it. I play with the dog. We talk. And sing. She's *expecting* me."

"Life is full of disappointments," Liz said. "You're not going back."

Dillie turned tragic eyes on Phin, and he said, "Do you want to say good-bye?"

Dillie nodded, tears starting in her eyes.

"I'll take you tomorrow when I pick you up at Junie's," he said, and Liz said, "No, you will not."

"Excuse me," he said to his mother. "I'm talking to my daughter. And she's going to say good-bye to her friend because it's the polite thing to do. Tuckers are always polite."

Liz pressed her lips together.

"Thank you, Daddy," Dillie said, blinking back the tears. Tuckers didn't cry.

"You're welcome." Phin met Liz's eyes across the table. "Anything else you want to say about this?"

The phone rang again, and Liz said, "I will get it." When she was gone, Dillie leaned forward and said, "Daddy?" in a half-whisper.

"What?"

"Remember how you said we could have sleepovers every Monday, and then I didn't get them?"

Phin winced. "Yeah. Sorry about that."

"That's okay," Dillie said. "Can I have something else? Just for one morning? Not a sleepover? Just once?"

"Probably," Phin said. "What?"

Dillie hesitated a long time, but when she heard Liz hang up the phone in the hall, she leaned forward and said fast, so the words ran together, "I want Sophie to come to my softball game today. It's my last one, and I don't get any sleepovers, and I want you and Sophie to come to my game. Please."

Liz came back in and sat down. "That was Virginia Garvey."

"There's a surprise." Phin finished buttering Dillie's muffin and passed it over, and Dillie took it, keeping her eyes on his face.

"Stephen's concerned you're up to something with those movie people," Liz went on.

"No he isn't," Phin said. "He *hopes* I'm up to something with those movie people."

"Well, you're going to stay away from them from now on," Liz said.

"Mother." Phin waited until Liz met his eyes. "You tell me what to do one more time, and Dillie and I are moving down to the bookstore."

"Phineas—"

"Back off or lose us." Phin watched her bite her lip, and then she got up from the table and went upstairs.

Dillie sat next to him, frozen, her muffin clutched in her hand.

"You okay?" he said to her.

She nodded. "Are we going to move?"

"Probably not. Grandma knows when to quit."

Dillie took a deep breath. "Can Sophie come to my game today?"

"Yes," Phin said. "At least we can call her and ask."

Dillie nodded and bit into her muffin, and Phin sat back.

"It will be exciting to have Sophie at my game," Dillie said around her muffin.

"You have no idea," Phin said.

Thirteen

he softball section of Temptation's tree-filled park had four neatly marked white diamonds, each with its own stand of seats, all filled with parents, grandparents, sisters, brothers, and friends of the family. It was like four Christmases without the turkeys, unless you counted some of the coaches and the more obnoxious of the parents.

"Bat country," Sophie said. "In every sense of the word."

"Yep," Phin said. "Temptation athletics at its finest."

Dillie nudged Sophie's arm. "Wish me luck, please."

She looked so determined in her red-and-white uniform, her red ball cap tilted over her little pointed face, that Sophie resisted to the urge to say, *You are cute as hell, kid*, and said, "You bet. Break a leg," instead.

"What?" Dillie said.

"It's an expression," Phin said. "One never used in athletics. Go do good."

"Okay." Dillie stretched up and Phin bent down to kiss her. Then she stretched up to Sophie, and Sophie bent down, too. Dillie's cheek was satin-smooth where Sophie kissed her, and she wrapped her arms around Sophie's neck and pulled her close for a moment.

"Thank you for coming to my game," she whispered, and Sophie whispered back, "Thank you for inviting me."

When Dillie ran off to join her team, Sophie turned back to the bleachers and faced a sea of fascinated faces, most of which were curious, some of which were disapproving, and at least one of which—Virginia Garvey's—was actively hostile. "Why is Virginia here?"

"Niece on the other team." Phin put his hand on the small of Sophie's back to steer her toward the bleachers, and Virginia flushed. Probably from the effort of trying to reach Liz by mental telepathy.

"So this is like dinner, only more so," Sophie said to Phin.

"This is dinner squared, cubed, and cloned."

"It's prom," Sophie said. "I finally made it."

Phin nodded. "They'll be talking about this ten years from now."

"They should get lives."

"They did," Phin said. "Ours. Go up to the top. We can see better up there."

Since the top was only a dozen rows up from the bottom, it was a short trip. It was also hot as hell, and by the middle of the first inning, Sophie was drenched in sweat.

Phin sat beside her, intent on the game, oblivious to the heat.

"So Tuckers don't have sweat glands?" she said, as she watched Dillie come to bat.

Dillie fanned the ball, and Phin winced and said under his breath, "Watch the ball, Dill," and a second later, the coach stood up and yelled, "Watch the ball, Dillie!"

"Uh, this doesn't really matter to you, does it?" Sophie said.

Dillie hit a single, and Phin said to himself, "Okay, that's not bad, not bad." Then, evidently realizing she'd been talking to him, he turned to her. "What?"

"Oh, jeez, you're one of those Sports Parents," Sophie said. "It's not just a game, it's a reflection of you and all of those in your bloodline who ever picked up a bat. It's—"

"We like to win," Phin said. "It's the American Way."

"Right," Sophie said. " 'We're ten and one.' "

"What?"

"It's from a movie," Sophie said. " 'We're Americans, we're ten and one.' The 'one' being Vietnam. Never mind."

He frowned at her. "Stop quoting. What do you have to be nervous about here?"

Sophie looked around at the various curious and hostile faces, with Virginia glaring in their midst like a basilisk. "Let's just say I'm not feeling the love." She started to twist her fingers where her rings had been, and Phin put his hand over hers.

"You're okay." He folded one of her hands into his and moved it to his knee, and she sat there in the sun, holding hands with the mayor, while Temptation parenthood looked at them from the corners of their eyes and whispered.

It was probably a nice change from talking about the murder and the video premiere.

The next batter grounded out, and Dillie went to play third base.

The pitcher wound up and threw the ball with her eyes closed and it sailed over the head of the batter and into the backboard.

"Oh, Christ," Phin said under his breath. When Sophie raised an eyebrow, he leaned closer and said, "This kid can't pitch, but she has low self-esteem so her mother insists."

"You're kidding," Sophie said. "Why are we whispering?"

Phin pointed to a tense woman in navy shorts sitting two rows in front of them. "That's Mom. President of the PTA. Nobody to mess with."

The pitcher wound up again and threw the ball almost straight up in the air. "Concentrate, Brittany!" the woman two rows down yelled, and when Brittany got the ball back, she screwed up her face in intense concentration and flung it as hard as she could. It went west and hit Dillie smack on the temple.

"Ouch," Phin said under his breath.

Dillie picked herself up and rubbed her head, and her coach went out to see her. Dillie nodded, and then the coach motioned somebody in from off the bench, and Dillie came up into the stands.

"I'm really okay," she said to Phin, blinking tears from her eyes. "Coach just thought I should sit down for a minute."

"Let me see, honey." Phin looked in her eyes and held up two fingers. "How many fingers?"

"Two," Dillie said, focusing on his hand. "I can go back in."

She sniffed once, and Sophie said, "Oh, take a break. Come here." She opened her arms and Dillie crawled into her lap and put her head on Sophie's shoulder. "We could use some ice here, Dad," Sophie said to Phin, as she took Dillie's cap off. "If you can't get that, get a cold can of pop."

"Actually she should probably go back—" Phin began, but Sophie met his eyes and he stopped.

"Ice," she said, "or there will be a scene."

"Okay," Phin said, and went.

"It kind of hurts," Dillie said.

"I can imagine." Sophie kissed Dill's forehead where the bruise was starting to come up. "Now you match your dad. He has one, too."

"So do you." Dillie looked up at her, as if she were gauging the moment, and then she said, "The whole family matches."

Sophie caught her breath.

"Don't we?" Dillie said, pressing closer, and Sophie thought, with more certainty than she'd ever dreamed possible, *This is what I want.*

"Yes," she said, and Dillie said, "Excellent," and cuddled closer.

Phin came back with some ice in a plastic bag. "Let's see, Dill." Dillie straightened a little and then winced as Phin put the cold bag against her bump. "Just hold it there a minute and then you go back."

"I don't think so," Sophie said, holding Dillie close and watching the field. Brittany had just whiffled one past the new third baseman, who was looking very uneasy.

"Back off," Phin said to Sophie. "This is my kid. She's a fighter. Right, Dill?"

Dillie straightened and nodded. "I'm a Tucker, and Tuckers are brave. We don't quit."

"Yeah?" Sophie said. "Well, I'm a Dempsey and Dempseys are smart. We don't go back on the field until the coach pulls the pitcher who's trying to bag her limit on third basemen."

"I beg your pardon," Brittany's mother said from two rows down.

"Sorry, Catherine," Phin said at the same time Sophie said, "Teach your kid to pitch before you force her out on the field." When Phin turned to give her the universal *Shut the fuck up* look, Sophie added, "Well, I don't think maiming her friends is helping Brittany's self-esteem. Look at her."

Down on the field, Brittany was sniffing back tears. That didn't stop her from pitching, of course, and with one mighty heave, she took out the new third baseman.

"I want to be a Dempsey," Dillie said.

"*What?*" Phin said, and Sophie said, "No, no, honey, you're a Tucker. You're just like your daddy. You need to defeat somebody on a regular basis or you'll start to twitch. Just wait until the coach disarms Brittany, and then you can go back."

Brittany's mother stood up, sent them a meaningful look, and stalked down the bleachers.

"Listen," Phin began, but out on the field, the coach was on her knees talking to Brittany, who was sobbing and nodding in what looked like relief.

"Yeah, sports are great for kids," Sophie said, and when the new pitcher came in, she said, "I don't know. This one looks wild, too."

Phin shook his head. "Tara Crumb. Her mother pitched the junior high to the semifinals and her father played high school baseball with me."

"Yes, but do they work with her?"

"Nightly," Phin said. "This one can pitch. Will you let go of my kid?"

Sophie opened her arms, and Dillie said, "Jeez, are we sure?"

"Oh, for crying out loud," Phin said, and Sophie said, "Yes. We have examined the family tree in detail, and they pass. You may go." She handed Dillie back her cap and added, "Put your cap on, though, it's hot out there."

Dillie nodded and started down the bleachers again.

"Clearly you do not understand athletics," Phin said.

"Clearly, I do," Sophie said. "Davy and Amy both played. And believe me, any pitcher who hit either of them lived to regret it. Dempseys get even."

"It's a game, not a war," Phin said, his eyes on his daughter as she went back on the field.

"Then why is your daughter wounded?" Sophie said, and then stopped.

Down at the foot of the bleachers, Brittany's mother was talking to Liz Tucker. While Sophie watched, Liz lifted her eyes to the top of the bleachers and stared, unblinking, at her son and the nightmare he'd brought to the game.

"Your mom's here," Sophie told Phin, who was still watching Dillie. "I know."

"Boy, are you in trouble now."

He leaned back and let his arm fall along the rail behind her. "I've been in trouble since I met you. This is just more of the same." He squinted at the field as Tara pitched a strike. "You're a pain in the ass, but you're worth it."

"Oh. That's good to know." Sophie tried not to look at Liz.

When Tara pitched her second strike and Dillie pounded her fist into her glove on third, Phin said, quietly so his voice didn't travel, "Thanks for taking care of my kid."

"My pleasure," Sophie said.

"But try to avoid my mother."

"Absolutely," Sophie said, keeping her eyes off Liz.

"And fuck my brains out later," Phin said, still staring at the field.

Sophie turned to see if anyone had heard. Evidently not; they weren't coming for her with pitchforks. "Are you trying to get me killed by a mob of softball moms?"

"They didn't hear," Phin said. "And it's your fault. You're sitting there driving me crazy."

Sophie looked down at her damp blouse and reddening arms. "I'm soaked in sweat and cranky."

"Doesn't matter." Phin did look at her then, and the smile he sent her pretty much telegraphed to everybody everything he'd said before. "All you have to do is breathe, and I fall."

Sophie felt herself flush. "Oh." She swallowed. "You're definitely getting lucky later." She turned away from him before she fell into his lap right there.

Out on the field, Tara struck out the batter, and Dillie jumped up and down with joy.

And down at the bottom of the bleachers, Liz stared up at Sophie, not joyful at all.

Phin pulled up in front of the farmhouse after the game and said, "I have to work until five and then Wes is coming by at seven. I'll be late coming out tonight."

"Or I could come buy a book between five and seven," Sophie said, and he met her eyes and she thought, *Oh, Lord, take me now.*

"I'd appreciate it," Phin said. "But you deserve more time than that so I'll see you at five, but I'll still come out when I get rid of Wes." Phin leaned to kiss her, stopping when she moved back and jerked her head a fraction of an inch toward the backseat and Dillie.

"I could look out the back window so you could kiss Sophie," Dillie said.

Sophie smiled at Dillie. "Oh, honey, he wasn't going to—"

"Look out the back window, Dill," Phin said, and when Dillie turned around, he kissed Sophie hard. "I'll see you at five," he said in her ear, and kissed her again, and when they drove away, she thought, *But that's six hours.*

She jumped the gun and got there at four-thirty, wearing her pink dress, and Phin said, "What kept you?"

"I'll be upstairs," Sophie said. " 'Take me to bed or lose me forever.' " She headed for the stairs and heard him come out from around the counter, and then she heard the CLOSED sign smack against the front window. "I can wait until five," she called back, and he hit the step behind her and said, "I can't."

But upstairs, he got a bottle of wine from the refrigerator—"It's safe to drink," he told her. "I bought it out of town"—and when she had her glass, he flipped on the stereo, and Dusty started to sing "I Only Want to Be with You."

Sophie sat up on the bed, delighted. "Why, *Mr.* Robinson, are you trying to seduce me?"

"Because that's so difficult? No. I've just developed a taste for Dusty. And you." She laughed up at him, and he looked at her for a long minute, and said, "My dad would have loved you."

"Oh," Sophie said.

"Scoot over," he said, and she did. He sat down and kicked off his shoes. "So how was your day?" he said, and leaned back on the pillows beside her.

Sophie cuddled up to him and sipped her wine. Good stuff. "My favorite part was when the coach threw Brittany's mother out of the game."

"That was good." Phin nodded. "You probably missed the part where Brittany's mother complained to the head of the Temptation Athletic Association to have the coach removed."

"Oh," Sophie said. "Is the president reasonable?"

"That would be Stephen Garvey."

"Oh, jeez, is there anything we can do?"

"The coach is staying," Phin said. "Drink your wine."

"Fixed it, did you?" Sophie said, and drank her wine.

"Yep."

"Do you have any idea how sexy power used for good is?" Sophie said, looking over her wineglass into his eyes.

"Really?" He settled deeper into the pillows. "Did I ever tell you how I battled Stephen to get Temptation new streetlights?"

Sophie put her wineglass down. "Take me."

He grinned at her, and then he put his wineglass down and leaned over and kissed her, slowly, and when they were naked under the quilt together, he still moved slowly, even though she'd said, "We'd better hurry if Wes is stopping by."

"The hell with Wes," he'd said. "Stay a while." Then he touched her everywhere she loved to be touched and when her breathing slowed to match his, she touched him, too, and the afternoon dissolved into soft laughter and heat and bone-deep pleasure. And when he finally took her, he moved so deliberately that he stretched minutes into eternity, and she stayed with him, looking into his eyes and sliding against his body and living in his kiss until she was so flooded with heat, she glowed. Then, after eons, he whispered, "Now," in her ear and rolled to bear down on her, and the heat fused and broke and she clung to him as every nerve she had went incandescent.

And when she stopped trembling, he was still holding on to her, shuddering and breathless and spent against her. She buried her face in his shoulder and thought about the day she'd had with him, and the laughter and the pleasure and the solid rightness of it all, and she felt so safe and satisfied and *better* that she held him tighter and when they were both calm again, she told him the truth: "I love you."

His breath went out on a *whoosh*. After a very long time, he pulled away from her, and when he smiled down at her, he looked as if he were trying to sell her a used car.

"Uh, thank you," he said.

Thank you? "You're welcome," Sophie said, disappointment and annoyance breaking nicely through her satisfaction. "What's the matter with you?"

"Why are you in such a hurry? Three weeks and you're throwing commitment around."

"That wasn't commitment, that was emotion," she said flatly.

"That was commitment," Phin said, just as flatly. "You know I'm crazy about you, why—"

"Say the *L* word and I'll know."

"What happened to 'You Don't Have to Say You Love Me'?"

"I'm not a fan of Dusty's masochist period," Sophie said. "You have to say it."

Phin rolled out of bed. "You know, you were right, Wes is going to be here anytime. We should probably get dressed." He grabbed his boxers and headed for the hall and the bathroom.

"Was it something I said?" Sophie called after him, but he was already down the hall, and it took all her self-control to keep from throwing his alarm clock at the wall.

Okay, she'd been stupid. But she really did love him. The middle of great sex probably wasn't the best place to have that realization, since great sex did tend to cloud a woman's mind, but now that she knew it, she also knew it had been there for a while.

She got out of bed and picked up her bra, determined to think of a way to make him admit he loved her because, of course, he did, the dummy, she had no doubts about that. The fair way would be to confront him and make him talk about it, but she'd just tried that and look where it had gotten her.

So, time to be a Dempsey. Time to throw away all her conscience and pride. Time to cheat and lie and get what she needed. She sat on the edge of the bed and thought about Phin's weak spots. He had so few. Sex. Shirts. Pool.

Pool.

She heard the shower go on in the bathroom and thought, *This boy is toast.* Then she got dressed, made one quick stop in the bathroom while he was still in the shower, and went downstairs to show him exactly what he was dealing with.

When Phin came out of the bathroom, Sophie had gone, which made him feel relieved and guilty until he heard balls knocking together on the pool table. He put his khakis and his shirt back on and went downstairs with dread in his heart.

The last thing he wanted to do was explain why he didn't love her back although he *cared* about her, of course, more than any other woman he'd ever known, but not "I love you," not after only three weeks—was she insane? They had such a great thing going here, and it could lead to commitment in a couple of years, maybe when Dillie wasn't so vulnerable and his mother got used to her, and until then they could keep things going if they were just careful, didn't expect too much, but no, she had to say it. Christ, *women.*

Then he hit the bottom of the stairs and saw Sophie.

She was bent over the table, racking balls and humming "Some of Your Lovin'," looking very hot in her pink dress, and the memory of where they'd just been and what they'd just done lessened his annoyance considerably.

"Hey, you," she said, and came around the table to kiss him, no hassles and no nagging, and when she broke the kiss and smiled lazily at him, he smiled back.

"How about a game?" she said. "We've got time for nine ball."

"You know nine ball?" he said, and she said, "Everybody knows nine ball, although I'm not in your league, of course. Do you want to play?"

"Yes," he said.

"Davy said you were really good," Sophie said. "Try not to beat me too bad."

"I'll go easy," he said, planning on blowing a few shots. It really wasn't fair to play her straight-on when she wasn't as good as he was.

She smiled at him again. "This is a magnificent table," she said, and the last of his tension eased away as he watched her stroke the rosewood rails. "But then, everything about you is magnificent."

He felt a faint stir of alarm, but then she came to the end of the table with cue in hand. She took a stance that dynamite couldn't have shifted, gripped the cue firmly with her thumb and two fingers and bent to sight down it in perfect form. Phin tilted his head to see her better. Perfect form and the world's best butt in a short pink dress.

She looked up at him, still smiling. "You playing, here?"

"Yeah." He picked up his cue and bent to shoot for the lag, but she was close beside him in that pink dress, and she shook his concentration and took the break away from him.

"I'll be damned," he said. "Very nice."

"Rack 'em." She chalked her cue, and then, while he watched, her smile evaporated and she pocketed the seven on the break with a power stroke that banished "cute" from his vocabulary for her forever.

"I never told you this before," she said, after she'd chalked and taken aim on the one. "But I come from a long line of felons."

"Really." Phin watched the ball fall into the pocket without hitting the back.

Sophie stood and chalked. "My father's on the lam right now on a fraud charge." She bent and fell into perfect position again, and Phin stifled a sigh. "He's a recidivist. A big one." She pocketed the two with a follow shot that left her exactly where she needed to be, and stood to chalk again. "Then there's my brother."

"Davy." Phin watched her bend again.

"He makes his living defrauding people who defraud people." Sophie pocketed the three. "They're not really in a position to go after him, so he gets away with it, although there are a considerable number of people who don't like him."

"Can't imagine why," Phin said, and Sophie chalked again.

"Amy had a few small problems with the law, but in general she's pretty straight now."

"That's good."

"And then there's me," Sophie said.

She pocketed the four on a beautiful stop shot, and Phin said, "You."

"Yeah." Sophie nodded and chalked again. "I've been ducking my destiny, trying to go straight and be good. But you know—"

She bent to take her shot, aimed carefully, and followed through with such perfect form that Phin went a little dizzy for a moment.

"—that's not really me," she said as she straightened. "I was born to be bad." She smiled at him. "I learned that from you. Thank you so much."

Phin swallowed. "You're welcome."

Then Sophie put away the six, and he thought, *Hell, she could beat me.* It was a strangely arousing thought.

But there was a limit.

"Actually, I already knew about your family," he said. "Zane told me."

She had chalked and bent to shoot again, but now she hesitated. "He did?"

Phin nodded. "He seemed a little annoyed that I didn't care."

"Oh," Sophie said, and sighted down the cue to the eight. When she missed the shot, it was by such a tiny miscalculation, hitting the ball just a fraction too hard, that he was almost sorry.

But not sorry enough not to put the eight and nine away. This was, after all, pool. He chalked his cue and looked at the eight. She'd left him a cut shot, not an easy one, but one he could make. He bent to shoot, and she said, "There's something else you should know."

"What?" he said, without raising his head.

"I'm not wearing any underpants." She sat down out of his sight line, and when he turned his head to look at her, she smiled at him innocently with her legs crossed, the slender, curving line of her thigh disappearing into her short, clinging pink dress. "Sort of like your fantasy."

His cue wavered, and he straightened. "You really think I'm going to fall for that?"

Sophie shrugged. "Check your back pocket."

Against his better judgment, he did, and felt the slippery slide of nylon and lace. He pulled it out and held it up in front of him. Definitely Sophie's pink lace drawers. He shrugged. "Big deal." He stuffed them back in his pocket and bent to take his shot, and then he thought about her bending over the table, making draw and follow shots with such elegance, hitting that one stop shot that had been so simply beautiful that he'd felt dizzy just looking at her. All without underpants.

Steady, he told himself.

Then he thought about the incredible things she'd just done to him in bed, and for the first time in his life, he thought seriously about having sex on his pool table. The hell with the felt. Great-grandpa would understand.

"You going to take that shot anytime soon?" Sophie asked, and he lined up the shot, thought of Sophie's naked butt, and miscued, just a fraction of a fraction of an inch, but a miscue just the same.

"So close," Sophie said as she stood up. "But then pool, like love, is not a forgiving sport." She went to the table, and he watched her make the cut shot with perfect draw and then pocket the nine with that stop shot that made his heart clutch.

"God almighty," Wes said from the doorway, and Phin looked up and said, "I know. It's a beautiful thing."

"Thank you." Sophie put her cue carefully back in the rack, and Phin followed the line of her back as she did, lingering on her naked-under-that-dress butt.

He had to do something to get some blood back to his brain. "I need to see you upstairs."

"I don't think so." She reached for his back pocket and pulled her underwear out as she walked past. "Turn around, Wes."

Wes raised his eyebrows at the underpants and then turned his back, and Sophie stepped into her drawers and pulled them up over her firm, round butt.

Phin said, "No, really. *Upstairs.*"

"No, really, *I can't.* If I go up there, I'll just lose my head and ask for commitment. So later for you." Sophie drifted past Wes, a vision of skill and sex, and Phin let his breath out as she went.

"I missed something, didn't I?" Wes said when she was gone.

Phin leaned on his cue, staring at the doorway where he'd seen her last, her pink dress imprinted on his retina. "I knew it. I knew it the first minute I saw her. The devil's candy."

"What?"

"She just fucked me six ways to Sunday."

"She beat you at pool, too," Wes said, looking at the table.

"That's what I mean," Phin said. "It's going to take me years to recover from this."

"It's just pool," Wes said. "She's leaving after the premiere on Tuesday. Get a grip. I need to talk to you."

Phin ignored him to replay Sophie's stop shot in his mind. Then he replayed her body in his bed. Then he remembered the way he needed to talk to her every night, and the way she'd stood up for Dillie at the game, and the way she laughed and made his heart pound harder every time she met his eyes, and he knew it wasn't just sex.

It wasn't even pool.

"Phin?" Wes said.

"I think I'm going to have to marry her," Phin said. "Dillie likes her. I could teach her to read. This could work."

Wes shook his head. "Your mind is clouded by pool. You've only known her three weeks. Wait until the game wears off and rethink this."

"Okay," Phin said, and thought about Sophie's stop shot again.

For that alone, he had to love her.

"Clea got to Rob," Wes told Phin, when they were sitting on the bookstore porch. "She's been telling him that the only thing standing in their way was Zane. She's got him convinced she's in love with him."

"Just like Dad," Phin said. "Helluva tradition, those Lutz boys."

"She gave him her cell phone and sent him out after Zane that night with instructions to call if Zane got into any trouble. She told Rob he was drunk and if he fell in the river, he'd drown."

"And Rob didn't get the hint."

"No, thank God. He followed him to the back of Garvey's, and then Zane stopped and waited there, so Rob called Rachel on the cell phone to come out and meet him."

Phin frowned, incredulous. "Why—"

"He thought Zane would make a pass and Rachel would scream and Stephen would come out and it would be all over. This is Rob, remember. No execution. For which we should all be grateful. So Rachel Maced him and shoved him in the river, and then Rob took her out to the Tavern and Zane climbed back to the path and met somebody with a gun." Wes sighed. "With the stuff I dragged out of Amy about the body, I've got a better time of death. Zane went into the water alive and unshot about nine forty-five. Amy came back from the Tavern and went upstairs a little after ten, but you and Sophie were . . . loud, so she went out to the dock to cool off and found Zane. Her best guess is ten-thirty."

"Forty-five minutes," Phin said. "Anybody have an alibi?"

"You and Sophie," Wes said. "Rob and Rachel at the Tavern. Leo in L.A. Hildy and Ed."

Phin raised an eyebrow. "Hildy and Ed?"

"Watching porn at his place," Wes said. "Police work turns up a lot of stuff you wish you didn't know."

"So that leaves . . . ?"

"Frank, who didn't go home. Georgia, who was home alone after you dropped her off. Your mom, who was home with Dillie in bed. Stephen, who was home, but who sleeps in a different room than Virginia."

"Christ, this guy can't catch a break," Phin said, and then thought about Virginia. "Or maybe he can."

"And Clea, Amy, and Davy," Wes said. "None of these people can find the guns that are supposed to be in their respective houses. All of them had access to Sophie's bedroom to plant the gun we found there, which, by the way, is now in Cincinnati for a ballistics test."

"Davy and Amy wouldn't put a gun under Sophie's mattress," Phin said.

"Amy might," Wes said. "She's used to Sophie carrying the can for her. And there was a good chance that gun would never be found. But Davy's the one I'm really interested in."

"I don't think Davy Dempsey is a killer."

"You're forgetting Clea. They were lovers five years ago until she dumped him for Zane, and I'm picking up some tension there now. It'd be like Clea to hedge her bets by sending two guys after Zane. What if she told Davy she'd made a mistake, that she'd come back to him if Zane were gone?"

"Davy Dempsey is not a killer," Phin said. "And if he decided to become one, he wouldn't shoot his victim in the shoulder with a pop-gun."

"Unless he knew his victim had heart problems," Wes said. "Then that becomes a smart thing to do. You can't be convicted of murder, but you can cause a man to die, just the same. That's devious enough for Davy. In fact, it's so devious I'm starting to think it can only be Davy."

"What are you going to do?" Phin said.

"Keep digging," Wes said. "Wait for the ballistics report on the gun in Sophie's bed. Watch Davy Dempsey. Pray for a miracle."

"You're doing a helluva job with this," Phin told him.

"One other thing," Wes said, and Phin tensed at the tone in his voice. "The gun in Sophie's bed was your dad's."

The worst part, Phin thought, was that neither of them was surprised. "I don't want to know this."

"Doesn't mean it's the gun that shot Zane," Wes said.

"No, but it is the gun that framed Sophie," Phin said. "I need to talk to my mother."

When Phin got home, Liz was waiting for him in the hall, glowering.

"Now what?" he said, and she said, "You took her to Dillie's softball game."

"Yes," Phin said, looking around for his daughter, and Liz said, "She's not here. I took her to Junie's so we could have this out."

"Good," Phin said. "You put Dad's gun under Sophie's mattress. A *loaded gun*, under Sophie's mattress. You could have killed her."

"I suppose she told you that," Liz stood stone-faced, framed by the big front door. "She lies. She's trying to destroy this family and you're letting her. You're going to have to choose. If you're going to continue to consort with her, you can't live under my roof. I won't let you destroy this family for sex."

"It's not sex," Phin said. "And I'm not destroying the family, but you might be."

"Choose," Liz said, and Phin said, "You're right. It's time anyway."

Her face relaxed and she smiled. "I knew you'd see—"

"I'll pack my stuff and move down to the bookstore tonight—"

"*No*," Liz said, her face twisting.

"What did you expect? I'll get one of the bedrooms cleared out tomorrow and come back for Dillie and her things then."

"*NO*," Liz said, and Phin said, "You can stop shrieking 'no' at me. This was your idea."

"If you have to move out to be with that—"

"Careful."

Liz drew a deep breath. "—that woman, that's your mistake, but you're not taking Dillie. You're not capable of—"

Phin took another step toward his mother so that he towered over her. "You have no idea of what I'm capable of when it comes to my daughter," he said softly. "Don't try to find out."

"You're being a fool," Liz said.

"You're being a bitch," Phin said, and Liz drew back as if she'd been slapped. "Stop harassing Sophie. I'll come get Dillie tomorrow." Then he turned and went up the stairs to pack, not looking back at all.

It took Phin and Sophie all Sunday to move the books from one of the bedrooms—the one with the window seat in the tower corner because Sophie insisted Dillie would love it—and when they were done, they were both covered in dust and sweat in spite of the air-conditioning.

"Dillie's going to go nuts for this room," Sophie said, wiping the sweat from her forehead and leaving a dirt streak behind. She looked at him cautiously. "Speaking of nuts, how's your mom taking this?"

"About as well as can be expected," Phin said, trying not to think about his mother. "Which is not well at all. Can I interest you in a shower?"

"I assume this is a twofer," Sophie said.

"Water conservation." Phin reached for her, knowing exactly how she'd feel against him and wanting her even more because of it. "Also sex. Come here."

"The things I give up for you." Sophie moved toward into his arms. "Private showers, vintage mattresses, money, my reputation—"

"So you're not losing anything you really needed." He smiled down at her as she cuddled close, and then what she'd said registered. "What money?"

She stopped to look up at him, caught, her eyes wide. "Money?"

He moved his hands up to her shoulders, exasperated with her and loving her anyway. "Sophie, listen to me, if you know where Zane's money is—"

"Oh, I don't," Sophie said, meeting his eyes without hesitation, clearly telling the truth. She slid her arms around his waist and pulled him close, and she felt great against him, but not great enough to distract him. "About that shower—"

"About that money," he said. "Whose money, and where is it?"

Sophie sighed. "It's your mother's, and it's in her bank account. That day she came out to the farm, she tried to buy me off. But that was two weeks ago so—"

"Buy you off?" Phin looked down at her, incredulous. "Who the hell does she think she is?"

"Liz Tucker," Sophie said. "She's just trying to protect you. Now, can I have that shower?"

There was something in her voice; she was talking too fast. "No." Phin guided her over to the window seat and pulled her into his lap. "There's more. I don't give a damn what it is, I'll forgive you anything, but I want it all."

Sophie pulled away from him. "I didn't do anything, you butthead. You can go forgive somebody else."

Phin winced. "Sorry. But you're not telling me everything. What else did my mother do?"

"I don't know," Sophie said, standing. "I haven't seen her since that day, I swear to God. Now, I'm going to shower. If you want to come, too, fine, but I'm going to be naked and wet with or without you."

He followed her into the bathroom, still suspicious, but when she took off her clothes, he decided he could wait to grill her again until they were both clean and satisfied.

An hour later, buttoning up his shirt as he sat on the edge of his bed and trying to think of what he was missing about his mother and money, Phin stopped on the second button and thought, *Diane.* "She bought off Diane, didn't she?" he said to Sophie, and Sophie zipped up her shorts and said, "How would I know?"

"But that's what you think."

"But I'm often wrong," Sophie said.

He thought about Diane and Dillie and the whole miserable mess. "Christ."

"It's over," Sophie said, coming to him. "Whatever really happened, it doesn't matter. It's over."

He put his arms around her and thought, *It's not over.* Two women had come between him and his family, and the first one was dead.

Family values weren't supposed to be lethal.

"What?" Sophie said.

"I have to take you home," he told her, standing up. "It's time for a little Tucker family time."

Phin found his mother sitting at her desk in her air-conditioned office on the Hill. She nodded when he came in, and then turned back to her desk, punishing him with her silence.

"You bought Diane off," he said, and she stiffened but didn't turn around. He went to her, grabbed the back of the chair and spun it around on its wheels so that she grabbed the arms.

"Phin!"

"How much?" he said, leaning over her.

She pressed her lips together, stony-faced, and he waited for what seemed like hours. "Fifty thousand," she said finally.

Phin straightened. "Not bad. What was that for, the first year?"

His mother nodded.

"As long as she stayed away from me and Dillie."

His mother nodded again.

"But she bought a car," Phin said. "New clothes, furniture for the river house. How long did it take her to run through it?"

"She was stupid," his mother said bitterly. "Thank God, Dillie got our brains."

"Right now, I'm wondering about yours," Phin said. "You really thought she'd leave us alone for fifty grand a year? Living right here in Temptation? She wasn't the only one who was stupid."

Liz flinched. "She was supposed to move away. As soon as she recovered from having Dillie, she was supposed to go away."

"And how were you going to make her do that?" Phin said. "Who do you think you are?"

"I'm your mother," Liz snapped. "I took care of you. That harpy would have ruined you. She made you miserable the whole time she was with you." She looked at him in disgust. "You're impossible when it comes to women. Diane was a greedy little slut and now this—"

"Careful." Phin's voice cut across the space between them. "You really don't want to make me choose again."

"The whole town's talking," Liz said, her voice shaking. "That woman killed Zane. They found the gun under her bed—"

"What?" Phin said. How the hell had the gossips gotten hold of that?

Liz nodded. "You don't know her. She killed him—"

"She was in bed with me," Phin said. "Wes has got the time of death narrowed down to forty-five minutes, and she was naked with me the entire time. Where'd you get this crap?"

"Virginia," Liz said. "But everybody knows. And now you're protecting her—"

"Could you just once listen to me?" Phin said. "Instead of spitting paranoia at me?"

Liz clenched her jaw. "I'm not paranoid. You need me. I got you free of Diane. I saved you."

"I'm just wondering *how* free," Phin said, looking at the steel in his mother's eyes. "She died when Dillie was three months old. That must have been about the time she ran out of money. Did she come back for more?"

"Yes," Liz said, her disgust palpable, and then his implication must have registered because her eyes widened, and she said, "No."

"Did you shove her down those steps?" Phin said, sick at heart. "Did you watch her bleed to death? Did Zane find out? Did you shoot him?"

Liz stood up. "I've given you my entire life and you say this to me."

"I didn't want your life," Phin told her bitterly. "I wanted mine. And Diane and Zane probably wanted theirs, too."

"I didn't kill them," Liz said.

"That's a pretty damn big coincidence, Mom." He turned to go. "I wouldn't want to have to explain it."

"Are you going to Wes?" Liz said from behind him, no emotion at all in her voice.

"No," Phin said, refusing to look back at her. "You're still my mother. Just stay away from Sophie."

"I didn't kill Diane, Phin," Liz said. "It really was a coincidence."

Her voice shook a little this time, and he turned back. "Remember that day in the courthouse when you said you'd do anything for me?"

She nodded.

"Don't."

He turned and walked out of his mother's house and down the Hill to the bookstore, not stopping until he was in front of the pool table.

It was a beautiful thing, massive in its elegance, impressive in its tradition. Just like his family.

He really did not believe his mother had killed people. His mother might be unhinged from his father's death but she wasn't a killer. There was still a human being in there somewhere, a cold, driven human being, but still a human being. She hadn't become a monster when he wasn't looking.

"Oh, Christ," he said, and sat down hard on the edge of the table. She really hadn't. Not his mother.

And now she was trying to pin Zane's death on Sophie.

He got up and went to the phone and dialed Hildy Mallow. "Hildy?" he said when she answered. "I've got some gossip for you to spread."

"I don't spread gossip," Hildy said primly.

"You will this gossip," Phin said. "Somebody's spreading the rumor that Sophie killed Zane."

"I'd heard that," Hildy said. "Didn't seem likely but people are strange."

"She was in bed with me," Phin said. "The entire time. Tell everybody."

"Oh," Hildy said. "All right. Your mother's not going to like this."

"Good," Phin said. "Tell her first."

When Sophie got home, Amy was waiting for her. "Where have you been?" she said. "I need—"

"Get it yourself," Sophie said, and went upstairs.

Amy followed her up. "What's with you? I just wanted your opinion on the cable cut of the video."

"Get all the sex out of it and bleep the foul language," Sophie said. "After that I don't care. I'm worried about Phin and Dillie. They—"

"Oh, sure," Amy said. "Phin and Dillie."

Sophie looked up at the tone in her voice. "You're jealous."

Amy shrugged. "I just think family—"

"That's why you called Brandon," Sophie said. "You don't like him, but you'd rather I was with him because you know I don't care about him. But Phin—"

"I don't care what you do with the mayor," Amy said. "Screw him all you want."

"It's really Dillie, isn't it?" Sophie said. "I can only have one kid in my life, and that's you?"

Amy's eyes filled with tears.

"Amy, I will always be here for you, but you're not getting my life anymore."

"No, *they* get it now." Amy sniffed. "Well, no problem. I can take care of myself."

"Actually, you can't." Sophie tried to smile to take the sting out of the words. "I wish you'd apologize to Wes and get him back. This is a man who not only fixed your funky sunglasses, he made them funkier. And he gave you a flexible showerhead that you've been using for immoral purposes ever since we got here. He may be the only man in the world who understands you and gives you what you need even before you know you need it. But you're giving him up for a dirty movie? Come on, Ame."

"This is my career, Sophie," Amy said stiffly.

"This is a home movie, Amy," Sophie said. "An amateur, direct-to-video skin flick. You are not Robert Rodriguez. Grow up and look at what matters in life."

Amy turned and walked out.

When Davy came up the stairs a few minutes later, he said, "What happened with Amy?"

"I picked Phin and Dillie," Sophie said. "Was that lousy of me?"

"No," Davy said. "It's past time for you to get a better plan than, 'I'll sacrifice my life for my grown brother and sister.' Way past time."

"What about you?" Sophie said.

"I have a plan of my own," Davy said, grinning. "Everything's going to be fine."

"Not for Amy," Sophie said, and Davy's smile faded.

"She'll be all right," he said, but he didn't sound convinced. The lights flickered, and he said, "Oh, great, she's plugged in all the computer stuff again. Didn't you tell her—"

"Over and over again," Sophie said, and got up to call down the stairs. "Amy? You're going to blow a—"

The lights went out downstairs.

"—fuse."

"I'll get it," Amy said coldly from the foot of the stairs. "How hard can this be if you do it?"

They heard her slam open the basement door and stamp down the stairs.

"You know, she needs smacked," Davy said. "Spoiled brat."

"She's just hurt," Sophie said. "She—"

The lights came on for a split second, and then there was a *crack* and they went out again.

"Amy?" Sophie said.

"*Amy?*" Davy ran for the stairs, Sophie on his heels.

"Somebody pulled loose a wire in the fuse box," Wes said, when Phin had come back from the hospital. "And poured water on the floor and set a trap for her."

"Not for her," Phin said, his voice grim. "Amy doesn't change the fuses. She doesn't do any scut work. She's the artist." He felt lousy even as he said it, remembering Amy's pale little face in the hospital bed, her fingers bandaged from the burns, her head shaved to stitch up the wound she'd gotten when the charge had blown her back against an old metal table.

"For Sophie," Wes agreed. "I got an anonymous phone call today. Somebody seemed to think there was a gun under Sophie's bed."

"Trace it?"

"The courthouse," Wes said. "Anybody in the world could have made it. And now this. Somebody wants Sophie out of the way pretty badly."

Phin closed his eyes. "I do not see my mother sneaking into a basement to fray a wire. Or putting a gun under a bed she knew I'd be sleeping in."

"Your mom is . . . upset that you moved out," Wes said. "Extremely."

"She'll get over it," Phin said. "So you going to the hospital to see Amy?" Wes turned away as he added, "She asked for you. I told her you were investigating the accident and you'd be out to talk to her later."

"She wants to see me?"

"Sounded like it," Phin said. "She pretty much got the spunk knocked out of her, and she's stuck in the hospital for the night. Good time to go talk to her."

Wes turned on him. "You think I'd ask her about Zane now?"

"I meant about the two of you," Phin said. "She's leaving tomorrow after the premiere."

"She'll be out that fast?"

"They're just watching her for the night. Go see her."

"Maybe," Wes said. "Is Sophie—"

"Sophie's staying with me tonight."

"I thought Dillie—"

"She's staying with me and Dillie," Phin said.

Wes raised his eyebrows. "Your mother—"

"Go see Amy," Phin said. "I'll take care of my mother."

When Wes brought Amy home from the hospital the next day, Sophie had the entire house cleaned, their things packed, and the car full of gas. "If you don't feel like leaving tonight after the premiere, we can stay," Sophie said, and Amy said, "Whatever you want," and went upstairs to bed.

"I'll come back later tonight," Wes told Sophie. "She's okay, she's just nervous about the video."

But when Sophie went upstairs to see her, she found Davy instead, packing his bag.

"You're leaving?"

"I've got a place I have to be, and somebody I have to finish things with." He closed the suitcase lid and locked it. "Harvard's watching your back here, probably better than I can. It's his turf, after all."

"I don't think—"

"Amy's okay and Clea's gone, so I'd say your problems—"

"Clea's gone?"

"Left about an hour ago," Davy said. His voice was light, but his face was grim.

"Is that why you're leaving?" Sophie felt sick. "You're not going off with her, are you? You don't want her back?"

"You ask too many questions." Davy sat down beside her and put his arm around her. "Listen to me: Marry the mayor and keep the dog and live happily ever after in this house. That's what you want. Forget about me and Amy and go for it."

"Just like that," Sophie said.

"Have you tried?" Davy said.

Sophie smiled faintly. "Well, actually, yeah. I kicked the mayor's butt at pool."

"Good girl," Davy said.

"By not wearing underwear," Sophie said.

"Even better," Davy said.

"I just don't think that's going to do it," Sophie said. "And I know that's not going to get me the house."

"I have a deal for you," Davy said, and Sophie said, "This should be good. Scamming your sister."

"No," Davy said. "This one's a promise. You stay here and marry the mayor and I'll get you this house."

Sophie blinked at him. "You have three-quarters of a million dollars?"

"Never ask people about money," Davy said. "It's rude."

Zane's bank book. Sophie went cold. "Where did you get three-quarters of a million dollars?"

"Sophie—" Davy said and hit her with the Dempsey smile.

Sophie sighed. "Call me for bail when you get caught."

"You have an attitude problem," Davy said, and kissed her cheek. "Don't go back to Cincy, stay here. I'll have the deed for you by Monday."

He picked up the suitcase, and she said, "Wait," and he caught her as she flung herself at him. "Be very, very careful," she whispered in his ear, not adding *especially with Clea*, and he held her tight and said, "Just for you, I always am." Then he kissed her cheek and was gone.

That night, Phin had just grabbed his car keys when Sophie knocked on the back door of the bookstore.

"I thought I was coming out to you," he said, letting her in.

"Amy is driving me crazy," Sophie said. "I left Wes to deal with her. She likes him better than me anyway." She slid her arms around his waist and he pulled her close and kissed the top of her head. "And unlike Amy, you are calm," Sophie said against his shirt. "I like that in a man."

"That's been harder lately," he said. "Dillie's at Jamie Barclay's. Want to come upstairs and watch TV in my bed?"

"I didn't even know you had a TV," Sophie said.

"ESPN2 has billiards on Wednesday nights," Phin said.

"Then of course you have a TV."

She piled his pillows at the head of the bed while he opened the cabinet that held his TV and flipped the channels to Temptation cable, and when he turned, she was propped up waiting for him, looking fairly comfortable and really good, even if she was back in khaki.

"Do I get popcorn?" she said, and Phin looked at the kitchen clock and said, "We have five minutes before showtime. You may get something else."

"Oh, gee, a whole five minutes." Sophie rolled her eyes. "That's what I need, a guy with staying power."

He stretched out on the bed next to her. "Before I forget, *Prizzi's Honor*." He patted the bed. " 'Right here on the Oriental.' "

"How'd you get that?"

"Amy," he said. "I asked her when she was in the hospital. Of course, she didn't know what I was going to do with it."

Sophie laughed and kissed him, and he fell into all her softness and the heat of her mouth.

"Funny you should mention that," Sophie said as she snuggled closer. "I went to Hildy's today to take her Dove Bars as a thank-you for rescuing me off her dock, and she had this book of ballads."

"Good," Phin said, and bent to kiss her again, sliding his arm behind her head.

"And 'Julie Ann' was in there," Sophie said, ducking him a little so that he stopped. "And I think you had it wrong."

He lifted his head. "Wrong? My grandmother sang that song to me for years. You're telling me my grandma was wrong?"

"The last line," Sophie said sternly, "says that they never found Julie, and they never found the bear."

"Right," Phin said.

"So they both disappeared," Sophie said.

"Right," Phin said.

"So it's a pretty patriarchal assumption that the bear got Julie." Sophie turned away from him a little and sliding her hand under the pillows. "I think Julie got the bear."

"Yeah, right," Phin said, and then he felt something cold snap on the wrist he'd put behind her head, and when he sat up, Sophie had him handcuffed to the headboard.

"Wes loaned them to me," she said. "I have to give them back later tonight, though."

Phin tugged once on the cuffs as he felt something closely akin to panic. "This isn't funny. Give me the key."

Sophie sat cross-legged on the bed and shook her head. "Nope. It's definitely Julie Ann's turn this time."

Phin closed his eyes. "At least tell me you *have* the key."

"Of course I have the key." He could feel Sophie leaning closer, and then he felt her working the buttons on his shirt open.

"Sophie, I don't th—" Phin began, but then her fingertips brushed his stomach, and every muscle he had tightened, and he shut up.

She popped open the button on his pants and said, soft and slow, "Let me give you an orgasm you don't have to work for," and he looked into her liquid brown eyes and said, "Just don't lose the key." She laughed and kissed his stomach, and then he forgot about the key, and the murder, and Temptation in general, and surrendered to Sophie's cool, searching fingers and her hot, hungry mouth.

Fifteen minutes later, he was staring contentedly at the ceiling, counting his blessings which now seemed numerous, when he heard somebody pound on the downstairs door. Sophie sat up beside him, and he tried to do the same, only to realize he was still handcuffed to the bed. "The key—" he began, and then he saw she was looking past him to the television, stunned. "What?" he said, and she said, "That's the wrong movie. That's *Cherished.*"

He turned and saw Rob on-screen, naked, reaching for Clea, also naked, and heard him say, " 'You definitely have discovery fantasies.' "

Phin froze as the dialogue rolled over him.

" 'We're going to be having a lot of sex in public places,' " Rob said. " 'You want to know why?' "

" 'No,' " Clea said and stretched for the camera.

" 'Because you like it,' " Rob said, and reached for her, and then the movie cut to grainier film of bodies writhing, and Sophie said, "Oh my God, that's *Hot Fleshy Thighs!*"

The pounding got louder downstairs, and Phin turned to her and said, *"Get me that key."*

Sophie scrambled for it on the bedside table and unlocked the cuffs with shaking fingers while he watched the film go into such a tight close-up that it was almost impossible to tell what body parts were being filmed.

Almost.

Phin rolled out of bed and grabbed his pants. "Call Wes at the farm and tell him to meet me at the cable station."

"That's not our movie," Sophie said, as she grabbed the phone and punched in the numbers, "that's Leo's movie, I swear to God."

"I really don't give a damn, Sophie," Phin said. "My kid is watching that."

The picture flipped back to a naked Rob who said to a naked Clea, " 'Your soul is a corkscrew.' "

"Phin—" Sophie's voice broke, and then the picture snapped and turned dark, and she shut up. Either his TV was broken, or somebody had stormed the cable station and shut it down. He flipped the channel and saw a blond teenager kicking the hell out of a vampire. His TV was fine.

His life, however, was broken.

"I'm sorry," Sophie whispered.

"Yeah, so am I," he said, and went downstairs to talk to the irate citizen pounding on the door.

Fourteen

Rachel sat across the table from Leo in Temptation's only diner, mired in misery, while Leo put on his glasses and read the receipt the waitress had just handed him with his Visa card.

He was leaving. He was going back to L.A. and leaving her stuck here in Temptation. And she loved him, damn it. That was the worst of it. It wasn't that he was leaving her in Temptation, although that was bad enough.

It was that he was leaving *her*. He didn't *love* her. She couldn't understand it at all. He'd kissed her that one glorious time, and he'd taken care of her when she'd gone to Wes, but that was it and now he was going and she was miserable.

Leo checked his watch. "The movie started fifteen minutes ago," he told her. "How long is it?"

"The clean version? About half an hour." Rachel leaned forward. "Leo, stop ignoring me."

Leo sighed. "I know you want to come to L.A., kid."

"I'm not a kid," Rachel said. "I'm a good worker. I learn fast. You're stupid not to take me."

"I'd be stupid *to* take you." Leo signed the receipt and pocketed his Visa. "Even assuming your father didn't come after me with a shotgun, I'd spend all my time looking after you. You stay here and have a normal life."

"I don't want a normal life," Rachel said. "If I wanted a normal life, I'd have done what my mother wanted and married Phin."

"Phin?" Leo scowled at her. "Phin's not right for you."

"I know that—" Rachel began, and then stopped as she realized somebody was standing by their table.

"You the guy that made that movie?" the man said, looking red in the face.

"No," Leo said. "Why?"

"Because whoever did that is a fucking pervert, that's why," the guy said.

"What?" Rachel said.

"Kids are watching that filth," the man said, and glared at Leo. "Are you sure you're not the guy?"

"I'm positive," Leo said mildly.

"Well, you should just be glad you took your daughter out for dinner tonight instead of watching that trash with her—"

"We have to go," Rachel said, getting up.

"My *daughter*?" Leo said, and Rachel leaned over and said, "*Now*, Leo."

Leo watched as the man stalked away. "She's not my daughter, you putz."

"*Leo.*"

"Showed the wrong movie, did they?" Leo said, and Rachel said, "I think they saw the old *Cherished* instead of the clean cut that Amy made, and I need to talk to Sophie *now*."

Leo dropped his napkin on the table. "Okay. But I'd still like to hear—"

"*Now*," Rachel said, and dragged him from the diner.

"I bagged the tape and sent it to Cincinnati," Wes said two hours later when he and Phin were finally alone in the bookstore. "Maybe we'll get some prints."

Phin shook his head, more tired than he could ever have imagined. It took a lot out of a mayor to have to deal with that many screaming citizens.

"Phin," Wes said. "Pay attention. We have to find out who took the tape. He violated the FCC up, down, and sideways, and we'll get him."

"I can't even think," Phin said. "I've been explaining the unexplainable all night. Where the hell did that tape come from?"

"From the farm," Wes said. "According to Amy, it was Leo's cut of a tape they'd made. I gather they made several versions."

"So whoever took that tape knew which one would do the most damage." Phin felt anger rise, cool and clean. "Somebody at the farm—"

"Not necessarily," Wes said. "Amy said when Rachel saw what Leo had done to the movie, she took the tape and wrote *'Smut, Smut, Smut'* on it in bright red marker. Anybody who wanted to sabotage the movie would have picked that one up."

"So somebody went out there and sorted through the tapes—"

"No," Wes said. "Somebody went out there and took all the tapes. As soon as the movie started, Amy went running to look. They're all gone, even the documentary she was working on. Somebody just backed up a car while we were all at the hospital this morning and took every one of them."

"Who?" Phin said, but even as he said it, he knew.

"Stephen's got this movie tied to your tail," Wes said. "This is a big break for him, just six weeks before the election. Six days would have been better, but six weeks isn't bad. And he's the only one I can see getting anything out of this."

Phin thought about Sophie. She'd gotten something out of it—out of making that damn movie at least. He heard his own stupid words coming out of Rob's mouth and felt like a fool.

Wes said, "You want to come to Stephen's with me?"

Phin thought of Stephen's smug, red face, and the pain cleared and his rage focused. "Yes."

"Thought so," Wes said.

———

Stephen answered the door, trying to look innocent and only looking smugger as a result. "I saw the premiere on television," he said to Wes. "That was a shocking thing. I certainly hope—"

"Forget it, Stephen," Phin said, as he pushed past him into the living room where Rachel sat on the couch in patent misery. "You knew all about it."

Across the room, Virginia looked up from the phone she was clutching and lowered her voice. Spreading the good word as usual.

Meanwhile Stephen was waxing indignant.

"What do you mean, I knew about it? You think if I'd known that kind of disgusting pornography was going to be broadcast to the people of this town—"

"Forget it, Stephen," Wes said. "The only voters here are the ones who know what really happened."

Rachel jerked her head up. "What did happen? I couldn't find Sophie to find out. That wasn't our film—"

"Young lady, you had nothing to do with that film," Virginia said from the phone.

"I worked on that film," Rachel said. "I'm proud of that film, but that film wasn't my film."

Virginia said, "I have to go," into the phone and hung up. "You had nothing to do with that disgusting movie, so you stop even pretending you did."

"I'm not pretending, I worked *hard* on that," Rachel said, and Virginia pointed her finger at her and said, "Enough. You've caused enough trouble acting up and from now on, you're going to be the daughter I raised. You're going to get married and settle down and be a good woman." Virginia's eyes slid to Phin.

"She's not marrying me," Phin said.

"She certainly isn't," Stephen said. "You're responsible for that porn going out to all of Temptation, corrupting—"

"Stephen," Wes said. "I told you. You can knock off the speeches. Everybody here knows you switched that tape—"

"Daddy?" Rachel said.

"That's the most ridiculous thing I ever heard of—" Stephen began.

"—and we're sending it to Cincinnati for a forensics check. The fingerprints will nail you if nothing else does."

"We'll just have to wait and see, then, won't we?" Stephen said, smug as ever, and Phin said, "Fuck. You wiped it before you played it, didn't you?"

"Phin!" Virginia said, and when Stephen said, "Well, that's the kind of language I'd have expected from somebody who'd consort with the *whores* who made that trash," Phin grabbed Stephen's throat and shoved him against the wall.

"About *Sophie*," Phin said, rage making his voice shake. "You damned near killed her, you bastard, and I never came after you for that—"

"I don't know what you're talking about," Stephen choked, wide-eyed.

"You shoved her in the river and almost drowned her," Phin said, gripping him tighter, and Rachel said, "Daddy!" at the same time that Wes said, "Let him go, Phin."

"You hurt her." Phin gripped his neck harder. "From now on, you come after *me*, you son of a bitch, not her, and not the people of this town—you do not show porn to kids to bring me down, do you understand? This is between *us*."

Stephen didn't say anything, but he turned blue, and from behind him, Phin heard Wes say calmly, "He's sick and smaller than you are and older than you are and not worth it. Let go of him, or I'll break your arm."

Phin looked into Stephen's sly, stupid, blue face and thought about all the crap Stephen had gotten away with because nobody had fought him—*because I didn't fight him, because I played it safe, because I was too damn lazy*—

Wes jerked Phin's left arm up hard behind him, and the pain knifed into his shoulder, and he let go of Stephen and his own pent-up breath at the same time.

"Thank you," Wes said, releasing his arm as Stephen slid down the wall, an interesting shade of purple.

"Ouch," Phin said, and eased his shoulder back.

"It would be bad if you killed him," Wes said. "Understandable, but bad." He looked at Stephen on the floor, trying to fill his lungs. "That 'whore' bit was a dumb move, Stephen. Don't do that again."

Phin rubbed his arm and watched Stephen get his breath back. "Well, at least the short-term pleasure was great." He leaned over and said softly to Stephen, "If you ever try to hurt Sophie again, I'll let Wes break every bone in my body before I let you go."

"I didn't hurt that woman," Stephen rasped. "I don't attack women. Have you lost your mind? Arrest him for assault, Wes. He's crazy. He almost killed me."

"I didn't see any assault," Wes said. "I did see two men in heated conversation but—"

"Well, my family saw." Stephen climbed to his feet. "Rachel—" He stopped when he realized Rachel was gone. "You better get a lawyer," he told Phin. "You're in big trouble."

Virginia stared at them from across the room, horrified. "You're a terrible man," she told Phin. "I'll never let you marry my daughter now."

"Well, at least something's going my way." Phin turned back to Stephen. "You shoved Sophie in the river, you stole that tape, and you played pornography on a public television station. Get your own lawyer, you son of a bitch."

"You can't prove any of that," Stephen said. "I wouldn't shove a woman anywhere." He looked genuinely insulted that Phin had suggested it, and Phin frowned at him. Then Stephen's face grew smug again. "And I certainly wouldn't show pornography to the good people of—"

"Here we go again," Wes said. "Stephen, we need the other tapes back. I don't think the women will prosecute if you give them their tapes back, but—"

"Nobody's going to prosecute me for anything," Stephen said. "You have no proof. And the last time I looked, you needed proof to arrest somebody, so—"

"Stephen," Phin said quietly. "Sophie came over one night when you were watching them film on the dock, and somebody pushed her into the river. Right here, at the end of your property." Stephen shut up and Phin watched him closely. "The river was high and she almost drowned. If she wasn't such a fighter, she'd have died."

"I don't know anything about that," Stephen said cautiously. "But I do know that the people *you* consorted with produced a *porno-graphic* movie in *clear* violation of the Temptation *film ordinance—*"

Phin tuned him out, and Wes said, "Okay, Stephen, you practice your speech, and we'll talk to you tomorrow."

"I want him arrested," Stephen said, and Wes said, "No, you don't, because if I arrest him, he'll get to explain why he went for you, and then people might get to thinking you'd played porn to their children just to get elected."

Stephen scowled. "That's ridiculous."

"No," Wes said. "That's the truth, and it's the lousiest thing I know about you. How many people had their kids in front of that TV set to watch Temptation in the movies? You set it all up. Anything to get elected. You and your family values."

"I didn't do it," Stephen said stubbornly, but his eyes slid away, and Phin gave up.

When they were back in car, Wes said, "If you ever attack another citizen in front of me, I will break your fucking arm and then move on to your head."

"Fair enough," Phin said. "I can't think of anybody else I want to attack, anyway, so it shouldn't be a problem."

"Because you pretty much threw away whatever leverage I had," Wes went on. "He can file assault charges, you know, and they'll stick. So I'm not exactly in a position to lean on him for this tape thing."

"I'm sorry," Phin said. "But we did get something out of that."

"Yeah," Wes said. "He didn't push Sophie."

"So who did?" Phin thought about Sophie and the movie, and shoved it aside as too painful to think about. He went back to every-thing Sophie had told them about the river. Somebody had shoved her really hard, she'd said. "Who else would do that?"

"You got me," Wes said, and started the car. "I'll put it on my list of things to do along with, 'Find out who shot Zane and tried to electrocute Sophie,' and 'Try to nail Stephen for pandering porn.' Jesus, I'm lousy at this job."

"No, you're not," Phin said. "You're just up against it right now."

Wes pulled back out onto the road and headed for the station. "I hate to point this out, but so are you."

"Yeah, I think that pretty well wraps it up for me as mayor." Phin settled back, rubbed his shoulder, and thought about how good it had felt to grab Stephen. "Thanks for waiting so long to pull me off."

"My pleasure. You know, this wasn't Sophie's fault, that was Leo's cut. She must be upset about all this. She worked pretty hard making that movie."

Phin heard his own dialogue coming at him from the screen again. "You have no idea how hard she worked."

"Am I missing something here?"

"Yes." Phin said.

"Am I going to continue missing it?"

"Yes."

Wes sighed. "Fine, be that way." He pulled up in front of the bookstore. "Get out. I got work to do."

"What work? It's after eleven. Go home."

"I'm not the only one here missing stuff," Wes said. "You go mope. I have things to do."

"Wait a minute," Phin said, but Wes pointed to the door, so he got out and let him drive away.

Fine. Whatever. He wasn't moping, he'd just had his entire future shot out from under him, and there was nobody to vent his annoyance on. Wes was gone, his mother was somewhere committing hari-kari, the Garveys were no doubt celebrating the coming mayoral victory, and Ed was probably trying to get a copy of *Hot Fleshy Thighs* for his porn collection even as Phin stood there.

And then there was Sophie.

"Fuck it," he said, and walked around the back of the bookstore to his car. Wes was right. He had things to do. Like demand an explanation. Like ask her what the hell she thought she was doing. Like make her feel guilty for all the hell she was leaving behind her.

If she thought she was leaving town without a reckoning, she didn't know him at all.

Rachel found Leo in his motel room, packing.

"Thank God," he said. "My ride to the airport and out of here. That guy in the restaurant was only the beginning. Did you hear those people in the lobby? I don't think I've ever seen that many people angry over soft porn before. Imagine what they'd do if they knew the kind of stuff I do."

"They do," Rachel said. "You missed that part. My dad switched tapes and the town watched *Hot Fleshy Thighs*."

"Oh," Leo said. "Well. Even so, it was just a movie. They overreacted."

"Forget them," Rachel said. "They're history. Think about the future."

Leo eyed her cautiously. "You seem fairly calm about this."

Rachel leaned against the wall and shrugged. "It'll be okay. Everybody's mad right now, which is good for them because not much happens in Temptation so this'll give them some exercise. They're not bad people and they won't go after Sophie or anybody, and even if somebody really lost it and tried, Phin and Wes would take care of it."

"I doubt Phin's going to take care of it," Leo said. "From the way those people downstairs are talking, he just lost the next election."

Rachel shrugged. "He'll get over it. He loves Sophie, and he'll keep her no matter what. Phin's determined like that. Love'll do that to a person." She met Leo's eyes and he flinched.

"Right." Leo shut his suitcase. "Well, I'm ready. You want I should call a taxi so you don't have to—"

"No," she said, and pulled her dress over her head.

Leo took a step back. "Rachel, stop it."

"I know you think you're leaving me." Rachel lifted her chin so it wouldn't quiver because that would ruin what she was pretty sure was the magnificent sight of her in Victoria's Secret red lace. "But you're not. I'm the best thing that ever happened to you, Leo. And I mean professionally, too. I stopped and talked to Sophie on my way here, and we worked it all out. You can teach me to run that new vanilla-porn section." She took a deep breath. "I think you should call it Rachel Films and use a cat for the logo that's like the lion on the Leo stuff. And I can do a lot of the promotion that you can't do, because I'm a woman. Sophie thinks it's a great idea."

"Rachel—"

"And I'm smart, Leo," Rachel said. "And I learn fast. Sophie says so. I'm going to do a lot for you, you'll see."

Leo looked at the ceiling. "Could we talk about this with you dressed?"

"No," Rachel said. "Because I'm going to sleep with you, too. I know you don't want to do this, but even just that one kiss with you was better than having sex with anybody else I've had sex with, and I'm coming after the rest of it now. And then we're going to go to L.A. and live happily ever after." She narrowed her eyes at him. "If you think I'm settling for anything less, you don't know me."

Leo closed his eyes.

"And you know me, Leo." She walked toward him while he kept his eyes closed. "Although, not nearly as well as you're going to."

Sophie was sitting on the porch swing waiting when Phin pulled up at the farm. Whatever he did, however much he yelled, she'd just take it. She deserved it.

When he came up on the porch and sat down beside her, he stopped the swing, and she curled her feet under her and sat there, suspended in air, not sure of where she was with him, or even where she wanted to be.

"Did Dillie see it?" she asked him, and he said, "No. Jamie Barclay's mother has a very fast hand with the remote."

"That was not our movie. That was Leo's movie. He took ours and cut the porn stuff into it."

"But you made a porn flick, didn't you?" Phin said, staring out across the yard.

Sophie thought about explaining vanilla porn and decided it was hopeless. "Yes. Not like that one, ours wasn't hard-core, and it was good, but yes."

"And you used the stuff I said in bed," Phin said.

"Yes," Sophie said.

"I wondered why you were so easy," he said. "Research."

"No," she said. "I was so easy because you were so good."

"Don't even try it," he said.

"You forget," she said. "We didn't start out like we are now. It was a game, remember? Julie Ann and the bear on the dock? You thought I was a one-night stand." She swallowed. "And I thought you were a safe chance to break some rules. I didn't think about writing that first scene until after you'd gone that night. And I didn't think you'd ever know. I didn't know you'd ever be important."

He closed his eyes. "You kept on doing it. When you knew we weren't a one-night stand."

"I stopped a long time ago," Sophie said. "Before Stephen caught us in the kitchen, even. Before it was more than you just exercising with me."

"Sophie, it was never just exercise."

"Well, you never told me that." Sophie felt her temper spurt even as she said it. "You make jokes and you stay cool and you do not get involved, and I'm supposed to feel guilty because I don't recognize your deep emotional involvement?"

"You're not supposed to betray the people you sleep with," Phin said.

"By the time I realized there might be something to betray, it was too late," Sophie said. "I owed Amy, too. And we didn't think anybody would ever know. Nobody does know, except for you and Amy. And now the tapes are all gone. There's nothing left of all that work." She lifted her chin. "So you're off the hook."

"Then why does it still feel like it's buried in my back?" Phin said.

He hadn't turned to look at her once, and she lost it and punched him hard on the shoulder so he jerked around. "What do you want from me?" she said. "An apology? I'm sorry, I really am. You want me to destroy the tapes? They're gone. You want me to feel guilty, to suffer? I do, I am. But you're part of this, too, you know. You never said, 'Sophie, you're important to me, Sophie, *this* is important to me.' You never even said, 'I love you.' You remember what you said when I said it on Saturday? You said, 'Thank you.' "

Phin turned away from her, and she said. " 'Thank you.' Yeah, that was a clear indication that you cared desperately about the sanctity of our relationship. You arrogant bastard."

"Wait a minute," Phin said. "Why are you yelling at me?"

Sophie stood up, and Phin grabbed the chain as the swing bounced. She said, "Because you betrayed me ten times more than I betrayed you. You knew you cared and you didn't tell me, and now you come out here all wounded, saying it was more than just playing around and *I should have known that*?"

"I'm just saying," Phin said quietly, "that it's pretty much a basic rule that you don't make public what a lover says to you in private."

"What 'private'?" Sophie waved her arm at the yard. "We weren't private. You went down on me on the *dock*. You threw a *lamp* against the wall so you wouldn't have to be alone with me. You did me on a *car*. It was all *a game*. And now you change the rules and you want me to feel guilty? Well, I'm not going to, so there. I've changed my mind. This is your fault."

"My fault." Phin stood up. "*My* fault. That's rich."

"Oh, that's good." Sophie nodded. "Now you can feel indignant and go back into town and lord it over the council meeting tomorrow and patronize everybody and think about how lucky you are to not be involved with somebody as irrational as me because you are clearly the cool one in control and—"

"Sophie, shut up." Phin leaned against the porch post, looking more tired than she'd ever seen him. "I'm so far out of control, I don't think there's anything left of my life."

"Well, then, do something about it instead of standing there all smug," Sophie said. "You're playing so many balls ahead, you don't even know there's a game in front of you."

"You know, I knew you were the devil's candy," Phin said, as if he weren't listening to her at all. "As soon as I set eyes on you, I knew you'd bring me down. You and that mouth."

Sophie stuck out her chin. "And I knew you were a town boy, out to get my virtue and leave me crying." She waited for him to say something snarky about her virtue, but all he did was shake his head.

"We should have gone with our instincts," he said, and started down the porch steps.

Sophie stared after him, nonplussed. "So what did you come out here for?" she called after him. "Vindication? Validation? Revenge? What?"

"I don't know," he said, as he jerked open his car door. "But I sure as hell didn't get it."

"Well, that's the first time you came out here and didn't get what you wanted," Sophie yelled. "You're long overdue to go home empty-handed, as far as I'm concerned."

He stood inside the open car door for a minute and then he said, "Do you know who pushed you into the river?"

"What?" Sophie looked at him incredulously. "What are you talking about? We're in the middle of a fight here." When he stood there, waiting, she said, "No, I've told you a million times, I don't know."

"Because it wasn't Stephen," Phin said. "Which means somebody else is gunning for you."

"It could be anybody," Sophie said. "The whole damn town hates me."

Phin shook his head. "No, they don't. Most of them don't even know you, and the ones that do, like you. Nobody'd want to kill you."

"After tonight they all do," Sophie said.

"Oh, I think they're pretty much concentrating on me, thanks to Stephen." Phin looked grim in the moonlight. "And you're leaving anyway. I'm the one facing the music. And it ain't Dusty Springfield, babe. Have a nice life." He got in the car and slammed the door and started the engine, drowning out anything else she might say, like, *Come back here and fight this out, you bastard.*

When he was gone, Amy came out on the porch and handed her a

Dove Bar. Sophie took it and followed her to the swing, which Lassie crawled out from under, now that the shouting had stopped.

"That's not over, you know," Amy said.

"It might be," Sophie said, trying not to sniff. "He's such an uptight jerk, it just might be."

"Nah," Amy said. "He's just trying to figure out what hit him. And what he's going to do with the pieces. He'll be back. He's like us that way. Gets what he wants."

They rocked in silence for a couple of minutes, and then Sophie said, "Are you okay with that? With Phin and me?"

"Yeah." Amy nodded. "Davy was right. And Wes likes him so he must be okay."

"What did Wes say about the video?"

"Not much." Amy bit into her ice cream. "He didn't care about the permit thing at all. He wants to know who switched the tapes and played porn to Temptation, and he wants to nail somebody for shooting Zane, preferably Clea or Davy. I don't know why he's so fixated on them, but he seems sure they know something."

"They're both gone, you know," Sophie said. "She left before he did. I don't think she even told Rob good-bye. So it's just us."

Amy nodded. "I'll stick with you through the council meeting to-morrow. And then I'm going to L.A. Unless we get arrested for violating the permit."

Sophie stopped the swing. "What?"

"Wes said it wouldn't be a big deal and we could come back to the farm. He said he and Phin would work it out because the whole permit thing was probably unconstitutional. But he also said we had to stay until they got it fixed. By Thursday, he said."

"Phin isn't going to fix anything for me," Sophie said. "And I was the only living Dempsey who'd never been in jail."

"Dad will be so proud," Amy said.

"There's a comfort," Sophie said, and rocked for a minute. "Phin said something else. He said Stephen wasn't the one who pushed me."

"And he got this information how?"

Sophie shook her head. "I don't know, but he was sure. And he hates Stephen so if he could have pinned it on him, he would have. So who did?"

"This doesn't make sense," Amy said. "I'd bet money Stephen switched the tapes. If he was out to get you—"

"Why would he be out to get me?" Sophie said. "Phin's the one in his way."

Amy stopped swinging. "So it really was somebody else?"

"Whoever it was, pushed me really hard," Sophie said slowly. "And then watched me fall into that river and get swept away. Somebody really had to hate me to do that. So who was it?"

" 'We all go a little mad sometimes,' " Amy said.

Sophie thought about Liz and Phin and Dillie, trapped together, tearing each other apart. "That has to end," she said. "I have to at least fix that before I go."

"You're not going to go see her, are you?" Amy said.

"I have to," Sophie said. "She's trying to kill me."

Fifteen

At noon the next day, Phin watched Wes climb the steps to the bookstore. "Good, it's you. I couldn't take one more person telling me how disappointed they were in me, what a loss I am as mayor to have let that happened, or how delighted they'll be not to vote for me in November. It's been a real stampede in here." He rubbed his neck. "And not one of them bought a book."

Wes sat down in his chair and put his feet on the rail. "So it's all over, huh?"

"Looks that way," Phin said. "I've still got six weeks before the election, but this is the kind of thing that sticks in people's minds."

"Yeah." Wes nodded sadly. "So how's Sophie?"

"Furious," Phin said, trying to sound detached about it. "She's decided it's my fault." He shrugged. "It's better this way. If I'd talked her around, I'd have had to listen to Dusty Springfield every day for the rest of my life."

"Yeah, and there'd have been all that sex, too," Wes said. "That would have gotten old."

"You can shut up anytime now," Phin said.

"And she could kick your ass at pool, too," Wes said.

"So, Amy still going to L.A.?"

"Shut the fuck up," Wes said.

"We did real well, didn't we?" Phin said, giving up on detached. "Christ, I haven't seen a crash-and-burn like this since . . ." He shook his head at the sky. "I've never seen a crash-and-burn like this. We're *good.*"

"Finest kind." Wes stood up, letting the legs of his chair hit the porch floor with a thud. "However, unlike you, I am not a quitter. I don't have a plan, but I'm not a quitter."

"I'm not a quitter," Phin said. "I just have no interest in going out there and having Sophie slam the door in my face to 'All Cried Out,' shortly followed by Davy trying to beat me up."

"He's gone," Wes said. "Hit the airport last night and flew to the Bahamas."

Phin straightened a little. "Did he, now?"

"Yep." Wes went down the steps. "So did Clea."

"And you let them go?"

"I can get 'em if I want 'em. I think they're both guilty as hell, but I can't figure out what they did. So I'm not sure I want them."

"But you want Amy," Phin said.

"I'll get Amy." Wes started down the street and then stopped and came back a couple of steps. "Almost forgot. The ballistics report came back. Zane's bullet did not come from your dad's gun."

Phin let his breath out. "Finally, something goes my way." Then he frowned. "So my mother used the gun to frame Sophie, not caring that the ballistics test would trip her up? That doesn't make sense. She's nuts but she's not stupid."

"I think the real gun's in the river," Wes said. "Everything about this yahoo so far says he's impulsive. It would make sense at the time for him to drop the gun in the water after he shot Zane. And with the current the way it's been, I don't think we're going to find it. If that's true, and somebody decided to frame Sophie as an afterthought, he'd have to get another gun. And if all he wanted to do was start gossip about Sophie he wouldn't care about the ballistics report."

"Or she."

Wes shrugged. "God knows, our women are as nuts as our men. Which reminds me, looked at the water tower lately?"

"The water tower?" Phin went down the steps to look up the Hill. "Oh. Nice."

The rain had done its work, washing off the bloody streaks of Stephen's cheap paint, but, as the Coreys had told him, red stains. It was flesh again, but it was a rosy flesh, a glowing flesh, round and full above the trees. Only, the catwalk at the top was still red. "A lipstick with a nipple," Sophie had said, but now it didn't look like a lipstick anymore.

"I like this even better," Wes said. "It's friendlier. And God knows I could use some 'friendly'."

"Stephen's really going to hate this," Phin said.

"Yeah," Wes said as he started back up the street. "It's going to be some council meeting. See you there."

Phin thought about the meeting and his neck tightened even more. Stephen would be after his butt, his mother would be even more homicidal over the tarnished Tucker legacy, the entire population would want him barbecued for contributing to the delinquency of their minors, and Hildy would ignore it all to protect her new mammary water tower.

And after all of that, Sophie wouldn't give him the time of day because he was a dickhead town boy.

She's a fucking nutcase, he told himself, and concentrated on the stuff that mattered in his life.

He was going to lose the election to that moron Stephen in six weeks, there was something to look forward to. His dad at least had gone down over the New Bridge, something civic. He was going down over a porn flick. And if he hadn't gone down in the first place, he wouldn't be in this mess. The devil's candy, and he'd bit. He closed his eyes against the memory. " 'I coulda been a contendah,' " he said, to nobody in particular, and then walked back up the steps to the bookstore.

"Wait a minute," his mother called from the street, and he turned as she reached at the bottom of the steps. "I'm on my way to Hildy's but I want to talk to you first."

"Oh, good," Phin said, and sat down.

"I realize we've had problems," Liz said, as she came up the steps. "But that's all behind us now that you're not going to see that woman again. Things are bad right now, but we have six weeks and if you stay away—"

"Mom, we're going to lose."

"We are *not* going to lose," Liz said. "Tuckers do not lose, we're not going to lose, I'm not going to lose you, we're going to—"

"What are you talking about?" Phin said. "You—" He stopped as what she'd said registered. "Fuck. *That's* what this is about?"

"Watch your language," Liz said. "Everything is—"

"Mom, You're not going to lose me," Phin said. "I'm not going to die if I don't win. My heart is fine, and even more important, I don't give a damn about being mayor. I care about winning, but not about being mayor. I'm not going to die if I lose."

"Well, of course you're not going to die," Liz said, but her voice shook a little. "Of course not. Now, we'll get everything back to normal. Dillie will forget, and you'll be reelected, things will be just the same. I think you were right about not getting married again, I won't bring it up anymore, we'll just go back to the way we were." She smiled at him, fiercely cheerful. "Just the three of us again."

Just the three of them. Trapped and frozen in the house on the Hill.

"No," Phin said, and Liz's smile evaporated and the cobra came back.

"Listen to me. I know you're blinded by your hormones on this, but will you just look at where this woman has left you?"

Phin nodded. "With nothing. She destroyed my life."

"Exactly." Liz bit off her words. "But we can get it back again. We—"

"Why the hell would I want to do that?" Phin shook his head at her startled face. "My life was a fucking wasteland; all Sophie did was clear the brush."

"What are you talking about?" Liz said.

"I don't want to be mayor," Phin said. "I never wanted to be mayor. I'll fight for the office this one last time, but don't expect me to give anything more for the Tucker legacy. I've already given too damn much for it."

"This is all because of that woman." Liz looked as if she were about to hyperventilate.

"Yep." *No more mayor*, he thought, and felt wonderful. No more council meetings, no more wrongheaded citizenry, no more fights over streetlights and bridges, just books and Dillie and pool.

And Sophie. The tension seeped from his muscles and he relaxed. Thank God for Sophie and her stupid fucking movie.

"She's corrupted you," Liz said, almost spitting in her frustration. "She's—"

"Well, it runs in her family," Phin said. "The rest of your grandchildren are going to be half-degenerate."

Liz froze.

Phin nodded at her sympathetically. "Yeah, I have to marry her. I'm sorry, Mom. I know this wasn't what you had planned. Any last words before you disown me?"

Liz swallowed and put on her Let's-be-reasonable-or-I'll-kill-you face. "You can't possibly be serious about marrying her. She's a known pornographer."

Phin nodded. "She beat me at pool, too."

"Oh, dear God," Liz said, and sat down on the step.

Sophie waited in front of the courthouse until Liz came into view. Then she got out of the car and said, "I need to talk to you."

Liz kept on walking. "I have *nothing* to say to you."

"Then I'll go to Wes," Sophie said. "He'll keep it quiet, but it would still be better if we just talked here. You know how this town finds out everything."

Liz stood very still for a long minute, her jaw clenched as she stared at Sophie. "In the car," she said finally. "I'd rather people didn't see us together."

Sophie nodded and got back in the car.

"Talk," Liz said, when she was in the car.

"I want you to stop trying to kill me," Sophie said, and Liz lost her frozen expression.

"What?"

"Somebody's been trying to kill me. And you're the only one in this town who hates me enough to do that."

Liz reached for the door. "That's ridic—"

"I understand. I'd do almost anything to protect my family, too. You want the best for Phin and Dillie, and I'm not it, and that's all right because I'm leaving." Sophie leaned forward, projecting sincerity and sanity. "But you have to stop attacking people, Mrs. Tucker. I think you should get help. I know a wonderful therapist in Cincinnati who is very discreet." Liz gaped at her, and Sophie said, "Look, I'm leaving, but sooner or later somebody else is going to get in your way, and this isn't a good method for handling it."

Liz found her voice. "You really think I'd try to kill you?"

"I think you'd do anything to protect Phin and win the election," Sophie said. "I'm not sure which you think is more important, and I don't like that part of you, but I can understand protecting Phin. Just not that way."

Liz sat back. "Exactly what's been happening to you?"

"Mrs. Tucker—"

"I didn't try to kill you." Liz's voice was so dry and matter-of-fact that Sophie began to have second thoughts. "If I'd wanted to hurt you, I have other ways. I'd never put my family in jeopardy by breaking the law."

"Oh," Sophie said.

"What happened?" Liz repeated, and Sophie hesitated and then told her about the river and the gun under the bed and the gossip and the electricity. "And you thought I'd be that stupid?" Liz said when she was finished. "To try to kill you that sloppily?"

"I knew you hated me that much," Sophie said uncertainly. "I didn't think about stupid."

"Whoever's doing this isn't thinking it through," Liz said. "He's stupid and impulsive."

"Stephen Garvey," Sophie said. "But he doesn't have a reason."

"Stephen wouldn't try to electrocute you." Liz stared into the distance, frowning. "He might push you in a rage, but he wouldn't *plan* to kill you. He's not insane."

"Well, nobody else hates me except for you and him," Sophie said. "I'm generally well-liked. Really."

The silence stretched out, and then Liz said, "No, there's somebody else who hates you."

Sophie swallowed. "Oh?"

"Do you know where Hildy Mallow lives?" Liz asked her. "Drive there."

"The Garveys will be here any minute," Hildy told them when they were sitting on her couch. "I still think this should wait until after the council meeting. Have you seen the water tower? There's so much—"

Her doorbell chimed, and Liz said, "Get it. We do this now." She sounded like Phin, and Sophie wasn't at all surprised when Hildy shut up and went.

Virginia Garvey came in, and Sophie could see past her to Hildy's porch, where Stephen checked his watch, bouncing on his heels in anticipation of his greatest council meeting ever. Virginia said, "Are you ready, Hildy? We're running a little—" and stopped dead when she saw Sophie. "What is she doing here?"

"Shut the door, Hildy," Liz said, and Hildy did, keeping her back against it. "Virginia, did you push Sophie into the river?"

"Liz!" Virginia looked outraged. "What a thing to—"

"I'll be damned," Hildy said. "Of course you did. It would be just like you. Impulsive and dumb as a rock. What did she do, wear white shoes after Labor Day?"

Sophie looked down at her white Keds and pulled her feet back a little.

"Hildy!" Virginia turned from one woman to the other. "This is ridiculous. I don't have to stand here—"

"Actually, you do," Liz said. "You tried to kill Sophie. Twice." The disgust in her voice was plain, and Virginia whipped her head around as if she'd been struck on the raw.

"Don't *you* defend her," she said. "You're on *my* side. You know what she is. If it hadn't been for her, Rachel would be married to Phin—"

"Phin is never going to marry Rachel," Liz said.

"Rachel was going to marry him until *she* showed up," Virginia said. "*She's* the one who introduced Rachel to that man who told her he'd find her a job in *Los Angeles.*" The way Virginia spit the words out, she might have been saying, "Gomorrah," which was fair, Sophie thought. "She's the one who *seduced* Phin away from Rachel."

"I swear to God, he seduced me," Sophie said.

"You think it's funny." Virginia took a step forward, and Sophie sank back a little into the sofa cushions. "You ruined my baby's life. I made sure Phin coached her at softball, I made sure she baby-sat his daughter, I made sure she got a job on the council, *I made sure he was going to marry her.*"

"Oh, Christ," Liz said. "*Virginia.*"

"And then you come in and you take Phin and you tell Rachel she should leave, and she does." Virginia shook with rage. "She called me. She's in *California.* And *it's all your fault.*"

Virginia was breathing hard now, and Sophie tensed to duck if she came after her, no longer doubting that Virginia was the one who'd shoved her into the river. Virginia would have shoved her into Hell if she could have.

Then Virginia got a grip. "But I didn't try to *kill* her," she said to Liz, with a tense little laugh. "That would be . . . insane."

"Exactly," Liz said.

Virginia laughed again, buddies. "Liz, our kind of people don't do that kind of thing."

"There is no kind of people that includes you and me," Liz said. "I always said Stephen married beneath him."

Virginia went white, only two spots of color high on her cheeks.

"Did you push Diane?" Liz said.

Virginia drew herself up. "If I had, it would have been just what she deserved, grabbing your son like that, ruining his life. If I had, you should be thanking me now. But I didn't. Nobody pushed her. She was a slutty little drunk who fell down her own steps."

"Here's what I know," Liz said. "I know you took my husband's gun from my house because you're the only one who visited me there. I know you put it in Sophie's bed because you started the gossip that it had been found. I know you know the farm and could have frayed that wire in the fuse box with no trouble at all."

"That's not proof," Virginia said. "You don't have any proof because I didn't do anything."

"I know you were out there watching with Stephen the night Sophie was pushed in the river," Liz said. "You wouldn't miss something like that. Sophie saw Stephen right before she was pushed—so it couldn't have been him—so you pushed her in, and when that didn't work, you stole my gun and put it in her bed, and when that didn't work you tried to electrocute her. You *are* dumb as a rock, Virginia, but what I still don't know is if you shot that man."

"He met somebody on the river path," Sophie said. "Wes got that far: that Zane had an appointment to meet somebody behind the Garvey house."

"He was trying to blackmail all of us," Hildy said, helpfully. "He must have had something on her."

"He had a file on Diane's death," Liz said. "He brought it to me and tried to convince me she'd been murdered. He said if we didn't stop the video, he'd do a human-interest piece on it, investigate it, solve the mystery, create a scandal. Except I didn't push Diane, and neither did my son, so I sent him away."

"My God," Sophie said, watching Virginia's face. "You did push Diane."

"You just shut up," Virginia said. "You're just like her, but I did *not* push her."

"You met him on the path because he was trying to blackmail you, and you shot him," Liz said. "How did you get him to the farm dock? He would have been heavy. Unless . . ." Liz frowned in thought. "Unless you convinced him to let you take him home." She nodded. "That was it, wasn't it? You told him you'd take care of him and you rowed him across the river, and when he got out onto the dock on his own, then you shot him. You *mothered* him to death. That would be like you. And you got Stephen to cover your car accidents, and me to harass my son about Sophie for you, so you could certainly get that stupid man to travel to his own death."

"You shot him from a boat?" Hildy looked at Virginia with disgust. "That's why you missed at close range and why the angle was so off. You shot him while you were *standing in a boat*. What kind of idiot are you?"

"I have no idea what you're talking about," Virginia said. "But I want you to know I'm deeply hurt by this. And I'm leaving."

She looked deeply enraged, to Sophie.

"Of course, we can't prove any of this," Hildy said gloomily to Liz, as Virginia reached past her to tug at the door.

She's going to get away with it, Sophie thought, and then she saw Liz smile her cobra smile.

"We don't have to prove it," Liz said. "We'll just talk."

"What?" Hildy frowned, and then brightened. "Oh. Yes. We will. We'll talk a lot, Virginia."

Oh, excellent, Sophie thought.

Virginia stopped tugging on the door.

"About how much you hate Sophie," Hildy went on happily. "About how you don't have an alibi for the shooting." Hildy let her eyes slide to Virginia's face. "About how Rachel ran to L.A. to get away from you."

Virginia's face went red. "She didn't. Rachel and I are very close. And—"

"We'll tell everybody what a lousy mother you are," Hildy said. "We don't have to take you to Wes. We're taking care of this ourselves."

"Unless," Liz said.

Virginia turned to her, seething.

"At the council meeting today," Liz said. "We're going to be watching your vote very closely."

"You can't—" Virginia began again.

"Yes, we can." Hildy was practically bouncing on her toes now. "One wrong vote and we hit the phones. And people will listen. They always listen, don't they, Virginia?"

Virginia eyes darted from Hildy to Liz. She looked like a trapped mink, and Sophie would have felt sorry for her if she hadn't been such a miserable excuse for a human being.

"Cross me again and I'll destroy you," Liz said to Virginia. "Don't ever come after my family again."

"I didn't—" Virginia said.

"And that includes Sophie," Liz said.

Sophie felt a catch in the back of her throat.

"Right, that's the other part of the deal," Hildy was saying. "You have to stop trying to kill Sophie. She gets a hangnail, and we pick up the phone."

Virginia drew a deep breath in through her teeth and looked at Sophie like death.

"Don't even think about it," Liz Tucker said. "You touch her, you say one word against her, and I'll bring you so low not even Junie Martin will give you the time of day."

"Jeez," Sophie said.

Liz looked at Sophie for the first time since they'd arrived. "Don't ever cross a Tucker."

"No ma'am," Sophie said.

The council hall was full by the time Phin got there, and the crowd was clearly not a happy one, but only Ed and Frank sat at the council table.

Amy and Sophie came in and sat down in the front row.

" 'This isn't the junior chamber of commerce, Brad,' " Sophie said to Amy.

Amy nodded, looking around at the marble and walnut. " 'Thank goodness we're in a bowling alley.' "

Nervous, Phin thought, and couldn't blame them.

Sophie turned and saw him. She stuck her chin out, and he thought,

Oh, good, still frosty. Then Stephen and Virginia came in followed by Hildy and Liz, and he ignored Sophie to concentrate on the problem at hand.

Stephen looked fat with satisfaction as he stopped to shake hands and nod to the populace, but Virginia looked tense and mad as hell. Hildy detoured around them and plopped down in the seat across from Phin. " 'Fasten your seat belts, it's going to be a bumpy night,' " she said, but she didn't look nervous at all.

"What are you up to?" he said, and she beamed and said, "Oh, I'm going to *enjoy* this."

Phin frowned at her, but then his mother sat down and shook his concentration. She had that look in her eye, the one she got right before she mutilated somebody: implacable will mixed with certainty of triumph.

"Mom?" he said, and she shook her head and said, "It's all right, Phin," and he sat back, wary as hell.

"All right," Phin said. "Now all we need is Rachel and we can get started. Where—"

"She's gone," Virginia said through her teeth, and Stephen looked at her, startled. "That woman—" She broke off as Hildy leaned forward and met her eyes. "She's not here."

"Okay." Phin nodded to Hildy. "Keep the minutes, please."

"Of course," Hildy said. "Although I'm only going to write down the intelligent things, so if anybody here was going to make a stupid speech, he can forget about getting it into the record."

"Hildy," Phin said, and Stephen said, "I don't need the record. I've got the whole town here, or most of it. And the ones that aren't here will hear about it later."

"Don't count on it," Hildy said, and Phin wondered what the hell was happening under his nose. Besides his political ruin.

"The first item of business," Phin said, when they were all settled and the crowd had stilled in anticipation, "is the streetlight vote that Stephen Garvey wants recalled." A soft murmur of disappointment went up from the crowd, and Phin knew how the lions had felt in the Coliseum. "The motion on the floor is from Hildy Mallow, to purchase vintage reproduction streetlights for Temptation. Hildy, do you want to address this again?"

"Just what I've said before," Hildy said. "It makes a difference to people when they're surrounded by beauty. We owe it to Temptation to look to the future."

"Anyone el—"

"But we also owe it to Temptation to be fiscally responsible," Stephen said, and waxed eloquent on fiscal responsibility for five minutes.

Phin tuned him out and felt uneasy. The crowd was restless, but his mother and Hildy sat back, calm. That was wrong. "Anybody else?" Phin said, when Stephen had wound down. "No? Call the roll, Hildy."

"Garvey."

"Certainly not," Stephen said.

"Garvey," Hildy purred, and Virginia turned to look at her.

Across the table from Phin, his mother shook her head and Hildy nodded.

Virginia smiled. "No."

Hildy turned to glare at Liz, who looked taken aback. "We need a little consensus here," Hildy hissed at Liz, who whispered back, "Well, Stephen's convinced people they're too expensive."

The vote split, three to three—Frank voting with Hildy and Ed because fancier streetlights would make his development look better—and Phin broke the tie, saying, "Yes. Let's go with posterity."

"Oh, sure," somebody from the crowd called. "You care about our kids."

"That's progeny," Phin said. "Posterity is your kids' kids."

"Phin," his mother said, and he shrugged.

"New business," he said.

"The water tower," Stephen said, taking him by surprise. "We're going to have to paint it again. It looks ... well, we're just going to have to paint it."

"I like it," Hildy said. "It's not as good as the original color, of course, but if somebody hadn't messed with it before, we wouldn't have this problem now. It's still pretty. Leave it be."

"You want that thing—"

"Can I have a motion?" Phin said.

"I move we paint the water tower *white*," Stephen said, and Virginia started to say, "I second," and then stopped.

"We need a second," Phin said to prod her.

"I second," Frank said. "What's going on here?"

"Call the roll, Hildy," Phin said, before Stephen could get into the water tower as a further corrupter of the town's children.

"Garvey," Hildy said, and Stephen said, "Yes!"

Hildy turned to Liz and whispered audibly, "It does *not* get painted."

"It looks *awful*," Liz hissed back.

"Hildy?" Phin said. "The roll?"

"Garvey," Hildy said, and Virginia looked down the table.

Liz nodded and Hildy shook her head.

"Oh, for crying out loud," Sophie said from behind them, and Liz and Hildy flinched.

The vote split again, and Phin broke the tie by saying, "No, we're not spending any more time or money on the water tower."

"Just what we'd expect from a porn mayor," somebody in the crowd called out, and Phin said to Hildy, "How come you paint it and I get the flack?"

"Because I'm a sweet old lady," Hildy said. "Let's get to it, shall we?"

"Oh, sure," Phin said. "If there's no other new businesses—"

Stephen opened his mouth.

"—I have some. It has come to my attention that this council passed an ordinance that is unenforceable because of the vagaries in its wording."

Hildy blinked at him, and his mother looked alarmed.

Phin said, "I move that the council repeal the antiporn ordinance it voted into effect two weeks ago before we get sued for overstepping somebody's constitutional rights."

The murmur from the crowd sounded angry, but Ed's "I second," cut right across it.

It was the first motion Ed had seconded in thirty years, and Phin looked at him appraisingly.

"Good to see you got your thumb out of your butt, boy," Ed said.

"Thanks, Ed," Phin said. "Discussion?"

"I have discussion," Stephen snapped. "Somebody clearly violated that ordinance—"

"Can't talk about that, Stephen," Hildy said briskly. "We can only talk about the issue on the table."

"It didn't violate anything," Stephen said.

"Yes, it did," Phin said. "You can't make a law against something you can't define. And we didn't define pornography. Therefore the ordinance is unconstitutional. We could get sued. For the protection of the town's treasury, we have to repeal it."

"That is the biggest—"

"I'll call the roll," Hildy said. "Garvey."

"*No,*" Stephen said. "This is—"

"Garvey," Hildy said over him, and turned razorlike eyes on Virginia.

Virginia looked down the table, and raised her eyebrows, as smug as her husband.

And Liz nodded with Hildy.

"Garvey," Hildy repeated viciously.

Virginia swallowed. "Yes."

"What?" Stephen turned on his wife, white-faced. "Have you lost your mind?"

"Virginia votes her conscience, Stephen," Hildy said crisply. "Now stop trying to intimidate a council member. Lutz."

"No," Frank said. "They ruined my life and I want them to pay."

"That's very adult of you, Frank," Hildy said. "Mallow—yes. Tucker."

"Yes," Liz said, and Phin thought, *I have no idea what's going on here, but I like it.*

"Yarnell," Hildy said, and before Ed finished his "yes," she said, "The motion passes."

"That pretty well wraps this up," Phin said, and Stephen said, "Oh, no it doesn't. Somebody showed pornography to our citizens and they should pay."

"And as soon as we find out who switched the tapes, Chief Mazur will arrest him," Phin said. "But until then—"

"What about the people who made the pornography?" Stephen said. "What about the person who *abetted* them? What about—"

"Okay, I've had enough," Sophie said, and Phin turned to see her standing up in the front row in her pink dress, looking like Gidget the Fury.

Don't do this, he thought, going tense in his chair. *We were almost out of here.*

"I can speak, can't I?" she said to Hildy. "As long as it's on the issue?"

"No, you can't," Stephen said, leaning forward to expound at the same time Hildy said, "Sure, go ahead." Hildy turned back to Virginia and said, "Shut your husband up before he violates her freedom of speech."

Virginia stiffened and then said viciously under her breath, "Shut up, Stephen. This is all your fault anyway."

Stephen sat back, stunned, and Phin sympathized. He didn't know what the hell was going on, either.

Sophie cleared her throat, and Phin thought, *Keep it short.* He'd save her from the mob if he had to, but it would be a lot easier if she just apologized and sat down.

"My name is Sophie Dempsey, and I'm responsible for the tape you saw last night." The crowd began to murmur, and Sophie raised her voice. "I'm responsible, because I knew somebody had cut those obscene parts into the beautiful love story we made here, and I didn't destroy that awful tape. And because I didn't destroy it, somebody broke into our farmhouse and stole it and played it to you all last night. That was a horrible thing, an unforgivable thing, but I believe that your police chief will ultimately find out who was to blame. You have a terrific police force here." The majority of the crowd stared back, hostile, but a couple of people nodded, and Amy folded her hands and put two fingers out, smiling to herself.

"So I apologize for my mistake," Sophie went on smoothly. "You see, I love Temptation so much and I feel so safe here, I didn't even lock my doors so it was easy to steal from me. That was stupid of me and I won't make that mistake again."

A couple more people shook their heads at how dumb she'd been, but they looked vaguely sympathetic, and Amy extended three fingers.

"If I could, I'd show you the real tape because Temptation looked wonderful in it, but unfortunately, whoever stole that vile tape to sabotage the premiere, also took everything we had. *Cherished* is gone forever."

Thank God, Phin thought, and kept a wary eye on the crowd.

"However, to make it up to you, my sister and I would be more than happy to tape your next theater performance so that can be shown on your cable channel."

Frank sat up at that, looking vaguely cheerful for the first time in weeks, and Amy looked surprised. She looked down at her hand and extended her fourth finger.

"The most important thing now, though," Sophie said, "is to help the police find the pervert who thought it would be a good idea to show pornography to schoolchildren." Sophie sounded outraged, and Phin wondered if that was real or con. He was pretty sure the rest of it was a con, but at least the populace wasn't trying to lynch her.

"So what I'm asking you all to do, is to think about who has the most to gain from this," Sophie said earnestly, and one or two people began to look interested.

"The mayor did it," the heckler said from the back, and Sophie said, "Why? That would be political suicide, I've even heard some people are so shortsighted that they're talking about not voting for him, but they can't be thinking this through. He'd have to be crazy to play that tape."

"He is," the heckler shouted back, and Sophie said, "No, he isn't, and you should be ashamed of yourself for just shouting things out instead of standing up for what you believe in, the way your mayor does. The people of this town don't like cowards and they don't like cheats, which is why they're not listening to you and why they're going to find out who really did this. The people of Temptation are too smart to fall for this. You're all upset now, but pretty soon you're all going to be asking yourselves the smart question: Who has the most to gain? It's your *civic duty* to ask that question, all of you."

She let the silence hang there, and Phin thought, *Don't look at Stephen, let them get there on their own.*

Sophie nodded. "You all know this town so much better than I do, you'll figure this out, and then I know you'll punish the culprit properly. Thank you." She sat down abruptly, and Phin could see her hands shaking.

Amy held out five fingers and said, "You got everything but the smile."

"I can't work miracles," Sophie said, and Phin thought, *The hell you can't.*

Because she'd made porn, and she was getting away with it. Stephen couldn't get her for it because he'd stolen the tapes, and if he produced them to get her, the townspeople would know he had been responsible for the debacle the night before.

Hell of a woman, his Sophie.

Phin leaned over. "Not bad," he told her, and she lifted her chin, still shaking, and said, "I was magnificent."

"I want to know what she was getting at," Stephen was blustering loudly, and Phin leaned back and said, "No, you don't, that's the last thing you want to know. I declare this meeting adjourned."

Hildy said, "Works for me," and stood up. "You can all go home now," she told the crowd. "Show's over."

"Wait a minute," Stephen said, and Virginia turned to him with loathing.

"This is all your fault, all of it," she told him, and got up and left, leaving her stunned husband behind her.

"Some days are like that, Stephen," Phin said, as he stood up to go.

"Sit down, I want to talk to you," Liz said, and Phin nodded as he watched the crowd. Most of them were still throwing him dirty looks, but one or two looked at Stephen with some curiosity.

Sophie went out with Amy and Hildy, and nobody said anything to her, nasty or otherwise, so she was going to be fine. Better than fine, if he had anything to do with it.

Then Wes came to stand in the doorway and caught his eye, motioning to him as people filed out around him.

"Make this fast," he told his mother as he nodded to Wes. "I have things to do."

Rachel sat by the garden at Leo's house, marveling at where she'd ended up. It looked like paradise. Leo's tiled pool sparkled blue in the sunlight, and there were palm trees, real palm trees, and blooming hibiscus, and up by the hot tub there was a lemon tree that really grew lemons.

She couldn't wait for Sophie to see that. She could pick them right off the tree and make lemonade.

Leo came out and sat down on the chaise next to her, still looking slightly stunned, and handed her a glass of what looked like sludgy orange juice.

"What is this?" Rachel said, looking at it with deep suspicion.

"Vitamin citrus smoothie," Leo said. "Drink it. It's good for you."

Rachel sipped it. It wasn't bad. "It's great." She looked at Leo over the glass. "Thank you."

"I'm going to hell for this," Leo said, and Rachel knew he wasn't talking about the smoothie. "Your father is going to come after me with a shotgun."

"He doesn't have a shotgun," Rachel said. "He has a nice rifle, though." Which he would probably use if he had any idea of the things Leo had done to her in his bedroom. Amazing, the things older men knew.

Not to mention how much longer they lasted.

She grinned again, the silly, satisfied grin that she couldn't keep off her face even though it made her look like a dork. She was in L.A. now. She was supposed to be sophisticated. A producer's mistress wasn't supposed to grin like somebody who'd just had the first great sex of her life.

"Twenty years old." Leo shook his head.

"I am not the first twenty-year-old you've slept with," Rachel said. "Cut me a break. How dumb do you think I am?"

"No, but you're the first twenty-year-old I'm going to marry," Leo said. "How dumb does that make me?"

Rachel straightened. "Marry?"

Leo sighed. "Yeah."

"You're going to marry me?"

"I think it's best for the kids. Especially if one of them's going to be mayor of Temptation someday. You know how those people are."

"Leo." Rachel felt tears come to her eyes, which was ridiculous because she hadn't even realized she wanted to be married. But she did. Her mother would be so happy.

Leo's face softened. "I'll take care of you, Rachel. You'll never be sorry."

Rachel nodded through her tears. "And I'll take care of you, too. You think you don't need it, but you do."

"I'm sure I do," Leo said, patting her hand.

"No, really." Rachel put the smoothie down and went into the house for her bag. When she came back out she said, "I was going to use this to convince you I should have that production job, but now it can be a wedding present. Although I still want that production job."

"You've got it, you've got it." Leo peered in the bag. "What have you got?"

Rachel pulled out a videotape and handed it to him and watched his face go slack with surprise.

"Don't tell me—"

"Yep." She patted his arm. "It's *Cherished*, the last version. I found it in Daddy's car, along with all the other tapes when I threw my bag in the trunk. I called Wes and told him where we left the car so he can find the others, but I knew you'd want this one."

Leo looked at her with wonder. "You're amazing."

Rachel nodded and crawled onto the chaise with him. "I'm beginning to see that. And that's just in Temptation. Imagine what I can do now that we're in L.A."

"Imagine," Leo said, putting his arm around her.

Rachel looked out over the lemon tree and the palm fronds and the hibiscus and thought, *This is all mine. I'm going to be Rachel*

Kingsley. A movie producer. Then she narrowed her eyes at the hibiscus.

"Leo, who weeds this place?" Rachel said.

"The gardener," Leo said.

"Fabulous," Rachel said, and relaxed into her new life.

At roughly the same time, Davy watched Clea come out of SuisseInvest Limited of the Bahamas, cross the street, and slump down onto one of the brightly painted benches that lined the edge of the beach. It had taken her long enough to get the bad news. If he'd thought he had a couple million in a bank somewhere, he wouldn't have dawdled.

She wasn't dawdling now, she was in shock. He was sympathetic. So were any number of men who slowed as they went by her. Time to get a move on. He crossed the street and sat down beside her. "Hey, Clea," he said. "Heard you're broke."

She jerked her head up and then her eyes narrowed. "What are you doing here?"

"Saving your life, which is more than you deserve," Davy said. "In fact, if you didn't have something my sister wants, I'd probably let you rot. You're a fairly miserable human being, you know."

"What are you doing here?" Clea said again.

"That's good. Focus." He put his hands in his pockets and stretched his legs out. "Let's see. You just went into that bank and found out that the bank book you took off Zane's body is for an empty account."

Clea looked around to see if anyone was listening. "I don't know what you're talking about."

"When Zane was fibrillating on the dock," Davy said slowly and distinctly, "you went through his pockets and found the bank book. And then you sat there and watched him die. And I stood on the back porch and watched you do it because I thought the poor son of a bitch was drunk." He felt his anger rise again, that he'd been that stupid, that she'd been that callous. "You can go to jail for that, Clea. It's called 'depraved indifference,' and you could go away for a nice chunk of time."

"You can't prove it," Clea said.

"I can do you a lot of damage," Davy said. "Temptation is the one place on earth where the mayor and the police chief will listen to me." She looked at him with unadulterated loathing and he shrugged. "Do what I tell you to and neither one of us will have to go back there."

Clea flopped back against the bench. "Great. Now I have to sleep with you."

"I wouldn't have you," Davy said, and Clea glared at him. "Okay, it's probably because I already have had you, but I like to think it's also because you're such a cold, conniving, murderous bitch. Pay attention. You're going to sign over the deed to that farmhouse to Sophie."

"No, I'm not," Clea said. "I'm selling it to Frank for three-quarters of a million."

"Sure," Davy said. "Go back to Temptation, explain why you let Zane die, deal with the police and the lawyers, and when you're done, how much of that three-quarters will there be left?"

"More than I'd have if I just give the damn thing to Sophie," Clea said.

"No, you'll have three-quarters of a million if you give it to Sophie," Davy said. "That's how much I'll transfer into an account for you once you send off the deed."

"And where would you get—" Clea began and then she turned on him. "You've got my money!"

"*My* money," Davy said. "It's been mine since the night Zane died and I copied the number and password out of the book in your bedroom while you were talking to the police. One wire transfer, and it was mine."

"How could you do that?" Clea said. "I had the bank book."

"It's not a passbook account, dummy," Davy said. "It's a pass*word* account. All you need is the account number and the password."

Clea looked at him with such venom, he almost moved back. "You son of a bitch."

"This is pretty easy, Clea," Davy said. "You give Sophie the farm, I give you seven hundred and fifty thousand dollars, you use it to find your next rich guy, and everybody lives happily ever after. Hell, you'll probably inherit more from Zane."

"There was a lot more than that in that account," Clea said.

"Sure was."

"I could have had all of that *and* the three-quarters from the farm," she said, and her voice had a vicious edge.

"The key words being 'could have had,' " Davy said. "That was then, this is now, and I'm bored with this conversation. You have one hour to bring me that deed transfer and the number of an account where I can transfer your money. After that, the price drops."

Clea's face smoothed out and became lovely again. "You know . . ." she said, leaning closer.

"Nope," Davy said warily. "I told you. I'm not interested."

"If you really thought I was a murderer, you wouldn't let me go," Clea said, sliding closer to him, and this time Davy did move back. "I know you. I know what you did to Chet in Iowa."

"Chad."

"You'd want me punished," Clea said silkily as she leaned closer. "Want to punish me, Davy?"

"I already did," Davy said flatly. "I took your money." He checked his watch. "Fifty-nine minutes."

"We could have it all," Clea said, putting her hand on his arm. "You and me." She was breathtaking in the sunlight, like human whipped cream.

"No, we couldn't," Davy said, trying to ignore his body's interest. "Sophie wants that farmhouse."

"Sophie?" Clea laughed low. "Sophie's just your sister. I—"

"You'll never get it, will you?" Davy said.

Clea drew back. "What?"

"Family," Davy said. "Strongest force in the world. Even trumps lust. Go get the deed."

Clea looked at him with undisguised malevolence. "This is not over, you bastard."

"Oh, yes it is," Davy said. "Because I'm sure as hell finished with it. Go get the deed."

Clea drew a deep breath and shoved herself off the bench, and Davy watched her stride back to the hotel, magnificent in her fury.

"Actually it doesn't trump lust," Davy said, when she was too far away to hear him. "It just trumps you."

"You're sure I can't talk you out of this?" Sophie said, as Amy threw her suitcase in the backseat with the rest of the camera equipment.

"Positive." Amy came back to the porch steps where Sophie stood. "I really need to just go. And maybe after a couple of months, I'll want to come back. This place has some good stuff in it."

Sophie tried to sound skeptical. "You think the good stuff is just going to sit around and wait until you come back?"

"If he's the good stuff, he will," Amy said. "But I'm not counting on it. He never even made a pass. Three weeks, and he never made a move on me."

"You didn't give him any openings."

"I didn't want to." Amy stepped back. "But he could have made one anyway. And he didn't talk to me today before the council meeting, he just took off to go to the airport for something."

"I'm sure it was important," Sophie said. "Things are a little hectic in Temptation these days."

Amy sighed. "Yeah, but he knows I'm leaving and he went to the airport anyway." She straightened her shoulders. "And I really do want to see L.A. Even if Davy says I'll hate it, I want to see it." She gave Sophie a weak smile. "I'll come back for Thanksgiving. You'll have me and Davy, just like always."

"Good enough," Sophie said, trying not to cry. She hugged Amy good-bye, holding on tight for a minute, and then Amy pulled away to walk to the car without looking back.

"Be *careful*," Sophie called after her, and Amy waved without turning and got in the car, and Sophie realized from the way she bent over the steering wheel that she was crying. "It's okay," she called out to

Amy, "you're doing the right thing. Stay out of bat country. Everything will be fine. Nothing but good times."

Amy nodded. She backed up the convertible and made her U-turn to get out of Temptation, and then she was gone.

This is good, Sophie told herself. *We needed our own lives. This is good.*

She sighed once and then walked through the house and out the back door, letting Lassie out with her this time. "So it's just us," Sophie said, as they walked down the hill. "A girl and her dog." Lassie barked and ran down to the dock, and Sophie followed her and kicked off her shoes to sit on the edge and dangle her feet in the water. The river was still high from the rain, and fast, and it flowed cool and sweet past her ankles.

"So here's the thing, dog," Sophie said. "We're out of a job, living in a house we're going to be evicted from at any minute, deserted by our siblings, discarded by our uptight lover, and with nothing to show for it because a creep of a politician stole all our work." Lassie lay down beside her, evidently overcome by the enormity of it all. "I'm looking for a bright side here, Lassie, I'm looking for a rainbow, but I am not seeing one." Lassie pricked up her ears. "Okay, forget the rainbow. What we need is a plan."

Lassie barked and bounded off the dock, and when Sophie turned around, she saw Dillie on the porch, crouched down to meet the dog, and Phin walking down the slope toward her, looking as perma-pressed as ever in his white shirt and khakis. "Hello," she said, and turned back to the river to get a grip. *Don't throw yourself at him*, she told herself, scrambling for a plan. *At least not for the first five seconds.*

Phin sat down behind her on the dock, and Sophie hugged herself to keep from reaching out and grabbing him. She could smell the sun on his shirt and feel the heat from his arm where it almost touched her.

"I'd have been here sooner, but we were waiting for Amy," Phin said. "Wes caught a ride with her to L.A."

Sophie forgot playing it cool and turned to look at him. "With Amy?"

Phin nodded, staring out over the river. "He's got so much vacation time, he can take it anytime he wants. So I suggested he take six weeks to go with her. He thought it was a good idea, and she didn't seem to mind." He stared out over the river. "It looked like the beginning of a beautiful friendship."

His sleeve brushed her bare arm, and she stifled her sigh and told herself, *Easy.* "Although six weeks is a long time," she said to make conversation, and then she frowned as she thought about it. "That's a really long time. Can Duane handle it that long?"

"No," Phin said. "Wes got somebody else to cover for him." He met her eyes, and his weren't as cool as they should have been. "Can we stop talking about Wes now?"

Sophie swallowed hard and gave up on cool. "Listen, I am really, really, really sorry about the premiere and the election, because we did make porn even though that wasn't our movie—"

"I know," Phin said. "You also helped Rachel elope with Leo, you didn't tell us Davy and Clea skipped, and you did something really vicious to Virginia Garvey. I'd love to know what that was."

He didn't seem angry as he went down her list of sins, and he was sitting awfully close to her just to give her a hard time. Maybe she didn't need a plan after all. "Right. So sue me."

"For what?" Phin said. "You don't have any money."

Sophie stuck her chin in the air. "I'm going to own this farm pretty soon."

"Really." Phin seemed interested. "And how are you going to do that?"

Sophie let her chin drop. "I don't know, exactly. Davy's going to fix it."

"Sure he is."

"Davy's never promised me anything he hasn't delivered," Sophie said. "I believe in Davy."

"As he does in you." Phin shook his head. "But he doesn't have the—" He stopped and she stole a look at him as she felt him straighten. He looked stunned. "Son of a bitch. He's got Zane's money."

Sophie blinked. "I don't think so. He didn't say anything about it."

Phin shook his head. "He's got it."

Sophie thought about it and decided he was right. It would be like Davy to find money and separate it from those who didn't deserve it. "Well, if he has it, I'm glad. At least somebody gets a happy ending out of this mess. Although, I'd be happier if the film we slaved over for a month still existed." *And if you were doing more than just sitting here.* "I still can't believe that lousy Stephen stole the tapes. And now they're gone and he's going to be mayor."

"Oh, you never know," Phin said. "Those tapes could be stashed somewhere, just waiting to be found. Anything can happen."

Sophie looked at him, exasperated. "You know, just once I'd like to see you sweat over something."

Phin scowled at her. "In the past three weeks, you've seen me sweat more than anybody else on the planet, woman."

Sophie waved her hand. "I meant—"

"I even yelled at you last night." Phin eased up. "For which I apologize."

"It was kind of nice," Sophie said. "At least you knew I was there."

"Oh, hell, Sophie, I always know you're there." Phin rolled toward her on one hip, and Sophie felt a flare of hope, but he was just digging something out of his back pocket. "Here." He held out an emerald-cut diamond ring the size of her head. "Marry me, Julie Ann. Ruin the rest of my life."

"Hello." Sophie gaped at the ring. "Jeez, that thing is huge. Where did you get it?"

"My mother gave it to me," Phin said, sounding bemused.

Then the other shoe dropped. "Marry you?" Sophie said, and the sun came out and the birds began to sing and the river sent up a cheer. Marriage was probably out—Liz as a mother-in-law was too terrifying to contemplate, and Phin would never get elected again if he was married to a pornographer—but suddenly everything else was looking pretty good.

Phin was still talking. "After the council meeting, she said, 'If you're going to marry that woman—'"

"'That woman'?" Sophie said. "Oh, gee, the holidays would have been swell."

"—'do it right,' and she took this off her finger, and handed it to me." Phin shook his head. "Surprised the hell out of me. She didn't seem upset about it at all."

"I thought you were never going to speak to me again," Sophie said.

"Then you haven't been paying attention," Phin said. "And the holidays are going to be fine. If I have to put up with Davy, you can put up with my mother. I already told her we'd be using 'I Only Want to Be with You' instead of 'The Wedding March,' and she took that pretty well, too. Concentrate. You want this ring or not?"

It was so gorgeous. Against her better instincts, Sophie took it to hold it up to the sunlight. Amy could have lit the entire house with it. "I don't think I can live up to this ring."

"You don't have any choice," Phin said. "All the Tucker brides get it. I thought I was going to have to ice-pick Mom to get it to you, but she came through after all. There's a question on the table here. Are you going to marry me?"

Sophie looked at the ring again and sighed. "No," she said and handed it back. "But I'll love you forever and you can come sleep with me whenever you want." She stretched to kiss him, so happy that she felt like bouncing.

Phin leaned away from her. "Why not?"

"Because I ruined your reputation," Sophie said. "And because I don't want to live in that damn big house on the Hill, I want to live here. And because we've only know each other three weeks and that's too soon. But I like everything else about you, so I don't see a problem here." She leaned toward him again. "Kiss me, you fool."

Phin shook his head. "My reputation will recover, we can live here, and three weeks is plenty of time when they're like the last ones. I doubt we'll have to survive this much stress again for the rest of our lives."

"You're missing some good stuff here," Sophie said, annoyed that she wasn't getting kissed.

Phin shook his head again. "You don't get me unless you marry me. I have standards. I'm the mayor."

"Only for another six weeks." Sophie pulled back, frowning at him.

"If I'm going to win the election," Phin said patiently, "I can't be cohabitating with a known pornographer. Weddings are popular. A big plus on the election trail."

"What trail?" Sophie gestured to yard. "We're in Temptation. You barely have an election bike path. And if you're really going to try to beat Stephen—"

"I'm not going to *try* to beat Stephen," Phin said, "I'm going to annihilate Stephen." He handed her the ring back. "Put that on and stop playing hard-to-get. God knows, you never have before."

"Hey," Sophie said, but the ring glinted like an arc light, so she held it up again just to see it sparkle.

"You'll like being the mayor's wife," Phin said. "You get to wear the ring all the time. And you can run for city council and torture Stephen."

"Mmmm." Sophie tilted the ring in the sun and watched it glow. It was huge. And politics might be fun. "Stephen's probably not going to be running for council—Stephen's going to be mayor, remember?" Sophie brought the ring into the shadow of their bodies and still it sparkled.

"Wes made Stephen acting police chief while he's gone."

Sophie tore her eyes from the ring. "What? Is he insane? Stephen with unlimited power will drive everybody in town craz—"

She stopped as the beauty of it hit her.

"Dear God. I've underestimated Wes."

"Many do," Phin said. "Will you please say yes, so I can have my last term as mayor *and* unlimited, headbanging sex? I don't think this is too much to ask. I've apologized for being a prick the other night, and I'm giving you a great ring."

"I haven't heard the *L* word, so I'm assuming this is really a political move," Sophie said, and Phin said, "Oh, for crying out loud," and kissed her, and he felt so good against her, his mouth hot against hers, that she kissed him back hard, gripping his shirt for dear life, as Dillie yelled, "Yes!" from the porch.

Phin pulled back and frowned at her. "Are you going to put that ring on? You have to now. Dillie thinks she's getting a mother."

Sophie caught her breath. "You really want to spend the rest of your life with the daughter of a thousand felons?"

"No," Phin said. "I just don't want to spend the rest of my life without you. I'll deal with the felons later. Put the ring on."

"Wait a minute," Sophie said. "Do you love me?"

Phin met her eyes and took her breath away. "More than you'll ever know."

"*Say* it," she said, and he said, "I love you. I'll always love you. Forever. It's a life sentence. Now put the damn ring on."

Sophie leaned against him and closed her eyes because he felt so good. *Don't ever let me go*, she thought, and then she opened her eyes and looked at the ring again. "Excellent." She put it on her finger, working it a little bit because it was tighter than her mother's rings had been and Phin said, "We'll have it resized to fit you."

The ring made her hand look important—heavier, adult. "This is a good ring."

"Try not to lose it," Phin said, his cheek against her hair. "That's pretty much the family fortune right there. That and four thousand *Tucker for Mayor: More of the Same* posters, which are going to be useless. I told my mother I'm finished with being mayor after this election. I have you to thank for that, too." He bent to kiss her again, and Sophie leaned toward him, thinking idly of what they could do with all those posters now that there were no Tuckers left to run—like paper their bedroom with them. *Tucker: More of the Same*, over and over again.

Or . . .

She straightened and bumped Phin's nose with her forehead. "What?" he said.

Four thousand *Tucker for Mayor: More of the Same* posters.

And Phin only had two more years of mayor before he retired in relief to concentrate on the bookstore and pool, which meant Stephen would be mayor then, unless somebody named Tucker stepped into the breach.

Hello.

"What?" Phin said.

She'd have two years to get to know everybody in town. That was only about two thousand people; she could do that. And she could make a difference, she was good at making people do what she wanted. She was born to make people do what she wanted.

"My God," she said, as the full meaning of her family's legacy for lying, cheating, and scheming hit her.

She was born to be a politician.

"Sophie?"

She leaned back against Phin. "I think I'll take your name," she said, smiling up at him sweetly. "Sophie Dempsey Tucker. It sounds . . ." She looked at the ring again. ". . . powerful."

"Why do I have a bad feeling about this?" Phin said, and she said, "Because your life just changed, but it's okay. You can trust me."

She pulled him close, and over his shoulder, she saw Dillie on the edge of the porch, holding the stick of her Dove Bar for Lassie to lick. Behind them, maple trees waved cheerfully in the breeze, cotton clouds bounced across the blue, blue sky, and the early-September sun glowed on everything in sight.

"Nothing but good times ahead," Sophie said, and kissed him.

Bet
Me

For
Monica Pradhan McLean

Because her price is above rubies
Which she knows how to invest,
And because every book she writes
is a diamond

Acknowledgments

My Thanks To

Meg Ruley
for selling this book against my better judgment
and for being right again,

Jen Enderlin
for buying this book against my better judgment
and for being right again,

St. Martin's Press
especially John Sargent, Sally Richardson, Matthew Shear,
Kim Cardascia, John Karle, and John Murphy,
for being supportive beyond the call of publishing
(and a big kiss to Sally for matchmaking the movie option),

Acknowledgments

Mollie Smith
for improving my Web site, organizing my business records,
critiquing my book, and illuminating my life,

Val Taylor
for working with me again
even though I promised her I'd never rewrite this one,

The Ladies of XRom
especially Jo Beverley for coming up with the pumpkin couch,

The Cherries
for critiquing the first scene, researching recipes,
putting up with my moaning, and being Cherries,

and
**The Nantucket Beach Patrol,
Police Department, Fire Department, and
Cottage Hospital Emergency Room Staff,**
whose speed and skill ensured that
this wasn't a posthumous book.
(If you're going to have an asthma attack in the surf,
I strongly recommend you do so in Nantucket.)

Women's total instinct for gambling
is satisfied by marriage.

—Gloria Steinem

Chapter One

*O*nce upon a time, Minerva Dobbs thought as she stood in the middle of a loud yuppie bar, *the world was full of good men.* She looked into the handsome face of the man she'd planned on taking to her sister's wedding and thought, *Those days are gone.*

"This relationship is not working for me," David said.

I could shove this swizzle stick through his heart, Min thought. She wouldn't do it, of course. The stick was plastic and not nearly pointed enough on the end. Also, people didn't do things like that in southern Ohio. A sawed-off shotgun, that was the ticket.

"And we both know why," David went on.

He probably didn't even know he was mad; he probably thought he was being calm and adult. *At least I know I'm furious,* Min thought. She let her anger settle around her, and it made her warm all over, which was more than David had ever done.

Across the room, somebody at the big roulette wheel–shaped bar rang a bell. Another point against David: He was dumping her in a theme bar. The Long Shot. The name alone should have tipped her off.

"I'm sorry, Min," David said, clearly not.

Min crossed her arms over her gray-checked suit jacket so she couldn't smack him. "This is because I won't go home with you tonight? It's Wednesday. I have to work tomorrow. You have to work tomorrow. I paid for my own drink."

"It's not that." David looked noble and wounded as only the tall, dark, and self-righteous could. "You're not making any effort to make our relationship work, which means . . ."

Which means we've been dating for two months and I still won't sleep with you. Min tuned him out and looked around at the babbling crowd. *If I had an untraceable poison, I could drop it in his drink now and not one of these suits would notice.*

". . . and I do think, if we have any future, that you should contribute, too," David said.

Oh, I don't, Min thought, which meant that David had a point. Still, lack of sex was no excuse for dumping her three weeks before she had to wear a maid-of-honor dress that made her look like a fat, demented shepherdess. "Of course we have a future, David," she said, trying to put her anger on ice. "We have *plans*. Diana is getting married in three weeks. You're invited to the wedding. To the rehearsal dinner. To the *bachelor party*. You're going to miss the *stripper*, David."

"Is that all you think of me?" David's voice went up. "I'm just a date to your sister's wedding?"

"Of course not," Min said. "Just as I'm sure I'm more to you than somebody to sleep with."

David opened his mouth and closed it again. "Well, of course. I don't want you to think this is a reflection on you. You're intelligent, you're successful, you're mature. . . ."

Min listened, knowing that *You're beautiful, you're thin* were not coming. If only he'd have a heart attack. Only four percent of heart attacks in men happened before forty, but it could happen. And if he died, not even her mother could expect her to bring him to the wedding.

". . . and you'd make a wonderful mother," David finished up.

"Thank you," Min said. "That's so not romantic."

"I thought we were going places, Min," David said.

"Yeah," Min said, looking around the gaudy bar. "Like here."

David sighed and took her hand. "I wish you the best, Min. Let's keep in touch."

Min took her hand back. "You're not feeling any pain in your left arm, are you?"

"No," David said, frowning at her.

"Pity," Min said, and went back to her friends, who were watching them from the far end of the room.

"He was looking even more uptight than usual," Liza said, looking even taller and hotter than usual as she leaned on the jukebox, her hair flaming under the lights.

David wouldn't have treated Liza so callously. He'd have been afraid to; she'd have dismembered him. *Gotta be more like Liza*, Min thought and started to flip through the song cards on the box.

"Are you upset with him?" Bonnie said from Min's other side, her blond head tilted up in concern. David wouldn't have left Bonnie, either. Nobody was mean to sweet, little Bonnie.

"Yes. He dumped me." Min stopped flipping. Wonder of wonders, the box had Elvis. Immediately, the bar seemed a better place. She fed in coins and then punched the keys for "Hound Dog." Too bad Elvis had never recorded one called "Dickhead."

"I knew I didn't like him," Bonnie said.

Min went over to the roulette bar and smiled tightly at the slender bartender dressed like a croupier. She had beautiful long, soft, kinky brown hair, and Min thought, *That's another reason I couldn't have slept with David*. Her hair always frizzed when she let it down, and he was the type who would have noticed.

"Rum and Coke, please," she told the bartender.

Maybe that was why Liza and Bonnie never had man trouble: great hair. She looked at Liza, racehorse-thin in purple zippered leather, shaking her head at David with naked contempt. Okay, it wasn't just the hair. If she jammed herself into Liza's dress, she'd look like Barney's slut cousin. "*Diet* Coke," she told the bartender.

"He wasn't the one," Bonnie said from below Min's shoulder, her hands on her tiny hips.

"Diet rum, too," Min told the bartender, who smiled at her and went to get her drink.

Liza frowned. "Why were you dating him anyway?"

"Because I thought he might be the one," Min said, exasperated. "He was intelligent and successful and very nice at first. He seemed like a sensible choice. And then all of sudden he went snotty on me."

Bonnie patted Min's arm. "It's a good thing he broke up with you because now you're free for when the right man finds you. Your prince is on his way."

"Right," Min said. "I'm sure he was on his way but a truck hit him."

"That's not how it works." Bonnie leaned on the bar, looking like an R-rated pixie. "If it's meant to be, he'll make it. No matter how many things go wrong, he'll come to you and you'll be together forever."

"What is this?" Liza said, looking at her in disbelief. "Barbie's Field of Dreams?"

"That's sweet, Bonnie," Min said. "But as far as I'm concerned, the last good man died when Elvis went."

"Maybe we should rethink keeping Bon as our broker," Liza said to Min. "We could be major stockholders in the Magic Kingdom by now."

Min tapped her fingers on the bar, trying to vent some tension. "I should have known David was a mistake when I couldn't bring myself to sleep with him. We were on our third date, and the waiter brought the dessert menu, and David said, 'No, thank you, we're on a diet,' and of course, he isn't because there's not an ounce of fat on him, and I thought, 'I'm not taking off my clothes with you' and I paid my half of the check and went home early. And after that, whenever he made his move, I thought of the waiter and crossed my legs."

"He wasn't the one," Bonnie said with conviction.

"You *think?*" Min said, and Bonnie looked wounded. Min closed her eyes. "Sorry. Sorry. *Really* sorry. It's just not a good time for that stuff, Bon. I'm mad. I want to savage somebody, not look to the horizon for the next jerk who's coming my way."

"Sure," Bonnie said. "I understand."

Liza shook her head at Min. "Look, you didn't care about David, so you haven't lost anything except a date to Di's wedding. And I vote we skip the wedding. It has 'disaster' written all over it, even without the fact that she's marrying her best friend's boyfriend."

"Her best friend's *ex*-boyfriend. And I *can't* skip it. I'm the maid of honor." Min gritted her teeth. "It's going to be hell. It's not just that I'm dateless, which fulfills every prophecy my mother has ever made, it's that she's crazy about David."

"We *know*," Bonnie said.

"She tells everybody about David," Min said, thinking of her mother's avid little face. "Dating David is the only thing I've done that she's liked about me since I got the flu freshman year and lost ten pounds. And now I have no David." She took her diet rum from the bartender, said, "Thank you," and tipped her lavishly. There wasn't enough gratitude in the world for a server who kept the drinks coming at a time like this. "Most of the time it doesn't matter what my mother thinks of me because I can avoid her, but for the wedding? No."

"So you'll find another date," Bonnie said.

"No, she won't," Liza said.

"Oh, *thank you*," Min said, turning away from the over-designed bar. The roulette pattern was making her dizzy. Or maybe that was the rage.

"Well, it's your own fault," Liza said. "If you'd quit assigning statistical probability to the fate of a union with every guy you meet and just go out with somebody who turns you on, you might have a good time now and then."

"I'd be a puddle of damaged ego," Min said. "There's nothing wrong with dating sensibly. That's how I found David." Too late, she realized that wasn't evidence in her favor and knocked back some of her drink to ward off comments.

Liza wasn't listening. "We'll have to find a guy for you." She began to scan the bar, which was only fair since most of the bar had been scanning her. "Not him. Not him. Not him. Nope. Nope. Nope. All these guys would try to sell you mutual funds." Then she straightened. "Hello. We have a winner."

Bonnie followed her eyes. "Who? Where?"

"The dark-haired guy in the navy blue suit. In the middle on the landing up by the door."

"Middle?" Min squinted at the raised landing at the entry to the bar. It was wide enough for a row of faux poker tables, and four men were at one talking to a brunette in red. One of the four was David, now surveying his domain over the dice-studded wrought-iron rail. The landing was only about five feet higher than the rest of the room, but David contrived to make it look like a balcony. It was probably requiring all his self-control to keep from doing the Queen Elizabeth Wave. "That's David," Min said, turning away. "And some brunette. Good Lord, he's dating somebody else already." *Get out now*, she told the brunette silently.

"Forget the brunette," Liza said. "Look at the guy in the middle. Wait a minute, he'll turn back this way again. He doesn't seem to be finding David that interesting."

Min squinted back at the entry again. The navy suit was taller than David, and his hair was darker and thicker, but otherwise, from behind, he was pretty much David II. "I did that movie," Min said, and then he turned.

Dark eyes, strong cheekbones, classic chin, broad shoulders, chiseled everything, and all of it at ease as he stared out over the bar, ignoring David, who suddenly looked a little inbred.

Min sucked in her breath as every cell she had came alive and whispered, *This one.*

Then she turned away before anybody caught her slack-jawed with admiration. He was not the one, that was her DNA talking, looking for a high-class sperm donor. Every woman in the room with a working ovary probably looked at him and thought, *This one.* Well, biology was not destiny. The amount of damage somebody that beautiful could do to a woman like her was too much to contemplate. She took another drink to cushion the thought, and said, "He's pretty."

"No," Liza said. "That's the point. He's *not* pretty. David is pretty. That guy looks like an adult."

"Okay, he's full of testosterone," Min said.

"No, that's the guy on his right," Liza said. "The one with the head like a bullet. I bet that one talks sports and slaps people on the back. The navy suit looks civilized with edge. Tell her, Bonnie."

"I don't think so," Bonnie said, her pixie face looking grim. "I know him."

"In the biblical sense?" Liza said.

"No. He dated my cousin Wendy. But—"

"Then he's fair game," Liza said.

"—he's a hit and run player," Bonnie finished. "From what Wendy said, he dazzles whoever he's with for a couple of months and then drops her and moves on. And she never sees it coming."

"The beast," Liza said without heat. "You know, men are allowed to leave women they're dating."

"Well, he makes them love him and then he leaves them," Bonnie said. "That is beastly."

"Like David," Min said, her instinctive distrust of the navy suit confirmed.

Liza snorted. "Oh, like you ever loved David."

"*I was trying to,*" Min snapped.

Liza shook her head. "Okay, none of this matters. All you want is a date to the wedding. If it takes the beast a couple of months to dump you, you're covered. So just go over there—"

"No." Min turned her back on everybody to concentrate on the black and white posters over the bar: Paul Newman shooting pool in *The Hustler*, Marlon Brando throwing dice in *Guys and Dolls*, W. C. Fields scowling over his cards in *My Little Chickadee*. Where were all the women gamblers? It wasn't as if being a woman wasn't a huge risk all by itself. Twenty-eight percent of female homicide victims were killed by husbands or lovers.

Which, come to think of it, was probably why there weren't any women gamblers. Living with men was enough of a gamble. She fought the urge to turn around and look at the beast on the landing again. Really, the smart thing to do was stop dating and get a cat.

"You know she won't go talk to him," Bonnie was saying to Liza. "Statistically speaking, the probable outcome is not favorable."

"Screw that." Liza nudged Min and sloshed the Coke in her glass. "Imagine your mother if you brought that to the wedding. She might even let you eat carbs." She looked at Bonnie. "What's his name?"

"Calvin Morrisey," Bonnie said. "Wendy was buying wedding magazines when he left her. She was writing 'Wendy Sue Morrisey' on scrap paper."

Liza looked appalled. "That's probably why he left."

"Calvin Morrisey." Against her better judgment, Min turned back to watch him again.

"Go over there," Liza said, prodding her with one long fingernail, "and tell David you hope his rash clears up soon. Then introduce yourself to the beast, smile, and don't talk statistics."

"That would be shallow," Min said. "I'm thirty-three. I'm mature. I don't care if I have a date to my sister's wedding. I'm a better person than that." She thought about her mother's face when she got the news that David was history. *No, I'm not.*

"No, you're not," Liza said. "You're just too chicken to cross the room."

"I suppose it might work." Bonnie frowned across the room. "And you can dump him after the wedding and give him a taste of his own medicine."

"Yeah, that's the ticket." Liza rolled her eyes. "Do it for Wendy and the rest of the girls."

He was in profile now, talking to David. *The man should be on coins*, Min thought. Of course, looking that beautiful, he probably never dated the terminally chubby. At least, not without sneering. And she'd been sneered at enough for one night.

"No," Min said and turned back to the bar. Really, a cat was a good idea.

"Look, Stats," Liza said, exasperated, "I know you're conservative, but you're damn near solidifying lately. Dating David must have been like dating concrete. And then there's your apartment. Even your furniture is stagnant."

"My furniture is my grandmother's," Min said stiffly.

"Exactly. Your butt's been on it since you were born. You need a change. And if you don't make that change on your own, *I will have to help you.*"

Min's blood ran cold. *"No."*

"Don't threaten her," Bonnie said to Liza. "She'll change, she'll grow. Won't you, Min?"

Min looked back at the landing, and suddenly going over there seemed like a good idea. She could stand under that ugly wrought-iron railing and eavesdrop, and then if Calvin Morrisey sounded even remotely nice—ha, what were the chances?—she could go up and say something sweet to David and get an intro, and Liza would not have movers come in while she was at work and throw out her furniture.

"Don't make me do this for you," Liza said.

Standing at a roulette wheel bar sulking wasn't doing anything for her. And with all she knew ahead of time, it wasn't likely that he could inflict much damage. Min squared her shoulders and took a deep breath. "I'm going in, coach."

"Do not say 'percent' at any time for the rest of the night," Liza said, and Min straightened her gray-checked jacket and said a short prayer that she'd think of a great pick-up line before she got to the landing and made a fool of herself. In which case, she'd just spit on the beast, push David over the railing, and go get that cat.

"Just so there's a plan," she said to herself and started across the floor.

Up on the landing, Cal Morrisey was thinking seriously about pushing David Fisk over the railing. *I should have moved faster when I saw them coming*, he thought. It was Tony's fault.

"You know, that redhead has great legs," Tony had said. "See her? At the bar, in the purple with the zippers? You suppose she likes football players?"

"You haven't played football in fifteen years." Cal had sipped his drink, easing into an alcohol-tinged peace that was broken only slightly when somebody with no taste in music played "Hound Dog." As far as he was concerned the only two drawbacks to the place were the stupid décor and the fact that Elvis Presley was on the jukebox.

"All right, it's been a while since I played, but she doesn't know that." Tony looked back at the redhead. "I got ten bucks says she'll leave with me. I'll use my chaos theory line."

"No bet," Cal said. "Although that is a terrible line, so that would shorten the odds." He squinted across the room to the roulette wheel bar. The redhead was flashy, which meant she was Tony's type. There was a little blonde there, too, the perky kind, their friend Roger's dream date. Behind the bar, Shanna saw him watching and waved, but she didn't smile, and Cal wondered what was up as he nodded to her.

Tony put his arm around Cal. "Help me out here, she's in a group. You go over and pick up her chubby friend in the gray-checked suit, and Roger can hit on the short blonde. I'd give you the short blonde, but you know Roger and midget women."

Roger jerked to attention at Cal's elbow. "What? What short blonde?" He peered across the room at the bar. "Oh. *Oh.*"

"Suit?" Cal looked back at the bar.

"The one in gray." Tony nodded toward the bar. "Between the redhead and the mini-blonde. She's hard to see because the redhead sort of dazzles you. I bet you—"

"Oh." Cal squinted to see the medium-height woman between the redhead and the blonde. She was dressed in a dull, boxy, gray-checked suit, and her round face scowled under brown hair yanked back into a knot on the top of her head. "Nope," he said and took another drink.

Tony smacked him on the back and made him choke. "Come on, live a little. Don't tell me you're still pining for Cynthie."

"I never pined for Cynthie." Cal glanced around the crowd. "Keep an eye out for her, will you? She's in that red thing she wears when she's trying to get something."

"She can get it from me," Tony said.

"Great." Cal's voice was fervent. "I'll even go pick up that suit if you'll marry Cyn."

Tony choked on his drink. "Marry?"

"Yes," Cal said. "She wants to get married. Surprised the hell out of me." He thought for a moment of Cynthie, a sweetheart with a spine of steel. "I don't know where she got the idea we were that close."

"There she is." Roger was looking over Cal's shoulder. "She's coming up the stairs now."

Cal got up and tried to move past Tony to the door. "Out of my way."

Tony stayed in his chair. "You can't leave, I want the redhead."

"So go get her," Cal said, trying to get around him.

"Cynthie's got David with her," Roger said, and there was great sympathy in his voice.

"Cal!" David's voice grated over Cal's shoulder. "Just who we were looking for." He sounded mad as hell, but when Cal turned, David was smiling.

Trouble, Cal thought and smiled back with equal insincerity. "David. Cynthie. Great to see you."

"Hello, Cal." Cynthie smiled up at him, her heart-shaped face lethally lovely. "How've you been?"

"Great. Couldn't be better. You, too, looking great." Cal looked past her to David, and thought, *Take her, please.* "You're a lucky man, David."

"I am?"

"Dating Cynthie," Cal said, putting all the encouragement he could into his voice.

Cynthie took David's arm. "We just ran into each other." She turned her shoulder to Cal and glowed up at David. "But it is nice seeing him again." Her eyes slid back to Cal's face, and he smiled past her ear again, radiating no jealousy at all as hard as he could.

David looked down into her beautiful face and blinked, and Cal felt a stab of sympathy for him. Cynthie was enchanting up close. And from far away. From everywhere, really, which was how he'd ended up saying yes to her all the time. Cal glanced at her impeccably tight little body in her impeccably tight little red dress and then took a step back as he jerked his eyes away, reminding himself of how peaceful life was without her. Distance, that was the key. Maybe a cross and some garlic, too.

"Of course," David was saying. "Maybe we can do dinner later." He glanced at Cal, looking triumphant.

"Well, don't let us keep you." Cal took another step back and bumped into the railing.

Cynthie let go of David's arm, her glow diminished. "I'll just freshen up before we go." Tony and David watched as her perfect rear end swung away from them, while Roger ignored her to peer across the room at the pixie blonde, and Cal took another healthy swallow of his drink and wished he were somewhere else. Anywhere else. Dinner, for example. Maybe he'd stop by Emilio's and eat in the kitchen. There were no women in Emilio's kitchen.

"So, David," Tony was saying. "How'd our seminar work out for you?"

"It was terrific," David said. "I didn't think anybody could teach some of those morons that new program, but everybody at the firm is now up to speed. We've even . . ."

He went on and Cal nodded, thinking that one of the many reasons he didn't like David was his tendency to refer to his employees as morons. Still, David paid his bills on time and gave credit where it was due; there were much worse clients. And if he took over Cynthie, Cal was prepared to feel downright warm toward him.

David wound down on whatever it was he'd been saying and looked toward the stairs. "About Cynthie. I thought that you and she—"

"No." Cal shook his head with enthusiasm. "She left me a couple of months ago."

"Isn't it usually the other way around?"

David arched an eyebrow and looked ridiculous. And still women went out with him. Life was a mystery. So were women.

"Aren't you supposed to be the guy who never strikes out?" David said.

"No," Cal said.

"He's losing his edge," Tony said. "I found an easy pickup for him, and he said no."

"Which one?" David said.

"The gray-checked suit at the bar." Tony motioned with his glass, and David looked at the bar and then turned back to Cal, smooth as ever.

"Maybe you *are* losing it." David smiled at him. "She shouldn't be that hard to get. It's not like she's a Cynthie."

"She's all right," Cal said, cautiously.

David leaned in. "After all, nobody says no to you, right?"

"What?" Cal said.

"I'm willing to bet you that you can't get her," David said. "A hundred bucks says you can't nail her."

Cal pulled back. *"What?"*

David laughed, but there was an edge to his voice when he spoke. "It's just a bet, Cal. You guys love risk, I've seen you bet on damn near everything. This isn't even that big a bet. We should make it two hundred."

That was when Cal had contemplated giving David a healthy push. Tony turned his back to David and mouthed, *Humor him*, and Cal sighed. There must be something he could ask for that would make David back down. "That baseball in your office," he said. "The one in the case."

"My Pete Rose baseball?" David's voice went up an octave.

"Yeah, that one. That's my price." Cal slugged back the rest of his scotch and looked around for a waitress.

David shook his head. "Not a chance. My dad caught that pop-up for me in seventy-five. But I like your style, upping the stakes like that." He leaned in closer. "Tell you what. The last refresher seminar you ran for us set me back ten grand. I'll bet you ten thousand in cash against a free seminar—"

Cal forced a smile. "David, I was kidding—"

"But for ten thou, you have to get her into bed. I'll play fair. I'll give you a month to get her out of that gray-checked suit."

"Piece of cake," Tony said.

Cal glared at Tony. "David, this isn't my kind of bet."

"It's *my* kind," David said, drawing his brows together, and Cal thought, *Hell, he's going to push this, and we need his business.*

Okay, clearly booze had shut down David's brain. But once it was back up and working again, David would back down on the ten thousand, that was insane, and David was never insane about money. So all he had to do was stall until David sobered up and then pretend the whole thing never happened. He stole a glance across the room to the bar and was delighted to see that the gray suit had disappeared some time during their conversation.

Cal turned back to David and said, "Well, I would, David, but she's gone." *And God bless you, gray suit, for leaving,* he thought and picked up his drink again.

Things were finally going his way.

Min had walked across the room, telling herself that it was a real toss-up as to which would be worse, trying to talk to this guy or enduring

Di's wedding unescorted. When she neared the landing, she edged her way under the rail, catching faint snatches of conversations as she went, not stopping until she heard David's voice faintly above her, saying, "But for ten, though, you have to get her into bed."

What? Min thought. It was noisy up there by the door, maybe she hadn't heard him—

"I'll play fair," David went on. "I'll give you a month to get her out of that gray-checked suit."

Min looked down at her gray-checked suit.

"Piece of cake," somebody said to David, and Min thought, *Son of a bitch, the world is full of sex-crazed bastards*, and forced herself to move on before she climbed the railing and killed them both.

She headed back to Liza and Bonnie, fuming. She knew exactly what David was up to. He assumed she wouldn't sleep with anybody because she'd turned him down. She'd warned him about that, about the rash assumptions he made, but instead of taking her advice, he'd kept asking her out.

Because he thought I was a sure thing, she realized. Because he'd looked at her and thought, *Overweight smart woman who'll never cheat on me and will be grateful I sleep with her.* "Bastard," she said out loud. She should have sex with Calvin Morrisey just to pay David back. But then she'd have no way of getting even with Calvin Morrisey. God, she was dumb. Fat and dumb, there was a winning combo.

"What's wrong?" Liza said when she was back at the bar. "Did you ask him?"

"No. As soon as you finish your drinks, I'm ready to go." Min turned back to the balcony and caught sight of them, just as they caught sight of her.

David's face was smug, but Calvin Morrisey clutched his drink and looked like he'd just seen Death.

"There she is," David crowed. "I told you she'd be back. Go get her, champ."

"Uh, David," Cal began, consigning the gray-checked suit to the lowest circle of hell.

"A bet's a bet."

Cal put his empty glass down on the rail and thought fast. The suit did not look happy, so the odds weren't impossible that she'd go for a chance to get out of the bar if he offered dinner. "Look, David, sex is not in the cards. I'm cheap, but I'm not slimy. You want to bet ten bucks on a pickup, fine, but that's it. Nothing with a future."

David shook his head. "Oh, no, I'll bet on the pickup, too, ten bucks if you leave with her. But the ten thousand is still on. If you *lose* . . ." He smiled at Cal, drawing out the 'lose,' "you do a seminar for me for free."

"David, I can't make that bet," Cal said, trying another tack. "I have two partners who—"

"I'm good for it," Tony said. "Cal never misses."

Cal glared at him. "Well, *Roger* isn't good for it."

"Hey, Roger, you in?" Tony said, and Roger said, "Sure," without looking away from the blonde at the bar.

"*Roger*," Cal said.

"She's the prettiest little thing I've ever seen," Roger said.

"Roger, you just bet that I could get a woman into bed," Cal said with great patience. "Now tell David you don't want to bet a ten-thousand-dollar refresher seminar on sex."

"What?" Roger said, finally looking away from the blonde.

"I said—" Cal began.

"Why would you bet on something like that?" Roger said.

"That's not the question," Tony said. "The question is, can he do it?"

"Sure," Roger said. "But—"

"Then we have a bet," David said.

"No, we do not," Cal said.

"You don't think you can do it," David said. "You're losing it."

"This is not about me," Cal said, and then Cynthie slid back into the group and put her hand on his arm. She leaned into him, and he felt his blood heat right on cue.

"She's over there waiting for you," David said, an edge in his voice.

"She?" Cynthie's glow dimmed. "Are you seeing somebody?"

Oh, hell, Cal thought.

"Cal?" David said.

"Cal?" Cynthie said.

"I *love* this," Tony said.

"What?" Roger said.

Cal sighed. It was the suit or Cynthie, the rock or the soft place who wanted to get married. He detached her hand from his arm. "Yes, I'm seeing somebody. Excuse me."

He pushed past Cynthie and David and headed for the bar, wishing them both the worst fate he could think of, that they'd end up together.

Min watched Calvin Morrisey move toward the stairs. The beast. He thought that he could get her in a month, that she was so pathetic she'd just—

Her brain caught up with her train of thought, and she straightened.

"Will you tell us what's wrong?" Liza said.

"A month," Min said.

He walked down the steps and made his way through the crowd, ignoring the come-hither looks of the women he passed.

He was coming to pick her up.

Suppose she let him.

Suppose for the next three weeks she made him pay by stringing him along and then took him to Di's wedding. He wouldn't leave her; he had to stick for a month to win his damn bet. All she had to do was say no to sex for three weeks, drag him to her sister's wedding, and then leave his ass cold.

Min settled back against the bar and examined the idea from all sides. He more than deserved to be tortured for three weeks. And in that three weeks she could figure out a way to make David suffer, too. And her mother would have somebody beautiful to point out to people at the wedding as her date. It was a plan, and as far as she could see, it was all good.

The bartender came back and Min said, "Rum and Diet Coke, please. A double."

"That's your third," Liza said. "And fourth. The aspartame alone will make you insane. What are you doing?"

"Was he mean to you?" Bonnie said. "What happened?"

"I didn't talk to him." Min waved them away. "Move down the bar a couple of feet will you. I'm about to get hit on and you're cramping my style."

"We missed something," Liza said to Bonnie.

"Move," Bonnie said, and pushed Liza down the bar.

Min turned away when the bartender brought her drink, so when The Beast spoke from beside her, she jerked her head up and caught the full force of him unprepared: hot dark eyes, perfect cheekbones, and a mouth a woman would betray her moral fiber to bite into. Her heart kicked up into her throat, and she swallowed hard to get it back where it belonged.

"I have a problem," he said, and his voice was low and smooth, warm enough to be charming, rich enough to clog arteries.

Dark chocolate, Min thought and looked at him blankly, keeping her breathing slow. "Problem?"

"Well, usually my line is 'Can I buy you a drink?' but you have one." He smiled at her, radiating testosterone through his expensive suit.

"Well, that is a problem." She started to turn away.

"So what I thought," he said, his voice dropping even lower as he leaned closer to her and made her heart pound, "was that we could go somewhere else, and I could buy you dinner."

The closer he got, the better he looked. He was the used car salesman of seducers, Min decided, trying to get her distance back. You could never get a good deal from a used car salesman; they sold cars all the time and you only bought a couple in a lifetime so they always won. Statistically speaking, you were toast before you walked on the lot. She could only imagine how many women this guy had mutilated in his lifetime. The mind boggled.

His smile had disappeared while he waited for her answer, and he looked vulnerable now, taking a chance on asking her out. He faked vulnerable very well. *Remember,* she told herself, *the son of a bitch is doing this for ten bucks.* Actually, he was trying to do *her* for ten bucks.

Cheapskate. Suddenly, breathing normally was not a problem.

"Dinner?" she said.

"Yes." He bent still closer. "Somewhere quiet where we can talk. You look like someone with interesting things to say. And I'm somebody who'd like to hear them."

Min smiled at him. "That's a terrible line. Does it usually work for you?"

He froze for a second, and then he segued from sincere to boyish again. "Well, it has up till now."

"It must be your voice," Min said. "You deliver it beautifully."

"Thank you." He straightened. "Let's try this again." He held out his hand. "I'm Calvin Morrisey, but my friends call me Cal."

"Min Dobbs." She shook his hand and dropped it before it could feel warm in her grasp. "And my friends would call me foolhardy if I left this bar with a stranger."

"Wait." He got out his wallet and pulled out a twenty. "This is cab fare. If I get fresh, you get a cab."

Liza would take the twenty and then dump him. There was a plan, but Liza didn't need a wedding date. What else would Liza do? Min plucked the twenty from his fingers. "If you get fresh, I'll break your nose." She folded the twenty, unbuttoned her top two blouse buttons, and tucked the bill into the V of her sensible cotton bra so that only a thin green edge showed. That was one good thing about packing extra pounds, you got cleavage to burn.

She looked up and caught his eyes looking down, and she waited for him to make some comment, but he smiled again. "Fair enough," he said, "let's go eat," and she reminded herself to ignore what a beautiful mouth he had since it was full of forked tongue.

"First, promise me no more lame lines," she said, and watched his jaw clench.

"Anything you want," he said.

Min shook her head. "Another line. I suppose you can't help it. And free food is always good." She picked up her purse from the bar. "Let's go."

She walked away before he could say anything else, and he followed her, past a dumbfounded Liza and a delighted Bonnie, across the floor and up onto the landing by the door, and the last thing she saw as they left was David looking outraged.

The evening was turning out *much* better than she'd expected.

Chapter Two

Liza scowled at the empty doorway. This was not good. When Calvin Morrisey came back in and spoke to David for a moment, it didn't get better.

"Do you suppose it was the booze?" Bonnie asked.

Liza thought fast. "I don't know what it was, but I don't like it. Why was he hitting on her?"

Bonnie frowned. "It's not like you to be jealous."

"I'm not jealous." Liza transferred her scowl to Bonnie. "Think about it. Min sends out no signals, he's never talked to her so he can't know how great she is, and she's dressed like a nun with an MBA. But he crosses a crowded bar to pick her up—"

"It's possible," Bonnie said.

"—right after he's talked to David," Liza finished, nodding to the landing where a red-faced David was now moving in on the brunette.

"Oh." Bonnie looked stricken. "Oh, no."

"There's only one thing we can do." Liza squared her shoulders. "We've got to find out what Calvin the Beast is up to."

"How—"

Liza nodded at the mezzanine. "He was with those two guys. Which one do you want, the big dumb-looking blond or the bullet head?"

Bonnie followed her eyes to the landing and sighed. "The blond. He looks harmless. The bullet head looks like all hands, and I'm not up to that tonight."

"Well, I am." Liza put her drink on the bar and leaned back. The bullet head was looking right at her. "The last time I saw a brow that low I was watching slides in anthropology class." She met his stare dead on for a full five seconds. Then she turned back to the bar. "Two minutes."

"It's a crowded room, Lize," Bonnie said. "Give him three."

David had watched Cal open the street door for Min and felt a flare of jealous rage. It wasn't that he wanted to kick Cal. He always wanted to kick Cal. The guy never broke a sweat, never made a bad business move, never lost a bet, and never hit on a woman and missed. *Your therapist warned you about this*, he told himself, but he knew it wasn't just his need to be first in everything. This time the jealousy had an extra twist.

This time Cal had taken Min. Min who was good, solid wife material except for that stubborn streak which he could have worn down, she'd have come back eventually. But now—

He stiffened as Cal came back through the door and motioned him over.

"We're going to dinner," Cal said, holding out his hand. "Ten bucks."

He sounded mad, which made David feel better as he took out his wallet and handed Cal the ten.

"Smart move not tipping me that she hates men," Cal said.

Then he was gone, and David went back to the railing and said, "I think I just made a mistake."

"You, too?" Cynthie said, her voice sad over her martini glass.

David glanced at the door. "So it wasn't your idea to break up with Cal?"

"No." Cynthie stared at the door. "I thought it was time to get married, so I said, 'Now or never.'" She smiled tightly up at David. "And he said, 'Sorry.'" She drew in a deep breath and David tried not to be distracted by the fact that she was braless under her red jersey dress.

"That's lousy." David leaned against the rail so he couldn't look down her dress since that would be crass, something Cal Morrisey would do. "Cal must be a moron."

"Thank you." Cynthie turned back to watch the bar as Tony got up from the next table and walked down the stairs with Roger following. Her hair moved like TV hair, a dark silky fall that brushed her shoulders. "I'd love to know how Cal met that woman. I could have sworn he wasn't dating anybody."

David considered telling her that Cal had picked up Min because of the bet and then thought, *No.* The bet had not been his finest hour. In fact, for the life of him, he couldn't think why he'd done it, it was as if some malignant force had whispered in his ear. No, it was Cal's fault, that's what it was, and it was a disaster because if Min ever found out he'd made that bet . . .

"Do you know her?" Cynthie said.

"She's my ex-girlfriend."

"Oh." Cynthie put her drink down. "Well, I hope Cal's sorry he picked her up. I hope he realizes what he's lost once he gets her back to his place."

"They're not going back to his place," David said. "She won't." Cynthie waited, and he added, "She doesn't like sex."

Cynthie smiled.

David shrugged. "At least, she wouldn't try it in the two months we were together. So I ended it."

Cynthie shook her head, still smiling. "You didn't give the relationship enough time. What does she do for a living?"

David stiffened at the criticism. "She's an actuary. And it strikes me that *two months—*"

"David," Cynthie said, "if you wanted sex in the first five minutes, you should have dated a stripper. If she's an actuary, she's a cautious person, her career is figuring out how to minimize risk, and in your case, she was right."

David began to dislike Cynthie. "How was she right?"

"You left her over sex." Cynthie leaned forward, and David pretended not to watch her breasts under the jersey. "David, this is *my* specialty. If you loved her, you wouldn't have given her an ultimatum over sex."

"What is it you do?" David said, coldly.

"I'm a psychologist." Cynthie picked up her drink, and David remembered some of the gossip he'd heard.

"You're the dating guru," he said, warming to her again. She was practically a celebrity. "You've been on TV."

"I do guest spots," Cynthie said. "My research on relationships has been very popular. And all of it tells me you do not give an ultimatum over sex."

"You gave Cal one."

"Not over sex," Cynthie said. "I'd never deny him sex. And it wasn't an ultimatum, it was strategy. We'd been together nine months, we were past infatuation and into attachment, and I knew that all he needed was a physiological cue to make him aware of his true feelings."

"That makes no sense at all," David said.

Cynthie smiled at him without warmth. "My studies have shown that the process of falling into mature love happens in four steps." She held up one finger. "When you meet a woman, you subconsciously look for cues that she's the kind of person you should be with. That's assumption." She held up a second finger. "If she passes the assumption test, you begin to get to know her to find out if she's appropriate for you. If she is, you're attracted." She held up a third finger. "If, as you get to know her, the attraction is reinforced with joy or pain or both, you'll fall into infatuation. And . . ." She held up her fourth finger. "If you manage to make a connection and attach to each other during infatuation, you'll move into mature, unconditional love."

"That seems a little clinical," David said, faking interest. After all, she was almost a celebrity.

"That doesn't mean it's wrong," Cynthie said. "Take assumption. Your subconscious mind scans women and picks out those that meet your assumptions about the kind of woman you're attracted to."

"I like to think I'm not close-minded," David said.

"Which is why I'm surprised Cal picked up your Min." Cynthie sipped her drink. "One of his assumptions is that his women will be beautiful."

"I always thought Cal was shallow," David said, and thought, *He picked her up for the bet, the bastard.*

"He's not shallow at all," Cynthie said. "Since they've passed assumption, they'll now subconsciously gauge attraction. For example, if they fell into step when they left the bar, that could be a strong psychological hint that they're compatible." She frowned. "I wish we could watch them at dinner."

"And see what?" David said, picking up his drink again. "Them eating in unison?"

"No," Cynthie said. "If they mirror each other in action, both crossing their legs the same way, for example. If she accepts his touch with pleasure. If they exchange a copulatory gaze."

David choked on his drink.

"It's a look that's held a few seconds too long," Cynthie said. "It's a clear sexual signal. All species do it."

David nodded and reminded himself not to stare in the future.

"If their conversation picks up a rhythm with no long silences, that will be attractive. If they develop enough of a relationship to use nicknames."

"Min hates nicknames," David said, remembering a disastrous "honey bun" incident.

"If they have the same tastes in music or film. If they establish shared secrets or private jokes. If they value the same things. Is Min self-employed?"

"No," David said. "She works for Alliance Insurance. Her father is a vice president there."

Cynthie's smile curved across her beautiful face. "Excellent. Cal likes to gamble, so he admires people who take risks. That's why he refused to go into his father's business and started his own company instead. He's not going to be impressed by somebody who's riding her father's coattails. He'll think she's dull."

"That's good," David said. *The superficial bastard.*

Cynthie nodded over her glass. "Even her attitude will make a difference. Someone who likes you and likes being with you is attractive." She looked woebegone for a moment. "And of course your Min will be delighted to be with him."

"No, she isn't," David said, feeling better. "She's mad at all men right now because I broke things off with her. And she's got a sharp tongue."

Cynthie brightened. "So he'll combine her bad temper with his analysis of her as someone who's too conservative. This is sounding very good, David. Will she let him pay for dinner?"

David shook his head. "Min insists on going Dutch. She's a very fair woman."

"Every species has a dinner date as part of courting ritual," Cynthie said. "A woman who won't let you pay for dinner is rejecting your courtship. She may think she's playing fair, or that she's being a feminist, but at a very deep level, she knows that she's crossing you off her list of possibilities."

"She won't let him pay," David said, rethinking his stance on that. When Min came back, he was going to pay for dinner.

"So they'll fight over the check. That's wonderful." She sat back, her face relaxed for the first time. "From what you've told me about her, Cal is already regretting asking her to leave with him."

"That's good," David said, cheering up at the thought.

Cynthie's smile wavered. "So did you want to go to dinner, or did you ask me out just to make Cal mad?"

Dinner. If he took Cynthie to dinner, Tony and Roger would tell Cal he and Cynthie had hooked up. That would serve Cal right. He could walk off with the hot brunette who'd dumped the legendary Calvin Morrisey. He'd win.

He put his drink down. "I asked because I wanted to have dinner with you."

Cynthie smiled and he was dazzled. Cal was a fool for letting this woman go.

"And you can tell me more about Min," Cynthie said.

"Of course," David said.

All about Min. Nothing about the bet.

Min had waited outside while the beast went back in to retrieve whatever he'd forgotten—his morals, maybe—and the cool air of the June night cleared her head and her anger a little. The bar was on one of her favorite streets, full of funky little shops and restaurants and a great revival theater, and a gentle breeze blew through the skinny trees that struggled to grow in their iron cages along the street edge. For a moment, Min watched the trees and thought, *I know just how you feel.* Well, she didn't know the skinny part. But the trapped? Yep.

Because she was stuck, no doubt about it. Stuck dateless in a stupid bridesmaid's dress for her sister's wedding to a dweeb with her mother sighing at her. Because the truth was, she wasn't going to be able to play somebody like Cal Morrisey for three weeks. It had been a dumb, dumb idea, fueled by rum and rage. For a moment, she wished that she was back in her attic apartment, curled up on her grandmother's old pumpkin-colored sofa, listening to Elvis's *Moody Blue* album. Maybe she wasn't the type to date, maybe she should just give in to her well-upholstered genes and become a kindly maiden aunt to Diana's inevitable offspring. It wasn't as if she wanted kids of her own. And what other purpose did men serve? Well, sex, but look how they acted about that. Honestly—

A cell phone rang behind her, and she started. When she turned, it was Calvin Morrisey, back again. He reached in his jacket and took out his phone, the kind that had more bells and whistles than any human being needed, and it confirmed her decision: There was no way in hell she was going to spend three weeks with a soulless yuppie just to get a date to Diana's wedding. She'd go Dutch on dinner and then say goodbye forever; *that* was a plan.

She crossed her arms and waited for him to impress her with a business call, but he turned the phone off.

Min raised her eyebrows. "What if it's important?"

"The only person I want to talk to is here," he said, smiling that *GQ* smile at her.

"Oh, for crying out loud," Min said. "Can you turn that off, too?"

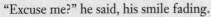

"Excuse me?" he said, his smile fading.

"The constant line." Min began to walk again. "You've got me for dinner. You can relax now."

"I'm always relaxed." He caught up to her in one stride. "Where are we going?"

Min stopped, and he walked a step past her before he caught himself.

"The new restaurant that everybody's talking about is this way. Serafino's. Somebody I used to know says the chef is making a statement with his cuisine." She thought of David and looked at Cal. Two of a kind. "I assumed that'd be your style. Did you have someplace else in mind?"

"Yes." He put one finger on her shoulder and gave her a gentle push to turn her around, and Min shrugged off his touch as she turned. "My restaurant's that way," he said. "Never go any place the chef is trying to talk with food. Unless you want Ser—"

"Nope." Min turned around and began to walk again. "I want to check out your taste in restaurants. I'm assuming it'll be like your taste in cell phones: very *trendy*."

"I like gadgets," he said, catching up again. "I don't think it's a comment on the real me."

"I've always wanted to do a study on cell phones and personality," Min lied as they passed the Gryphon theater. "All those fancy styles and different covers, and then some people refuse to carry them at all. You'd think—"

"Yours is black," he said. "Very practical. Look out for the glass." He reached to take her arm to steer her around a broken beer bottle, but she detoured on her own, rotating away from him.

He looked at her feet and stopped, probably faking concern, and she stopped, too. "What?"

"Nice shoes," he said, and she looked down at her frosted-plastic open-toed heels tied with floppy black bows.

"Thank you," she said, taken aback that he'd noticed.

"You're welcome." He put his hands in his pockets and started walking again, lengthening his stride.

"But you're wrong." Min took a larger step to catch up. "My cell phone is not black. It's green and it's covered in big white daisies."

"No, it's not." He was walking ahead of her now, not even pretending to keep pace with her, and she broke into a trot until she was even with him. "It's black or silver with a minimum of functions, which is a shame because you never know when you're going to get stuck somewhere and need a good poker game."

When she glanced up at him, he looked so good that she stopped again to make him break stride. The key was to keep him off balance, not gape at his face, especially when he was being so annoyingly right about her black cell phone. "I beg your pardon," she said stiffly, folding her arms again. "I know what my cell phone looks like. It has daisies on it. And I know I'm wearing a suit, but that doesn't mean I'm boring. I'm wearing scarlet underwear."

"No, you aren't." His hands were still in his pockets, and he looked big and broad and cocky as all hell.

"Well, with that kind of attitude, you'll never find out," Min said and walked on until she realized he wasn't following her. She turned back and saw him watching her. "Uh, dinner?"

He ambled toward her while she waited for him, and when he was beside her again, he leaned down and said, "I will bet you ten dollars that your cell phone does not have daisies on it."

"I don't gamble," Min said, trying not to back up a step.

"Double or nothing you're wearing a plain white bra."

"If you think I'm that boring, what are you doing with me?"

"I saw the bra when you put the twenty in it. And you have conservative taste, so there's no way you have a phone with daisies on it. The only exciting thing about you is your shoes."

Ouch. Min scowled. "Hey—"

"And what I'm doing with you," he said, clearly at the end of his patience, "is trying to take you to a great restaurant, which is just up ahead, so if we could call a truce until we're there—"

Min started to walk again.

"No bet?" he said from behind her.

"No bet." Min walked faster, but he caught up with her anyway, with no visible effort. *Long legs*, she thought and then kicked herself for thinking about any part of his body. Or the fact that he'd noticed how great her shoes were. Which was *just* the kind of thing his kind of guy would do. *Think about the bet,* she told herself. *He's a beast and a gambler.*

The beast and gambler stopped in front of a dimly lit storefront window that was covered with red velvet café curtains. Above the curtains, EMILIO'S was written in gold script.

"This is the restaurant?" Min said, surprised he hadn't picked something flashier.

"Yep." He reached for the door.

"Wait." Min squinted at the card on the door. "It closes at ten on weekdays. It must be close to that now. Maybe we should—"

"I'm Emilio's favorite customer," he said, pulling the door open. "At least until he meets you."

"Another line?" Min said, exasperated.

"No," he said with great and visible patience. "Keep busting my chops all the way through dinner, and Emilio will give you a free dessert."

"I thought you were his favorite customer," Min said.

"I am," he said. "Doesn't mean he won't appreciate the show. You coming in or not?"

"Yes," Min said and walked past him into the restaurant.

It was a minute and a half by Liza's watch before the bullethead tapped her on the shoulder. "Excuse me," he said, "but I believe you were staring at me."

Liza blinked at him. "That was disbelief. I couldn't believe you were so slow."

"Slow?" He looked insulted. "Nobody could have gotten through that crowd faster than me. I didn't even have blockers."

Liza shook her head. "You spotted me a good hour ago. What did you do, sit down and think about it?"

He rolled his eyes. "I heard redheads were hard to handle." He leaned on the bar. "I'm Tony. And you owe me."

Okay, here we go, Liza thought, and leaned on the bar, too, mirroring him. "I owe you?"

"Yes." He grinned at her. "Because of chaos theory."

Liza shook her head. "Chaos theory."

He moved closer to her. "Chaos theory says that complex dynamical systems become unstable because of disturbances in their environments after which a strange attractor draws the trajectory of the stress."

Liza looked at him, incredulous. "This is your line?"

"I am a complex dynamical system," Tony said.

"Not that complex," Liza said.

"And I was stable until you caused a disturbance in my environment."

"Not that stable," Liza said.

Tony grinned. "And since you're the strangest attractor in the room, I followed the trajectory of my stress right to you."

"That's not what you followed to me." Liza turned so that her back was against the bar, her shoulder blocking him. "Give me something better than that, or I'll find somebody else to amuse myself with."

From the corner of her eye, she saw the other guy, the vacant-looking blond, lean down to Bonnie. "Is she always like this?" he said to Bonnie, and Liza turned to size him up. Big. Husky. Boring.

"Well, your friend isn't exactly Prince Charming," Bonnie said, giving him her best fluttery smile.

He beamed back down at her. "Neither am I. Is that okay?"

Oh, come on, Liza thought, and caught Tony-the-bullethead's eye.

"He means it," Tony said. "Roger has no line."

"After the chaos theory debacle, that's a plus," Liza said.

"Poor baby," Bonnie was saying as she put her hand on Roger's sleeve. "Of course, that's okay. I'm Bonnie."

Roger looked down at her with naked adoration. "I'm Roger, and you are the most beautiful woman I've ever seen in my life."

Bonnie's smile widened, and she moved closer to him.

"Which doesn't mean he's bad with women," Tony said, sounding bemused.

"I begin to see his appeal." Liza turned back to Tony. "What's yours?"

"I'm great in bed," Tony said.

"Right," Liza said. "You're hopeless, but you can buy me a drink and tell me all about yourself. And your friends."

"Anything you want," Tony said, and waved to the curly-headed bartender. When she came down the bar, he said, "Hey, Shanna, you playing on my side of the street yet?"

The bartender shook her head. "No, but when I do, you'll be the last to know."

"Just so I'm somewhere on the list," Tony said. "Shanna, this is Liza. We need refills all around here."

"You know him?" Liza said to Shanna.

"He hangs out with my next-door neighbor," Shanna said. "I get him by default because of Cal."

"Cal?" Liza said, and thought, *Damn, I could have just asked the bartender about him without picking up this yahoo. Well, later for her.*

"You don't want to know about Cal," Tony was saying. "He's no good. Women should stay far away from him."

Shanna rolled her eyes and moved away.

"That's interesting," Liza said, smiling at him. "Tell me all about Cal and why he's no good."

"I lied. He's great," Tony said. "We met in summer school—"

"You went to high school together?" Liza said, taken aback.

"We went to third grade together," Tony said. "Although why you think this is interesting—"

"I want to know everything about you, sugar," Liza said. "I find you fascinating."

Tony nodded, accepting this as fact. "I was born—"

"You and *your friends*," Liza said. "So you and Roger and *Cal*—"

Tony began to talk, while behind her, she heard Bonnie say, "You know my mama would like you," and Roger answer, "I'd love to meet your mother."

Liza jerked her head toward Roger. "Does he say that to every woman?"

"What?" Tony said, startled out of his story about being a football star in the third grade.

"Never mind," Liza said. "Let's fast forward to puberty. You and Roger and *Cal* . . ."

Cal watched the shock on Min's face as she caught the full force of Emilio's for the first time, seeing his favorite restaurant in all its funky glory, the wrought-iron chandeliers with the amber flame bulbs, the old black and white photos on the walls, the red and white checked table-cloths on the square tables, the candles in the beat-up Chianti bottles, the hand-lettered menus and mismatched silver. He waited for her lip to curl and then realized it couldn't because her mouth had fallen open. Well, she deserved it for being such a pain in the—

"This is *great*," she said, and started to laugh. "My God, how did somebody like you ever find this place?"

"What do you mean, somebody like me?" Cal said.

She walked over to look at the photos of Emilio's family for the past eighty years. "Where did they get this stuff?" She smiled, her soft lips parted and her dark eyes alight, and then Emilio came up behind him.

"Ah, Mr. Morrisey," Emilio said, and Cal turned to meet his old roommate's glare. "How excellent to see you again."

"Emilio," Cal said. "This is Min Dobbs." He turned back to Min. "Emilio makes the best bread in town."

"I'm sure you make the best everything, Emilio," Min said, offering him her hand. She looked up at him from under her lashes, and her wide smile quirked wickedly.

Emilio cheered up, and Cal thought, *Hey, why didn't I get that?*

Emilio clasped her hand. "For you, my bread is poetry. I will bring my bread as a gift to your beauty, a poem to your lovely smile." He kissed the back of her hand, and Min beamed at him and did not pull her hand away.

"Emilio, Min is my date," Cal said. "Enough kissing already."

Min shook her head at him, with no beam whatsoever. "I'm not anybody's date. We don't even like each other." She turned back to Emilio,
smiling again. "Separate checks, please, Emilio."

"Not separate checks, Emilio," Cal said, exasperated beyond polite-
ness. "But a *table* would be good."

"For you, anything," Emilio said to Min and kissed her hand
again.

Unbelievable, Cal thought, and kicked Emilio on the ankle when Min
turned to look at the restaurant again. The guy was married, for Christ's
sake.

"Right this way," Emilio said, wincing. He showed them to the best
table by the window, slid Min into a bentwood chair, and then stopped
by Cal long enough to say under his breath, "I sent the servers home
half an hour ago, you bastard."

"You're welcome," Cal said loudly, nodding to him.

Emilio gave up and went back to the kitchen, while Cal watched Min
examine the room in detail.

"It's like an Italian restaurant in the movies," she told Cal. "Except
not. I love it. I love Emilio, too."

"I noticed," he said. "You're the first woman I ever brought here who
was on a kissing basis with him before we sat down."

"Well, he's going to feed me." She picked up her napkin. "That's
always a good sign in a man." She spread the napkin in her lap, and then
her smile faded and she looked tense again. "Except . . ."

Cal braced himself for her next shot.

She leaned forward. "I can't eat the bread or pasta, but I don't want
to hurt his feelings. Can you order something else?"

"Sure," Cal said, surprised. "Salad. Chicken marsala, there's no pasta
with that."

"Thank you." Min smiled at him. "I wouldn't want to ruin his evening."

"I think you just made his evening," Cal said. Her lips were full and
soft, and when she smiled her gratitude at him, her face changed from
grim prison warden to warm baby doll, but the wicked glint she'd had in
her eyes when she'd flirted with Emilio was gone, which was a real
shame.

Emilio brought the bread, and Min leaned forward to see it. "Oh, that smells good. I missed lunch so this is wonderful."

"It is good," Cal said. "Emilio, we'll have the house salad to start and then the chicken marsala."

"Excellent choice, Mr. Morrisey," Emilio said, and Cal knew it was because everything was simple to make. "And a nice red wine to accompany?"

"Excellent," Cal said, knowing they were going to get whatever Emilio had left over and open in the kitchen.

"Ice water for me," Min said with a sigh, still looking at the bread.

When Emilio was gone, Cal said, "The bread's excellent. He makes it here."

"Carbs," Min said, her scowl back in place, and Cal had heard enough about carbs in his nine months with Cynthie so he let it drop.

"So," he said, picking up one of the small loaves. "What do you do for a living?" He broke the bread open and the yeasty warmth rose and filled his senses.

"I'm an actuary," Min said, the edge back in her voice.

An actuary. He was on a dinner date with a cranky, starving, risk-averse statistician. This was a new low, even for him.

"That's . . . interesting," he said, but she was watching the bread and didn't notice. He held half the small loaf out to her. "Eat."

"I *can't*," she said. "I have this dress I have to fit into three weeks from now."

"One piece of bread won't make that much difference." He waved it, knowing that the smell of Emilio's bread had driven stronger Atkins people to their knees.

"No." She closed her eyes and her lips tight, which was useless because it wasn't looking at the bread that was going to bring her down, it was smelling it.

"This might be your only chance to eat Emilio's bread," he said, and she took a deep breath.

"Oh, hell." She opened her eyes and took the bread from him. "You really are a beast."

"Who, me?" Cal said, and watched her tear off a piece of the bread and bite into it.

"Oh," she breathed, and then she chewed it with her eyes shut, pleasure flooding her face.

Look at me like that, he thought, and felt something nudge his shoulder. He looked up to see Emilio standing with a half bottle of wine, staring at Min. He nodded at Cal and whispered, "Keeper."

Min opened her eyes and said, "Emilio, you are a genius."

"The pleasure is all mine," Emilio said.

Cal took the wine from him. "Thank you, Emilio," he said pointedly and Emilio shook his head and went back to the kitchen for the salads.

When he'd brought them and was gone again, Cal said, "So you're an actuary."

She looked at him with contempt again. "Please. You don't care what I do. Take the night off, Charm Boy."

"Hey." He picked up his bread. "I don't do this nightly. It's been a while since I picked up anybody."

Min looked at her watch as she chewed. She swallowed and said, "It's been twenty-eight minutes."

"Besides you. My last relationship ended a couple of months ago, and I've been enjoying the peace and quiet." She rolled her eyes and he added, "So of course, when I decide to start dating again, I pick up somebody who hates me. What's all the hostility about?"

"Hostility? What hostility?" Min stabbed her fork into her salad and tasted it. "*God,* this is good."

She chewed blissfully, and Cal watched her, trying to figure out what he was doing wrong. She should be *liking* him. He was charming, damn it. "So what are your interests in life besides great shoes?"

"Oh, please," Min said, when she'd swallowed. "You talk. I know why I picked you out, tell me why you picked me."

He stopped with his glass halfway to his mouth. "You picked me up?"

Min shook her head. "I picked you *out.* I saw you on the landing. Well, my friend Liza saw you first, but she gave you to me."

"Thoughtful of her," Cal said. "So you were expecting me when I showed up?"

"Pretty much." Min shoved the bread toward him. "Take this bread basket away from me, I'm making a fool of myself."

He pulled the basket toward his plate. "Then why did you give me such a hard time?"

Min snorted. "You think that was a hard time? You must not get much grief from women."

"Well, not in the first five minutes," Cal said. "They save that for the future."

"Yes, but we don't have a future," she said, looking longingly at the bread. "I had to be proactive."

Cal pushed the basket back to her. "Why don't we have a future?" he said, even though he'd come to the same conclusion about thirty seconds after he'd said hello in the bar.

"Because I'm not interested in sex." Min tore off another piece of bread and bit into it, and Cal watched while the pleasure spread across her face.

You lie, Cal thought.

"And that means you're not interested in me," Min said when she'd finished chewing.

"Hey," he said, insulted. "What makes you think I'm only interested in sex?"

"Because you're a guy." She picked up the bread again. "Statistics show that men are interested in three things: careers, sports, and sex. That's why they love professional cheerleaders."

Cal put his fork down. "Well, that's sexist."

Min licked a crumb off her lip, and his irritation evaporated. She was fun to look at when she wasn't scowling: smooth milky skin, wide-set dark eyes, a blob of a nose, and that lush, soft, full, rosy mouth. . . .

"Yes, I know," she said. "But it's true, isn't it?"

"What?" Cal tried to find his place in the conversation. "Oh, the sports and sex thing? Not at all. This is the twenty-first century. We've learned how to be sensitive."

"You have?"

"Sure," Cal said. "Otherwise we wouldn't get laid."

She rolled her eyes, and he picked up the bottle and filled her wineglass.

"I can't," she said. "I had too much to drink at the bar."

He slid her glass closer. "I'll make sure you get home okay."

"And who'll make sure I get away from you okay?" she said and he put the bottle down.

"Okay, *that* was below the belt," he said, more sharply than he'd intended.

She met his eyes, and he thought, *Oh, hell, here we go again.* Then she nodded and said, "You're right. You've done nothing to deserve that. I apologize." She frowned, as if thinking about something. "In fact, I apologize for the whole night. My boyfriend dumped me about half an hour before you picked me up—"

"Ah *ha*," Cal said.

"—and it made me insane with rage. And then I realized that I'm not even sure I *liked* him anymore, and that the person I'm really mad at is me for being so stupid about the whole thing."

"You're not stupid," Cal said. "Making mistakes isn't stupid, it's the way you learn."

She squinted at him, looking confused. "Thank you. Anyway, this evening is not your fault. I mean, you have your faults, but you shouldn't pay for his. Sorry."

"That's okay," he said, confused, too. *What faults?* "Now drink your wine. It's good."

She picked up her glass and sipped. "You're right. This is excellent."

"Good, we'll come here often," he said, and then kicked himself because they weren't going anywhere again.

"Another line," Min said, without venom. "We're not going anywhere again and you know it. What is it with you? You see a woman and automatically go into wolf mode?"

Cal sat back. "Okay, was that because of the ex-boyfriend, too? Because I'm usually not paranoid, but you are definitely out to get me."

"Don't be a wimp," Min said as she tore the bread. "You've got that gorgeous face, and a body that makes women go weak at the knees, and then you whine."

Cal grinned at her. "Do I make you go weak at the knees?"

Min bit into her bread and chewed. "You did until you whined," she said when she'd swallowed. "Now I know. The magic is gone."

Cal watched her lick her full lower lip, and two months of celibacy plus a lifetime of habit kicked in. "Give me a chance," he said. "I bet I can get the magic back."

She stopped with the tip of her tongue on her lip, and her eyes met his for a long, dark, hot moment, and this time that glint was there, and sound faded to silence, and every nerve he had came alive and said, *This one.*

Then her tongue disappeared, and he shook his head to clear it and thought, *Not in a million years.*

"I never bet," Min said. "Gambling is a statistically impractical form of generating income."

"It's not a method of generating income," Cal said. "It's a way of life."

"Could we be any more incompatible?" Min said.

"Can't see how," Cal said, but then her eyes went past him and he watched while she drew in her breath.

Cal turned and saw Emilio, this time with a fragrant platter of chicken marsala, golden-brown filets and huge braised mushrooms floating in luminous dark wine sauce.

"*Oh, my Lord,*" Min said.

Emilio beamed at her as he served. "It's a pleasure to serve someone who appreciates food. Taste it."

Min cut into the chicken and put a forkful in her mouth. She looked startled and then she closed her eyes and began to chew, her face flushed with pleasure. When she'd swallowed, she looked up at Emilio, her eyes shining. "This is *incredible*," she said, and Cal thought, *Me, look at me like that.*

"Try the mushrooms," Emilio said, happy as a half-Italian clam.

"Go away," Cal told him, but Emilio stayed until Min had bitten into one of the huge mushrooms and told him with heartfelt passion that he was a genius.

"Can I get some credit for bringing you here?" Cal said when Emilio was gone.

"Yes," Min said. "You are a genius at restaurants. Now be quiet so I can concentrate on this."

Cal sighed and gave up on the conversation for the rest of the meal. There was a skirmish at the end when Min tried to insist on separate checks, but Cal said, "I invited you, I pay. Back off, woman." She looked as though she were going to argue for a moment, and then she nodded. "Thank you very much," she told him. "You've given me a lovely meal and a new favorite restaurant," and he felt appreciated for the first time that night.

When they left, she kissed Emilio on the cheek. "Your bread is the greatest, Emilio, but the chicken is a work of art." Then she kissed him on the other cheek.

"Hey," Cal said. "I'm right here. I *paid* for the chicken."

"Don't beg," Min told him and went out the door.

"Morrisey, I think you just met your match," Emilio said.

"Not even close," Cal said, grateful to be without her for a moment. "This was our first, last, and only date."

"Nope," Emilio said. "I saw the way you looked at each other."

"That was fear and loathing," Cal said, opening the door.

"God, you're dumb," Emilio said, and Cal ignored him and went out into the dark to find Min.

Chapter Three

"Infatuation is the fun part of falling in love," Cynthie said to David when they were ensconced in Serafino's and the waiter had brought their very expensive filets and departed.

David smiled at her and thought, *I bet Min isn't talking psychology with Cal.* God knew what Min was doing with Cal. Whatever it was, he was going to have to find a way to stop it.

"Infatuation triggers a chemical in the brain called PEA," Cynthie said. "Your heart races, and you get breathless and dizzy, you tremble, and you can't think. It's what most people think of when they think of falling in love, and everybody goes through it." She smiled a lovely, far-away smile. "Our infatuation was wonderful. We couldn't resist each other."

"Hmm." David picked up his blue-frosted margarita glass. "Tell me again how it's not working out for them."

"Well," Cynthie said, "about now, he should be realizing it's time to cut his losses. He'll take her to her car to make sure she's safe, and then he'll shake her hand and say, 'Have a nice life,' and that'll be it."

"What if he was attracted to her?"

"I told you, he wasn't," Cynthie said, but her smile faded. "But if he was, which he wasn't, then he'd ask her out again and look for more cues, more evidence that she's somebody he should love. Like whether his family and friends like her. But she's not Roger's type, he likes giggly little blondes, and I doubt Tony even saw her since he's pretty much a breast-butt-legs man, so it wasn't his friends who prompted him to pick her up."

"Hard to tell what made him do that," David said, trying to sound innocent.

"And she's not going to meet his family, but even if she did, his mother would hate her, his mother disapproves of everything, so that wouldn't be a cue, since Cal needs his family to approve of him."

"So you're saying that's all it would take for them to reject each other?" David said. "Friends and family disapproving?"

"Unless she doesn't like her family or wants to rebel against them. Then their disapproval would push her into his arms, but it doesn't sound like that's the case."

"No," David said, thinking of two dinners with Min's parents in the past two months. "They're very close."

"Then family and friends are very powerful," Cynthie said. "Which is why I've been nice to Tony for nine months. But, David, it's not going to happen. Cal is in the mature love and attachment stage with me, which means he won't be attracted to Min."

"Mature love. That would be the, uh, fourth stage," David said, trying to show he'd been listening.

"Right," Cynthie said. "Infatuation doesn't last because it's conditional and conditions change, but if it's real love, it turns into mature, unconditional love, and new chemicals are released in the brain, endorphins that make you feel warm and peaceful and satisfied and content whenever you're with the one you love." She took a deep breath. "And miserable when you're without him because if he's not there, the brain won't produce the chemicals."

"Oh," David said, understanding now. "So you're going through endorphin withdrawal."

"Temporarily," Cynthie said, her chin up. "He'll be back. He's going without sex, which is pain, a physiological cue to deepen his attachment to me."

"Pain," David said, thinking anything that hurt Cal was a good idea.

Cynthie nodded. "In order to move from infatuation to attachment, Cal will have to feel joy or pain when he's with Min. The joy could be great conversation or great sex, the pain could be jealousy, frustration, fear, almost anything that adds stress. The pain cue is the reason there are so many wartime romances. And office romances."

"Right," David said, remembering an intern from his earlier years.

"But I don't think that's going to happen tonight. I think he's going to be bored. I must say that it's a great comfort to know that your Min is dull and frigid."

"I didn't say she was dull and frigid," David said. "I wouldn't date somebody who was dull and frigid."

"Then you should have stuck it out," Cynthie said. "Infatuation lasts anywhere from six months to three years, and you can't know you've found the right person until you've worked your way through it. You quit at two months so you couldn't have reached attachment and neither could she." She shrugged. "Mistake."

"Six months to *three years?*" David said. "And you pushed Cal after nine months?" He shrugged. "Mistake."

Cynthie put down her fork. "Not a mistake. I know Cal, I have written articles on Cal, and he is in the attachment stage, we both are."

David stopped eating, appalled. "You wrote about your lover?"

"Well, I didn't call him by his real name," Cynthie said. "And I didn't say he was *my* lover."

"Isn't that unethical?"

"No." Cynthie pushed her plate away, most of her dinner untouched. "That's how we met. I'd heard about him through a couple of my clients. He had quite a reputation."

"I know," David said, thinking vicious thoughts about Cal Morrisey, God's Gift to Women. "Totally undeserved."

"Are you kidding?" Cynthie said. "I was *studying* him, and he got me." Her mouth curved again. "Nature gave him that face and body, and his parents gave him conditional affection as a child. He's been trained to please people to get approval, and the people he likes to please most are women, who are more than willing to be pleased by him because he looks the way he does. So his looks guarantee assumption and his charm guarantees attraction. He's one of the most elegant adaptive solutions I've ever observed. The papers I wrote on him got *a lot* of attention."

David tried to picture Cal Morrisey as a child, trying to earn affection. All he could come up with was a good-looking dark-haired kid in a tuxedo, leaning on a swing set and smiling confidently at little girls. "Did he know you wrote papers on him?"

"No," Cynthie said. "He still doesn't. He never will. I finished that work, it's over. I'm writing a book now, already under contract. It's almost done." She smiled, a satisfied feline smile. "The point is, I'm not some silly woman moaning, 'But I thought he loved me,' I have clinical proof he does love me. And he'll come back to me soon, as long as your Min doesn't distract him."

"So," David said, leaning closer. "If we wanted to make sure they didn't get to—what was it? Attraction?—what would we do?"

Cynthie's eyes widened. "Do?" She put her wineglass down and thought about it. "Well, I suppose we could talk to their friends and families, poison the well, so to speak. And we could offer them joy in different forms to counteract whatever happens between them. But that wouldn't be . . . David, we don't have to do anything. Cal loves me."

"Right," David said, sitting back. *Family*, he thought. *I have an in with the family.*

Cynthie smiled at him. "I'm tired of talking about them," she said. "What is it that you do for a living?"

David thought, *It's about time we got to me.* He said, "I'm in software development," and watched her eyes glaze over.

Outside Emilio's, Min took a deep breath of summer night air and thought, *I'm happy.* Evidently great food was an antidote to rage and humiliation. Good to know for the future.

Then Cal came out and said, "Where's your car?" and broke her mood.

"No car," Min said. "I can walk it." She held out her hand. "Thank you for a lovely evening. Sort of. Good-bye."

"No," Cal said, ignoring her hand. "Which way is your place?"

"Look," Min said, exasperated. "*I can walk—*"

"In the city alone at night? No, you can't. I was raised better than that. I'm walking you home, and there's nothing you can do about it, so which way are we going?"

Min thought about arguing with him, but there wasn't much point. Even one short evening with Calvin Morrisey had taught her that he got what he wanted. "Okay. Fine. Thank you very much. It's this way."

She started off down the street, listening to the breeze in the trees and the muted street noises, and Cal fell into step beside her, the sound of his footfalls matching the click of her heels in a nice rhythm.

"So what is it you do for a living?" she asked.

"I run a business seminar group with two partners."

"You're a teacher?" Min said, surprised.

"Yes," he said. "So you're an actuary. I have a great deal of respect for your profession. You do it for money. I do it for recreation."

"Do what?"

"Figure out whether something's a good bet or not." He looked down at her. "You're a gambler. You do it with millions of dollars of an insurance company's money. I do it with ten-dollar bills."

"Yeah, but I don't lose any of my own money," Min said.

"Neither do I," Cal said.

"You win *every* bet?" Min said, disbelief making her voice flat.

"Pretty much," Cal said.

"Hell of a guy," Min said. "Is that why you went into business for yourself? So you could control the risk?"

"No, I just didn't want to work for anybody else," Cal said. "That didn't leave me any other options."

"We turn here," Min said, slowing as they came to the corner. "Look, I can—"

"Keep walking," Cal said, and Min did.

"So what's the name of this company?"

"Morrisey, Packard, Capa."

"Packard and Capa being the other two guys on the landing with you," Min said. "The big blond and the bull—uh, the jock-looking one."

"Yeah." Cal grinned. "Bull?"

"One of my friends mentioned his head looked like a bullet," Min said, wincing. "She meant it as a compliment."

"Bet she did," Cal said. "That would be the redhead, right?"

"You noticed her," Min said, and felt a twinge.

"No, the bullet-head noticed her," Cal said.

"Don't tell him she said that," Min said. "She wouldn't want to hurt his feelings."

"It takes a lot to bring Tony down," Cal said. "But I won't mention it."

"Thank you."

The farther they got from the busier streets, the darker it became, even with the streetlights, and Min began to feel grateful he was there. "So why do people hire you to teach? I mean, you specifically. Instead of somebody else."

"We tailor the programs," Cal said. "In any instructional situation, a certain percentage of the student population will fail to master the material. We guarantee one hundred percent and we stay until it's achieved."

"That sounds like promotional literature."

"It's also the truth."

"And you do this how?" Min said. "Charming them?"

"What have you got against charming?" Cal said.

"It so rarely goes hand in hand with 'honest,' " Min said.

Cal sighed. "People shut down because of fear. The first thing we do is analyze the students to find out who's afraid and how they're coping with it. Some of them freeze up, so we put them with Roger. Very gentle guy, Roger. He can reassure anybody into learning anything."

"That's a little creepy," Min said, trying to picture Roger as one of those slick self-help gurus.

"You are a very suspicious woman," Cal said. "Then some people hide their fear in wisecracks, disrupting class. Tony takes them. They joke around together until everybody's relaxed."

"And who do you get?" Min said.

"I get the angry ones," Cal said. "The ones who are mad that they're scared."

"And you charm them out of it," Min said.

"Well, I wouldn't put it that way, but yes, I suppose that's one interpretation."

The angry ones. They walked on in silence, their footsteps echoing together.

Min looked up at him. "You must have felt right at home with me tonight."

"Nope," Cal said. "You're not mad because you're scared. I doubt that much scares you. You're mad because somebody was lousy to you. And there's not enough charm in the world to get you out of that until you've resolved the deeper issue."

"And yet you kept on trying," Min said.

"No, I didn't," Cal said. "Once you'd told me you'd been dumped, I backed off."

Min thought about it. "I guess you did. Pretty much."

"Now aren't you sorry you were such a grump all night?" Cal said.

"No," Min said. "Because you were pouring on the charm before that which means you were trying to get something from me, God knows what—" *Sex to win a bet, you beast.* "—and you deserved to be called on that."

A few steps later Cal said, "Fair enough."

Min smiled to herself in the darkness and thought, *Well, he does have an honest bone in his body. Too bad it's just one.* They walked on in silence until they reached the steps to her house. "This is it. Thank you very much—"

"Where?" Cal said, looking around. "I don't see a house."

"Up there," Min said, pointing up the hill. "The steps are right there. So we can—"

Cal peered up the hill into the darkness. "Christ, woman, that looks like Everest. How many steps are there?"

"Thirty-two," Min said, "and another twenty-six after that to get up to my apartment in the attic." She held out her hand. "So we'll say goodnight here. Thank you for the walk home. Best of luck in the future."

He ignored her to look up the hill again. "Nope. I'm not leaving you to climb up there in the dark."

"It's okay," Min said. "Seventy-eight percent of women who are attacked are attacked by men they know."

"Is that another shot at me?" Cal said.

"No. I don't know any men who would climb thirty-two steps to attack me, so I'm safe. You can go home with a clear conscience."

"No," he said patiently. "I can't. Get moving. I'll be right behind you."

Behind her? Thirty-two steps with him looking at her butt? "No, you won't."

"Look, it's late, I'm tired, can we just—"

"It'll be a cold day in hell when you follow me up those steps. You want to go up, you go first."

"*Why?*" he said, mystified.

"You're not looking at my rear end all the way up that hill."

He shook his head. "You know, Dobbs, you look like a sane person, and then you open your mouth—"

"Start climbing or go home," Min said.

Cal sighed and took the first step. "Wait a minute. Now you'll be looking at my butt all the way up the steps."

"Yes, but you probably have a great butt," Min said. "It's an entirely different dynamic."

"I can't even see yours," Cal said. "It's dark and your jacket is too long."

"Climb or leave," Min said, and Cal started up the steps.

When they got to the top, he hesitated, and she saw the mid-century stone and stucco house through his eyes, dark and shabby and overgrown with climbing rosebushes that were so ancient they'd degenerated into thornbushes. "It's nice," she said, on the defensive.

"It's probably great in the daytime," he said, politely.

"Right." Min pushed past him to climb the stone steps to the front porch. She unlocked the door. "There, see? You can go now."

"This is not your door," he said. "You said you live twenty-six steps up."

"Fine, climb all the way to the attic." She waved him in front of her into the square hall of the house. With him there, the faded blue wallpaper and dull oak woodwork looked shabby instead of comfortable, and that irritated her. "Up," she said, pointing to the narrow stairway along one wall, looking even narrower now that he was at the bottom with what looked like several yards of shoulder blocking her way, and he climbed two more flights of stairs to the narrow landing with her following.

He had a great butt.

And that's all that's nice about him, Min told herself. *Be sensible, keep your head here. You're never going to see him again.*

"Well, at least you know anybody who walks you home twice is serious about you," he said, as he reached the top.

He turned as he said it, and Min, still two steps down scoping out his rear end, walked into his elbow and clipped herself hard over the eye, knocking herself enough off balance that she tripped back, grabbed the railing, and sat down on the step.

"Oh, *Christ*," he said. "I'm sorry." He bent over her and she warded him off.

"No, no," she said. "My fault. Following too close." *Ouch*, she thought, gingerly feeling the place he'd smacked her. *That's what you get for being shallow and objectifying the beast.*

"Just let me see it," he said, trying to look into her eyes. He put his hand gently on the side of her face to tip her chin up.

"No." She brushed his hand away as her skin started to tingle. "I'm fine. Aside from being part of the seventy-eight percent of women who are attacked by—"

"Oh, cut me a break," he said, straightening. "Are you all right?"

"Yes." She stood up again and detoured around him to unlock her door. "You can go now."

"Right." He picked up her hand and shook it once. "Great to meet you, Dobbs. Sorry about the elbow to the head. Have a nice life."

"Oh, I'm going to," Min said. "I'm giving up men and getting a cat."
She slipped inside and shut the door in his face before he could say anything else. *Have a nice life. Who is he kidding?*

She turned on her grandmother's china lamp by the door, and her living room sprang into shabby but comforting view. The light on her machine was blinking, and she went over and pressed the button, and then rubbed her temple while she listened.

"Min," her sister's voice said. "Just wanted to make sure you didn't forget the fitting tomorrow. It'll be nice to see you." Diana sounded a little woebegone, which was not like her, and Min replayed the message to hear her again. Something was wrong.

"The Dobbs girls cannot win," she said, and thought about Calvin Morrisey. She went over to her battered mantel and looked over the snow globes lined up there into the tarnished mirror that had once hung in her grandmother's hall. A plain round face, plain brown hair, that's what Cal Morrisey had looked at all night. And now it had a nice bruise. She sighed and picked up the snow globe Bonnie had given her for Christmas, Cinderella and her prince on the steps of their blue castle, doves flying overhead. Cal Morrisey would look right at home on those steps. She, on the other hand, would be asked to try the servant's entrance. "Just not the fairy tale type," she said and put the globe down to go turn on her stereo, hitting the up button until Elvis started to sing "The Devil in Disguise."

"And let's not forget that's what Calvin Morrisey is, Dobbs," she told herself, and went to put arnica on her bruise and take a hot bath to wash the memory of the evening away. At least the part with David in it. There were some moments after David that weren't entirely horrible.

But she definitely wasn't going to see Calvin Morrisey again.

When Cal got to work the next morning, the sun was shining through the tall windows in the loft office, the smell of coffee permeated the room, Roger waved to him from his desk by the window, and Elvis Costello was singing "The Angels Wanna Wear My Red Shoes" on the

CD player. *All right*, Cal thought. He dropped a folder on the frosted glass desktop, poured himself a cup of coffee, and pulled out his Aeron chair, ready to make the world a better place for people trapped in business training seminars.

Tony came through the door and slapped him on the back. "Nice going last night. Tell me you won."

"What are you talking about?" Cal said.

"The bet with David," Tony said. "The one about the gray-checked suit. Tell me you won it."

"Sure." Cal dropped into his desk chair. "You saw me leave with her."

"You're right, you're right, I should have had faith. You want to tell David or should I?"

"Tell him what?" Cal turned on his Mac and hit the GET MESSAGE button for his e-mail.

"That you had sex with the suit," Tony said.

"What?" Cal said, squinting at the screen while Elvis sang backup to his morning. "Of course I didn't."

"Oh." Tony nodded. "Well, you've still got a month."

"Tony," Cal said as the list of messages showed up in the window. "I don't know what you're talking about, but I'm positive it's wasting my time."

"David bet you that you could get the suit into bed in a month," Tony was saying with obvious patience. "I could use the money, too, so if you'd—"

"No," Cal said. "I did not make that bet."

"David thinks you made the bet," Tony said.

"No, he doesn't," Cal said. "Now that he's sober he does not think that he bet me ten thousand dollars I could get a strange woman into bed. Now could we get some work done? There's money in it for you. They pay us to do this stuff."

He slid the folder on his desk across to Tony, who picked it up and leafed through it. "Piece of cake," he said, and began to move away. "Oh, just so you know, Cynthie left with David last night."

"Good for them." Cal turned back to his e-mail.

"This doesn't bother you?" Tony said.

"Why are you harassing me this morning?" Cal said, putting an edge on his voice.

"I just want to make sure you're not going back to her," Tony said. "My future is on the line here."

"How?" Cal said.

"Well, you'll get married first," Tony said, coming back to sit on the corner of Cal's desk. "You always do everything first. And then Roger will get married and you'll both move to the suburbs. And Roger is going to marry somebody as uptight as he is, which means I'll have to live with you, and since Cynthie never did like me, she'd be a problem to convince on that."

"So would I," Cal said. "Get off my desk."

"It wouldn't be *with* you, not in the house," Tony said. "I figure a nice apartment over the garage. It'd be convenient for you. You could come over and watch the game and get drunk and not have to drive home. And I could baby-sit the kids when you and the wife wanted to go out."

"First," Cal said, "I'm not getting married, so forget the wife. Second, if I was insane enough to get married, I wouldn't have kids. Third, if I was insane enough to get married and have kids, it would be a cold day in hell I'd let you baby-sit."

"Well, we'll both have matured by then," Tony said. "I wouldn't let me baby-sit now, either."

"I'm getting married first," Roger said.

They both turned to him, and he smiled back, big, blond, and placid in the sunlight from the big loft windows.

"I'm going to marry Bonnie," Roger said.

Cal frowned at him. "Who's Bonnie?"

"The mini-blonde he met last night," Tony said, disgust in his voice.

"Her name is Bonnie," Roger said, his voice like ice, and both Cal and Tony straightened.

"He's serious," Cal said to Tony. "What happened?"

"The redhead wanted me," Tony said. "So I went over. And Roger followed and hooked up with the mini . . . with Bonnie. And sometime between then and now he lost his mind." He shook his head at Roger.

"This is a woman you've known less than twelve hours. It took you a year to pick out a couch, but you're seriously—"

"Yes," Roger said. "She's the one."

"Maybe," Cal said, thinking, *The hell she is.* "You didn't tell her that, though. Right?"

"No," Roger said. "I thought it was too soon."

"You *think?*" Tony said. "Jesus."

"I'm going to marry her," Roger said, "so stop yelling and get used to it. She's perfect."

"No woman is perfect," Tony said. "Which is why we must keep looking. You going to see her tonight?"

"No," Roger said. "They have some Thursday night thing they do every other week. Bonnie called it their 'If Dinner.'"

"They?" Tony said.

Roger nodded. "Bonnie, Liza, and Min."

"Who's Min?" Tony said, lost again.

"The one I'm not going to sleep with," Cal said. If Bonnie was anything like Min, Roger was in big trouble.

"You seeing Bonnie on Friday?" Tony said to Roger, sticking to the basics.

Roger nodded. "She said they'll be at The Long Shot. It's not their regular hangout, but she said she'd look for me there. And she's coming to the game Saturday. And we might go to dinner Saturday night."

"She's coming to watch you coach a kid's baseball game?" Cal said. "She must love you a lot."

"Not yet," Roger said. "But she will."

"Friday," Tony said, ignoring them. "That's good. I can hit on Liza, and Cal can move on the suit."

"No," Cal said.

Roger looked sympathetic. "What happened?"

Cal went back to his computer. "She's a conservative, antigambling actuary who spent dinner bitching at me. Then I took her home, climbed fifty-eight steps to her apartment to make sure she didn't get mugged, and elbowed her in the eye. It was the worst date of my life, and I'm sure it was in her bottom five."

"You hit her?" Tony said.

"By accident," Cal said. "I'd send flowers to apologize, but she's anticharm, too. It's over. Move on."

"So you're going to give up on another one," Tony said, shaking his head.

Cal looked up at him, annoyed. "Now tell me about your deep and lasting relationships."

"Yes, but that's me," Tony said. "I'm shallow."

"Bonnie lives on the first floor of that house," Roger said, as if they hadn't spoken, "so I just had to make the first thirty-two steps. And then she felt bad for me, so she invited me in for coffee. I can get used to the steps."

"Does that mean Liza lives on the second floor?" Tony said.

"No, Liza lives over on Pennington," Roger said. "She moves every year to a new place, about the time she changes jobs. Bonnie says Liza likes change."

Cal looked at Tony. "You didn't walk her home?"

"She ditched me while I was in the john," Tony said. "I think she's playing hard to get."

"Sounds like Min," Cal said, going back to the computer. "Except I don't think she's playing."

"Bonnie and I walked Liza home," Roger said. "It was nice. It gave me more time with Bonnie."

"Jesus, man, pull yourself together," Tony said.

"You're serious about this?" Cal said, turning back to Roger.

"Yes."

Cal saw determination on his face. "Congratulations," he said, deciding to check Bonnie out. "Wait a month to propose. You don't want to scare her."

"That's what I thought," Roger said.

"You're both nuts," Tony said.

"We're all going to be unemployed if we don't get to work," Cal said. "Start with the Batchelder refresher."

"Bonnie says Min is great," Roger said. "She looked nice."

"Min is not nice," Cal said. "Min is mad at the world and taking it out on whatever guy is standing next to her. Now about the Batchelder refresher—"

"Are you sure David knows there's no bet?" Tony said.

"Positive," Cal said. "I'm never seeing that woman again. Now about the *Batchelder refresher* . . ."

At half past four that afternoon, Min walked into the ivory moiré–draped fitting room of the city's best bridal emporium, well aware she was late and not caring much. Her mother was probably so absorbed in harassing Diana and the fitter that—

"You're late," Nanette Dobbs said. "The appointment was for four."

"I work." Min crossed the thick gold carpet and detoured around the dark-haired bundle of exasperation that had given birth to her, dropping her jacket on an ivory-upholstered chair. "That means the insurance company gets first dibs on my time. If you want me here on the dot, schedule this for after work."

"That's ridiculous," Nanette said. "Your dress is in the second dressing room. The fitter is with Diana and the other girls. Give me your blouse, you'll just drop it on the floor in there." She held out one imperious, French-manicured hand, and Min sighed and took off her blouse.

"Oh, *Min*," her mother said, her voice heavy with unsurprised contempt. "Wherever did you get that bra?"

Min looked down at her underwear. Plain cotton, but perfectly respectable. "I have no idea. Why?"

"White cotton," Nanette said. "Honestly, Min, plain cotton is like plain vanilla—"

"I like plain vanilla."

"—there's no excitement there at all."

Min blinked. "I was at work. There's never any excitement."

"I'm talking about men," Nanette said. "You're thirty-three. Your prime years are past you, and you're wearing white cotton."

"I was at *work*," Min said, losing patience.

"It doesn't matter." Her mother shook out Min's blouse, checked the label, saw it was silk, and looked partly mollified. "If you're wearing white cotton lingerie, you'll feel like white cotton, and you'll act like white cotton, and white cotton cannot get a man, nor can it keep one. Always wear lace."

"You'd make a nice pimp," Min said, and headed for the dressing room.

"*Minerva,*" her mother said.

"Well, I'm sorry." Min stopped and turned around. "But honestly, Mother, this conversation is getting old. I'm not even sure I want to get married, and you're critiquing my underwear because it's not good enough bait. Can't you—"

Nanette lifted her chin, and her jawline became even more taut. "This is the kind of attitude that's going to lose David."

Min took a deep breath. "About David . . ."

"What?" Her mother's body tensed beneath her size four Dana Buchman suit. "What about David?"

Min smiled cheerfully. "We're no longer seeing each other."

"Oh, *Min,*" Nanette wailed, clutching Min's blouse to her bosom, the picture of despair in the middle of a lot of expensive gold and ivory décor.

"He wasn't right for me, Mother," Min said.

"Yes," Nanette said, "but couldn't you have kept him until after the wedding?"

"Evidently not," Min said. "Let's cut to the chase. What do I have to do to keep you from mentioning his name ever again?"

"Wear lace."

"That will get you off my back?"

"For a while."

Min grinned at her and headed for the dressing room door. "You are a piece of work."

"So are you, darling," Nanette said, surveying her eldest. "I'm very proud of you, you know. You have a blotch of makeup over your eye. What is that?"

"Oh, for crying out loud." Min closed the door behind her. She unzipped her skirt, let it fall to the gold carpet, and studied herself in the gold-framed mirror. "You're not that bad," she told herself, not convinced. "You just have to find a man who likes very healthy women."

She unclipped the long lavender skirt from the gold hanger and stepped into it, being careful not to rip the knife-pleated chiffon ruffle at the bottom, and sucked in her stomach to get it buttoned. Then she shrugged on the lavender chiffon blouse and buttoned the tiny buttons, stretching the fabric tightly across her bust so that her white bra showed at the corners of the low, squared bodice. She shook out the sleeves, and the chiffon fell over her hands in wide double ruffles that she would drag through everything at the reception. The blouse also erupted around her hips in more ruffles at the side. "Oh, yes," she said. "More width at the hip. Can't ever get enough of that."

Then she picked up the corset, a blue and lavender watercolor moiré tied with lavender ribbons. The fabric had been so beautiful when Diana had chosen it six months before that Min had hired the seam-stress to make a comforter for her bed with it, and she looked at the nar-row corset now and thought, *I'm going to have to wear the comforter. This is never going to fit.* She took a deep breath and wrapped the corset around her. It shoved her breasts up to a dizzying height and then failed to meet in the middle by almost two inches. *Carbs.* She thought vicious thoughts about Cal Morrisey and Emilio's bread. Then she tried to smooth out the extra foundation without showing the bruise and went out into the dressing room to face her mother.

Instead, she found Diana, standing on the fitting platform in front of the huge, gold-framed mirror, flanked by her two lovely bridesmaids, the women Liza called Wet and Worse, while the Dixie Chicks played on Diana's portable CD player.

"'Ready to Run,'" Min said to Diana. "And so not appropriate."

"Hmmm?" Diana said, staring into the mirror. "No, it's *Runaway Bride*."

"Right," Min said, remembering that Diana had decided to score her wedding to music from Julia Roberts's movies. Well, at least it was a plan.

"I loved that movie," Susie said. She looked blond, bilious, miserable, and, well, wet in corseted green chiffon, the loser in the bridesmaid dress lottery.

"I thought it was ridiculous," dark-haired Karen, a.k.a. Worse, said, looking sophisticated and superior in corseted blue chiffon.

Min waved her hand at Worse. "Scoot over so I can see my sister."

Worse moved, and Min got her first look at Diana. "Wow."

Diana looked like a fairy tale come to life in ivory chiffon and satin. Her dark curling hair fell from an artfully messy knot into pearl-strewn tendrils around her pale oval face and her neck rose gracefully above the perfect expanse of skin revealed by a very low, square-necked bodice identical to the one flashing Min's white bra. Her neckline had chiffon ruffles cascading over the beaded ivory corset that cinched her slim waist, and more ruffles fell from her wrists and flowed out from under the corset, parting to reveal a straight skirt flounced with more ruffles along the side like panniers and ending in a knife-pleated border that touched the toes of her satin buckled pumps. She turned on the platform to look into the mirror and Min saw the bustle of gathered chiffon at the base of her spine that erupted in more and more ruffles and pleats until the back of the dress took on a life of its own, quivering when Diana moved.

"What do you think?" Diana said, no expression at all on her face.

I think you look like a sex-crazed princess on heroin, Min thought, but she said, "I think you look beautiful," because that was true, too.

"You look gorgeous," Worse said, straightening Di's skirt, which didn't need straightening.

"Uh huh," Wet said. Min wanted to feel sorry for her—it couldn't be easy watching your best friend marry your ex-boyfriend, especially when you looked like hell in green—but Wet was so spineless that it was hard to sympathize.

"It wouldn't do for a morning wedding," Diana said, touching the ribbon bow at her breasts. "It wouldn't work for evening, either. But my wedding is at dusk. That's magic time. It changes everything."

"You look like magic," Min said, hearing the same strain in Diana's voice that she'd heard on her answering machine the night before. "Are you all right?"

Diana turned back to the mirror. "You wouldn't be caught dead in this, would you?"

"If I looked like you, I might."

Worse surveyed Min from head to toe, taking in the bursting corset and white bra along the way. "It's not Min's style."

"You think?" Min said. "Because I was going to wear the corset to the office when this whole deal was done. Could I talk to my sister alone for a minute, please?"

Worse raised her eyebrows, but Wet escaped into the dressing rooms gladly, and when Min folded her arms and stared, Worse gave up and left, too.

"What's going on?" Min asked Diana, as the Dixie Chicks finished and Martina McBride began to sing the impossibly chipper "I Love You."

"Nothing," Diana said, watching herself in the mirror. "Well, the cake, we're having problems with the cake, but everything else is perfect."

"Is it Greg?" Min said, thinking, *I wouldn't want to marry a wimp no matter how cute and rich he was.* If she ever got married, it'd be to somebody with edge, somebody who'd be tricky and fast and interesting forever—

"Greg is perfect," Diana said, fluffing the ruffles that somehow made her hips looks slimmer.

"Oh, good," Min said. "What about the cake?"

"The cake . . ." Diana cleared her throat. "The cake didn't get ordered in time."

"I thought Greg knew this great baker," Min said.

"He does," Diana said. "But he . . . forgot, and now it's too late, so I have to find a new baker."

"Who can do a huge art cake for three weeks from now?"

"It's not Greg's fault," Diana said. "You know men. They're not dependable on stuff like that. It was my fault for not checking."

"Not all men are undependable," Min said. "I met a real beast last night, but he'd have gotten that cake."

"Well, Greg isn't a beast," Diana said. "I'd rather have a good man who forgets cakes than a beast who remembers them."

"Good point," Min said. "Look, I'll find you a cake. It's the least I can do to make up for my screwups."

Diana gave up on her ruffles and turned around. "What's wrong? You're not a screwup. What's the matter?"

"I lost David, and I'm too fat for this corset thing," Min said, holding up the ribbon ends.

"You're not fat," Diana said, but she stepped down off the platform. "They probably sent the wrong size. Let me see."

Min untied the corset and handed it over and then watched as Diana flipped it inside out with expert hands.

"What happened with David?" Diana said as she frowned at the tag.

"I wouldn't sleep with him so he left."

"What a dumbass." Diana looked up, mystified. "You know, this is an eight, it should fit."

"In what universe?" Min said, outraged. "I wasn't an eight at birth. Who ordered this thing?"

"I did," Nanette said from behind her. "I assumed you'd be losing weight for your sister's wedding. You're still on your diet, aren't you?"

"Yes," Min said, biting the word off as she turned to face her mother. "But let's be realistic here. You bought a blouse that fit." She looked down to where the tiny buttons stood at attention as they crossed her bustline. "Sort of. Why not—"

"You've had a year," her mother said, clutching a lot of lace from the lingerie department. "I thought the corset could cinch you in if you missed your target by a few pounds, but you've had plenty of time to lose that weight."

Min took a deep breath and popped the button on her skirt. "Look, Mother, I am never going to be thin. I'm Norwegian. If you wanted a thin daughter, you should not have married a man whose female ancestors carried cows home from the pasture."

"You're half Norwegian," Nanette said, "which is no excuse at all because there are plenty of slim Nordic beauties. You're just eating to rebel against me."

"Mother, sometimes it's not about you," Min snapped as she held her skirt together. "*Sometimes it's genetics.*"

"Not your loud voice, dear," her mother said, and turned to Diana as she held up the corset. "We'll just have to tie it tighter."

"Good idea," Min said. "Then when I pass out at the altar, you can point out how slim and Nordic I am."

"Minerva, this is your *sister's wedding*," Nanette said. "You can sacrifice a little."

"It's okay, it's okay," Diana said, holding out her hands. "There's time to have one made in Min's size. Everything will be fine."

"Oh, good." Min stepped up on the platform to look at herself in the trifold mirror. She looked like the blowsy barmaid who worked in the inn behind the castle, the one who'd trash-picked one of the princess's castoffs. "This is so not me."

"It's a great color for you, Min," Diana said softly as she came to stand behind her on the platform, and Min leaned back so their shoulders touched.

"You're going to be the most amazing bride," she told Diana. "People are going to gasp when they see you."

"You, too," Diana said, and squeezed Min's shoulder.

Yeah, when my corset explodes and my breasts hit the minister.

"What happened to your eye?" Diana said in Min's ear, low enough so that Nanette couldn't hear.

"The beast hit me last night," Min said, and then when Diana straightened she added, "I walked into his elbow. Not his fault."

"That's the wrong bra for that dress," Nanette said from behind them.

"You're not by any chance my stepmother are you?" Min said to her mother's reflection. "Because that would explain so much."

"Here, darling," Nanette said and handed her five different colored lace bras. "Go in there and put one of these on and bring me that cotton thing. I'm going to burn it."

"What cotton thing?" Diana said.

"I'm wearing a plain white bra," Min told her as she stepped off the platform, her hands full of lace.

Diana widened her eyes and looked prim. "Well, you're going to hell."

"*Diana,*" Nanette said.

"I know," Min said as she headed for the dressing room. "That's where all the best men are."

"*Minerva,*" Nanette said. "Where are you going?"

"It's Thursday," Min said, over her shoulder. "I'm meeting Liza and Bonnie for dinner, and I don't want to talk about my underwear anymore." She stopped in the doorway to the dressing room. "Order the bigger corset—*much bigger, Mother*—and we'll try this again when it comes in."

"No carbs," her mother called after her as she went into the dressing room. "*And no butter.*"

"I know you stole me from my real parents," Min called back. "They'd let me eat butter." Then she shut the door behind her before Nanette could tell her to avoid sugar, too.

Chapter Four

When Cal got home from work, he flipped on the white overhead light, kicked off his shoes, and went into the white galley kitchen behind the white breakfast bar to pour himself a Glenlivet. Even as he poured, Elvis Costello blared out in the next apartment, reverberating "She" through the wall.

"Oh, Christ," Cal said, and put his glass on his forehead. Shanna's rocky romance must have crashed. He tossed back the drink and went to pound on her door.

When Shanna opened the door, her pretty face was tear-stained under her tangled mop of soft kinky hair. "Hi, Cal," she said and sniffed. "Come on in."

He followed her into the Technicolor version of his apartment, wincing until she'd turned Elvis down to a reasonable volume. "Tell me about it."

"It was awful," she said, going to her bright red bookcase and moving aside a madly colored tiki god doll to get the bottle of Glenlivet she kept for him.

"I just had one," he said, warding her off.

"I thought this was it." Shanna put the tiki back and changed course to the big old couch she'd covered with a purple Indian bedspread. "I thought it was forever."

"You always think it's forever." Cal sat down beside her and put his arm around her. "Who was it this time? I lost track."

"Megan," Shanna said, her face crumpling again.

"Right." Cal put his feet on the ancient trunk she used for a coffee table. "Megan the bitch. You know, maybe you should try dating for fun instead. Or take a break, that's what I—"

"Megan was fun," Shanna said.

"Megan was a humorless pain in the ass," Cal said. "Why you always fall for women who make you feel guilty is beyond me. That kind makes me run."

Shanna looked at him with watery contempt. "All kinds make you run."

"This is not about me," Cal said as Elvis finished with a last big, "She!" and began again; Shanna had put him on replay. "You have to get a new breakup song."

"I love this song," Shanna said.

"I used to like it," Cal said. "But that was many months ago before you bashed me over the head with it every time your latest disaster left. You're ruining Elvis Costello."

"Nobody can ruin Elvis. Elvis is a god," Shanna said.

"Isn't Megan the one who hated Elvis?" Cal said.

"No, that was Anne," Shanna said. "Although Megan wasn't a fan, either."

"Well, there it is," Cal said. "Play Elvis on the first date, and if she doesn't like him, get rid of her before you get attached."

"Is that what you do?" Shanna let her head fall back on his arm. "Is that how you go through all those women unscathed?"

"This is not about me," Cal said. "This is about you. Stop dating people you think you should like and spend time with somebody who's fun to be with."

"There are people like that?" Shanna said.

"They all are in the beginning," Cal said, and then remembered Min. "Well, except for the woman I had dinner with last night. She was pretty much a pain in the butt from the start."

"Of course you picked up a woman last night." Shanna rolled her head to look at him. "They could drop you in the middle of a guy's locker room and you'd come out with a woman. How do you do it?"

Cal grinned at her. "My natural charm." He could almost see the actuary rolling her eyes as he said it.

Shanna rolled her head away. "And the sad thing is, that's true. I have no natural charm."

"Yes, you do," Cal said. "You just don't use it."

Shanna looked back at him. "I do?"

"When you're not worried about impressing some snobby twit, you're great," Cal said. "You're smart and funny and a good time."

"I am?"

"I hang out with you, don't I?"

"Well, yeah, but you're just being nice."

"I'm not nice," Cal said. "I'm selfish as all hell. And since you've made it clear you'll never sleep with me, I must be spending time with you because you're fun, right? Not counting these wet Elvis nights."

"Right," Shanna said, brightening some.

"Well, my standards of fun are very high," Cal said. "So you must be great. You just date the biggest bitches I've ever met in my life."

"Oh, and the women you date are all sweethearts." Shanna got up and moved away from him.

"This is not about me," Cal said. "The reason you keep crashing and burning is that you have no confidence and you keep picking women who like that about you."

"I know." Shanna sat down on the red barstool next to her breakfast bar and shoved back the yellow curtain she'd draped in the opening to reach for her Betty Boop cookie jar.

"So you should pick somebody who makes you feel good."

Shanna opened the cookie jar and took out an Oreo. "I know."

"How many times have we had this talk?"

"A thousand." Shanna bit savagely into her cookie.

"And every time, you abuse Elvis. That was a good song and you ran it into the ground. Sooner or later, you're going to pay for that."

"I know," Shanna said around her Oreo.

"Pick something that has some fight to it," Cal said. "There must be a pissed-off breakup song."

"I've always liked 'I Will Survive,'" Shanna said, cheering up a little.

"Oh, Christ." Cal stood up. Behind him, Elvis began to sing "She" again. "Set him free, will you?"

Shanna crossed to the bookcase and turned Elvis off. "They're not mean when I meet them, you know."

"Remember your first date with Megan?" Cal said. "You introduced us in the hall?" Shanna nodded. "She apologized for your clothes. I would have bitch-slapped her then but she looked like she could take me."

"She had very high standards."

"She was a bitter, controlling snob," Cal said. "You should have cut your losses after the first date."

"Is that what you did last night?" Shanna said.

"Hell, yes," Cal said.

"Well, I can't do that," Shanna said, going back to her cookie jar. "I'm not like you. I have to give it a fair shot."

Cal sighed. "All right. Why did she leave?"

Shanna's face crumpled again. "She said I was too much of a doormat."

"Well, she wiped her feet on you often enough to know," Cal said. Shanna burst into tears, and he went to her and put his arms around her. "Get mad at her, Shan. She was not a nice person."

"But I loved her!" Shanna wailed into his chest, spitting Oreo crumbs on his shirt.

"No, you didn't," Cal said, holding her tighter. "You wanted to love her. It's not the same thing. You only knew her a couple of weeks."

"It can happen like that." Shanna looked up into his face. "You can just know."

"No," Cal said. "You do not look at somebody, hear Elvis Costello singing 'She' on the soundtrack in your head, and fall in love. It takes time."

"Like you'd know." Shanna pulled away and picked up her cookie jar. "Have you ever stayed with anybody long enough to love her?"

"Hey," Cal said, insulted.

"That's no answer," Shanna said, retreating to her couch with her cookies. "Is that why you keep walking away so fast? Because at least I *try*."

"This is not about me," Cal said.

"I know, I know," Shanna said, fishing out another Oreo. "God, I'm a mess. Want a cookie?"

"No," Cal said. "Get your act together and try again tomorrow. If you swing by the office, I'll take you to lunch before you go to work."

"That would be nice," Shanna said. "You're a good person, Cal. Sometimes I wish you were a woman—"

"Thank you," Cal said doubtfully.

"—and then I remember you have that commitment phobia and I'm glad you're a guy. I have enough problems."

"This is true." Cal put his hand on the doorknob. "Can I go home now?"

"Sure," Shanna said. "Take me someplace expensive tomorrow."

"I'll take you to Emilio's," Cal said. "He needs the business and you like the pesto."

While Cal was trying to prop up Shanna, Min stopped by Emilio's to pick up salad and bread.

"Ah, the lovely Min!" he said when she tracked him down in his kitchen.

"Emilio, my darling," Min said. "I need salad and bread for three right now and a kickass wedding cake for two hundred three weeks from Sunday."

"Oh." Emilio leaned against the counter. "My grandmother makes wedding cakes. They taste like . . ." He shut his eyes. ". . . heaven. Light as a feather." He opened his eyes. "But they're good, old-fashioned cakes, they don't have marzipan birds or fondant icing."

"Could she make a cake and decorate it with fresh flowers?" Min said. "I can get some real pearls. Maybe if the cake is covered with real things instead of sugar imitations, people will be impressed."

"I don't know," Emilio said. "But what matters is how it tastes, and it will taste—"

"Emilio, that's sweet," Min said, imagining Nanette's reaction to that one. "Unfortunately, in this case, what matters is how it looks."

"How about this," Emilio said. "I'll see if she'll do the cake. If she says yes, she'll ice it plain, and you can put the flowers and the pearls on it."

"Me," Min said doubtfully. "Well, not me, but Bonnie can do it, she has fabulous taste. It's a deal. Call your grandma."

Emilio picked up the phone. "So you taking Cal to this wedding?"

"I'm never seeing Cal again," Min said.

"God, you guys are dumb," Emilio said as he punched the numbers into the phone. In a moment, his face brightened. "Nonna?" he said and began to talk in Italian. The only word Min recognized was "Cal" which was worrying, but when Emilio hung up, he was smiling.

"It's all set," he said. "I told her you were Cal's girlfriend. She loves Cal."

"All women do." Min kissed him on the cheek. "You are my hero."

"That's the food," Emilio said, and packed up bread and salad for three for her. Then she went home and walked up thirty-two steps to Bonnie's apartment on the first floor.

"So," Liza said when she answered Bonnie's door. "You want to explain last night?"

"Can I come in first?" Min said, and slid past Liza into Bonnie's bright, warm apartment.

Bonnie had set her mission table with her Royal Doulton Tennyson china and a cut glass vase of grocery roses. It looked so pretty that Min thought, *Okay, my apartment will never look this good, but I could set a better table. I could even cook. I could get my grandmother's kitchen things out of the basement.* It would be nice to do kitchen stuff like her grandmother had. Maybe bake cookies.

That she couldn't eat.

Min sighed and put the Styrofoam boxes down on Bonnie's table.

"What's that?" Bonnie said, poking at the Styrofoam.

"The best salad you'll ever eat, and even better bread," Min said, and Bonnie went to get serving bowls.

"Bread?" Liza said to Min. "You're going to eat bread?"

"No," Min said. "I ate bread last night and then paid for it today. You're going to eat bread, and I'm going to live vicariously."

Liza made a face as she pulled out one of Bonnie's tall dining room chairs. "Like dessert. Stats, you—"

"What did you bring?" Min said, dreading the answer.

"Raspberry Swirl Dove Bars," Liza said, as she sat down.

"Rot in hell," Min said, pulling out her own chair. "Why can't you ever bring fruit?"

"Because fruit is not dessert," Liza said. "Now explain to us why you left the bar with Calvin Morrisey last night."

Min shoved the bread box Liza's way. "David bet him ten bucks he couldn't get me into bed in a month." She watched them freeze in place, Bonnie with a platter of chicken and vegetables in her hands, Liza opening the bread.

"You are *kidding me*," Liza said, her face dangerous with anger.

"I let him pick me up because I had a plan to get a date to the wedding, and then I realized I couldn't put up with that smarmy charm for three weeks, so I ate an excellent dinner and left."

Bonnie's face crumpled. "Oh, honey, that's awful."

"No," Min said. "Let's forget Cal Morrisey and eat. I want to talk about Diana. She's not happy."

"Wet and Worse." Liza gave Min a look that said they'd be talking about Cal again soon. "They'd bring anybody down."

Min closed her eyes. "Do not call them that. I almost called Susie Wet this afternoon at the fitting. She looked like she was about to sob through the whole thing."

"Well, that's understandable," Bonnie said, sympathy in her voice. She put the platter in the middle of the table and sat down, too.

Liza dumped the bread into a bowl. "Maybe Di shouldn't have asked Wet to be a bridesmaid. That's almost cruel."

"It would be worse not to be asked," Bonnie said. "Is that why she's upset, Min?"

"I think it's Greg," Min said, starting on her salad, "but she won't admit it. He's the one who forgot to order the wedding cake."

"Whoa," Liza said. "This is a man who's resisting his own wedding. And let's face it, your mother and Diana railroaded him into it."

"He proposed on his own," Bonnie said.

"I think he wanted a longer engagement," Min said. "But he said yes when they set the date. He's not incapable of speech. He could have said 'No.'"

"To Nanette and Diana?" Liza said as she started on her salad. "Fat chance. Worse will do a kind deed before Greg will grow a spine. Now you talk about Calvin Morrisey and this damn bet. We want to know *everything*."

Half an hour later, the salad was gone, the leftover chicken was in the refrigerator, and Bonnie was unwrapping a Dove Bar as Min finished her recap of the evening.

"At least he walked you home," Bonnie said. "That was nice." She sounded doubtful.

"Yes. And then he hit me in the head, said, 'Have a nice life,' and left me," Min said. "I didn't like him, you guys don't like him, and he didn't like me. I think that's a perfect score."

"I think that whole good-bye thing is a trick," Liza said around a mouthful of Dove Bar. "I think he's putting you off guard, and he'll be back. If you're not careful, he'll charm you into bed and break your heart."

Min frowned at her in exasperation. "How naïve do I look? I know about the bet. Anyway, I have a new plan."

"Oh, good," Liza said. "Because you don't have enough plans."

Min ignored her. "I was listening to Elvis singing 'Love Me Tender' last night, and it occurred to me that if he'd been reincarnated, he'd be about twenty-seven now, and I'm open to younger men. Statistically, the most successful marriages are those in which the woman is eight years older than the man. So I've decided to wait for Elvis to find me."

"You'd only be six years older," Bonnie said.

"Yes, but it would be Elvis, so I'd try harder," Min said.

"Why Elvis?" Liza said.

"Because he always tells the truth when he sings. Elvis is the only man in my life I can trust."

"So let me get this straight," Lisa said, pointing with her half-eaten Dove Bar. "Bonnie is waiting for a fairy tale character to make her life complete, and you're holding out for the reincarnation of a guy who ate fried banana sandwiches."

"Yep," Min said, and Liza shook her head.

"I might have found my prince," Bonnie said. "Roger's good."

"Roger?" Min asked, trying not to watch Liza consume her Dove Bar.

"We picked up the beast's friends last night," Liza said around her ice cream. "Bonnie got the one that walks upright."

"Roger is a sweetheart," Bonnie said. "I'm thinking of breaking my date Saturday night and going out with him instead. I'll wait and see how Friday night with him works out."

"He asked you out?" Min said, relieved to be off the subject of Cal. "Tell all."

"He asked her out for every night for the rest of her life," Liza said. "He's blind for her."

"That's nice." Min picked a last salad leaf out of her bowl to compensate for her lack of sugar. "So he has potential, Bon?"

"Maybe." Bonnie came as close to frowning as she ever did. "I think if I keep seeing him for a couple of weeks and it's working, I'll take him home to Mama and let her scope him out."

Min raised her eyebrows. "You think he'll cross three states to meet your mother after two weeks?"

"He would cross the Andes to get her a toothpick," Liza said. "It's pathetic."

"No, it's not." Bonnie frowned over her ice cream stick. "It's sweet. And he thinks Cal is great, which is confusing."

"So Bonnie met a good one," Min said to Liza, ignoring the Cal reference. "Who'd you get?"

"The village idiot," Liza said. "He also thinks Cal is the man. They're like the Three Stooges. Only not funny."

"The Three Stooges aren't funny," Bonnie said.

"Too true," Min said. "Are you seeing the idiot again?"

"Yes." Liza licked the last of her ice cream off the stick. "I think your beast is coming back, and my idiot babbles nicely when I ask him questions. Plus, there is a bartender who lives next door to the beast with whom I must bond."

"Well, don't ask questions for me," Min said. "Calvin Morrisey is not part of my future."

"He will be tomorrow night," Bonnie said. "He'll be at The Long Shot with Roger and Tony."

Min shook her head. "Then I'll stay home."

"No," Bonnie said, stricken. "We don't have to go there. We'll go somewhere else so you can come, too."

"And make you miss Roger?" Min reconsidered. "No. Not even I am selfish enough to cross True Love. I'll go. I want to see this Roger up close anyway."

"Are you sure Cal made that bet?" Bonnie said.

"I was standing right there," Min said. "I heard it. With my own ears. He said, 'Piece of cake.'" That rankled more than anything.

"Because Roger thinks the world of him," Bonnie said. "He told me all about him, about the three of them. It's kind of sad. They met in summer school when they were in the third grade. Roger said he was a slow thinker, and Tony didn't care about school, and Cal was dyslexic, so everybody thought they were dumb."

"Cal's dyslexic?" Min said, surprised.

"Tony *is* dumb," Liza said at the same time.

"No," Bonnie said, with the heavy patience that meant "back off." "Tony is not dumb. When he cares, he's very smart. And Roger isn't dumb, either, he's just very methodical, you can't hurry him. He's like my uncle Julian."

"Oh, God," Liza said to the ceiling. "He's like family. I will bet you anything that Roger is her If this week."

"I don't bet," Min said. "Bonnie? What's your If?"

Bonnie stuck her chin out. "If Roger turns out to be as sweet as I think he is, I'm going to marry him."

"Oh, good grief," Liza said.

"Leave her alone," Min said to Liza. "She gets whatever If she wants. What's yours?"

Liza straightened. "If my job doesn't get any more interesting, I'm quitting next week."

"Get the calendar," Min said to Bonnie.

"I don't have to," Bonnie said. "It was August when she quit the last time because she said nobody should work in a heat wave."

"Ten months," Min said. "That's not good. Her attention span is getting shorter."

"It's an If," Liza said to Min. "I'm keeping an eye on my options. I think I might want to waitress again if I can find someplace fun. What's your If?"

Min thought of Cal Morrisey, and her head began to throb. "If I can find the reincarnation of Elvis, I'll date again. Until then, I'm taking a break from inter-gender socialization. It's just too painful."

"I am the only sane woman in this room," Liza said.

"Sanity is overrated," Min said, and went home to get an aspirin.

The next night, Cal was back at The Long Shot, as far away from the landing as possible to give himself a wide escape path. Roger was ten feet away, looking at Bonnie as if she were the center of the universe. Bonnie was looking at Roger as if he were a very nice man she didn't know very well. Cal shook his head. Watching Roger date was like watching a toddler in traffic.

Tony sat down beside Cal and slid his Scotch over. "I think you should go for it," he said, nodding toward the bar.

"What?" Cal looked past Bonnie, to see a tall, slender redhead. Tony's Liza. Then she shifted and he saw Min standing behind her, draped in a loose red sweater. It had some kind of hood hanging down the back, and Roger tugged on it and said something that made her smile. "Great." Now he'd have to put up with Min slanging at him for another evening.

"It's not like you to stare and not do anything about it," Tony said. "You are losing it."

"I was watching Roger and Bonnie," Cal said.

"Oh." Tony looked over at Roger and shrugged. "Yep, he's a goner. Well, we all gotta die sometime."

"Yeah, you're the guy I want watching my back," Cal said.

"Well, what are you gonna do?" Tony looked past him and straightened. "What the hell? Where do they think they're going?"

Cal turned back to see the four of them commandeer a poker table on the other side of the bar. "Not here," he said, cheering up. Evidently Min had had as bad a time as he'd had. Which was her own fault because she was impossible to please. God knew he'd tried. Well, except for clipping her there at the end.

She sat down beside Liza, and he watched her as she leaned back and stretched out her black-clad legs. Her legs were pretty good, strong full calves, sturdy, like Min in general.

"She'll be over here in five minutes," Tony said.

"Ten bucks says she won't," Cal said, turning back to his Glenlivet.

"You're on," Tony said. "She wants me."

"You?" Cal said, startled. "Oh, you mean Liza." He looked back at the redhead who was laughing with Min and giving no evidence whatsoever that she knew Tony existed. "Nope, she won't, either."

"Oh, you were talking about the chub?" Tony said.

"Don't call her that," Cal said. "Her name is Min. She's a good woman, apart from her rage." He watched her as she leaned sideways in her chair to say something to Bonnie. "She's not chubby. She's just got a really round body. Everywhere."

"Nice rack," Tony said, trying to be fair. "So you struck out, huh?"

"No," Cal said, turning his back on them again. "I asked her to dinner and she went. Then I walked her home and said good-bye. I did not strike out."

"Finally, a woman you can't get," Tony said, satisfaction in his voice. "That's kind of depressing because it's like an era is passing—"

"I didn't *try*," Cal said.

"—but it's good to know you put on your pants one leg at a time like the rest of us."

"I've never understood that," Cal said. "How else would you put on your pants?"

Tony leaned over. "Ten bucks says you can't get Min to go out with you tomorrow night."

"I don't want to go out with her tomorrow night," Cal said.

"Take her to the movies," Tony said. "You won't have to talk to her."

"Tony . . ."

"Ten bucks, hotshot. I don't think you can do it."

Cal looked over his shoulder at Min. All the laughing aside, she didn't look any more relaxed than she'd been Wednesday night. And she was ignoring him. He shook his head at Tony. "She won't go. No bet."

"This is hard to believe," Tony said. "You chickening out."

"Tony, she hates men right now. She just broke up with somebody."

"Well, there you go. She's on the rebound," Tony said. "That gives you an edge. You could get her into bed."

"I don't want her in bed," Cal said. "She'll probably ice pick the next guy she sleeps with to get even with the guy who dumped her. Trust me, this is not a woman you close your eyes around."

"Wuss," Tony said. "I'll make it easy. Lunch. Ten bucks says you can't get her to lunch."

Cal looked over at Min again. What would get her to lunch? She was sitting back in her chair now, smiling at Roger, as if she were sizing him up. Protective of her friend. She could relax about Roger. If Bonnie got him, she'd be a lucky woman.

Of course, Min didn't know that.

"You in?" Tony said.

So if he went over and said—

"Cynthie just came in," Tony said.

"*Hell.*" Cal sat up but didn't look toward the door. "She hates this bar. Why—"

"She's stalking you," Tony said. "She must really want to get married. And she's headed this way."

"Right." Cal stood up. "Come on."

"Where?" Tony said, not rising.

"Over there so you can harass your redhead while I get a lunch date and duck Cyn. You're on."

"You just lost ten bucks, old buddy," Tony said, practically chortling. "I saw Min's face when you came in, and she was not happy to see you." He stood up, too. "I can't believe you went for that. You hit her in the head, you dork. Why would she go anywhere with you?"

"Ten bucks first," Cal said, holding out his hand.

"You have to get the date first," Tony said. "Which ain't happening."

"No, this is for the redhead who did not come to get you in five minutes," Cal said, and Tony sighed and got out his wallet.

Min was ignoring Cal and checking out Roger, when Liza pulled up the chair to her right and sat down.

"So," Liza said, sliding over a Diet Coke and rum. "What's new with Di?"

"I called her today," Min said, picking up her drink. "I asked her if everything was okay with Wet—" She closed her eyes. "—with *Susie*, and she said, yes, Susie's dating a very nice man and she's fine with the wedding. And Worse . . . and *Karen* has talked to Susie and has assured Diana that Susie's fine with it."

"Is she delusional?" Liza said, as somebody pulled up a chair to Min's left.

"Who? Wet, Worse, or Diana?" Min said.

"All of them," Liza said.

"My guess is that Wet's being brave, Worse is being a bully, and Diana's in denial," Min said, turning to see who was on her left. "Oh," she said, when she saw Cal sitting there with two glasses in front of him. He was as beautiful as he'd been two nights before, and her DNA went wild again.

"Hello, little girl," he said and flipped the hood on her sweater.

Liza snorted and turned to talk to Bonnie on her other side.

"Oh, that's good," Min said. "You're definitely the first person to make a Red Riding Hood crack to me tonight. I'm never wearing this sweater again."

"Hostility," Cal said. "It's déjà vu all over again. How's your head?"

"The pain comes and goes," Min said. "And then there are the voices."

"Good. Now you have someone to talk to. Who are Wet, Worse, and Diana, and how did they get those terrible names?"

"Nobody you want to know." Min picked up her drink. "What are you up to?"

"Let me guess," Cal said, his voice heavy with scorn. "That's a rum and Diet Coke. The breakfast of dieters."

"Don't you have somewhere else to be?"

"No, Buffy. Fate sent me over here to teach you to drink with dignity." He took her rum away from her and slid one of his glasses over to her. "Glenlivet. Drink it slowly."

Min frowned at him. "This is your idea of charm?"

"No," Cal said. "I don't waste charm on you. I'm trying to help you grow. Real women do not screw up good booze with diet soda."

"Peer pressure," Min said. "It never stops."

"Try it," Cal said. "One sip. You hate it, I'll give you this slop back."

Min shrugged. "Okay." She picked it up and took a drink and then choked as the Scotch seared her throat.

"I said, *sip*, Dobbs," Cal said over her gasping. "You're supposed to savor it, not guzzle it."

"Thank you," Min said when she had her breath back. "You can go now."

"No, I can't." He leaned closer, and Min started to feel too warm in her sweater. "I have a deal for you."

Min picked up the Scotch again and sipped it. It was nice when you sipped it.

Cal leaned closer until he was almost whispering in her ear. "I want to know about Bonnie."

His breath was warm on her neck, and Min blinked at him. "Bonnie? I think Roger's got dibs on Bonnie."

"I know. That's why I want to know about her. Roger is . . ." Cal looked across the table. ". . . not adept with women. I want to know about your friend."

"Well," Min said, prepared to give Bonnie a perfect report card.

"Not here," Cal said, still too close. "I think they'll notice. I'll meet you for lunch tomorrow. You know where Cherry Hill Park is?"

"I've heard of it," Min said. "I don't have the bank account to go up there and hang around."

"There's a picnic area on the north side," Cal said. "I'll meet you at the first table tomorrow at noon."

"Why do I feel like there should be a code word?" Min said, finally pulling away from him. "I'll say 'pretentious' and you say 'snob.' "

"You want to know about Roger or not?" Cal said.

Min looked back at Bonnie. If you didn't know her, she looked detached, but Min knew her. Bonnie was glowing. "Yes."

"Good," Cal said. "Let me see your shoes."

"What?" Min said, and Cal looked under the table. She pulled her foot out, and he looked down at her open-toed high-heeled mules, laced across her instep with black leather thongs that contrasted with her pale skin and bright red toenail polish. "Liza calls them 'Toes in Bondage,'" she said helpfully.

"Does she?" Cal sat very still, looking at her toes for a long moment. "Well, that's made my evening. See you tomorrow at noon." He pushed back his chair and left, taking his Scotch and her rum and Diet Coke with him.

"Okay, I couldn't hear the part at the end," Liza said, leaning over to her. "What was he asking you?"

"I'm going to lunch tomorrow," Min said, not sure how she felt about that. If he whispered in her ear again, she was going to have to smack him, that was all there was to it.

"Where?"

"Cherry Hill Park."

"Jeez," Liza said. "Softball of the Rich and Famous. What time?"

"Noon."

Liza nodded. Then she raised her voice and called, "Tony."

Min looked around for him and saw him at the roulette bar, handing Cal a ten-dollar bill. "I don't *believe* it," she said, straightening in outrage. The sonofabitch had bet on lunch and she'd fallen for it.

Tony looked up, and Liza crooked her finger. He walked over and said, "You know, I'm not the kind of guy you can do that to."

"You and I are having lunch at noon tomorrow in Cherry Hill Park," Liza said.

"Okay," Tony said. "But only because I've gotta coach a softball game there in the morning anyway."

"Good," Liza said. "You can go now."

Tony shook his head at her and went back to the bar and Cal.

"Well, at least he's obedient," Min said.

"Don't get any ideas about saying yes at lunch," Liza said.

"It's *lunch*," Min said. "In broad daylight. In a public park."

"You said you weren't going to see him, and he still got you to lunch."

"I had a reason for that," Min said, casting a bitter glance at the bar. Cal was still there, but now the brunette from Wednesday was there, too, moving closer to him in a blue halter top. That figured. Beast. "I'll be fine, believe me, I know what he is." She cast another look at the bar where Cal appeared to be sliding away from the halter top. Playing hard to get, the jerk.

"Yeah, well, I'm watching your back just the same," Liza said. "And if it hits the grass, Calvin's going to lose a body part."

"Boy, you really don't like him, do you?" Min said.

"I think he bet Tony he could get that lunch date," Liza said.

"I think so, too," Min said.

"See if you can do something horrible to him tomorrow," Liza said.

"Already planning it," Min said.

After another excruciating Saturday morning forcing fourteen eight-year-olds to play baseball against their better judgments, Cal was not in the mood to put up with Min, but he grabbed his cooler from the car, stopped by the charity hot dog stand for the main course, and went to meet her at the picnic table he'd told her about. She wasn't there, so he threw an old blanket across the massive teak table—Cherry Hill did not stint on the amenities—put the basket on it, and then sat on top of the table, feeling cheerful about being stood up. It was a beautiful day, the park was thick with shade trees, the kids were gone, and nobody was bitching at him.

Then Min came into the park through the trees, following the curving crushed gravel path. She was wearing her long red sweater again, but this time she had on a red-and-black-checked skirt that floated when the breeze blew. Her hair was still wound in a knot on the top of her head, but her stride was long and loose as she came toward him, and the sun picked up glints of gold in her hair, and she smiled at him as she drew closer, and it suddenly seemed better not to have been stood up. And when he offered her his hand to help her up on the table, she hesitated and then took it, and her fingers were pleasantly, solidly warm as she boosted herself up beside him on the table.

"Hi," she said and he grinned at her.

"Hi," he said. "Thank you for coming."

"Thank you for inviting me." Min dropped her bag on the bench below them. "Give me ten bucks."

Cal blinked. "What?"

Min smiled at him, cheerful as the sun. "I was going to make your lunch a living hell, but it's such a beautiful day, I've decided to enjoy it. You bet Tony ten bucks you could get me to lunch."

"No, I didn't," Cal said.

Min's smile disappeared.

"Tony bet me ten bucks I could get you to lunch."

Min rolled her eyes. "Whatever. Give me ten bucks or I'm leaving you cold and you'll have to give Tony his ten bucks back plus ten more because you've lost."

"I think I won when you said, 'Yes,'" Cal said, suddenly a lot more interested in Min.

"Try explaining that to Tony," Min said.

"Okay," Cal said. "How about we split it?"

Min held out her hand and wiggled her fingers. "Ten bucks, Charm Boy."

Cal sighed and dug out his wallet, trying not to grin at her. She took the ten, picked up her bag, stuffed the bill in it and then pulled out a twenty and handed it to him.

"What's this?" Cal said.

"That's the twenty you gave me for cab fare on Wednesday," Min said. "I forgot to give it back to you."

"So now I'm up ten bucks," Cal said.

"No, now you've broken even. It was your twenty to begin with. I had no right to it since you didn't get fresh."

Cal looked up at the sun. "The day's young."

"I don't see you making your move on a picnic table," Min said. "In fact, I don't see you moving on me at all, so tuck that away and tell me everything you know about Roger."

"I'm glad to see you, too," he said, and her smile widened.

"Sorry. I forgot your lust for small talk. And how have you been in the fourteen hours since we last spoke, eight of which you were sleeping?"

"Fine. And you?"

"Wonderful. How much of this before we get to Roger and Bonnie?"

"You're a very practical woman," Cal said, and then Min pulled her legs up to tuck them under her and he caught sight of her shoes, ridiculous sandals made mostly of ribbons with a single bright red flower over the instep. "Except for your shoes."

"Don't make fun of my shoes." Min wiggled red-tipped toes under the flowers. "I love these shoes. Liza gave them to me for Christmas." She untied the ribbons and pulled them off and put them on the table behind her, patting the flowers before she turned back to him.

"I can see why you love them," Cal said, distracted by her toes, and then she pulled her skirt over them and he added, "They're very Elvis."

She raised her eyebrows. "*You* are an Elvis fan?"

"Best there is," Cal said. "You, too?"

"Oh, absolutely." Min looked perplexed and then said, "Well, I guess it does makes sense. You are the devil in disguise."

"What?" Cal said, and then it hit him. "Elvis *Presley*?"

"Well, of course, Elvis Presley," Min said. "What other . . . *oh*. The angels want to wear my red shoes. Elvis Costello." She shrugged. "He's good, too."

Cal shook his head in disbelief. "Yes, he is."

"Good thing this isn't a date," Min said cheerfully. "Or there'd be a really awkward silence while we tried to come back from that one."

Cal grinned at her. "Have you ever had an awkward silence in your life, Dobbs?"

"Not many," Min said. "You?"

"Nope." Cal dumped the bag of wrapped hot dogs out on the blanket. "Okay. Roger and Bonnie. Have a hot dog while we talk."

"A hot dog?" Min said, in the same tone of voice she'd have used to say "Cocaine?" "Those aren't good for you."

"They're protein," Cal said, exasperated. "You can have them. Just lose the bun."

"Fat," Min said.

"I thought fat was okay on no-carb diets," Cal said, remembering Cynthie chowing down on buttered shrimp.

"It is, but I'm on a no-fat Atkins," Min said.

Cal looked at her, incredulous. "Which leaves you *what* to eat?"

"Not much," Min said, looking at the hot dogs with patent longing.

"They're brats," Cal said.

"Oh, just hell," Min said.

"It's Saturday," Cal said. "Live a little."

"That's what you said Wednesday at Emilio's. I've already sinned this week."

"Saturday is the first day of the new week. Sin again."

Min bit her lip, and the breeze picked up again, rustling the trees and lifting the edge of skirt, floating it closer to him.

"I brought you Diet Coke to compensate," he said, opening the cooler. "Also, this conversation is boring."

"Right. Sorry." She took the can he handed her and popped it open. "Really sorry. There's nothing more boring than talking about food."

"No," Cal said. "Talking about food is great. Talking about not having food is boring." He picked up one of the wax-paper-wrapped sandwiches and handed it to her. "Eat."

Min looked at the hot dog, sighed, and unwrapped it. "You are a beast."

"Because I'm feeding you?" Cal said. "How is that bad? We're Americans. We're supposed to eat well. It's the American Way."

"Hot dogs are the American Way?" Min said, and then stopped. "Oh. I guess they are, aren't they? Right up there with baseball and apple pie."

"Baseball you can have," Cal said and bit into his hot dog.

Min squinted at his team shirt. "Isn't that shirt sort of baseball-ish?"

"Yes," Cal said. "For my sins, I teach children to run around bases on Saturday mornings. Someday, your husband will be doing this, too, while you sit in the bleachers and cheer on little whosis. It's the price you pay for liberty."

"I'm not having kids," Min said, and bit into her hot dog.

"You're not?" Cal said, and then was distracted by the look of bliss on her face while she chewed. The brats were good, but they weren't that good.

She swallowed and sighed. "This is wonderful. My dad used to sneak us out for brats every time there was a festival anyplace within driving distance. My mother would have killed him if she'd known. Do you know how long it's been since I tasted one of these? It's heaven."

"It looks like heaven," he said, and then she leaned over to take another bite, keeping the sandwich over the waxed paper to catch the drippings, and he looked down the v-neck of her loose red sweater and saw a lot of lush round flesh in tight red lace. *Tony would have a heart attack*, he thought and then realized he was a little lightheaded himself. The breeze blew again and wafted her skirt against the hand he had braced on the table, and it tickled, soft and light.

"So," he said, moving his hand. "All right. Why don't you want to be part of the American Way?"

She chewed with her eyes closed, and he looked down her sweater again and had impure thoughts. Then she swallowed and said, "I have to give birth to be a good American? No. There are more than four million babies born in this country every year. The American Way is covered. If it worries you, you can have extra to make up for mine."

"Me?" Cal sat back away from distraction. "I don't want kids. I'm just surprised that you don't. You'd make a great mom."

"Why?" Min stopped with the sandwich halfway to her mouth.

Because she looked soft all over. Because she looked like she'd age into the kind of mother he'd have killed for. "Because you look comfortable."

"Oh, God, *yes*," Min said, glaring at him. "That's *exactly* the compliment every woman longs for."

She leaned forward to bite into her sandwich, and he watched transfixed as her breasts pressed against the lace again.

"It's a very sexy comfortable if that makes it better," he said.

"Marginally better," she said, following his eyes down. "You're looking down my sweater."

"You're leaning over. There's all that red lace right there."

"Lace is good, huh?" Min said.

"Oh, yeah."

"My mother wins again," Min said and bit into her hot dog.

Cal picked up his hot dog. "How'd your mother get into this?"

"She's pervasive." Min swallowed, frowning. "So if you don't like kids, how'd you end up coaching?"

"I didn't say I didn't like kids," Cal said, trying to think of something beside Min's red lace. "I said I didn't want kids. There's a difference."

"Good point. And yet I ask, why coach?"

"I got shanghaied," Cal said. "We both did. Harry hates baseball as much as I hate coaching."

"Who's Harry?"

"My nephew."

"Why don't the two of you go AWOL?"

"Turns out there are other kids on the team besides Harry," Cal said. "Who knew?"

"Funny. So you're out here every Saturday morning?" Min shook her head. "That must have been some shanghai."

"I got hit by the best." He picked up a pickle and bit into it. "It's not that bad. Roger and Tony do most of the work. They like it."

"Roger," Min said. "Ah yes, Roger. I have some questions about Roger."

"Not Tony?" Cal said.

"Tony is seeing Liza," Min said. "If Tony turns out to be a rat, Liza will exterminate him."

"Tony's hard to put down," Cal said, "but I get your drift. So Bonnie's not like that?"

"Bonnie is no pushover," Min said. "She's smart and she's tough but she has this one blind spot. She believes in the fairy tale, that there's one man in the world for her. And she thinks your friend Roger is her prince on very little evidence. So tell me about Roger."

"Roger's the best guy I know," Cal said. "And he's crazy about Bonnie. He's going to get banged up if she walks away. Tell me about Bonnie."

Min shifted on the blanket as she reached for her Coke can, and Cal watched her, aware of every move she made, of the smooth curve of her neck as her sweater slipped toward her shoulder, the ease in her round body as she leaned back and smiled at him, the swell of her calf under her checked skirt as it blew toward him again. "Bonnie," she said, bringing him back to the subject at hand, "spent a year and a half looking at couches. Couches are very important, they're right up there with beds in hierarchy of furniture, but even I thought a year and a half was a long time looking for a couch."

"Yes," Cal said, trying to think of Roger instead of curves. "But—"

"Then one night we were on the way to the movies and she stopped in front of a furniture store window and said, 'Wait a minute,' and went in and bought this horribly expensive couch in about five minutes." Min leaned forward again, and Cal looked down her sweater again and thought, *Don't do that, I'm getting a headache from the blood rush.* "She had to put it on two different credit cards," Min went on, "and it took her two years to pay it off, but it's a great couch and she's never regretted it, and when she had it reupholstered, the upholsterer said it would last forever."

"Great," Cal said, still looking down her sweater. She was breathing softly, just enough for the rise and fall to—

"*Hello,*" she said and he jerked his head up. "Not that I'm not flattered, but I'm making a point here. Roger is Bonnie's new couch. She's always been sure that some day her prince would show up, and she's done a lot of dating looking for him, and now she's taken one look at Roger and she's sure he's the one, and she's going to buy him in about a minute. So if he isn't a good guy, I want to know now so I can break it to her. Tell me he's not a rat."

"Roger took a year to buy a couch, too," Cal said, regrouping.

"What kind of couch?" Min said.

"Sort of a La-Z-Boy with a thyroid problem," Cal said. "I think it's brown."

Min nodded. "Bonnie bought a reproduction mission settle with cushions upholstered in a celadon William Morris print."

"I think I know what 'mission' is," Cal said. "Everything else, you were speaking Chinese."

"Roger's couch is toast," Min said. "Will he mind?"

"She can chop it into kindling in front of him and he won't blink," Cal said.

"Can he take care of her?" Min said. "She probably won't need it, but in a crunch—"

"He will throw his body in front of her if necessary. You have nothing to worry about with Roger. He's the best guy I know. If I had a sister, I would let Roger marry her. It's Bonnie I'm worried about it. She's got that efficient look that usually means she likes to boss people around. And since she's so little, there's probably a Napoleon complex—"

"Nope," Min said. "She's solid. Roger's a lucky guy." She finished the last of her hot dog and then licked a smear of ketchup off her thumb, and Cal lost his train of thought. "So they're okay and we don't have to worry," she said when she'd wiped her hands on a napkin.

"Yep," Cal said. "How about dessert?"

"I don't eat dessert," Min said.

"Really?" Cal said. "What a surprise."

"Oh, bite me," Min said. "I told you there's this bridesmaid's dress—"

Cal pulled a waxed paper bag from the cooler. "Doughnuts," he said, but before he could go on, a too-familiar piping voice came from behind him.

"Can I have one?"

He sighed and turned around to see his skinny, grubby, dark-haired nephew standing at the end of the picnic table. "Shouldn't you be home by now?"

"They forgot again," Harry said, putting a lot of pathetic in his voice. It helped that he wore glasses and was small for his age. He peered around Cal. "Hello," he said cautiously to Min.

"Min," Cal said, glaring at Harry. "This is my nephew, Harry Morrisey. He was just leaving. Harry, this is Min Dobbs."

"Hi, Harry," Min said cheerfully. "You can have all the doughnuts." Harry brightened.

"No, you can't." Cal took out his cell phone. "You'd just throw them up again."

"Maybe not." Harry sidled closer to the doughnut bag.

"You do remember the cupcake disaster, right?" Cal said as he punched in his sister-in-law's number.

"Can't he have *one*?" Min smiled at Harry as he drew closer, her face soft and kind, and Cal and Harry both blinked at her for a moment because she was so pretty.

Then while Cal listened to the phone ring, Harry looked at Min's skirt and poked it with his finger.

"*Harry*," Cal said, and Min pulled out one of her sandals.

"Here," she told Harry, and he poked at the flower.

"Those are *shoes*," Harry said, as if he were observing an anomaly.

"Yep," Min said, watching him, her head tilted.

Harry poked the flower again. "That's not real."

"No," Min said. "It's just for fun."

Harry nodded as if this were a new idea, which, Cal realized, it probably was. Not a lot of floppy flowers on red toes in Harry's world.

Min reached in the bag and handed him a doughnut.

"Thank you, Min," Harry said, still channeling abused orphans.

"Don't buy his act," Cal said to Min.

"I'm not." Min grinned at Harry. "You look like you're doing fine, kid."

"I had to play baseball," Harry said bitterly. "Are those hot dogs?"

"No," Cal said. "You know you're not allowed to have processed meat. Go over there on that bench and eat your doughnut."

"He can eat it here," Min said, putting her arm around him protectively.

Harry, no dummy, leaned into Min's hip.

Bet that's soft, Cal thought, and then realized he was close to being jealous of his eight-year-old nephew. "Harry," he said warningly, but then his sister-in-law answered her phone. "Bink? You forgot to pick up your kid."

"Reynolds," Bink said in her perfectly modulated tones. "It was his turn."

"He's not here," Cal said.

Bink sighed. "Poor Harry. I'll be right there. Thank you, Cal."

"Anything for you, babe." Cal shut off his phone and looked over at Harry. "Your mother is coming. Look on the bright side, you get a doughnut and your mother, instead of nothing and your father."

"Two doughnuts," Harry said.

"Harry, you barf," Cal said. "You can't have two doughnuts. Now go away. This is a date. Seven years from now, you will understand what that means."

"This isn't a date," Min said. "He can stay."

Harry nodded at her sadly. "It's okay."

"Oh, come off it, Harrison," Cal said, knowing Harry was milking the situation. "You have a doughnut. Go over on that bench and eat it."

"All right." Harry trailed disconsolately across the grass to a nearby Lutyen bench, his doughnut clutched in his grubby little hand.

"He's so cute," Min said, laughing softly. "Who's Bink?"

"My sister-in-law," Cal said, watching Harry, who still looked skinny, grubby, and bitter to him. "I don't see the cute part. But he's not a bad kid."

"Bink," Min said, as if trying to get her head around the name.

"It's short for Elizabeth," Cal said. "Elizabeth Margaret Remington-Pastor Morrisey."

"Bink," Min said. "Okay."

Cal picked up a doughnut. "Your turn, Dobbs."

Min leaned back. "Oh no. No, no, no."

He leaned forward to wave it under her nose. "Come on, sin a little."

"I hate you," Min said, her eyes on the doughnut. "You are a beast and a vile seducer."

Cal lifted an eyebrow. "All that for one doughnut? Come on. One won't kill you."

"I am not eating a doughnut," Min said, tearing her eyes away from it. "Are you crazy? There are twelve grams of fat in one of those. I have three weeks to lose twenty pounds. Get away from me."

"This is not just a doughnut," Cal said, tearing it in two pieces under Min's eyes, the chocolate icing and glaze breaking like frost, the tender pastry pulling apart in shreds. "This is a chocolate-iced Krispy Kreme glazed. This is the caviar of doughnuts, the Dom Perignon of dough-nuts, the Mercedes-Benz of doughnuts."

Min licked her lips. "I had no idea you were a pastry freak," she said, trying to pull back farther, but the wind blew her skirt over to Cal again, and this time he moved his knee to pin it down.

He broke a bite-size piece from one of the halves. "Taste it," he said, leaning still closer to hold the piece under her nose. "Come on."

"No." Min clamped her lips shut, and then shut her eyes, too, screwing up her face as she did.

"Oh, that's adult." He reached out and pinched her nose shut, and when she opened her mouth to protest, he popped the doughnut in.

"Oh, God," she said, and her face relaxed as the pastry melted in her mouth, her smile curling across her face.

Cal relaxed, too, and thought, *Feeding this woman is like getting her drunk.*

Then she swallowed and opened her eyes, and he held out another piece so he could see that expression again. "Come here, Dobbs."

"No," Min said, pulling back. "No, no, *no.*"

"You say that a lot," Cal said. "But the look in your eyes says you want it."

"What I want and what I can have are two different things." Min leaned back farther, stretching her skirt, but her eyes were on the doughnut. "Get that thing away from me."

"Okay." Cal sat back and bit into it while she watched, the sugar rush distracting him for a moment until Min bit her lip, her strong white teeth denting the softness there. His heart picked up speed, and she shook her head at him.

"Bastard," she said.

He bit into the doughnut again, and she said, "That's enough, I'm out of here," and leaned forward to pull her skirt out from under him. "Would you get off—" she began, and he popped another piece of doughnut in her mouth and watched as her lips closed over the sweetness. Her face was beautifully blissful, her mouth soft and pouted, her full lower lip glazed with icing, and as she teased the last of the chocolate from her lip, Cal heard a rushing in his ears. The rush became a whisper—*THIS one*—and he breathed deeper, and before she could open her eyes, he leaned in and kissed her, tasting the chocolate and the heat of her mouth, and she froze for a moment and then kissed him back, sweet and insistent, blanking out all coherent thought. He let the taste and the scent and the warmth of her wash over him, drowning in her, and when she finally pulled back, he almost fell into her lap.

She sat across from him, her sweater rising and falling under quick breaths, her dark eyes flashing, wide awake, her lush lips parted, open for him, and then she spoke.

"More," she breathed and he looked into her eyes and went for her.

Chapter Five

Cal's eyes were as dark as chocolate, and Min panicked as he leaned close again. She put her hand on his chest, and said, "No, wait," and he looked down and said, "Right," and picked up another piece of doughnut. She opened her mouth to say, "No," and he slipped the piece in and the heat of her mouth dissolved the icing as she closed her eyes, and the tang went everywhere, melting into pleasure. And when she opened her eyes, he was there.

He leaned forward and kissed her softly, his mouth fitting hers so perfectly that she trembled. She tasted the heat of him and licked the chocolate off his lip and felt his tongue against hers, hot and devastating, and when he broke the kiss, she was breathless and dizzy and aching for more. He held her eyes, looking as dazed as she felt, but she wasn't deceived at all, she knew what he was.

She just didn't care.

"More," she said, and he reached for the pastry, but she said, "No, *you*," and grabbed his shirt to pull him closer, and he kissed her hard this time, his hand on the back of her head, and she fell into him, as glitter exploded behind her eyelids. She felt his hand on her waist, sliding hot under her sweater, and her blood surged, and the rush in her head said, *THIS one.*

Then he jerked forward and smacked into her.

"Ouch?" she said, and he looked behind him, still clutching her with both hands.

"What the *hell?*" Cal said.

"I said," Liza said, holding up her leather purse, "what are you doing?"

"What does it look like I'm doing?"

"I cut my mouth," Min said, touching her finger to her lip.

Cal turned back to her and pulled her finger away, his face flushed and concerned, and he was so close to her that she leaned forward as her heart pounded, and he did, too, his eyes half closed again, and she thought, *Oh, God, yes.* Then Liza jerked at Min's arm and almost pulled her off the table.

"Get *down* from there, Stats," Liza said as Min's head reeled.

"*Tony,*" Cal said through his teeth.

"Sorry, pal," Tony said. "She's uncontrollable."

"We were just having dessert." Min scooted back as far as she could with Cal still sitting on her skirt. *I know that was dumb*, she thought, trying not to look at him, *but I want that again.*

"Dessert?" Liza looked down at the table. "You're eating *doughnuts?*"

"Oh," Min said, guilt clearing some of her daze.

"What are you?" Cal glared at Liza. "The calorie police? Go away."

"No," Liza said. "I think she should eat all the doughnuts she wants. I just don't want you feeding them to her."

"*Why?*" Cal said savagely.

"Because you are Hit-and-Run Morrisey, and she's my best friend." Liza tugged on Min's arm again. "Come on. Bonnie's waiting."

"I'm *what?*"

Min tried to scoot back a little more, but Cal was still on her skirt. *Which is all right, really.*

"Bonnie's over there on a park bench talking to Roger," Tony said to Liza. "She could care less."

"Couldn't care less," Liza said. "And she could." She fixed Min with a stare. "We've talked about this. Get off that table."

Right, Min thought. *I don't want to.*

Across from her, Cal looked even more gorgeous than usual, enraged in the sunlight, but as her daze lifted, she remembered why she wasn't supposed to be there. "Could I have my skirt back, please?" she said, faintly, and he rolled back enough that she could pull the fabric free. "Thank you very much. For lunch. I had a wonderful time."

"Stay," he said, and she looked into his eyes and thought, *Oh, yes.*

"*No,*" Liza said and pulled Min off the table so that she stumbled onto the grass.

"She can make up her own mind," Cal said.

"Yeah?" Liza took a step closer to him. "Tell me you know her. Tell me you care about her. Tell me you're going to love her until the end of time."

"*Liza,*" Min said, tugging on her arm.

"I just met her three days ago," Cal said.

"Then *what are you doing kissing her like that*?" Liza turned her back on him. "Come on, Min."

"Thank you for lunch," Min said as Liza tightened her grip. She reached back for her sandals on the table and caught the ribbons, and then Liza dragged her away through the trees.

When they were gone, Cal turned to Tony and said, "I can't decide whether to have you killed or do it myself."

"Not me, Liza," Tony said. "And she did call Min's name and poke you in the side a couple of times before she whacked you in the back of the head with her purse." His eyes went to the table. "Hey, hot dogs." He sat on the table and reached for a sandwich.

"That woman is insane," Cal said, rubbing the back of his head. The heat was subsiding now that Min was gone, but it wasn't making him any happier. "That was assault."

"She's insane?" Tony said, as he unwrapped a brat. "How about you?"

"It wasn't that big a deal." *Ten minutes more and we would have been naked.* That *would have been a big deal.*

"Tell that to Harry," Tony said. "That was probably more than he needed to know about what Uncle Cal does with his free time."

"Harry?" Cal said and looked over to where Harry had been sitting. He was still there, only now there was a thin blonde with him. Bink. Cal closed his eyes and the memory of Min's heat vanished. "Tell me Bink wasn't watching us, too."

"Don't know. She wasn't there when we got here so she may just have caught the big finish. What the hell am I sitting on?" He pulled a red-flowered shoe out from under the blanket.

"Min's," Cal said, getting a nice flashback to her toes. "Give it to Liza when you get the chance. Down her throat, if possible."

"Yeah, like I'll remember," Tony said and tossed it in the cooler.

Cal dug it out again before the ice could get the flower wet and tried to get his mind off Min. "It turns out that Bonnie's a good deal, so Roger's okay." He turned Min's sandal around in his hand. It was a ridiculous thing with a little stacked heel that probably sank into the ground when she walked across the grass and that dopey flower that would get screwed up if she wore them in the rain, and that was a turn-on, too.

"Roger's not okay," Tony said around a mouthful of brat. "He's going to get married."

"It's not death," Cal said, trying to imagine why anybody as practical as Min would wear a shoe like that. But then Min clearly had an impractical streak or she wouldn't have frenched him on a picnic table. The rush he got from that blanked out sound for a moment. "What?" he said.

"I said, yes, that's why you're running like a rabbit from Cynthie," Tony said.

"Well, marriage is not for me, but it's probably for Roger," Cal said, dropping the shoe on the table. "He's never been big on excitement."

"True," Tony said. "And if Bonnie is a nice woman, maybe I'll live over their garage after all."

"More good news for me," Cal said, and thought of Min again, full and hot under his hands— *No.* He didn't need any more hostility in his life. If he wanted great sex, he could always go back to Cynthie, who at least was never bitchy. He tried to call up Cynthie's memory to blot out Min's, but she seemed gray and white next to Min's lush, exasperating, heat-inducing, open-toed Technicolor.

"What?" Tony said.

"Are there any hot dogs left?" Cal said. "That you haven't sat on?"

Tony found one under a fold in the blanket and passed it over, and Cal unwrapped it and bit into it, determined to concentrate on a sense that wasn't permeated with Min. Then he remembered her face when she'd tasted the brat, and imagined her face like that with her body moving under his, hot and lush, her lips wet—

Oh, hell, he thought.

"So what are you going to tell Harry?" Tony said.

"About what?"

"About you doing Min on a picnic table," Tony said. "You guys looked pretty hot."

"I'm going to tell him I'll explain it when he's older," Cal said, and thought, *We were hot. And now we're done.* "Much older," he said, and went back to the cooler for a beer.

"Okay, *why* did we have to leave?" Bonnie said when they were in Liza's convertible and Min was banished to the backseat.

"Because Min was swapping tongues with a doughnut pusher." Liza looked back over the seat at Min the sinner and shook her head.

Bonnie turned so she could see over the seat, too. "You ate doughnuts?"

"Yes," Min said, still trying to fight her way back from dazed. "Big deal."

Bonnie nodded as Liza started the car. "Was he a good kisser?"

"Yes," Min said. "Pretty good. Very good. World class. Phenomenal. Woke me right up. Plus there were the doughnuts, which were *amazing*." She thought about Cal again, all that heat and urgency, and as Liza started down the curving drive to the street, Min lay down on the back seat before she fell over from residual dizziness. It felt good to lie down but it was such a shame she was alone.

"Have you lost your mind?" Liza said, over the seat.

"Just for that minute or two," Min said from the seat, watching the treetops move by overhead. "I kind of enjoyed it." *A lot.*

"You know," Bonnie said to Liza, "he might be legit. He looked really happy with her. Roger even said so."

"Oh, well if *Roger* says so," Liza said.

"Don't make fun of Roger," Bonnie said, warning in her voice.

"Okay," Min said, sitting up again as her world steadied. "I'm fine now. Very practical." She picked up her shoe to untangle the ribbons. "So how was Tony?"

"Mildly amusing," Liza said. "Stop changing the subject. What are you going to do about Cal?"

"Not see him again," Min said, looking for her second sandal. "Oh, for heaven's sake. I left a shoe behind. We have to go back."

"No," Liza said and kept driving.

"They're my favorite shoes," Min said, trying to sound sincere.

"All your shoes are your favorite shoes," Liza said. "We're not going back there."

"Are you okay, honey?" Bonnie said to Min.

"I'm great," Min said, nodding like a maniac. "Cal told me all about Roger. You have my blessing."

"Based on Calvin the Beast's say-so," Liza said.

"I have ways of telling," Min said. "I know how to handle him."

"Yeah, I saw you handling him," Liza said. "You're weak."

"Oh, come on," Min said, guilt making her exasperated. "I heard the bet. I know what's going on. I'm not seeing him again. Especially since you yelled at him and called him names." She thought about Cal leaning close, how hard his chest had been against her hand, how hot his mouth had been on hers, how good his hand had felt on her breast. "I found out how he gets all those women, though," she said brightly. "Turns out it's not just the charm."

"Maybe you should see him again," Bonnie said, sounding thoughtful. "I think sometimes you just have to believe."

That might be good, Min thought.

"*Bonnie,*" Liza said. "Do you *want* her to get mutilated by the same guy who broke your cousin's heart and made that bet with David?"

That would be bad, Min thought.

"No," Bonnie said, doubt in her voice.

"Then no more pep talks about believing in toads," Liza said.

"Don't they turn into princes when you kiss them?" Bonnie said.

"That's frogs," Liza said. "Entirely different species."

"Right," Min said, trying to shove Cal out of her mind. "Toad not frog. Beast. Absolutely." Then she sighed and said, "But he really had great doughnuts," and lay back down on the seat again to recover her good sense.

David was settling down in front of the television on Sunday afternoon when the phone rang. He picked it up and heard Cynthie's voice.

"Cal and Min were in the park today," she said. "He kissed her. That's joy, it's a physiological cue, that could push them into—"

"*Wait,*" David said, and took a deep breath. It was that damn bet. Cal would do anything to win that bet.

"He fed her doughnuts," Cynthie said. "He took her on a picnic and—"

"Min ate doughnuts?" David went cold at the thought. "Min doesn't eat doughnuts. Min doesn't eat carbs. She never ate carbs with me."

"And every time he fed her a piece, he kissed her."

"Sonofabitch," David said, viciously. "What do we do?"

"We have to work on their attraction triggers, create joy, make them remember why they wanted *us*," Cynthie said. "Take her to lunch tomorrow. Make it perfect. Make her feel special and loved, give her joy, and *get her back*."

"I don't know," David said, remembering Min's face when he'd dumped her. The idea was for her to come crawling back to him, not for him to go to her.

"I'll have lunch with Cal," Cynthie said as if he hadn't spoken. "I've been lying low, hoping he'd come back on his own, but there's no time for that now. I'll have him in bed before dessert, and that should finish the whole thing."

"Min's mad at me," David said. "I think it's too soon for a lunch."

"Oh, that's very aggressive." There was a long silence and then

Cynthie said, "Her family. Did you say she needs them to approve of her lovers?"

"Yes," David said. "Her mother was crazy about me."

"There you go," Cynthie said. "Call her mother and tell her the truth about Cal and women."

"No," David said, remembering Nanette's lack of focus on anything not involving calories or fashion. "Her sister's fiancé. Greg. I'll call him tonight."

"How will that help?"

"He'll tell Diana right away," David said. "He sees her every night. And she lives with her parents, so she'll tell her mother and father. Her father is very protective."

"That's good," Cynthie said.

"He fed her doughnuts?" David said, wincing at the thought.

"One piece at a time," Cynthie said.

Bastard. He was doing it for that damn bet. After all that big talk about being cheap but not slimy, he was going to seduce Min with doughnuts and then come back to collect his ten thousand bucks. The great Calvin Morrisey wins again.

Not if I have anything to do about it.

"David?" Cynthie said.

"Trust me," David said, grimly. "Min just ate her last doughnut."

On Monday, Roger came in late to work. *Bonnie*, Cal thought, which made him think of Min, which was ridiculous.

"What is this?" Tony said. "I'm the last one in to work. It's tradition."

"Bonnie." Roger yawned as he sat down at his desk. "We talked pretty late last night."

"Talked," Tony said, sitting on the edge of the work table. "The least you could do is get laid."

Roger narrowed his eyes.

"Okay, now that we're all here—" Cal said.

"I'm going to marry Bonnie," Roger told Tony. "You don't talk like that about the woman you marry."

"Sorry," Tony said. "I'm never getting married so I wouldn't know."

"—we need to block out the Winston seminar—"

"You'll know when you find the right woman," Roger said.

"No such animal," Tony said.

"—and get *the packets done*," Cal said, raising his voice.

"She has a perfect kiss," Roger said, looking out the window, probably in what he thought was Bonnie's direction. "Did you ever kiss like that, where everything was exactly right and it just blew the top of your head off?"

"No," Tony said, looking revolted.

"Yes," Cal said, Min coming back to him in all her hot and yielding glory. They both turned to look at him, and he said, "Can we go to work now? Because we're about a minute away from breaking out the ice cream and talking about our feelings, and I don't think we can come back from that."

"I'll get on the invoices," Roger said and went to his desk.

Cal leaned back in his desk chair, opened a computer file, and thought about Min. He'd had no intentions of kissing her and then he'd jumped her, some insane impulse shoving him into her lap. And she'd been no help. She should have slapped him silly and instead there she was, saying "More," egging him on—

The phone rang and Tony picked it up. "Morrisey, Packard, Capa," he said and then rolled his eyes at Cal. "Hey, Cynthie."

Cal shook his head.

"He's not here," Tony said. "I think he's gone for the morning." He scowled at Cal, who sighed and leaned back in his chair to look at the ceiling.

"Lunch?" Tony said. "Sorry, he's got a lunch date. At Emilio's. With his new girlfriend."

Cal sat up so fast his feet that hit the floor hard. *No*, he mouthed at Tony and made a slicing motion across his throat with his hand.

"So you don't have to worry about him being depressed over losing you," Tony said. "He got right back on the horse."

Cal stood up, rage in his eyes, and Tony said. "Gotta go," and hung up.

"Are you insane?" Cal said.

"Hey, it got rid of her, didn't it?" Tony said. "I did you a favor." He frowned. "I think. The whole thing sort of came to me in a flash." He looked at Roger. "Was that a bad move?"

"I'm not sure," Roger said. "You might want to stay away from flashes in the future."

"I don't want to see Min again," Cal said, and thought about seeing Min again.

"So? Cynthie doesn't need to know that," Tony said.

"So now I have to take Min to Emilio's because Cynthie will check," Cal said.

"I don't see why," Roger said. "If Cynthie asks, you can say you went someplace else."

"I try to tell as few lies as possible." Cal sat down again, trying to feel exasperated about the whole mess. He picked up the phone and dialed Min's company, tracking her down through the switchboard operator, but her phone was busy and voice mail was not an option. Nobody ever talked anybody into lunch on voice mail.

He hung up the phone and saw Roger and Tony watching him. "What?"

"Nothing," Roger said.

"Nothing," Tony said.

"Good," Cal said and ignored them to go back to his computer screen.

When her office phone rang, Min thought *Cal*, and then kicked herself. The beast must have the power to cloud women's minds if she was thinking about him at 9 A.M. on a Monday morning in the middle of a prelim report.

"Minerva Dobbs," she said into the phone, tapping her red pen on the frosted glass top of her desk.

"Tell me about this man you're dating," her mother said.

"Oh, for crying out loud." Min leaned back in her Aeron chair, exasperated.

"Greg says he has a horrible reputation with women," Nanette said. "Greg says he uses them and leaves them. Greg says—"

"Mother, I don't care what Greg says," Min said over her mother's panic. "And I'm not dating him. We went to dinner and had a picnic in the park and that's it." She wrote Cal's name in block letters on the cover sheet of her report and then drew a heavy red line through it. Gone, gone, gone.

"Greg says—"

"Mother."

"—that he's a heartbreaker. He's worried for you."

Min started to say, *Oh, please,* and stopped. Greg probably was worried about her. Greg worried about everything.

Why was Greg worried about her?

"How does Greg even know this guy exists?" Min said as she wrote "Greg" in red block letters and drew two heavy lines through it. Then she wrote "Dweeb" below that and "Snitch" below that.

"*I'm* worried for you," her mother was saying. "I know you're being brave about losing David, but I just hate it. I can't stand it if you're hurt."

Min felt her throat close. "Who are you and what did you do with my mother?"

"I just don't want you hurt," Nanette said, and Min thought she heard her voice shake. "I want you married to a good man who will appreciate you for how wonderful you are and not leave you because you're overweight."

Min shook her head. "You had me right up to the last line." She wrote "Mother" in block letters, drew a heart around it, and then, while Nanette talked on, she drew four heavy lines across it.

"Marriage is hard, Min," Nanette was saying. "There are a million reasons for them to cheat and leave, so you have to work at it all the time. You have to look good all the time. Men are very visual. If they see something better—"

"Mom?" Min said. "I don't think—"

"No matter how hard you work, there's always somebody younger, somebody better," Nanette said, her voice trembling. "Even for Diana, for everybody. You can't start with a handicap, you can't—"

"What's going on?" Min said. "Is Greg cheating on Diana?"

"No," her mother said, sounding taken aback. "Of course not."

Min tried to imagine Greg betraying Diana, but it was ridiculous. Greg didn't have the gumption to cheat. Plus, he loved Diana.

"Why would you say that?" her mother said. "That's a horrible thing to say."

"You were the one who brought up cheating," Min said. So if not Greg, then who? *Dad?* Min rejected that thought, too. Her father had three interests in life: insurance, statistics, and golf. "The only thing Dad would leave you for is the perfect four iron, so that's not it. What's going on?"

"I want you married and happy and this Cabot isn't—"

"Calvin," Min said.

"Bring him to dinner Saturday," Nanette said. "Wear something black so you'll look thinner."

"I'm not seeing him, Mother," Min said. "That's going to make it doubtful that he'll want to meet my parents."

"Just be careful," her mother said. "I don't know how you find these men."

"He looked down my sweater and saw that red lace bra," Min said. "It's all your fault."

She spent a few more minutes reassuring Nanette, and then she hung up and went back to editing for another five minutes until the phone rang again. "Oh, great," she said and answered it, prepared to argue with her mother again. "Minerva Dobbs."

"Min, it's Di," her sister said.

"Hi, honey," Min said. "If this is about Greg ratting out my picnic date, it's okay, it's over, I'm never going to see him again." She drew another line through Greg's name. As far as she was concerned, there couldn't be too many lines through Greg's name.

"Greg says David says he's awful," Diana said.

Min sat up a little straighter. "David said that, did he?" The rat fink didn't even play fair on his bets. She wrote "David" in big block letters and then stabbed her pen into it.

"He told Greg not to tell me he'd told him," Diana said.

"Right," Min said, not bothering to follow that.

"He just doesn't sound like part of your plan," Di said.

Min stopped stabbing. "My plan? What plan?"

"You always have a plan," Di said. "Like me. I've planned my wedding and my marriage very carefully and Greg fits perfectly. He's perfect for me. We're going to have a perfect life."

"Right," Min said, and drew another line through Greg's name.

"So I know you must have a plan and this wolf—"

"Beast," Min said.

"—frog, whatever, can't fit your plan."

"He's not a frog," Min said. "I kissed him and he did not turn into a prince." *He turned into a god. No, he didn't.* "Look, I'm never going to see him again, so everybody can relax."

"Good," Di said. "I'll tell Mom you're being sensible as usual and she won't worry anymore."

"Oh, good," Min said. "Sensible as usual. Nobody mentioned this to Dad, did they?"

"Mom might have," Diana said.

"Oh, hell, Di, why didn't you stop her?" A vision of her overprotective father rose up before her like a big blond bear. "You know how he is."

"I know," Di said. "I'm still not sure he likes Greg."

Are you sure you like Greg? Min wanted to say, but there wasn't any point since Diana would insist it was True Love to the death. "Well, good news, I got you a cake—"

"You did?" Di's voice went up a notch. "Oh, Min, thank you—"

"—but it won't be decorated so Bonnie and I are going to do that with Mom's pearls and a lot of fresh flowers." Min began to draw a wedding cake.

"You're going to decorate my cake?" Di said, her voice flat.

"People are going to love it when they taste it," Min said, adding some doves to the top.

"Taste?" Di said. "What about when they look at it?"

"Are you kidding? Fresh flowers and real pearls? It'll be a sensation." Min drew in some pearls. They were easier than doves, and she was experiencing enough difficulty with her morning.

"What does Mom say?"

"Why don't we ask her at the wedding?" Min said, keeping her voice chirpy.

"Okay," Di said, taking a deep breath into the phone. "I really am grateful. And it's good that it'll taste good, too. For the cake boxes and everything."

"Cake boxes?" Min said.

"The little boxes of cake that the guests take home for souvenirs," Diana said. "To dream on."

"Cake boxes," Min said and began to draw little squares. "Two hundred. You bet."

"You didn't get cake boxes?"

"Yes," Min said, drawing boxes faster. "I got cake boxes. Will you relax? You sound like you're strung up on wires. How are you doing?"

"I'm *fine*," Diana said, with too much emphasis.

"No trouble with Wet and Worse?" Min said and then winced. "I mean Susie and Karen?"

Diana laughed. "I can't believe you said that."

"I'm sorry," Min said. "It's . . ."

"Min, we know about it. Karen overheard Liza say it back when we were in high school. She calls Bonnie and Liza Sweet and Tart."

Min laughed in spite of herself.

"Don't tell them," Diana said. "I'll go on pretending you don't call Susie and Karen Wet and Worse if you'll go on pretending we don't call Bonnie and Liza Sweet and Tart."

"Deal," Min said. "God, we're horrible people."

"Not us," Diana said cheerfully. "It's our friends who make this stuff up. We're those nice Dobbs girls."

"I think that depends on who you ask," Min said, thinking of Cal. She had to remember to be nicer to him. Except she wasn't going to see him again so it didn't matter. Also, when she was nice to him in the park, it went badly. "I've been really bitchy lately. . . ." Her voice trailed off as her father loomed in the doorway, looking like an anxious Viking. "Hi, Daddy."

"Oh, no," Diana said.

"I'll talk to you later," Min said to Diana and hung up. "So, what brings you down here?" she said to her dad. "Air get too thin on the fortieth floor?"

"About this man you're seeing," George Dobbs said, glowering at his daughter as he came into her office.

"Don't even try it," Min said. "I know you have junior account executives for breakfast, but that doesn't work with me. I'm not seeing Cal anymore, but if I were, it would be my choice. Come on, Dad." She smiled at him, but his face stayed worried. "Two and a half million people get married every year in this country. Why not me?"

"Marriage isn't for everybody, Min," he said.

"Daddy?" Min said, taken aback.

"This man is not a good man," George said.

"Now wait just a minute," Min said. "You don't even know him. He was a perfect gentleman both times we went out—" *Well, there were hands in the park.* "—and since we've decided not to see each other again, it's pretty much not a problem."

"Good." Her father's face cleared. "Good for you. That's smart. Why take chances with a man you know isn't a good risk?"

"I'm not selling him insurance," Min said.

"I know, Min," he said. "But it's the same principle. You're not a gambler. You're too sensible for that."

He smiled at her, patted her hand, and left, and Min sat at her desk and felt dull, frumpy, and boring. Not a gambler. Sensible as usual. She let herself think about kissing Cal in the park, his mouth hot on hers, his hands hard on her, and she felt the heat rise all over again. That hadn't been sensible, that hadn't been a plan. And now she was never going to see him again.

She looked down at her report and realized she'd perforated it. She must have been stabbing it, the Norman Bates of statistical analysis. "Great," she said, and tried to pull the pages apart. The top sheet ripped, and her phone rang, and she picked it up and snarled, "Minerva Dobbs," ready to perforate the caller this time.

"Good morning, Minerva," Cal said, and all the air rushed out of Min's lungs. "How did you get that godawful name?"

Breathe. Deep breaths. Very deep breaths.

"Oh," she said. "This is good. Grief about my name from a guy named Calvin." *I do not care that he called. I am totally unaffected by this.* Her heart was pounding so loudly she was convinced he could hear it over the phone.

"I was named after my rich uncle Robert," Cal said, "which turned out to be a total waste when he left everything to the whales. What's your excuse?"

"My mother wanted a goddess," Min said faintly.

"Well, she got one," Cal said. "I take it back, it's the perfect name for you."

"And my father's mother was named Minnie," Min said, trying to get back to offhand and unfazed. "It was a compromise. Why isn't your name Robert?"

"I got his last name," Cal said. "Which is good. I don't see myself as a Bob."

"Bob Morrisey." Min leaned back in her chair, pretending to be cool. "That weird guy in the shipping department."

"The insurance agent you can trust," Cal said.

"The used car salesman you can't," Min said.

"Whereas Calvin Morrisey is the old fart who started the company in 1864," Cal said. "Or in this case, the guy who has your shoe."

"Shoe?"

"Red ribbons, funky heel, big dopey flower."

"My *shoe.*" Min sat up, delighted. "I didn't think I'd ever see it again."

"Well, you won't unless you come to lunch with me," Cal said. "I'm holding it for ransom. There's a gun to its heel right now."

"I have lunch at my desk," Min began, and thought, *Oh, for crying out loud, could I be any more pathetic?*

"Emilio is experimenting with a lunch menu. He needs you. I need you."

"I can't," Min said while every fiber in her being said, *Yes, yes, anything.* Thank God her fiber couldn't talk.

"You can't let Emilio down," Cal went on. "He loves you. We'll have chicken marsala. Come on, live a little. A very little."

A very little. Even Cal knew she was a sensible, non-gambling, plan-ridden loser. "Yes," Min said, her heart starting to pound again. "I would love to get my shoe back and have chicken marsala for lunch."

"Keep in mind, you have to eat it with me," Cal said. "You're not seeing that shoe until you eat."

"I can stand that," Min said, and felt lighter all over. Then she hung up and looked at her report.

She'd been drawing hearts on it, tiny ones, dozens of them.

"Oh, my Lord," Min said and put her head on her desk.

When Min got to Emilio's, a dark-haired teenage boy at the door said, "You looking for Cal?" and when she nodded, said, "He's at your table," and jerked his head into the restaurant.

"I have a table?" Min said, but then she saw Cal sitting by the window at the table they'd had Wednesday night, and she lost her breath for a minute. *I keep forgetting how beautiful he is*, she thought, and watched as he sat relaxed in his chair, his dark eyes fixed on the street outside, his profile perfect. He was tapping his fingers on the table, and his hands looked strong, and Min remembered how good they'd felt on her and thought, *Get out of here*. Then he saw her and straightened and smiled, his eyes lighting as if he were glad to see her, and she smiled back and went to meet him. *Charm Boy*, she thought, and slowed down again, but he already had her chair pulled out for her.

"Thanks for coming," he said, and she slid into the chair thinking, *He's up to something, be careful*. Then she noticed him looking at the floor and said, "What?" her voice cracking with nerves.

"Shoes," he said. "What are you wearing?"

"You sound like an obscene phone call," she said, trying to keep her treacherous voice steady, but she stuck her foot out so he could see her blue reptile slides, open-toed to show off the matching blue nail polish.

He shook his head. "You can do better. The toes are nice, though."

"These are work shoes," she said, annoyance clearing up her nerves. "Also, you have my red shoe so I couldn't wear those. Can I have my shoe back?"

"Not until after lunch," he said, sitting down across from her. "It's my only leverage."

"Have you had this foot fetish long?" she said, as he passed her the bread basket.

"Just since I met you," he said. "Suddenly, there's a whole new world out there."

"Glad to know I've made an impact," she said, and was appalled to realize that she really was. It was enough to make her nerves come back. *He doesn't matter.* She shoved the bread basket back to him, determined to be virtuous in consumption if not in thought, and said, "So who's the charmer at the door? He needs lessons from you."

"Emilio's nephew." Cal picked up a piece of bread and broke it. "His tableside manner could use some work."

"Doesn't Emilio have somebody else to put up front?" Min picked up her napkin to keep her hands off the bread. "He can't be good for business."

"Brian's the socially adept one in the family," Cal said. "His brothers are back in the kitchen where they won't hurt anybody. Fortunately, they can cook. I already ordered. Salad, chicken marsala, no pasta."

"Oh, good," Min said, "because I'm starving. Did you know that forty percent of all pasta sold is spaghetti?" *Geek,* she thought, and tried to suppress her statistical instinct while she smiled at him. "I think that shows a huge lack of imag—"

Brian slung a salad in front of her and another in front of Cal. "Your chicken's up in about fifteen," he told Cal. "You want wine with that?"

"Yes, please," Cal said to him. "I thought you were working on your finesse."

"Not with you," Brian said. "I know it's chicken, but for you, red wine, right?"

"Right," Cal said. "Now ask me what kind of red."

"Whatever Emilio puts in the glass," Brian said, and left.

"Just a little ray of sunshine," Min said. "But enough about him. Give me the ten bucks."

"Ten bucks?" Cal looked beautifully blank and then shook his head. "There wasn't a bet. Stop harassing me for cash."

"You asked me out without a bet?" Min said.

"No money will change hands," Cal said. "Except for me paying the tab."

"We can go Dutch," Min offered.

"No, we can't."

"Why not? I can afford it. We're not dating. Why—"

"I invited you, I pay," Cal said, his face beginning to set into that stubborn look that exasperated her.

"That means if I invite you, I pay," Min said.

"No, I pay then, too," Cal said. "So tell me who Diana, Wet, and Worse are."

"That's why you invited me to lunch?" Min said, infusing her voice with as much skepticism as possible.

"No." Cal put his head in his hands. "Could we just for once meet like regular people? Smile at each other, make small talk, pretend you don't hate me?"

"I don't hate you," Min said, shocked. "I like you. I mean, you have flaws—"

"*What* flaws?" Cal said. "Of course I have them, but I've been on my best behavior with you. Except for hitting you in the eye and attacking you on a picnic table. How are you?"

"I'm fine," Min said, putting as much chipper as she could into her voice. "I'm turning over a new leaf. Taking risks. Like having lunch with a wolf."

"I'm a wolf?" Cal said.

"Oh, please," Min said. "You picked me up on Friday with 'Hello, little girl.' Who did you think you were channeling, the prince?"

Emilio appeared with wine before Cal could say anything, and Min beamed at him, grateful for the rescue. "Emilio, my darling. I forgot to mention cake boxes. Two hundred cake boxes."

"Already on it," Emilio said. "Nonna said you'd need them. She said to get four-inch-square boxes for three-inch-square cakes."

"I'm getting the boxes," Min said, nodding. "Sure. Great. Fine. Your grandmother is an angel and you are my hero. And of course, a genius with food."

"And you are my favorite customer." Emilio kissed her cheek and disappeared back into the kitchen.

"I *love* him," she told Cal.

"I noticed," Cal said. "Been seeing him behind my back, have you?"

"Yes," Min said. "We've been having conversations about cake."

"Whoa," Cal said. "For you, that's talking dirty."

"Funny." Min stabbed her salad again and bit into the crisp greens. Emilio's dressing was tangy and light, a miracle all by itself. "God, I *love* Emilio. This salad is fabulous. Which is not a word I usually use with 'salad.'"

"Tell me about the cake," Cal said, starting on his own salad.

"My sister Diana is getting married in three weeks," Min said, glad to be on a topic that wasn't dangerous. "Her fiancé said he knew this great baker and that he would order the cake as a surprise. And then the surprise turned out to be that he hadn't ordered the cake."

"And the wedding's still on?" Cal said.

"Yes. My sister says it's her fault for not reminding him."

"Your sister does not sound like you," Cal said.

"My sister is my exact opposite," Min said. "She's a darling."

Cal frowned. "Which makes you what?"

"Me?" Min stopped eating, surprised. "I'm okay."

Cal shook his head as Emilio appeared with a steaming platter of chicken marsala. When he and Min had assured each other of their undying devotion, he left, and Cal served chicken and mushrooms. "So how do Wet and Worse figure in this cake story?"

"They don't," Min said. "Except that they're my sister's bridesmaids. But do *not* tell anybody I called them that." She ate her first bite of chicken, savoring it, and then teased an errant drop of sauce from her lower lip. "Do you think—"

"Don't do that," Cal said, his voice flat.

"What?" Min blinked at him. "Ask questions?"

"Lick your lip. What were you going to ask me?"

"Why? Bad manners?" Min said, dangerously.

"No," Cal said. "It distracts me. You have a great mouth. I know. I was there once. What were you going to ask me?"

Min met his eyes, and he stared back, unblinking. *Oh*, she thought and tried to remember what they'd been talking about, but it was hard because all she could think about was how he'd been there once, and how good he'd felt, and how hot his eyes were on her now, and how much she—

"You guys okay?" Brian said.

"What?" Cal said, jerking his head up.

"Is there something wrong with the chicken?" Brian frowned at them both. "You guys looked strange."

"No," Min said, picking up her fork again. "The chicken is wonderful."

"Okay," Brian said. "You need anything else?"

"A waiter with some class?" Cal said.

"Yeah, right, like I'd waste that on you," Brian said, and wandered off.

"So anyway," Min said, scrambling for a safer topic, "when Diana told me about the cake, I turned to Emilio in my hour of need, and he called his grandmother. So he's my hero."

"Wait'll you taste the cake," Cal said. "She only makes it for weddings and it's like nothing else in this world."

"When did you eat wedding cake?" Min said.

"When Emilio got married," Cal said. "When my brother got married. When everybody I've ever known got married. Tony, Roger, and I are the last hold-outs, so there have been a lot of weddings. And now Roger's going down for the count."

"Well, at least you and Tony will have each other," Min said brightly. "So you have a brother. Younger or older?"

"Older. Reynolds."

Min stopped eating. "Reynolds? Reynolds Morrisey?"

"Yes," Cal said. "Husband to Bink, father to Harry."

"Isn't there a fancy law firm called Reynolds Morrisey?"

"Yes," Cal said. "My father, his partner John Reynolds, and my brother." He didn't sound too thrilled about any of them.

"Cozy," Min said. "So how is Harry?"

"Permanently scarred from watching us on a picnic table."

Min winced. "Really?"

"Hard to say. I haven't seen him since. Bink probably has him in therapy by now. So what's your take on Bonnie and Roger?"

"They'll be engaged before fall," Min said, and they began to discuss Bonnie and Roger and other safe topics for the rest of the meal. When they were finished and Cal had signed the charge slip, he said, "So lunch with me is risky. Does that mean you need an apology for our last lunch?"

"No." Min smiled and tried to look unfazed. "I've been working on the theory that if we don't talk about it, it didn't happen. Although a lot of people seem to know about it. Greg, for example. He ratted us out, and now my mother wants you to come to dinner." Cal looked taken aback for a minute, and she said, "I told her you were a complete stranger so dinner was unlikely." Then out of the blue, she blurted, "So what was that on Saturday?"

"Well." Cal took a deep breath. "That was chemistry. And it was phenomenal. I'd be more than interested in doing that again, especially naked and horizontal, but—"

Min's pulse picked up, but she slapped herself in the forehead to forestall him and her own treacherous imagination.

"What?" he said.

"I'm remembering why you never ask guys to tell you the truth," she said. "Because sometimes they do."

"My point is," Cal said, "that Liza was right, I had no business kissing you like that because I don't want anything that serious. I just got out of a relationship that was a lot more intense than I'd realized and—"

Min frowned. "How could it have been more intense than you'd realized?"

"I thought we were just having a good time," Cal said. "She thought we were getting married. It ended okay, there are no hard feelings—"

Min looked at him in amazement. "She wanted to get married, you didn't, but there are no hard feelings."

"She said if I wasn't ready to commit, she'd have to move on," Cal said. "It was pretty cut and dried."

"And you're the guy who's supposed to be a wizard at understanding women. It was not cut and dried. She either hates you, or she thinks you're coming back."

Cal shook his head. "Cynthie's very practical. She knows it's over.

And so are we because, even though it was great, this is not something either one of us wants to pursue."

"Right," Min said, understanding completely if not happily. "It would be different if we were at all compatible. I'm not averse to commitment especially if it'd be that much fun, but the last thing I need is to fall for somebody I already know is no good for me just because he kisses like a god. Also, I'm waiting for the reincarnation of Elvis and you are not him. But—"

She stopped because Cal had a strange look on his face.

"What?" she said. "I was kidding about Elvis."

"I'm no good for you," he said, "but I kiss like a god?"

Min considered it. "Pretty much. Why? Did you have a different take on it?"

Cal opened his mouth and then stopped and shrugged. "I guess not. I don't think you'd be bad for me, I just can't take the hassle. You're not a restful woman."

"This is true," Min said. "But you ask for it. You're such a wolf."

"I'm retired," Cal said. "All I want now is some peace and quiet. I just need a break."

"That's my plan," Min said. "I'm taking a break from dating."

"Until Elvis shows up," Cal said.

"Right. As far as I can see, there's no downside to this at all."

"No sex," Cal said.

"I can stand that," Min said.

"Yeah, you're good at denying yourself things."

"Hey," Min said, insulted. "We were doing just fine there and then you had to take a shot at me."

"Sorry," Cal said.

They got up to go, Min kissed Emilio good-bye, and they went out into the street.

"Okay, it's broad daylight and my office is only six blocks away," Min said. "You don't have to walk me."

"Fair enough." Cal held out his hand. "We'll probably meet again at Roger and Bonnie's wedding. In case we don't, have a nice life."

Min shook his hand and dropped it. "Likewise. Best of luck in the future."

She turned to go and he said, "Wait a minute," and made her heart lurch. But when she turned around, he was holding her shoe, the red ribbons fluttering in the light breeze.

"Right," she said, taking it. "Thank you very much."

He held on to it for a moment, looking into her eyes, and then he shook his head and said, "You're welcome" and let go, and she set off down the street without looking back, full of excellent food but not nearly as happy as she should have been.

Charm Boy, she thought, and put him out of her mind.

On Tuesday, Min looked at the salad on her desk at lunch and thought, *There has to be more to life than this*. It was Cal's fault; she'd had real food in the middle of the day and it had tainted her. Until Cal, she'd never thought about food except as something she couldn't have. Even before she'd started dieting for the bridesmaid's dress, there'd been no butter in her life. *There should be butter*, she thought, and then realized the folly of that.

But there could be chicken marsala.

Min shoved her salad to one side, logged onto the net, and did a search for "chicken marsala" because doing a search for "Cal Morrisey" would not have been helpful to her damn plan.

"Very popular dish," she said when she got 48,300 matches. Even allowing for the weird randomness that more than 48,000 of them would demonstrate if she ever got that far, that was still a lot of recipes. There was one with artichokes, that was insane. One had lemon juice, which couldn't be right, another peppers, another onions. It was amazing how many ways people had found to garbage up a plain recipe. She printed off two that sounded right and went to log off the net, but instead, on a random impulse, Googled for "dyslexia" instead. An hour later, she logged off with a new respect for what Calvin Morrisey had accomplished.

When she got off work, she stopped by the grocery. There was something about having a plan for dinner, a recipe in hand, that made her feel much less hostile about food. Of course, she was going to have to adapt the recipe. It called for the chicken to be breaded in flour, which was just extra calories, and carb calories no less. Skip the breading. Salt and pepper she already had, and parsley had no calories, so she picked up a jar of that. Skinless, boneless chicken breasts she was familiar with, no problem there, but butter and olive oil? "It is to laugh," she said and got spray olive oil in a can. Mushrooms were mostly water, so she could have those, and then there was the marsala. She found it in the cooking wine section. Resolutely passing by the bread section, she checked out feeling triumphant, went home and changed into her sweats, cranked up the CD player, and sang her head off to her *Elvis 30* album as she cooked.

An hour later, Elvis was starting all over again and she was staring at the mess in her only frying pan trying to figure out what had gone wrong. She'd browned the chicken in the non-stick skillet and then followed all the other directions but it looked funny and tasted like hell. She tapped her spatula on the edge of the stove for a few moments and thought, *Okay, I'm not a cook. I still deserve great food*, and dropped the spatula to pick up the phone.

"Emilio?" she said when he answered. "Do you deliver?"

The Parker seminar was turning into the worst mess Morrisey, Packard, Capa had ever seen, mostly because the idiot who was in charge of training kept changing the seminar information. "I'm faxing some information over," she'd say when she called. "Just slot it in somewhere."

"That bitch must die," Tony said when she called at ten till five on Tuesday. "I've got a date with Liza tonight."

"I'll stay for the fax," Roger said. "Bonnie will understand."

"You go, I'll stay," Cal said. "I'm dateless and too tired to move anyway."

Tony and Roger left, both heading for warm women, and Cal read the fax and tightened the seminar packet one more time, trying to feel grateful that there wasn't any place he had to be, no woman demanding his time and attention. At seven, he turned off the computer with relief and realized he was starving.

Emilio's seemed like an excellent idea.

"Don't tell me," Emilio said when Cal came through the swinging doors into the kitchen. "Chicken marsala."

"I've had enough chicken marsala for a while," Cal said as the phone rang. Emilio turned to get it and Cal added, "Something simple. Tomato and basil on spaghetti—" No. Forty percent of all pasta sold was spaghetti. No imagination. "Make that fettuccine—"

He stopped when Emilio held up his hand and said, "Emilio's," into the phone. Emilio listened and then looked back over his shoulder at Cal and said, "We usually don't, but for such a special customer, we'll make an exception. Chicken marsala, right? No, no, no trouble at all. You can overtip the delivery boy."

He hung up and smiled at Cal. "That was Min. She wants chicken marsala. You can deliver it to her."

"What?" Cal said, dumbfounded.

"You know the way. It's probably on your way home."

"It's not on my way home, it's not on anybody's way home except God's, the damn place is vertical. What gave you the idea I'd do this?"

Emilio shrugged. "I don't know. She called, you were here, you two are great together, it seemed like a good idea. Did you have a fight?"

"No, we didn't have a fight," Cal said. "We're not seeing each other because I'm all wrong for her and she's waiting for Elvis. Call her back and tell her your delivery boy died."

"Then she won't have anything for dinner," Emilio said. "And you know Min. She's one of those women who eats."

Cal thought about the look on Min's face when she ate chicken marsala. It was almost as good as the look on her face when she ate doughnuts. Which wasn't anywhere near as good as the look on her face when he'd kissed her, that had been—

Emilio shrugged. "Fine. Brian can take it to her."

"No," Cal said. "I'll take it to her. Hurry up, will you? I'm hungry."

Chapter Six

Forty-five minutes later, Cal was climbing the steps to Min's place when something small and orange streaked past him and almost knocked him down the hill. He finished the climb cautiously, but when he looked around at the top, nothing was there. He rang the doorbell, and Bonnie came to let him in.

"Hi," he said. "Min ordered takeout." He held up the bag, feeling stupid, his least favorite feeling in the world.

"And you're delivering?" Bonnie said as she stepped back.

"Well, you can never have enough extra cash," Cal said and hit the stairs, knowing she was watching him. When he got to the top, he heard Elvis Presley singing "Heartbreak Hotel" through Min's door and sighed.

Min looked surprised when she opened the door at his knock, and he felt pretty stunned himself: as far as he could see, all she was wearing was a very long, very old blue sweatshirt and lumpy sweatsocks. Her hair was down in frizzy waves, and she was wearing no makeup, so the only color on her face was the fading yellow bruise from where he'd clocked her.

"What the hell?" she said. "How did you get in the front door?"

"This is how you open the door to delivery guys?" Cal said, staring at the good strong legs he'd scoped out in the bar on Friday.

"No, this is how I open the door to Bonnie," Min said. "Stop ogling. I have shorts on under this." She pulled up the edge of her shirt and he saw baggy plaid boxers that were only marginally less ugly than her shirt and socks. "*Why* did you get in the front door?"

Then something orange streaked past both their legs and into the apartment.

"What is *that?*" Min said, and Cal came in, leaving the door open behind him.

"I don't know." Cal put Emilio's bag down on an old cast iron sewing machine table beside a couch that looked like a moth-eaten, overstuffed pumpkin. "It ran past me on the steps—"

"Oh, *Lord,*" Min said and Cal turned to look where she was looking.

The mangiest-looking animal he'd ever seen was glaring at them from the end of the couch, its left eye closed and sinister. It was mottled all over in browns and oranges so that, in general, it matched the couch.

"What *is* that?" Min said.

"I think it's a cat," Cal said.

"What kind?" Min said, an awful fascination in her voice.

"Not a good kind," Cal said. "Although you did say you wanted one."

"No, I didn't," Min said.

"When I brought you home last week," Cal said. "You said you were going to get a cat."

"That was a *joke,*" Min said, keeping an eye on the cat. "That's what every woman in her thirties who's been screwed over by men says. 'I'm going to give up the bastards and get a cat.' It's *a cliché.*"

"You know," Cal said, watching the cat, too, "if you're going to talk in code, you have to warn me."

The cat didn't seem to be moving, so Cal looked around the rest of her apartment. It appeared to be the entire attic, its crazy angles punctuated by dormers, and it was furnished in ancient pieces, none of them antiques. He frowned and thought, *This doesn't look like her.*

Min tilted her head at the cat, nonplussed. "Why is its eye shut?"

"My guess is, that one's missing," Cal said.

"Hard life, huh, cat?" Min sighed. "I have extra chicken. I tried the marsala and screwed it up. Maybe the cat will be desperate enough to eat it."

"If you feed it, it'll stay forever," Cal said. "Yo, cat, the door's open. Leave."

The cat curled up on the back of the couch and stared at him haughtily.

"It looks very Cheshire," Min said. "Like it could disappear a little bit at a time."

"And it's already started with the eye," Cal said. "Min, this cat probably has every disease in the Cat's Book of Death."

"I can at least feed it," Min said and went to get some chicken.

"It does go with the couch." Cal closed the door and moved Emilio's bag from the sewing machine table to a battered old round oak table behind the couch. The cat watched his every move while pretending not to care.

Min brought some chicken slivers on a paper towel. She put it under the cat's nose and then stepped back. It sniffed at the chicken and then looked at her. "I know," she said, despair in her voice. "It's awful. You don't have to eat it."

The cat lifted its nose and then nibbled at the closest piece.

"That's a very brave cat," Min told Cal and went to the mantel to get her purse. "Let me pay you or Emilio or whoever."

"No," Cal said, still looking around. The furniture was all comfortable, but none of it was interesting or attractive, nothing like Min. It was almost as if it were somebody else's apartment. "Are you subletting?"

"No," Min said, fishing in her purse. "How much do I owe you?"

"Nothing." There were snow globes on the mantel, lined up on both sides of a kitschy old clock made from fake books, and he went over beside her to look at them, saying, "You didn't pick out this furniture."

"It was my grandmother's," Min said. "Look, you're not going to pay for my dinner. You did me a favor by bringing it, so—"

"You collect these?" Cal said, picking up Rocky and Bullwinkle.

"Cal," Min said.

"There's enough food there for an army," he said. "If you want company, I'm staying and eating half of it. If you don't, I'll take half with me, although I am reluctant to leave you alone with that animal." Cal put Rocky down and looked at the next one. Chip and Dale. "Where did you get these?"

"Friends," Min said. "Family. Flea markets." She paused. "You can stay." She looked at the cat which, having wolfed down the chicken, now seemed to be considering sleep. "You I don't know about," she said, and it regarded her gravely, its right eye closed. "Wasn't the other eye closed before?" Min said to Cal. "The left one?"

"I can't remember," Cal said. "I wouldn't be surprised. It's a very shifty cat. You know, this furniture is not you, that clock is not you, and you don't seem like the snow globe type."

"I know it's not me," Min said, looking around at it. "But it's good furniture, so it doesn't make sense to buy new. Besides, it reminds me of my grandmother. And the snow globe thing started by accident." She turned back to him. "At least let me pay for half of dinner."

"No." Cal picked up a massive piece that had a globe with Lady and the Tramp sitting on top of a detailed Italian restaurant. "What kind of accident?"

"My Grandma Min had a Mickey and Minnie Mouse snow globe. They were dancing and Minnie was wearing a long pink dress and Mickey was dipping her." Min's voice softened as she spoke. "My grandpa gave it to her for a wedding anniversary, but I loved it so much that she gave it to me when I was twelve."

Cal scanned the mantel. Christine and the Phantom, Jessica and Roger Rabbit, Blondie and Dagwood, Sleeping Beauty and the Prince, Cinderella and her prince in front of a castle with white doves suspended in air, even Donald and Daisy were there, but no Mickey and Minnie. "Where is it?"

"I lost it," Min said. "In one of the moves when I was in college. You know how it is, you move every year and stuff disappears. I was upset about it so people started giving me other ones on my birthday and for

Christmas to make up for it. I tried to tell them I didn't want any more, you know, 'Thank you, it's lovely, but you shouldn't have,' but by then it had taken on a life of its own." She looked at the mantel and sighed. "I have boxes of them in the basement. These are just my favorites. Never collect anything. People never let you quit."

Cal looked over the assortment again. There was one big, dark one at the end of the mantel that looked like monsters. "What's this?" he said, picking it up.

"Disney villains," Min said. "Liza and Bonnie each got me one for Christmas two years ago."

"Liza got you that one," Cal said, putting it back.

"How do you know it wasn't Bonnie?" Min said.

"Because that's not Bonnie." He pointed to the Cinderella globe with the doves. "She got you that one."

"Yes," Min said. "I still don't see—"

"Bonnie wants the fairy tale," Cal said. "Liza's a realist, she sees the bad guys. Also Bonnie wouldn't have missed the important part. She got you a couple."

"A couple of what?" Min said.

"A couple," Cal said. "Twosome. These are all couples. Look. Lady and the Tramp, Christine and the Phantom, Jessica Rabbit and Roger . . . except for Liza's, they're all couples."

"I wouldn't call Rocky and Bullwinkle a couple exactly," Min said, looking at them doubtfully. "And Chip and Dale. I mean, I know there have been rumors, but—"

"C'mon, Minnie," Cal said. "You started with a couple."

"Don't call me Minnie," Min said, her eyes flashing at him.

"You can call me Mickey," Cal said, grinning at her, wanting that flash again.

"I'm going to call you a cab if you don't stop annoying me," Min said. "Can we just eat?"

Cal gave up and went back to the table to unpack Emilio's bag, detouring around the cat in case it decided to go rogue and start on him. "That guy really did a number on you."

"What guy?"

"The one who dumped you the night I picked you up. You must have loved him a lot."

"Oh." Min blinked. "Him? No. Not at all."

Good, Cal thought, even though it didn't make any difference. "Do you have plates?"

She went around the table and into an alcove that anybody else would call a closet, but that her landlord evidently thought was a kitchen.

"Get wineglasses, too," Cal said as he opened the box with the bread in it.

"What?" Min said, leaning out of the alcove.

"Glasses," Cal said. "For the wine."

Min came out of the alcove with two wineglasses and set the table while he pulled the cork from the wine and poured, trying not to look at her sweats. It was nice of her to dress so badly. If she'd been wearing that red sweater again, he might have had a problem. Then she opened the carton with the salad in it, and tried to plate it using a tablespoon. "Damn," she said, as the dressing spilled onto the table.

"You don't cook, do you, Minerva?" Cal said.

"Oh, and you do?" Min said.

"Sure." He took the spoon from her. "I worked in a restaurant while I was in college. You need a big spoon, Minnie. This one is for eating."

"Or I could just jab you with it," Min said.

He shook his head and went around her into the kitchenette to look for a larger spoon and instead found a frying pan with something horrible in it.

"What is this?" he said when she came in for a paper towel.

"None of your business," Min said. He raised his eyebrows at her and she said, "I thought I could make it on my own. I got the recipe. But it didn't—"

Light dawned. "This is chicken marsala?"

"No," Min said. "That is a mess, which is why I called Emilio's."

"What did you do?" Cal said.

"Why?" Min said. "So you can make snarky comments?"

"Do you want to know how to make chicken marsala or not?" Cal said, exasperated. She was such a pain in the ass.

She scowled up at him. "Yes."

"What's the first thing you did?" Cal said.

"Sprayed the pan with olive oil," Min said.

"Sprayed?" Cal said. "No. Pour. A couple of tablespoons."

"Too much fat," Min said.

"It's good fat," Cal said. "Olive oil is good for you."

"Not for my waistline," Min said.

"You're going to have to pour, Minnie," Cal said. "It's part of the flavor."

"Okay," Min said, but she looked mutinous. "Then I browned the chicken."

"Too fast," Cal said. "Pound the chicken breasts first. Use a can if you don't have a mallet, put them in a plastic bag, and pound them thin. Then dredge them in flour mixed with ground black pepper and kosher salt."

"You're kidding," Min said. "Flour just adds calories."

"And seals the chicken," Cal said. "So it doesn't get . . ." He picked up a fork, jabbed one of the petrified slabs in the pan, and held it up. ". . . dry. Then what did you do?"

Min folded her arms. "When they were browned, I put the mushrooms in and poured the wine over and let it reduce."

"No butter?"

"No butter," Min said. "Are you insane?"

"No," Cal said, dropping the chicken back in the pan. "But anybody who makes chicken marsala without olive oil, butter, or flour may be. If you wanted broiled chicken, you should have made broiled chicken." He dipped his finger in the sauce and tasted it. It was so vile he lost his breath, and Min ran him a glass of water and handed it to him.

"I don't know why that part didn't work," she said.

"What marsala did you use?" Cal said when he'd gotten the taste out of his mouth, and she handed him a bottle of cooking wine. "No, no, no," he said and then relented when she winced. "Look, honey, when you make wine sauce, you're cooking the wine down, concentrating it. You have to use good wine or it'll taste like . . . He looked down at the pan. ". . . this. It's a wonder the cat's not dead."

"Ouch," Min said. "Could you write that down for me?"

"No," Cal said, and then they heard a crash from another room. He looked around. "Your cat's gone, Minnie. You leave a window open anywhere?"

"I have one of those cheapo sliding screens in the bedroom," Min said and went through a doorway beside the mantel to look. "Oh, this is good," she said when she was inside, and Cal followed her in.

Her sliding screen was gone from the dormer window, which was now open to the night air. Cal went over and looked out. The screen was halfway down the roof, and the cat was sitting in a tree branch that tapped the shingles, washing its paws. Its left eye was closed.

"It does switch eyes," Cal said, pulling his head back in. "Maybe it's conserving . . . " His voice trailed off as he saw Min's bedroom.

Most of it was filled with the most elaborate brass bed he'd ever seen, a huge thing covered with a watery lavender-blue satin comforter and lavender satin pillows that were piled against a headboard that curved and twined, erupting in brass rosettes and finials, until he grew dizzy just looking at it. "How do you keep from falling out of bed?"

"I just hold on and try not to look at the headboard," Min said. "I love it. I bought it last month even though it was completely impractical. . . ."

She went on, but Cal had stopped listening when she said, "I just hold on," imagining her lying back on the soft blue satin comforter, her soft gold-tipped curls spread out on the pillows, her soft lips open as she smiled at him, her soft hands gripping the headboard, her soft body—

"Cal?" Min said.

"It smells good in here," Cal said, trying to find a thought that didn't have "soft" in it. Or "hard," for that matter.

"Lavender pillows," Min said. "My grandmother always put lavender in her pillowcases. Or maybe it's the cinnamon candles."

Cal cleared his throat. "Well, it's . . . nice. It's the first thing I've seen in this apartment that looks like you." The thought of tipping her onto that blue comforter was entirely too plausible, so he said, "We should go eat. Now."

"Okay," Min said and started for the door.

"You want the window closed?" Cal said.

"Then how will the cat get back in?" Min said.

"Good point," Cal said, thinking, *Oh, Christ, I gave her a feral cat*, and followed her out.

When they were eating Emilio's salad, Min said, "So chicken marsala is not heart smart or weight friendly."

"Heart smart?" Cal said, picking up his tumbler of wine. "Does that mean good for your heart? Because it is. I told you, olive oil is good for you. And a little bit of flour and butter won't kill you."

"Tell that to my mother." Min tasted her salad again. "This is so good. You know, the lesson here is, I shouldn't be cooking."

"Why?" Cal said. "It was the first time you tried. Everybody makes mistakes." He picked up the chicken carton and filled the two plates, managing it so that nothing spilled.

"Except you," Min said, watching him. "You do *everything* well."

"Okay," Cal said, putting the carton down. "You just got dumped, I get that, but you didn't care about the guy, so why are you still so mad and taking it out on me?"

Min cut into her chicken. "He was sort of the last straw." She put the chicken in her mouth and chewed, and got the same blissful look she always got when eating good food.

"You should never diet." Cal picked up his fork and began to eat. "So what did he do that you can't get over?"

"Well." Min stabbed a mushroom with more antagonism than it deserved. "It was mostly my weight."

"He criticized your weight?" Cal shook his head. "This guy has the brains of a brick."

"He didn't criticize, exactly," Min said. "He just suggested that I should go on a diet. And then he left because I wouldn't sleep with him."

"He told you to go on a diet and then asked you to bed?" Cal said. "I take it back. Bricks are smarter than this dipwad."

"Yes, but he has a point," Min said. "I mean, about my weight." She looked at him, defiant. "Right?"

"There is no way I can answer that without getting all that rage put back on me," Cal said. "Keep it on the loser who dumped you. I'm the good guy."

Min stabbed another mushroom, and then put the fork down. "Okay, I'll give you a free pass on this one. No matter what you say, I won't get mad."

Cal looked at her stormy face and laughed. "How are you going to work that?"

Min nodded. "Okay, I'll get mad, but I'll play fair. The thing is, you're the only man I trust enough to tell me the truth."

"You trust me?" Cal said, surprised and flattered. "I thought I was a beast."

"You are," Min said. "But you do tend to tell me the truth. On most things."

Cal stopped eating. "On all things. I've never lied to you."

"Yeah," Min said dismissively. "So what am I supposed to do about my weight?"

Cal put his fork down. "All right. Here's the truth. You're never going to be thin. You're a round woman. You have wide hips and a round stomach and full breasts. You're . . ."

"Healthy," Min said bitterly.

"Lush," Cal said, watching the gentle rise and fall of her breasts under her sweatshirt.

"Generous," Min snarled.

"Opulent," Cal said, remembering the soft curve of her under his hand.

"Zaftig," Min said.

"Soft and round and hot, and I'm turning myself on," Cal said, starting to feel dizzy. "Do you have anything on under that sweatshirt?"

"Of course," Min said, taken aback.

"Oh," Cal said, ditching that fantasy. "Good. We should be eating. What were we talking about?"

"My weight?" Min said.

"Right," Cal said, picking up his fork again. "The reason you can't lose weight is that you're not supposed to lose weight, you're not built that way, and if you did manage through some stupid diet to take the weight off, you'd be like that chicken mess you just made. Some things are supposed to made with butter. You're one of them."

"So I'm doomed," Min said.

"Another problem is that you don't *listen*. You want to be sexy, be sexy. You have assets that skinny women will never have, and you should be enjoying them and dressing like you enjoy them. Or at least dressing so that others can enjoy them. That suit you were wearing the night I picked you up made you look like a prison warden." He remembered looking down the front of her red sweater and added, "Your underwear's good, though."

"There are no clothes that look good on me," Min said.

"Of course there are," Cal said, still making his way through dinner. "Although you're the kind of woman who looks better naked than dressed." His treacherous mind tried to imagine that and he blocked it. "I'm assuming. Eat, please. Hunger makes you cranky."

"I look better naked?" Min said, picking up her fork again. "No. Listen—"

"You asked, I told you," Cal said. "You just don't want to hear it. The truth is, most guys would rather go to bed with you than with a clothes hanger, you're a lot more fun to touch, but most women don't believe that. You keep trying to lose weight for each other."

Min rolled her eyes. "So I've been sexy all these years? Why hasn't anybody noticed?"

"Because you dress like you hate your body," Cal said. "Sexy is in your head and you don't feel sexy so you don't look it."

"Then how do you know I am?" Min said, exasperated.

"Because I've looked down your sweater," Cal said, flashing back to that. "And I've kissed you, and I have to tell you, your mouth is a miracle. Now *eat something*."

Min looked at her plate for a moment and then dug in. "God, this is good," she said a few minutes later.

"Nothing better than good food," Cal said. "Well, except for—"

"There's got to be a way to make this heart smart," Min said.

Cal shook his head. "Good to know I've been talking to myself here. Did you hear anything I said?"

"Yes," Min said. "So I looked like a prison warden when you picked me up, huh?"

"No," Cal said. "You had great shoes on. You do let yourself go on shoes." *Nice toes, too.*

"So the reason you crossed the bar to pick me up even though I looked like a prison warden was because of my shoes?"

The question sounded pointed, so he tried to remember why he had picked her up. The dinner bet. He winced. That stupid dinner bet with David. "Oh, hell."

"There was a bet, wasn't there?" Min said, sounding disgusted.

Cal took out his wallet and put a ten on the table. "There you go, it's all yours. Can I finish dinner before you throw me out?"

"Sure," Min said. "You know, you're taking losing that bet pretty well."

"I didn't lose," Cal said, stabbing another mushroom. "I don't lose."

"You collected on that bet?" Min said, sounding outraged.

Cal frowned at her. "You walked out the door with me. I won."

"And everybody just *assumes* . . ."

"Assumes what?" Cal said, exasperated. "Somebody bet me ten bucks I could get you to leave with me. You left with me. I got the ten bucks. Now you've got the ten bucks. Can we move on?"

"So the bet's over," Min said, disbelief palpable in her voice.

"Yes," Cal said, moving beyond exasperation. "Okay, it wasn't the best start to a relationship, but we don't have a relationship, what with you waiting for Elvis and both of us with our non-dating plans. Plus I'm feeding you. Again. Why are you mad?"

"No reason at all," Min said, flatly, and went back to her chicken.

"I'm missing something big here, aren't I?" Cal said.

"Yep," Min said. "Keep eating."

Cal offered to help with the dishes, but Min shoved him out the door, fed up with him because of the bet and with herself for caring. She put the leftovers from Emilio in the fridge and dumped the mess she'd made into the trash, and then she went into her bedroom and crawled under the satin comforter. Cal had said the bed was the only thing that looked like her. In an apartment full of plain lumpy furniture, he'd picked out the one beautiful, rich, sexy thing and said, "That's you." The bastard.

The cat jumped up on the bed and padded across to her. "Hey," she said as it curled up by her side. She petted it, feeling its skinny little body under its fur, and it opened both eyes. They were different colors, one of them stained with a blotch that matched the blotch of its fur. "Patch-work cat," she said, and it snuggled next to her, incredibly comforting. She turned on her bedside stereo and listened to Elvis sing about how lousy life had been since his baby left him. The cat pricked up its ears for about a verse, and then relaxed into the comforter again. "Moving into Heartbreak Hotel, are you?" Min said to it, and scratched it behind the ears. It lifted its head to press closer to her fingers, and she looked at its weird little face, screwed up in ecstasy with both eyes shut, and felt a rush of affection for it. It began to purr, and the sound was more comforting that she could have imagined. "It would not be sensible to keep you," she told it, and it opened its eyes slowly and then closed them again, and she kept petting it as it curled close, warm and peaceful and comforting. No wonder all those single women kept cats. They certainly beat charming, lying, compulsive gamblers who kissed like gods and had hands like— "Oh, I'm so lonely, baby," Elvis sang, and Min reached over and punched the UP button. The cat picked up its head, but it seemed to like "Don't Be Cruel" as well as "Heartbreak Hotel" and curled up again, warm against her stomach. "You can stay," she told it, and they lay together in companionable silence, listening to Elvis, until they both fell asleep.

"There's a real babe waiting in your office," David's assistant said when David came in on Wednesday. "Very nice."

Min, David thought and then realized with disappointment that it couldn't be. Nobody described Min as a babe.

When he opened the door, Cynthie was sitting across from his desk, looking phenomenal in a red suit.

"There you are," she said, standing up.

"That's a great suit," he said, closing the door behind him. He walked around her, impressed by the way the skirt curved under her tight little butt without hugging it.

"David," Cynthia said. "Forget the suit. Why is Cal still dating the woman you love?"

"Dating?" David lost interest in Cynthie's suit and sat down behind his desk.

"He took her to lunch on Monday which meant he couldn't go with me. He took her dinner last night at her place." Cynthie leaned closer, her lovely little face tense. "I thought you were going to call Greg. Why is he still with her?"

"I did call Greg." David moved some papers around while he thought fast. "I don't know why it didn't work. Maybe Cal had a good time when he was with her." *Maybe he wants to win ten thousand dollars.*

"But no sex," Cynthie said.

"No," David said, praying Min was still frigid. "They will not be having sex."

"I think you're right." Cynthie began to pace. "She doesn't sound like a woman who would do it that fast, and he wouldn't push it. He has great instincts."

"Well, hooray for him," David said. "Is there anything else you wanted?"

Cynthie leaned over the desk. "I want you to call Min. Ask her to lunch, ask her to dinner, pay for it, and *get her back*."

David looked down the neckline of her suit and revisited her cleavage. "You do this on purpose, don't you?"

Cynthie took a deep breath, her jaw rigid. "David, I am a dating expert who is losing the man she loves. This isn't just about my private life, this is about my public life, it's about my *whole* life. I have a potential bestseller on my hands, my editor wants to put our wedding picture on the back cover, everything is riding on this, and I am not going to see it go down the drain because *you're too spineless to get your girlfriend back*." She leaned closer. "I'll go away when you promise me you'll call her for lunch, and you tell me who her best friends are. I saw two in the bar on Friday. A little blonde and a tall redhead. Are they close to her?"

Her perfume wafted toward him, very faint, a whisper of a scent that made him dizzy. "What perfume are you wearing?" he said, trying to ignore the "spineless" crack.

"It's a special blend made just for me," Cynthie said, her voice lower now. "It's made of the scents that most strongly activate a man's libido. I put it on for you, David. Who's her best friend?"

David shook his head to clear it and slid his chair back, away from her. "What's in that stuff?"

"Lavender and pumpkin pie." Cynthie straightened. "I need to know her best friend. I'm helping you, David. You want the actuary back, right?"

She stood in front of him, lithe and lean in red wool crepe, smelling like lavender and cinnamon, and it took him a minute to remember who the actuary was.

"I don't even *like* you," he told her. "Why am I so turned on?"

She rolled her eyes. "Because you're male. Who's her friend?"

"Why do you want to know?"

Cynthie exhaled through her teeth. "I told you this. Attraction. If I can tell her best friend about Cal's pathology with women, I can ensure that the friend finds out enough to worry, and then she will tell Min she dislikes him. And that will help to ward off the infatuation stage. It's all science, David. Nobody is going to get mugged in an alley."

"Okay," David said, still fixated on her breasts. "Are you wearing anything under that jacket?"

"If I show you, will you give me a name?" Cynthie said.

"Yes," David said, knowing he was low and weak and not caring.

Cynthie popped the two buttons on her jacket and opened it. Her red silk bra matched the lining of the suit, and her breasts were perfect B cups, high and taut and, from where he sat, real.

"Oh, God," David said, freezing in his seat.

"Damn right," Cynthie said, buttoning back up again. "Now give me the name."

"The redhead," David said. "Liza Tyler. She thinks all men are bastards anyway."

"She's right," Cynthie said. "Call Min for lunch."

Then she left and David watched her go, the afterimage of her perfect breasts imprinted on his retinas, trying to tell himself that he'd done the right thing because somebody had to stop Cal Morrisey. And save Min, that was important, too.

"Very hot," his assistant said from the doorway. He sniffed the air. "Wow. Is that her perfume?"

"Yes," David said, picking up his phone. "It's brimstone. Don't let her in here again."

At eight that night, Liza was sitting with Tony and Roger in The Long Shot waiting for Bonnie and Min to come back from the bathroom when Tony said, "Uh oh," and turned away from the bar.

"What?" Roger followed his gaze. "Oh." He shrugged. "She's clear across the room."

"She who?" Liza squinted through the dim light. A brunette lounged at the bar, looking expensive, lean, and bored while the guy next to her made his pitch. "Old girlfriend?"

"Nope," Tony said as Bonnie came back from the bathroom. "I don't date the insane. Well, not until you."

"Do you date the insane?" Bonnie said to Roger with interest as she sat down.

"No, no, Cal, not me," Roger said, almost falling off his chair. "I hardly ever date."

"It's all right, baby." Bonnie patted his knee. "You're allowed to date."

"I don't want to date," Roger said and Tony rolled his eyes.

"So that's Cal's old girlfriend." Liza stood. "I'll be right back."

"Wait a minute," Tony said and caught her arm. "Why do you care about Cal's love life?"

"He's dating my best friend," Liza said, trying to sound innocent. "I'm curious."

"What I meant by the not-dating thing," Roger said to Bonnie, "was not dating anybody but you."

"I really don't expect monogamy on the third date," Bonnie said.

"Okay," Roger said. "But it's here anyway."

"Am I going to have to put a chain on you?" Tony said to Liza. He stopped to contemplate that for a moment and then shook his head. "Forget the chains. Stay away from Cynthie. She has psychology on the brain. Probably because she's a psychologist, but still, she comes up with some very whacko stuff."

"Analyzed you, did she?" Liza said, looking back across the bar.

"The not-dating-other-people is just for me, of course," Roger said to Bonnie. "You don't have to just date me. Unless you want to."

Tony shook his head. "She has this insane four-steps-to-love theory that she thinks explains all relationships."

"Oh," Liza said, taken aback.

"Which is dumb because chaos theory explains relationships," Tony said, tugging her back into her seat.

"What?" Liza said, trying to pull her arm away.

"Human relationships, like the weather, cannot be predicted," Tony said, holding on, and Liza sat down again to relieve the pressure on her arm. "Take, for example, Min and Cal. Cal's a complex dynamical system who's trying to maintain stability by not dating."

"He's not dating?" Liza said.

"No," Tony said. "Can you believe it? That alone is making him unstable. The man is not good at celibacy. Then he meets Min, a disturbance in his environment. He begins to move at random because of the disturbance, trying to find stability, but he's caught in the field of her attraction, and starts bouncing off the sides of that field at random, never repeating himself but still caught in her pattern. She's the strange attractor."

"Uh huh," Liza said. "And what good is all of this?"

Tony leaned closer. "Cynthie thinks relationships follow a pattern and that you can predict them. But how can you? People are complex, the disturbances in their lives are complex, and the attractors in their lives are complex. People in love are pure chaos theory."

"Okay," Liza said, still confused.

"That's why Cynthie is crazy," Tony said, letting go of her. "She thinks love can be analyzed and explained. It can't."

Liza sat back and considered Tony for the first time. Somehow he didn't look dumb anymore, and it wasn't because of whatever the hell chaos theory was. It was because he was interested in what he was saying. When he cared, he was smart.

"What?" Tony said.

"Have you ever been in love?" Liza said.

"No," Tony said. "I don't think it's going to happen." He grinned at her. "It would cause too much disturbance in my environment."

Liza frowned. "So why don't you like Cynthie?"

"She tried to pin Cal down. She analyzed him and thought she knew him. He deserves better than that. He should be with somebody who's willing to face the chaos. No rules, no conditions, no theories, no safety nets. The way Bonnie is with Roger."

Liza looked over at Bonnie, laughing with Roger. "You're right. We all deserve that."

"Good," Tony said. "Then you don't have to talk to Cynthie."

Roger said something, and Tony turned away to answer him, and Liza got up and went to meet Cynthie.

When Liza slid into a seat and said, "Hi, I'm Liza," Cynthie looked up and did a double take.

"Hi," she said, sounding surprised, almost as if she recognized her. "I'm Cynthie. Do we know each other?"

"No," Liza said. "But your ex is dating a friend of mine. Tell me everything you know about Calvin Morrisey."

Fifteen minutes later, Liza sat back and thought, *Chaos theory, my ass, Calvin Morrisey has a pattern*. "I knew it," she said to Cynthie. "I knew he was going to break her heart. How many times has he done this?"

Cynthie shrugged. "I was at a party one night after we broke up, and I started talking to a woman who had dated him, too. Then somebody else drifted over. By the end of the night there were four of us, all the same story. A couple of months, life is good, you think 'he's the one' and then he kisses you on the cheek, says 'Have a nice life,' and he's gone."

"You're kidding," Liza said. "And nobody's hunted him down with a tire iron?"

"You can't," Cynthie said. "What are you going to say, 'You dated me for two months, how dare you leave me?' You'd sound demented." She sipped her drink. "And he doesn't do it on purpose," she added, for what must have been the thousandth time.

"You know, I don't care," Liza said. "I just don't want him hurting Min."

"Maybe they're not that serious," Cynthie said. "Do they have anything in common?"

"Not that I can tell," Liza said.

"Are they relaxed together?"

"No," Liza said. "Mostly they fight."

"Do they have shared secrets? In-jokes?"

Liza shook her head. "They don't know each other that well."

Cynthie drew her fingertip around her glass. "Do you like him? I mean, have you told Min you don't like him?"

"Hell, yes," Liza said. "Bonnie and I have both warned her."

"Hmmm." Cynthie smiled at Liza. "Does he have a nickname for her yet?"

"A nickname?" Liza tried to remember. "He calls her by her last name sometimes. Never anything like 'pookie' or 'baby doll.'"

"How about her?" Cynthie said. "Does she have a nickname for him?"

"The beast," Liza said. "I don't think it's affectionate."

Cynthie laughed. "Then why is she dating him?"

"I'm not sure she is," Liza said. "But I think she's going to. I think she's falling for him even though she doesn't want to."

Cynthie stopped laughing.

"And that worries me," Liza said. "She's a terrific person, she doesn't deserve to be dallied with. Can you give me some pointers on how he works?"

Cynthie straightened and nodded. "Sure. Has he given her anything yet?"

"He's only known her a week," Liza said. "I don't . . ." She stopped when Cynthie shook her head.

"If he's serious at all about her, he'll give her something. He'll find out what she wants most, and he'll make sure she gets it. He has to, it's this pattern he's fallen into because of his mother."

"His mother?" Liza said.

"She's withholding," Cynthie said. "He only knows conditional love. So he acts out the same pattern with every woman he meets, trying to win her love. And then when he gets it, the pattern breaks because if she loves him, she's not a stand-in for his mother, and he moves on, to make somebody else love him."

"He's got an Oedipus complex?" Liza said, appalled.

"No," Cynthie said. "She just set up the pattern. He's not in love with her."

"So that means the more Min rejects him . . ." Liza said.

"The more he'll chase her," Cynthie said, all traces of amusement gone. "He can't help it. He doesn't even know he does it. Does she collect anything?"

"Snow globes," Liza said, and then when Cynthie tried to hide her contempt, added, "It's not her fault. It was a family thing that got out of hand."

"He'll buy her a snow globe," Cynthie said. "And it'll be the perfect one, the one she's been missing or always wanted or maybe didn't even know she wanted until he gives it to her. And when he does, you get her out fast, or it'll be all over but the weeping."

"Snow globe," Liza said, looking back at the table where Cal had joined the group after working late.

"He's not a bad person," Cynthie said again. "He'd never hurt anyone on purpose. He's just got this . . ."

"Pathology where he mutilates women because of his mother," Liza said. "I think that was Norman Bates's story, too."

"He'd *never* hurt her physically," Cynthie said, shocked.

"Well, he's not going to hurt her emotionally either," Liza said. "Thank you very much, I appreciate this."

"My pleasure," Cynthie said. Liza thought, *Your pleasure?*, and she must have looked at her oddly, because Cynthie added, "To help. Out. Your friend." She looked down at her drink. "I don't want her to get hurt."

"Me, either," Liza said, and headed back to the others.

When she got back to the table, Tony was saying to Min, "I don't believe it."

"Believe it," Min said. "There are ways you can tell."

"Tell what?" Liza said, sitting down beside Tony but keeping an eye on Cal.

"If a guy is worth dating early in the game," Min said. "We were talking about the old dating tests we used in college."

"Tests," Cal said, leaning his head back and closing his eyes. "I *hate tests*."

"Like what?" Tony asked Liza.

Liza shrugged. "Like you ask him over to watch a video."

"This is good," Tony said. "Videos are good."

"And you show him *Say Anything*," Bonnie said.

"Chick flick," Tony said.

"You flunked this test before it started," Liza said.

Bonnie went on. "And then you wait until he's watching the scene where John Cusack brushes the broken glass out of Ione Skye's path."

Liza watched Cal grin at Min, and Min shake her head at Cal. *Secrets*, she thought, and straightened a little in her chair.

"And then what?" Tony said.

"And if you say . . ." Bonnie deepened her voice. " '*What the hell? She's wearing shoes, ain't she?*' you're gone."

"Well, she was," Tony said, exasperated.

"But they were open-toed," Roger said.

"You get extra points for noticing they were open-toed," Bonnie told him.

"Great," Tony said. "The guy with the foot fetish gets extra points."

"Okay, Minnie," Cal said to Min, "the guy says that and then what happens?"

Minnie? Liza thought and waited for Min to savage him.

"I become ill with something communicable," Min said, trying not to smile.

"How ill?" Cal said, grinning at her.

Damn it, Liza thought.

"There will be retching," Min said, and grinned back.

"And in your case, I will throw up on your shoes," Liza said to Tony, needing to yell at somebody.

"What happens to me?" Roger asked Bonnie.

"Wonderful things," Bonnie said, slipping her arm into his.

"I hate you," Tony said to Roger. "You keep fucking up the curve."

Min laughed, and Cal watched her laugh, and Liza thought, *Oh, no.* He looked like a man with a goal, and she knew what it was. *I catch you with a snow globe, buddy*, she thought, *and you are dead meat.*

Cal glanced over at her and froze. "What?" he said.

"Nothing," Liza said and smiled at him with intent. "Nothing at all."

"Who's the lucky woman tonight?" Shanna said when Cal went to the bar for refills.

"No woman," Cal said. "I'm resting. How's Elvis? Still singing 'She' on permanent rotation?"

"Don't knock Elvis. If he was a girl, I'd marry him." She craned her head to look around Cal. "I see the Goon Brothers and two women. Let me guess. The tall skinny redhead is yours."

"No," Cal said. "Refills all around for them, Scotch for me."

Shanna looked past him again. "You're with the little blonde in the blue? She looks vacant to me."

"Misleading," Cal said. "But no, not her, either. She's Roger's."

"Then where—" Shanna began.

"Hi," Min said from behind him, and he turned, smiling automatically. "I completely understand your need to flirt with the bartender, but Tony sent me to remind you to hurry."

Shanna leaned over the bar and stuck her hand out to Min. "Hi, I'm Shanna, Cal's next-door neighbor."

Min looked surprised but took it. "I'm Min." She hesitated, and then she leaned over the bar. "Can I ask you something personal?"

"Oh, please do," Shanna said, looking deep into her eyes.

"Excuse me?" Cal said, not sure whether he was annoyed or turned on that Shanna was hitting on Min in front of him.

"You have the most beautiful hair," Min said, ignoring him. "How do you keep it from frizzing?"

"I don't wash it," Shanna said. "Just rinse and condition it. It'll never frizz on you again."

"You're kidding," Min said. "I'm going to try that. I'm so sick of pinning my hair up that I'll try anything."

"Well, come back in when you let it down," Shanna said. "I want to see it."

Me, too, Cal thought.

"I will do that," Min said. "Thank you." She turned back to Cal. "Do you need help carrying the drinks?"

"Yes," Cal said before Shanna could say "No" and hand him a tray.

"I'll be right back then," Min said, and went over to the jukebox.

Cal leaned on the bar as he watched her cross the room. "Get those drinks, babe."

"Tell me she's bi," Shanna said, watching Min, too. "The things she could do with that mouth . . ."

"The things I could do with that mouth," Cal said. *The things I have done with that mouth*. He felt a little dizzy again. Well, it was warm in the bar.

"I'll get those drinks," Shanna said and left while Cal watched Min flip cards on the jukebox. He focused on the gorgeous curve of her neck as she read the song titles. She looked juicy, bitable there, and that set off a whole new train of thought that he told himself was all right as long as he didn't *do* anything about it.

When Shanna came back with six glasses and mugs on a tray, she said, "So how long have you been seeing her?"

"I met her a week ago, but we're not—"

"Early yet." Shanna nodded. "She's got another month, probably two before you wander off. Tell her nice things about me so I can lay a foundation."

"For what?" Cal said.

"She's going to need comforting when you tell her to have a nice life. I will be that comfort. Are you sleeping with her yet?"

"I'm not even dating her," Cal said as Min fed some coins into the jukebox and punched in some numbers. "Give me my Scotch. I think we're going to be listening to Elvis Presley and I will need it."

"Not dating her, huh? Good news for me." Shanna slid his glass across to him.

Cal shook his head. "No. She does not play for your team. And you're still grief-stricken, remember?"

"I'm feeling much better," Shanna said, as "The Devil in Disguise" boomed out of the jukebox. "How do you know she doesn't play for my team?"

"I kissed her. She plays for mine. Although not for me."

"Not for you, huh?" Shanna took two fives from her pocket and slapped them on the bar. "I got ten bucks says you can't kiss her again right here."

"No kidding." Cal laughed at the thought of the damage Min would do to him if he tried. "Also no bet."

Shanna tilted her head. "Okay. I got ten bucks says you *can* kiss her right here."

"I've explained this to you," Cal said. "You have to figure the odds and then take the side that's probable. You don't just flip a coin."

Shanna tapped her finger on the two fives. "Ten says you can do it."

"What's with you?" Cal said. "When did you turn into somebody who likes to watch?"

"I'm just—" Shanna began.

"Hey," Min said, from behind Cal, startling them both. "I thought you weren't going to bet on me anymore."

Cal looked down at her exasperated face. Her lush lower lip stuck out a little, not enough for a pout but enough to remind him of why he'd been staying away from her. "I never said that. Besides, what makes you think I'm—"

"You're both staring at me and there's money on the bar," Min said. "We've been here before." Her eyes were dark, crackling with heat now as she scowled at him, and he began to breathe a little faster, remembering.

"He didn't make the bet," Shanna said. "I did. In fact, he—"

Cal took a ten out of his pocket and slapped it on the bar over Shanna's two fives. "You're on," he said, and leaned down to Min.

Chapter Seven

"Oh, yeah, he's innocent," Min said and then stopped as Cal leaned closer, giving her plenty of time to back away.

Her eyes widened and her lips parted, and she said, "Uh," and then he kissed her, gently, wanting to remember every second this time, the way she felt and tasted, soft and sweet, and he felt her suck in her breath, and then she kissed him back, giving him everything again, and the voice in his head said, *THIS ONE*, and he forgot his good intentions and cradled her face in his hand and lost himself in her.

When he broke the kiss, her eyes were half-closed and her cheeks were flushed. "Did you win?" she said, breathless, and he said, "Yes," and kissed her again, harder this time, feeling her hand clutch his shirt, and then something smacked him on the back of the head and knocked him into her, and she jerked away and said, "Ouch. Ouch."

"Damn it," he said, swinging around to face Liza. *"Stop doing that."*

"I will if you will," she said.

"No, really," Min said, sounding dazed. "It was okay. It was just another bet."

"Scum," Liza said.

"Look," Cal said, trying to catch his breath. "Min can take care of herself."

Liza stepped closer. "Yeah, tell me you know her. Tell me you care about her. Tell me you're going to love her until the end of time."

"What *is it* with you?" Cal said. "I kissed her. It happens."

Shanna picked up the twenty bucks on the bar. "And I, for one, am very grateful you did. Thank you very much."

"I thought you won," Min said to Cal. Her eyes were hot, and she was breathing faster, too.

"I did," Cal said, falling back into her. "I just lost the bet."

"Come on, Stats," Liza said, pulling on her arm.

"Right," Min said, shaking her head a little as if to clear it. "Did anybody see that?"

"The entire bar was holding up numbers," Liza said. "It was like the Olympics."

"How'd we do?" Cal said, putting an edge on his voice as he cooled off.

"The Russian judge thought you needed work," Liza said. "There was hooting."

"Well, the Russians are tough," Cal said. "Could you let go of her, please?"

"I don't think so," Liza said and tugged Min's arm again.

"I should go back," Min said to Cal. "You know. Because of the plan."

"What plan?" Cal said.

"Not dating. Taking a break. Remember? Both of us?"

"Right," Cal said, thinking, *Why did I think that was a good idea?* "The plan. Waiting for Elvis. Great." He picked up his Scotch again. "Here's to the plan."

"Yeah, well, have a nice life." Min picked up the tray of drinks and followed Liza back to the table.

"So the tall redhead hates you," Shanna said.

"Liza," Cal said. "I have never done a thing to that woman."

"I think it's what you want to do to her friend," Shanna said. "Still, it does seem like an overreaction. Is there something you're not telling me?"

"Like what?" Cal said. "I am innocent on this one." *No, I'm not.*

"No, you're not," Shanna said. "I saw that kiss. And you're right. She plays for your team."

"Not anymore," Cal said, feeling the back of his head. "We agreed on a plan. Not dating." He gestured with his glass. "I'm going to drink this and then go home for aspirin."

"That's not going to help," Shanna said. "Try a cold shower, too."

"Good to see you've got your sense of humor back," Cal said, and went home to find some peace and painkillers.

That week, Min began screening her calls to duck David, who had developed a pressing need to talk to her, but she didn't need to screen for Cal, who remained annoyingly silent. It was really frustrating avoiding the calls of somebody who didn't have the decency to pick up a phone. Even the If Dinner turned annoying when Liza told them about meeting Cal's ex-girlfriend.

"Cynthie says he's a great guy," Liza said. "He's just caught up in some kind of pathology where he has to make women love him and then leave him. He got conditional love as a child and now he's desperate for it."

Min frowned. "He does not strike me as desperate."

Bonnie shook her head. "Me, either. The ex sounds sort of over the top."

"Well, she's a psychologist," Liza said. "You know how they are. But it does explain why he'd leave such a string of broken hearts behind him and still be the guy we know. I'm suspicious of him but I don't think he's cruel. He wouldn't enjoy dumping them." She looked back at Min. "Cynthie said one of the things he'd do would be to find things you needed and give them to you. I told her about your snow globes, and she said you should brace yourself for incoming."

"He brought me a cat," Min said, and Liza put down her fork.

"A cat?" Liza said. "He must be losing his touch. That should have been a snow globe. Where is this cat?"

"Bedroom," Min said and Liza got up and went to look. When she came back she said, "It's the cat from hell. What was he thinking?"

Min shrugged, not wanting to argue. "He brought me takeout from Emilio's and it followed him in. And then he saw the snow globes."

"And?" Liza said.

"And he told me I collect couples," Min said. "Which I had never seen before, but he's right."

Liza opened her mouth to object and then got up and went to the mantel. "I'll be damned," she said after a moment. "They're all couples except mine, unless Captain Hook is dating Maleficent on the sly. How'd I miss this?"

"Better question is how'd he get it?" Bonnie said.

Min shook her head. "I think he's just really, really, *really* good with people. Empathetic." She hesitated and then said to Bonnie, "After you said he was dyslexic, I researched it on the net. There are all kinds of barriers—"

"Do not feel sorry for him," Liza said.

"I don't," Min said. "Are you kidding? Look at him, he has it all. But he's had to work for it. Anyway, one of the aspects of dyslexics is that they're often very empathetic. That's Cal. He spends all his time looking outward, making sure he understands other people. I don't think he has much self-knowledge, but he makes sure he knows the people in his world. He knows me."

Liza put the villains down with a clunk and came back to the table. "No, he doesn't. He's trying—"

"No," Min said, losing patience with her. "We talked about my weight. He said I dress like I hate my body."

"Good for him," Liza said. "I mean, he's a beast, but he's right on that one. What did he say exactly?"

Min pushed her plate away. "Lots of things, but the gist was that I had a sexy body and I should dress like I'm proud of it."

"Then he asked you to bed," Liza said.

"No, then he said we should eat," Min said. "Oh, and he told me what I was doing wrong on the chicken marsala, so I'm going to try it again."

"He brought you food, understood your snow globes, taught you to cook, said you had a sexy body, and left without making a pass," Bonnie said.

Min nodded.

Bonnie looked at Liza. "He *is* a beast."

"No, this is what Cynthie was talking about," Liza said. "He will fulfill her every need until she falls for him and *then he'll leave*."

Min bit her lip. "Look, I'm not falling for him, although I swear every time he kisses me, I hear voices and see stars. If nothing else, there's that bet. Which I asked him about and which he lied about, so it's over. Really."

"Uh huh," Liza said, clearly not convinced.

Neither was Min, so on Friday afternoon while she was at work, she very sensibly decided not to go to The Long Shot that night and called her sister instead. "I want to go shopping."

"Shopping?" Di said.

"Somebody told me that I dress like I hate my body."

"You do," Di said. "You want to change? *Yes*."

"Just a little," Min said, hastily. "I—"

"I know where we'll go," Diana said. "We're going to *transform* you!"

"No," Min said. "Soften a little, maybe, but not—"

"I'll be waiting out front at five," Di said. "This is going to be *so much fun*."

"Well," Min said, but Di had already hung up. "Oh. Well. All right."

She hung up and decided not to worry about transformation until she was actually in Diana's clutches. She went back to finishing up her work week, and then, as she was putting on her jacket to go meet Di, the phone rang. When she answered, a woman said, "My name is Elizabeth Morrisey, and I'm looking for a Min Dobbs who met my son Harrison at Cherry Hill Park a week ago."

"Bink?" Min said, dumbfounded.

"Yes," the woman said. "Oh, good. I'm so sorry to bother you at work, but I couldn't find a home listing. Just a moment." Min heard the phone clunk a little, and then Harry came on. "Min?" he said, breathing hard into the phone.

"Yes," she said, grinning. "How are you, Harry?"

"I'm fine. Are you coming to the park tomorrow?"

"Well, I wasn't—"

"Because you could come to my game," Harry said, showing an ability to focus that was much like his uncle's. "It's at ten o'clock. In the morning. And we could have a doughnut."

"Well," Min said, taken aback.

Harry breathed into the phone again. He sounded like Darth Vader, only smaller.

"Sure," she said. "Why not? I'll get the doughnuts—"

"My mom'll get them," Harry said. "I told her what kind."

"Well, good," Min said, regrouping. "Thank you for—"

Harry dropped the phone, and Min heard Bink say, "Say good-bye politely, Harry," and Harry came back on and said, "Good-bye," and dropped the phone again.

"Hello?" Bink said when she'd picked it up.

"Hello," Min said, trying not to laugh.

"We're still working on our phone skills," Bink said.

"He did pretty good," Min said. "Except for the breathing."

"I appreciate this," Bink said. "Harry has spoken of you often this week."

"He has?" Min said, surprised.

"And your shoes," Bink said.

"He's a lot like his uncle," Min said.

"We can only hope," Bink said. "Tomorrow at ten, then?"

"Tomorrow at ten," Min said and sat for a moment after Bink hung up.

That hadn't been Cal's idea. If he'd wanted her there, he'd have called her. He probably didn't even know she was coming. She finished putting on her jacket and thought about surprising him the next day. It would be good to take *him* off guard for a change, catch *him* flatfooted.

She picked up her purse and went down to meet Diana, suddenly interested in being transformed.

The next morning, Cal was watching a particularly hopeless outfielder named Bentley try to throw a ball when two cool hands covered his eyes from behind. He smelled lavender and cinnamon and felt a rush of pleasure so intense, he almost sighed. "This is not like you, Minnie," he said, and then he turned and saw Cynthie, like a cold shower, pulling her hands back. "Cyn?"

"Hi," Cynthie said.

"Sorry," Cal said, taking a step back. "You wear the same perfume as a friend of mine. Except she doesn't wear perfume, come to think of it." *Nor does she come to these damn games*, he thought, mad at himself for making such a stupid mistake.

"Perfume," Cynthie said, looking poleaxed.

"So," Cal said, taking another step back. "How've you been?" A ball rolled past his feet and he bent to pick it up. "You should get back to the other side of the fence. These kids have no control."

"Right," Cynthie said, swallowing. "I just wanted to say, 'Hi!'"

"Hi," Cal said. Something in the bleachers caught his eye and he looked past her to see Harry climbing up to the top. "Where the hell is he—" Cal began and then he looked past Harry and saw Min, sitting at the top, her hair cut short in loose curls that glinted in the sun. She was wearing a filmy, flowing white shirt, and her face lit up when she saw Harry so that she looked positively angelic, and he lost his breath for a moment. "She cut her hair," he said out loud, and Cynthie said, "What?" and followed his eyes.

Cal nodded to the bleachers, recovering. "Go up there and send Harry back down here, will you? He's supposed to be playing ball, not flirting with older women."

"Right," Cynthie said, in that brittle tone that Cal knew meant "I'm very upset, but I'm going to be an adult about it."

"You okay?" he said to her.

"Just fine," Cynthie said, even more brittle, and went around the fence to climb the bleachers.

What's her problem? Cal thought and then forgot her to look back at Min again, glowing in the sunlight while Harry wiped his nose on his arm and adored her. *I am not interested in Minerva Dobbs*, he told himself. *She's too high maintenance. She's never peaceful. And, oh yeah, she hates me.* Then Min smiled at Harry, and Cal thought, *Damn, she's pretty*, and kept staring.

———

When Min got to the park, the kids were warming up, and she saw Harry out on the field, smaller than the other kids and grubby as usual, and felt a twinge for him. Then he saw her and smiled the Morrisey smile at her, and she thought, *Oh, he's going to be fine,* and smiled back. She climbed up to the top of the bleachers and felt the wind ruffle her newly short curls and the fluttery sleeves of her organdy blouse as she sat down. She tried to watch Harry, but it was hard because Cal was there, and her eyes kept going to him. *It's purely physical,* she told herself, but it wasn't; she loved the way he was with the kids. He hated coaching, but he was doing it right. That was Cal.

Oh, stop it, she thought. *You don't even know him.*

A slender brunette walked up behind Cal and put her hands over his eyes, and Min thought, *Of course,* and felt all her ludicrous happiness deflate. It didn't matter that he was good with kids, since she didn't want any. But it did matter that he was a beast with women, so—

Someone sat down beside her and said, "Hello," in a beautifully modulated voice, and Min turned and saw a pale-haired, paper-thin woman smiling faintly at her. She had a heart-shaped face and huge gray eyes, her platinum hair was razor cut close to her finely boned head, and she couldn't have weighed more than ninety pounds. "I'm Bink," she said.

"Right," Min said. "Hi. I'm Min."

"It's so sweet of you to come for Harry," Bink said. "I do appreciate it."

"Well, Harry's a sweet kid," Min said, looking back to find him, only to discover that he'd escaped from the field and was climbing the bleachers toward them, looking even grubbier as he came closer.

"Most people don't notice that," Bink said, looking at him with love.

"Hi, Min," Harry said when he was one row down. He was beaming at her and she smiled back because anybody would.

"Hey, Harry," she said. "How's it going?"

"I have to play baseball," Harry said. "Otherwise, pretty good."

"Well, live through this and we'll celebrate with a doughnut afterward," Min said.

"Cool," Harry said, bobbing his head.

"You're looking good down there on the field," Min lied.

"Thanks," Harry said, still bobbing.

"You can really throw that ball," Min said, guessing.

"Not really," Harry said, but he didn't seem depressed by that.

He sniffed and kept nodding, and Bink said, "I think Uncle Cal wants you, Harry," and he turned around and saw Cal and the brunette watching him.

"Yeah," he said and sighed.

"Just keep thinking about that doughnut," Min said.

"Cool," Harry said again, beaming at her.

Min smiled back.

"I gotta go," Harry said, not going anywhere.

"Good luck," Min said.

"Yeah," Harry said, nodding for another minute or so. Then his smile faded and he trailed down the bleachers, avoiding his uncle's gaze.

"That was nice of you," Bink said, and Min looked at her, surprised.

"No, it wasn't," she said. "I like Harry."

The wind picked up before Bink could answer, and Min half expected her to blow away. *I'm so glad she's sitting beside me*, she thought bitterly. *Because I didn't look hefty enough sitting up here by myself.* Then she kicked herself. Bink might turn out to be nice, she was certainly polite, and Cal had warned her about hating her body. *Okay*, she thought. *I'm one of those heavy cream wedding invitations, the kind you have to touch because it's so beautiful, and she's the expensive tissue paper that's wrapped around me.*

"Are you all right?" Bink said.

"Yes," Min said. "Why?"

"You were frowning," Bink said.

"I have to work on my metaphors," Min said. "So Harry plays baseball."

"Unfortunately," Bink said, and Min thought, *She's not one of the people who shanghaied Cal and Harry. I wonder—*

"Hi!" somebody said brightly from Min's other side, and this time when she turned she saw the brunette who'd been flirting with Cal. She had a heart-shaped face and big gray eyes, and her dark hair was thick and silky.

Kill me now, Min thought as the paragon sat down beside her. *I've been bookended by the thin and rich.*

"How *are* you, Bink?" the woman said, and Bink smiled at her faintly—Bink evidently did everything faintly—and said, "Hello, Cynthie."

Cynthie. Min turned back to the brunette with renewed horror. Cal's ex. Wearing, Min now noticed, a black halter top that wasn't appropriate for a kids' baseball game. Except that Cynthie was wearing it with no self-consciousness at all, probably because her breasts were those perfect perky kind men were always going on about. *Bite me,* Min thought and looked down on the field to see Cal staring up at the three of them with a very strange expression on his face. Probably realizing with horror that he'd been kissing a woman who was never going to wear a size eight. That hurt a lot more than it should have.

"There's Cal," Bink said.

"What's wrong with him?" Min said. "Besides the fact that he hates this."

"He doesn't hate this," Cynthie said. "He agreed with me that this was great for Harry."

"Oh," Min said. "This was your idea?"

"Yes," Cynthie said, smiling.

Min turned to Bink. "Cynthie got Harry into baseball."

"Yes," Bink said. "Cynthie discussed it with Harry's grandmother and they agreed it would be good for him. Harry's grandmother can be very forceful."

"Oh," Min said, and turned back to the field to see a batter hit a wobbly shot into left field where a kid on Harry's team bobbled the ball. Cal missed all of it, staring up into the bleachers at them.

Then Cal began to turn away, and the kid in the outfield picked up the ball and threw it with desperation and an impossible force for an eight-year-old. It smacked Cal on the back of the head, knocking him off balance so that he fell to his knees and then to the ground.

"No," Min said and zapped down the bleachers and around the chain

link fence. "Cal?" she said, going down on her knees beside him as he tried to sit up. "Cal?"

He looked dazed, so she stared into his eyes, trying to see if the pupils were different sizes. They weren't, his eyes were the same hot, dark depths they always were, and she fell into them again, growing breathless, as music swelled behind her, Elvis Costello singing his heart out on "She," and the voice in her head said, *THIS ONE*.

Then she heard Tony say, "Turn that damn thing off," and when she looked up, she saw two girls with a radio next to the fence and Cynthie coming around it to kneel beside Cal, too.

"Sorry," one of the girls said, and the other said, "Is he dead?"

"Go away," Min said and they left, taking the music with them.

"Cal, are you all right?" Cynthie said, and Min looked down at him again to see him still staring at her.

"Cal?" she said.

The assassin from the outfield came running up. "Did you see that, Mr. Capa? I really threw it."

"Yeah, you did, Bentley," Tony said, looking down at Cal. "You okay, there, buddy?"

"I knew I could do it," Bentley said. "I saw Wyman getting close to third base, and something just *told me* I could do it, and I really *threw* that sucker, boy."

"Cal, *say something*," Cynthie said, panic in her voice.

"Boy, I really *threw that sucker,*" Bentley said.

"Yeah," Tony said. "Too bad you missed third base by a mile and took out Mr. Morrisey." He crouched down next to Cal. "Say something or Min takes you to the ER now."

"Did you hear music?" Cal asked, still staring into Min's eyes.

"I really *threw* that sucker," Bentley said.

Tony handed Min his car keys. "Go. The Cherry Hill ER is up the road a mile."

"I know the way," Cynthie said, standing. "I have a car."

Min helped Cal to his feet, trying to steady him as he lurched, and Tony took his other side.

"I'll take him," Cynthie said. "My car is just—"

"No," Cal said as he righted himself. "If I'm going to throw up, it'll be in Tony's clunker."

"Drive fast," Tony said to Min, and helped them both to the car.

Cal lay on the table in the ER, trying to remember what had happened. He'd been staring at Min, watching the breeze flutter the ends of her blouse and tousle her curls, and he'd been telling himself that she was a pain in the ass and that he didn't want anything to do with her, and then that ball had come out of nowhere and—

"Cal?" Min said, leaning over him. The fluorescent light above back-lit her hair and she looked like an angel again.

"Hi," he said.

"The doctor said you're going to be all right," she said, trying to look cheerful. "I just filled your prescription." She held up an amber plastic pill bottle. "For the pain. In case you have headaches. Do you have a headache?"

His head felt like a vise. "Yes."

She opened the bottle and dumped out two pills into her palm. "Here," she said, handing them to him. "I'll get water."

Cal thought about telling her that he'd already had a pain pill and then decided that since the damn thing wasn't working, two more would be good.

"You *scared* me," she said, when she came back with the water. "You got hit in the head. People get killed that way. I don't know how many a year. I haven't had time to look it up."

Cal propped himself up to take the pills. "Bentley," he said bitterly.

"I'm sure he'll be sorry," Min said. "When he gets over how hard he threw the ball."

"Little bastard," Cal said without heat. "Was there music? I could swear I heard—"

"—Elvis Costello singing 'She.'" Min nodded. "You did. Some kids had it on a radio. Which is weird because I don't think it gets a lot of airplay. My sister's using it in her wedding." She sounded as if she were babbling, which was so unlike Min that Cal chalked it up to his general dizziness. "I called Bink on her cell and told her you were okay and I was taking you home."

"Your sister likes Elvis Costello?" Cal said.

"No," Min said. "My sister likes music from Julia Roberts movies."

"Oh," Cal said and focused on her. "You cut your hair."

"Diana took me to her stylist," Min said. "To go with the new clothes. I did what you said."

"I didn't tell you to cut your hair." His eyes dropped to her blouse, looking through the thin fabric to the equally thin camisole underneath, and he almost fell off the table.

"Easy," Min said, breathless as she tried to prop up his weight, and he looked down the open neck of her blouse and saw pink lace under the camisole.

"Pink," he said.

"Oh, good, you're feeling better," Min said, relief in her voice. "Come on. I'll take you home."

"Okay," Cal said. "I like your hair."

Half an hour later, Min pulled up in front of Cal's apartment, having followed his increasingly groggy directions. "Let's go," she said, and opened the car door for him.

"I can get up there myself," Cal said, weaving a little as he got out. "Take the car—"

"You're not going up there alone." Min pulled his arm across her shoulders. It felt good there, if heavy. "My mother raised me better than that."

"Well, then you're going up first so you can't look at my butt."

"There's an elevator, Charm Boy," Min said, kicking the door shut behind them. "Move it."

"Wait a minute," he said, and she stopped so he could get his bearings, but he put his hand on her curls again, patting them. "Springy."

"Right," Min said and herded him upstairs to a white, slightly battered apartment that looked like something he would have lived in during college. She steered him through a living room furnished with

Danish modern furniture that would have made all of Denmark cringe, into an even bleaker, uglier bedroom. "How are you feeling?" she said as she guided him toward his headboardless bed.

"Better," he said, sounding groggy. "The drugs kicked in and I'm not coaching baseball."

"There you go," she said, "Always a bright side." She shouldered him toward the bed, and he bounced when he sat down.

"You're a lot more aggressive than I thought you'd be." He fell back onto the pillows, but his feet still hung off the side.

"You're a lot heavier than I thought you'd be," Min said, and realized that was probably because he moved so well when he was conscious. Semiconscious, he moved like a lurching glacier. She pulled off his Nikes, and her heart skipped a beat. "You're an eleven-D."

"Yes," Cal said, sleepily. "Tell me that proves I'm a beast. You haven't said anything lousy to me all day."

"Elvis wore an eleven-D," Min said, and Cal mumbled, "Good for him."

She picked up his feet and threw them on the bed, and then realized that he was way too close to the edge; if he rolled off in his sleep, he'd hit his head on the battered bedside table. She shoved at him to get him to the center of the bed.

"What are you doing?" he said, half asleep as she tried to rock him over.

"Trying to keep you safe," she said between her teeth as she put one knee on the bed and shoved again. "Roll over, will you?"

He rolled just as she shoved and knocked them both off balance. She grabbed at him to save herself, and he pulled her down with him.

"I should be awake in about eight hours," he yawned into her hair. "Stick around."

"Fine," she said into his chest. "Fall on the floor. Get a concussion. See if I care." He didn't say anything, so she shoved at him again, but it was like shoving at a wall. She stopped to consider the situation. There was something very protective in the way he held onto her. Thoughtful.

He began to snore.

Instinctive.

"Okay," she said, and squirmed around until she got one foot on the floor and shoved off, toppling him over onto his back in the middle of the bed, which stopped his snoring. Then she stood up and looked at him, sprawled out on an ugly, generic bedspread in a plain, cheap bedroom with lousy, awkward lighting. He looked like a god.

"It is *so* unfair," she said to him. "Couldn't you at least drool or something?"

He began to snore again.

"Thank you." She opened his closet door and found a blanket folded on the top shelf, over a tasteful collection of expensive suits. "You are so weird," she said to him as she snapped the blanket over him. "This place does not look like you at all."

He breathed deeper, and she looked down at the beautiful strong bones of his face, his lashes like smudges on his cheeks as he slept, and thought, *I could love you.*

Then she straightened and returned to reality. Every woman in the city thought that when she looked at him so it wasn't as if . . . *Oh, the hell with it*, she thought, and put his shoes where he wouldn't trip over them, got him a glass of water for his bedside table, made sure his pills were within reach, and pulled the blanket up so he wouldn't get chilled. Then, at a loss as to what to do next, she patted his shoulder and left.

On Monday, David picked up the phone and heard Cynthie say, "I talked to Cal. He thinks she smells like lavender. He noticed she cut her hair. His nephew loves her. *There was a copulatory gaze in the park.*"

"Isn't that illegal?"

"Don't make *fun*, David. This isn't *amusing*. We could *lose them*." He heard her take a deep breath over the phone. "The best thing for you to do right now is to ask her to lunch. Evoke joy. Did you even call her?"

"She's not returning my calls," David said, trying not to sound annoyed.

"How do you feel about that?" Cynthie said. "A little angry?"

"A little," David said. "But—"

"And you're angry that she never let you pay for dinner, too. She was rejecting your sexual advances, just as she's now rejecting your phone calls. So now—"

"This is ridiculous," David said, moving beyond annoyed.

"Your problem is that you're angry with her and she can sense that, so you're going to have to get over it. *Now*."

"I'm not angry, damn it," David snapped.

"Ask her to lunch and insist on paying. You'll feel much better, the anger will go away, she'll see you as a potential mate, and then you can make your move."

"This is such crap," David said.

"I don't care," Cynthie said. "*Do it*. Or she's going to end up with Cal."

Cal. Cal was going to win that damn bet. He always won, the bastard. "I'll call her," David said. "We'll have lunch. I'll play it by ear."

"Don't screw this up, David," Cynthie said. "My life is riding on it. My *career* is riding on it. *I need that wedding picture on my book cover*."

"You know—" David began, but Cynthie had already hung up. "Wonderful," he said, and began to dial Min.

Min was sitting at her desk, trying to be sensible, when the phone rang. *Cal*, she thought, and then kicked herself. They had a good sensible plan that would prevent either one of them from getting hurt, they were logical, rational people, so that certainly wasn't him calling. The phone rang again, and she picked it up and said, "Minerva Dobbs," and waited for Cal to say, "Hi, Minnie, how's the cat?"

"Min," David said. "Have lunch with me. We need to talk."

"No, we don't," Min said, trying hard not to be disappointed. "But I do need lunch. We can go Dutch."

"No, *I'll pay*," David said. "I mean, I'd like to pay."

"Sure, fine," Min said, confused.

"I'll meet you at Serafino's at noon then?" David said.

"Is that the place where the chef is trying to make a statement with food?"

"It's the hottest place in town," David said.

"This should be good," Min said and hung up, chalking the whole thing up to the general weirdness of her life lately.

When she got to the restaurant, David was waiting. He stood and smiled when he saw her, and then he stared. Min looked down and realized he was focusing on the blue gauze top beneath her gray-checked jacket.

"You look wonderful," he said.

"I'm evolving," Min said, sitting down at the inlaid table. "I'm also starving. What's good here?" She looked around at the silver and blue. "Besides the decorating."

"I already ordered," David said. "I didn't want you to have to wait."

"Thoughtful of you." Min called the waiter back and changed her order to salad and chicken marsala. Might as well see what Emilio's competition was doing.

"I think I made a mistake," David said, when the waiter had placed his bowl of chilled chestnut watercress soup in front of him.

"I think so, too," Min said, looking at the beautifully garnished sludge in his bowl. "You're going to hate that soup. There's a hot dog vendor outside. Maybe we should—"

"Not the order." David took a deep breath and smiled. "Min, I want you back."

Min stopped fishing overly artistic vegetable flourishes out of her salad. "What?"

"I was hasty," David said, and went on while Min thought, *The bet. That damn bet. You're afraid you're going to lose the bet.*

She sat back and considered the situation as David rambled on. Somehow, David had gotten the idea she was going to sleep with Cal. Now where would that have come from? The thought that it might be Cal gloating to him made her ill for a moment, but then common sense came back. Cal wasn't a gloater. Also, he wasn't dumb, and it would take somebody really dumb to tip off an opponent that he was about to lose. And anyway, Cal wouldn't.

"Are you listening to me?" David said.

"No," Min said. "Why are you doing this?"

"That's what I was just telling you—"

"No," Min said, "you were telling me about you. You were hasty, you were thoughtless, you were stupid—"

"I didn't say stupid," David said, sounding testy.

"Where am I in all of this?" Min said.

"In my life, I hope," David said, and he sounded so sincere, Min was taken aback. "I asked you out in the beginning because I thought you'd make a good wife, and I still think that, but what I missed was how . . ." He stopped and took her hand and Min let him, just to see what would happen next. ". . . how *sweet* you are."

"No, I'm not," Min said, trying to take her hand back.

"And how . . ." He looked at her gauze blouse. ". . . *sexy* you are. You've changed."

Min yanked her hand back. "David, this is buyer's remorse, or the opposite of buyer's remorse. If you got me back, you'd dump me again. Go date one of those skinny women you like to look at."

David started to say something but stopped as the waiter brought his veal whatever and her chicken marsala. Min sliced into the chicken and tasted it. "Bacon. And *tomato*. What kind of fool puts bacon and tomato in chicken marsala?"

"Min . . ."

"You can even see the bacon pieces in the sauce. Emilio would spit."

"You're not taking me seriously," David said.

"I know," Min said, putting down her fork. "Honest to God, what were they *thinking*?"

"What I'm trying to tell you," David said, "is that I think we should date again."

"No, you don't," Min said. "You're panicking because I'm dating somebody else. Taste your soup."

"I'm not—"

"The soup," Min said.

David tasted the soup and made a face. "What the hell?"

"I told you." Min pushed her plate away. "Never go anyplace the chef is trying to talk with food. You'll end up paying for his ego. Sort of like dating." She picked up her purse. "I'm sorry, David, but we have no future. We're not even going to finish this lunch, although I do appreciate you paying for it. Thank you."

"Where are you going?" David said, outraged as she stood up.

"To get a hot dog," Min said. "I think that vendor had brats."

Emilio called Cal on Tuesday night at six. "Min ordered takeout again," he said. "You taking it to her?"

"Yes," Cal said automatically and then remembered they weren't seeing each other. "No." Which didn't mean they couldn't be friends. "Yes." Which was a huge rationalization. "No."

"Uh huh," Emilio said. "So that's a no?"

On the other hand, he had to eat. And he should thank her for taking care of him on Saturday. And he wanted to see her. "No," Cal said. "That's a yes. I'll take it to her."

Chapter Eight

Min answered the door in her godawful sweats again, no makeup and her curly hair going every which way. She looked wonderful. "Hi," she said, sounding surprised, and then she grinned. "Emilio shanghaied you, huh?"

"He said you were starving," Cal said, smiling back in spite of himself. "You took me to the ER. You put a glass of water by my bed. I owe you."

"That's lame," she said, but she stood back and he walked in, glad to see her ugly cat staring one-eyed at him from the back of her ugly couch.

"I can't believe you still have that cat," Cal said, unpacking the bag onto the table. "What did you name it?"

"I can't believe you brought me that cat," Min said, heading for her kitchen alcove. "And I haven't named it anything yet. We're still trying to decide if we want to make a commitment. Although he does come home every night and sleep with me."

"Smart cat," Cal said.

"I was thinking about trying to make him an indoor cat because cats live longer if they're kept indoors, but he's a guy, so I'm assuming he'd hate being tied down."

"Depends on what you tied him to," Cal said, thinking of her brass bed.

Min brought plates to the table. "You know, if you'd brought me a snow globe I could understand, but a cat?"

"You said you didn't want a snow globe."

"I don't," Min said. "Well, I want my grandma's Mickey and Minnie globe back. Bring my grandma's back to me, and I'll love you until the end of time. Bring me another cat, I'm going to rethink the whole chicken marsala thing."

"Speaking of which," Cal said, "what happened this time?"

Min groaned and went back to the alcove and Cal followed her, feeling right at home. "It doesn't look bad," he said when he saw her latest effort. "It just doesn't look like chicken marsala."

"I was trying to avoid the olive oil and butter," Min said, and then held up her hand before he could speak. "I know, I know, I'm learning my lesson. I used chicken broth instead. It smells good but it doesn't look right."

"That would be because olive oil and chicken broth are not the same thing," Cal said. "You're all right. Just make a roux to thicken the broth and serve it over fettuccine."

"A roux," Min said.

"Melted butter and flour," Cal said. "I don't suppose there's a chance in hell you have butter."

"Bonnie might," Min said. "I don't have fettuccine or flour, either. I'll go borrow them from her."

"Do you have a big pot for the noodles and a colander?" Cal said, looking around the spare alcove. *She's got to find a better place.*

"In the basement," Min said.

"That's convenient. Where's the lid?"

"Lid?" Min said.

"Something that will keep the cat from going headfirst into this pan while we're down in the basement?"

"We're going down to the basement?"

"Do you want to learn to cook, Minnie?" he said with more affection than he'd intended.

Min blinked. "Yes. Yes, I do."

"Then you'll need pots and pans," Cal said.

They went to the basement, and Cal picked out one of the half-dozen unmarked boxes at random and opened it with his pocketknife. Min unwrapped the first package in the box: her grandmother's green colander. "This is the box," she said as she dropped the colander back in the box. "You went right to it. You're good."

"Hell, yes." Cal grinned at her and picked up the box. "Move it, Minnie, and don't forget to stop for butter, flour, and pasta."

Teaching Min how to make a roux should have been pretty innocuous, but the kitchenette was tiny, and she was close, and her curls smelled like lavender, and there wasn't anything about her that wasn't round, and there was that brass bed with a satin comforter just a room away, so after he'd explained the basics of roux, Cal retreated to unpack the box.

The cat was sitting in it. "Out," he said, and it switched eyes on him, lolling among the lumpy packages. He reached in and picked it up and put it on the floor, and it rubbed up against his leg, purring. "Very affectionate cat," he told Min.

"I know, I love the damn thing," Min said. "He curls up beside me every night and purrs along to Elvis. He's smart, too. He's learned how to hit the stereo button so he can play Elvis without me."

Cal pulled out the first package and unwrapped a thick, clear glass, angular bowl that looked as though it might have a specific function. "What's this?"

Min looked back. "It's an egg-beater bowl. There should be a metal lid for it with a beater in it."

Cal dug around the box until he found it. The lid sat on the bowl with the crank for the beaters above it, and the beaters below. "That's pretty neat," he said, and picked up the next wrapped package, a heavy one which turned out to be nested mixing bowls, thick white china with a blue stripe.

"Oh," Min said, "I *remember* those, my grandma used to make cookies in the big one. That was back when I ate cookies."

"The good old days." Cal picked up the next package. It was heavy and round and as he unwrapped it, he began to realize what it was. When he pulled the last of the paper away, he wasn't that surprised to see a snow globe with Mickey inside, dipping Minnie in her pink dress. But he was appalled.

"So, how long does this cook?" Min said. "I mean, before the flour loses the raw flavor? Cal?" She looked back at him. "What's wrong?"

He held up the snow globe, and she froze over the chicken pan.

It was heavy in his hand, heavier than a snow globe should be. He tipped it and saw the key on the bottom. "Music box?" he said to her and she nodded. "What's it play?"

" 'It Had to Be You,' " she said, faintly.

"Of course." Cal looked at Mickey and Minnie, trapped forever in the globe. *Bring my grandma's snow globe back to me and I'll love you until the end of time.*

"I've been looking for that for fifteen years," Min said, her voice flat. "And then you go right to it. How do you do that?"

"It's not me." Cal put it down on the counter.

"You didn't make a deal with the devil, did you?" Min said, staring at it.

"What?"

"You know, some kind of bargain where everything you did would be perfect so that every woman you met would be unable to resist you, only you forgot to mention that should work only with women you wanted, and now we're stuck in this loop with each other?"

Cal took a deep breath. "Okay, leaving aside the fact that you think the devil exists and is making deals, I'm a little upset that you think I'd be hanging out with him."

"Well, hell, Cal, you're practically his first cousin," Min said. "You're tall, you're dark, you're handsome, you're charming, you wear suits, you never sweat, and you always show up with whatever I'm needing at the moment. That snow globe has been lost for *fifteen years*. I keep getting this feeling that if I say yes to you, I'll go straight to hell."

Cal nodded. *Why did I come back here?* "Okay. You know, I'm not hungry anymore. I think I'll be going."

"That might be good," Min said, staring at the snow globe.

He picked up his jacket and headed for the door and then paused as he opened it. "Have a—" he started to say and then stopped.

"Nice life?" Min said, still staring at the globe.

He shook his head. "It just doesn't have the same ring to it," he said, and went down the stairs.

When he was gone, Min walked over to the snow globe and wound it. It began to tinkle the first bars of "It Had to Be You," and she looked into it, and tried to get her breath back. The dome was heavy and perfect, sitting atop a black art deco base, and inside silver glitter and tiny silver stars swirled as Minnie beamed out at her, happy to be in Mickey's arms, and Mickey beamed at Minnie.

Maybe that's what I loved, she thought. *That she was so happy and he thought she was wonderful.* Plus there was that swirling pink dress Minnie was wearing and the great pink shoes to match. Well, the shoes were a little plain. Min tipped the globe to see, and the glitter and stars swirled again as the song slowed down and ran out.

It's not me, Cal had said, but it was him. She'd been going along, perfectly happy, and then he'd walked into the bar and shaken up her life and suddenly it was all glitter and stars everywhere. And every time things calmed down, every time she got things back to normal, he came back and shook—

Something furry nudged her leg and she jumped. The cat meowed at her and she picked him up and thought about the situation logically. Of course it wasn't him. Coincidences happened all the time. That was life. As long as nothing else happened . . .

"We'll just stay away from him," she told the cat. "We won't go to The Long Shot unless we know he won't be there, and this will all pass and we'll be normal again. No more goddamn glitter."

The cat switched eyes again, and Min realized that talking to an animal using "we" was probably not normal, either. "Chicken?" she said to the cat, and gave up on logic to eat dinner.

On Wednesday, Liza was at the bar trying to signal Shanna when Cynthie sat down next to her and smiled at her. "Hi. Where's your friend?"

"She said she had to stay home with her cat," Liza said, "but I think she's avoiding Cal."

"That's a good idea," Cynthie said. "The best way to resist him is to stay away from him." She looked around the bar. "Do you see him?"

"No," Liza said. "Tony said he's working late. Why?"

"Because if she's not here, he should be working on you."

"Me?" Liza said, appalled. "She's gone so he's going to pick me up?"

"No," Cynthie said. "It's important to the health of a relationship that her friends and family approve of him. I'm surprised he hasn't tried to charm you yet."

"He's not dumb," Liza said. "And we're not buddies."

"Well, your friend is doing the right thing by avoiding him," Cynthie said. "I don't think he's going to get to her at all."

"He got to you, though, huh?" Liza said.

Cynthie lifted her chin. "I . . ."

Liza waited.

"Yes," Cynthie said. "He got to me."

"Rat bastard," Liza said.

"No, he's not," Cynthie said. "He just—"

"Needs approval from women because of Mommie Dearest," Liza said. "You know, with all you know about him, you could write a book."

Cynthie sipped her drink.

"Ah," Liza said. "You are writing a book."

"Yes," Cynthie said. "But not about . . . well, not entirely about . . ."

"Boy," Liza said. "So when he left, you lost a lover and a research subject. I don't understand this. You're an expert in this relationship stuff and he still got to you?"

Cynthie bit her lip. "What you know logically doesn't help if you're feeling something emotionally."

The pain on her face was real, and Liza put her hand on Cynthie's arm. "I'm sorry."

"You know," Cynthie said, sticking her chin out, "it's not a problem. There are people with much worse problems than mine."

"Doesn't make yours any more fun to bear," Liza said.

"No," Cynthie said. "But it does help with the self-pity." She shoved her glass away. "If I've made Cal seem like a bad guy—"

"You haven't," Liza said. "In fact, I think you have a pretty rosy view of him."

"No," Cynthie said. "He's a good—"

"I don't care. I just want him to stay away from Min."

"Me, too," Cynthie said.

She finished her drink and left, and Shanna came down the bar and said, "Refill?"

Liza smiled. "Tell me about Cal Morrisey."

"Why?" Shanna said, warily.

"Because he's been kissing my best friend, and I've heard he has a commitment problem."

Shanna shrugged. "Him and half the male population."

"Half of the male population isn't kissing Min," Liza said. "He's not serious about her, is he?"

Shanna bit her lip. "He's the best guy I know. If I was ever in trouble, I'd call Cal, and he would come and get me out, I know that in my soul."

"And yet, not an answer to my question," Liza said.

Shanna was quiet for a moment and then she said, "Tell your friend not to get invested. He doesn't stay."

"Thank you," Liza said.

"But he's a really good guy," Shanna said.

"I keep hearing that," Liza said, getting up. "I'm just having trouble believing it."

At seven, Cal decided that one more minute of looking at the seminar packet would make him beat his head against the desk and he'd had enough cranial injury for the month. On the other hand, looking at Min at The Long Shot would only lead to being called the devil again. Or, if she was having a good day, a beast. He stood up and stretched, and then set out for home, slowing down as he passed the Gryphon Theater. They were doing the last week of the John Carpenter revival, and there was a short line out in front for *Big Trouble in Little China*.

Kurt Russell beats the bad guys, he thought. *Haven't seen that since I was a kid*. The last person left the box office, and he went up and bought a ticket. Better than spending the night alone, concentrating on not thinking about . . . anyone.

As he walked in, the previews were running for an Elvis Presley series, and he thought of Min. *Forget her*, he told himself, and found a place a few rows down and a few seats over, surrounded by empty seats. But as the movie began and Kurt started talking trash in his truck, a family of five came in and asked him to move down. The person to the right of his new seat was quiet, so he slouched down and lost himself in the movie, peaceful for the first time since the night before.

When the lights came up, he stood up to go at the same time as the woman on his right. Medium height, short curly brown hair tipped with gold, turning now to get her gray-checked jacket . . .

They stared at each other for a long, dumbstruck moment, and then she walked out of the theater and he followed. When they were outside she turned and looked at him.

"What are the odds?" Cal said.

"I don't even know how to calculate the odds," Min said, and started walking, and he fell into pace beside her because she shouldn't walk home alone in the dark in the city.

Coincidence, Cal told himself. *Happens all the time. No big deal. Means nothing*.

When they got to her apartment, she climbed the steps without any arguing about who was going first, and for once he was too stunned to think about her rear end. At her door she turned and said, "Thank you for walking me home," and he said, "You're welcome." They looked at each other for one long moment, and Cal felt breathless, falling into her eyes, and he thought, *Oh, Christ*, no, *not you*. Then she shook her head and went inside and closed the door, and he turned and walked down fifty-eight steps to the street, not sure whether to be relieved or not.

He paused and looked up at the dormer that was her bedroom window. The cat sat there, silhouetted against the light from her lamp, staring down at him, probably shutting one eye in the darkness. He imagined Min sitting down on that satin comforter, lying back on embroidered pillows that smelled of lavender, her gold-tipped curls against the blue satin, and he put himself there, beside her, pulling her to him, her arms around him, all her warm roundness against him, soft and yielding, imagined taking her lush mouth, feeling the swell of her breast under his hand, the rise of her hips to his, imagined pushing into all that softness, shuddering into the hot wetness of her, hearing her moan and sigh as he moved, and he realized that he wanted her more than he could ever have imagined wanting anything or anyone.

The light went out in her bedroom and broke the spell, and he closed his eyes against the darkness and the cold shock of reality. Then he turned and started back to the main street, to light and noise and safety.

On Thursday, when Liza showed up at Min's apartment for the If Dinner, Bonnie answered the door looking cautious. When Liza lifted her eyebrows to ask *What?*, Bonnie shook her head and stood back to let her in.

"Hi," Min said, a little too quietly, and Liza thought, *That rat bastard Cal.*

"What did he do?"

"Nothing," Min said. "Sit down. I made a huge Cobb salad and I'm starving. Let's eat."

Liza turned back to the couch and saw a one-eyed animal looking at her. "You still have the cat."

"I love that cat," Min said. "He's always there for me, he pats me with his paw when I'm depressed, he keeps me warm at night, and he has a beautiful voice. I've decided he's the reincarnation of Elvis."

"The long wait is over," Liza said. *He gave her something she didn't even know she needed. The bastard.*

After ten minutes of bread, salad, and stilted conversation about the cat, Liza had had enough. "I talked to Cynthie last night. She said Cal would try to—"

"I like him," Bonnie said.

Liza sat back in her chair. "What?"

"I like him," Bonnie said.

"That doesn't mean you should encourage—"

"It doesn't matter," Min said, and they both turned to look at her. "I'm trying to get away from him, but it's not working. Remember that snow globe I lost? He found it. He came over on Tuesday and went straight down to the basement and picked out the one box there that the snow globe was in."

"Dumb luck," Liza said.

"And then last night, I decided to go to the movies," Min said. "And when the lights came up, guess who was sitting beside me?"

"Now *that's* creepy," Liza said, going cold. "He's stalking you."

"No," Min said. "I picked up the paper, and the movie page fell out, and I saw *Big Trouble in Little China* was at the revival theater, and I thought, 'Oh, good, Kurt Russell beats the bad guys' and I went on an impulse. I didn't tell anybody. I didn't even mention it to the *cat.* And there he was. It's like he's magic."

"It's like he's the devil," Liza said.

"It's like he's the prince," Bonnie said.

Liza and Min looked at her.

"In the fairy tale," Bonnie said. "He has to go on quests to get you. And the snow globe was one."

"Bonnie, honey," Min said, jarred out of her numbness. "Let's do the Ifs instead. If I were a sane person, I wouldn't be so freaked out by this. So I'm going to be a sane person and not be freaked out. Liza? What's your If?"

"If I find out Cal Morrisey is stalking you, I'm going to tear him limb from limb," Liza said. "Bonnie?"

"If you two get any dumber, I'm going to have to find new friends," Bonnie scowled at Min. "Cal's winning you. Just like in the fairy tale. You said his kiss woke you up."

"I said his kiss turned me on," Min said. "Not the same thing." She leaned forward a little. "I was fine with using the fairy tale as a sort of metaphor, Bon, but this is real life. No prince, no stepmother, no poisoned apple."

"And no happy ending if you think like that," Bonnie said. "True love is beating you over the head to get your attention, and you're rejecting it because you don't want to believe. You have the fairy tale *right in front of you*—"

"*Wait* a minute," Liza said, trying to head off disaster.

"And you're *worse*," Bonnie said, turning on her. "Min doesn't believe in love for her, but you don't believe in it for anybody. You're a love nihilist."

"A love nihilist." Liza thought about it. "I kind of like that."

"Well, I don't," Min said. "I believe in love. I think. I just don't believe in fairy tales."

"I have known my whole life that sooner or later my prince would come," Bonnie said to Min. "How many times have you told me that everybody gets lucky breaks in business but not everybody is ready for them? Well, it's true about love, too. I've been planning my marriage my whole life because I'm smart enough to know that's the most important decision I'll ever make, and now Roger's here, and I'm ready to go. And you two are going to miss it when it comes for you because you don't want to believe because if it isn't true, you'll be disappointed."

Liza rolled her eyes. "Oh, come *on*—"

"You're *planning* on being disappointed, you'd be disappointed if you weren't disappointed, your whole world view depends on men disappointing you." Bonnie picked up her plate. "Well, that's just cowardly. Especially *you*," she said, scowling at Min. "You've got Cal right in front of you, loving you so much he can't see straight, you've got fate sending you so many signals even I can see them, and you're holding on to that bet like a shield. You haven't even asked him about the bet, have you?"

"What's he going to say?" Min said. "'Yeah, but I'm really your prince and I love you truly, come to bed'?"

"You're not usually this slow," Bonnie said, "so it must be just chicken-hearted fear. What if this is real? What if this is the happily ever after and he truly loves you so much that it's forever? Then what are you going to do?" She shook her head. "You don't know. You never prepared for that. You've thought about everything in your life, but you never thought about that. You're hopeless." She took her plate out to the kitchen and came back to shove her chair under the table. "I'll see you tomorrow at The Long Shot. I'm going to go see Roger and remember why I believe."

"Bon, wait," Min said, getting up, but Bonnie was already at the door.

When she slammed it behind her, Min sat down across from Liza.

"Well, at least we're sane," Min said.

"Yeah," Liza said. "How's that working out for you?"

"Not that well," Min said. "Did you bring dessert?"

"Cherry Dove Bars," Liza said.

"Give me one," Min said. "I'll be sensible tomorrow."

On Friday, Cal was settling in to stay home for a change on the theory that if he didn't leave the apartment, nothing weird would happen to him, when he heard "She" go on next door.

"Oh, for crying out loud," he said and then stopped because that was what Min always said. "No," he told himself and went next door to distract himself with Shanna. "You got dumped again?" he said when she opened the door.

"No," she said, serious, but not tear-stained. "I'm trying to figure out my life. Come on in."

"Figure out your life?" Cal said, following her.

"I keep thinking if I listen to this song, there'll be a clue," Shanna said, getting out her bottle of Glenlivet.

"If you're planning your life based on a popular song, you need that Scotch more than I do," Cal said.

"It's not that." Shanna poured his drink. "I've always gone on the theory that one day the right woman would show up and I'd know."

"You've pretty much disproved that one," Cal said, taking the glass she handed him.

"So I thought since Elvis Costello had already made a list of things the perfect woman would have, I'd start there, and sort of figure out what kind of person I'd want to spend the rest of my life with. And then if I met somebody who didn't fit the list . . ."

"That's very organized of you." Cal sat down on the couch and thought, *That's very Min of her.*

"But the thing is," Shanna was saying, "Elvis is not saying she's perfect. So I'm thinking maybe I just need a few key things. Like she should be kind."

"Yes," Cal said, remembering Min with Harry.

"And smart," Shanna said. "Somebody I don't have to explain everything to."

"Maybe," Cal said, thinking about explaining chicken marsala to Min. "It's no crime not to know everything. I'd make that somebody who was open to new ideas, willing to learn. And who had things to teach you."

"See, this is good," Shanna said, sitting down on her coffee table trunk. "And I thought a sense of humor would be important."

"Right," Cal said. "If you can't laugh at the screwups, what's the point?" He thought of Min saying, "Good thing this isn't a date," when they'd confused their Elvises, and—

"And because I'm superficial, I put down physically attractive," Shanna said.

"Me, too," Cal said, trying not to think of Min in all her hot glory. "And great shoes."

"What?" Shanna said.

"Nothing. What else?"

"That was it," Shanna said. "I didn't want to make too long a list. Kind, smart, funny, attractive. How's that?"

"Damn good if you can find it," Cal said.

"Didn't you?" Shanna said. "Min? She seemed—"

"Not dating her," Cal said. "Barely know her."

"Uh huh," Shanna said. "And why is that? She's pretty, she's kind, she's smart, she makes you smile, and you get all dazed when you kiss her. What is it that she doesn't have?"

"Well," Cal began and stopped. "She bitches at me a lot."

"Chicken," Shanna said. "You could walk away from all the other ones because they weren't right. This is the real thing, so you're running."

"This from a woman who just made a shopping list for love." Cal stood up and handed the Scotch back to her. "I'm going now. Best of luck with that list."

Shanna clucked at him as he went out the door, and he went home to ignore her. Once there, he realized that he hadn't had dinner, and he wasn't going out because if he did, he'd fall over Min.

"Not a problem," he told himself and went out to the kitchen. He had bread and peanut butter and not much else, so he plugged in the toaster and put the bread in and then he leaned against the refrigerator and waited for the toast to pop.

His kitchen was ugly, he realized as he looked around. And through the archway, his living room was worse. Maybe if he fixed the place up a little, he'd want to stay home more. He was getting too damn old to be hanging out in bars anyway. The phone rang and he grabbed it, grateful to have a distraction.

"Calvin?" he heard his mother say, but even she was better than the silence.

"Mother," he said. "How are you?" His toast popped, and he cradled the phone between his shoulder and his ear as he opened the peanut butter.

"I'm calling about dinner on Sunday," she said.

"I will be there, Mother," Cal said, thinking, *I'm there the third Sunday of every month, Mother.* Definitely in a rut.

"I'd like you to pick up our guest."

"Guest?" Cal said, as he got out a table knife to spread the peanut butter.

"Minerva Dobbs," his mother said.

"What?" Cal said and dropped the knife.

"I called her because Harrison has been speaking of her often, and it occurred to me that it would be nice for him to have her there."

Cal sighed. "What did she say when you called?"

"She seemed surprised," his mother said. "But when I explained that Harrison would be so pleased if she came—"

"She said yes," Cal said, reaching for his toast. "However, I cannot bring her because I will not be seeing her ever aga—" His fingers brushed the metal top of the toaster and he burned himself and dropped the phone. *"Damn it,"* he said and put his scorched fingertips in his mouth.

"Calvin?" his mother said from the phone.

He picked up the receiver. "I burned myself on the toaster. Sorry." Cal turned on the cold water and stuck his fingers underneath the stream. "Anyway, I will not be seeing Minerva Dobbs again." He stepped away from the sink onto something hard and his foot slipped out from under him and smacked into the cabinets. "Ouch."

"Calvin?" his mother said.

"I stepped on a knife." Cal bent to pick up the peanut butter knife and smacked his head into the counter. *"Hell."*

"Did you cut yourself?" his mother asked.

"No. I . . ." He put the knife in the sink. "I'll call you tomorrow, Mother."

"Calvin?" his mother said, and he hung up on her and considered the situation.

He was sabotaging himself, that had to be it. He was distracted, he was tired, he was hungry, he was careless. He picked up the phone again and called Tony's cell.

"Hello?" Tony yelled over the noise of the bar.

"Is Min there with you?" Cal said.

"Wait a minute," Tony said, and came back on a minute later without the background noise. "Sorry. What?"

"Is Min with you? I'm trying to make sure that wherever I go next, she won't be." He frowned. "She's driving me to incoherence."

"She's stalking you?" Tony said, sounding skeptical.

"No, she doesn't want it, either," Cal said. "It's like we're stuck inside a box. We try to go our separate ways and then we end up with each other anyway. You're not going to Emilio's, are you?"

"Chaos theory," Tony said. "Min's a strange attractor."

"This is true," Cal said. "Are you going to Emilio's tonight, or can I go eat in the kitchen there?"

"You can go," Tony said. "Seriously, the box you're talking about is the field of your attraction. You and Min try to get away and you hit the sides of the box at random because you're unstable, never repeating, but making a pattern."

"Good for us," Cal said. "Just keep Min away from Emilio's, will you? I'm starving."

"I think she and Liza are going someplace," Tony said. "They've been talking all night about some job Min wants Liza to take, and I think Min's going to drag her there to show it to her. Unless Emilio's been advertising for help, it's not there."

"He hasn't," Cal said. "He's full up on nephews. Thanks, Tony. I'll see you tomorrow."

He hung up, changed out of his work clothes, and started for Emilio's, trying not to think about Min. That didn't work, so he switched over to chaos theory, of which he had only vague memories. The Butterfly Effect, he remembered that, the idea that a butterfly flapping its wings in Hong Kong could cause a hurricane ten years later in Florida or prevent a tornado ten years later in Texas, take your pick because it was unpredictable. That was Min; she'd looked harmless that first night, and then she flapped her wings two weeks ago and now he was a mess. She was a goddamn stealth butterfly.

He looked down the block at the front of the Gryphon Theater, half expecting to see Min standing there since it was the first night of the Elvis revival week. Nope. Which made sense, since events did not repeat in chaos theory. Somehow, the idea that it was science made the whole thing a lot less worrisome. He wasn't insane, fate wasn't stalking him, he was just standing on the edge of chaos. Much better.

He turned down the street to Emilio's, trying to remember what "the edge of chaos" meant. It was something about flipping a coin, something about the edge being the moment when the coin was in the air. The point at which the system was pure potential, about to choose a path. Or something about a pile of sand, adding sand a grain at a time, and the edge of chaos being the point at which the critical grain landed and the pile either shifted or turned into an avalanche . . . Cal slowed as he remembered a grad assistant in a baggy blue sweater, his hair standing on end from his complete earnestness about the subject, saying that the edge of chaos was a time of turbulence, mental chaos if the system was a human being, but also the time of greatest potential, possibly the place where life starts. "The place," the grad student had said, "where the system cascades into a new order and moves from being to becoming."

Cal shook the grad student out of his head, and pulled open the door to Emilio's. When he got inside, he heard Roger say, "Cal!" and he stopped, frozen, knowing before he turned that Min would be there, strange attractor, effective butterfly, locus of fate. He turned and saw her, sitting at a table with everybody else, looking like a startled cherub, her beautiful lips open in surprise, her dark eyes wide, and he felt his breath go again, felt his blood heat, his entire system rushing about insanely, bouncing off the inside of his skin, his future impossible to predict, everything riding on his next lurch through chaos.

Min bit her lip and smiled at him ruefully, and without another thought, he walked across the room to her, feeling almost relieved as the avalanche began.

Chapter
Nine

Cal pulled a chair from another table, and Min scooted over to let him in. She was wearing another soft shirt, this one in panels of different colored sheer prints, and she looked pretty and warm and more desirable than he could have imagined.

Beyond her, Tony shrugged and looked apologetic.

"Tony said you'd told him you were going to work late tonight," Min said as he sat down.

"I lied."

Min shifted a little more to give him room, and he caught the faint scent of lavender and felt dizzy again. "Well, at least you're honest about your dishonesty."

" 'I was raised to be charming, not sincere,' " Cal said, and relaxed as she smiled at him.

"You know *Into the Woods?*" Min said, "That's my favorite Sondheim."

"Mine, too," Cal said, watching her face. "Tony likes *Sweeney Todd*, and Roger's is *Sunday in the Park with George*, but—"

"You're kidding me," Min said, blinking those dark eyes at him. "You're all Sondheim fans?"

"We roomed with a drama minor in college." *God, you look good.*

"There was a fourth roommate?" Min said, and then she closed her eyes. "Of course there was. Emilio. It was his restaurant you worked in when you were in college."

"No," Cal said. "It was his grandpa's restaurant. He went out on his own about two years ago."

"And he's not setting the world on fire." Min nodded. "That's why I brought Liza here. It took me all night to talk her into it, but I think she likes the place."

"Good," Cal said, not following and not caring. It felt too damn good to be sitting next to her again to insist on clarity, too.

"Liza's a fixer," Min said. "She finds businesses that need help and then she . . . helps them."

"So, she advertises that she can fix things," Cal said, not caring.

"No," Min said. "She chooses. There are a lot of places that need a kick in the butt to get going, and Liza gets a job and provides the kick. She's not good for the long term, once things are good she leaves, but for the year she stays, magic happens." She grinned at him. "Sort of like you and women."

"Hey," Cal said, but then he caught sight of Emilio, gesturing to him from the kitchen door. "Be right back."

Emilio dragged him through the door when he got there. "There's a woman out there," Emilio said. "The redhead with Tony. She just told me she's thinking about working here. Is she delusional?"

"Not even a little bit," Cal said. "Tony knows her better than I do, but if you're asking, I vote you hire her. It can't hurt, and Min says she's a genius at what she does."

"What does she do?" Emilio said.

"I'm not sure," Cal said, looking through the round window on the door to see Min. "I'm just going on what Min says."

"Min." Emilio nodded. "Min I trust."

"Me, too," Cal said and followed Emilio back to the table in time to hear Min say, "So here's something I just found out. These guys are Sondheim freaks."

"What?" Liza said, turning to Tony in amazement.

"What?" Tony said back. "I can't have facets?"

"Because of Emilio," Min said. "Which I bring up because I want to hear his voice."

"Uh," Emilio said.

"Don't fight it," Cal said, sitting down next to Min again. "She gets what she wants, too."

"I like the 'Moments' song," Min said, grinning at Emilio. "Or 'Into the Woods.' That's peppy."

"Nah," Tony said. "'Sweeney Todd.'" He sang the first line of "Sweeney Todd" in a surprisingly true bass, and Roger joined in on the next line, and they sang until Emilio gave up and helped them finish on "the demon barber of Fleet . . . *Street*," while Cal watched Min smile and thought, *Kiss me*.

"Probably not the best thing to sing in a restaurant," Cal said when Min was done clapping, and Emilio winced.

"You don't sing?" Min said to Cal.

"Only in the shower," Cal said, and imagined Min in the shower.

"Wuss," Tony said, breaking the moment. "He can sing, he's just a coward."

"But you are not," Liza said, turning back to Tony. "You are multi-talented. Who would have guessed it?"

"What else does he do?" Bonnie said, and Tony grinned at her.

"He has skills we'll discuss later," Liza said. "This is excellent pasta, Emilio. This place should be packed every night."

"Which is your job," Min said to her. "Save Emilio. I love him."

"I think so," Liza said. "Let me check out the kitchen first."

She got up, walked past Emilio, and pushed her way through the swinging doors.

"Is she—" he said to Min.

"She's the best waitress you'll ever have," Min said. "And she will get you business. She's checking out your kitchen now. If you pass muster, you've got her."

Emilio went to protect his kitchen from Liza, and Cal poured more wine into Min's glass. "Drink this. I'm about to try to talk you into something, and I need you juiced."

"I kind of miss the charm," Min said, picking up her glass. "Listen, I was thinking about the snow globe and the movies and everything, and I apologize for calling you the devil. They were all coincidences."

"Yeah," Cal said. "Tony thinks it's chaos theory."

"Bonnie thinks it's the fairy tale," Min said, and sipped her wine.

"Fairy tale?" Cal said, lost again.

"You know, you're a prince, it's meant to be, we'll live happily ever after. It's okay, she's sane on everything else." Min smiled at him. The point is, we'll be fine as long as we stick to the plan."

"Right," Cal said. "The plan." Her lips were soft and full, curved in that comforting smile, and he started to get dizzy again. *Kiss me.* "I think we should start dating. Want to go to the movies?"

Min blinked at him and put down her glass. "Did you hear anything I said?"

"Everything was a coincidence, we should stick to the plan," Cal said. "That's not going to work for me."

Min folded her arms. "Why not?"

"Because if we don't date, the universe is going to maim me."

"*What?*"

"The universe, fate, chaos theory, fairy tales, the spirit of Elvis, I don't know what it is, but I'm not fighting it anymore." Cal leaned closer and caught the faint scent of lavender again as Min looked at him as if he were insane. "You hate me, you're high maintenance, you're pathological about food, and your best friend will kill me someday, but it doesn't matter. I'm going to give this a shot. Does your mother still want to check me out at dinner? I'll go."

"Why, if I'm that awful?" Min said, looking annoyed.

He smiled down into her beautiful face. "Because you're smart and kind and funny, and my nephew is crazy about you, and you wear great shoes, and you look like a depraved angel." *Because I'm going to go crazy if I don't touch you.*

"Uh huh." Min nodded. "And because of that, you're going to dinner at my parents' house tomorrow night so my mother can see you're harmless?"

"Tomorrow?" He nodded, trying not to look appalled. "Good. We'll get that out of the way fast. Tomorrow night it is. So about tonight—"

"On the dating thing? No, so you're off the hook with my mother, you do not need to go to dinner. But if you want to do a friends-night-out thing, we could go to the movies. *Blue Hawaii* is playing at ten o'clock."

"*Blue Hawaii*," Cal said. "I don't suppose that's porn."

"It's part of the Elvis revival," Min said. "You don't have to go."

Cal sighed. "Yes, I do. And I'm going to your parents' tomorrow, too."

"I'm not understanding this at all," Min said, and he took her hand, happy to be touching her again, and said, "Come with me, Minnie. I will explain."

He pulled her out of her chair and across the restaurant to the front door, and when they were out on the darkened street, he leaned down, his heart pounding, and he kissed her with no reservation at all. The familiar rush was fast and hot as always, hotter because he wasn't fighting it, but there was comfort there, too, she felt so right under his hands, against his mouth, and when she slipped her arms around his neck, he kissed her harder, falling into her helplessly, not even trying to save himself. He felt her move closer, and her perfect mouth opened as her lush body pressed against him, and years passed, and he saw paradise, and the voice in his head whispered, THIS ONE, YOU IDIOT. Then something smacked him hard on the arm and jarred them both out of the kiss.

"What the—" he began, still holding on to her, and then saw Liza, standing on the sidewalk with her purse. "You know, if Bonnie is right, a leprechaun will be by any minute to kneecap you."

"*Liza*," Min said, stepping away from him a little, and he felt cold where she'd been touching him and held on to her.

"I didn't hit him on the head," Liza said.

Cal looked at Min. "Forget her. You want to know why? This is why. It really is bigger than the both of us, and I, for one, am not fighting it anymore." She opened her mouth to say something and he said, "And you want this, too."

Liza scowled at him. "Oh, tell me you know her. Tell me—"

"Yes, I do know her, although not as well as I'm going to," Cal said, facing her down. "And yes, I care about her. A lot. And I don't know the rest, but I'm going to find out. Is that all right with you?"

Liza looked at him for a moment. "Yes. But I'm watching you."

"All right then," Cal said, feeling relieved in general. The just-friends bit wasn't good, but that was okay, he was good at courting women. *We're playing my game now*, he thought and looked down at Min with great affection.

"Don't look at me like that," Min said and turned to Liza. "We're going to the ten o'clock movie, just as friends. Want to come?"

"Yes. Tony?" Liza said as Tony came out of the bar to find her. "We're going to the movies at ten."

"It's *Blue Hawaii*," Cal said to Tony.

"I don't suppose that's porn," Tony said.

"It's Elvis," Cal said.

"Why?" Tony said.

"Because it's time to make my move," Cal said, looking down at Min.

"Hey," Min said.

"Oh, well, hell, then," Tony said. "Let's go."

Min had started her Saturday by calling her mother to tell her that Cal would, in fact, be dining with them that night.

"We'll see what kind of man he is," Nanette said, her tone boding no good for Cal.

"You're going to love him," Min said. "He's gorgeous and successful."

Nanette sniffed. "Probably the kind who thinks he's an eight and you're a four. Men are shallow and treacherous. Wear something slimming."

"He's a ten, Mother," Min said. "And I'm not slim."

After that, baseball seemed an improvement, at least until she got to the park.

"You're sticking with me," she told Liza. "Bonnie always wanders off with Roger, but you are staying so you can jab me if I start to act goofy around Cal."

"There's not that much jab in the world," Liza said, but she followed Min to the bleachers anyway.

"*Min*," Harry yelled when he saw her, and she stopped to smile at him as he came running up.

"Hey, you," she said as he skidded to a halt in front of her. "How's it going?"

"Good," he said, nodding his head. "Thanks for coming." Then he looked down and said, "Whoa. Cool shoes."

"Thank you," Min said as Harry bent closer to see the blue plastic fish that overlapped across the toes of her sandals. "You know, you're a lot like your uncle."

"Harrison, your instincts are right," Cal said from behind them, and Min jumped. "Women are more important than baseball, but get your butt back to the outfield anyway." Then she turned and he grinned at her, his face softening, and her heart rate bumped up again. "Minnie, you're getting freckles on your nose."

"I know." Min rubbed the bridge of her nose, trying not to care about the affection in his voice. "It's these Saturday mornings. I never go out in the sun so I keep forgetting to get sunscreen."

"I like them," Cal said, and Min felt her heart bump again.

"Me, too," Harry said from below.

"I don't," Min said, trying to keep a grip. "But I'm stuck with them because I keep forgetting—"

Cal took off his cap and put it on her head. "Problem solved." His grin widened. "Very cute. You can play for my team any time."

"Stop that," Min said, and tried to adjust the hat so it wouldn't squash her curls. It felt warm from him, and she kept her hand on it a minute longer just to feel it. *You're worthless*, she told herself.

"Harry!" somebody called, and Min turned and saw Cynthie walking toward them in a fluttery pink dress, smiling beautifully at Harry. "How are you, buddy?"

Harry scowled. "Hi."

"Hi, Cynthie," Min said, trying not to hate her, and turned back to Harry. "We're going to go get good seats. Knock 'em dead, kid." She looked past Cal's ear, avoiding eye contact. "Thanks for the hat. I'm sure it makes me look like hell."

"Nah." Cal tapped it on the brim. "It makes you look like a butch angel. Shanna should be here."

Min smiled at him in spite of herself, warm all over, and then Tony yelled, "Hey, we're playing *baseball* here," and Cal dragged Harry onto the field.

"How'd I do?" she said to Liza.

"As well as could be expected under the circumstances," Liza said.

"Do at what?" Cynthie said.

"I'm practicing my cool," Min said.

"Oh," Cynthie said. "Well, good job."

Min followed Liza and Cynthie over to where Bonnie was sitting and watched Harry's team get killed in the first three innings, trying not to watch Cal. When he looked up and caught her looking at him, he grinned, and she thought, *Oh, for heaven's sake, Minerva,* and turned to Liza to distract herself. "You'd think Tony would be apoplectic by now," Min said to Liza.

"No," Liza said. "He just wants them to have a good time. He yells at them so they'll get better, but he doesn't care if they win. He says all their games are practice for the future."

"Really?" Min said. "He does have layers."

"Only about three," Liza said. "I was wrong about him being dumb, though, he's actually quite bright. He's a nice guy."

"That's all?" Min said.

"Yes," Liza said. "That's all. He is not The One. Speaking of which, nice ball cap you got there, Stats." She tapped the brim. "Maybe he'll buy you a soda after the game."

Min shook her head. "We're just—"

"It's the fairy tale," Bonnie said. "He's winning you."

"What?" Cynthie said. "Fairy tale?"

"Yes," Bonnie said. "Min and Cal, they're a fairy tale. She's the girl who doesn't have the life she deserves, so her fairy godmother got her a prince to rescue her."

"Fairy godmother?" Min said.

"Liza," Bonnie said. "She picked Cal out for you."

"*Wait a minute*," Liza said. "I am *not* accepting responsibility for Calvin Morrisey."

Min started to laugh. "You did pick him out. You sent me over there to meet him. Now, *that's* funny."

"A fairy tale," Cynthie said, sounding as if she wasn't sure they were serious.

Bonnie nodded. "Cal gave her the ball cap because it's part of his quest."

"No, he gave her the ball cap because he's courting," Cynthie said, a little sharply. "It's part of the attraction stage."

"Attraction stage," Liza said.

"He is not attracted—" Min began.

"There are four stages to mature love," Cynthie said. "Assumption, attraction, infatuation, and attachment."

"Now, see, I would have called the way he looks at her infatuation," Liza said.

"Excuse me?" Min said, looking at her best friend, the betrayer.

"It's the fairy tale," Bonnie said.

"It's attraction," Cynthie said flatly.

"It's love, a random reaction," Liza said. "Chaos theory."

"Hey," Min said, and they looked at her. "It's a kind act by a friend because I don't want freckles. Not everything is a theory."

"The fairy tale is not a theory," Bonnie said. "Even if you won't believe it's happening to you, it's happening to me." She smiled at them all, too happy to be smug.

"So how's Roger?" Min said, more than willing to have somebody else be the topic at hand.

"He is The One," Bonnie said. "He's going to propose in a couple of weeks and I'll say yes. I told my mama to plan the wedding for August."

"He told you he's going to propose?" Cynthie said, and when Bonnie looked at her, surprised, she said, "I'm writing a book on this. It's none of my business, but I am interested."

"Oh," Bonnie said. "Well, no, he hasn't told me. I just know."

Min tried to look supportive, but the silence that settled over them must have reeked of skepticism because Bonnie turned back to the field and called Roger's name. When he came trotting over to them, she said, "Honey, are you going to ask me to marry you?"

"Yes," he said. "I didn't want to rush you, so I thought I'd wait till our one-month anniversary. It's only eleven days."

"Very sensible," Bonnie said. "Just so you know, I'm going to say yes."

Roger sighed. "That takes a lot of the worry out of it." He leaned over and kissed her and went back to the field.

"That was either really sweet or really annoying," Liza said.

"It was sweet," Min said, trying to imagine Cal saying any of that. *Stop thinking about him.* "And annoying."

"I told you," Bonnie said. "It's the fairy tale. You have to believe."

"Positive thinking," Cynthie said, nodding. "There's good evidence for that. Could I interview you? For my book. Because this is fascinating. You've moved into the infatuation phase very quickly."

"Sure," Bonnie said. "But it's not infatuation. This is True Love. Like Cal and Min."

"Will you stop that?" Min said.

"Of course," Cynthie said to Bonnie with no conviction whatsoever, and they began to talk.

Min took a deep breath and turned back to Liza. "Cynthie seems nice," she said quietly, hoping for a conversation that didn't have Cal in it.

"She is," Liza said. "But I think she wants Cal back."

Min gave up and stared out at the field where Cal was talking to somebody on third base. His face was serious again, and the kid nodded, hanging on his every word. *What a darling*, she thought and then remembered, *No, beast*, but that wasn't working anymore. Well, it had never worked, really.

"Are you going out tonight?" Liza asked.

"Yes, but just as friends," Min said. "He's doing me a favor. We're going to my mother's so she can stop worrying about him being a vile seducer."

Liza shook her head, looking doubtful. "I don't think meeting Cal is going to reassure your mother."

"Why not? Elvis likes him. And Elvis has very good instincts."

"Elvis?" Liza said, sounding alarmed.

"The cat. I named him Elvis," Min said.

Liza sighed. "Thank God. I thought you'd finally cracked."

"Hey, I'm not the one who believes in the fairy tale," Min said. "Or in chaos theory, for that matter."

"Or the four-step program to love," Liza said, jerking her head toward Cynthie, who was listening to Bonnie finish up the theory of fairy tale love.

"Right," Min said. "That's all garbage. You don't need a theory, you just have to be practical, figure out what it is you want in a man, and then find one who has those things. Make a plan. Stick to it." Her eyes went to Cal. "Don't get distracted."

Liza rolled her eyes. "Or you could just fall the fuck in love."

"Oh, *right*," Min said, looking away from Cal. "That's like saying you could just fall off a building. Because it won't hurt until you *land*."

Liza drew back. "I just meant—"

"*No,*" Min said as several people turned to look at her. "You have to be sensible. It's not silly love songs and sloppy kisses, it's dangerous. People die for it. People die *from* it. Wars are fought. *Empires fall.*"

"Uh, Min . . ."

"It can *ruin your life*," Min said, shutting her eyes so she wouldn't look for Cal. "Which is why I'm staying friends with Cal, nothing more. I'd have to be insane to think there could be anything permanent. Masochistic. Suicidal. Delusional."

"Uh huh," Liza said.

"So that's my plan," Min said. "And I'm sticking to it."

"Right," Liza said.

When the game was over, Harry came up and said, "Uncle Cal said we can go to lunch if you'll come," and Min said, "Well . . ." and thought *Calvin, you nephew-exploiting bastard.* Still, lunch wouldn't kill her. It was okay to have lunch with a friend. And his nephew. Like a chaperone.

"Uh huh," Liza said, even though Min hadn't spoken.

She made him take them to a retro diner where she and Harry played Elvis all the way through lunch, a new experience for Harry, who'd been raised on Chopin. Cal didn't seem to mind. When they dropped her off, Harry said, "I'll see you tomorrow, Min," and she said, "Yes, you will. Dinner at Grandma's." Harry looked a little confused, and Cal said, "Harrison, I will pay you fifty bucks if you'll call your grandmother that tomorrow." "I don't think so," Harry said, and Min got out of the car feeling that tomorrow was going to explain a lot about Calvin Morrisey, assuming he lived through dinner that night with her parents.

"Keep the cap, Minnie," Cal said when she tried to hand it back to him through the window. "You look good in it. I'll pick you up at eight." Then he drove off and left her feeling ridiculously happy, which couldn't be good.

"You're a mess," she told herself, and went to get ready for dinner with her mother.

That evening, Cal picked up Min in his ancient Mercedes. She was sitting on the bottom step when he got there, dressed in a plain black dress that she'd pulled over her knees. She looked like a cranky nun.

"What are you doing down here?" he said when he got out of the car.

"You have to put up with my parents," she said, standing up. "It didn't seem fair to make you do those steps, too."

"I don't mind climbing as long as you're at the top." Cal looked down at her feet. She was wearing plain black flats, no toes showing at all. "Why the awful shoes?"

"They're not awful," Min said. "They're classic. Like your car, which is very nice and yet somehow not what I'd pictured you in."

"Graduation present." Cal opened the door for her. "Never look a gift car in the mouth. Get in, Minnie, we do not want to be late."

When he was in the driver's seat, Min said, "For the MBA?"

"What?" Cal said as he started the car.

"The car. A graduation present for the MBA? I got a briefcase, so I'm trying to put things into perspective here."

"High school," Cal said and pulled out into the street.

"High school," Min said, nodding. "What did they get you for the MBA? A yacht?"

"A place in my dad's firm."

"But—"

"I declined the gift," Cal said. "How's Elvis?"

"Really healthy," Min said, sounding mystified. "I took him to the vet and he says he's in great condition. Just weird."

"Like so much of my life lately," Cal said. "Speaking of which, is there anything I should know about your family before I get there?"

"You don't have to do this," Min said.

"Minerva, I am going. Prep me for your parents, please."

"There's nothing, really," Min said. "My mother is always polite, and my father is not talkative unless you hit a nerve. Don't hit a nerve."

"Right," Cal said. "Could I have a list of nerves?"

"Insurance fraud, younger men who want his job, music after 1970, and sex with his daughters."

"Sex with his daughters," Cal said.

Min nodded. "My father will assume you're trying to debauch me."

"Your father is a keen judge of character," Cal said. "How about your mother?"

"Well, normally, she'd be scoping you out for son-in-law potential. There would be a quiz by dessert."

"Written or oral?"

"Oral."

"Good. Oral I'm good at." The silence stretched out until he said, "I didn't mean that the way it came out."

Min stared straight ahead. "Perfectly all right. There won't be a quiz. My mother has other things on her mind at the moment."

"Does she have any other issues I should know about?"

"Yes, but they're all about me."

Cal shook his head. "I don't care. Give me that list, too."

"Eating carbs, wearing white cotton underwear, not losing weight, failing to hold onto my ex-boyfriend whom she loved," Min said. "I don't think any of those are going to come up in your conversation with her."

"My mother likes my ex, too," Cal said. "I think it's laziness. She just doesn't want to learn a new name. Who else is going to be there?"

"My sister, Diana. You're safe with her. She's nuts right now because she's getting married in a week, but she's great just the same. If things get too awful, you can sit and look at Di. She's beautiful."

"Good to know," Cal said. "Mom, Dad, Diana, you, me. Cozy group."

"And Greg," Min said, trying to keep her voice from going flat. "My sister's fiancé."

"Right. Greg of the faulty memory. How's that going?"

"Something's wrong," Min said. "I don't know what it is but he's not helping. The thing is, he's not a bad guy, except for dumping Wet which he had every right to do, and he adores Diana, so I can't figure it out." She looked over at Cal. "See what you think of him."

"Me?" Cal said, surprised.

"You're a good judge of character," Min said. "Intuitive. Intuit Greg for me."

"The chances of me figuring out what's wrong over dinner are slim," Cal said as Min's cell phone rang.

When she pulled it out of her purse, he said, "A plain black cell phone. You lied to me that first night, Minnie."

"Which you knew," Min said, and answered the phone. "Hello. What?" She listened for a minute and then said, "Oh, for crying out loud." She listened again and said, "Di, it's Saturday evening. I don't know where . . . Wait a minute." She turned to Cal. "Greg promised to get the wine for dinner."

"Let me guess," Cal said.

"You wouldn't have a bottle or two at your apartment, would you?" Min said.

"Emilio's," Cal said, and made a U-turn.

Min turned back to the phone. "Cal's going to fix it." There was a note of pride in the way she said it, and Cal grinned. Then she turned off her phone and said, "You are a prince."

"Thank you," Cal said. "Say something bitchy to me, will you? You're confusing me."

He stopped and got the wine, and when he was back in the car, Min looked at the labels on the bottles. "These were expensive, weren't they?"

"Not really," Cal said. "About forty bucks each."

Min started to laugh. "Serves Greg right, the dumbass."

Ten minutes later, Cal had followed Min's directions and parked in front of a fairly large, fairly new house. Min said, "You know, you can still get out of this. Drop me off and I'll tell—"

"Nope." Cal opened his car door. "Stay there."

"Stay where?" Min said, reaching for her door handle.

Cal came around the car and caught the door for as she opened it. "You cannot leap out of cars without assistance." He caught her hand and pulled her to her feet as she got out, and she ended up closer to him than he'd planned, which was fine by him. "It makes me look weak and powerless when you get out without me," he said, watching the breeze ruffle her curls.

"Yeah, weak and powerless," she said. "I bet you get that a lot." She detoured around him as he shut the car door, and he caught sight of someone vanishing from a window. "Well, the good news is, you just made points with my mother. She was scoping you out from the window."

"Great," Cal said, taking her elbow. "Now all we have to do is survive dinner."

Min's father met them in the hall, a lumbering man with a shock of blond hair and heavy white eyebrows who should have been hearty and welcoming but instead had the vaguely paranoid look of a sheepdog whose sheep were plotting against him.

"Dad, this is Calvin Morrisey," Min said. "Cal, this is my father, George Dobbs."

"Pleased to meet you, Calvin." George's gruff voice was firm as if to belie any indication that he wasn't pleased, but his eyes telegraphed, *What are you up to?*

"Pleased to be here, sir," Cal lied, and Min patted him on the back, which was more comforting than he could have imagined.

"You're late," George said to Min. "We've already had cocktails."

"Sorry, sir," Cal said, and Min said, "No, you're not. It was my fault, Dad, we had to go back for something."

"Well, come in now," George said, and Min sighed and went into the dining room, and Cal followed and met Min's dragon of a mother.

The house was a showplace, clearly done by a decorator, and Min's mother, standing in her perfect living room, matched it: Both were designer creations with no warmth whatsoever. The house at least had some color, but Min's mother was small, thin, dark-haired, dressed in black, and groomed to within an inch of her life, the exact opposite of Min. "This is my mother, Nanette," Min said, practically chirping. "Mother, this is Calvin Morrisey," and Nanette Dobbs said, "Welcome, Calvin," in a voice that could have flash-frozen fish.

"Did I do something?" Cal whispered when she'd turned to speak to George.

"You frenched me in the park on a picnic table," Min whispered back.

"How do they know that?" Cal said.

"Greg ratted us out," Min said. "He also mentioned your hit-and-run past."

"And I got him wine," Cal said.

"And here he is," Min said. She lifted her voice and said, "Greg! This is Cal Morrisey."

Greg was young and smooth, clearly polished by prep schools and buffed in the gym until his surface gleamed. He smiled at Cal and then realized who he was shaking hands with. "Oh," Greg said.

Cal waited for something more, but that was it. "Yep," he said and leaned forward. "The wine is in the front seat of my car."

Greg exhaled in relief. "Thanks, man," he said, clasping Cal on the arm. "Be right back," he said in a voice that was a fraction too loud. "Left the wine in the car."

"And this is my sister, Diana," Min said, her voice softening, and Cal looked up to see a younger, sweeter version of the dragon. Diana was slender, dark, and lovely, and clearly the princess in the family. She beamed when she saw Min, and welcomed Cal with more warmth than everyone else in the room put together, and asked about his baseball team.

"Nice kid," he told Min when Diana had gone to find the amnesiac she was marrying.

"Kid?" Min said.

"Cute," Cal said. "But she's not you."

"You're not the first to have noticed," Min said. "Listen, don't let the 'rents get you down. They're just . . ." Her voice faded away as she tried to think of something to call them.

"Fine," Cal said, and then Nanette called Min away as Greg showed up with the wine.

When Min came back a few minutes later, all her curls were pulled back in combs, and they went in to dinner.

"What's with the hair?" Cal said in her ear when they were seated.

"It's not flattering to my round face when it's left loose," Min said. "I knew better."

"I liked it," Cal said, and Min said, "I did, too," and then dinner started.

"So what is it you do for a living, Calvin?" George asked when the soup had been dispatched with small talk and the prime rib had been served.

"Training seminars," Cal said, keeping a wary eye on Nanette, who had been staring at him throughout the soup course. He couldn't call it a frown since her forehead wasn't furrowed, but it was not warm.

"So you're a teacher," George said. "There much money in that?"

"Dad," Min said.

"There's enough," Cal said, distracted because Min had discreetly begun to pat his back again. He was grateful to her for the support, but it felt way too good to be something he should be enjoying in front of her father.

"What firm are you with?" George said.

"Morrisey, Packard, Capa." Cal smiled at Min's mother. "This beef is excellent, Mrs. Dobbs."

"Thank you." Nanette Dobbs did not look appeased.

"Morrissey," George said. "So you work for the old man. Not too hard getting that job, huh?"

"Uh, no," Cal said. "I'm the old man. It's my company."

Min stopped patting and glared at George. "I wonder what the statistics are on the number of daughters who return home to visit after their guests *are harassed by their fathers.*"

"You inherited it?" George said.

"I started it," Cal said.

"I'm guessing they're *pretty low,*" Min said.

"But your old man bankrolled you," George said.

"No, he didn't," Cal said. "He wanted me to go into his business, so I went outside the family for capital."

"For crying out loud, Dad, that's enough," Min said, taking her hand away from Cal's back. "Let's talk about something else. I got a cat."

"So it's a start-up," George said. "Thirty-three percent of start-ups fail in the first four years."

"It's sort of a *mutant* cat," Min said.

"It was a start-up ten years ago," Cal said to George. "It's up."

"It annoys all my friends," Min said. "*I'm thinking of calling it George.*"

"*Minerva,*" Nanette said. "Not your loud voice."

"Bread?" Min said, shoving the basket under Cal's nose.

"Yes, thank you." Cal took a roll and handed her the basket back. She took one, too, and her mother spoke again.

"Min."

"Right," Min said and put the roll back.

"So you own your own business," George said, skepticism heavy in his voice.

"Yes." Cal frowned down at Min. "Why can't you have a roll?"

"I told you, I have this dress I have to fit into," Min said. "It's all right. I can eat bread again in July."

"Min is Diana's maid of honor next weekend," Nanette said. "We don't want her to get too big for the dress."

"I'm already too big for the dress," Min said.

"You should come," Diana said to Cal, leaning across the table. She hadn't touched the bread, the butter, or her beef, Cal noticed. Her water glass was getting quite a workout, though. "To the wedding. And the rehearsal dinner. Min needs a date."

Before Cal could answer, George said, "Who are some of your clients?," and Nanette said, "How long have you and Min been dating?," and Min tugged on his sleeve. When he looked down at her, she said, "Do you have family?"

"Yes," Cal said, trying to sound noncommittal about it.

"Are they this awful?" Min said.

"*Minerva,*" Nanette said, warning in her voice.

"Well, they do let me eat bread," Cal said, keeping an eye on Nanette. "Other than that, pretty much."

"I beg your pardon?" George said.

"Look, I don't mind you grilling me about what I do for a living," Cal said. "Your daughter's brought me home and that has some significance. And I don't mind your wife asking about my personal life for the same reason. But Min is an amazing woman, and so far during this meal, you've either ignored her or hassled her about some dumb dress. For the record, she is not too big for the dress. The dress is too small for her. She's perfect." Cal buttered a roll and passed it over to Min. "Eat."

Min blinked at him and took the roll.

Cal looked past her to her mother. "I've never been married. I've never been engaged. My last relationship ended about two months ago. I met your daughter three weeks ago." He turned back to Min's father. "The business is in the black and has been for some time. I can give you references if you'd like to check. Should things between Min and me ever grow serious, I can support her."

"Hey, I can support me," Min said, still holding her roll.

"I know," Cal said. "Your dad wants to know that I can. Eat." Min bit into the roll, and he looked around the table. "Anything else anybody wants to know?"

Diana held up her hand.

"Yes?" Cal said.

"Are you Min's date for the wedding?"

Min tried to swallow the bite she'd just taken.

"She hasn't asked me." Cal looked down at Min. "Want to go to your sister's wedding with me?"

Min choked on her roll and he pounded her on the back.

"Of course she wants to go with you," Nanette said, smiling for the first time. "We'd be delighted to have you. The rehearsal dinner, too."

"Good," Cal said, feeling progress had been made as Min gasped for air.

"This wine is excellent," George said to him.

"Thank—uh, thanks to Greg," Cal said. "Knows his wine."

"Uh huh," George said, looking at Greg, who smiled back at him feebly.

"You have a *cat?*" Nanette said to Min, and the evening rolled on while she harangued Min about cat diseases, and George asked questions about the seminar business, and Greg glowered, and Diana smiled, and Cal's head pounded. He'd had worse evenings, but not many.

Then Min smiled up at him and said, "I'm sorry" so softly he almost missed it. He said, "For what? I'm having a great time," and felt better about everything.

After dessert, which only the men ate, Min dragged Diana into the hall. "Are you out of your mind," she whispered. "Why in the name of God did you ask that man to the wedding?"

"Why not?" Diana said. "You needed a date. He's darling. I don't see a problem."

"That's because you don't know our history," Min said.

"Well, at least you have a date now," Diana said. "I think it was a pretty good idea."

Min stabbed her finger at her. "Don't do anything like that again. Ever. *Ever.*"

"Okay," Diana said. "But you've still got a really hot date."

Her really hot date came out in the hall, said a pleasant good-bye to her parents, walked her down the front steps, handed her into his car, got in the driver's side, reached over and pulled the combs out of her hair.

"These are ugly, Minnie," he said, and threw them out his car window into the street.

"I know," she said, trying not to feel rescued. "Thank you."

The next day, Min dressed very carefully for her dinner with the Morriseys, pulling out her plain black dress again, polishing her black flats, and trying to make her hair lie down. Things didn't get better when Nanette called.

"Darling, your Calvin is lovely," Nanette said.

"Thank you, Mother," Min said, bracing herself for whatever was coming next.

"And Daddy checked his financials and he's very solvent," Nanette went on.

"He checked on a Saturday night?" Min said. "How?"

"You know your father," Nanette said in a tone that said she wished she didn't. "And your Calvin seems very taken with you. That was very sweet, the thing with the bread and butter. You won't eat it again, of course, but still . . ."

"A man who will feed you is a good thing," Min agreed.

"So don't ruin this one," Nanette said. "I was upset about you losing David, but that's all right now. Just don't lose Calvin, too."

"Mother, I don't want him," Min lied.

"Of course you want him," Nanette said. "You'll have beautiful children."

"I don't want those, either," Min said. "New subject. I'm thinking about quitting my job to become a cook."

"Don't be ridiculous, dear," Nanette said. "You around food? You'd blow up like a balloon."

"Thank you, Mother," Min said. "I'm going to go now."

"Go where?"

"I'm having dinner with Cal's parents."

"That's nice. Who are they?"

"Jefferson and Lynne Morrisey. I don't know—"

"You're having dinner with Lynne Morrisey?"

"Yes," Min said. "Because she gave birth to my date, otherwise, I wouldn't be."

"Min," her mother said, her voice dropping in respect. "Lynne Morrisey is *huge* in the Urban League."

"I'm so sorry," Min said, thinking that was the first time she'd ever heard Nanette say "huge" with approval.

"No carbs, darling," Nanette said. "And tell me *everything* when you get home."

"Oh, dear Lord," Min said and hung up to go back to her hair problem.

When Cal knocked on her door, she and Elvis were contemplating a headband without much confidence.

"Do you think a headband?" she said to Cal when she opened the door.

"Christ, no," he said, reaching down to pet the cat, who had come to purr at his feet. "Look at you, you're in mourning again."

"Don't even try to talk me out of this dress," she said.

He looked down. "At least give me your feet. How about the shoes with the black bows, the ones you wore the first night?"

"Cal," Min said.

"It's not a lot to ask," he said, leaning in the doorway grinning at her. "Go change your shoes, Minnie, and then we'll face the dragons together."

She smiled back in spite of herself. "That charm stuff doesn't work on me," she told him and went to change her shoes.

Chapter Ten

When they were in the car, she said, "Okay, give me the cheat sheet for your parents."

"There is none," Cal said. "They will be very polite but not warm. We don't have to chill the wine at home, the atmosphere does it for us."

"Oh, good," Min said, "this is exactly the time I want to hear jokes."

But when they arrived at his parents' home, she realized he wasn't being funny. The house was large, one of the Prairie mansions that always looked to Min like ranch houses on steroids; the maid at the paneled door was polite, the paneled hall was cool, and when they went into what Min doubted they called the living room, Cal's parents were downright frigid.

"We're so pleased to have you," Lynne Morrisey said to Min, taking her hand. She didn't look pleased; she didn't look anything but darkly, stunningly, expensively beautiful, as did her husband, Jefferson, and her son, Reynolds, possibly the only man on the planet who made Cal look a little plain.

"*Min!*" Harry said from behind her, and she turned and saw him towing Bink into the room.

"Hey, you," she said, bending down to him. "Thanks for the dinner invitation. I was *starving.*"

Harry nodded and then leaned forward and whispered, "I like your shoes. The bows are neat." He nodded at her, grinning maniacally.

"Thank you," Min whispered back, and stole a glance at Cal. His face was expressionless, and she realized he hadn't said a word since they'd arrived. *O-kay,* she thought. *Welcome to hell.*

She did her best to make politely chilly conversation until they were all seated and served with a series of plates beautifully presented with syrup swirls. Then she gave up and just ate.

"What is it that you do, Minerva?" Jefferson said when they'd reached the filet-and-piped-potatoes course.

Min swallowed and prayed she didn't have anything in her teeth. "I'm an actuary."

"I see," he said, not impressed but not scornful, either. "Who's your employer?"

"Alliance," Min said, and went back to her rare beef. The food was both beautiful and excellent, she had to give the Morriseys credit for that, but it wasn't Emilio's. They needed a few comic ethnic photos on the wall to liven things up. Not that they'd ever admit to being ethnic. She glanced around the table. Irish, she'd bet, and not just because of the name. Dark and beautiful, all of them, in that austere, tragic way. She looked down at her lavishly presented plate. Although the potato famine was clearly behind them.

"Dobbs," Cal's father said, and Min realized he'd been silent for a while. "George Dobbs is a vice president there."

"That's my father," Min said.

Jefferson Morrisey smiled at her. "You went to work for your father's firm."

"Well, it's not as if he owns it," Min said, positive there was a land mine somewhere in the conversation. "But he was a help in getting me the job."

"You didn't need any help," Cal said, his voice flat. "You're an actuary. You must have had forty offers."

"There were a lot," Min said, wondering what the hell was going on. "But there weren't a lot of great offers. My dad helped."

"That was very wise of you," Lynne Morrisey said.

Min turned to meet her cold dark eyes and thought, *I don't want you approving of me, lady.*

"To take the help your father offered," Lynne went on. "Very wise."

"Well." Min put down her fork. "It came with no strings attached, so there wasn't a down side."

Across the table, Reynolds smiled and became even better looking. *I don't like you, either,* Min thought. Bink sat frozen, not in terror so much as in watchfulness, and between them, Harry clutched his fork and plowed his way through his piped potatoes, keeping an eye on everybody.

"And many benefits, no doubt," Jefferson was saying. "I'm sure your father helped you along the way."

"She made it on her own," Cal said, his voice still flat. "Insurance companies are not sentimental. She holds the record for promotions within her company and nobody's saying it's because of her father. She's smart, she's hardworking, and she's excellent at what she does."

There was something bleak and awful in his voice, out of proportion to the tension in the conversation, and Min discreetly put her hand on his back. Even through his suit coat, his muscles were so rigid that it was like patting cement. She felt him tense even tighter for a moment at her touch, and then his shoulders went down a little.

"Of course she is," Jefferson was saying, but he was looking at his wife, a half smile on his face. "We think it's admirable of her that she followed in her father's footsteps."

"My father's not an actuary," Min said.

"Of course not, dear," Lynne said, a little edge to her voice. "We admire you for making the right choice and staying in your father's business." She smiled past Min to Cal. "Don't you think so, Cal?"

"I don't think Min ever makes a mistake," Cal said. "This filet is excellent."

"Cal didn't go into the family business," Reynolds said, smiling at

Min, pseudo-pals, and Min thought, *And you are dumb as a rock to be the one who says that out loud.*

"Well, for heaven's sake, why would he?" Min said brightly. She took her hand away from Cal's back, thought, *I'm never going to see these people again so screw 'em all.*

"Why would he go into the family business?" Lynne echoed, raising one eyebrow, which annoyed Min because she was pretty sure she couldn't do it. "Because it's his legacy."

"No," Min said, and across from her Bink's eyes widened even farther. "It would be completely wrong for him. He's clearly doing what he should be doing." She turned to smile at Cal and found him staring straight ahead, at the space between Bink and Harry. *Okay, he's gone,* she thought, and looked at Harry. He was still clutching his fork, checking faces. No wonder the kid threw up all the time.

Jefferson cleared his throat. "Wrong for him to go into a well-respected and established law firm? Nonsense. It's the Morrisey tradition."

Min blinked. "You went into your father's business? I thought you and your partner started the firm."

Across the table, Bink did the impossible and made her little owl face even more impassive.

"They did," Reynolds said from across the table, indignation in his voice. "They began the tradition."

"I don't think you can call two generations a tradition," Min said, trying to make her voice speculative, as if she were considering it. She looked at Harry. "You want to be a lawyer, Harry?"

Harry blinked at her. "No. I want to be an ichthyologist."

Min blinked back. "Fish?"

"Yeah." Harry lifted his chin and grinned.

"Good for you," Min said.

"Harrison is a child," Lynne said. "Next week, he'll want to be a fireman." She smiled at Harry, almost with warmth.

"No, next week, I'll want to be an ichthyologist," Harry said, and finished his potatoes.

I love you, kid, Min thought.

"Harrison," Lynne said to him. "Why don't you have your dessert in the kitchen with Sarah?"

"Okay." Harry scooted back his chair. "May I be excused?"

"Yes, dear," Lynne said, and Min watched him trot out of the room, thinking, *Harry, you lucky dog.*

"Now," Lynne said, turning back to the table with her lizard smile. "I apologize for interrupting you, Minerva. What were you saying?" She looked at Min as if to say, *You have a chance to back down; take it.*

Min smiled back at her. *Bite me, lady.* "I was saying that if you analyze the situation, you'll see it was always impossible that Cal would go into the firm."

Jefferson put down his fork.

Min picked up her wineglass. "To begin with, he's the younger child. Older children tend to follow in the family footsteps because they're pleasers." She smiled across the table at Reynolds. "That's why they're so often successful." She took a sip of excellent wine, while they all watched her with varying degrees of frigidity. "Also, they tend to get the lion's share of attention and respect so their success is a kind of self-fulfilling prophecy. But youngest children learn that they have to be more demanding to get attention, so they become rule breakers."

"I suspect your psychology is less than professional," Jefferson said, smiling at her with no warmth whatsoever.

"No, it's pretty much a given," Min said. "The colloquial evidence is even there. All the way back to myth and legend. After all, it's always the youngest son who goes out to seek his fortune in fairy tales."

"Fairy tales," Reynolds said, chuckling like a fathead, while Bink continued her imitation of a frozen owl.

Min turned back to Jefferson. "Then consider Cal's personality. His friends tell me that he rarely makes a bet he doesn't win. The knee-jerk reaction to that is that he's a gambler, but he's not. If he were a gambler, he'd lose half the time. Instead, he calculates the odds, and only takes the risks he knows he can capitalize on." She looked across the table at Reynolds. "As the younger son in the family firm, he'd never make it to the top. That's such a bad risk, I doubt he ever considered joining the firm."

"He'd have made partner," Jefferson said, all pretense of light conversation gone.

"Third partner, maybe, after he'd followed you and Reynolds around," Min said. "Plus there'd be your partner and his children to contend with. Within the family, he's always going to be the baby. He had to get out. And then, of course, there's the dyslexia."

The silence that settled over the table that time was so complete that Min was amazed there wasn't hoarfrost on all of them. She picked up her knife and fork and cut into her filet again, wishing she could ask for a Styrofoam box and go home.

"We prefer not to discuss Cal's handicap," Lynne said with finality.

Min took her time with the filet, but when she'd swallowed, she said, "Why? It's part of who he is, it helped shape him. It's not shameful. Over ten percent of the population is dyslexic, so it's not rare. And it's a large part of why he started his own firm. Ninety-two percent of dyslexics go into business for themselves. They need to control the environment in which they work because the regular working environment isn't sympathetic to their needs. And they generally do very well because they are generally intelligent, empathetic people." She picked up her water glass. "You have a son who's smart, hardworking, successful, popular, healthy, charming, and extremely pleasant to look at. I'm surprised you're not passing his picture around to all your friends, bragging about him." She turned to smile up at Cal and found him watching her, his face wooden. "I'd brag about him if he were mine and I had a picture."

"We are, of course, quite proud of Calvin," Lynne said, her voice bleak.

"Oh, good," Min said, going back to her plate. "He's right about the filet, too. It's fabulous."

"Thank you," Lynne said, and then she turned to Reynolds and asked him about work. Fifteen minutes later, dessert was served; Reynolds, Lynne, and Jefferson were discussing the firm; Cal was still silent; Bink had eaten three slivers of carrot and sucked down all her wine; and Min had had enough.

She put her napkin down by her plate, and said, "You know, I'm

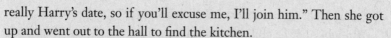

really Harry's date, so if you'll excuse me, I'll join him." Then she got up and went out to the hall to find the kitchen.

When she got there, Harry was finishing off his ice cream under the watchful eyes of the woman who'd served dinner.

"Hey, fish guy," she said. "Is there any more of that?"

Harry nodded at the woman. "She's the one, Sarah."

"Huh," Sarah said, surveying Min from head to toe. "What would you like on your ice cream?"

"Chocolate," Min said, sitting down across from Harry. "Chocolate is always good."

Harry scraped the bottom of his bowl with his spoon, and then sat silently looking at Min, as owlish as his mother, until Sarah put Min's ice cream in front of her. There was a lot of it.

"Thank you," Min said, taken aback. "I'm Min, by the way." She held out her hand to the maid.

"Sarah," the woman said, shaking it. "Eat it before it melts."

Min nodded and scooped up a spoonful. The ice cream was heavenly, superfatted and smooth, and the chocolate exquisitely light and bittersweet. She had to hand it to Lynne Morrisey: The woman provided excellent food.

Sarah leaned back against the sink. "So you talked back to the Snow Queen?"

Min thought about pretending she didn't understand and then shrugged. "I disagreed with her."

Sarah nodded. "You won't be back."

"Lord, no," Min said.

Harry put down his spoon, alarmed. "Are you still coming to the park?"

"Yes," Min said. "Although I'm not sure your uncle Cal is still speaking to me."

"He seems like a nice guy," Sarah said. "Quiet. We don't see him much."

"I can imagine," Min said, and then Cal came into the kitchen. "Hi, there," she said, waving her spoon at him. "Turns our your mom has great taste in ice cream, too." Which figured, come to think of it.

Cal nodded, expressionless. "You ready to go?"

Min looked at her full bowl of premium sugar and fat, and sighed. "Yes," she said obediently and put her spoon down. If she were Cal, she'd be screaming to get out of here, too.

Cal went out into the hall and Harry said, "Can I have your ice cream?"

"Will you barf?" Min said.

Harry shook his head. "Not ice cream."

Min pushed the bowl across to him. "Knock yourself out." She stood up. "It was very nice meeting you, Sarah."

"Yeah," Sarah said. "Good luck."

She met Cal in the hall, and he opened the door for her without speaking. They'd almost made it to the steps when Bink appeared in the doorway. "Well?" she said to Cal.

Cal shook his head at her, and she smiled at Min and said, "It was so nice to see you again," sounding as if she meant it. Cal turned and walked down the steps as Bink slipped away again, and Min followed him, fairly sure they were about to fight.

Well, she had no regrets. She slid into the front seat of Cal's car and settled into the leather seat. Okay, she'd miss the car. And the food, although she could still go to Emilio's without him. And—

Cal got in the car and slammed the door and then sat there for a moment, and Min looked at his rigid profile and thought, *And you. I'm going to miss you.*

"What did Bink want?" she said, trying to stave off whatever was coming.

Cal turned to her, and when he spoke, his voice was so strained it almost broke. "I am so sorry about that."

"What?" Min said, taken aback.

"My family." He closed his eyes, and then said viciously, "They usually behave *very well* in front of strangers."

"I don't think I was their type," Min said, keeping her voice light. "And then I was rude. But the good news is, I got great food and I never have to see them again. Do you know what kind of ice cream that was? Because it was phenomenal, although I'm guessing it wasn't nonfat."

"You don't care?" Cal said.

"That your mother is a witch and your father is a bastard and your brother is a supercilious moron?" Min said. "No. Why should I? They're not my family. Who are looking pretty damn good right about now, so I owe you for that. Now about the ice cream—"

He leaned forward and kissed her, hard, and she put her hand on his cheek and kissed him back, falling into that same hot, glittery rush she got every time, so glad to be touching him, to have his hand laced through her curls, to be *with him*. When he broke the kiss, she stayed close to him, not ready to let him go. "Was that because I insulted your mother?" she said, a little dazed. "Because I have lots of other horrible things to say about her."

Cal grinned, and she relaxed because he looked like Cal again. "Nah, I just like kissing you."

"Oh, good," Min said, recovering. "Except, stop that because we're not doing that. I was just relieved because I thought you were never going to want to see me again. I'm positive your family doesn't want to."

Cal put the key in the ignition and started the car. "Oh, some of them do."

"Harry." Min leaned back in her seat, and tried to think about something else besides kissing him. "That's just because I gave him my ice cream."

Cal slowed the car. "He had yours and his?"

"Yes," Min said. "He said he didn't throw up ice cream."

"He lied." Cal stopped the car. "It's sugar in general that makes him sick."

"Do we have to go back?" Min said, alarmed.

"Christ, no." Cal pulled out his cell phone. When he'd warned Bink about the imminent vomiting, he started the car again.

"Great, I poisoned her kid," Min said. "Now she hates me, too."

"No. She knows Harry and the cons he pulls for sugar. She likes you."

"She didn't look like it."

"No, she really likes you," Cal said as he pulled out into the street. "She offered me a hundred thousand dollars to marry you."

"What?" Min laughed. "I didn't think she had a sense of humor."

"She does, but she wasn't joking. She can afford it." Cal picked up speed as they left his parents' street and sighed. "Thank *God*, we're out of there."

"Wait a minute," Min said, not laughing. "She honestly offered you—"

"She's been going to dinner there every Sunday for ten years," Cal said. "That was the first one she enjoyed. When you figure that my parents are in their fifties and likely to be around for at least another thirty years, she's looking at a minimum of sixteen hundred more miserable Sundays. That's her estimate. Add in holiday dinners, and she says a hundred K would come out to about sixty dollars a dinner, which is a real bargain in her book." He thought about it. "Actually, that's a bargain in my book, too, although nothing on this earth could get me there every Sunday."

"My Lord," Min said.

"Plus Harry's been singing 'Hunka hunka burning love' since we went to lunch yesterday. She said the expressions on my parents' faces alone were worth a hundred grand."

There was a smile in his voice now, and Min said, "Well, that's a mind-boggler."

"It wasn't the only one this afternoon." They drove on for a while and then he said, "How did you know I was dyslexic?"

"Roger told Bonnie so I looked it up on the net. And then you wouldn't write the recipe for chicken marsala down when I asked. You never say no to me, so I knew it had to be something you couldn't do." Min rolled her head on the back of her seat to look at him. "Are you upset?"

"No," Cal said. "Is that true, about dyslexics starting their own businesses?"

"Yes," Min said. "Everything I told them was true. How'd you know about my promotions?"

"Bonnie told Roger," Cal said, and turned into a parking lot.

Min squinted at the storefront. It looked expensive and snotty. "Be right back," he said, and went inside. Fifteen minutes later he came back with a glossy shopping bag embossed in gold, which he tossed in her lap as he got in the car.

"What?" she said, catching it. It was heavy, so she peered inside at the square white cartons sealed with gold labels.

"The ice cream my mother serves," he said as he pulled out of the lot. "Eight flavors. I'll send flowers, but you deserved this now."

"Oh." Min clutched the bag tighter. He really wasn't mad. Relief swept over her, and she realized just exactly how much she didn't want him out of her life. It was not a good realization.

"Everything okay?" Cal said, and she forced a smile at him.

"Well, no," she said, trying to sound exasperated. "Where's the spoon?"

Without taking his eyes from the road, he took a plastic spoon from his suit pocket and handed it to her.

"I'm crazy about you," she said without thinking.

"Good," he said. "I'm crazy about you, too."

"In a friendly kind of way," she said, hastily.

"Right," Cal said, shaking his head.

"Just so you know," Min said, and opened the first carton.

"He calls her Minnie," Cynthie said when David picked up the phone that evening. "He gave her his ball cap."

"Well, if he gives her his class ring, let me know," David said. "Could I have one Sunday in peace?"

"I don't know, David," Cynthie said, her voice dangerous. "You want any of them in the future to be with Min?"

"Yes," David said. "But she hated lunch, and she won't return my calls. Look, Cal always dumps his girlfriends after a couple of months. It seems to me the smartest thing to do is wait until he dumps her and then comfort her."

"And it doesn't bother you that he's going to be fucking her blind for those two months?" Cynthie said.

"Hey." David sat up. "That's—"

"You have no idea what that man can do to a woman in bed,"

Cynthie said. "What makes you think you're going to be able to please her once she's slept with him?"

"I do just fine in bed," David said, outraged.

"Cal does more than fine," Cynthie said. "If I were you, I wouldn't wait until she finds out how much more."

"Cynthie, this is distasteful."

"Fine," Cynthie said. "Let him win."

Her voice was like a fingernail down a blackboard. "It's not about winning," David said and thought, *The bastard's going to win.*

And he'd lose Min. It was all her fault, really. She was the kind of woman who just asked to be taken for granted, and now that Cal Morrisey was showering attention on her to win a bet, she was flattered. He thought about how grateful Min would be if he went back to her and paid attention. She was such a simple woman. Which was why Cal could get to her. Which meant it was his duty to stop Cal. And save her.

"David?" Cynthie said, prompting him. "You do want her back, don't you?"

"Yes," David said.

"Then go over to her apartment and dazzle her," Cynthie said. "Tell her how important she is. Take her a gift, she likes snow globes, take her a snow globe. Give her joy, damn it."

"Snow globe," David said, recalling there had been some on Min's mantel.

"And if she resists, leave something there so you can go back and get it and try again the next day," Cynthie said. "Your tie or something."

"Why would I take off my tie?" David said.

There was a short silence, and then Cynthie said, "Just *do it*, David. I don't have time for remedial seduction lessons."

"All right," David said. "I'll go over after work. I'll surprise her. We'll talk about marriage."

"*Talk?*" Cynthie said, exasperated. "For once in your life, could you do more than talk?"

"Well, I'm not going act like a caveman with her," David said.

"Ever tried that?" Cynthie said.

"No, of course not."

"Then how do you know it doesn't work?"

"Well," David said. "Oh, hell, all right. I'll kiss her. She's a good kisser."

"Good to know," Cynthie said. "Don't screw this up, David."

"I won't," David said, but she'd already hung up. "God, you're a witch," he said to the dial tone, and then he hung up, too.

On Monday morning, Nanette called Min to find out how dinner at the Morriseys had gone. "Tell me everything," she said.

"Mother, I'm at work," Min said.

"Yes, but your father would never fire you," Nanette said. "He'd never betray *you.*"

"Mom?" Min said.

"What was their house like?" Nanette said. "Did his mother like you?"

"It was very beautiful," Min said, "and his mother hated me."

"Min, if she's going to be your mother-in-law—"

"She's not going to be my mother-in-law."

"—you're going to need her. For when you hit the bad times. Not that your grandmother ever helped me in the slightest—"

"When did you ever need help with Daddy?" Min said.

"Well, *now,*" Nanette said, goaded.

"Well, she's dead now," Min said. "She can't help. What's wrong?"

There was a long silence, and then Nanette said, very dramatically, "He's having an affair."

"Oh, he is not," Min said. "Honestly, Mom, when would he? You know where he is every moment of the day."

"It's those lunches," Nanette said darkly.

"He has lunch with Beverly," Min said. "Beverly who adores her husband and would really like not to work through lunch. He is not having an affair with her."

"You're so naïve, Min," Nanette said.

"You're so paranoid, Mother," Min said. "What's going on that makes you think he's cheating?"

"It's not the same. We never talk anymore."

"All you ever talk about is clothes and the wedding and my weight," Min said. "He's not interested. Take up golf. You'll be chattering away in no time."

"I should have known you wouldn't understand," Nanette said. "You have your Calvin, after all."

"I do not have a Calvin," Min said, fishing in her drawer for a paper clip. "I'm not seeing—ouch." She pulled her hand out to see a staple stuck in the end of her finger.

"You don't have time to think about your mother," Nanette said.

"Oh, for crying out loud," Min said. "Go back to worrying about the wedding and do not do anything dumb like leaving Dad, because there is nothing going on. As God is my witness, the man is innocent."

"The daughters are always the last to know," Nanette said, and hung up.

"Nuts," Min said, and hung up the phone to blot her fingertip on a piece of scrap paper.

The phone rang again, almost right away, and she answered it to hear Diana say, "Hi," in a wavery little voice.

"What's wrong?" Min said, blotting more blood on the scrap paper.

"I'm just a little . . . down," Diana said. "Could we do something together?"

"Absolutely," Min said. "How about tonight?"

"I can't," Di said. "I have to go to Greg's parents' house for dinner. How was it at Cal's parents?"

"Very bad," Min said. "How about tomorrow night?"

"I can't," Di said. "Susie and Karen are throwing a sex toy shower for me."

"Sorry I'm going to miss that," Min lied, trying not to think about Worse with a vibrator in her hand.

"How about Wednesday?" Diana said. "I know you go out with Sweet and Tart that night, but can I come along?"

"Yes," Min said, trying not to laugh. "Especially if you promise to call them Sweet and Tart."

"Liza would *kill* me," Diana said, but her voice sounded lighter.

"Come here first," Min said. "And then we'll go out and you can come back and spend the night. It'll be like old times. Except we'll be folding your cake boxes because they have to be assembled, I've just found out."

"Okay," Di said. "Okay. I feel better. It's just pre-wedding jitters."

"Right," Min said. "You haven't talked to Mom recently, have you?"

"Well, yes," Diana said. "I live with her."

"No, I mean *talk*. Because she just called to tell me Dad's cheating on her."

"Oh," Diana said, sounding taken aback. "No, she hasn't mentioned that."

"Well, good," Min said, and reassured Diana that their father was not sleeping with his secretary—"It would mean he'd have to skip lunch, Di, and do you really see that happening?"—and hung up with a renewed promise that they would have a wonderful time on Wednesday.

Then she sat and looked at the phone and waited for it to ring again. She'd told Cal not to call her, that she wanted Monday to herself, but he was not good at taking directions, so maybe . . .

By five that evening, it had become clear that the bastard had learned to take directions. Min went home and heard Elvis playing on the stereo before she opened the door. She went in and saw the cat splayed out on the back of her couch, his ears close to the speakers. "Turned it on again, did you?" she said, and went over and cuddled him to make up for leaving him all day, something that didn't seem to bother him much at all. Then she made spaghetti and began the pleasant evening she'd planned with her cat, keeping one ear cocked for a knock at the door, just in case. When it came, she felt equal parts exasperated and happy. Okay, Cal wasn't good at listening, that was bad, but she was still glad he was there.

Then she opened the door and he wasn't, it was David, and her feelings simplified down to just exasperated.

"What are you doing here?" she said.

"I need to talk to you." He walked in and stopped dead, staring at the end of her couch. "My God, what is that?"

"That's Elvis," Min said closing the door behind him. "My cat. I love him. Insult him and you're history."

David sat down on the couch, as far away from Elvis as he could get. "I've been thinking about us," he began as he loosened his tie.

"There is no us," Min said. "There never was an us. The best thing you ever did for me was dump me. I'd be grateful but I'm still mad at you for it."

"I know, I know, I deserve it." David pulled the knot out of his tie, looking more undone than Min could ever remember seeing him. "It was the dumbest thing I ever did." He patted the couch beside him. "Come here and let me talk to you."

Min went over and sat down on the couch. "Make this fast," she told him. "Elvis and I have a big evening ahead of us." At the sound of his name, Elvis crept forward on the back of the couch and sat beside her, growling softly, and she put her hand up and rubbed him behind the ears. "Easy, tiger," she told him. "He's leaving."

David leaned closer, keeping one eye on the cat. "I want to marry you, Min."

Elvis reached out a claw and buried it in David's sleeve.

"*Hell*," David said, scooting back on the couch. "What was that for?"

"Elvis doesn't want to get married," Min said. "I think Priscilla broke his heart. He always loved her, you know."

"It's not funny," David said.

"Who's laughing?"

"Look, I'm serious," David reached in his coat pocket and handed her a package. "This is how serious I am."

"That's not a ring, is it?" Min said with horror.

"No," David said, so she unwrapped the box. Inside was an expensive, three-inch snow globe with the Eiffel Tower inside.

"The Eiffel Tower?" Min said. *This guy doesn't know me at all.*

"That's where we'll honeymoon," David said, edging closer. "In Paris. We'll have a wonderful life, Min. And I don't mind starting a family right away, we can—"

"I don't want kids," Min said, peering into the snow globe. "David, this isn't my kind of—"

"Of course you want kids," David said. "You were born to be a mother."

Min put the snow globe on the end table and looked at the cat. "There are two men, Elvis. One calls you a depraved angel and the other calls you a natural born mother. Which one do *you* pick?"

"Well, you're more than that, of course," David said. "But—" He stopped when the cat jumped down from the back of the sofa, brushing against him and leaving a smudge of rusty cat hair on his sleeve. "Your cat just got cat hair on me."

"It's only fair," Min said. "Your suit just got expensive suit lint on him."

"Min, I know you're seeing Cal Morrisey," David said.

"You do?" Min said, thinking, *You miserable son of a bitch, you're still trying to win that bet.* It was enough to make her sleep with Cal just to get even with David. The thought was much more exciting than it should have been.

"You shouldn't see Cal," David said seriously. "Ever again."

The cat jumped up on the end table and nosed the snow globe off with enough force that it landed on the stone hearth in front of the fireplace and smashed, water running everywhere.

"Elvis!" Min shoved herself off the couch to shoo him away. "Stay away from there. There's broken glass."

"He did that on purpose," David said, outraged.

"Yes, David, the cat is plotting against you." Min fished the base out of the water and glass shards and put it on the table. Then she went to get her wastebasket and began to put the glass pieces in it.

"That cat—" David said.

"Yes?" Min said as she picked up the biggest piece.

"Never mind," David said. "You don't know what Cal Morrisey's up to."

"Sure, I do," Min said, picking up another piece. "He's trying to get me into bed."

"Well, yes," David said. "But it's more than that."

"I know." Min picked up the third and last large piece and then looked at the rest. "Give me that magazine on the table, will you?"

David passed the magazine over and she tore off the cover while he said, "You don't know. He's capable of anything."

"That was the impression I got." Min slid the cover under the glass while using the rest of the magazine as a broom. She dumped the glass in the basket and then saw one more large piece, a little beyond her sweeping area. "Look, David, you don't have to worry about me. I am not in love with Cal Mor—*ow!*" She pulled back her hand as the blood welled up. "What the hell?" She picked up the last piece and dropped it in the basket and then went out to the kitchen to wash off the blood.

"Are you listening to me?" David said.

"No," Min said over the running water. "I'm injured. Go away. I don't want to marry you." She turned off the water, wrapped a paper towel around her finger, and went back to get rid of him.

"Min," David said, standing up. "You're not taking me seriously."

"Lord, no," Min said, opening her front door. "You're a nice man, David. Well, not really. Go—"

"No, Min, I'm staying," he said, his voice deep and serious.

Then he grabbed her and kissed her hard.

Chapter Eleven

David was holding Min's head in his hands too tightly for her to pull away, so she drew back her hand to slap him, only to have him yank away and scream before she could complete the smack.

At his feet, Elvis snarled, his front claws planted in David's shin.

Min wiped her mouth off as David kicked Elvis off his leg. "Well, that was *gross*. As I was saying, go find some woman who meets your criteria for a good mate and marry her. I have an attack cat, and I'm accessing my inner bitch all the time now, so you'll never survive here."

"I'm sorry," David said. "I just want you so much."

"Yeah," Min said. "Do that again and I'll Mace you. Now get out."

"Promise me you won't see Cal Morrisey again," David said, and Elvis lowered his head on the back of the couch and growled.

"No, David, I will not promise you anything." Min pointed to the door. "Out or I get a restraining order."

"At least think about it," David said.

"No," Min said and pushed him out the door. When she had it shut behind him, she looked at Elvis, now stretched out on the back of the couch, his head close to the stereo he loved. He batted the stereo with his paw until he connected with the ON button, and "Heartbreak Hotel" boomed out of the speakers.

"Turn that down," Min said and then remembered she was talking to a cat. She went over and moved the volume lever down. "That was weird, Elvis."

Elvis patted the UP button over and over again until "Love Me Tender" came on.

"Well, it could be worse," Min said, looking at him sprawled on the back of her couch. "You could like music from Julia Roberts movies."

Elvis's tail began to twitch to the music, and Min gave up and went to get a Band-Aid.

Cal didn't call Tuesday either, and Min was congratulating herself that night that she was finally free of him and feeling lousy about it when somebody knocked on her door. She stirred her chicken marsala one more time and went to answer it, picking up her Mace on the way. After forty-eight hours and no phone call, she was hoping it was a mugger so she could release some tension. But when she opened the door, Cal was leaning in the doorway, holding the usual sack from Emilio's and another, smaller shopping bag, looking more tired than she'd ever seen him. His shirt collar was open, his tie ends hanging down, his shirtsleeves were rolled up, and he was rumpled and sloppy and the sexiest thing she'd ever seen, and her heart lurched sideways just because she was so damn glad he was there.

He said, "Hi," and saw the Mace. "You can just say no," he said, and she opened the door wider, and he came in and kissed her on the forehead. She leaned into him because he looked so solid and because she was so glad to see him and then, on an impulse, she stretched up and kissed him gently, a hello-how-are-you kiss that felt like exactly the right thing to do.

When she pulled back, Cal looked stunned.

"What?" she said. "That was a friendly kiss."

He shook his head and closed the door behind him with his shoulder.

"That was . . . nice. Here." He handed her the small shopping bag. "I'm courting. You get gifts."

Min took the bag and felt deflated. "Bad kiss? Did I do it wrong?"

"No." He grinned tiredly at her. "You couldn't possibly do it wrong." Then his smile faded. "That's just the first time."

"Oh, please," Min said. "We've been kissing for days."

"I've been kissing you for days," Cal said, tossing his jacket on the armchair as he went to put Emilio's bag on the table. "That's the first time you've kissed me. What smells so good?"

"Chicken marsala," Min said. "I think I got it. What do you mean, that's the first time? I . . ." Her voice trailed off as she thought about it. He was right. He always kissed her.

"Don't worry about it," Cal said as he came back to her. "So—"

Min dropped the shopping bag and went up on her toes and kissed him again, this time giving it everything she had. The rush made her dizzy, and she grabbed his shirt to steady herself, and he held her, kissing her back until she was hot and trembling.

"That's two," Cal said, breathlessly. "Not that I'm counting."

"There should have been more," Min said, trying to get her breath back. "I mean, we're not doing this anymore, but I shouldn't have made you do all the work."

"I didn't mind," Cal said, pulling her closer, and she knew she should pull back but she didn't want to because he felt so damn good against her. "Although I'm liking this."

"I just didn't want you to get the wrong idea," Min said, putting her forehead against his chest.

"Which would be what?"

She felt him kiss the top of her head again, and smiled. "That I wanted, you know, more."

"Right," Cal said. "Just friends. You bet. Kiss me again."

Min grinned and lifted her head. "It doesn't count if you tell me to."

"It always counts," Cal said and kissed her, and she let herself fall into him until she lost track of time and everything but the way he felt wrapped around her. Then he came up for air and said, "I may be getting the wrong idea."

"No," Min said, backing away. "Don't do that. Forget any of that happened." She held up the Mace can. "I have Mace."

"Right," he said and let go of her to collapse onto the couch. "Elvis, old buddy, how are you doing?" He reached up to scratch Elvis behind the ears and Min almost said, "Don't," remembering what had happened to David. But Elvis flattened his head so Cal could get closer and purred his appreciation. "You know, this is a nice cat."

"I know." Min tried to calm her pounding heart as Elvis rolled to his feet. "I don't know how I ever lived without him." She picked up the bag she'd dropped and went to sit next to Cal on the couch. "So. I've heard about this," she said, pulling open the bag. "You're going to give me something I didn't even know I needed."

"What do you mean, you heard?" Cal said, but Min was pulling out a shoe box and ignored him.

"I have very specific tastes in shoes," she said, shaking her head. "The possibilities for disaster here are huge."

"I live on the edge," Cal said.

Min opened the box. Inside were mules with her favorite French heel, but they were covered in white fur. "What the hell?" she said but when she pulled them out, she saw the bunny faces on the furry insteps. "You got me *bunny slippers?*" she said, holding them up. The bunnies looked back her, dopey and sweet. "*Open-toed bunny slippers?* These are *incredible.*"

"I know," Cal said, scratching Elvis's stomach now. "There's music in there, too."

"Let me guess," Min said, reaching in the bag again. "Elvis Costello." She pulled out the CD and read the title: "Elvis Presley, Fifty Greatest Love Songs." She looked at Cal. "You got me Elvis *Presley.*"

"It's what you like," Cal said, as the cat rolled away from him. "Why would I get you what I like?"

"Boy, you *are* good at this," Min said, looking back at the bunnies. "I *love* these shoes."

"Every woman needs bunny slippers," Cal said, taking one of them. "Especially women with toes like yours." He reached down and picked up her foot and stripped her sweat sock off, and Min wiggled her suddenly cool, pink-tipped toes at him. "Very hot toes, Minnie," he said, rubbing his thumb along the bottom of her foot.

"Ticklish," Min said, trying to pull her foot back, but he slipped the shoe on before she could move, and she closed her eyes and sighed at how good the fur lining felt on her skin. "Oh, lovely," she said and then looked down at her foot again, and wiggled her toes under the bunny's mouth. "These are perfect."

"I know," Cal said, and let go of her foot.

Min stripped her other sock off and slid into the other bunny slipper. "You're a genius at this. I'll wait to play the CD when you're gone so you don't have to suffer."

"I like Elvis," Cal began, but Elvis the cat had crept his way down the chair arm, and now he pushed something off the sewing machine table at the end of the couch.

"Hey." Cal leaned out to retrieve it. "Careful, cat, you'll—" He stopped as he picked it up. "Why do you have a statue of the Eiffel Tower?"

"Somebody brought me an Eiffel Tower snow globe last night," Min said, watching her toes wiggle under the bunnies' chins. "Elvis broke it."

"Good for Elvis." Cal handed her the tower and she dropped it in the wastebasket and went back to looking at her bunnies. "So who was clueless enough to give you a snow globe without people in it? Greg?"

"No," Min said cheerfully as she saw trouble loom. "You know what? I think I made the chicken right." She stood up. The slippers felt wonderful. "These fit *perfectly*."

"Minerva," Cal said. "You're keeping something from me."

"Many things," Min said, and went out to the kitchen, concentrating on the way the slippers tapped on her hardwood floor. "I may never take these shoes off again."

Behind her, "Love Me Tender" began to play, and Cal said from the couch, "The cat knows how to turn on the stereo?"

"He knows the power button," she called back. "And replay, unfortunately. I heard 'Love Me Tender' four times last night before I took the CD out." She stirred the chicken one more time, tasted it, and thought, *I really think this is it.* She smiled to herself and tasted it again to make sure before she called back, "I think you should taste this."

"I will," Cal said from behind her. "First tell me who this belongs to."

She turned and saw him holding up David's tie.

"Where'd you get that?" she said.

"Elvis was playing with it," Cal said.

She took it from him and dropped it in the kitchen trash. "It's none of your business who that belongs to."

"I know," Cal said.

"You can't be jealous," Min said.

"And yet, much to my own disgust, I am," he said, folding his arms. "All right, I have no business asking."

"This is true," Min said.

"So who was it?"

She leaned against the stove and realized she was glad he was jealous. *You're a mess*, she told herself.

"Minnie," Cal said.

"My ex-boyfriend. He dropped by and proposed."

"He did?" Cal said calmly, but his jaw tightened.

"Yes, he did," Min said, enjoying herself. "He brought the paper-weight because we were going to honeymoon in Paris."

"Thoughtful of him," Cal said, biting off the words.

"Not really." Min straightened. "I don't want to honeymoon in Paris."

"Did you tell him that?"

"No," Min said, her patience at an end. "I told him I didn't want to get married, and then I kicked him out."

"Uh huh," Cal said.

"That's it," Min said. "He's gone."

"No, he's not," Cal said.

"I assure you—"

"He left his tie, Min."

"So?"

"So he left it so he could come back for it."

"That's . . ." Min thought about it. ". . . entirely possible."

"Give me the tie," Cal said.

"Why?" Min said, exasperated.

"So I can messenger it back to the son of a bitch tomorrow," Cal said. "Who is he?"

"Have you lost your only mind?"

Cal closed his eyes. "Yes."

"There we go," Min said. "The first step in solving your problem is admitting you have one."

"Don't see him anymore," Cal said, making it a request, not an order.

"I won't," Min said. "I don't even like him much."

"Can I return the tie, please?" Cal said, holding out his hand.

Min fished it out of the trash. "Here. His name is David Fisk. He runs a soft—" She stopped at the look on Cal's face. "What?"

"Your ex is David Fisk?" Cal said, and Min remembered the bet.

"Yes," she said. "Do you know him?"

"Yes," Cal said. "He's —" He stopped and she waited. "He's a client."

"Oh," Min said, and thought, *The bet, he's not going to tell me about the bet. Damn it.*

Cal crumpled up the tie. "I'll send it back to him. How's the chicken?"

"I think it's excellent," Min said, feeling depressed as Elvis sang about true love.

"It looks great." Cal picked up a spoon from the dish drainer and scooped up some sauce. He tasted it and Min waited, caring way too much about what he thought. "Damn, that's good," he said, looking at her with surprise. "I think that's better than Emilio's. Did you do something different?"

"Yes," Min said. "But that's my secret. You have secrets, I have secrets."

"I don't have secrets," Cal said.

"Dinner," Min said and went to set the table as "Love Me Tender" began again.

They talked through dinner and the dishes, and Min tried not to enjoy it, tried to remember the bet, but it was so comfortable being with him that she kept forgetting. Somehow he'd slipped into her life and under her skin, and she was happy about that even though she knew that was his plan. *I don't have a plan*, she thought, and that was so good that she gave up and smiled at him and when he left, she kissed him good night without reservation, and he leaned in the doorway and said, "Minnie, about this friends thing," and she pushed him out gently and closed the door to keep from saying, "I hate that, forget that, make love to me."

Because that, she told herself as she went back to Elvis, would be bad.

At seven Wednesday night, David was in his shirtsleeves, trying to find two shipments that had gone astray and thinking about how to get to Min, who'd once brought him a Caesar salad (no croutons), when his office door banged open and Cynthie stood here in another tailored suit, this one pink.

"Oh good, it's you," he said flatly.

"They're still dating." Cynthie came in and closed the door. "You were supposed to make your move."

"I did," David said. "She said no. And I left the tie but Cal messengered it back to me so that didn't work. But she also said she wasn't going to sleep with him, so I'm thinking if we wait—"

"Well, wait for this. He took her home to meet his mother."

David sat up straighter as the cold hit his spine. "What?"

"He took her home to meet his mother," Cynthie said again. "It took me seven months to get Cal to take me home to his parents. She did it in *three weeks*. David, *I'm losing him*."

"His mother," David said, and thought, *The bastard. He'll do anything to win that bet. "Fuck."* He looked up, startled that he'd said it out loud. "Sorry."

"No," Cynthie said, stopping in front of him. "You are not sorry. You are *mad*."

"Yeah, I am." David thought about Cal Morrisey and got madder. Somebody should stop guys like him. He stood up. "So what am I supposed to do about it?"

"Fight for her," Cynthie said. "She's your girlfriend. Get her back."

"I tried," David said, losing some steam. "She likes Cal."

"You are the most *passive* son of a bitch," Cynthie said. "No wonder she never slept with you. You probably never asked her."

"Thank you," David said. "That's great coming from somebody who got turned down after putting out for nine months. Don't see that being aggressive worked for you, sweetheart. Maybe you're the one with the heat problem."

"Listen, you," Cynthie said. "I have a perfect body and I am *great* in bed."

"You know, I doubt it," David said, coming around his desk. "Don't bother to open your jacket again. I already saw that commercial."

Cynthie gaped at him. "You *bastard*."

"Well, hell, Cynthie, what do you expect? You come in here screaming at me and calling me names because your ex took the woman I love home to meet his mother. If you want to stop it, go get him. Unbutton your jacket at *him*." David stopped and closed his eyes. "Look, I'm tired, I'm miserable, and I haven't had sex in three months. Take your perfect body back to the guy who was having perfect sex with you. I have work to do."

When she didn't say anything, he opened his eyes. She was frowning at him.

"They're not sleeping together," Cynthie said.

"I know," David said. "So nobody's getting any. Great. Go away."

"You can tell by the way they act together," she said, and he stopped. "I was just at The Long Shot. Min was there with Cal. I watched them. They haven't done it. You can tell, people touch differently when they've had sex, they relax, they . . ." Cynthie took a step closer. "They haven't done it. We can still get them back. And I know a great aphrodisiac."

"Right," David said. "You unbutton your jacket."

"No," Cynthie said, so close now she was almost touching him. "Pain. If joy doesn't work, try pain. Like jealousy. It's a physiological cue, a very powerful one. They're going to Emilio's now, I heard them say so. We're going to go."

David stepped back and bumped into his desk. "Cynthie, I don't—"

"But first," Cynthie said. "We're going to have sex."

David froze.

"It's been three months for me, too," Cynthie said. "So we are going to have incredible, athletic, sweaty sex right here, and then we're going to go to dinner. And Cal will know. People look different when they've just had sex."

David swallowed. "Well, thank you, but I don't think it's going to—"

Cynthie unbuttoned her jacket, revealing a shiny pink bra that was so sheer it was probably illegal in several states.

"—accomplish anything beyond making us both feel foolish—"

She dropped her jacket to the floor and unzipped her skirt.

"—after the shallow physical thrill—"

Her skirt slid down her remarkable legs, and David was left looking at the most perfect body he'd ever seen in the flesh.

"—subsides," he finished lamely.

She walked up to him. "You're not going to say no to me."

"I guess not," David said and let her drag him to the floor.

It was odd having Diana with her, Min realized when they were in The Long Shot. Like two different worlds colliding. Di looked around at everything with new eyes, smiled her delight at Shanna, laughed at everything Tony said, watched Cal with approval, and asked where Liza was, as if she wanted the complete cast of Min's life there.

"Working," Tony said. "She's decided that she's going to revamp Emilio's night shift first and save lunch for later. I haven't seen her since she started."

"We should go to Emilio's," Roger said. "That way you could see Liza."

"I don't want—" Tony said, but Min said, "You know, that's a good idea. I'm hungry and Di's never been there," and they migrated the two blocks to Emilio's.

"These guys are so great," Di whispered to her. "I didn't know you had such a great group."

"Well, I don't know that I have a group," Min said and then realized that Di was right, that she was as relaxed with Tony as she was with Cal and that she'd long ago accepted Roger as the honorary brother-in-law that Bonnie was about to make him.

Liza met them at the door, in a little black dress that looked like a million dollars but probably cost her ten in a thrift store somewhere. "Welcome to Emilio's," she said, winking at Di. "You're going to love it here."

"I don't know," Cal said, sotto voce from behind Min and Di. "I heard the service was Tart."

Di elbowed Min, and said, "You weren't supposed to tell anybody," and then Cal grinned at her and she laughed.

"Charm Boy," Min said.

Brian showed up, impeccably dressed, as Liza led them to the table by the window. "Hello," he said. "I'm Brian, and I'll be your server tonight."

"Brian?" Cal said.

"Mr. Morrisey," Brian said, glaring at him.

"Don't let the consumers get you down, Brian," Liza said, putting her hand on his arm. "Remember, you're better than they are."

"Yes, Liza," Brian said, adoration oozing from his pores.

"Oh, God," Cal said.

"You have my permission to be rude to Mr. Morrisey," Liza told Brian.

"Good," Brian said, and slapped Cal on the back of the head with the menu, making Di laugh again.

"What is this place?" she said, looking around.

"Home," Cal said, and Min nodded, seeing her life through Di's eyes. It was a damn good life but somehow it had gotten tangled up in Cal's. *What am I going to do when he leaves?* The thought chilled her, that she'd let things get this far, that she was in this much danger, and she stayed silent through most of dinner, listening to Diana chatter on with everybody else, watching Cal, his tie loosened and his sleeves rolled up, completely at home and smiling at her. He looked solid sitting there, not like David's fashionable leanness or Greg's gym-toned obviousness, but broad and strong and real and infinitely desirable. *I could say yes to him before he goes*, she thought and felt a wave of heat roll over her, and even though she knew she'd never do it, she let herself have one brief fantasy of falling back with his solid weight on top of her, his hands hot on her again, her arms wrapped around the broad bulk of him, one visceral moment that made her half close her eyes and bite her lip, and when she shook it off, he was watching her, not smiling anymore.

"Come here and tell me what you're thinking, Minerva," he said, leaning toward her.

"I don't think so, Calvin," she said, regrouping.

"*Hel*-lo," Tony said, and the rest of the table looked where he was looking.

David and Cynthie had come in, looking flushed. Brian gestured them to a table like a pro, and David put his hand on Cynthie's lower back as they followed. Cynthie didn't seem to mind.

"Why don't they just wear T-shirts that say, 'We did it'?" Tony said.

"Shhh," Cal said. "Don't ruin this beautiful moment."

Min looked at him. "You don't mind?"

"Why would I?" Cal said.

"Well, she . . ." Min let the word trail off.

"Is history," Cal said.

"Okay," Min said, trying very hard not to feel glad about that.

"How about David?" Cal said.

"Not even history," Min said. "The man brought me an Eiffel Tower snow globe, for heaven's sake."

"We should send them a nice bottle of wine," Cal said.

"Why?" Tony said.

"So they'll get drunk and go back to bed," Cal said. He caught Liza frowning down at him and said, "What now?"

"Nothing," Liza said. "I'm just thinking."

"Well, think about somebody else," Cal said. "Think about Tony."

"I have Tony figured out," Liza said. "You, however, are a mystery."

"I'm a mystery," Tony said, wounded.

"Want to have sex tonight?" Liza said.

"Yes," Tony said.

"No mystery," Liza said, and turned back to Cal. "Do you have any weaknesses?"

"Min," Cal said, smiling at Min.

Liza closed her eyes in disgust. "I'm trying to think if I've ever seen you caught off guard."

"Well, there was the time Bentley hit me with the ball," Cal said.

"I know." Liza straightened behind Cal's chair. "Singing. You're not shy but you won't sing. Why is that?"

"Lousy voice," Cal said.

Liza looked at Tony. "True?"

"Nope," Tony said. "Quit hassling him."

"You take care of your friends, I'll take care of mine," Liza said to him and turned back to Cal. "So why not?"

"Stage fright," Cal said. "I can't perform in public. Too self-conscious."

"You?" Liza said. "I would never have guessed it." She folded her arms. "So what would it take to get you to sing?"

"A gun pointed at my head," Cal said.

"*Liza,*" Min said, seeing a light in Liza's eyes that boded no good for anyone. "Why are you pushing this?"

"Here's the deal," Liza said, leaning over Cal's shoulder, her mouth close to his ear. "You sing right now, here, in front of everybody—"

"No," Cal said.

"—and I will never say or do another thing to keep you away from Min."

Cal sat very still for a minute, and then he said to Min, "Does she keep her deals?"

"Of course she does," Min said. "Which doesn't mean—"

Cal looked up at Liza. "What do you want to hear?"

"Oh, I'll let you pick," Liza said, straightening. "That should be interesting all by itself."

"Why are you doing this?" Min said to Liza, exasperated.

"Because up until now, he's had it easy," Liza said, still watching Cal. "I want to see if he'll break a sweat for you."

"It hasn't been all that easy," Cal said.

"You don't have to do this," Min said to Cal. "I mean it."

"Why?" Cal said. "Men have been singing to women for centuries. It's right up there with giving them jewelry."

"Buy me a nice keychain," Min said.

He put his hand on the back of her chair and leaned forward. "Pay attention, Minnie, because you'll never hear me do this again."

"Cal," she said, but then he began to sing "Love Me Tender," his snarky grin in place as he oversold the song, deepening his voice in a not-bad Elvis impression.

"Not *Elvis*," Tony groaned, and Roger shook his head and laughed at the ceiling, but Min lost her breath because Cal's voice was beautiful and because, after the first verse, his grin faded, and he began to sing it for real. All other sound stopped, and it was just the two of them as he looked into her eyes and asked her to love him, and she felt dizzy because he meant it, whatever else was going on, whatever else was happening between them, this was real. Even if it was just for this moment, *and it's just for this moment,* it was real, and he loved her, and it was better than anything she could have dreamed of, and she felt her heart ache, felt it clench in her chest because she loved him so much she couldn't stand it. *Don't do this to me,* she thought as he sang, *don't break my heart, I don't deserve this, please don't,* and when he finished, perfectly on key with "I love you, and I always will," the silence around them was deafening. *Oh, God,* Min thought, and looked in his eyes and saw the same surprise there, and regret and confusion, and she thought, *It wasn't him, it's this* thing *that's haunting us, he didn't mean it.*

Then Diana said, "Wow," and Liza said, "All right, I am impressed," and Min grabbed her purse and walked out of the restaurant.

Chapter Twelve

Min let the restaurant door bang behind her and crossed the sidewalk, blind with the need to save herself. She stepped off the curb and a horn blared and somebody yanked her back from the street, and she turned and barged into Cal.

"I'm sorry," he said, holding on to her. "Whatever it was that I did—"

"You're going to hurt me," she said, breathless.

"What?" he said, looking appalled. "*No*. I'd never—"

"You're going to break my heart," Min said, taking a breath like a sob. "I'm going to love you, and you're going to leave, you always do, it's what you do, and I don't think I can get over you, if I ever let go and love you, I think it'll be forever because it's so deep, it already hurts just the little bit I let myself—"

"Min, I'd *never* hurt you," Cal said.

"Not on purpose," Min said. "But you have the right to leave. You've never promised me you'd stay. That's the way it always is. You're wonderful, you know us, and we love you, and you leave. I can't do that. I could tell myself that David was an idiot who didn't know me, but you know *me*."

"Min, wait," Cal said, trying to put his arms around her.

"*No,*" Min said, slipping away. "Nobody in my life has ever known me the way you do. Nobody in my life has ever made me feel as good as you do. You know me, you know everything about me, and when you leave me, you're going to be leaving the real me, the me nobody else has ever seen, that's who you're going to be rejecting."

"What makes you so sure I'm going to leave you?" Cal said, his voice sharp.

"Because that's *what you do.* You *always leave.* Are you going to promise me right now that you'll stay forever?"

"I've known you three weeks," Cal said. "That'd be a little impulsive, don't you think?"

"*Yes,*" Min said. "So why the full court press? Why the perfect shoes and the perfect song and . . ." She shook her head, helpless. "I *told you* we should start as friends, *I told you*—"

"You want more than friends," Cal said flatly. "That's the dumbest line you ever pulled on me."

"Look, I'm not *ready* for you," Min said. "I'm not *prepared.* I don't have any defenses when you're around. I make these plans and I mean it, I really do, and then I kiss you because I'm crazy about you which would be fine if I didn't fall in love with you but there that is, just standing there, and you know it, you know you've got me." She stopped because she was sounding hysterical.

"All right," Cal said, setting his jaw. "Maybe we—"

"I need to go home," Min said.

"All right," Cal said again. "We can—"

"*No,*" Min said. "Diana will be out to find me in a minute and she'll walk me. We'll walk each other."

"Min," Cal said.

"I just wasn't expecting that song," Min said. "Not the way you sang it."

"Neither was I," Cal said grimly.

"I know," Min said. "I could see it in your eyes. You didn't mean it."

"Of course I meant it," Cal snapped, as Diana came out into the street. "I just didn't know I meant it until I sang it. Fucking Elvis and his love songs."

"Well, that's the thing about Elvis," Min said, finally losing her temper. "You make all the fun you want of the fried bananas and the sequined jumpsuits, but he never lied when he sang, he always meant it. There weren't any damn secrets—"

"*What* secrets?" Cal said.

"—and there weren't any damn lies. So the next time you want to snow somebody, *don't channel Elvis.*"

Min turned away and started off down the street, making her heels click on the pavement like a backbeat.

"You know, all I wanted was a little *peace and quiet*," Cal yelled after her. "But no, I had to get *you.*"

Diana hurried behind her to catch up.

"Why are you upset?" Diana said when she was beside her. She looked back over her shoulder at Cal. "That was the most romantic thing I've ever heard."

"I know," Min said and walked faster.

"What's *wrong?*" Diana said.

Min stopped. "I'll tell you if you tell me what's wrong with you and Greg."

Diana bit her lip. "You first."

"The first night Cal picked me up?" Min said.

Di nodded.

"He did it because David bet him ten bucks he couldn't get me into bed in a month," Min said.

"No, he didn't," Diana said, positive. "He wouldn't do that."

"I heard him, Di," Min said. "He did it. And I know there's more there now, but I've only known him three weeks, and I'm already lost whenever he's around, and it's just too big a gamble. He's just . . . he leaves women all the time. Greg was right about that. I don't want to be in a place where I'll die if he leaves me because he's going to leave me." She felt tears start and blinked them back. "And then the son of a bitch sings to me like that, and I just . . . He's just too . . ."

"Dangerous," Di said. "That's why I picked Greg. I knew he'd never be dangerous."

"What happened?" Min said.

"I don't think he wants to get married anymore," Di said, and Min heard the tears in her voice. "I asked him, I told him if he wasn't ready we could postpone it, but he keeps saying he's ready, he wants to, and I think it's just because he can't stand disappointing everybody but he's—"

"What are you guys doing?" Tony said, coming up out of the dark and scaring them both into shrieks. "Standing around waiting to get mugged?"

"And now our wait is over?" Min said, trying to get her breath back.

"Cal sent me," Tony said. "He doesn't like you walking home alone. So you get me."

"You don't have to," Min said.

"Are you kidding? I'm with two hot women in the dark," Tony said. "By the time I'm finished retelling this in my head, it's going to be phenomenal."

"Is he joking?" Di said to Min.

"I don't think so," Min said. "Could you picture me about twenty pounds lighter in this fantasy?"

"No," Tony said. "I'm picturing you just the way you are, babe. Don't tell Cal or he'll break my teeth."

"Your teeth are safe," Min said, and began to walk again.

"So what would we be doing in this fantasy?" Di said to Tony as they fell into step beside Min.

"Well, first we'd read a good book because I know that classy women like you go for guys who read," Tony said.

Min took his arm. "Thank you for walking us home."

"Anything for you, kid," Tony said, patting her hand, and then he went on with his fantasy, and Min held on to him and tried not to think about what she was walking away from.

Back in the restaurant, David looked at Cynthie triumphantly and said, "We did that."

"No," Cynthie said, her face white. "That wasn't us."

"Min was jealous," David said, feeling better than he had in weeks. "And then Cal made a fool of himself with that stupid song and embarrassed her. You were right about us . . ." He waved his hand and added silently, . . . *having the best sex in the history of the world. God, I'm good.*

"I wish that were true," Cynthie said, still staring at the door.

"You know they're out there fighting," David said. "Why aren't you happy?"

"There's a certain kind of fight that is . . . a relationship adjustment," Cynthie said, her voice dull. "You fight, and then reconcile and move closer together. And then fight again, and reconcile. Each time there's a compromise. Each time you grow closer."

"Fighting is good?" David said. "That's nonsense."

"What's the best kind of sex there is, David?" Cynthie said. "Make-up sex. It's because you've come back even closer. If it's the right kind of fight. You're going to have to move fast if she truly is upset with him."

"I'll call her tomorrow," David promised. "She's emotional right now. Better to let her calm down."

Cynthie looked back at the door. "All right. Be careful."

"Stop it," David said, covering her hand with his. "We won."

Cynthie shook her head. "Nobody won tonight."

Later that night, after Min and Diana had folded two hundred cake boxes and talked about the wedding but not Greg or Cal, Diana went to bed, and Min sat alone on the couch with Elvis in her lap, and tried to figure out where she'd gone wrong. Maybe if she hadn't said yes to that picnic in the park, if she hadn't kissed him back, if he hadn't kissed her at all, if she hadn't met Harry. Definitely before she met Harry. Maybe if she hadn't thought she was so damn smart that she could play David and Cal in the beginning. Maybe if she'd had enough sense not to cross the damn bar in the first place, if she'd looked at him and known nothing good could come of him and had never overheard that damn bet. It was hard to pinpoint exactly where she'd moved past reckless and into insanity, but she kept thinking if she could just figure out where she'd gone wrong, she'd understand what happened, and then she'd be done with it—

Somebody knocked on the door, and when Min opened it, Bonnie was standing there in her chenille robe holding a teapot. "I made cocoa," she said, and Min felt the tears start. "Oh, baby," Bonnie said and came in, putting her arm around Min, balancing the cocoa pot in her other hand. "Come on. We just need to talk about it."

"I thought I was so smart," Min said, fighting to keep her voice steady. She took a shuddery breath. "I kept thinking I had it all under control."

"I thought you did pretty well," Bonnie said, putting the cocoa pot down on the sewing machine table. She took a cup out of each pocket, and Min laughed at her through her tears.

"Where's Roger?" Min said. "I don't—"

"He's asleep downstairs," Bonnie said, picking up the pot. "He's worried about you, but it gets to be midnight and he clonks right out for a solid eight hours."

Min laughed again and then sniffed. "If I'd had any brains, I'd have grabbed Roger that first night."

"Roger would bore you to tears," Bonnie said, handing her a filled cup. "Just like I'd have shoved Cal under a bus by now."

"You would have?" Min sniffed again.

"Oh, please, that master of the universe act?" Bonnie said. "That's one scared man you've got there. I don't have the time for that. I want kids, I don't want to marry one."

"He's a good guy, Bon." Min sipped her cocoa and began to feel better.

"I know," Bonnie said. "And some day he'll grow up and be a good man. In the meantime, he broke your heart so I'm mad at him."

"No, he didn't," Min said. "He tried not to be with me."

"No, he didn't." Bonnie sat down next to her on the couch with her own cup. "He had every opportunity in the world to get away from you and he passed up every one of them to be with you."

"That's because he couldn't charm me," Min said. "It wasn't—"

"Oh, stop being such a baby," Bonnie said, and Min jerked her head up and startled Elvis. "Well, listen to yourself. You're miserable, but it's not his fault and it's not your fault. Well, screw that."

"*Bonnie,*" Min said, scandalized.

"What do you want, Min?" Bonnie said. "If life were a fairy tale, if there truly was a happy ending, what would you want?"

"I'd want Cal," Min said, feeling ashamed even as she said it. "I know that's—"

"Don't," Bonnie said, holding up her hand. "Why do you want him?"

"Oh, because he was *fun*," Min said, smiling as she blinked the tears away because she was so shallow. "He was so much fun, Bonnie. And he made me feel wonderful. I was never fat when I was with Cal."

"You're never fat when you're with Liza and me," Bonnie said.

"I know," Min said. "He was almost like you except I couldn't trust him and he really turned me on."

"Maybe that's why he turned you on," Bonnie said. "Somebody you couldn't handle."

"Yeah." Min let her head drop back against the couch. "He was exciting. I never knew what was coming next. And neither did he. We fed off each other. What dummies we were."

"I wouldn't rush to use the past tense," Bonnie said. "So back to the fairy tale. Tell me your happily ever after."

"I don't have one," Min said. "Which is why I'll never get one."

"Mine," Bonnie said, "is that I marry Roger, and we have four kids. We live in a nice house in one of the suburbs with good schools, but not one where everybody wears plaid."

"Makes sense," Min said, and sipped her cocoa again.

"I'm a stay-at-home mom," Bonnie said, "but I do keep a few clients, my favorite clients, and I watch their portfolios like a hawk so I don't lose my edge. And word gets out, and as the kids get older, I add to my client list because there are so many people who are dying to get me."

"That's not a fairy tale," Min said, putting her cocoa cup down. "That can all happen."

"And our house," Bonnie said, as if she hadn't heard, "becomes the place everybody comes home to, for the holidays and everybody's birthdays, everybody comes to us. And we have these big dinners and everybody sits around the table and we're family by choice. And you and Liza and Cal and Tony are all godparents to our kids, and every time there's a big school thing, you all come out and cheer our kids on—"

"I'll be there," Min said, trying not cry.

"—and none of us will ever be alone because we'll have each other," Bonnie said. "You're going to like my grandchildren, Min. We're going to take them shoe shopping."

"Oh, *Bonnie*," Min said and put her head down on the couch cushion and howled, while Bonnie stroked her hair and drank her chocolate.

When Min had subsided to a few gasping, shuddering sobs, Bonnie said calmly, "Now you."

"I *can't*," Min said.

"Well, you're gonna," Bonnie said. "It starts with Cal, right?"

"Why?" Min sat up and wiped her face with the back of her hand. "Why does it always have to start with some guy?"

"Because it's a fairy tale," Bonnie said. "It all starts with the prince. Or if you're Shanna, with the princess, but still. It starts with the big risk. You're all alone sitting on a tuffet, on in your case, an Aeron, and this guy rides up and there it is, your whole future right there before you—"

"What if he's the wrong one?" Min said. "Accepting for the moment, which I don't, that the whole thing starts with the prince, how do you tell the prince from—"

"The beast?" Bonnie said. "Honey, they're all beasts."

"Roger isn't," Min said.

"Oh, please," Bonnie said. "He's down there snoring like a bear now," and Min laughed in spite of her tears. "You really think Cal's a mistake?"

Min swallowed. "Well, logically—"

"Do not make me dump my cocoa on you," Bonnie said.

"I don't have anything else to go on," Min said. "How am I supposed to know?"

"Tell me your fairy tale," Bonnie said. "It's just between you and me, nobody else will ever know. If you could have anything you wanted, no explanations, no logic, just anything you—"

"Cal," Min said. "I know that's stup—"

"Stop it," Bonnie said. "God, you can't even dream without qualifiers. Tell me your fairy tale."

Min felt the tears start again, and she gathered Elvis up and petted him to distract herself. "It's Cal. And he loves me, so much that he can't stand it, as much as I love him. And, uh," she gulped back tears, "we, uh, we find this great house, here in the city, maybe on this street, one of the old bungalows like the one my grandma used to live in. I'd like that. With a yard so Elvis could stalk things. And maybe a dog, because I like dogs."

Bonnie nodded, and Min sniffed again.

"And I keep working because I like my work, and so does Cal because he loves what he does." She sighed. "And sometimes he calls me up and says, 'Minnie, I've been thinking about you, meet me at home in twenty minutes' and I do and we make love and it's wonderful, right in the middle of the day. . . ." She stopped to sniff and Bonnie nodded.

"And sometimes we go to Emilio's, we meet all you guys at Emilio's, like every Wednesday, we all meet, and we laugh and catch up on what's happening, and when you and Roger have your kids, Emilio adds more tables, and he and his wife and kids eat, too, and Brian serves us, and sometimes we go out to your house . . ."

Bonnie smiled and nodded.

". . . and the guys watch the game and hoot and moan, and you and I and Liza and Emilio's wife sit out in the kitchen and eat chocolate and talk about all the things we've done and they've done and laugh. . . ." Min took another deep breath and realized she was still crying.

"And then Cal and I go home," she said, her voice breaking, "and it's just the two of us, and we laugh some more and hold each other and eat and make love and watch dumb movies and just . . . be with each other. We just feel good because we're with each other." She wiped her eyes again. "That's all I'd need. The two of us, talking and cooking and laughing. It's so simple."

She took a deep shuddering breath and met Bonnie's eyes. "I can have that, can't I?"

"Yes," Bonnie said.

"But only if Cal is who I need him to be," Min said.

Bonnie nodded.

"So I just have to trust that he's who I think he is and not who he thinks he is," Min said.

"Big gamble," Bonnie said.

"Do you ever wonder what happened after the happily ever after?" Min said. "After the wedding was over and the townspeople went home, and they finished opening all the stuff that was monogrammed with a gold crown? Because the story's over then. All the questing and the courting and the trauma. From then on it's just sitting around the castle, polishing all the toasters they got for wedding gifts."

"That would pretty much depend on the prince," Bonnie said. "I can see David polishing a lot of toasters."

Min laughed in spite of herself.

"But Tony would hot wire them all together and calibrate them so they'd shoot toast at varying intervals," Bonnie said and Min laughed harder.

"And Cal would bet on it," Min said, smiling and crying at the same time now, "but only after he'd seen Tony shoot the toasters a thousand times and calculated the odds."

"And Roger would put out stakes and yellow tape so that nobody got hit by flying bread," Bonnie said with affection.

"And Liza would figure out how to make the whole thing pay," Min said. "And you'd make sure Tony bought the bread at cost and invested the profits wisely."

"And you'd look at the whole thing and gauge the risk and tell us what we'd missed," Bonnie said.

"You know this toaster thing might be worth looking into," Min said. "Tony's nuts, but his ideas are always good."

Bonnie nodded.

Min bit her lip and swallowed more tears. "I want the fairy tale."

"Okay," Bonnie said. "Now all you have to do is figure out how."

"Yeah," Min said. "I can do that. I just have to think it out." She looked at Bonnie. "Are you going to dump cocoa on me?"

"No," Bonnie said. "The only illogical thing you have to do is believe. After that, you need brains."

"Oh, good," Min said. "Brains, I got. Leap of faith, taken. Plan, still in the works."

Bonnie nodded again. "Can you sleep now?"

"Uh huh," Min said, tearing up again. "Why can't I stop crying?"

"When was the last time you cried?" Bonnie said.

"I can't remember," Min said.

"When was the last time you cared enough to cry?" Bonnie said.

"I can't remember that, either," Min said, appalled.

"So you've got some catching up to do," Bonnie said, standing up. "I have to go downstairs and sleep with a bear."

Min gave her a watery grin. "Do not expect me to feel sorry for you because you've got Roger."

"I don't," Bonnie said airily. "I expect you to envy me beyond measure."

"I do," Min said, thinking of the man she'd left enraged in the moonlight. "But I want Cal."

Cal didn't call, and that was all right, Min told herself, because she'd see him at the rehearsal dinner since he hadn't called to cancel, plus she didn't have time to think about him with the wedding only four days away, especially since she found herself fielding a dozen calls a day from her increasingly frantic sister, and anyway she was better off without him as a distraction.

She missed him.

Sunday, she kept telling herself, *on Sunday this will all be over, Diana will be married, and I can fix my own life then.* The only part she wasn't sure about was the "Diana will be married," but since Diana was insistent that her romance was a fairy tale, there wasn't much Min could do besides hold her hand, make supportive noises, and listen. So she propped Diana up, went to the If Dinner on Thursday night and brought the rest of the hand-packed quarts of ice cream that Cal had given her, told Liza there was no need to apologize for making Cal sing since their fight had been inevitable, and tried to figure out a way to make things right without actually talking to him or seeing him.

But on Saturday morning, she had to go to baseball for Harry, so she put on her newest sandals—clear plastic mules with French heels and cherries on the toes—and got to the park a couple of minutes after the game started. She found a seat to one side, trying to stay inconspicuous and wave to Harry at the same time, but Bink saw her and motioned her up. Min smiled at her and then realized that the man sitting next to her wasn't just a miscellaneous father, he was Reynolds. Cynthie was on Bink's other side, wedged in next to another parent, which meant Min was going to be stuck sitting beside Reynolds. *This has to be payback for something*, she thought, and climbed to the top and sat down.

"So how we doing?" she asked him.

"These kids can't play," Reynolds said, shaking his head. "No discipline."

"Well, you know, they're *eight*," Min said.

"Discipline starts young," Reynolds said, looking at her with contempt, and Min thought, *There goes our chance at bonding*.

Down on the field, Bentley bobbled a catch and the ball rolled over to Harry, who picked it up and threw it in the general direction of a base he thought might be appropriate.

"Oh, God, *Harry*," Reynolds said loudly.

Min saw Cal off to one side of the field and felt her stomach lurch. *Ridiculous*, she told herself and swallowed hard. He spread his arms out at Harry as if to say, *What?* and Harry shrugged and crouched down again. Cal shook his head but Min could tell from the set of his shoulders that he wasn't mad. When he turned around he was grinning, and then he caught sight of her and his grin vanished, and she felt the rejection in the pit of her stomach.

Oh, ouch, she thought and looked away to the dugout where Tony was eating a hot dog and shaking his head, and Liza was sitting next to him with her chin on her hand. Down at the bottom of the bleachers, Bonnie was keeping some kind of tally for Roger who would use it to explain to the kids later the importance of something or other. *Lucky kids*, she thought and wished she were down there with Bonnie, or with Liza, or better yet, shoe shopping somewhere. Anywhere but here, looking at what she couldn't have. Or didn't have the guts to go after. Same thing, really.

Throughout the rest of the game, Reynolds continued to express his disgust at the general ineptness of the team in general, winning no friends among the parents in the bleachers, and making an already jittery Min long to hit him with something. Bink grew more and more owl-like, and Min wondered why she put up with him. *I'd have left his ass a long time ago.*

Down on the field, Harry came up to bat. He looked up at them, and Min waved to him, smiling. He pounded his bat on the ground a couple of times and then put it on his shoulder, dead serious. And when the pitch came, he missed it by a mile.

"Come on, Harry," Reynolds yelled. "You can do better than that. You're not trying."

Shut up, Reynolds, Min thought.

Down on the field, Harry's shoulders hunched a little, and up in the bleachers, Bink grew even stiller.

Harry fanned the next one, too, and Reynolds yelled, "Concentrate, Harrison! You can't swing at anything like a *dummy. Think*," and Min saw Cal look up at his brother, his face set.

Might want to ease back on that, Reynolds, Min thought, and then Harry stiffened up and swung at a pitch that was so bad it didn't even cross the plate, and Reynolds stood up and yelled, "Harry, that was *stupid*, damn it, can't you do anything right?," and Harry froze, his little shoulders rigid, and Cal left the field, coming straight for his brother, murder in his eyes.

"No, no," Min said, panicking as Cal hit the bleachers. She stood up and stepped in front of Reynolds and hit him hard on the arm with her fist.

"Hey!" Reynolds said, grabbing his arm.

"You miserable excuse for a parent," she said to him under her breath. "You do *not* humiliate your kid like that." She raised her voice and yelled, "Harry is really smart, he's always smart," and then she whispered, "But you are the dumbest son of a bitch I have ever seen in my life."

"I beg your pardon," Reynolds said, outraged.

"It's not my pardon you need, you miserable butthead," Min whispered, leaning closer. "It's your kid's, the one you just humiliated in front of all his friends, and if you think that made you look good to anybody here, your head really is up your butt."

"You're out of line," Reynolds said, but he looked wary now, darting a glance at the other parents, who were clearly not amused. He shook his head, trying for bluster. "Who the hell do you think you are?"

"Well, for starters, she's the woman who just saved your ass," Cal said from behind her. "Because I was going to throw it off the bleachers until she got in my way."

"You," Reynolds said, looking past Min. "Like you could do anything about it. You can't even coach these kids—"

"Oh, give it up," Min said. "You know you screwed up, and the best you can do is blame your brother?"

"Listen," Reynolds said, raising a finger. "You are not—"

"You know, Reynolds," Cal said. "When you get home, you're going to figure out that you just gave your kid the same kind of flashback you and I have been having all our lives. And while you are a butthead, you're not a mean butthead, so that should give you some good nightmares about your parenting skills. In the meantime, you're picking a fight with somebody who takes no prisoners. I'd back away slowly if I were you."

"We're going home," Bink said.

"I don't see why—" Reynolds began and then Bink looked at him, her gray eyes steely cold.

"We," she said, "are going home where we will discuss this. Min, will you and Cal see that Harry gets home safely?"

"Yes," Cal said from behind her, and Min nodded, shaking now that the first adrenalin rush had passed. She stepped sideways, back to her own seat, feeling incredibly rash, not to mention rude, and when she turned and sat down, Cal had already started back down the bleachers, Reynolds and Bink following him.

Out on the field, Harry had his back to them, but Tony was talking to him, so that was all right. Of course, Tony was probably telling him that his father was a jerk, but as far as Min was concerned, that was all right, too.

She glanced over at Cynthie, who looked thoughtful. "Hi," Min said, taking a deep breath. "Enjoy the show?"

"I wouldn't have done it," Cynthie said, "but good for you anyway. You have more guts than I have."

"It wasn't guts," Min said. "I probably overreacted."

"No," Cynthie said. "Cal overreacted, but he couldn't help it. Reynolds played that family script and it makes Cal insane. He can't stand being called stupid."

"They get that a lot when they were kids?" Min said.

"I think they both had lousier childhoods than we can imagine," Cynthie said. "That doesn't mean you get to hit your brother in front of your nephew."

"He probably wouldn't have," Min said.

"I don't know," Cynthie said. "But now you're the bad guy for the family, not him. So you did him a favor there."

"I was already the bad guy," Min said. "His parents hated me."

"I don't think they like anybody much," Cynthie said. "They're very self-absorbed people. Not cruel. They just don't pay attention."

"So," Min said. "You're the psychologist, right? What do we do for Harry?"

"Cal will take care of it," Cynthie said, nodding down at the field, where Harry and Cal were now sitting in the dugout. She tilted her head at Min. "It was doubly bad because you were here, you know. Harry has such a crush on you that to be embarrassed like that . . ." She shook her head and sighed. "You're right. Reynolds is a butthead."

"Is that the clinical term?" Min said.

"In Reynolds's case, yes," Cynthie said.

Down in the dugout, Tony sat down next to Liza and said, "You know, I used to think that if I was ever in a bar fight, I'd want you backing me up, but I think Min just moved ahead of you in the ranking."

"I wouldn't cross her," Lisa said. "That man is a complete loss."

"Yeah," Tony said, his eyes on the field. "But Harry'll be okay. He has Cal and Bink and Min on his side. I'd take that team any day. Christ, look at that." He raised his voice. "Hey, Soames, look where you're throwing the ball." He shook his head but kept watching Soames anyway, ready to help.

That was Tony all over, Liza thought. He acted like a big lug but if anybody needed him, he was there.

She was really going to miss him.

"Tony," she said as he bit into his hot dog, waiting until he was eating on the theory that it would soften the blow. "We are not going to work out."

"What was your first clue?" Tony said around his hot dog, his eyes still on the field.

Liza let out her breath in relief. "It's not that you're not a great guy—"

"I know." Tony swallowed and bit into his sandwich again. Out on the field, a kid bobbled a catch, and he closed his eyes. "*Jesus.*"

"We just got caught up in that threesome thing," Liza said, and Tony stopped chewing and looked at her. "I mean, the three of us, the three of you. You know."

"Right." Tony resumed chewing and watching the field.

"Bonnie and Roger," Liza said, "that's a little spooky, but Bonnie doesn't make mistakes."

Tony swallowed. "Neither does Roger. They'll be okay."

Liza nodded. "And Min and Cal . . . well, I don't know, but he's not taking her for a ride, so I'm butting out of that one."

"Good." Tony took another bite, squinting at the field.

"But you and I are toast," Liza finished.

"Yep." Tony shook his head at the field. "That kid has no arm."

"I'm glad to see you're taking this so well," Liza said, annoyed.

Tony shrugged. "I like you, but you're always charging someplace, creating disturbance, and I like my stability."

"Chaos theory," Liza said.

"Yep," Tony said. "Disturbed systems move to a higher order or disintegrate. We disintegrated. Also, you hate sports. Big deal. Nobody's mad. What's not to take?"

"Then why didn't *you* end it?" Liza said, annoyed.

"I liked the sex. Oh, hell." Tony scowled at the field where a hapless child had just missed a grounder. "You know, some kids should not play baseball."

"Actually, I liked the sex, too," Liza said, thinking about it.

"Anytime," Tony said. "Now *that's* an arm." He lifted his chin and shouted, "Nice one, Jessica!"

Jessica waved back at him and then forgot Tony and crouched down, waiting for whatever came next.

Jessica is no dummy, Liza thought. "I do like you," she told Tony, and he looked at her and grinned.

"I like you, too, babe," he said. "If you ever need a guy beat up, call me."

"Thank you," Liza said, touched. "If you ever need a woman slapped, you have my number."

"Really?" Tony perked up a little. "Can I watch?"

"And this is why we're no longer having sex," Liza said. "So you're okay?"

"Yes," Tony said, and then yelled, "No, no, no," at the field.

Liza stood up and kissed him on the top of the head. "Don't be mean to these kids," she told him before she left him. "They're going to grow up to own the companies you'll be working for."

A few minutes before the game ended, Min went down to the fence where Cal was leaning on the dugout. She stood there for a minute, not sure what to do, and then she cleared her throat.

"That was good, what you said to Reynolds," she said, hooking her fingers in the chain link. "Really good."

Cal looked out at the field.

Look at me, damn it, Min thought, and searched for something that would get his attention. "And . . . really hot," she lied, and swallowed hard. "I was very turned on. If there hadn't been so many people here, I'd have done you in the dugout."

Cal stood very still and then turned to her, his face still wooden.

Uh oh, she thought.

"Give me five minutes," he said. "I'll clear the place."

Min exhaled in relief. "You had me worried."

"Sorry." Cal walked over to her and leaned on the fence to talk to her, looping his fingers through the chain link so they touched hers. "That was a bad flashback."

"Your dad." Min crossed her fingers over his because touching him again felt so right. "I got that. Is Harry okay?"

"No," Cal said. "But he'll live."

"I don't know if Reynolds will," Min said. "Bink looked like the Angel of Death."

"His ass is grass," Cal said. "Doesn't help Harry much."

"Why did she marry him?" Min blurted. "I'm sorry, but—"

"He blinded her with charm." Cal smiled at her tightly. "He met her in college and took one look at her money and threw everything he had at her. She never had a chance."

Min thought of Bink, probably a frightened little owl in college, running into the glamorous and gorgeous Reynolds. "Why does she stay?"

"Because he loves her now," Cal said. "Harry's birth changed him. He's a lot better than he used to be."

"Damn," Min said. "What was he before?"

"A charming bastard," Cal said, his face grim again as he looked down at her. "Just like all the Morriseys."

"That's not you," Min said.

"Oh, honey, it is sometimes," Cal said miserably. "More than you know."

"I've never seen it," Min said.

"That's because I wasn't a bastard with you," Cal said. "You beat that out of me early."

Min grinned. "Well, you asked for it, Charm Boy."

"Thanks for coming down here," he said softly, and then Tony called him and he went back to the field.

Min went to sit beside Bonnie, and it wasn't until Bonnie reached over and covered Min's hands with hers that she realized she was shaking.

"How's it going there?" Bonnie said.

"This fairy tale thing," Min said. "It's not for kids."

Min went out to the parking lot after the game and found Harry in the backseat of Cal's car, and Cal leaning against the passenger door, waiting for her. *Don't lunge for him*, she told herself. *Harry will notice.*

"How are we doing?" she said.

"We're going to have lunch," Cal said, straightening. "And hear a lot of Elvis because thanks to you, that's now Harry's favorite music." He opened the car door for her.

"That's because Harry has great taste," Min said, sticking her chin out. She got in the car and said, "Hey, fish guy, I hear we're going to the diner for lunch. All Elvis, all the time."

Harry nodded.

"If I were you, I'd ask for processed meats," Min said. "In fact, ask for a brat. Milk this sucker for everything you can get."

Harry looked surprised and then he nodded.

"Ready, Harry?" Cal said as he got in.

Harry nodded at him, soberly. "May I have a brat for lunch?"

"What?" Cal said and turned to look at him.

Harry peered back, woebegone.

"Minerva," Cal said, looking straight into her eyes. "You're corrupting my nephew."

"Me?" Min lost her breath and smiled at him. "No, no. It's just that Americans eat twenty billion hot dogs a year and I think Harry should have one of them."

"Yeah," Harry said from the backseat.

"Twenty billion," Cal said and started to laugh, and Min relaxed a little.

When they were on the road, Min looked over the seat at Harry. "So what's new in the world of fish?"

"Are you wearing those fish shoes?" Harry said.

"No," Min said. "I found another shoe sale. I am wearing glass slippers with cherries on the toes."

Cal looked down at her feet. "They're okay," he said after a moment. "But they're not fish."

Harry nodded.

"So explain to me about ichthyology," Min said, and for the next two hours, Harry did, while Min tried to be fascinated but mostly thought about ways to get Cal to touch her. Anywhere. She'd take a pat on the head. To start with. But even with the distraction of Cal, by the time they were finished with lunch, Min knew more about fish than she thought possible.

"I may never eat seafood again," Cal said, as he held the car door for her.

"Yes, but if there's any money in fish, Harry will support you in your old age," Min said, trying to ignore how close he was, and got in.

When Cal was in the car, too, Min said, "So, Harry, how you doing back there?"

"Can I have a doughnut?" Harry said, looking woebegone again.

"Harrison," Cal said. "You are pushing it."

"Drive to Krispy Kreme," Min told Cal, who rolled his eyes and drove.

When they got there, the "Hot" sign was on, and Harry turned his owl eyes on Min. "Can I have two?"

"Harry," Cal said.

"Yes," Min said. "Today you can have two."

"This is a mistake," Cal said, but he went inside with them and they drank milk and ate warm chocolate-iced glazed doughnuts and talked about fish, and Min remembered the picnic table and tried not to breathe faster. By the time Harry was done with his second doughnut, he didn't look woebegone anymore.

When they got back to the car, Cal said to Min, "You're in the back-seat."

"Okay," Min said, and got in the backseat, not sure why she'd been banished. Maybe Cal had seen the lust in her eyes and was trying to protect himself.

Harry looked happy as a clam riding shotgun for about five minutes. Then he turned green.

"Yep," Cal said and pulled over.

Harry opened the door and lost two doughnuts and a pint of milk into the gutter.

"Oh, honey," Min said, wincing with guilt. "I'm sorry."

"It was worth it," Harry said, wiping his mouth. "And I kept the brat."

Cal passed him a bottle of Evian. "Rinse and spit. At least twice."

"Where'd you get that?" Min said while Harry rinsed and spat.

"I bought it when I paid for the doughnuts," Cal said. "I've been here before."

Harry sat back in his seat. "It's pretty gross out there. Should I pour the rest of the water on it?"

"Sure," Cal said, and met Min's eyes in the rearview mirror. "We Morriseys always wash out gutters with Evian."

"You people are pure class," Min said.

When they pulled into Harry's driveway, which was a clone of

Cal's parents' drive, Harry turned to Cal and said, "Thank you very much."

"You're welcome, Harry," Cal said.

Then Harry leaned between the seats and whispered, "Thank you for the doughnuts."

"My pleasure," Min whispered back, and then she leaned closer and whispered in his ear, "I love you, Harry."

He grinned at her, and then shot a superior look at his uncle.

"Harrison, if you're making time with my girl, you're in big trouble," Cal said.

Harry grinned wider and got out of the car. "See ya," he said and slammed the door.

"He's a little young for you, don't you think?" Cal said, meeting her eyes in the rearview.

Min swallowed. "Yes, but he's a Morrisey. You can't resist that charm."

"Yeah, I thought it was particularly charming the way he barfed in the gutter," Cal said. "You going to move back up here with me?"

"I kind of like it back here," Min said, faking unconcern. "Home, Morrisey."

"Get your butt up here, Dobbs," Cal said, and Min laughed and got out of the car.

When she was in the front seat and Cal had pulled out of the driveway, she said, "Is he okay?"

"Sure," Cal said. "Harry's used to throwing up."

"I mean about the game."

"Yeah," Cal said. "It'll come back to haunt him at odd moments from now on but he'll handle it. He got rescued. The people around him told him he was fine. And Bink will handle it for him at home. It's just tough when it's your dad telling you that you're stupid."

"Yeah," Min said, hating Jefferson Morrisey with a passion. "How are you doing?"

"Me? I'm fine."

"Good," Min said, and took a deep breath. She'd been on simmer for way too long. She had him alone, it was time for a plan. The smart thing to do would be to get everything out in the open, beginning with telling him she knew about the bet, discuss it like adults, and then maybe she could jump him—

"What?" Cal said into the silence.

"What?" Min said, jerking back in guilt.

"You went quiet," Cal said. "Spill it."

"Oh." Maybe a full frontal approach wasn't the way to go. "Well," Min said. "I was thinking . . ."

"Uh huh," Cal said.

". . . that we have some issues to, uh, settle. I think. I would like to settle them."

"Yes," Cal said, sounding as if he didn't have a clue what she was talking about but was willing to play along anyway.

"Because I think . . . maybe . . . we could . . . you know . . . give this a shot," she said. "If we talked."

Cal's hands tightened on the wheel, but he kept his eyes on the road. "All right."

You're not helping, Min thought. "Did you know that seventy-eight percent of couples keep secrets from each other?"

"I wouldn't be surprised," Cal said.

Min nodded.

"You made that up, didn't you?"

"Yes," Min said. "Although I bet it's close. Is there something you're not telling me? Something from . . ." She shrugged. ". . . oh, before you met me?"

Cal didn't say anything, and when she looked over he had that *Oh, hell* look on his face. "You already know," he said, "or you wouldn't ask."

"Well, yes," Min said, every muscle she had tensing. *Why'd you have to ask? All those people who say, "Just talk about it," they're idiots.*

"Min, it was years ago. My life was hell, and she was so great, and Reynolds was treating her like dirt—"

What? Min thought, her stomach plummeting.

Cal shook his head. "She's a good person. I fell pretty hard."

"Oh," Min said, and told herself, *Next time be more specific about the confession you want, you dumbass.*

"Nothing happened, Min," Cal said, glancing at her as he drove. "Bink isn't a cheater, and as much as I want to smack my brother every time I see him, I wouldn't do that to him. We just talked. A lot."

"Uh huh," Min said, trying to sound bright and encouraging.

"It was years ago," Cal said. "She said I was the only person who didn't care about her money. You've met her. You know what she's like. She's wonderful."

"Uh huh," Min said. *I'm going to kill myself now.*

"Are you okay?"

Min turned to look at him and blurted, "Did you love her?"

Cal slowed the car and Min thought, *Oh, just hell, when will I learn not to ask what I don't want to know?*

He pulled over and shut off the ignition and turned to her. "Yes."

"Oh." Min nodded. "Okay. From now on, when I ask you something, just refuse to answer, okay?"

"All right," he said.

"Do you still love her?" Min said.

"Yes," Cal said.

"You don't *listen*," Min said.

"Min, it's not like that. I haven't been in love with her for a long time. I think we both saw where it was going and neither of us wanted that nightmare, and Reynolds starting paying attention to her again, and I dated other women, and over time, it went away."

"Not really," Min said. "There's something nice between you. More than in-law affection."

Cal nodded. "Yes, she's special. But it's not . . . romantic. That was over a long time ago. Years and years ago."

"Uh huh," Min said, still coping.

Cal stared out the window. "Cynthie," he began, and Min thought, *Oh, kill me now.* "She never caught that. She's the psychologist, we were together for nine months, and she never saw that I'd felt like that about Bink. How did you?"

"I'm very acute," Min lied.

Cal slid a little way down in his seat and stared out the windshield, and Min watched the ease in his broad body and wanted him more than she thought was possible. "You know, Cyn spent months trying to figure out why I was a serial dater."

"A what?" Min said, trying to find her way back from lust and misery.

"That's what she called it. The hit and run thing you keep busting me on. She decided it was because I was trying to make up for my mother, that I was trying to get love from all these women, and then when they gave it to me, I'd leave them to try to earn it from somebody else."

"That Cynthie, a theory for every occasion," Min said, feeling bitter and wanting somebody to take it out on. Cynthie seemed good.

"I wasn't looking for my mother," Cal said. "I was looking for Bink." He turned and Min smiled at him so he wouldn't see she was about to open the car door and throw up in the gutter. "I wanted somebody I could talk to, somebody I didn't have to charm and please, somebody it just felt good to be with." He shook his head. "I just didn't realize it until now."

"Well, good luck on that," Min said brightly.

"Pay attention, Minnie," he said. "I was dead in the water the minute you sat down on my picnic table."

Suddenly Min realized there was no air anywhere. That would account for the dizziness.

"It took me a while to figure it out," he said. "I wasn't used to anybody like you. Because there isn't anybody else like you."

Keep breathing, Min thought.

"And then you ripped up at me in the street in front of Emilio's, and I thought, *Well, the hell with you*. For about five minutes. Then I just wanted you back. You're the only woman I've ever wanted back. And I've been trying to figure out a way to get you back ever since."

Min sucked in some air before she passed out.

"I love you," Cal said. "I know it's insane, we've only known each other a few weeks, we need more time, I get all of that, but I love you and it's not going to change."

Min took another deep breath. You needed air to talk.

"For God's sake, Min, *say something*," Cal said.

"I love you," Min said on a breath. "I've loved you forever."

"That'll do it," Cal said and reached for her.

Chapter
Thirteen

Min wrapped her arms around his neck, so grateful to be back in his warmth that she dragged him over the stick shift to get him closer to her.

"Ouch," Cal said.

"Sorry," Min said, trying to pull back.

"Not a problem," Cal said, holding on. "God I've missed you." He kissed her and the glittering heat flared low just like always, except that this time she wasn't fighting it and it went everywhere. She clutched at him, amazed that he was kissing her again, breaking the kiss to kiss him again, over and over until he stopped to breathe.

"Listen," she said. "About my heart. Don't break it."

"Right. Me, too." Cal pulled her back, and she fell into him and lost herself, drunk on the knowledge that she could have him, would have him, that everything was going to be wonderful. She felt his hand slide under her shirt and touch her breast, and she shuddered against him and bit his lip, and his hand tightened on her, and then her cell phone rang.

He pulled back, breathing hard, his eyes dark for her, and she held on to him.

"Ignore it," she said, gasping, "it's Diana, she calls twelve times a day, *come back here and love me*," and he shook his head.

"Answer it," he said, between breaths. "We have to stop. We're parked on a public road."

"I *don't care*," she said, reaching for him again.

He put the car in gear. "Your place or mine, Minnie, *not* in a car."

"Whatever's *closer*," Min said, and answered the phone to stop the ringing as Cal pulled out into traffic.

"*Min*," Diana said, her voice tight. "Oh, *Min*, we're in *trouble*."

"Okay," Min said, trying not to sound dizzy with lust. "What?"

"The *rehearsal dinner*," Di said. "Greg was going to get the caterers because he could get us this deal."

"Oh." Min looked at Cal, who was much too far away. "Greg was going to get the caterers for the rehearsal dinner. In four hours."

"I hate Greg," Cal said.

Diana sounded as breathless as Min felt. "Mom's going to *crucify* Greg and he's already *a nervous wreck. This is my perfect wedding*."

"Okay," Min said. "Let me think." *Cal, naked, in my bed, in me.* No, not that thought.

"What are we going to do? There's *nothing*," Di said.

"I'm trying to think," Min said and met Cal's eyes for a long moment, until the car drifted and hit the edge of the pavement and Cal yanked it back.

"Where is this dinner?" he said, keeping his eyes on the road.

"At some bed and breakfast near the chapel," Min said. "Down by the river. Why?"

"How many people?" Cal said.

"Fourteen, I think," Min said and spoke into the phone. "Dinner for fourteen, right?"

"*Yes*," Diana said.

"We can do it," Cal said. "Tell her it's okay."

"We can?" Min said. "We who?"

"Tony and Roger and I worked in a restaurant, remember? We'll get supplies from Emilio's, you make chicken marsala, and they'll plate it and serve it. Your parents don't know Tony and Roger so they'll buy them as servers. It'll work."

"I'm making chicken marsala?" Min said, and then thought, *What the hell.* "Okay, I'm making chicken marsala." She spoke into the phone. "We've got it covered. Relax. Your job is to give Mom a story if Cal and I are late and to make sure the back door to that kitchen is open. We'll do everything else."

"Oh, thank God," Di said. "I didn't interrupt anything, did I?"

"Yes," Min said. "But it's okay. We have a couple of hours before we have to cook. You can do a lot in a couple of—"

"*No, you don't,*" Diana said. "*Are you crazy?* You've got the *last fitting right now.* We thought *you were on your way.* We're here *now.* We're *waiting for you.* You can't miss *the fitting.* Mom will *kill you.* I *need you.* You *can't*—"

"Right. Now," Min said. "I forgot."

"Don't tell me," Cal said as he slowed the car.

"Fitting," she said to him. "I have a fitting right now. I have to—"

"Not a problem," Cal said, taking a deep breath. "I'll drop you off at the fitting, I'll get the food for the dinner, we'll cook, we'll go to the dinner, and *then*—"

"I have to spend the night with my sister," Min said, closing her eyes. "I hate it, but it's the night before her wedding, I promised—"

"Fine," Cal said. "Not a problem."

"*Maybe not for you,*" Min said, and thought, *Loud voice, loud voice.* She took a deep breath. "I want you *now.* I want—"

"Oh, *Christ,*" Cal said. "I'm trying to be—"

"Min?" Diana said from the other end of the phone.

"I'll be there," Min told her and hung up.

"Where's the fitting?" Cal said, his voice resigned.

"Bridal department at Finocharo's," Min said bitterly. "Why couldn't Greg have been in charge of the dresses?"

Cal drove to the store, kissed her several times, and then drove off to get the dinner supplies, and it wasn't until he was gone that she realized that he still hadn't mentioned the bet.

We didn't have time, she thought. *There's a good reason, I didn't give him a chance, and even if there's not a good reason,* I don't care, *nothing is going to screw this up for me.*

Then she went to face her mother and that damn corset.

"You're late again," her mother said as she came through the door.

"Hi, Mom," Min said, prepared to savage her if she said anything nasty.

"Eat this," Nanette said and handed her an apple.

"Why?" Min said.

"Because God knows what those caterers that Greg got will make. He is completely unreliable. And you know he didn't tell them not to use butter. So fill up on that."

"On this." Min looked at the apple, shook her head, and put it down to go jam herself into the corset. Half an hour later, the fitter left Min's dressing room, and Min stared at herself in the mirror, all heat gone, and thought, *I'd kill myself, but this is not the last thing I want to see before I go.*

She was once again in the blue skirt that zipped up only when she sucked in all the air in the room, the lavender chiffon blouse that still pulled across the bust, and the new blue corset that only laced shut when Min gave up breathing and the fitter used the force of ten. And she wasn't going to be taking any deep breaths now that the damn thing was on: one good heave and she'd pop out the top of it.

Why would Cal want to sleep with somebody who looks like this?

Min came out of the dressing room, and Nanette said, "It still doesn't fit," in a tone that did not bode well for her fat daughter.

"As God is my witness, I have followed that diet," Min said to her, feeling depressed. "Mostly."

"You've had a year," her mother said bitterly. "And now you're going to ruin Diana's beautiful wedding."

"Here's an idea." Min tried to tug the corset up. "Why don't I sprain an ankle and Karen can be the maid of honor? That way the entire wedding party will be beautiful and thin, and—"

"*No*," Diana said from the doorway, and they both turned to her.

"Not your loud voice, dear," Nanette said.

Di pointed at Min. "You're *my sister* and you're going to be my *maid of honor* and you're going to look *beautiful* because that lavender is *just your color* and it's all going to be *perfect*." She had the same maniacal look in her eye that Nanette did, so Min shut up.

"Well, there's nothing we can do about it now." Nanette stood up, disgusted. "You were late, and we have a million things to do. The dinner's in three hours, for heaven's sake. You'll have to try on the rehearsal dinner dress without us."

"Rehearsal dinner dress?" Min said. "Why—"

"I found something for you that will be slimming." Nanette shook her head at her eldest daughter, the disappointment. "Make sure the hem is in the right place. If it cuts you at the knees, your legs will look like fence posts."

"Thank you, Mother," Min said, figuring this was a fight she didn't care about. She just felt tired.

Her mother stopped and met her eyes. "I know you think I'm awful. But I know how the world works. And it's not kind to fat people, Min. It's especially not kind to fat women. I want to see you happy and safe, married to a good man, and it's not going to happen if you don't lose that weight."

"She's *not fat*," Diana said from behind her. "*She is NOT FAT.*"

"Not your loud voice," Nanette said, and Diana glared at her.

"*Screw* my loud voice, stop telling her she's *fat*." Diana stopped, looking as surprised as Nanette and Min that she'd said it. She went on, in a calmer voice. "Leave her alone."

Nanette shook her head and leaned forward to grip Min by the upper arms. "I just want you to be happy," she said, and then stopped and squeezed Min's arms again. "Have you been lifting weights the way I told you to? Because if your arms aren't toned, those chiffon sleeves—"

"We have to go now," Diana said, pushing her mother toward the door. "We'll be late as it is." She turned back at the door and said, "You look *great*," before she left, too.

"Yeah," Min said and turned back to look at herself in the mirror. The chiffon blouse wasn't too bad, but her breasts were just obnoxious.

"Oh, Lord," she said, and tried to sit down but the skirt was too tight.

"Wait a minute, wait a minute," the fitter said and scurried around behind her to unzip the skirt before it split.

"I hate this," Min said as she stepped out of the skirt.

"The color is wonderful on you," the fitter said, and Min looked back into the mirror and thought, *She's right. Diana has a perfect eye for that kind of thing.* "You're lucky you didn't get the green one," the fitter went on as she unlaced the corset and Min began to breathe again. "The colors are going to look lovely going down the aisle, green and blue and your blue-violet, but the little blonde who has to wear the green is so unhappy about it."

Wet, Min thought. Well, that's what you get for dating the groom.

"Now, I'll bring you the dinner dress, and we'll get you all fixed up."

"Yeah," Min said. She took the blouse off and stood looking at herself in the mirror. Full breasts, full hips, full thighs . . . She tried to remember what Cal had said but her mother's voice was louder.

"Here we go," the fitter said, coming back. "We'll just slip this over your head . . ."

Min looked at herself in the mirror as the dresser zipped her up. Her mother had chosen black, of course, a sheath dress with a vertical white insert down the front that made her look vaguely like a penguin. V-shaped inserts at the waist were supposed to give the illusion of a waistline but instead made her look like a penguin whose bow tie was riding low.

"It's very slimming," the fitter said.

"Right," Min said, and picked up her mother's apple. "Slimming."

From behind her Cal said, "*God*, that's an ugly dress," and she turned to see him leaning in the doorway, holding a bottle of wine and two glasses.

Min's heart gave a leap. "Oh, good, it's you."

"What were you thinking, Minnie?" Cal said, coming into the room, his eyes on hers. "Take that thing off. It's an insult to your body."

"Only one of many today," Min said. "My mother picked this out. She has excellent taste."

"I don't think so." Cal put everything on the low table by the couch. "I could pick out a better dress than that."

"You're on," Min said. "I'll give you five minutes while I eat this apple, and then we're hemming this thing so my legs don't look like fence posts. Did you bring a corkscrew? I could use the wine, too."

Cal took the apple out of her hand. "Apples and wine? I don't think so." He tossed the apple in the small gold wastebasket beside the table and pulled a corkscrew out of his pocket. "Your legs are great. Take that dress off. There must be a better one someplace."

"Downstairs," the fitter said eagerly, looking at Cal as if he were the best thing she'd ever seen.

Min looked at Cal and remembered he was gorgeous.

"Hi." Cal smiled at the fitter. "I'm Cal."

"Hi," she said back, smiling wider. "I'm Janet."

Oh, for crying out loud, Min thought.

"Janet, you look like you have exceptional taste," Cal said to her. "I know you didn't pick that thing out."

"No, no," Janet said, disavowing all knowledge.

"I bet you could find her the perfect dress," Cal said, looking right into her eyes, sincerity made flesh. "Maybe something bright red."

"Blue," Janet said. "She looks wonderful in blue or violet."

"So she does. Go find a great blue dress and we'll celebrate with a drink."

Janet hesitated. "Mrs. Dobbs was very clear . . ."

"I'll take care of Mrs. Dobbs," Cal said. "You take care of the dress."

When Janet was gone, Cal screwed the corkscrew into the cork and yanked it, and the cork popped out without a fight. Then he poured her a glass. "Here. You're tense."

"My mother was here," Min said, taking the glass and wishing he was touching her. Except she was fat.

"That explains why Janet looked like a deer caught in headlights." Cal looked over his shoulder. "She's not here and you haven't kissed me in an hour, Minerva. Come here."

Min stepped down off the platform and went to him, loving the way his arms went around her, trying not to think about how fat she must feel under his hands, and then he kissed her hard, and she sighed against him, grateful to have him even if she didn't know why he wanted her.

The bet.

Nope, never, that was not it, she believed in him.

"What's wrong?" he said.

Min shook her head. "Rough fitting."

"Let me guess," he said. "Your mother. Ignore her. Think about me."

She smiled in spite of herself, and he kissed her again, his mouth gentle on hers, and she felt the tension in her body begin to ease.

"There you go," he said, patting her back. "Now drink your wine. I'm going to get you drunk and then have my way with you under the table at the rehearsal dinner."

"Oh, if only," Min said and sipped her wine.

Half a glass of wine and several kisses later, Min was feeling much better, and Janet came back with a hanger full of something dark purple and slinky.

"You're kidding me," Min said. "This is for *me*, remember?"

"No, this one's for me," Cal said, looking at it on the hanger. "I'm taking you to this thing and I'm not going to look at a butt-ugly dress all night."

"Leave," Min said. "I'm not undressing in front of you." *Yet.* She thought of Nanette grabbing her arm and squeezing. *Maybe never.*

"Well, a guy can hope," Cal said, and took his wine out the door with him.

When he was gone, Janet said, "*That's* your boyfriend?"

"Yes," Min said, surprised to realize he was.

"My God, he's *beautiful*," Janet said.

"He's nice, too," Min said. "But about this dress—"

"No, it'll be good," Janet said, shaking the dress out as she held it up. "Your boyfriend likes it. Does he know anything about women's clothes?"

"I think he's removed a lot of them," Min said, stripping off the penguin dress.

"He could remove mine," Janet said and then froze. "Sorry. I didn't mean—"

"Not a problem," Min said, handing her the penguin dress. "I'm used to it. How does this one go on?"

"You pull it over your head," Janet said, giving her the purple dress. "It's a draped surplice top."

"I don't know." Min held the dress up.

"Try it on," Janet said. "*He* likes it."

"And he brought me wine," Min said. "Where's my glass?" She tossed back the rest of her glass and then, with a sigh, pulled the dress over her head and looked in the mirror.

There were many things right with the dress. The surplice neck made her look thinner and the way it draped over her breasts was downright sexy as long as she didn't slump. And the drape made her hips look voluptuous instead of buslike. But still, this was the kind of dress that thin women wore, this was—

"The handkerchief hem is genius," Janet said. "He's right, you do have good legs. They're just . . . curvy."

"Thank you," Min said. "The rest of me is curvy, too."

"You look really sexy in this," Janet said. "I'll go get him so he can see."

"I'll have some more wine," Min said, but the dresser was already gone, Cal-hunting. Min poured a second glass and sipped it while she stared into the mirror. The dress was a vast improvement over the penguin dress. Plus her mother would be annoyed, which served her right. Even better, she wouldn't be able to say anything because Min could tell her that Cal liked it. "So, okay," Min said, toasting her reflection, and knocked back the entire glass. The warmth of the wine spread through her, melding nicely with the warmth from Cal's kisses, and she sighed.

She was bending over the table to get a third glass of wine when Cal came back.

"I hear you look—" he began and stopped.

"What?" Min said, looking up from the wine.

"Uh," he said and she followed his eyes to her cleavage, most of which was displayed because the surplice was gaping. "You look good," Cal said with enough tension in his voice to make it an understatement.

"It's not a fat dress," Min said, turning back to the mirror. "It doesn't hide anything."

"Haven't we talked about this?" Cal said, coming to stand behind her.

"Yes, but my mother has talked since then," Min said. "Also, there's this mirror which tells me I don't have much of a waistline."

"You have a waistline." Cal put his hands on her hips. "It's right here." He slid his hands across her stomach and she shivered, watching him touch her in the mirror. With Cal's hands on her, she looked different, good, and when he pulled her back against his chest, she relaxed into him and let her head fall back on his shoulder. "Very sexy dress," he whispered into her ear, and then kissed her neck. She drew in her breath and he whispered, "Very sexy woman," and moved his hand up to her neckline, drawing his finger down the edge of the silky fabric, making her shudder as the heat spread and she began to feel liquid everywhere.

"I have to stop drinking wine when I'm with you," she whispered to him in the mirror. "I start believing all this garbage you tell me."

He grinned at her, his reflection warming her as much as his body against her back.

She bit her lip. "It feels so good to be alone with you. And I can't because we have to go to this rehearsal dinner, we have to *make* this rehearsal dinner, and then tomorrow I've got to go to this wedding in a ridiculous dress and I'm feeling fat again."

"That's because you're not paying attention," Cal said in her ear. "Look at yourself."

"I am," she said, and he said, "Not the way I look at you." His hand moved up her side and he whispered, "Look at the beautiful curve of you, how full you are," and as his voice in her ear made her dizzy, his hand moved up around her breast.

She turned her head and said, "Hey!" and brought her hand up to move his, and he stopped her breath with his mouth, kissing her hard, catching her hand to press her open palm against the warm heaviness of her breast, and she thought, *That feels so good*, and let the heat wash over her.

"Look how *beautiful* you are," he whispered in her ear as he laced his fingers in her other hand. "There's not a man alive who could see you like this and not want to touch you." He rolled her other hand so her palm was against her stomach and slid it up to her breast. "You're a fantasy, Min. You're my fantasy."

He pressed both her palms against her breasts and she felt the fullness there and shuddered under his hands and believed him. She turned in his arms and kissed him with everything she had, pressing herself against him with no other thought than to get close, loving how hard his body felt against hers, the way her body yielded to him, the heat of his hands on her as they slid down and pulled her to him. She arched her hips against him, bit his lip and licked his mouth, felt him shaking as she whispered, "*I want you,*" and heard his breath shudder as he kissed her on the neck and then softly bit the place he'd kissed.

"Whoops," Janet said from behind them, and Min pulled back, dizzy and breathless.

"We'll take the dress," Cal said, without looking around, his voice husky.

"This is a very dangerous dress," Min said, trying to catch her breath.

"That's why we're taking it," Cal said, and kissed her again before he let her go.

When they got to the bed and breakfast, Diana had left the back door unlocked as promised. "It's a decent kitchen," Cal said when they'd unloaded the car. "We can work here."

"It's a great kitchen," Min said with envy. She turned to Cal and said, "I think—" and he kissed her while she smiled against his mouth and moved closer to him. "What was that for?"

"Because I can," Cal said and pulled her closer. Her cell phone rang, and he leaned back. "What did Greg forget now?"

Min clicked her phone on. "Hi."

"Where are you? We're at the B and B. Mom's fussing over my dress," Diana said, all in frantic whisper. "She wants to know where you are."

"We're downstairs getting ready to cook," Min said, as Cal kissed her on the neck. She stifled a giggle and said, "Stall her."

"She's going to be mad at you," Di said.

"And this is news," Min said. "She'd have been mad when she saw my dress anyway. Cal picked it out. I look like a ho." She felt Cal laugh against her hair.

"Really?" Di said. "What color is it?"

"*Di—*"

"I'll stall Mom," Di said. "*Thank you!*"

"You don't look like a ho," Cal said when Min clicked off her phone. "You look like an expensive call girl." He slid his hand down to her rear end. "And I have money."

"Try to think of cooking as foreplay," Min said, and Cal sighed and started to unpack the food.

Fifteen minutes later, Min had the bottoms of four frying pans covered in hot olive oil, Cal had pounded sixteen chicken breasts flat as flounders and was washing mushrooms, and Diana had stuck her head in to say, "No butter. And thank you, thank you, thank you."

"Where am I, by the way?" Min said as she began to dredge the chicken breasts.

"Cal's car broke down and you're somewhere on 275," Di said.

"My car did *not* break down," Cal said, stopping in mid-mushroom. "I keep that car in—"

"Thank you, that'll work," Min said, and Diana left. "I know, but can you park your male pride for the night?"

"What's in it for me?" Cal said.

"My eternal gratitude," Min said and leaned over the table and kissed him on the mouth, loving the way his mouth fit hers.

"How much gratitude?" Cal said, leaning to follow her as she pulled away.

"More than I can express in a single night," Min said. "Slice some of those, will you? We need some for the salad." She held the first chicken piece over the hot oil and stopped.

"Problem?" Cal said.

"No," Min said and put down the chicken. She rummaged in one of the bags and pulled out a pound of butter. "You know," she said as she opened the box, "you really can't cook without a *little* butter."

"Yep," Cal said and grinned at her.

Min dropped a healthy pat into each of the four pans and inhaled the sweet smell. Then she smiled and dropped the chicken breasts in.

"They'll never know anyway," Cal said.

"My mother can smell butter on me three days after I've eaten it," Min said. "She'll know. I just don't care. Tear up the romaine next, will you? I've got to steam beans."

Half an hour later, Tony and Roger showed up in white shirts and black bow ties with Bonnie behind them.

"What?" Min said, trying not to laugh at the ties.

"Yeah, you snicker now, but you're going to be impressed later," Tony said, and did water goblets faster than she could have imagined, as Roger slung fourteen plates in a row and squirted raspberry sauce on them in a pattern and then plated salads that looked like they'd come from the Ritz.

"I'm impressed," Min said.

"So am I," Bonnie said from her stool at the end of the table where she was cutting scallions into strips, and Roger beamed at her as Tony carried the glasses out.

When Tony came back, he said, "They're all out in the parlor, being polite. Di looks bored. Well, she did until she saw me in this tie."

"Must be hell," Min said over the steaming pan of beans. "I'd much rather be in here with you guys. From now on, I'm catering all my mother's dinners."

"Not once she tastes the butter," Cal said, and helped Tony lay out another fourteen plates for the entrée.

Ten minutes later, the plates were ready for the chicken, the chicken looked like heaven simmering in its dark wine sauce, the green beans were tossed with the almonds and tied into bundles with the scallion strips, and Min was talking to herself.

"Salad, done," she said to herself. "Meat, beans, done. Emilio's corn relish, ready to plate. Rolls out of oven and in baskets. What have I missed? Oh, damn. Dessert."

"I got dessert." Cal picked up the last bag and pulled out two boxes that said KRISPY KREME.

"*Doughnuts,*" Min said, appalled.

"Get me a cake plate," Cal said, and Bonnie rummaged in the cupboard and found one. Then while they watched, he made a ring of seven chocolate-iced cake doughnuts with one in the middle topped by a ring of five chocolate cake doughnuts, topped by a ring of three vanilla-iced glazed, topped by one beautiful chocolate-iced Kreme on top, all stuck together with the white glaze icing that Bonnie had dribbled between the layers.

Min's mouth began to water.

"I read about this," Bonnie said, standing back. "It was in *People* magazine. People do this all the time."

Cal picked up a box he'd set to one side, ripped it open, and dumped out a very small bride and groom under a plastic arch. It looked like hell until he shoved it into the top doughnut, and then it looked funky.

"This is the cake I want at my wedding," Min said. "Of course, my mother is going to go into cardiac arrest."

Cal grinned at her, and she laughed as she took off her apron. "You're a genius, Calvin. I need one moment in the closet to put on my dress, and then it's showtime."

She changed as fast as she could, and when she came back she heard Tony say to Cal, "Okay, we got it. You can go—" He stopped when he saw her, and then Roger turned to follow his eyes and stopped, too, and Bonnie peered out from behind Roger.

"Oh, Min," she said. "You look *wonderful*."

"*Very* hot," Tony said, staring at her, and Cal clipped him on the back of the head. "I'm just *saying*," Tony said.

Cal handed the cake to Roger. "You guys can handle everything now?"

"Piece of cake," Tony said, and Min stopped, startled. "What?" he said.

"Nothing." Min shook her head and then checked her face in the mirror by the door to make sure she wasn't wearing flour as foundation. The heat from the kitchen had flushed her skin and kinked her hair and she looked . . .

"You look beautiful," Cal said, and Min turned and saw Roger and Tony with him, and realized that a month before, she hadn't known any of these guys, and now they'd all come together to bail her sister out of trouble.

"This is so *great* of you," she said to them. "This is so above and beyond the call of friendship."

"Anything for you, babe," Tony said. He bent down and kissed her cheek, and Min blushed, and Cal said, "Enough with the flirting with other men, Minerva," and took her hand, and Roger patted her shoulder as Cal pulled her out the back door.

"Those are the best people," she said to him, as they hit the gravel path around to the front of the house.

"Yes," Cal said. "And now we get to have dinner with your family."

"Oh, hell," Min said.

Looking back on the rehearsal dinner later, Min was hard put to choose the low point of the evening.

There was the moment when Nanette spotted them coming through the door and was so caught off guard by Min's purple dress that she stopped after "You're late . . ." and just glared while Min braced herself.

But then Cal patted her on the back and Greg's best man said, "Whoa," and nodded at her.

"Thank you," Min said.

"I told you so," Cal said in her ear. "Stay away from him."

Or there was the moment when Min saw Greg, who had decided to have his hair cut in a Caesar cut the day before his wedding, and looked, if possible, dumber than ever.

"Don't ever do that," Min whispered to Cal and Cal said, "No, I don't think so."

Or the moment when Roger and Tony were serving the salads, and Di grinned and said, "Gee, such *cute* waiters," and Roger almost dropped Greg's salad in his lap.

"Watch it," Greg said sharply, and Di lost her smile.

"*Very* cute," Min said, and frowned at Greg, who blinked back at her.

Or the moment when Greg's mother said, "This chicken is delicious. Who did you say catered this?" and all eyes turned to Greg. Min let him flounder for a couple of seconds and then said, "Emilio's, wasn't it?", throwing him a rope that he grabbed onto so gratefully she almost felt sorry for him.

That was followed by the moment when Nanette said, "There's *butter* in this."

"Yep," Min said and kept eating while Cal patted her back.

But the low point probably came toward the end of the meal when Min's cell phone rang. She looked over at Diana, startled, since Diana was the only one who would be calling her, and then remembered the trio in the kitchen. "I'll be right back," she said, and slipped outside to answer it. "Hello?"

"Min," David said. "I've been trying to get you all day."

"Why?" Min said. "Never mind, I don't care. This is my sister's rehearsal dinner, David. Go away."

"It's about Cal," David said, and Min grew still. "I still care for you, Min, and you need to know something about Cal Morrisey."

"Do I," Min said flatly.

"That night he picked you up?" David said. "He did it because he made a bet that he could get you into bed in a month."

"He did," Min said, thinking, *What a waste you are.*

"The bet's up next Wednesday, Min," David said, sincerity oozing through the phone. "And Cal Morrisey does not lose. He'll do anything to win that bet. I thought you should know. I don't want you to get hurt."

"Gee, thanks," Min said.

"You don't sound upset," David said.

"Boys will be boys," Min said.

"I thought you'd be shocked," David said, sounding shocked himself.

"David, I knew," Min said. "I overheard you. Which is why I also know that Cal didn't make the bet, you did. It was your idea, which makes you the chief slimeball in this."

"No," David said hastily, "no, I was upset because we'd broken up—"

"David, *you* dumped *me*," Min said. "What the hell were you upset about?"

"—I've regretted that bet a thousand times since, but Cal won't call it off."

"Asked him to, have you?" Min said, not believing him.

"Over and over," David said.

"David?" Min said.

"Yes?" David said.

"Rot in hell," Min said, and clicked off the phone.

She stood on the porch of the bed and breakfast and looked out over the river beyond. It was very pretty. "Damn," she said. She believed in Cal, she really did, but that bet . . .

I'll ask him after the wedding, she told herself. When she was out of that awful corset, when they were alone, when they could talk it out without Diana tugging on her arm for help, she'd ask him then.

Tomorrow night, she told herself and went back inside in time to catch what was definitely the high point of the evening, Nanette's face when she saw the Krispy Kreme cake.

"Hey," David said when Cynthie picked up the phone on Sunday afternoon. "I haven't heard from you. What's—"

"It's over," Cynthie said, and she sounded as if she been crying. "They're in infatuation. It could be years before he comes to his senses. We lost, David."

"No, we didn't," David said. "I don't lose."

"Cal loves her. He's being honest with her. There's nothing—"

"No, he isn't," David said, fed up with hearing about Cal. "He's chasing her to win that damn bet."

"What?" Cynthie said.

"Uh," David said, trying to find a way to explain that without looking like slime.

"Tell me," Cynthie said, her voice brooking no nonsense.

"That first night," David said. "I was mad. And hurt. And—"

"David, *I don't care about you*," Cynthie said. "Tell me about the bet."

"I bet Cal that he couldn't get Min into bed in a month," David said.

"Cal would not make that bet," Cynthie said, her voice sure.

"Oh, because he's too noble."

"He distracted you with something else."

"He bet me he could take her to dinner."

"She left with him because *you made a bet?*" Cynthie said, fury in her voice.

"It wasn't my fault," David said.

"It doesn't matter now anyway." Cynthie's voice dropped back into misery. "Even if you told her about the bet, she'd check with Cal."

"She already knew," David said, resentfully. "I called her and told her last night. She said she'd overheard us."

Cynthie didn't say anything.

"I think she went to dinner with him to make me mad," David said. "He sounded like she was pretty snippy, so she must have made him pay, too." The silence stretched on until David said, "Cynthie?"

"Does he know?" Cynthie said, her voice tight. "Does he know that she went out with him to make him pay?"

"I don't think so," David said. "He hasn't called me to tell me the bet's off, and once he knows that she knows, it's off."

More silence.

"Cynthie?"

"Do you know where Cal is now?" Cynthie said.

"No, but he'll be at Diana's wedding tonight," David said. "What diff—"

"I know how to break them up," Cynthie said, her voice like lead.

"How?" David said.

"Take me to the wedding. If she hasn't slept with him yet, he's frustrated to the breaking point. I'll watch them, and if something makes him tense, if she turns him down again, if something goes wrong . . ." Cynthie paused again, and then he heard her take a deep breath. "I'll tell you, and you go tell him that Min's been making a fool of him all along. Tell him that everybody thinks he's stupid."

"That's enough to break them up?" David said.

"That's enough to give Cal nightmares for years," Cynthie said, her voice miserable. "It's illogical, but it's been his trigger since he was a kid. Push that button and he explodes. If he does it in front of her family and friends—"

"Wow," David said, impressed with her once again.

"What time is the wedding?" Cynthie said.

"Seven," David said. "Diana wanted it at twilight. Some fairy tale garbage."

"Pick me up at six," Cynthie said, and hung up.

Min had spent the night with Diana, who'd been so manic that she'd still been up, fixing bows on cake boxes, when Min gave up and went to bed, too tired even to miss Cal. But the next day, Di was quiet, still tense but not manic with energy anymore.

"I just didn't get enough sleep," she told Min.

When they got to the chapel dressing room, Wet, Worse, and Nanette were waiting, and Min ducked Nanette and her hair combs ("Min, you look awful with your hair like that"), took the cake boxes to the reception hall next door, and then went into the bathroom at the chapel to put her dress on. She was not going to struggle into the damn thing while Nanette made comments and Worse smirked.

Something was very wrong, she thought as she tried to get the corset tied around her. Something besides her insane mother and the idiot wet and weeping bridesmaid in green, something beyond the cake Bonnie was now trying to decorate in orchids and pearls, something, she was pretty sure, much like the groom. *I've got to talk to Di*, Min thought, but what was she going to say? "You're miserable and your groom is a moron and I think we should eat the cake and go home"?

"Oh, hell," she said and left the bathroom to go back to her sister.

"You're late," Worse said, patting her ornate chignon as Min came into the room.

"Bite me," Min said, and went to stand beside Di. "Hey, baby, what's up?"

"Nothing," Di said. "I'm just . . . glad you're here."

"Yes, I am in all my glory," Min said, holding her arms out to show off her gaping corset.

"That corset's not tight enough," Nanette said, and turned her around. "Honestly, Min." She untied the bow at Min's neckline and then began to tighten the laces, working up from the bottom.

"Uh," Min said, as her lungs constricted. "Mother." She put her hand on the back of Di's chair to stabilize herself as Nanette yanked on the ribbons. "I have to be able to . . . breathe . . . during . . . the ceremony."

Nanette gave the ribbons a final excruciating pull at the top, tied them with a knot that would have had Boy Scouts staring in awe, and stood back to consider her work.

"Well, it's the best I can do," Nanette said, and Min thought, *That pretty much sums up our entire relationship*, and turned away from her, her hand on her side, trying to breathe and see Diana at the same time.

"Di?" Min said, and when Di didn't say anything, she leaned over to see her sister's face, constricting her lungs even more.

Di was staring into the mirror, her eyes huge, the line of her beautiful jaw rigid, and Min forgot she couldn't breathe.

"Di? Are you all right?"

"Fine," Di said faintly, not taking her eyes off the mirror.

"You look beautiful," Min said. On Di, even the corset looked right. "Swanlike," Min added, hoping to get a flicker.

"She's just got pre-wedding jitters," Wet said as she settled her wreath of ivy and white baby orchids on her smooth, blond hair. She looked miserable.

Worse nudged Min aside. "Go put your wreath on straight." Her own wreath of cornflowers and orchids was perfectly centered on her head, balanced in back on her chignon.

"Oh, *Min*," Nanette said. "Your *wreath*."

Min picked up her wreath of lavender and orchids and slapped it on her head. At least it smelled good. She jammed a couple of hairpins in to hold it, watching Diana in the mirror the whole time.

Di met her eyes and sat up straighter. "Go away."

"Okay," Min said.

"Not you," Di said. "Everybody but you."

"What?" Worse said, stopping with her hands in midair, reaching for Diana's wreath.

"*Diana*," Nanette said, shocked.

Min took a look at Di's frozen face. "Sister time. We'll see you all outside in a minute."

"Hey," Worse said. "I'm a *bridesmaid*—" Then she saw Diana's face and stopped.

"Out," Min said, jerking her thumb toward the door.

"Well, I'm not going," Nanette said. "This is my daughter's wedding."

"So go to it," Min said. "Weren't the pews all supposed to have flowers?"

"Honestly, Min," Nanette said and stopped. "Of course they're all supposed to have flowers."

"Better check," Min said, and Nanette took off for the chapel.

Wet picked up her bouquet of orchids, leaned over, and kissed Di's cheek. "You look wonderful," she whispered. "You look like a size two!" She handed Worse's bouquet to her and pushed her toward the door, and Worse looked back, not so cocky anymore.

Then Min and Di were alone.

Min leaned against the counter and tried to work her fingers under the edge of the corset to gain a millimeter more of air so she could say what need to be said. "Okay," she said. "This is it. You tell me what's wrong now, or I'm stopping this wedding."

"I want a Krispy Kreme doughnut," Di said, the threat of a sob under the words.

"I'll get you one," Min said, regrouping. "I'll go out and—"

"I can't have one," Di said. "There are twelve grams of fat in every Krispy Kreme."

"Well, yes," Min said, "but I'm thinking since it's your wedding day—"

"Everything is perfect," Di said.

"Not even close," Min said. "Listen, if you want out of this wedding, I'll get the car keys from Cal, and you and I can go back to the apartment and drink champagne and eat many Krispy Kremes."

"Want out?" Di straightened. "No. No."

"Okay," Min said. "But if you change your mind, I'm not kidding about the car keys and the doughnuts."

"I won't change my mind," Di said. "This is my fairy tale wedding."

"Then it's time to go," Min said, hoping action might jog something loose in Di's brain.

Di stood up and Min held out her arms again to show her the corset. "So what do you think?"

"This was a dumb idea," Di said, her voice unsteady as she looked at Min. "Why would I put you in a corset?"

"So I'd have a waistline," Min said.

"You have a waistline," Di said. "It's not a small waistline, but there's nothing wrong with it." She stood looking into Min's eyes, breathtakingly beautiful, cold as ice.

"Okay," Min said, taking her hand. "You *have* to tell me what's wrong."

"Nothing is wrong," Di said. "Everything is perfect."

Worse knocked on the door and poked her head in. "Are you ready?" she asked, sounding more tentative than Min had ever heard her. "Because we're supposed to be lining up."

Di ignored her, and Min said, "We'll be right out."

Worse opened the door farther. "You look wonderful, Di."

Di picked up her bouquet.

"Wreath," Min said, and Di reached down for the wreath of white orchids and roses and slapped it on her head, the fingertip-length veil askew. "Oh. Okay. I can just pin—"

But Diana was already crossing the room.

"I'll fix it," Worse said, giving Min her usual "you're impossible" stare.

"I don't think you can," Min said, and picked up her bouquet and followed Diana out.

Chapter Fourteen

The setting sun flooded the vestibule, but Di's face was pale and cold under her now perfect wreath and veil. George stood beside her, uncomfortable in his morning suit, darting anxious glances at her. He frowned a question at Min, and she shrugged. She felt for him, but he was low on her list of people to save at the moment.

Wet stood in front of them beside the arch, and then the processional started, and she gave her bustle one final twitch, sniffed, broke into a rigid smile, took a step forward, and turned into the chapel.

Worse moved forward, stood counting until it was her turn, blew a kiss to Di, took a step, smiled a broad cheerleader smile, and turned into the chapel.

Min looked back at Di. "You are my sister, and I am with you no matter what. If you want out of this, *I will get you out.*"

"Min?" her father said, startled, and Di shook her head.

"Okay." Min picked up the count from the music, plastered a smile on her face, took a step, and turned into the chapel.

Something caught at her bustle and left her stuck, leaning into the archway in midstep. She looked behind her and saw Di's hand clutching the lavender chiffon ruffles on her butt.

"Diana?" her father said, bewilderment in his voice.

Min stepped back. "Daddy, go smile in the archway so they know everything's all right." She pried Di's hand off her ruffles and towed her out onto the church steps into the waning light. "Talk."

Di's bouquet trembled in her hands. "Greg slept with my brides-maid."

"*Susie?*" Min said, not surprised but sick just the same. "I knew she—"

"Worse," Di said.

"How could it be worse?" Min said and then the other shoe dropped. "*Karen?*"

Di nodded.

"Oh," Min said, trying to think of what to say as her rage rose. "Oh, *honey.*" She put her arm around Di. "Tell me this was before he proposed to you and not—"

"Last night," Di whispered, and Min took a deep breath, corset or not.

"*Son of a fucking bitch.*"

"Thank you," Di said, and sniffed.

"That *whore*, I swear I'll rip out *every hair on her goddamn head.*" Min held Di tighter. "I'll nail her fucking chignon *to the church door,* the miserable *bitch*. And Dad will take Greg apart. He's been wanting to for months."

Di sniffed back a sob.

"We'll take care of you," Min said. "You are *not alone.* Liza and Bonnie—" She broke off, realizing that flaunting her friends wasn't the best move now, trying to imagine how she'd feel if either of one them betrayed her, if Liza slept with Cal, and it was incomprehensible, it couldn't happen, they'd never—

"I watched you and Cal last night," Di said, tears blurring her eyes, "and you were so perfect for each other, you were just you, laughing and whispering together, you didn't have to be anybody else, thin or anything, he loves you just for being you, and I wanted to talk to Greg, I wanted to be that with him, too, so when you fell asleep, I drove over to his apartment, and they were in the bedroom." Her face crumpled. *"They weren't even on the bed."*

Min put both arms around her and held her close. "And Karen's blowing you kisses today. The skanky *whore.*"

"They don't know I know," Di said into her shoulder. "They didn't see me. I backed out."

"That was very mature," Min said, gritting her teeth. "I would have put blood on the walls. Okay, I'll go stop the wedding—"

"No," Di said, straightening fast. Her pearl-studded corset rose and fell as she sucked in air. "No, no. No."

"What?" Min said.

"No," Diana said. "I'm ready to go."

"Okay, I admire how you've handled this," Min said, trying to sound calm, "but I think actually *marrying* the son of a bitch may be carrying maturity *too far.*"

"I have to," Di said, breathless. "It's all planned. There are presents. Bonnie put pearls on a cake."

"I'll eat the cake," Min said. "I'll send the presents back. I'll even maim the groom for you."

"No," Di said. "It wasn't . . . He wasn't . . . It was just pre-wedding jitters. We'll be fine."

"Di." Min took as deep a breath as possible and tried to sound calm. "Pre-wedding jitters means he panics at the bachelor party. *It doesn't mean he fucks your best friend.*"

Di shook her head. "No, no. Not everybody finds a Cal. Greg is a good man. He just . . . panicked. I'm getting married." She swallowed. "I just had to tell somebody. It's a relief to tell somebody."

"Oh." Min felt sick. "Okay. But if you change your mind *at any time,* in the middle of the ceremony, in the middle of your honeymoon, in the middle of the *birth of your first child,* I will be there to help you leave. You say the word and we're *gone.* You are *not alone.*" She tried to take another breath and her corset fought back. "Listen, are you sure? Because I—"

Di nodded. "I just had to tell somebody. I'm okay."

"Wonderful," Min said, "I'm not." She waited another beat for her to back down, but Di walked past her into the vestibule, leaving her nothing to do but follow.

Min smiled at her father, who looked crazed, took her place in the arch, and started down the aisle, vaguely aware that David and Cynthie were in a pew together looking tense, that Bonnie and Liza were in the third pew from the altar sending her "What the hell?" looks, that Cal was in the second row staring fascinated at her neckline, and that Greg-the-bastard was up at the front looking annoyed. *Die, you treacherous scum-sucking pig*, she thought, and that was so inadequate she began to think of other things, not realizing she was scowling until she saw Cal's eyes widen and Greg take a step back.

She smoothed out her face. Okay, there was that "show just cause or hold your peace" moment for stopping weddings, the escape clause. She could say something there. But if she did, she'd ruin Di's wedding, and she had a feeling the wedding was more important to her sister than the marriage. And even if it wasn't, it was Di's choice. She was not going to be her mother, running Di's life for her.

She took her place beside Worse at the front of the church and thought about smacking her in the face with her bouquet. Maybe she could say she'd slipped. A couple of times.

Worse sighed and shook her head at Min, pointing at her own wreath.

Bitch whore, Min thought, and straightened her wreath.

The wedding march kicked in, and Min turned and watched as Diana started down the aisle, a Hollywood vision with the sun shining behind her like a blessing.

Her face was lost, and Min's heart broke for her.

Min turned away and saw Cal frowning at her. He mouthed "What?" at her and she shook her head, almost in tears. Not even he could fix this one.

Di reached the front of the church, the ceremony began, and after a while people began to stir in their seats. *They know something's wrong*, Min thought. They weren't getting that happiness buzz people were supposed to get at weddings. Even Di's bustle looked tragic.

Then the minister said, "If any man can show just cause why they may not lawfully be joined together, let him now speak," and Min took a step closer to her sister.

Di turned to look at her, and Min met her eyes. "Do it."

After a moment, the minister nodded, and began the vows.

Di reached out and clutched Min's arm and whispered, "I do," and Min sighed in relief.

"Not yet, dear," the minister whispered back.

"*No,*" Min said to him. "That's not what she means." She nodded at Diana again. "*Do it.*"

Di swallowed. "I object," she said, but her voice was so faint that the minister leaned forward.

"She *objects,*" Min said loudly.

"To *what?*" Greg said.

"To *you,* you *traitorous son of a bitch,*" Min said, and heard a gasp from the front pews. *Loud voice, loud voice,* she told herself. *Not your loud voice.* Then she looked at Greg again, and thought, *Hell, yes, my loud voice.*

"I object," Di said, her voice up to room temperature again. She turned so she was facing the pews. "I object to the groom sleeping with my bridesmaid last night. I object to the groom being a—" Her voice broke.

"*Cheating, scum-sucking pig,*" Min said to Greg behind Di's back, definitely in her loud voice.

"*Yes,*" Di said, and walked down the steps, her bouquet quivering.

"Also, your hair is *stupid,*" Min said to Greg, and started down the chapel steps after her sister. Greg caught her arm, and said, "*Wait a minute—*" and she swung back to let him have it, and then Cal was between them, shouldering Greg aside. Behind them Wet said to Worse, "You slept with *Greg?,*" and then somebody tapped Greg on the shoulder just as Wet lunged for Worse, and Greg turned around and met George's fist as Wet yanked hard on Worse's chignon, and Worse went ass over elbow into the front pew.

Cal caught Greg by the shoulders just before he hit the ground, and they both looked up to see Nanette, coming at them, exquisite in pearl gray.

"You're a *horrible* man," she said to Greg, and kicked him in the ribs with her pointed Manolo Blahniks.

"*Mother,*" Min said.

Nanette said, "*Thirty-seven goddamn years,*" kicking him on every word, until Min pulled her away. She staggered sideways and ended up facing George, who was trying to get past Cal to hit Greg again. "*And you, too,*" Nanette said and smacked him in the head with her purse.

George put his hands up to ward her off and said, "*What did I do?*" and she stormed down the aisle, her head held high.

Behind George's back, Wet said, "You *bastard,*" to Greg and began to hit him in the face with her bouquet while Worse tried to crawl out of the pew.

"I have to go to Di," Min said to Cal. "Step on his head, will you?"

"Go," Cal said, and the last thing she saw as she turned for the door was Cal dropping Greg on the carpet to block George from hitting him again while Wet whaled on him with her orchids.

Cal found Min at the reception, since Di had insisted on going to meet anybody who might show up. They were sitting in the mostly deserted ballroom with Liza, Bonnie, and an entirely too cheerful Wet, while Roger ferried champagne back and forth and Nanette consoled Di with the news that all men were cheating scum.

"*Mother,*" Min said, and Cal took her hand and pulled her out into the hall with him.

"My mother is *insane,*" Min said to him.

"You just noticed?" Cal said, trying not to be distracted by her bulging neckline. "That looks like it hurts."

"It does," Min said. "I've spent the entire day in bondage." She peered back through the archway. "Look at Wet. She's in there *giggling.* To think that I ever felt sorry for that wench. Did you need me for something?"

"Yes," Cal said, getting a little dizzy as her cleavage rose and fell. "Especially now that you brought up bondage. When can you take that off?"

"I think I could lose it now, except the knots are so tight I can't get them undone." She ran her finger around the top of the corset, and Cal thought, *Let me do that.* "It's killing me."

"Wait," Cal said, and fished in his pocket for his pocketknife.

He slipped the knife under the bow and sliced through the ribbon, and Min took a deep breath as the rest of the corset began to unlace itself from the pressure. "Oh, Lord, that feels good."

Cal watched the rise and fall of her loosened corset. "Looks good, too." Even though he knew better, he drew his finger down the slope of her breast and felt the need for her that had been simmering for weeks flare up again.

If he didn't have her soon, he was going to lose his mind.

She said, "Hey," and caught his hand.

"Not my fault," he said, close to her mouth. "You were flaunting."

Her mouth melted under his, warm with familiarity, and her breath came faster as his hand curled around the firmness of her breast. "Oh," she said, and he kissed his way down the smooth curve of her neck and felt her sigh under his hand. "Oh, that feels so good. But I have to—"

"I know," he said, holding on to her. "I shouldn't have—" He kissed her again, wanting her so much that he couldn't let go.

"Yes, you should have," Min said, against his mouth. "But Di—"

"Right," Cal said, remembering his mission. "That's what I came to tell you. One of the ushers has Greg out in the car. Does Diana want to see him before he goes? He wants to apologize."

"Hell, *no*," Min said, pulling away from him. "What can he possibly say?"

" 'I'm the biggest cliché in bad wedding stories'?" Cal said, missing her warmth. "If it helps, the ushers are disgusted with him, too."

"I hate him," Min said, looking back into the ballroom.

"How is she?" Cal said, following her eyes to her sister, feeling guilty that he was having carnal thoughts while Di was in misery.

"I think she's almost relieved," Min said, watching her. "Not happy, and she's going to cry, but I think she knew she wanted the wedding and not Greg."

"Very sensible of her," Cal said. "Who would want Greg?"

Min stretched up and kissed him. "I'm staying with her tonight."

"I figured," Cal said, hating it anyway. He wrapped his arms around her and hugged her close. "I want you, Minerva."

"I'm free tomorrow night," she said, smiling up at him. "Go get rid of that jerk and come back for champagne."

"Be right back," Cal said, and kissed her again, surprised all over again that it was so easy, that everything with her had become so easy. *That can't be right*, he thought, but he grinned anyway as he went to tell the ushers they could remove Greg.

On his way back from the car, Cal ran into David.

"I think the reception's over, David," Cal said, trying not to snarl. "You can go home now."

"I can't," David said, looking noble. "There's something you should know."

Oh, hell, Cal thought and said, "What?"

"That bet we made," David said, "the one where you could get Min into bed in a month."

"What?" Cal looked at him, confused. "What bet? We didn't make that bet. That was you, being drunk and reckless."

"Min knows," David said, and Cal felt a chill. "She overheard it that night, that's why she went out with you, to pay us both back and to get a date to this fiasco. They all knew, Liza, Bonnie, her sister, she told everybody. They've all been laughing at us."

The hallway suddenly seemed too narrow, not enough air, and it was much too cold for June.

"I had to tell you because if she knows about it, the bet's off. You never had a chance to win. She's been playing you the whole time."

"No," Cal said, his throat tight. "She wouldn't." The familiar slug of shame and self-loathing hit him—*how stupid can you be*—even while common sense told him this was David making trouble, that Min wouldn't do that—

"Face it," David said, clapping him on the shoulder. "She made fools of us. Well, you more than me because I wasn't trying to get her into bed, but I feel pretty stupid, too."

Cal looked at him with loathing. "At last, some self-knowledge." *She knew. She thinks I'm stupid.*

"Hey." David held his hands up. "Don't turn on me. *I'm* not the one who's been making you look *stupid* for a month."

Cal flinched and then turned and walked away, back into the reception hall. It wasn't true, Min wasn't like that, she wouldn't do that, except that suddenly a lot of things that had been inexplicable now made sense.

He walked across the almost-deserted reception hall to where Min was trying to shield Diana from Nanette. "Could I talk to you for a minute?" he said.

Min looked up from Diana and said, "Now isn't—"

"*Now*," Cal said, and Min's eyes widened and she nodded. "I'll be right back, baby," she said to Diana, and let him draw her out into the hall, casting anxious looks back to her sister as she went.

"Is it Greg?" she said when they were in the hall where she could still keep an eye on Diana. "Did he—"

"Why did you go to dinner with me that first night?" Cal said.

"*What?*" Min said, so surprised she stopped looking at Di.

"Tell me the truth."

Min straightened. "I went . . ." She looked away from him and shook her head. "I went because you made a bet with David you could get me into bed in a month, and I needed a date for this wedding. And then we went out and you were so slick I knew I couldn't stand that for three weeks and I thanked you for dinner and went home. And why we have to talk about this now is beyond me."

"Why in hell would you keep going out with me if you thought I'd do that?" Cal said, a month's worth of frustration morphing into anger. "For the *sport?* Was it *funny?*"

"*No,*" Min said, sounding annoyed. "That's why I kept turning you down. Could we discuss this la—"

"So," Cal said. "You turned me down to make a fool of me, and you and Bonnie and Liza sat around and laughed about it."

"No," Min said, exasperated. "We thought you were slime. It wasn't funny at all."

"Ah," Cal said, nodding at her. "*This* is why Liza kept hitting me."

"Yes. But I don't *care.*" She spat the last word from between her teeth. "It doesn't *matter.*"

"You care," Cal said, grimly. "You're mad as hell. That's why you've been playing me, making me crazy for you, making me look like—"

"Hey," Min said, pointing her finger at him. "I have been completely honest with you."

"You never asked me about the bet," Cal said.

"Yeah, I did," Min said, folding her arms. "And you ducked it every time I asked."

"No, you didn't ask." Cal folded his arms. "And you know how I know? Because I'd have told you I didn't make that bet."

"I was *standing right there*," Min said.

"Then *you didn't listen very well*," Cal said. "*I told him no.*"

"You said, 'Piece of cake,'" Min snapped.

"I have never said 'Piece of cake' in my life," Cal said. "It's a *stupid* thing to say." He took a deep breath and thought, *Fuck it.* "How *stupid* do you think *I am?*" he said savagely, and Min froze. "How *stupid* does *everybody* think I am?"

"Not stupid," she said, watching him warily now. "What's going on?"

"They all thought I'd made that bet with a *sleaze* like David." Cal shook his head at the breadth of her betrayal. "Because *you told* them I made that bet. And they watched you play me, and like a fool I fell for it."

"You did make it," Min said, but she sounded uncertain. "Look, I didn't think you were stupid, I thought you were . . . awful. But then you weren't awful so I . . . Where is this coming from? You know how I feel about you. I love you. The bet doesn't matter—"

"It doesn't matter?" Cal said. "How *stupid are you?*"

"Hey," Min said, her face darkening. "Okay, look, I know this is pushing all your buttons, but get a grip. I love you, you know I love you, but I don't have time to baby-sit you right now—"

"*Baby-sit me?*" Cal clenched his jaw to keep from screaming at her, because she'd betrayed him and because he still wanted her, desperately. *Get out of this*, he thought, and said, "Well, you'll never have to baby-sit me again."

"*What?*" Then she started to nod, her face twisted in anger. "Oh. I get it. *Of course.* You're running. *You bastard.* You got what you wanted, I said 'I love you,' the game is over, and now you're out the door. I knew you'd do this. *I knew you'd do this.*"

"This is not about me," Cal said, not meeting her eyes.

"Oh, *please*," Min snapped. "This is all about you. One hundred percent of your relationships end with you running away. This is you grabbing any excuse to get—"

"*Hey*," Tony said, and they both turned to see him standing in the doorway, looking madder than Cal had ever seen him. "I don't know what the fuck you're doing, but whatever it is, it's not as important as what that kid in there is going through. You've got the rest of your lives to fight, she needs you now."

"Tell Min I didn't make that damn bet with David to have sex with her," Cal said.

Tony looked at Min, exasperated. "He didn't make that bet."

"I heard him make the bet," Min said. "David said that he'd have to get the gray-checked suit into bed in a month and he said, 'Piece of . . . cake.'" She looked from Tony to Cal. "Oh."

"I said 'Piece of cake,'" Tony said. "I was wrong. I don't care. Fight about it later. Right now, get your ass back in there and help your sister. Your mother took her champagne away because it has too many calories, and that damn bridesmaid in the green dress keeps laughing."

"You're right," Min said, stepping toward the door. "But we won't be fighting about it later because *Calvin* has decided it's time to *go*."

"You're kidding me," Tony said, looking at them both with contempt. "You two are the biggest babies I've ever seen."

"What?" Min said, stopping.

"Here's the short version," Tony said to Min. "You're a man-hating bitch and he's a woman-fearing coward." He looked at Cal. "Get over that, will you?"

"*The hell with both of you*," Min said and went back to her sister, as Cal turned on Tony.

"They're all like that," Nanette was saying to Di when Min got back to them, seething. "You can't trust any of them." She gestured with the champagne glass she was holding. "They tell you they love you and then—"

Min grabbed the glass out of her hand. *"Here,"* she said, handing it to Di. "We're drinking about twelve bottles of this tonight, so get started."

"Do you know how many calories—" Nanette began.

"Listen, you," Min said to her. "You're going home and throwing out every damn fashion magazine in the house. You're going cold turkey, it's the only thing that's going to save you."

Nanette straightened. "Just because you won't lose the weight, doesn't mean Diana has to be fat."

"I'm not *fat,* Mother," Min said. "But while we're on the subject, I don't see where not eating for fifty-five years has made *you* particularly happy. Go home and eat something, for Christ's sake." She looked around. "Where are those goddamn cake boxes?"

"I'll get them," Roger said, and went fast.

"I think that's very sensible," Wet said, beaming at Min.

"And *you,*" Min said. "Go someplace else and gloat. In fact, go find Greg. You deserve each other. He's a selfish bastard and you love to be beat."

"That's not fair," Wet said, back to her familiar whine.

"Hit the road, Wet," Liza said. "You've been laughing ever since you stopped hitting Worse. If you're not going to be a comfort, have the decency to be an empty space."

"Well, at least I'm not *Tart,*" Wet said and stalked off.

"Did she just call me a tart?" Liza said to Bonnie.

Min sat down next to Diana in Wet's vacated chair.

"Here's what we're going to do," she said, taking her hand. "We're going to get those cake boxes and a case of the champagne, and we're going back to my place."

"Okay," Diana said, her voice breaking again.

"And we're going to eat cake and get drunk," Min said.

"Oh, *Min,*" Nanette said. "It'll take you weeks to work off those calories."

Min looked at her mother for a moment and thought, *This is what Diana lives with every damn day.* "And then," she said to Diana, "since you have the week off for your honeymoon, I'm going to take the week off, too, and we're going to go house-hunting."

Diana stopped crying. "House-hunting?"

"Yes," Min said. "I'm going to buy a great two bedroom Arts and Crafts bungalow. And you're going to move in with me."

"I am?" Diana said, sitting up a little.

"Yes," Min said. "You've lived with the calorie police for too long."

"That's ridiculous," Nanette said. "She is not going to move."

"But there are some rules," Min said, and Diana swallowed and nodded. "There will always be butter in the refrigerator. There will be no sound tracks from Julia Roberts movies. And from now on," she said, looking toward the door where Cal was glaring at Tony, "we only date ugly men."

Diana was nodding at Min. "And I'll get out of the way on Thursday nights."

"Why?" Min said, mystified.

"So you guys can have your If Dinner," she said, and Min realized that the worst thing that had happened to Di wasn't that she'd lost Greg, it was that she'd lost her best friends. She thought again of what it would be like if Bonnie and Liza had betrayed her, and she lost her breath at how far beyond horrible that would be.

As bad as losing Cal.

"You'll come, too," Bonnie said, putting her arm around Di.

"Hell, yes," Liza said, as Roger came back with a tray of cake boxes and the cake topper. She ripped the bride and groom off the cake top and put it in front of Diana and said, "Pay attention, Little Stats, we're about to have a moment." Diana looked up and Liza stomped on the head of the groom, shattering it into dust. "Now," she said. "He is officially history. And if there's a God, he has a splitting headache."

"I think you can count on that," Roger said. "He got hit a lot."

"Good," Liza said. "Now we're going back to Min's and get drunk."

Diana looked at Min through her tears. "Can I wear your bunny slippers?"

"You can *have* my bunny slippers," Min said, thinking of Cal in furious misery.

She looked toward the door and saw him standing there, watching her, and then Tony was in her way, spreading out his hands, saying to

Liza, "Nice job on the cake topper, ace. I suppose you had to kill the groom," and Liza said, "Defend him and die," and Tony said, "No, he was an asshole even without the haircut," and Diana laughed and then cried again.

Out in the hall, Cal turned and Min saw Cynthie standing behind him. He stopped for a moment, and then he left, and Cynthie went with him.

Right. You wouldn't stay to help because it's not about you, is it, buddy? Min thought and then shoved him out of her mind and turned back to Diana.

"I'm a coward?" Cal had said to Tony when Min had gone, pleased to be fighting with somebody he could hit.

"I can't believe you're running away from this one," Tony said. "Hell, Cal, you're thirty-five, aren't you tired of that shit by now?"

"You're thirty-five, too," Cal said grimly.

"And I have never in my life looked at a woman the way you look at Min," Tony said. "I'd be pissed at her, that all-men-are-pigs bit is a pain in the ass, but I'd *tell* her that, I wouldn't walk away from her. What's wrong with you?"

"This is not about me," Cal said.

"Jesus," Tony said and turned back to the ballroom.

"Where are you going?" Cal said.

Tony shook his head. "Back to where there's real trouble. We're all in there. Why aren't you?"

Then he walked away and Cal looked past him to where Min had her arms around Diana, and Bonnie was leaning close to them, and Roger was holding a tray of cake in one hand and patting Diana on the back with the other, and Liza was smashing something with her foot, and as Tony got closer, he spread his hands out, and Diana looked up and gave him a watery smile and Cal knew he was clowning again, doing his bit. *Fuck*, he thought. *I should be in there.* Then Min looked up and saw him, her face set and stormy, and he flinched and thought, *The hell with you*, and turned, furious and miserable to see Cynthie, looking lovelier than ever.

"Are you all right?" she said.

"No," Cal said.

She smiled at him. "I know a place we can get a drink."

"Where's that?" Cal said.

"My place," Cynthie said.

"Let's go," Cal said, and left, knowing Min was watching.

Cal spent most of Monday fuming about what a bitch Min had been, and Tuesday wasn't much better. It didn't help that in the same two days, Cynthie had called twice to talk him into the drink he'd turned down when he'd dropped her off at her place, every client had become intensely stupid, and his partners kept looking at him as if he'd been drowning puppies. Worst of all, he missed Min so much, wanted her so much, that it was making him sick. The crowning touch to his day was his mother, calling him at work to find out if he was seeing Cynthie again.

"No," he said. "I'm never going to see her again, so *get off my ass about her*."

"*Calvin,*" his mother said, in a voice that would have stopped him cold any other day.

"In *fact*," he said, "since I'm such an *overwhelming disappointment* to you, I'm never going to see *you* again, either."

"Calvin?" his mother said, a new note in her voice.

"*Forget it,*" Cal said, and hung up.

Tony came over and unplugged his phone. "You get this back when you call her," he said. "Until then, you don't talk to people."

"I'm never calling her again," Cal said. "She's been a bitch my whole life and I'm done with her."

"Not your mother, you dumbass," Tony said. "Min."

"She's been a bitch for a month and I'm done with her, too," Cal said. "The hell with both of them."

"That's very mature," Tony said, sounding just like Min.

Roger shook his head and went back to work, and Cal ignored them both to savagely edit a seminar packet.

When he got home, he threw his suit coat on the couch, picked up his Glenlivet and then stopped as Elvis began to sing "She" next door.

"Jesus fucking Christ," he said and slammed the Glenlivet down.

When he pounded on Shanna's door, a strange woman answered, brown-haired, a little below medium height. "Oh," he said. "I thought . . . Shanna . . ."

"Oh, she's here." The woman smiled at him, a sweet smile that reminded him of Min, her eyes huge in her round face as she stepped back. "Shanna?"

Cal looked past her to Shanna, carrying two ruby goblets out of the kitchen.

"Cal!" she said, smiling. "This is Linda. Linda, this is my next-door neighbor, Cal." Her smile widened and she jerked her head toward the stereo. "First date music."

"Oh," Cal said, taking a step back. "Hell, I'm sorry . . ."

"Don't you just love Elvis?" Linda said.

"Yeah," Cal said. "Good for you, Shan. I'll see you later."

"Stay for a drink," Shanna said, with a look that telegraphed, *Get lost*.

"Can't stay," Cal said. "I have to . . ." He jerked his head toward his apartment, at a loss for what he might have to do over there besides fume.

"Is Min there?" Shanna said, putting the glasses down on the breakfast bar. "Maybe later we could—"

"No," Cal said, his rage back on the surface again. "Min is not there." Shanna stopped, reading his face. "Oh, no. What did you do?"

"Strangely enough, *nothing*," Cal said. "Why do you assume—"

"I don't care," Shanna said. "Get her back."

"It's *done*," Cal said.

"No, it is not," Shanna said. "You really lost something this time."

"This is not about me," Cal said.

"Yes, it is," Shanna said. "This time it is. What happened?"

Cal shook his head. "Nope. Not interesting." He nodded at Linda. "Very nice to meet you." He turned to go but Shanna grabbed the back of his shirt in her fist and yanked.

"Sit down and tell me everything," she said. "Or I will track you back to your apartment and bitch at you until you tell me there."

Fifteen minutes later she said, "Well, it's a toss-up as to which of the two of you is dumber."

"*Hey*," Cal said.

"You're desperately in love with each other and you're playing footsie with it. Do you know how rare what you have is?"

"Christ, I hope so," Cal said. "I'd hate to think there was an epidemic of this garbage."

"Stop it," Shanna said. "You want her back."

"*Why* would I—"

"*Stop it!*" Shanna said. "You want her back."

Cal sat back on the couch and the memory of Min he'd been fighting for two days came back. He put his head in his hands. "Oh, Christ, I want her back. Which shows you how stupid I really am."

"Oh, for heaven's sake, *call her*," Shanna said. "Tell her you're sorry."

Cal jerked his head up. "Hey, *I'm the injured party here*."

"Yeah," Shanna said. "That been keeping you warm at night, has it? Call her. Tell her you want to talk to her tomorrow night. Take a nice bottle of wine, tell her you love her, work out this non-problem, and live happily ever after."

"Why tomorrow?" Cal said, confused. "If I'm going to apologize for something I *did not do*, I could go over there now—"

"Because by then you'll have lost the bet," Shanna said.

"*I didn't make the bet*," Cal said.

Linda moved a little farther away from him on the couch.

"Stop yelling," Shanna said. "It doesn't matter. You hit her where it hurts."

"What—"

"She's not beautiful," Shanna said over him. "She's not thin. She knows that everybody who sees you with her wonders how she got you."

"That's not true," Cal said. "She's amazing."

"Right," Shanna said. "We see that, but there are many people who don't. Including, I believe, her ex-boyfriend who dumped her and then tried to make that bet with you."

"*Ouch*," Linda said.

"And then you come along, gorgeous and perfect, and you convince her you love her—"

"I do love her, damn it," Cal said.

"—only it turns out you made a bet—"

Cal stood up. *"I did not make that bet—"*

"—that you could take her to dinner," Shanna went on.

Cal sat down.

"And she thought you were trying to get her into bed for a bet, and then in the end, when things got tense, instead of standing by her, you walk out with your gorgeous ex-girlfriend."

"Not good," Linda said.

"Oh, hell." Cal put his head in his hands again. "I can't believe I fell for this. I can't believe I let that asshole David Fisk do this. I *am* stupid."

"Only this once," Shanna said. "It's going to be okay. All you have to do is throw the bet. Big deal, you lose a little pride and ten bucks."

"Ten thousand bucks," Cal said.

"Whoa," Linda said, straightening. "This is like cable."

"You bet David ten thousand dollars you could get Min into bed?" Shanna said, incredulous.

Cal looked at the ceiling. "Does *anybody* here listen to me?"

"He didn't make the bet," Linda told Shanna.

"Thank you," Cal said.

"Everybody knows about the bet," Shanna says. "It exists in everybody's minds and if you sleep with her before . . . when is the bet up?"

"Tomorrow at nine, nine-thirty, I don't know," Cal said, trying to remember when they'd made the damn thing. *Hadn't* made the damn thing. Christ, even he was doing it.

"Is she worth losing ten thousand dollars?"

"Hell, yes," Cal said.

"Well, there you are. Go call her and tell her you'll see her after you lose the bet." Shanna folded her arms, implacable. "Don't make me come over there and do it for you."

"Do it," Linda said to Cal. "It's romantic in a perverse sort of way."

"Thank you," Cal said to her. "On that note, I'm going home." He got up and left, ignoring Shanna's *"Cal."*

Shanna was *wrong*, he told himself as he poured himself another Scotch, but the thought didn't have much conviction. He closed his eyes and thought of Min and tried to remind himself that it was all treachery, but he kept hearing her say, "I love you," and he knew it was true.

"Oh *fuck*," he said and when the doorbell rang, he yanked it open, prepared to deck Shanna if she was going to yap about Min anymore.

It was Cyn, looking hot as hell in her blue halter top and short black skirt. She tilted her head up at him and her glossy black hair swung back. "I know you're upset," she said, softly. "I don't want you to be alone."

"I'm all right," he said, as she stepped closer.

"No, you're not," she said. "She hit you hard." She held up a bottle of Glenlivet. "Come on, talk about it. You'll feel better."

She'll do anything I ask, Cal thought. *And the world is full of women like her. Why do I need Min?*

Cynthie smiled up at him, lovely and warm. "Do I get to come in?"

"No," Cal said. "I have to make a phone call."

Chapter Fifteen

Cynthie said, "I can wait," and he remembered Min saying, "You get to know the real us and then you leave us." Cynthie smiled up at him, her heart in her eyes, and he thought, *Oh, hell.*

He shook his head at her. "I'm sorry. Somebody explained to me what I've done to you. I'm sorry. I never meant to hurt you, I never meant to hurt anybody, but I never meant to marry you, either."

Cynthie took a deep breath and nodded. "That's all right, I can wait—"

"There's somebody else," Cal said, as gently as he could. "I'm sorry, but I'm in love with somebody else."

She flinched. "No. You love me."

"I never said that. You know that."

"Yes, but you do." Her hands gripped the bottle tighter. "You don't realize it, but you do. We're perfect for each other."

He closed his eyes so he wouldn't see how desperate she was.

"It's Min," Cynthie said. "I know it's Min. Look, she's a nice woman, but she's not me."

"I know," Cal said. "That's the problem." Cynthie's face twisted, and he said, "I'm sorry, Cyn."

He shut the door in her face and leaned against the door for a moment, trying not to think about how much damage he'd done to her, not even wanting to think about anybody else.

Except Min.

Fix this, he told himself and sat down to figure out a way.

At about the same time Shanna was reading Cal the riot act, Min was listening to Liza say, "This is really good," as she speared the last marsala-soaked mushroom at Min's dining room table. Then Liza said, "Tell me again why we're doing this."

"Because we always had chicken marsala on Tuesday nights," Min said, stabbing her chicken with no enthusiasm as Elvis prowled about her ankles, impatient for leftovers. "I'm trying to cloud the association."

"Very practical," Lisa said. "Except you're miserable, so there's not enough cloud in the world, babe."

"May I have the butter, please?" Diana said, picking up another piece of bread from Emilio's. '

Bonnie pushed the butter dish her way. "Have you heard from him?" she asked Min.

"Of course not," Min said, revving up her anger again so she wouldn't have to think about how she'd been waiting for a phone call for two days. "He's *mad at me.* Can you believe it? *He's* mad at *me.* Did I make a bet? Noooo. But *he's*—"

"Oh, *please,* no more of this," Liza said. "You've bitched about him for two days. Face it, the man has a point."

Min put down her fork, and Diana stopped buttering her bread.

"He does not have a point," Min snapped. "This whole mess is because he does not have a point and now you're turning on me? It's not enough that Bonnie sandbagged me with that fairy tale garbage, now you—"

"It's not garbage," Bonnie said. "You got the fairy tale. You got the handsome prince who loved you. It worked."

"It did not work," Min said, slamming her hand down on the table. "He went into a snit and *left*. Just my luck, I get a *snitty prince*. Which is why he wasn't *a prince*. Which is why I don't believe *that garbage. I do not believe in the fairy tale, okay?*"

"I don't think it matters," Bonnie said, mild as ever. "The fairy tale believes in you."

Min turned to Liza. *"Tell her."*

Liza leaned her elbow on the table. "She's right."

Min flopped back in her chair. "Oh, for crying out loud. If this wasn't my apartment, I'd leave."

"Well, look at it from his point of view," Liza said. "He didn't make the bet. He tried not to date you, but he had to keep coming back because he was nuts about you, and you kept kissing him and then turning him down. He was patient, he charmed your parents, he was good to your friends, he found your snow globe, he taught you to cook, he got you a *cat*, for Christ's sake, and then it turns out that while he was knocking himself out for you, you were playing him for a fool."

"No, I wasn't," Min said, but her anger cooled considerably.

"He really is a sweetie," Diana said, licking butter off her lip.

"Liza's right," Bonnie said. "You know how awful school was for all three of these boys. They're all sensitive about being dumb. You hit Cal right on his sore spot, in front of his friends, in front of Cynthie, in front of David."

"Ouch," Min said faintly. She tried to summon up her old outrage over the bet, but after two days of venting, she'd been running out of steam anyway.

"I know you needed to be mad to deal with the pain," Liza said. "I do that, too. But if you want him back, get over it. Because if there wasn't a bet—"

"There wasn't," Min said miserably. "I believe him on that."

"Then he's given you everything and you haven't given him a damn thing."

"That's pretty harsh," Bonnie said to Liza.

"Why didn't you just ask him about the bet?" Liza said.

"I did," Min said.

"You said, 'Did you make a bet with David that you could sleep with me in a month?'"

"No," Min said, not meeting her eyes. "I asked him if there was anything he wasn't telling me."

Bonnie nodded. "And what did he say?"

Min sat back. "He kept confessing to things that weren't the bet."

"That must have been fun for everyone," Liza said. "Why didn't you flat out ask him?"

Min put her head in her hands. "I was afraid, okay? You know how all those people say, 'If they just *talked* about their problems, they'd all go away'? Well, I bet none of those people talk about *their* problems. I mean, it *sounds* good, but it's a terrible gamble." She looked up at Liza. "I knew he made that bet. I *heard him*. And I . . ." She stopped and swallowed. "I knew I only had a month and I wanted that month with him." She shook her head. "Not everybody faces life head-on the way that you do."

"Well, they should," Liza said. "You screwed up. So now you're going to have to grovel."

"What?" Bonnie said, while Min gaped at Liza, and Diana watched them all, fascinated.

Liza got up from the table, picked up Min's phone, and brought it over to her. "Call him. Tell him you were wrong, he was right, and you'll do anything to make it up to him."

Min swallowed. "*You* want me to grovel?"

"Yes," Liza said. "I'm not going to watch you lose him because of your dumb pride. Call and offer him anything he wants if he'll take you back."

Min looked at Bonnie, who nodded.

Min looked at the phone. If she called Cal, she'd at least get to hear his voice. How pathetic was that? "Pathetic," she said out loud.

"Only if you let this go," Liza said. "For once in your life, do the irrational, reckless thing. Call him."

Min sat there, frozen in fear. Then she took a deep breath and picked up the phone.

Cal was rehearsing his "How about a late dinner tomorrow?" speech when the phone rang, but when he picked it up and heard Min's tentative "Hi?" he forgot it all.

"Hi," he said and sat down hard on the couch.

"Don't say anything," she said, her words coming out in a rush. "Let me get this out. I was wrong not to tell you I knew about the bet. I was wrong not to trust you. Everything you said at the wedding was right. It's my fault. I want you back. I want us back. I love you and I need you—"

Relief made Cal dizzy.

"And I want you to see you now," she went on, and Cal thought, *Christ, yes*, and then the other shoe dropped. "Now?" he said and looked at the clock. Twenty-six hours before the bet was up. *Just tell her yes,* he thought, *she doesn't care about the bet anymore, she said so,* and then he remembered how she'd sounded when she'd said it at the wedding.

"It's been driving me crazy saying no to you all these weeks," Min was babbling, "but if you're not ready for that, that's okay, I just want to see you. I haven't seen you for two days, and I miss you so much. Can I come over right now? Just to talk? Or, you know, we could do other things. I can think of several. If you want more than talk. More would be good with me. Or not. Whatever."

More would be great with me, Cal thought and shook his head to clear it.

"I'm on my knees here," Min said, her voice straining to be chipper. "And not in a good way. Can I come over?"

"No," Cal said. "I'll come to you. Later." He swallowed. "Tomorrow. Nine-thirty. Tomorrow night, nine-thirty."

"Not *now*?" Min said, her voice cracking.

"*No,*" Cal said. "No. Nine-thirty. Tomorrow. I'll bring dinner."

"I can cook now," Min said. "I can make dinner. I can make it now."

"I'll bring dinner tomorrow," Cal said, thinking, *Christ, I've been stupid.*

"Fine, whatever." Min waited for a moment and then added, "I'm kind of hungry now, though."

"Tomorrow, nine-thirty, your place," Cal said, gritting his teeth.

"Okay," Min said. "All right. Tomorrow night it is." He was about to say good-bye when she said, "Are you seeing Cynthie?"

"Christ, no," Cal said, casting a guilty look at the door.

"Because you left with her. And David said you were. Or I wouldn't have asked. I mean, it's none of my business."

"It's your business," Cal said. "And David is an idiot. Stop talking to him."

"I'm trying," Min said.

Cal felt all his tension morph into a much more convenient anger. "What does that mean, you're trying?"

"He calls. For some reason, this whole mess has convinced him that he and I should get married."

"He's wrong," Cal snapped.

"I *know that*," Min said, her voice not placating anymore.

"You've got caller ID. Stop picking up the phone."

"Look, I'm not completely stupid."

"You're not stupid at all," Cal said, "your past month's performance notwithstanding." He winced. *Stupid. Stupid.*

"Hey, you made the bet."

"*I did not—*"

"The second one. The take-me-to-dinner one. I screwed up but I'm not going to pay for it for the rest of my life. You're culpable here, too. You made that dinner bet."

There you go, Cal thought. Shanna was right, damn it.

"Not that I'm assuming you're going to be around for the rest of my life," Min said, tentative again.

"*Tomorrow night*," Cal said and hung up, before either one of them said something even dumber, pretty sure he'd done the right thing. *Christ, I'm in a Doris Day movie*, he thought, and went to tell Shanna that he'd done what she said.

"I love you," Min said forlornly to the dial tone.

"What happened?" Liza said. "What was all that stuff about Cynthie and David? I told you to grovel, not fight."

Min put the phone down and picked up Elvis for comfort. "He doesn't want to see me until tomorrow."

"That's strange," Liza said. "If I'd promised Tony sex like that, he'd have been here before I hung up the phone."

"I didn't actually promise him sex," Min said.

"Oh, please," Liza and Bonnie said together, and even Diana nodded and said, "Yes, you did."

"Could I keep some shred of dignity here?" Min said. "He just said no to sex, the bastard."

"No, he didn't," Bonnie said, patting her hand. "He just said, not until tomorrow." She frowned. "I don't get him."

"Tell us what he said," Liza said.

"He said he'd come over here tomorrow at nine-thirty, and he'd bring dinner. Like I want to eat." Min sniffed. "I hate this. This is dumb."

"What's so special about nine-thirty tomorrow night?" Liza said. "What's tomorrow? It's just Wednesday."

"It's Roger's and my anniversary," Bonnie said. "He's ordering champagne, and then he's going to pick me up at the bar the way he did four weeks ago, and then he's going to propose."

"Cute," Min said.

"That's it," Liza said, straightening. "Tomorrow night it's four weeks since David made the bet."

"But Cal didn't take the bet," Min snapped. "I'm tired of this conversation. He didn't—"

"But everybody knows about it," Liza said. "So if you give in before the time's up, he wins. And he loves to win. He always wins. He lives to win."

"Not seeing your point," Min said.

"He's throwing the bet," Liza said.

"Why?" Min stood up and Elvis leaped for the floor. "Why in the name of *God*—"

"It's sort of gallant," Bonnie said.

"If you ask me, it's a control thing, too," Liza said, disdain in her voice. "He gets to call the shots. What happened at nine-thirty?"

Min shrugged, confused. "We got to the restaurant a little before ten so we were probably leaving the bar about then."

Liza nodded. "He's giving himself some leeway." She frowned.

"Although more than he needs if he's bringing dinner. Then there'll be foreplay. It's going to take some time to get you—"

"He can have me when he walks in the door," Min said.

Diana picked up her bread again. "I'll go to the movies tomorrow night. You're going to need this place to yourself, and I'm not going back home. Mom's still mad I moved in here. She's convinced I'm eating carbs." She bit into the bread, and Min laughed in spite of herself and then began to consider the situation.

So what if Cal lost the bet? Ten bucks. He could afford it. "No," she said. "I'm not going to be the bet he lost, that's not how I want us to start. He's going to win that bet tomorrow night, and he's going to be *very* happy doing it."

"Why tomorrow?" Liza said.

"Because I'm going to need a really hot nightgown," Min said. "And a lot more courage than I have right now. And a plan."

"Explain," Liza said, and Min leaned in and they began to talk.

"What the hell is going on?" David said the next evening when he called Cynthie. "I thought you said that fight at the wedding would end it."

"We lost," Cynthie said, her voice sounding tired. "He loves her so much, he's forgiven her."

"I just talked to Min," David said, reliving the experience in vivid detail. "She told me she's going to make sure he wins so I should get my checkbook out. She sounded mad *at me*."

"David, it's done," Cynthie said. "The only thing we can do is wait and hope infatuation wears itself out and they come to their senses."

"Six months to three years? I'm not waiting on Calvin Morrisey." David thought of Cal with loathing. He had Min so snowed she believed he'd actually throw that bet. He'd probably set it up so she'd insist on his winning. He'd probably . . . David sat back. "Wait a minute. What if Min found out *he* was playing *her*? What if he tricked her into sleeping with him so he could win the bet?"

"He's not," Cynthie said, tiredly. "It's *done*, David."

"No, it's not," David said. "Not if the bet's for midnight. What if her family and friends found out he made that bet?"

"*It's done, David,*" Cynthie said.

"I'm not done," David said. "I'm going to win."

At eight, Cal had a bottle of wine and a box of Krispy Kremes ready to take to Min's apartment, and an hour and a half of rabid sexual frustration to kill when the phone rang.

"*Cal,*" Diana said when he answered. "You have to *get over here.* Min's *in trouble.*"

"What—" Cal said, and then all he heard was a dial tone. "Okay," he said, and headed over to Min's apartment, deeply suspicious.

When he knocked on the door, Diana opened it. "Thank God you're here," she said, and hauled him inside. Then she slipped out the door and left, slamming it behind her.

"What is this?" Cal turned around and saw Min, dressed in a short black trench coat, her back against the door, that glint in her eyes. "Oh, funny," he said, trying to sound mad. "Did you ever hear the story about the actuary who cried 'Wolf'?"

"Yes," Min said. "The wolf ate her." She grinned at him, and his pulse kicked up. "I have news for you, Charm Boy. You are not going to throw this bet."

"Oh, yes, I am," Cal said, retreating around her couch while Elvis watched with contempt. "If we sleep together now, there will come a day when we're arguing about the electric bill, and you'll say, 'You only dated me for the bet.' I'm not paying for this for the rest of my life when all I have to do is wait an hour and a half." He looked at the clock on the mantel. "Eighty minutes."

"The rest of your life, huh?" Min said.

"Yes, Minerva, the rest of my life. You think I'd go through the hell this month has been just for the sex?"

Min blinked. "Well, yes."

Cal thought about it. "Okay, you have a point."

"Did I mention I'm not wearing underwear." Min slid around the couch and he backed around to the other side.

"You do this to torture me, don't you?" Cal said.

"No, I'm doing it to get you into bed," Min said. "The torture is just a perk."

"Min," Cal said.

"No," Min said. "I don't want to spend the rest of my life as the bet you lost. Plus I'm tired of hearing about how I'm not a risk-taker. So I'm taking a risk on you." She pulled a ten-dollar bill out of her trench coat pocket. "I've got ten bucks says I'm going to have you naked and inside me before nine-thirty."

Cal went dizzy for a moment and when he'd shaken his head to clear it, she'd slapped the ten on the table by the couch.

"There it is, sport," Min said. "You going to be a wimp, or are you going to play?"

She was smiling at him, heat and love in her eyes, and he started to laugh. "Min, it's eighty minutes, not a month. You really think I can't hold out that long?"

"Yep," Min said, her hands on her hips.

He got out his wallet, took out a ten, walked over to the table, and slapped it on top of her ten. "You're on," he said, keeping the table between them. "Let's see what you've got, Minnie."

She unbuckled her trench coat, dropped the belt onto the couch, and took off the coat. She was wearing a strapless black lace nightgown, and as far as Cal could see, there was nothing holding it up. "I know it would have been better if I'd been naked," she said, rocking on her heels so that everything bounced. "I'm just not that confident yet."

"Actually," Cal said, staring at her, "now I'm going to think about ripping that off you for the next eighty minutes, so this may be the way to go." He looked at the top of the nightgown where the lace cut into her flesh. "It doesn't look that hard to get off."

Min put her finger inside the top of the lace and snapped it. "Elastic. One good tug and—"

"Not for eighty minutes." He looked at the clock. "Seventy-seven minutes. But I want to make it clear that when the time's up, you're mine."

"Oh, yeah," Min said, nodding.

"Well, then," Cal said. "Read any good books lately?"

"No," Min said, beginning to move around the table. "I can't read because all I can think about is you."

Cal moved away from her, toward the other end of the couch. "That must be boring."

"No, you're always doing the most amazing things to me," Min said, moving closer.

Cal moved around to the front of the couch. "You know, I'm not that good in bed."

Min reversed direction and surprised him, grabbing his shirt. "That's all right. I'm fantastic."

She pushed him onto the couch and straddled him, her soft weight pinning him down, and Cal thought, *I should do something about this*, but even as he thought it, his hands were on her, feeling her heat through the scratch of the lace. "I've been told my mouth is a miracle," she whispered, leaning into him, and he closed his eyes as her breasts pushed softly against his chest.

She kissed him, and her mouth was hot and sweet, and he tightened his hands on her and pulled her close. "Christ, I've missed you," he said against her mouth.

"I missed you, too," she said, not playing anymore. "I don't ever want to be without you again."

"You never will," Cal said. "I'm not walking away from you again. Ever."

"Thank you." Min sat back and took a deep breath and Cal watched, heat rising. "Listen, there's something I have to tell you."

His hands cupped her rear end and pulled her tighter. She really wasn't wearing underwear. "Talk slow." He bent his head to kiss her neck and bit it softly instead.

Min shivered. "Remember, I said, 'Don't break my heart'? Well, I changed my mind. You can break it."

"Hey," Cal said, his hands tightening on her. "I'm not—"

"It doesn't matter, I'll love you anyway," Min said, "I loved you when I thought you'd made that bet, I loved you when I thought you were playing me, I loved you while I was screaming at you in the street, I loved you when you left the wedding with Cynthie, you rat bastard—"

"I took her home and left," Cal said, alarmed. "I swear to God, I—"

"It doesn't matter," Min said. "That's what I'm trying to tell you, it doesn't matter what you do or say. I'm going to love you till the end of time."

Cal looked at her, stunned.

"I know," Min said. "It's really un-PC. I just thought you should know that you can't screw this up."

"I can't?" Cal said, wanting to believe her.

"No," Min said. "Which doesn't mean I'm not going to yell if you make me mad again. I will shout and slam doors. I just won't be on the other side of the door when I slam it. You've got me for life."

He lost his breath and put his forehead against her shoulder. "God, I love you."

Min sighed. "That's good because there's something else I have to tell you."

Cal nodded, still dazed.

Min swallowed. "The thing is, I'm going to spread. Hips, thighs—"

"Not till nine-thirty," Cal said, trying not to picture her.

"—waist," Min said, and then stopped. "What? Nine-thirty? Not till my *forties*, probably, I think I can fight it off that long, but then—"

"What?" Cal said.

"I'm going to get fat," Min said, and he blinked. "Er. I'm going to get fatter." She frowned at him. "What did you think I meant?"

"For future reference," he said, starting to laugh. "If you're sitting half naked on my lap and you tell me you're going to spread—"

"*No,*" Min said and tried to push him away, and he toppled her so she landed, lush and hot beneath him. "I would never say that," she said, looking up at him as her arms slid around his neck. "That would be crude."

"I liked it," Cal said and kissed her.

"What I'm trying to tell you," Min said when she came up for air, "is that I'm going to grow up to be one of those chubby old ladies. It's in my genes. Like self-rising flour. I'm going to pouf."

"That's going to work out well for me," Cal said. "Because I'm going to grow up to be one of those horny old men who chases chubby old ladies around the couch."

"I'm *serious*," Min said, but she was smiling, her soft lips open for him.

"So am I," Cal said. "You think I care what you weigh? Hell, woman, you've called me a beast, a wolf, the devil, and a vile seducer. Plus your best friend has beaten me up three times—"

"You hit me in the eye," Min said.

"—and you yelled at me in public, and I'm still here. If you think you getting softer is going to get rid of me—"

"Men are visual," Min said.

"Yeah." Cal slid his finger under the elastic edge of her nightgown. "That's why I like this thing you're not wearing. But I still want a chance to rip your sweats off you, too." He stopped smiling, trying to give her what she'd given him. "It's just you, Minnie. That's all I want. I just want to spend the rest of my life with you."

"Oh." Min reached up for him, and he remembered the bet and sat up, hating to let her go.

"Starting at nine-thirty." He looked at the clock. "Which is in seventy minutes. What do you want to do for seventy minutes, Minnie? Got a Scrabble board?"

"I'll use dirty words," Min said.

"Yeah, like 'spread,'" Cal said, and laughed.

Min looked at the ceiling. "See, this is one of those things that doesn't matter, I love you anyway."

"I love that part," Cal said. "So what's new with you?"

"That would be saying 'yes, you can have me any way you want me' to you." She sat up and pulled him to her again, and he shifted on the couch to make room for her and felt something dig into his hip. Min kissed his neck, and he shivered as he reached behind him and pulled out her coat belt, buckle first. Then she bit him, and he said, "Ouch," and she leaned back and smiled at him.

"You're going to win the bet with David and lose the bet to me, hotshot," she said. "Think of it as breaking even."

He looked at her and thought, *she's right*, and then looked at the belt in his hand. "Just for the record, no matter what I do, you'll love me?"

"Yes," she said.

"Good." He tipped her back onto the couch and stretched her wrists over her head. "I like being in control, Minnie."

"I know." Min smiled up at him. "I can work with that."

He kissed her again, and while she was distracted, he wrapped the belt around her wrists.

"Hey," she said, breaking the kiss, but he'd already wrapped the ends of the belt around the arm of the couch.

She stretched up to see her wrists as he tied the knot. "This is a little kinky, Calvin."

"Not really," Cal said, getting up. "You know, I had a dozen doughnuts to bring over here, and then you cried wolf, and now we don't have them. But I forgive you because that's the kind of relationship we have." He moved to the kitchen alcove. "So what do you want to talk about for . . ." He stretched to see the clock. ". . . sixty-seven minutes."

"*Cal,*" Min said.

There was a familiar green and white sack on the kitchen counter. "Krispy Kremes," he said. "Great minds think alike." He brought the sack back into the living room. "You know, Minnie, you tortured me for a month, looking so good I lost my mind every time I saw you. I wanted you so much I was insane from it." He looked down at her, tied to the couch. "Still am, evidently."

"Okay, I'm sorry about that," Min said, tugging on the belt.

"So now it's your turn." He sat down across from her. "Now I'm going to torture you."

Min stopped tugging. "This could be good. What are you going to do?"

He took a Krispy Kreme out of the bag.

"I'm going to eat this in front of you," Cal said, and bit into the doughnut.

David went down to the street to the pay phone on the corner because damn near everybody had caller ID these days. He dialed Min's parents' number, and when the phone stopped ringing, he said, "You should know this," only to be overrun by their answering machine. Well, that was all right, they never stayed out longer than nine anyway. Plenty of time. When he heard the beep, he said, "You should know this. Calvin Morrisey is seducing your daughter to win a bet. They're at her apartment right now." Then he hung up and considered what he had just done. As far as he could see, it was flawless.

Feeling pretty good about himself, he began to look through the directory wired to the pay phone for the Morriseys' number.

Min scowled at Cal, but all the bastard did was grin back, looking desirable as all hell while he finished his second doughnut. Slowly.

"And you wonder why I wouldn't sleep with you," Min said. "It was because I sensed the sadist in you." She shifted to get more comfortable and watched his jaw tense. *Hello*, she thought, and shifted again.

"I haven't see Elvis for a while," he said, watching her. "He must have gone out the window again. What are the statistics on outdoor cats?"

"You know," Min said, trying a new strategy. "This is scaring me. There's a strange man in my apartment, and I'm tied to my couch. I'm *terrified*." She tried to put some fear into her voice, but it was hard since it was soaked with lust.

"Funny, you just look pissed off." Cal picked up the remote. "TV?"

Min gritted her teeth. "Men get arrested for this."

"Only if they get caught. I usually check CNN about this time." Cal looked down at her. "Of course, I usually don't have something better to look at. You have a great body."

"Oh, please," Min said. "I know you want to get laid but—"

"Guys buy magazines to look at breasts like yours," Cal said, "and here I am with a pair tied to a couch." He tossed the remote back on the coffee table. "CNN has lost its appeal."

"If I ever get off this couch," Min said through her teeth, "you're never seeing these breasts again. Now untie me."

"You didn't think that through," Cal said. "Try again."

"*Calvin*—"

"Do you have any idea," he said conversationally, "how hard it is for me to keep my hands off you?"

"So untie me and let's go," Min said, starting to feel cheerful again.

"Forty-five minutes," Cal said. "What do you want to talk about?"

Okay, Min told herself. *You're not thinking. You have the upper hand here, aside from being tied to the couch. He wants you. He can have you. He just needs jump-started.* "I've wanted you, too," she said, relaxing back against the pillows.

"Right," Cal said, picking up another doughnut. "That's why you kept walking away."

"That was the bet," Min said. "Remember that picnic in the park? I wanted to knock you down and rip off your shirt and bite into you."

Cal stopped with the doughnut halfway to his mouth.

"I used to close my eyes and imagine you naked against me, all the things you'd do to me." He drew back a little and she said, "Especially my breasts. I have really sensitive breasts, did I mention that? I could almost come just imagining your mouth on my—"

"You don't play fair," Cal said.

"*I* don't?" Min said, trying to rise up. "I'm *tied to the couch.* How is that fair?"

"It's not," Cal said. "One of the many reasons I like it."

She exhaled in frustration, and he watched her, and then he got up and moved around the table to sit beside her. He scooped some chocolate icing off the doughnut with his finger. "Do you know how many fantasies I've had about your body?" He drew his finger around the slope of her breast, smearing the chocolate under the lace, and Min sucked in her breath. "This wasn't one of them," he said, marking her other breast the same way. "But it should have been."

"Sticky," Min said, complete sentences escaping her for the moment.

"Not a problem," Cal said, bending over her. "It's coming right off."

"Pervert," Min said, closing her eyes as she felt his tongue on her.

"Yep," he said, moving the lace lower. "But you like it."

"Ha," Min said.

Cal straightened enough to look into her eyes. "Want me to stop?"

he said, and Min felt his hand under her breast, felt his thumb move across the heat there to the edge of the lace.

"I want everything you've got," Min said and watched his eyes darken as his hand tightened on her. "Untie me."

"Nope," Cal said.

Min arched against him and he pushed her back, his breath coming faster, and bent down to her again, and this time he pulled down the lace, and when she felt his mouth on her, she arched as every nerve she had flared in relief.

He pulled back as she jerked and looked down at her, breathing hard, and just as she realized he was staring at her naked breast, he stripped the rest of the nightgown down so she was naked to the waist. "Hey," she said and moved instinctively to cover herself and remembered she was tied.

"God, you're beautiful," he said, still staring at her breasts.

Min tugged at the belt, torn between embarrassment and lust, and then he slid his hands up to cup her breasts, and lust won. She closed her eyes and felt the heat of his mouth on her again, felt herself tighten and shudder, and pressed against him, praying he wouldn't stop.

The Morriseys weren't in the book, so David called Cynthie. "I need the number for Cal's parents."

"Why?" Cynthie said flatly.

"It doesn't matter why," David said. "What matters is that Cal would be furious if he found out that you told me how to start that fight on Sunday. Give me the number or I tell him."

There was a long silence, and then Cynthie put down the phone. When she came back, she gave him the number.

"Thank you," David said, and hung up and dialed the number. When the ringing stopped, he said, "You should know this," only to be overridden by the Morriseys' answering machine. "This is ridiculous," he said, but when the beep sounded, he said, "You should know this. Your son is seducing a woman right now to win a bet. Her name is Min

Dobbs and she is litigious and vindictive." Then he gave her apartment address and hung up.

"Not bad," he told himself and picked up the phone again, feeling pretty good about himself in general.

Because he was going to win.

Fifteen minutes later, Cal picked up the rest of the third doughnut, and Min tried to remember her name.

"What are you *doing?*" she said.

"Pacing myself," Cal said, sounding ragged. He bit into the dough-nut. "I figure," he said after he'd swallowed, "that as long as I have this in my mouth, I won't put you there." He looked at the clock. "We've got half an hour. I don't think you bought enough doughnuts."

"Could you at least pull my nightgown up?" Min said, feeling a blush start as the heat receded.

"Nope." Cal finished the doughnut. "I'm thinking you should always go topless."

"That'll perk things up at work," Min said, and then remembered that there was nothing perky about her. "I meant—"

"Not in public, dummy," Cal said. "Just at home. We'll put it in the wedding vows. You can promise to love, honor, cherish, and be naked from the waist up every night."

"Married?" Min said, trying to sit up.

"Well, of course, married," Cal said, watching her with interest. "You think I'd tie up somebody I wasn't serious about?"

"You haven't *asked,*" Min said, yanking on the belt.

"Will you marry me?" Cal said, still watching her breasts.

"*No,*" Min said, torn between love and murder.

"Right," Cal said. "Because years from now when Harry asks how I proposed, you don't want to say, 'Well, he tied me to the couch and ripped off my nightgown and ate doughnuts off my breasts and then he asked me.'" He bit into the doughnut again.

"All I want is to make love so we can put this dumb bet behind us and start a real relationship, although maybe not after this." She yanked on the belt again. "This could set us back some."

"Nope," Cal said, insufferably calm. "We agreed that nothing could hurt this relationship now. It's a little bent, but I like that about us."

"You're a little bent," Min said. "I am completely normal. Now untie me and fuck my brains out."

Cal caught his breath for a minute, and Min thought, *Take me*, and then he bit into the doughnut again, and she exhaled through her teeth in frustration.

"Maybe I'm filling the wrong mouth," he said, and tore off a piece of the doughnut. "Open up."

"Look, I don't—" Min said, and Cal slipped the pastry into her mouth, and the sugar flooded everywhere. "Oh," she said and let the chocolate melt into her senses.

"My goal in life is to put that look on your face without chocolate," Cal said.

Min swallowed. "You do. You're just never looking at me when it's on there."

"Really." Cal cupped her breast and began to stroke her with his thumb, and Min felt herself tighten under him again, but this time, when she opened her eyes, he was staring at her, watching her, and she blushed, from embarrassment and from heat and from wanting him. "Damn, you're right," he said and bent to kiss her, and Min forgot to be embarrassed and rose to taste him as he caressed her, sighing against his mouth.

"Untie me," she whispered, and he looked over her head.

"Nope, we still have half an hour to kill." He slid his hand down her calf. "I think I'll start with the toes this time. It's never been toes for me before, so this will be new."

"You're going to suck my toes for half an hour?" Min said in disbelief.

"I'm going to start at your toes," Cal said. "And work up."

"Up?" Min said.

"And in about fifteen minutes, you're going lose the rest of this nightgown."

"With the lights on?" Min said, outraged, and he laughed and bent to her toes.

David dialed Diana's cell phone on the theory that after what had happened to her on Sunday, Diana would be ripe to maim any man in her path, especially one hurting her sister. When the ringing stopped, he said, "You should know this," only to be overridden by Diana's voice mail. "Don't any of you people stay home on Wednesdays?" he snapped, but when the beep sounded, he said, "You should know this. Calvin Morrisey is seducing your sister right now to win a bet." Then he hung up and thought about the last call he had to make. The scary one.

It's anonymous, he told himself. *She'll never know.*

He went back up to his apartment to have a drink first anyway.

At quarter after nine, having been touched everywhere she could imagine and a couple of places she hadn't thought of, Min felt Cal untie her.

She sat up and slugged him on the arm. "Don't *ever* do that again."

"Ouch?" Cal said, and she pushed him back and climbed onto his lap and kissed him hard, wrapping herself around him as tightly as she could.

When she came up for air, she slapped him on the shoulder again. "I *mean it*, never again," she said, and then went for his mouth again, hungry for it. A minute later she broke the kiss, breathing heavily, slugged him again, and said, "*Never* ever again."

"Really?" he said, as breathless as she was, and she looked back at the arm of the couch, the belt still tangled around it, and shivered.

"Well, not in the living room," she said. "And not for so long, and not with all these lights—"

He dumped her back on the couch, pressing her against the pillows. "When we do it again," he told her, his hands hot on her, "it'll be where I want, when I want, with spotlights if I want."

"I don't think so," she said and he kissed her again and she thought, *Oh, hell, whatever you want,* and kissed him back.

"Whatever I want," he whispered in her ear.

"Okay," she whispered back. "But can I have you now?"

"Almost," Cal said into her neck. "Fifteen—"

"You know what my favorite fantasy is?" she whispered in his ear, and he groaned. "It's you, sliding hard inside me." His hand tightened on her, and she said, "I love that part of sex, the first part, the way it feels, and it's going to be the best with you because everything else with you has been the best I've ever had, the way I feel when you touch me, the way you kiss me, that's why I know the way you—"

He kissed her hard, pushing her back on the pillows, taking her voice and her breath away, and when he stopped, he said, "Shut up, we've got fifteen minutes yet," and began to lick his way down her body.

"Uh," Min said, as he set every nerve she had alight again. "What are you going to do for fifteen minutes?" and he bit into her thigh as he moved her legs apart with his hand.

"Oh, *God*," Min said, as he licked inside her. *"I'm going to lose ten dollars."*

Liza's cell phone rang in the kitchen at Emilio's, and Tony got it out of her purse and handed it to her, never dropping the fork he had buried in his spaghetti.

"You sure we're not seeing each other?" Liza said as she took the phone. "Because you sure show up here at lot."

"I eat here," Tony said, twirling more spaghetti on his fork. "I pre-date you."

"Right," Liza said, clicked her phone on. "Hello?"

"Liza?" a man's voice said. "You should know this. Cal Morrisey is tricking Min into winning that bet."

"What?" Liza said. "Who is this?"

"The bet's over at midnight," the voice said, sounding smugly familiar. "And he wants to win."

"David?" Liza said.

The phone clicked off and Liza was left with a dial tone.

"David?" Tony said, looking up from his spaghetti.

"Hey, Emilio?" Liza yelled over the kitchen noise. "I'm taking a break."

"Oh, no," Tony said.

"Eat your pasta," Liza said, moving toward the door.

"Oh, hell," Tony said and dropped his fork to follow her.

Chapter

Sixteen

When Min was wound so tight, she was shaking, Cal laced his fingers in her hair and turned her head to show her the mantel clock. "It's nine-thirty-five," he said, his voice husky. "I lost the bet to David. It's over."

"We wasted five minutes?" Min said wildly.

"You weren't complaining," Cal said, resting his head on her stomach.

"Take me to bed or do me on this couch," Min said, breathing hard. "I want you *now.*"

"I'm definitely marrying you," Cal said, and pulled her up off the couch and toward the bedroom.

She tripped behind him and then gasped as he toppled her onto her satin comforter, her body sizzling against the cool fabric as he stripped and found a condom, and then he was beside her, pressed hotly against her, and she closed her eyes to savor him, bone and muscle hard against her. *"Don't wait,"* she said, and felt his hands on her again, sliding over her, making every nerve she had scream, and when his fingers slipped inside her again, she opened to him, shaking under him, and when she felt his body between her thighs, she arched to meet him, desperate to feel him hard inside her. His eyes were hot on her and she stared back, caught, crazy for him, and then he kissed her and slipped his tongue in her mouth as he slid into her, slick and hot, and she gasped and clutched at him as the shock of him went everywhere.

He pulled back and then slid deeper, and she bit her lip, weak with pleasure as heat thickened in her, and then she began to move with him, catching his rhythm, dizzy with the rightness of him, of them together. He whispered in her ear as he moved against her, telling her that he loved her, that she was beautiful, that she was his, over and over and over, until she could feel him everywhere, his voice and his breath and his hands and his body, all loving her, making her drunk with love and lust. She licked her tongue across his lips and she told him she loved him, forever, for-ever, no end, forever, and she felt him build in her blood, felt him every-where, in her fingertips, behind her eyes, and deep and low where they were locked together, where the heat and the pressure and the tension twisted and tightened, glitter and stars, fusing into brightness sharper than anything ever before. He rocked higher, sharper, and she dug her fingernails into him and cried his name as he rocked again and again and then she broke, arching under his hands as he held her down, spasming helplessly as his body surged against hers. And then, while she was still clutching him, still gasping from shattering ecstasy, he shuddered, too, and collapsed into her arms.

"Oh, *God*," Min said, when she could speak again.

"Good?" he said, breathless, and she shook her head.

"Very good. World class. Phenomenal." She took a deep breath to stop the gasping and he slid his hand up to her breast where it belonged. She put her hand over his and pressed it tighter to her, and drew in another deep breath. "God, I love you."

"Good," Cal said, looking exhausted. "I love you, too. Sorry we didn't have time to talk about what you wanted."

"I wanted that," Min said between breaths.

"You got it," Cal said, and rolled his head and caught sight of her clock. "Oh, Christ."

Min looked up at her curling brass headboard and drew in a deep sighing breath. "I think I might want to be tied to this headboard some-day."

"Just for the record," Cal said, "I usually last more than seven min-utes." He let his head fall back onto her pillow. "Of course, foreplay usually doesn't last a month." He took a deep breath. "Go ahead, tell me the statistics on how long foreplay usually lasts."

"Not long enough," Min said. "You're the exception. Maybe I'll tie you to this headboard. And *I'll* do the chocolate icing."

Cal closed his eyes. "Thank you. I'd like that. Make a list. We'll do it all. Probably not tonight, but eventually."

Min curled into him as her pulse began to slow. "I'm so happy. I'm so crazy about you, and I'm so happy."

He rolled closer to her and kissed her, and she settled into him, safe and warm and satisfied.

"I love you," he said, and she opened her mouth to tell him that she loved him, too, when someone began to pound on her door.

"What the hell is that?" Cal said.

"My door?" Min said.

"Did Diana forget her key?" Cal eased himself up into a sitting posi-tion. "Ouch. You're a very athletic woman, Minerva."

"Not really," Min said as the phone rang. "I got C's in gym."

"They were giving you the wrong assignments." Cal patted her on the hip and reached for his pants. "You get the phone. I'll get the door. I'll meet you back here. Stay naked."

Cal buttoned his shirt as he crossed Min's living room, reminding him-self that yelling at his future sister-in-law would be bad. That made him almost glad when he yanked open the door and saw David instead. He could yell anything he wanted at that dickhead.

"Is Min here?" David said, looking smug.

"Yes, go away." Cal started to close the door and then remembered. "You won. I'll send you a check tomorrow. Now go away."

"I don't think so." David blocked the doorway. "I have to see Min."

"David?" Min said from behind them, and when they turned, Cal lost his breath.

She had her blue-violet comforter wound around her and Elvis twining around her ankles, but her shoulders were bare, and she looked disheveled and rumpled, her gold-tipped curls tousled, her baby-doll cheeks flushed, and her full lips bruised and rosy, and Cal thought, *I did that,* and wanted her again so much that he took a step toward her.

"God," David said, slackjawed.

"Mine," Cal said. "Go away."

"You won," David said, and shoved the check at him.

"What?" Cal frowned at him. "No."

"The bet was for midnight," David said, still staring at Min. "You've got more than two hours left." He smiled at Min. "Guess Calvin the Great is also Calvin the Fast."

"Oh, for crying out loud," Cal said as Elvis hissed at David and David took a step back.

"It was for midnight?" Min's voice was too high as she came closer to them, tripping over the comforter on the way.

Minerva, what are you up to? Cal thought, and watched her with interest and rebounding lust.

"Of course it was." David smiled triumphantly at Cal. "All bets end at midnight."

Min hauled the comforter up again. "Do you mean to tell me," she said, her voice breaking, "that Cal *won this bet*?"

"Oh, yes," David said, smugly.

"Well, gee, thanks," Min said in her normal voice as she took the check out of his hand. "I can always use ten bucks."

"What?" David said, losing his smug.

Min smiled cheerfully at David. "I know Cal won it," she said, "but we have this unwritten rule that I get all the money he wins on me. I'm picking up quite a bit of spare change that way, so this—" She looked at the check and almost dropped her comforter. *"Oh, my God."*

"Not ten bucks," Cal said, yanking up the comforter before she lost it.

Min looked up at him, appalled. "You bet *ten thousand dollars* you could get me into bed?"

"No," Cal said. "I'm going to get a T-shirt made that says, 'I did not make that bet.'"

"Ten thousand dollars," Min said, looking at the check again. "If you'd told me about this the first night and offered to split it, I'd have slept with you then."

"Really?" Cal said.

"No," Min said.

"I didn't think so." Cal took the check out of her hand and pushed it at David. "You can go now."

"What is that?" David said, pointing to the couch.

Cal looked back and saw Min's belt still draped over the arm.

"He tied me to the couch," Min said helpfully. "Then he ripped off my nightgown and smeared chocolate icing on me and licked it off. It was a *nightmare*." She grinned. "If you leave, we can do it again." She looked at Cal. "We're not out of doughnuts, are we?"

"If we are, I will run out and get more," Cal said. "Run being the operative word."

David looked floored. "That's . . ."

Min waited.

". . . so not like you," he finished.

"Well, it wasn't," Min said. "It is now."

"But—" David began, and then Nanette and George pushed him out of the doorway to get into the room.

"Oh, great," Cal said, lust evaporating as George caught sight of him.

"That's what I came to tell you," Min said, clutching her comforter more tightly. "David called Di, who called to warn me that he'd probably called some others."

"*You,*" George said, heading for Cal, and Min stepped between them.

"You're overreacting," Min said to George.

"I've never liked your apartment, dear," Nanette said, looking around. Then she saw the green and white bag on the table. "*Dough-nuts?*"

"You should have been feeding me cocaine," Min said to Cal. "I understand that's slimming."

George stuck to his guns. "Min, David says this man made a wager that he could—"

"No," Min said. "*David* tried to get him to make that bet but Cal said no. Go yell at David."

"Then what's this?" George ripped the check out of Cal's hand. "This is—" He caught sight of the amount. "—for ten thousand dollars." He looked at Cal. "You're not only immoral, you're reckless with money."

"I didn't make the bet," Cal said. "And no one will ever believe that."

"I believe it," Min said, smiling up at him.

"Then the hell with everybody else," Cal said, and moved closer to her.

George drew himself up. "Minerva, get your clothes on, you're coming home."

"Dad, I'm thirty-three," Min said. "No." She reached out and took the check out of his hand. "Go home now. Take Mother with—"

"Calvin," a voice like ice said from the doorway.

Cal looked around George to see his mother. "Oh. Wonderful." He looked down at Min. "This is pretty much my fantasy. I finally make love to the woman of my dreams, and my mother shows up for the afterglow."

"Well," Min said, trying to keep the comforter up. "It really isn't a party until somebody brings the ice."

"Excuse me," Nanette said, trying to push George out of the way. "You're Lynne Morrisey, aren't you?"

Lynne looked at Nanette as if she were part of the work force.

Nanette held out her hand. "I'm Min's mother, Nanette? So pleased to meet you."

"How do you do," Lynne said, without taking the hand, and turned back to Cal. "Calvin."

"Hello, Mother," Cal said. "This is the woman I'm going to spend the rest of my life with. If you don't approve, we'll spend the third Sunday of the month listening to Elvis at the diner. Your call."

Lynne looked at him for a long frozen moment, and then Cal saw Cynthie come through the doorway behind her, looking sheet white. "Cynthie?"

"I called her," Lynne said. "I felt that—"

"No," Cal said to them both.

"You cannot be serious—" Lynne began.

"Don't push him," Cynthie said, quietly. "That's what I came to tell you. This is infatuation. It'll pass. Give him time."

Cal shook his head and pulled Min toward the couch, away from the loons.

"I'll give him time," George said, still scowling. "I'll give the bastard—"

"Oh, *you'll give him time*," Nanette snapped. "Like you're not worse than he is."

"What?" George said.

Min curled up next to Cal on the couch and laced her fingers with his. "So I owe you ten dollars since you made me wait until after nine-thirty."

"Yep," Cal said, tightening his grip on her. "Except I won it on a bet on you, so you'll just take it away from me again."

"I *know what you're doing*," Nanette said to George, rage in her voice.

"I'm . . . yelling at the bastard who seduced my daughter," George said, knocked off stride.

"*I know what you're doing on your lunch hour,*" Nanette said, murder in her eye.

"I'm eating," George said, perplexed.

"Yes, *but who?*" Nanette yelled, and Min cringed and said, "Oh, God, *Mother,*" and Lynne looked at Nanette in contempt, and Cynthie closed her eyes, and David looked frustrated and confused and mad as hell, and then Liza walked in with Tony behind her and stopped, scowling at all of them.

"What the hell is this?" she said.

"Tony," Cal said, an edge to his voice.

"For the record," Tony said to him, "I tried to stop her."

"Why didn't you lock the door so these people couldn't get in?" Liza said to Min.

"I did," Min said. "Cal opened it. Yell at him."

"Just hit me," Cal said. "Save us all some time."

"What did you mean by that?" George said to Nanette, his face red.

"Your *lunches*," Nanette said, her voice rising. "*You take your secretary to lunch every damn day.*"

"Loud voice," Min said, thinking of her neighbors. "Not your loud voice."

"They're *working lunches*," George said. "I need a secretary *to work.*"

"*You never take me to lunch*," Nanette yelled.

"*You don't EAT,*" George yelled back.

Min craned her neck to see around them to Liza. "You know, that bet was for ten thousand dollars."

"You're kidding." Liza looked at Cal, surprised. "You bet ten thousand dollars on—"

"*No,*" Cal said. "Damn it, *look.*" He took the check out of Min's hand and tore it in two. "See? *No bet.*"

"We could have used that," Min said, but she didn't sound upset.

They all began to talk, and Cal looked at Min and thought, *all I want is to be alone with her for the rest of my life.*

"Hey!" he said, and they all looked at him with various degrees of contempt, despair, and rage. He picked up a doughnut and turned to Min. "Minerva Dobbs, I love you and I always will. Will you marry me?"

"This is so sudden," Min said, grinning at him.

"We got an audience, Minnie," Cal said. "You in or not?"

"I'm in," Min said, and he took her left hand, spread her fingers out, and slipped the doughnut over her ring finger, knowing with a certainty he'd never felt before that this was exactly the right thing to do.

"I'll get you a better ring later," he said, looking into her dark, dark eyes. "I'll do this better, too. This is just to get these people off our backs."

"Well, when you do this better, I'm going to say yes again," Min said.

"Thank you," Cal said and kissed her, falling into her heat all over again. "God, I love you," he whispered in her ear. "I can't believe how much I love you."

"Okay," Liza said. "Show's over." She looked at Lynne. "You have to be the mother. Don't mess with Min. If Cal has to choose—"

"Elvis," Lynne said, her voice flat. She turned and walked out of the apartment.

"*Lovely* woman," Liza said, and turned to Nanette. "Now you. Your husband is not cheating on you. I know men and he's not the type." She looked at George. "Stop working through lunch and take your wife out to eat instead." She turned back to Nanette. "And you. Eat."

Nanette's face crumpled, and George put his arm around her. "I'm not cheating," he said. "I don't have the time."

"*Dad,*" Min said, but Nanette sniffed and said, "Really?"

"I didn't think I'd find you here," Liza said to Cynthie, not unkindly. "It's the book, isn't it?"

"No," Cynthie said, staring hopelessly at the doughnut squashed between Min's fingers. "No."

"Listen," Liza told her, "nobody wants to hear an incredibly beautiful woman tell about how she landed an incredibly beautiful man. That's just smug. Write a book about how you lost the love of your life and recovered. People could *use* that."

"I—"

"It's over, Cynthie," Liza said. "He's gone. Forever."

Cynthie's face fell, and Liza turned to David.

"And you are a worthless piece of garbage," she said. "So do something decent and take Cynthie home."

"This is a mistake," David told Min. "Do you know what this man is?"

"Yep," Min said, pulling a piece of chocolate icing off her engagement ring. "It's okay. We're going to evolve together."

"*Out,*" Liza said to him, and Cynthie left. Liza glared at David. "Well, go *after her*, you vicious dork. Do something nice for a change instead of anonymous phone calls."

David drew himself up. "I didn't—" he began, but Liza folded her arms, so he transferred his attention to Min. "He's a terrible user, Min."

"No, he's not," Min said. "He's a prince. And you're a toad who makes anonymous phone calls."

"You never did understand me," David said, and walked out.

"What a fathead," Liza said.

"You're going to marry this man?" George said to Min, sounding incredulous.

"Yes," Min said. "Don't be mean to him, or you'll lose us to Elvis, too."

George shot Cal a look that said, *I'm watching you, buddy*, and then turned on his heel and left.

"Well, you'll have beautiful children," Nanette said, cheering up.

"We're not having kids," Min said, and when her mother's eyes narrowed, she added, "because you know I'd never lose the weight afterward."

"That's true," Nanette said, and then George came back and dragged her out the door.

"All right then," Liza said, looking around the emptied apartment. "My work here is done."

"Who are you again?" Cal said. "Because you look like this woman who keeps hitting me, but you seem to be on my side. Do you have an evil twin?"

"I'm Min's fairy godmother, Charm Boy," Liza said, frowning down at him. "And if you don't give her a happily ever after, I'm going to come back and beat you to death with a snow globe."

"What happened to 'bibbity bobbity boo'?" Cal asked Min.

"That was Disney, honey," Min said. "It wasn't a documentary."

Liza went to the door and stopped when she saw Tony there, his arms folded. "Come on. You can yell at me on the way back to the restaurant."

"Nope," Tony said. "That was good what you did." He leaned closer. "Very hot."

"I'm not going to sleep with you," Liza said, and went out the door.

"Can't blame a guy for trying," Tony said and followed her out, closing the door behind them.

Silence settled over the apartment.

"I'll never forget my first time with you," Min said as she edged the doughnut off her finger. "The earth moved, and then my mother asked my father who he was going down on at lunch."

"Yes, there were some moments there," Cal said.

Min shook her head. "We're never going to be rid of those people."

"I know," Cal said.

"Thank God we have each other." Min looked up at him. "I love you."

"Thank you," Cal said and kissed her.

"So I'm buying a house," Min said when she came up for air. "How do you feel about an Arts and Crafts bungalow like my grandma used to live in?"

"Are you in it?" Cal said.

Min nodded.

"I'm there," Cal said. "Can we go back to bed now?"

"Yes," Min said. "Bring the doughnuts."

An hour and a half later, Min lay curled beside Cal with Elvis asleep at the foot of the bed, looking like rusty velvet on the lavender blue satin. Cal was breathing almost loudly enough to be called snoring, and she patted his shoulder. *A month ago, I didn't know him*, she thought dreamily. *And now he's the rest of my life.*

Then she pulled back a little. That sounded ridiculous. Completely irrational, in fact. *Screw rationality*, she thought, but the thought didn't go away. You'd have to be insane to pin the rest of your life on somebody you'd only known a month, especially somebody with a past like Cal's.

She slid out from under his arm, and picked up his shirt from the floor. When she put it on, it failed to meet in the middle over her chest. *That always works in the movies*, she thought, disgusted, and dropped it on the floor. Instead, she pulled the comforter off the bed, annoying Elvis but leaving Cal asleep under the sheet. It was June. He wasn't going to freeze.

Then she went out and sat on her grandmother's couch, wrapped in her comforter, and tried to make sense of everything. Elvis padded out to join her and curled up on the back of the couch, and she moved her head a little bit to rub against him and make him purr.

So, she thought, *essentially what we have here is that I'm looking at the biggest player in town and thinking he's True Love That Will Last Forever. What are the odds on that?* Across from her, the clock on the mantel clicked as the hands hit midnight.

"Hey," Cal said, and she looked up to see him in the doorway, stifling a yawn. "What are you doing?"

"It's midnight," she said, trying to sound cheerful. "I'm turning back into a pumpkin."

"That explains the couch," he said and came to sit beside her. He put his arm around her and pulled her close and kissed her on the forehead, and she closed her eyes and leaned into him, loving him so much she was weak with it. *I'm in big trouble here*, she thought.

"Something wrong?" he said. "I thought everything was pretty much perfect once the loons left."

"It is," she said. "I'm just trying to figure out what's next."

"Next." Cal nodded. "Okay. Well." He took her hand and yawned again. "Tomorrow, I'll call my mother so she doesn't put a curse on us, and we'll go have dinner with your parents and make sure they're not still nuts."

"There's a hope," Min said. The comforter slipped down over her shoulder, and Cal put his hand there, making lazy circles on her skin with his fingertips as he talked.

"And then we'll go looking for that house you were talking about, one with only six steps up from the street." He shifted a little to avoid a spring and added, "And we'll get a new couch."

Min felt herself start to smile, the happiness bubbling up in spite of the odds, and he held her tighter. "And then we'll get married, and we'll live happily ever after."

Min went cold as he brought her hand to his mouth and kissed her knuckles. "Yeah. That's the part I'm wondering about."

Cal's hand tightened on hers. "You think we're going to have prob-lems?"

"I don't know," Min said, looking into his eyes. "I think we're going to love each other till the day we die, but I don't know if that's enough. Life is not a fairy tale."

"Okay," Cal said. "It's midnight, I've had a very full evening, and I'm a little slow here. What are you worried about?"

"The happily ever after," Min said, knowing she was sounding like an idiot. "All the stuff we just did, the romance part, the fairy tale stuff, I know how that works, I read the stories."

"Fairy tale stuff?"

"But they don't tell you about the happily ever after. And as far as I can see, that's where it all breaks down. Fifty percent of marriages end in divorce, and yes, I know those statistics are skewed by repeat divorcers—"

"It's midnight, and I'm listening to statistics," Cal said to the cat.

"—but I'm worried. There aren't any happily ever after stories. That's where it ends. Where the hard part starts."

"All right," Cal said. "So?"

"So," Min said, meeting his eyes. "What are we going to do?"

"You want me to be philosophic about the future now?" Cal said. "I'm not even sure where I left my pants."

Min looked at him for a moment, loving him in spite of the fact that he had bed hair and was making jokes and wasn't helping. *In spite of everything*, she thought and smiled at him. "No." She clutched the com-forter around her. "I don't know what I was thinking. Let's go back to bed."

"We're going to take it one day at a time," Cal said, holding on to her. "I don't know anything about this, either, I didn't plan for this, but I think we just stick together. Take care of each other. Pat each other on the back when things get tight." When she still looked unsure, he smiled at her with so much love in his eyes that she went dizzy, and then he said, "Bet you ten bucks we make it."

What are the odds? she thought, and realized with sudden, blinding clarity that she wouldn't take the other side of that bet, that only a loser

would bet against them. *This is really it*, she thought, amazed. *This is really forever. I believe in this.*

"Min?" he said, and she kissed him, putting all her heart into it.

"No bet," she said against his mouth. "Your odds are too good."

"*Our* odds are too good," he said, and took her back to bed.

Chapter Seventeen

In case you were wondering . . .

David got over Min pretty quickly, although the fact that Cal won bothered him for years. Four months later, he met a woman who agreed with everything he said and slept with him on the third date. They were married six months later. She never cooks with butter.

Cyn took longer to get over Cal because she really did love him. She holed up in her apartment, subsisting on carrots and nonfat ranch dressing, until Liza dragged her out into the sun, made her write about her breakup, and called in a favor from one of her many former bosses to get the book to another editor. The editor, a guy with glasses who was two inches shorter than Cynthie and slightly overweight, made her rewrite it four times and then threw all the promotional power of his publishing house behind it. He married Cynthie the day before the book hit number one on the *NYT* list. They have a penthouse in New York and eat only in the very best restaurants.

Emilio let Liza tell him what to do and within the year Emilio's was the hottest restaurant in town. He offered her a partnership if she stayed, but things were running well and she was bored, so she introduced him to a friend of hers with an MBA in management and left to go save somebody else.

George stopped taking his overworked secretary to lunch, for which she was grateful even though she missed the expensive food. He now has lunch with Nanette three times a week. She eats.

Reynolds spends so much time with Min, Cal, and Bink on social occasions that, given their willingness to say, "Reynolds, you're being a butthead," he has stopped being a butthead when he's with them. At all other times, he continues being a butthead. Bink loves him anyway.

Shanna and Linda parted company after a year with no hard feelings. Shortly after that, Shanna went to work for Emilio, where she met the MBA who, it turned out, adored Elvis Costello. Four months later they moved into a lavish loft in the city, and a year later they went to China and adopted a little girl. Shanna is a stay-at-home mom except when Emilio gets swamped and needs the help. Her Betty Boop cookie jar always has Oreos.

Harry got a growth spurt at fourteen, shot up and filled out and became a carbon copy of his father and uncle, except that his hair still flops over his forehead and he still wears glasses. He became an ichthyologist, met a zaftig girl on a dive in the Bahamas, fell in love, and married her a month later. She has brown hair with gold highlights, a logical mind, and a penchant for shoes. He still can't eat more than one doughnut.

Roger and Bonnie got married, moved to the suburbs, and had four kids. Everybody goes to their house for the holidays.

Diana got engaged twice more and broke off both engagements, crying in Tony's arms each time. He told her she had lousy taste in men and to try picking a good one next time, so she proposed to him. He said no, appalled. Six weeks later they eloped to Kentucky because Tony had tickets for the Derby. They have three kids, all big-boned, beautiful girls who dominate whatever field or court they play on, probably because they eat carbs.

Liza continues to have an exciting, varied, constantly changing life that is much too complicated to synopsize here.

Cal bought Min an engagement ring made of six perfect diamonds set in a circle. It looks nothing like a Krispy Kreme, but Min knows. They got married and bought an Arts and Crafts bungalow one block from Min's apartment. It has thirty-seven steps up from the street. They also bought a mission couch like Bonnie's, and occasionally somebody gets tied to it. They go to the If Dinner at Emilio's every Thursday night with Roger and Bonnie and Tony and Diana and Liza and whomever Liza's seeing that week. His mother tolerates her. Her mother adores him. They don't have kids, but they did get a black lab mix puppy from the pound that they named The Beast. Elvis is coping.

They all lived happily ever after.